Praise for T̶

"Poignant . . . funny . . .   . is one of her
best. . . . [Tyler] has never been stronger."
—*The New York Times*

"Tyler has given us an endlessly diverting book whose strength
gathers gradually to become a genuinely thrilling one."
—*Los Angeles Times*

"Bittersweet . . . evocative . . . It's easy to forget this is the warm
lull of fiction; you half-expect to run into her characters at the dry
cleaners. . . . Tyler [is] a writer of great compassion."
—*The Boston Globe*

"A rarely equaled richness and depth . . . delicious humor . . .
Without Anne Tyler, American fiction would be an immeasurably
bleaker place."
—*Newsday*

Praise for *Ladder of Years*

"A page-turner in the best sense. . . . One wants to lightly caress the
pages of the story because one cares for Ms. Tyler's touchingly
flawed characters. . . . Both madcap and genteel, Anne Tyler
knows as well as anyone that 'human beings lead many lives.'
Casually, delightfully, *Ladder of Years* will tell you just how we
humans manage this trick."
—*The Baltimore Sun*

"Fresh, funny, and poignant."
—*The Christian Science Monitor*

"*Ladder of Years* has charm galore. . . . Tyler does a lovely job
painting Delia's entry into her new world."
—*Newsweek*

The Accidental Tourist

&

Ladder of Years

The Accidental Tourist

&

Ladder of Years

TWO NOVELS

Anne Tyler

BALLANTINE BOOKS
NEW YORK

2005 Ballantine Books Trade Paperback Edition

Published in the United States by Ballantine Books, an imprint of The Random House Publishing Group, a division of Random House, Inc., New York.

BALLANTINE and colophon are registered trademarks of Random House, Inc.

Originally published as two separate works entitled *The Accidental Tourist* and *Ladder of Years* in the United States by Alfred A. Knopf, a division of Random House, Inc., in 1985 and 1995 respectively.

ISBN: 0-345-48764-8

Printed in the United States of America

www.ballantinebooks.com

The Accidental
Tourist

o n e

They were supposed to stay at the beach a week, but neither of them had the heart for it and they decided to come back early. Macon drove. Sarah sat next to him, leaning her head against the side window. Chips of cloudy sky showed through her tangled brown curls.

Macon wore a formal summer suit, his traveling suit—much more logical for traveling than jeans, he always said. Jeans had those stiff, hard seams and those rivets. Sarah wore a strapless terry beach dress. They might have been returning from two entirely different trips. Sarah had a tan but Macon didn't. He was a tall, pale, gray-eyed man, with straight fair hair cut close to his head, and his skin was that thin kind that easily burns. He'd kept away from the sun during the middle part of every day.

Just past the start of the divided highway, the sky grew almost black and several enormous drops spattered the windshield. Sarah sat up straight. "Let's hope it doesn't rain," she said.

"I don't mind a little rain," Macon said.

Sarah sat back again, but she kept her eyes on the road.

It was a Thursday morning. There wasn't much traffic. They

passed a pickup truck, then a van all covered with stickers from a hundred scenic attractions. The drops on the windshield grew closer together. Macon switched his wipers on. Tick-*swoosh*, they went—a lulling sound; and there was a gentle patter on the roof. Every now and then a gust of wind blew up. Rain flattened the long, pale grass at the sides of the road. It slanted across the boat lots, lumberyards, and discount furniture outlets, which already had a darkened look as if here it might have been raining for some time.

"Can you see all right?" Sarah asked.

"Of course," Macon said. "This is nothing."

They arrived behind a trailer truck whose rear wheels sent out arcs of spray. Macon swung to the left and passed. There was a moment of watery blindness till the truck had dropped behind. Sarah gripped the dashboard with one hand.

"I don't know how you can see to drive," she said.

"Maybe you should put on your glasses."

"Putting on my glasses would help you to see?"

"Not me; you," Macon said. "You're focused on the windshield instead of the road."

Sarah continued to grip the dashboard. She had a broad, smooth face that gave an impression of calm, but if you looked closely you'd notice the tension at the corners of her eyes.

The car drew in around them like a room. Their breaths fogged the windows. Earlier the air conditioner had been running and now some artificial chill remained, quickly turning dank, carrying with it the smell of mildew. They shot through an underpass. The rain stopped completely for one blank, startling second. Sarah gave a little gasp of relief, but even before it was uttered, the hammering on the roof resumed. She turned and gazed back longingly at the underpass. Macon sped ahead, with his hands relaxed on the wheel.

"Did you notice that boy with the motorcycle?" Sarah asked. She had to raise her voice; a steady, insistent roaring sound engulfed them.

"What boy?"

"He was parked beneath the underpass."

"It's crazy to ride a motorcycle on a day like today," Macon said. "Crazy to ride one any day. You're so exposed to the elements."

"We could do that," Sarah said. "Stop and wait it out."

"Sarah, if I felt we were in the slightest danger I'd have pulled over long ago."

"Well, I don't know that you would have," Sarah said.

They passed a field where the rain seemed to fall in sheets, layers and layers of rain beating down the cornstalks, flooding the rutted soil. Great lashings of water flung themselves at the windshield. Macon switched his wiper blades to high.

"I don't know that you really care that much," Sarah said. "Do you?"

Macon said, "Care?"

"I said to you the other day, I said, 'Macon, now that Ethan's dead I sometimes wonder if there's any point to life.' Do you remember what you answered?"

"Well, not offhand," Macon said.

"You said, 'Honey, to tell the truth, it never seemed to me there was all that much point to begin with.' Those were your exact words."

"Um . . ."

"And you don't even know what was wrong with that."

"No, I guess I don't," Macon said.

He passed a line of cars that had parked at the side of the road, their windows opaque, their gleaming surfaces bouncing back the rain in shallow explosions. One car was slightly tipped, as if about to fall into the muddy torrent that churned and raced in the gully. Macon kept a steady speed.

"You're not a comfort, Macon," Sarah said.

"Honey, I'm trying to be."

"You just go on your same old way like before. Your little routines and rituals, depressing habits, day after day. No comfort at all."

"Shouldn't I need comfort too?" Macon asked. "You're not the only one, Sarah. I don't know why you feel it's your loss alone."

"Well, I just do, sometimes," Sarah said.

They were quiet a moment. A wide lake, it seemed, in the center of the highway crashed against the underside of the car and slammed it to the right. Macon pumped his brakes and drove on.

"This rain, for instance," Sarah said. "You know it makes me nervous. What harm would it do to wait it out? You'd be showing some concern. You'd be telling me we're in this together."

Macon peered through the windshield, which was streaming so that it seemed marbled. He said, "I've got a system, Sarah. You know I drive according to a system."

"You and your systems!"

"Also," he said, "if you don't see any point to life, I can't figure why a rainstorm would make you nervous."

Sarah slumped in her seat.

"Will you look at that!" he said. "A mobile home's washed clear across that trailer park."

"Macon, I want a divorce," Sarah told him.

Macon braked and glanced over at her. "What?" he said. The car swerved. He had to face forward again. "What did I say?" he asked. "What did it mean?"

"I just can't live with you anymore," Sarah said.

Macon went on watching the road, but his nose seemed sharper and whiter, as if the skin of his face had been pulled tight. He cleared his throat. He said, "Honey. Listen. It's been a hard year. We've had a hard time. People who lose a child often feel this way; everybody says so; everybody says it's a terrible strain on a marriage—"

"I'd like to find a place of my own as soon as we get back," Sarah told him.

"Place of your own," Macon echoed, but he spoke so softly, and the rain beat so loudly on the roof, it looked as if he were only moving his lips. "Well," he said. "All right. If that's what you really want."

"You can keep the house," Sarah said. "You never did like moving."

For some reason, it was this that made her finally break down. She turned away sharply. Macon switched his right blinker on. He pulled into a Texaco station, parked beneath the overhang, and cut off the engine. Then he started rubbing his knees with his palms. Sarah huddled in her corner. The only sound was the drumming of rain on the overhang far above them.

t w·o

After his wife left him, Macon had thought the house would seem larger. Instead, he felt more crowded. The windows shrank. The ceilings lowered. There was something insistent about the furniture, as if it were pressing in on him.

Of course Sarah's personal belongings were gone, the little things like clothes and jewelry. But it emerged that some of the big things were more personal than he'd imagined. There was the drop-leaf desk in the living room, its pigeonholes stuffed with her clutter of torn envelopes and unanswered letters. There was the radio in the kitchen, set to play 98 Rock. (She liked to keep in touch with her students, she used to say in the old days, as she hummed and jittered her way around the breakfast table.) There was the chaise out back where she had sunbathed, planted in the only spot that got any sun at all. He looked at the flowered cushions and marveled at how an empty space could be so full of a person—her faint scent of coconut oil that always made him wish for a piña colada; her wide, gleaming face inscrutable behind dark glasses; her compact body in the skirted swimsuit she had tearfully insisted on buying after her fortieth birthday. Threads of her exuberant hair showed up at the bottom of the sink. Her shelf in the medicine cabinet, stripped, was splashed with drops of liquid rouge in a particularly plummy shade that brought her instantly to Macon's mind. He had always disapproved of her messiness but now those spills seemed touching, like colorful toys left on the floor after a child has gone to bed.

The house itself was medium-sized, unexceptional to look at, standing on a street of such houses in an older part of Baltimore. Heavy oak trees hung over it, shading it from the hot summer sun but also blocking breezes. The rooms inside were square and dim. All that remained in Sarah's closet was a brown silk sash hanging on a hook; in her bureau drawers, lint balls and empty perfume bottles. Their son's old room was neatly made up, as sleek as a room in a Holiday Inn. Some places, the walls gave off a kind of echo. Still, Macon noticed he had a tendency to hold his arms close to his body, to walk past furniture sideways as if he imagined the house could barely accommodate him. He felt too tall. His long, clumsy feet seemed unusually distant. He ducked his head in doorways.

Now was his chance to reorganize, he told himself. He was struck by an incongruous little jolt of interest. The fact was that running a house required some sort of system, and Sarah had never understood that. She was the sort of woman who stored her flatware intermingled. She thought nothing of running a dishwasher with only a handful of forks stacked inside. Macon found that distressing. He was opposed to dishwashers in general; he believed they wasted energy. Energy saving was a hobby of his, you might say.

He started keeping the kitchen sink filled at all times, adding some chlorine bleach for disinfectant. As he finished using each dish, he dropped it in. On alternate days he pulled the plug and sprayed everything with very hot water. Then he stacked the rinsed dishes in the empty dishwasher—which had become, under his new system, a gigantic storage area.

When he hunkered over the sink to let the spray attachment run, he often had the feeling that Sarah was watching. He sensed that if he slid his eyes just slightly to the left, he would find her with her arms folded across her chest, her head tipped and her full, curved lips meditatively pursed. At first glance she was simply studying his procedure; at second glance (he knew) she was laughing at him. There was a secret little gleam in her eyes that he was all too familiar with. "I see," she would say, nodding at some lengthy explanation of his; then he'd look up and catch the gleam and the telltale tuck at one corner of her mouth.

In this vision of her—if you could call it a vision, considering that he never did glance over at her—she was wearing a bright blue dress from the early days of their marriage. He had no idea when she had given that dress up, but certainly it was years and years ago. He almost felt that Sarah was a ghost—that she was dead. In a way (he thought, turning off the faucet), she *was* dead, that young, vivid Sarah from their first enthusiastic apartment on Cold Spring Lane. When he tried to recall those days, any image of Sarah was altered by the fact that she had left him. When he pictured their introduction—back when they were barely out of childhood—it seemed nothing more than the beginning of their parting. When she had looked up at him that first night and rattled the ice cubes in her paper cup, they were already moving toward their last edgy, miserable year together, toward those months when anything either of them said was wrong, toward that sense of narrowly missed connections. They were like people who run to meet, holding out their arms, but their aim is wrong; they pass each other and keep running. It had all amounted to nothing, in the end. He gazed down at the sink, and the warmth from the dishes drifted gently up into his face.

Well, you have to carry on. You have to carry on. He decided to switch his shower from morning to night. This showed adaptability, he felt—some freshness of spirit. While he showered he let the water collect in the tub, and he stalked around in noisy circles, sloshing the day's dirty clothes underfoot. Later he wrung out the clothes and hung them on hangers to dry. Then he dressed in tomorrow's underwear so he wouldn't have to launder any pajamas. In fact, his only real laundry was a load of towels and sheets once a week—just two towels, but quite a lot of sheets. This was because he had developed a system that enabled him to sleep in clean sheets every night without the trouble of bed changing. He'd been proposing the system to Sarah for years, but she was so set in her ways. What he did was strip the mattress of all linens, replacing them with a giant sort of envelope made from one of the seven sheets he had folded and stitched together on the sewing machine. He thought of this invention as a Macon Leary Body Bag. A body bag required no tucking in, was unmussable, easily changeable, and the perfect weight for summer nights. In winter he would have to devise something warmer, but he couldn't think of winter yet. He was barely making it from one day to the next as it was.

At moments—while he was skidding on the mangled clothes in the bathtub or struggling into his body bag on the naked, rust-stained mattress—he realized that he might be carrying things too far. He couldn't explain why, either. He'd always had a fondness for method, but not what you would call a mania. Thinking then of Sarah's lack of method, he wondered if that had got out of hand now too. Maybe all these years, they'd been keeping each other on a reasonable track. Separated, demagnetized somehow, they wandered wildly off course. He pictured Sarah's new apartment, which he had never seen, as chaotic to the point of madness, with sneakers in the oven and the sofa heaped with china. The mere thought of it upset him. He looked gratefully at his own surroundings.

Most of his work was done at home; otherwise he might not have cared so about the mechanics of the household. He had a little study in the spare room off the kitchen. Seated in a stenographer's chair, tapping away at a typewriter that had served him through four years of college, he wrote a series of guidebooks for people forced to travel on business. Ridiculous, when you thought about it: Macon hated travel. He careened through foreign territories on a desperate kind of blitz—squinching his eyes shut and holding his breath and hanging on for dear life, he sometimes imagined—and then settled back home with a sigh of relief to produce his chunky, passport-sized paperbacks. *Accidental Tourist in France. Accidental Tourist in Germany. In Belgium.* No author's name, just a logo: a winged armchair on the cover.

He covered only the cities in these guides, for people taking business trips flew into cities and out again and didn't see the countryside at all. They didn't see the cities, for that matter. Their concern was how to pretend they had never left home. What hotels in Madrid boasted king-sized Beautyrest mattresses? What restaurants in Tokyo offered Sweet'n'Low? Did Amsterdam have a McDonald's? Did Mexico City have a Taco Bell? Did any place in Rome serve Chef Boyardee ravioli? Other travelers hoped to discover distinctive local wines; Macon's readers searched for pasteurized and homogenized milk.

As much as he hated the travel, he loved the writing—the virtuous delights of organizing a disorganized country, stripping away the inessential and the second-rate, classifying all that remained in neat, terse paragraphs. He cribbed from other guidebooks, seizing small kernels of value and discarding the rest. He spent pleasurable hours dithering over questions of punctuation. Righteously, mercilessly, he weeded out the passive voice. The effort of typing made the corners of his mouth turn down, so that no one could have guessed how much he was enjoying himself. *I am happy to say,* he pecked out, but his face remained glum and intense. *I am happy to say that it's possible now to buy Kentucky Fried Chicken in Stockholm. Pita bread, too,* he added as an afterthought. He wasn't sure how it had happened, but lately pita had grown to seem as American as hot dogs.

. . .

"Of course you're managing," his sister told him over the phone. "Did I say you weren't? But at least you could have let us know. Three weeks, it's been! Sarah's been gone three weeks and I only hear about it today. And by chance, at that. If I hadn't asked to speak to her, would you ever have told us she'd left you?"

"She didn't *leave* me," Macon said. "I mean it's not the way you make it sound. We discussed it like adults and decided to separate, that's all. The last thing I need is my family gathered around me saying, 'Oh, poor Macon, how could Sarah do this to you—' "

"Why would I say that?" Rose asked. "Everybody knows the Leary men are difficult to live with."

"Oh," Macon said.

"Where is she?"

"She's got a place downtown," he said. "And look," he added, "you don't have to bend over backwards, either, and go asking her to dinner or something. She does have a family of her own. You're supposed to take my side in this."

"I thought you didn't want us to take sides."

"No, no, I don't. I mean you shouldn't take *her* side, is what I'm trying to say."

"When Charles's wife got her divorce," Rose said, "we went on having her to dinner every Christmas, just like always. Remember?"

"I remember," Macon said wearily. Charles was their oldest brother.

"I suppose she'd still be coming, if she hadn't got remarried to someone so far away."

"What? If her husband had been a Baltimore man you'd have gone on inviting them both?"

"She and Porter's wife and Sarah used to sit around the kitchen — this was before Porter's wife got *her* divorce — and they'd go on and on about the Leary men. Oh, it was the Leary men this, the Leary men that: how they always had to have everything just so, always so well thought out beforehand, always clamping down on the world as if they really thought they could keep it in line. The Leary men! I can hear them still. I had to laugh: One Thanksgiving Porter and June were getting ready to leave, back when their children were small, and June was heading toward the door with the baby in her arms and Danny hanging onto her coat and this load of toys and supplies when Porter called out, 'Halt!' and started reading from one of those cash-register tapes that he always writes his lists on: *blanket, bottles, diaper bag, formula out of the fridge* . . . June just looked over at the other two and rolled her eyes."

"Well, it wasn't such a bad idea," Macon said, "when you consider June."

"No, and you notice it was alphabetical, too," Rose said. "I do think alphabetizing helps to sort things out a little."

Rose had a kitchen that was so completely alphabetized, you'd find the allspice next to the ant poison. She was a fine one to talk about the Leary men.

"At any rate," she said. "Has Sarah been in touch since she left?"

"She's come by once or twice. Once, actually," Macon said. "For things she needed."

"What kind of things?"

"Well, a double boiler. Things like that."

"It's an excuse, then," Rose said promptly. "She could get a double boiler at any dimestore."

"She said she liked ours."

"She was checking to see how you're doing. She still cares. Did you talk at all?"

"No," Macon said, "I just handed her the double boiler. Also that gadget that unscrews bottle tops."

"Oh, Macon. You might have asked her in."

"I was scared she'd say no," he said.

There was a silence. "Well. Anyhow," Rose said finally.

"But I'm getting along!"

"Yes, of course you are," she told him.

Then she said she had something in the oven and hung up.

Macon went over to his study window. It was a hot day in early July, the sky so blue it made his eyes ache. He rested his forehead against the glass and stared out at the yard, keeping his hands stuffed deep in the rear pockets of his khakis. Up in one of the oak trees, a bird sang what sounded like the first three notes of "My Little Gypsy Sweetheart." "Slum . . . ber . . . on . . ." it sang. Macon wondered if even this moment would become, one day, something he looked back upon wistfully. He couldn't imagine it; he couldn't think of any period bleaker than this in all his life, but he'd noticed how time had a way of coloring things. That bird, for instance, had such a pure, sweet, piercing voice.

He turned away from the window, covered his typewriter, and left the room.

. . .

He didn't eat real meals anymore. When he was hungry he drank a glass of milk, or he spooned a bit of ice cream directly from the carton. After the smallest snack he felt overfed and heavy, but he noticed when he dressed in the mornings that he seemed to be losing weight. His shirt collar stood out around his neck. The vertical groove between his nose and mouth had deepened so that he had trouble shaving it. His hair, which Sarah used to cut for him, jutted over his forehead like a shelf. And something had caused his lower lids to droop. He used to have narrow gray slits of eyes; now they were wide and startled. Could this be a sign of malnutrition?

Breakfast: Breakfast was your most important meal. He hooked up the percolator and the electric skillet to the clock radio on his bedroom windowsill. Of course he was asking for food poisoning, letting two raw eggs wait all night at room temperature, but once he'd changed menus there was no problem. You had to be flexible about these matters. He was awakened now by the smell of fresh coffee and hot buttered popcorn, and he could partake of both without getting out of bed. Oh, he was managing fine, just fine. All things considered.

But his nights were terrible.

It wasn't that he had trouble getting to sleep in the first place. That was easy. He'd watch TV till his eyes burned; then he'd climb the stairs. He would start the shower running and spread his clothes in the tub. At times he thought of skipping this part, except there was such a danger in falling behind with your system. So he carried out each step: hanging the laundry, setting up the breakfast things, flossing his teeth. He couldn't go to bed without flossing his teeth. For some reason, Sarah had found this irritating. If Macon were condemned to death, she'd said once, and they told him he'd be executed by firing squad at dawn, he would no doubt still insist on flossing the night before. Macon, after thinking it over, had agreed. Yes, of course he would. Hadn't he flossed while in the depths of pneumonia? In the hospital with gallstones? In a motel the night his son was killed? He checked his teeth in the mirror. They were never entirely white, in spite of all his care. And now it seemed his skin was taking on a yellowish cast as well.

He turned off the lights, moved the cat over, helped the dog up onto the bed. The dog was a Welsh corgi, very shortlegged, but he did love to sleep in a bed, and so every night he stood erect and propped his elbows on the mattress and gazed at Macon expectantly till Macon gave him a boost. Then they'd all three settle themselves. Macon slipped into his envelope, the cat fitted her shape to the warm spot under his arm, and the dog plopped down near his feet. Then Macon closed his eyes and drifted off.

But eventually he found himself conscious of his dreams—not borne along by them but tediously constructing them, quibbling over details. When it dawned on him that he was awake, he would open his eyes and squint at the clock radio. But it was only one a.m. At the latest, two. There were all those hours still to be survived.

His brain buzzed with little worries. Had he left the back door unlocked? Forgotten to put the milk away? Made out a check for his bank balance instead of his gas bill? He remembered all in a rush that he'd opened a can of V-8 juice and then put the can in the icebox. Oxidation of the metal seams! Resulting in lead poisoning!

The worries changed, grew deeper. He wondered what had gone wrong with his marriage. Sarah had been his first and only girlfriend; now he thought he should have practiced on someone else beforehand. During the twenty years of their marriage there'd been moments—there'd been months—when he didn't feel they had really formed a unit the way couples were supposed to. No, they'd stayed two distinct people, and not always even friends. Sometimes they'd seemed more like rivals, elbowing each other, competing over who was the better style of person. Was it Sarah, haphazard, mercurial? Was it Macon, methodical and steady?

When Ethan was born, he only brought out more of their differences. Things they had learned to ignore in each other resurfaced. Sarah never got their son on any kind of schedule at all, was lax and unconcerned. And Macon (oh, he knew it, he admitted it) had been so intent on preparing him for every eventuality that he hadn't had time to enjoy him. Ethan at two, at four floated up into his vision as clearly as a color film projected upon the bedroom ceiling. A chortling, sunny little boy, he'd been, with Macon a stooped shape above him wringing his hands. Macon had been fierce in teaching him, at age six, how to swing a bat; it would have wrenched his soul to have Ethan chosen last for any team. "Why?" Sarah had asked. "If he's chosen last, he's chosen last. Let it be, why don't you." Let it be! Life was so full of things you couldn't do anything about; you had to avert what you could. She laughed when Macon spent one fall collecting Wacky Packs, which had these jokey stickers inside that Ethan liked to plaster his bedroom door with. He'd have more than anyone in the whole third grade, Macon vowed. Long after Ethan lost interest, Macon was still doggedly bringing them home. He knew it was absurd, but still, there was this one last sticker they had not yet managed to get hold of . . .

Ethan went away to camp when he was twelve—a year ago, almost exactly. Most boys started earlier, but Macon had kept delaying it. Why have a child at all, he asked Sarah, if you were only going to ship him off to some godforsaken spot in Virginia? By the time he finally gave in, Ethan was in the top age group—a tall blond sprout of a boy with an open, friendly face and an endearing habit of bouncing on the balls of his feet when he was nervous.

Don't think about it.

He was murdered in a Burger Bonanza his second night at camp. It was one of those deaths that make no sense—the kind where the holdup man has collected his money and is free to go but decides, instead, first to shoot each and every person through the back of the skull.

Ethan wasn't even supposed to be there. He had snuck away from camp with a cabinmate, who waited outside as a lookout.

Blame the camp for not supervising. Blame Burger Bonanza for poor security. Blame the cabinmate for not going in too and altering, perhaps, what took place. (Lookout for what, for God's sake?) Blame Sarah for allowing Ethan to leave home; blame Macon for agreeing; blame even (hell, yes) Ethan. Blame Ethan for wanting to attend that camp and for sneaking off from it, and for entering Burger Bonanza like some headstrong fool while a holdup was in progress. Blame him for so meekly moving to the kitchen with the others, for placing his hands flat against the wall as he was ordered and no doubt bouncing slightly on the balls of his feet . . .

Don't think about it.

The director of the camp, not wanting to break the news on the phone, had driven to Baltimore to tell them in person. Then he'd driven them back to Virginia. Macon often recalled that director. Jim, his name was, Jim Robinson or maybe Robertson—a burly, white-whiskered man with a crew cut, wearing a suit coat, as if in respect, over a Redskins T-shirt. He'd seemed uncomfortable with silence and did his best to fill it with abrupt little fragments of chitchat. Macon hadn't listened, or he'd thought he hadn't; but now all the fragments came back to him. How Jim's mother had been a Baltimorean herself, born the year Babe Ruth was playing for the Orioles. How Jim's tomato plants had been acting queerly, producing only tiny green marbles that fell off the vines before they ripened. How Jim's wife was terrified of driving in reverse and avoided any situation that required it. Macon gave a lot of thought to that now, lying in his bed at night. Could you really drive a car without reversing? What about at intersections, where a bus driver pokes his head out his window and asks you to roll on back a few yards so he can turn? Would she refuse? Macon imagined her, staunch and defiant, glaring straight in front of her and pretending not to notice. The driver escalating into curses, horns blowing, other drivers shouting, "Aw, lady!" It made a nice picture. He kept it firmly in mind.

Finally he would sit up and wriggle out of his sheet. The dog, sighing, roused himself and dropped off the bed to pad downstairs behind him. The floorboards were cool underfoot, the kitchen lino-leum cooler still; there was a glow from the refrigerator as Macon poured himself a glass of milk. He went to the living room and turned on the TV. Generally some black-and-white movie was running—men in suits and felt hats, women with padded shoulders. He didn't try to follow the plot. He took small, steady sips of milk, feeling the calcium traveling to his bones. Hadn't he read that calcium cures insomnia? He absently stroked the cat, who had somehow crept into his lap. It was much too hot to have a cat in his lap, especially this one—a loose-strung, gray tweed female who seemed made of some unusually dense substance. And the dog, most often, would be lying on top of his feet. "It's just you and me, old buddies," Macon would tell them. The cat made a comma of sweat across his bare thighs.

At last he would slip out from under the animals and turn off the TV. He would put his glass in the chlorine solution in the kitchen sink. He would climb the stairs. He'd stand at the bedroom window looking over the neighborhood—black branches scrawled on a purple night sky, a glimmer of white clapboard here and there, occasionally a light. Macon always took comfort if he found a light. Someone else had trouble sleeping too, he assumed. He didn't like to consider any other possibility—a party, for instance, or a heart-to-heart talk with old friends. He preferred to believe that someone else was on his own, sitting up wide awake fending off his thoughts. That made him feel much better. He returned to his bed. He lay down. He closed his eyes and without even trying, he dropped off the edge into sleep.

t h r e e

Sarah telephoned Macon and asked if she could come get the navy blue rug from the dining room.

"Navy blue rug," Macon repeated. (He was stalling for time.)

"I wouldn't mention it except you never liked it," Sarah told him. "You said it was a mistake to have a rug where people were eating."

Yes, he had said that. A crumb catcher, he'd said. Unsanitary. Then why did he feel this sudden, wrenching need to keep the rug for himself?

"Macon, are you there?"

"Yes, I'm here."

"So would you mind if I came and got it?"

"No, I guess not."

"Oh, good. My apartment has these bare floors and you've no idea how—"

She would stop by for the rug and he'd invite her in. He'd offer her a glass of sherry. They would sit on the couch with their sherry and he would say, "Sarah, have you missed me?" Or no, he'd say, "I've missed you, Sarah."

She would say . . .

She said, "I thought I'd drop over Saturday morning, if that's convenient."

But people don't drink sherry in the morning.

And besides: He wouldn't even be here then. "I leave for England tomorrow afternoon," he said.

"Oh, is it time for England again?"

"Maybe you could come this evening."

"No, my car's in the shop."

"Your car? What's wrong with it?"

"Well, I was driving along and . . . you know that little red light on the lefthand side of the dash?"

"What, the oil pressure light?"

"Yes, and so I thought, 'Well, I'll be late for the dentist if I stop and see to it now and anyway, the car does seem to be running all right, so—'"

"Wait. Are you saying the light lit up? And then you went on driving?"

"Well, nothing sounded any different and nothing *acted* any different, so I figured—"

"Jesus, Sarah."

"What's so terrible about that?"

"You've probably ruined the engine."

"No, I did not ruin the engine, for your information. I just need this single, simple repair job but unfortunately it's going to take a few days to do it. Well, never mind. I've got a house key. I'll just let myself in on Saturday."

"Maybe I could bring the rug over."

"I'll wait till Saturday."

"That way I could see your apartment," Macon said. "I've never been inside, you know."

"No, it's not fixed up yet."

"I don't care if it's fixed up."

"It's a disaster. Nothing's been done."

"How could nothing be done? You've been living there over a month."

"Well, I'm not so wonderfully perfectly efficient as you are, Macon."

"You wouldn't have to be efficient to—"

"Some days," Sarah said, "I can't even make it out of my bathrobe."

Macon was silent.

"I should have agreed to teach summer school," Sarah said. "Something to give some shape to things. I open my eyes in the morning and think, 'Why bother getting up?' "

"Me too," Macon said.

"Why bother eating? Why bother breathing?"

"Me too, sweetheart."

"Macon, do you suppose that person has any idea? I want to go see him in prison, Macon. I want to sit on the other side of the grid or the screen or whatever they have and I'll say, 'Look at me. Look. Look at what you did. You didn't just kill the people you shot; you killed other people besides. What you did goes on and on forever. You didn't just kill my son; you killed me; you killed my husband. I mean I can't even manage to put up my curtains; do you understand what you did?' Then when I'm sure that he does understand, that he really does realize, that he feels just terrible, I'm going to open my purse and pull out a gun and shoot him between the eyes."

"Oh, well, sweetheart—"

"You think I'm just raving, don't you. But Macon, I swear, I can feel that little kick against my palm when I fire the gun. I've never fired a gun in my life—Lord, I don't think I've ever *seen* a gun. Isn't it odd? Ethan's seen one; Ethan's had an experience you and I have no notion of. But sometimes I hold my hand out with the thumb cocked like when kids play cowboy, and I fold my trigger finger and feel what a satisfaction it would be."

"Sarah, it's bad for you to talk like this."

"Oh? How am I supposed to talk?"

"I mean if you let yourself get angry you'll be . . . consumed. You'll burn up. It's not productive."

"Oh, productive! Well, goodness, no, let's not waste our time on anything unproductive."

Macon massaged his forehead. He said, "Sarah, I just feel we can't afford to have these thoughts."

"Easy for you to say."

"No, it is not easy for me to say, dammit—"

"Just shut the door, Macon. Just walk away. Just pretend it never happened. Go rearrange your tools, why don't you; line up your wrenches from biggest to smallest instead of from smallest to biggest; that's always fun."

"Goddammit, Sarah—"

"Don't you curse at me, Macon Leary!"

They paused.

Macon said, "Well."

Sarah said, "Well, anyhow."

"So I guess you'll come by while I'm gone," he said.

"If that's all right."

"Yes, certainly," he said.

Although he felt a curious uneasiness when he hung up, as if he were letting a stranger come. As if she might walk off with more than just the dining room rug.

.   .   .

For his trip to England, he dressed in his most comfortable suit. *One suit is plenty,* he counseled in his guidebooks, *if you take along some travel-size packets of spot remover.* (Macon knew every item that came in travel-size packets, from deodorant to shoe polish.) *The suit should be a medium gray. Gray not only hides the dirt; it's handy for sudden funerals and other formal events. At the same time, it isn't too somber for everyday.*

He packed a minimum of clothes and a shaving kit. A copy of his most recent guide to England. A novel to read on the plane.

Bring only what fits in a carry-on bag. Checking your luggage is asking for trouble. Add several travel-size packets of detergent so you won't fall into the hands of foreign laundries.

When he'd finished packing, he sat on the couch to rest. Or not to rest, exactly, but to collect himself—like a man taking several deep breaths before diving into a river.

The furniture was all straight lines and soothing curves. Dust motes hung in a slant of sunlight. What a peaceful life he led here! If this were any other day he'd be making some instant coffee. He would drop the spoon in the sink and stand sipping from his mug while the cat wove between his feet. Then maybe he'd open the mail. Those acts seemed dear and gentle now. How could he have complained of boredom? At home he had everything set up around him so he hardly needed to think. On trips even the smallest task required effort and decisions.

When it was two hours till takeoff, he stood up. The airport was a thirty-minute drive at the most, but he hated feeling rushed. He made a final tour of the house, stopping off at the downstairs bathroom—the last *real* bathroom (was how he thought of it) that he'd see for the next week. He whistled for the dog. He picked up his bag and stepped out the front door. The heat slammed into him like something solid.

The dog was going with him only as far as the vet's. If he'd known that, he never would have jumped into the car. He sat next to Macon, panting enthusiastically, his keg-shaped body alert with expectation. Macon talked to him in what he hoped was an un-alarming tone. "Hot, isn't it, Edward. You want the air conditioner on?" He adjusted the controls. "There now. Feeling better?" He heard something unctuous in his voice. Maybe Edward did, too, for he stopped panting and gave Macon a sudden suspicious look. Macon decided to say no more.

They rolled through the neighborhood, down streets roofed over with trees. They turned into a sunnier section full of stores and service stations. As they neared Murray Avenue, Edward started whimpering. In the parking lot of the Murray Avenue Veterinary Hospital, he somehow became a much smaller animal.

Macon got out of the car and walked around to open the door. When he took hold of Edward's collar, Edward dug his toenails into the upholstery. He had to be dragged all the way to the building, scritching across the hot concrete.

The waiting room was empty. A goldfish tank bubbled in one corner, with a full-color poster above it illustrating the life cycle of the heartworm. There was a girl on a stool behind the counter, a waifish little person in a halter top.

"I've brought my dog for boarding," Macon said. He had to raise his voice to be heard above Edward's moans.

Chewing her gum steadily, the girl handed him a printed form and a pencil. "Ever been here before?" she asked.

"Yes, often."

"What's the last name?"

"Leary."

"Leary. Leary," she said, riffling through a box of index cards. Macon started filling out the form. Edward was standing upright now and clinging to Macon's knees, like a toddler scared of nursery school.

"Whoa," the girl said.

She frowned at the card she'd pulled.

"Edward?" she said. "On Rayford Road?"

"That's right."

"We can't accept him."

"What?"

"Says here he bit an attendant. Says, 'Bit Barry in the ankle, do not readmit.' "

"Nobody told me that."

"Well, they should have."

"Nobody said a word! I left him in June when we went to the beach; I came back and they handed him over."

The girl blinked at him, expressionless.

"Look," Macon said. "I'm on my way to the airport, right this minute. I've got a plane to catch."

"I'm only following orders," the girl said.

"And what set him off, anyhow?" Macon asked. "Did anyone think to wonder? Maybe Edward had good reason!"

The girl blinked again. Edward had dropped to all fours by now and was gazing upward with interest, as if following the conversation.

"Ah, the hell with it," Macon said. "Come on, Edward."

He didn't have to take hold of Edward's collar when they left. Edward galloped ahead of him all the way across the parking lot.

In that short time, the car had turned into an oven. Macon opened his window and sat there with the motor idling. What now? He considered going to his sister's, but she probably wouldn't want Edward either. To tell the truth, this wasn't the first time there had been complaints. Last week, for instance, Macon's brother Charles had stopped by to borrow a router, and Edward had darted in a complete circle around his feet, taking furious little nibbles of his trouser cuffs. Charles was so astonished that he just turned his head slowly, gaping down. "What's got into him?" he asked. "He never *used* to do this." Then when Macon grabbed his collar, Edward had snarled. He'd curled his upper lip and snarled. Could a dog have a nervous breakdown?

Macon wasn't very familiar with dogs. He preferred cats. He liked the way cats kept their own counsel. It was only lately that he'd given Edward any thought at all. Now that he was alone so much he had taken to talking out loud to him, or sometimes he just sat studying him. He admired Edward's intelligent brown eyes and his foxy little face. He appreciated the honey-colored whorls that radiated so symmetrically from the bridge of his nose. And his walk! Ethan used to say that Edward walked as if he had sand in his bathing suit. His rear end waddled busily; his stubby legs seemed hinged by some more primitive mechanism than the legs of taller dogs.

Macon was driving toward home now, for lack of any better idea. He wondered what would happen if he left Edward in the house the way he left the cat, with plenty of food and water. No. Or could Sarah come see to him, two or three times a day? He recoiled from that; it meant asking her. It meant dialing that number he'd never used and asking her for a favor.

MEOW-BOW ANIMAL HOSPITAL, a sign across the street read. Macon braked and Edward lurched forward. "Sorry," Macon told him. He made a left turn into the parking lot.

The waiting room at the Meow-Bow smelled strongly of disinfectant. Behind the counter stood a thin young woman in a ruffled peasant blouse. She had aggressively frizzy black hair that burgeoned to her shoulders like an Arab headdress. "Hi, there," she said to Macon.

Macon said, "Do you board dogs?"

"Sure."

"I'd like to board Edward, here."

She leaned over the counter to look at Edward. Edward panted up at her cheerfully. It was clear he hadn't yet realized what kind of place this was.

"You have a reservation?" the woman asked Macon.

"Reservation! No."

"Most people reserve."

"Well, I didn't know that."

"Especially in the summer."

"Couldn't you make an exception?"

She thought it over, frowning down at Edward. Her eyes were very small, like caraway seeds, and her face was sharp and colorless.

"Please," Macon said. "I'm about to catch a plane. I'm leaving for a week, and I don't have a soul to look after him. I'm desperate, I tell you."

From the glance she shot at him, he sensed he had surprised her in some way. "Can't you leave him home with your wife?" she asked.

He wondered how on earth her mind worked.

"If I could do that," he said, "why would I be standing here?"

"Oh," she said. "You're not married?"

"Well, I am, but she's . . . living elsewhere. They don't allow pets."

"Oh."

She came out from behind the counter. She was wearing very short red shorts; her legs were like sticks. "I'm a divorsy myself," she said. "I know what you're going through."

"And see," Macon said, "there's this place I usually board him but they suddenly claim he bites. Claim he bit an attendant and they can't admit him anymore."

"Edward? Do you bite?" the woman said.

Macon realized he should not have mentioned that, but she seemed to take it in stride. "How could you do such a thing?" she asked Edward. Edward grinned up at her and folded his ears back, inviting a pat. She bent and stroked his head.

"So will you keep him?" Macon said.

"Oh, I guess," she said, straightening. "If you're desperate." She stressed the word—fixing Macon with those small brown eyes—as if giving it more weight than he had intended. "Fill this out," she told him, and she handed him a form from a stack on the counter. "Your name and address and when you'll be back. Don't forget to put when you'll be back."

Macon nodded, uncapping his fountain pen.

"I'll most likely see you again when you come to pick him up," she said. "I mean if you put the time of day to expect you. My name's Muriel."

"Is this place open evenings?" Macon asked.

"Every evening but Sundays. Till eight."

"Oh, good."

"Muriel Pritchett," she said.

Macon filled out the form while the woman knelt to unbuckle Edward's collar. Edward licked her cheekbone; he must have thought she was just being friendly. So when Macon had finished, he didn't say good-bye. He left the form on the counter and walked out very quickly, keeping a hand in his pocket to silence his keys.

.   .   .

On the flight to New York, he sat next to a foreign-looking man with a mustache. Clamped to the man's ears was a headset for one of those miniature tape recorders. Perfect: no danger of conversation. Macon leaned back in his seat contentedly.

He approved of planes. When the weather was calm, you couldn't even tell you were moving. You could pretend you were sitting safe at home. The view from the window was always the same—air and more air—and the interior of the plane was practically interchangeable with the interior of any other.

He accepted nothing from the beverage cart, but the man beside him took off his headset to order a Bloody Mary. A tinny, intricate, Middle Eastern melody came whispering out of the pink sponge earplugs. Macon stared down at the little machine and wondered if he should buy one. Not for the music, heaven knows—there was far too much noise in the world already—but for insulation. He could plug himself into it and no one would disturb him. He could play a blank tape: thirty full minutes of silence. Turn the tape over and play thirty minutes more.

They landed at Kennedy and he took a shuttle bus to his connecting flight, which wasn't due to leave till evening. Once settled in the terminal, he began filling out a crossword puzzle that he'd saved for this occasion from last Sunday's *New York Times*. He sat inside a kind of barricade—his bag on one chair, his suit coat on another. People milled around him but he kept his eyes on the page, progressing smoothly to the acrostic as soon as he'd finished the crossword. By the time he'd solved both puzzles, they were beginning to board the plane.

His seatmate was a gray-haired woman with glasses. She had brought her own knitted afghan. This was not a good sign, Macon felt, but he could handle it. First he bustled about, loosening his tie and taking off his shoes and removing a book from his bag. Then he opened the book and ostentatiously started reading.

The name of his book was *Miss MacIntosh, My Darling*, and it was 1,198 pages long. (*Always bring a book, as protection against strangers. Magazines don't last. Newspapers from home will make you homesick, and newspapers from elsewhere will remind you you don't belong. You know how alien another paper's typeface seems.*) He'd been lugging around *Miss MacIntosh* for years. It had the advantage of being plotless, as far as he could tell, but invariably interesting, so he could dip into it at random. Any time he raised his eyes, he was careful to mark a paragraph with his finger and to keep a bemused expression on his face.

There was the usual mellifluous murmur from the loudspeaker about seatbelts, emergency exits, oxygen masks. He wondered why stewardesses accented such unlikely words. "*On* our flight this evening we *will* be offering . . ." The woman next to him asked if he wanted a Lifesaver. "No, thank you," Macon said, and he went on with his book. She rustled some little bit of paper, and shortly afterward the smell of spearmint drifted over to him.

He refused a cocktail and he refused a supper tray, although he did accept the milk that was offered with it. He ate an apple and a little box of raisins from his bag, drank the milk, and went off to the lavatory to floss and brush his teeth. When he returned, the plane was darker, dotted here and there with reading lamps. Some of the passengers were already asleep. His seatmate had rolled her hair into little O's and X-ed them over with bobby pins. Macon found it amazing that people could be so unselfconscious on airplanes. He'd seen men in whole suits of pajamas; he'd seen women slathered in face cream. You would think they felt no need to be on guard.

He angled his book beneath a slender shaft of light and turned a page. The engines had a weary, dogged sound. It was the period he thought of as the long haul—the gulf between supper and breakfast when they were suspended over the ocean, waiting for that lightening of the sky that was supposed to be morning although, of course, it was nowhere near morning back home. In Macon's opinion, morning in other time zones was like something staged—a curtain painted with a rising sun, superimposed upon the real dark.

He let his head tip back against the seat and closed his eyes. A stewardess's voice, somewhere near the front of the plane, threaded in and out of the droning of the engines. "We just sat and sat and there wasn't a thing to do and all we had was the Wednesday paper and you know how news just never seems to happen on a Wednesday . . ."

Macon heard a man speaking levelly in his ear. "Macon." But he didn't even turn his head. By now he knew these tricks of sound on planes at night. He saw behind his eyelids the soap dish on the kitchen sink at home—another trick, this concreteness of vision. It was an oval china soap dish painted with yellow roses, containing a worn-down sliver of soap and Sarah's rings, her engagement ring and her wedding band, just as she had left them when she walked out.

"I got the tickets," he heard Ethan say. "And they're opening the doors in five minutes."

"All right," Macon told him, "let's plan our strategy."

"Strategy?"

"Where we're going to sit."

"Why would we need strategy for that?"

"It's you who asked to see this movie, Ethan. I would think you'd take an interest in where you're sitting. Now, here's my plan. You go around to that line on the left. Count the little kids. I'll count the line on the right."

"Aw, Dad—"

"Do you want to sit next to some noisy little kid?"

"Well, no."

"And which do you prefer: an aisle seat?"

"I don't care."

"Aisle, Ethan? Or middle of the row? You must have some opinion."

"Not really."

"Middle of the row?"

"It doesn't make any difference."

"Ethan. It makes a great deal of difference. Aisle, you can get out quicker. So if you plan to buy a snack or go to the restroom, you'll want to sit on the aisle. On the other hand, everyone'll be squeezing past you there. So if you don't think you'll be leaving your seat, then I suggest—"

"Aw, Dad, for Christ's sake!" Ethan said.

"Well," Macon said. "If that's the tone you're going to take, we'll just sit any damn place we happen to end up."

"Fine," Ethan said.

"Fine," Macon said.

Now he did turn his head; he rocked it from side to side. But he kept his eyes tightly closed, and in time the voices stopped, and he found himself in that edgy twilight that passes for sleep when you're traveling.

. . .

At dawn he accepted a cup of coffee, and he swallowed a vitamin pill from his bag. The other passengers looked frowsy and pale. His seatmate dragged an entire small suitcase off to the lavatory and returned all combed, but her face was puffy. Macon believed that travel causes retention of fluids. When he put his shoes on, they felt too tight, and when he went to shave he found unfamiliar pillows of flesh beneath his eyes. He was better off than most people, though, because he hadn't touched salted food or drunk any alcohol. Alcohol was definitely retained. Drink alcohol on a plane and you'd feel befuddled for days, Macon believed.

The stewardess announced what time it was in London, and there was a stir as people reset their watches. Macon adjusted the digital alarm clock in his shaving kit. The watch on his wrist—which was not digital but real time, circular—he left as it was.

They landed abruptly. It was like being recalled to the hard facts—all that friction suddenly, the gritty runway, the roaring and braking. The loudspeaker came on, purring courteous reminders. The woman next to Macon folded her afghan. "I'm so excited," she said. "I'm going to see my grandchild for the very first time." Macon smiled and told her he hoped it went well. Now that he didn't have to fear being trapped, he found her quite pleasant. Besides, she was so American-looking.

At Heathrow, there was the usual sense of some recent disaster. People rushed about distractedly, other people stood like refugees surrounded by trunks and parcels, and uniformed authorities were trying to deal with a clamor of questions. Since he didn't have to wait for his luggage, Macon sailed through the red tape far ahead of the others. Then he exchanged his currency and boarded the Underground. *I recommend the Underground for everyone except those*

afraid of heights, and even for them if they will avoid the following
stations, which have exceptionally steep escalators . . .

While the train racketed along, he sorted his currency into
envelopes that he'd brought from home—each envelope clearly
marked with a different denomination. *(No fumbling with unfamil-*
iar coins, no peering at misleading imprints, if you separate and clas-
sify foreign money ahead of time.) Across from him a row of faces
watched. People looked different here, although he couldn't say just
how. He thought they were both finer and unhealthier. A woman
with a fretful baby kept saying, "Hush now, love. Hush now, love,"
in that clear, floating, effortless English voice. It was hot, and her
forehead had a pallid shine. So did Macon's, no doubt. He slid
the envelopes into his breast pocket. The train stopped and more
people got on. They stood above him, clinging not to straps but to
bulbs attached to flexible sticks, which Macon on his first visit had
taken for some kind of microphone.

He was based in London, as usual. From there he would make
brief forays into other cities, never listing more than a handful of
hotels, a handful of restaurants within a tiny, easily accessible radius
in each place; for his guidebooks were anything but all-inclusive.
("Plenty of other books say how to see as much of the city as possible," his boss had told him. "You should say how to see as little.")
The name of Macon's hotel was the Jones Terrace. He would have
preferred one of the American chain hotels, but those cost too
much. The Jones Terrace was all right, though—small and well
kept. He swung into action at once to make his room his own, stripping off the ugly bedspread and stuffing it into a closet, unpacking
his belongings and hiding his bag. He changed clothes, rinsed the
ones he'd worn and hung them in the shower stall. Then, after a
wistful glance at the bed, he went out for breakfast. It was nowhere
near morning back home, but breakfast was the meal that businessmen most often had to manage for themselves. He made a point of
researching it thoroughly wherever he went.

He walked to the Yankee Delight, where he ordered scrambled eggs and coffee. The service here was excellent. Coffee came

at once, and his cup was kept constantly filled. The eggs didn't taste like eggs at home, but then, they never did. What was it about restaurant eggs? They had no character, no backbone. Still, he opened his guidebook and put a checkmark next to the Yankee Delight. By the end of the week, these pages would be barely legible. He'd have scratched out some names, inserted others, and scrawled notes across the margins. He always revisited past entries—every hotel and restaurant. It was tedious but his boss insisted. "Just think how it would look," Julian said, "if a reader walked into some café you'd recommended and found it taken over by vegetarians."

When he'd paid his bill, he went down the street to the New America, where he ordered more eggs and more coffee. "Decaffeinated," he added. (He was a jangle of nerves by now.) The waiter said they didn't have decaffeinated. "Oh, you don't," Macon said. After the waiter had left, Macon made a note in his guidebook.

His third stop was a restaurant called the U.S. Open, where the sausages were so dry that they might have been baked on a rooftop. It figured: The U.S. Open had been recommended by a reader. Oh, the places that readers wrote in to suggest! Macon had once (before he'd grown wiser) reserved a motel room purely on the strength of such a suggestion—somewhere in Detroit or was it Pittsburgh, some city or other, for *Accidental Tourist in America*. He had checked out again at first sight of the linens and fled across the street to a Hilton, where the doorman had rushed to meet him and seized his bag with a cry of pity as if Macon had just staggered in from the desert. Never again, Macon had vowed. He left the sausages on his plate and called for his bill.

In the afternoon (so to speak), he visited hotels. He spoke with various managers and inspected sample rooms where he tested the beds, flushed the toilets, squinted at the showerheads. Most were maintaining their standards, more or less, but something had happened to the Royal Prince. The fact was that it seemed . . . well, foreign. Dark, handsome men in slim silk suits murmured in the lobby while little brown children chased each other around the spittoons. Macon had the feeling he'd got even more hopelessly lost than usual and ended up in Cairo. Cone-shaped ladies in long black veils packed the revolving doors, spinning in from the street with shopping bags full of . . . what? He tried to imagine their purchasing stone-washed denim shorts and thigh-high boots of pink mesh—the merchandise he'd seen in most shop windows. "Er . . ." he said to the manager. How to put this? He hated to sound narrow-minded, but his readers did avoid the exotic. "Has the hotel, ah, changed ownership?" he asked. The manager seemed unusually sensitive. He drew himself up and said the Royal Prince was owned by a corporation, always had been and always would be, always the same corporation. "I see," Macon said. He left feeling dislocated.

At suppertime, he should have tried someplace formal. He had to list at least one formal restaurant in every city for entertaining clients. But tonight he wasn't up to it. Instead, he went to a café he liked called My American Cousin. The diners there had American accents, and so did some of the staff, and the hostess handed out tickets at the door with numbers on them. If your number was called on the loudspeaker you could win a free TV, or at least a framed color print of the restaurant.

Macon ordered a comforting supper of plain boiled vegetables and two lamb chops in white paper bobby socks, along with a glass of milk. The man at the next table was also on his own. He was eating a nice pork pie, and when the waitress offered him dessert he said, "Oh, now, let me see, maybe I will try some at that," in the slow, pleased, coax-me drawl of someone whose womenfolks have all his life encouraged him to put a little meat on his bones. Macon himself had the gingerbread. It came with cream, just the way it used to at his grandmother's house.

By eight o'clock, according to his wristwatch, he was in bed. It was much too early, of course, but he could stretch the day only so far; the English thought it was midnight. Tomorrow he would start his whirlwind dashes through other cities. He'd pick out a few token hotels, sample a few token breakfasts. Coffee with caffeine and coffee without caffeine. Bacon underdone and overdone. Orange juice fresh and canned and frozen. More showerheads, more mattresses. Hair dryers supplied on request? 110-volt switches for electric shavers? When he fell asleep, he thought anonymous rooms were revolving past on a merry-go-round. He thought webbed canvas suitcase stands, ceiling sprinklers, and laminated lists of fire regulations approached and slid away and approached again, over and over all the rest of his days. He thought Ethan was riding a plaster camel and calling, "Catch me!" and falling, but Macon couldn't get there in time and when he reached his arms out, Ethan was gone.

.   .   .

It was one of Macon's bad habits to start itching to go home too early. No matter how short a stay he'd planned, partway through he would decide that he ought to leave, that he'd allowed himself far too much time, that everything truly necessary had already been accomplished—or almost everything, almost accomplished. Then the rest of his visit was spent in phone calls to travel agents and fruitless trips to airline offices and standby waits that came to nothing, so that he was forced to return to the hotel he'd just checked out of. He always promised himself this wouldn't happen again, but somehow it always did. In England, it happened on his fourth afternoon. What more was there to do? he started wondering. Hadn't he got the gist of the place?

Well, be honest: It was Saturday. He chanced to notice, entering the date in his expense book, that at home it was Saturday morning. Sarah would be stopping by the house for the rug.

She would open the front door and smell home. She would pass through the rooms where she'd been so happy all these years. (Hadn't she been happy?) She would find the cat stretched out on the couch, long and lazy and languid, and she'd settle on the cushion next to her and think, *How could I have left?*

Unfortunately, it was summer, and the airlines were overbooked. He spent two days tracking down faint possibilities that evaporated the instant he drew close. "Anything! Get me anything! I don't have to go to New York; I'll go to Dulles. I'll go to Montreal! Chicago! Shoot, I'll go to Paris or Berlin and see if they have flights. Are there ships? How long do ships take, nowadays? What if this were an emergency? I mean my mother on her deathbed or something? Are you saying there's just no way out of this place?"

The people he dealt with were unfailingly courteous and full of chirpy good humor—really, if not for the strain of travel he believed he might actually have liked the English—but they couldn't solve his problem. In the end he had to stay on. He spent the rest of the week huddled in his room watching TV, chewing a knuckle, subsisting on nonperishable groceries and lukewarm soft drinks because he couldn't face another restaurant.

So he was first in line, naturally, at the check-in counter on the day of his departure. He had his pick of seats: window, nonsmoking. Next to him was a very young couple completely absorbed in each other, so he didn't need *Miss MacIntosh* but sat staring out at the clouds all the long, dull afternoon.

Afternoon was never his favorite time; that was the worst of these homeward flights. It was afternoon for hours and hours, through drinks and lunch and drinks again—all of which he waved away. It was afternoon when they showed the movie; the passengers had to pull their shades down. An orange light filled the plane, burdensome and thick.

Once when he'd been away on an unusually difficult trip—to Japan, where you couldn't even memorize the signs in order to find your way back to a place—Sarah had met his plane in New York. It was their fifteenth anniversary and she had wanted to surprise him. She called Becky at the travel agency to ask his flight number and then she left Ethan with her mother and flew to Kennedy, bringing with her a picnic hamper of wine and cheeses which they shared in the terminal while waiting for their plane home. Every detail of that meal remained in Macon's memory: the cheeses set out on a marble slab, the wine in stemmed crystal glasses that had somehow survived the trip. He could still taste the satiny Brie. He could still see Sarah's small, shapely hand resolutely slicing the bread.

But she didn't meet him in New York today.

She didn't even meet him in Baltimore.

He collected his car from the lot and drove into the city through a glowering twilight that seemed to promise something—a thunderstorm or heat lightning, something dramatic. Could she be waiting at home? In her striped caftan that he was so fond of? With a cool summer supper laid out on the patio table?

Careful not to take anything for granted, he stopped at a Seven-Eleven for milk. He drove to the vet's to pick up Edward. He arrived at the Meow-Bow minutes before closing time; somehow, he'd managed to lose his way. There was no one at the counter. He had to ring the service bell. A girl with a ponytail poked her head through a door, letting in a jumble of animal sounds that rose at all different pitches like an orchestra tuning up. "Yes?" she said.

"I'm here for my dog."

She came forward to open a folder that lay on the counter. "Your last name?"

"Leary."

"Oh," she said. "Just a minute."

Macon wondered what Edward had done wrong this time.

The girl disappeared, and a moment later the other one came out, the frizzy one. This evening she wore a V-necked black dress splashed with big pink flowers, its shoulders padded and its skirt too skimpy; and preposterously high-heeled sandals. "Well, hi there!" she said brightly. "How was your trip?"

"Oh, it was . . . where's Edward? Isn't he all right?"

"Sure, he's all right. He was so good and sweet and friendly!"

"Well, fine," Macon said.

"We just got on like a house afire. Seems he took a shine to me, I couldn't say why."

"Wonderful," Macon said. He cleared his throat. "So could I have him back, please?"

"Caroline will bring him."

"Ah."

There was a silence. The woman waited, facing him and wearing a perky smile, with her fingers laced together on the counter. She had painted her nails dark red, Macon saw, and put on a blackish lipstick that showed her mouth to be an unusually complicated shape—angular, like certain kinds of apples.

"Um," Macon said finally. "Maybe I could pay."

"Oh, yes."

She stopped smiling and peered down at the open folder. "That'll be forty-two dollars," she said.

Macon gave her a credit card. She had trouble working the embossing machine; everything had to be done with the flats of her hands, to spare her nails. She filled in the blanks in a jerky scrawl and then turned the bill in his direction. "Signature and phone," she said. She leaned over the counter to watch what he wrote. "Is that your home phone, or your business?"

"It's both. Why? What difference does it make?" he asked.

"I was just wondering," she told him. She tore off his copy, in that splay-fingered style of hers, and put the rest of the bill in a drawer. "I don't know if I mentioned before that it so happens I train dogs."

"Is that right," Macon said.

He looked toward the door where the first girl had disappeared. It always made him nervous when they took too long bringing Edward. What were they doing back there—getting rid of some evidence?

"My speciality is dogs that bite," the woman said.

"Specialty."

"Pardon?"

"Webster prefers 'specialty.' "

She gave him a blank look.

"That must be a dangerous job," Macon said politely.

"Oh, not for me! I'm not scared of a thing in this world."

There was a scuffling sound at the door behind her. Edward burst through, followed by the girl with the ponytail. Edward was giving sharp yelps and flinging himself about so joyfully that when Macon bent to pat him, he couldn't really connect.

"Now, stop that," the girl told Edward. She was trying to buckle his collar. Meanwhile, the woman behind the counter was saying,

"Biters, barkers, deaf dogs, timid dogs, dogs that haven't been treated right, dogs that have learned bad habits, dogs that grew up in pet shops and don't trust human beings . . . I can handle all of those."

"Well, good," Macon said.

"Not that he would bite *me*, of course," the woman said. "He just fell in love with me, like I think I was telling you."

"I'm glad to hear it," Macon said.

"But I could train him in no time not to bite other people. You think it over and call me. Muriel, remember? Muriel Pritchett. Let me give you my card."

She handed him a salmon-pink business card that she seemed to have pulled out of nowhere. He had to fight his way around Edward to accept it. "I studied with a man who used to train attack dogs," she said. "This is not some amateur you're looking at."

"Well, I'll bear that in mind," Macon said. "Thank you very much."

"Or just call for no reason! Call and talk."

"Talk?"

"Sure! Talk about Edward, his problems, talk about . . . anything! Pick up the phone and just talk. Don't you ever get the urge to do that?"

"Not really," Macon said.

Then Edward gave a particularly piercing yelp, and the two of them rushed home.

. . .

Well, of course she wasn't there. He knew it the instant he stepped inside the house, when he smelled that stale hot air and heard the muffled denseness of a place with every window shut. Really he'd known it all along. He'd been fooling himself. He'd been making up fairy tales.

The cat streaked past him and escaped out the door, yowling accusingly. The dog hurtled into the dining room to roll about on the rug and get rid of the scent of the kennel. But there was no rug—only bare, linty floor, and Edward stopped short, looking foolish. Macon knew just how he felt.

He put away the milk and went upstairs to unpack. He took a shower, treading the day's dirty clothes underfoot, and prepared for bed. When he turned off the light in the bathroom, the sight of his laundry dripping over the tub reminded him of travel. Where was the real difference? *Accidental Tourist at Home*, he thought, and he slid wearily into his body bag.

four

When the phone rang, Macon dreamed it was Ethan. He dreamed Ethan was calling from camp, wondering why they'd never come to get him. "But we thought you were dead," Macon said, and Ethan said—in that clear voice of his that cracked on the high notes—"Why would you think *that*?" The phone rang again and Macon woke up. There was a thud of disappointment somewhere inside his rib cage. He understood why people said hearts "sank."

In slow motion, he reached for the receiver. "Yes," he said.

"Macon! Welcome back!"

It was Julian Edge, Macon's boss, his usual loud and sprightly self even this early in the morning. "Oh," Macon said.

"How was the trip?"

"It was okay."

"You just get in last night?"

"Yes."

"Find any super new places?"

"Well, 'super' would be putting it a bit strongly."

"So now I guess you start writing it up."

Macon said nothing.

"Just when do you figure to bring me a manuscript?" Julian asked.

"I don't know," Macon said.

"Soon, do you figure?"

"I don't know."

There was a pause.

"I guess I woke you," Julian said.

"Yes."

"Macon Leary in bed," Julian said. He made it sound like the title of something. Julian was younger than Macon and brasher, breezier, not a serious man. He seemed to enjoy pretending that Macon was some kind of character. "So anyway, can I expect it by the end of the month?"

"No," Macon said.

"Why not?"

"I'm not organized."

"Not organized! What's to organize? All you have to do is retype your old one, basically."

"There's a lot more to it than that," Macon said.

"Look. Fellow. Here it is—" Julian's voice grew fainter. He'd be drawing back to frown at his flashy gold calendar watch with the perforated leather racing band. "Here it is the third of August. I want this thing on the stands by October. That means I'd need your manuscript by August thirty-first."

"I can't do it," Macon said.

In fact, it amazed him he'd found the strength to carry on this conversation.

"August thirty-first, Macon. That's four full weeks away."

"It's not enough," Macon said.

"Not enough," Julian said. "Well. All right, then: mid-September. It's going to knock a good many things out of whack, but I'll give you till mid-September. How's that?"

"I don't know," Macon said.

The dullness of his voice interested him. He felt strangely distant from himself. Julian might have sensed this, for after another pause he said, "Hey. Pal. Are you okay?"

"I'm fine," Macon told him.

"I know you've been through a lot, pal—"

"I'm fine! Just fine! What could be wrong? All I need is time to get organized. I'll have the manuscript in by September fifteenth. Possibly earlier. Yes, very possibly earlier. Maybe the end of August. All right?"

Then he hung up.

. . .

But his study was so dim and close, and it gave off the salty, inky smell of mental fidgeting. He walked in and felt overwhelmed by his task, as if finally chaos had triumphed. He turned around and walked out again.

Maybe he couldn't get his guidebook organized, but organizing the household was another matter entirely. There was something fulfilling about that, something consoling—or more than consoling; it gave him the sense of warding off a danger. Over the next week or so, he traveled through the rooms setting up new systems. He radically rearranged all the kitchen cupboards, tossing out the little bits of things in sticky, dusty bottles that Sarah hadn't opened in years. He plugged the vacuum cleaner into a hundred-foot extension cord originally meant for lawn mowers. He went out to the yard and weeded, trimmed, pruned, clipped—stripping down, he pictured it. Up till now Sarah had done the gardening, and certain features of it came as a surprise to him. One variety of weed shot off seeds explosively the instant he touched it, a magnificent last-ditch stand, while others gave way so easily—too easily, breaking at the topmost joint so their roots remained in the ground. Such tenacity! Such genius for survival! Why couldn't human beings do as well?

He stretched a clothesline across the basement so he wouldn't have to use the dryer. Dryers were a terrible waste of energy. Then he disconnected the dryer's wide flexible exhaust tube, and he taught the cat to go in and out through the empty windowpane where the tube had exited. This meant no more litterbox. Several times a day the cat leapt soundlessly to the laundry sink, stood up long and sinewy on her hind legs, and sprang through the window.

It was a pity Edward couldn't do the same. Macon hated walking him; Edward had never been trained to heel and kept winding his leash around Macon's legs. Oh, dogs were so much trouble. Dogs ate mammoth amounts of food, too; Edward's kibble had to be lugged home from the supermarket, dragged out of the car trunk and up the steep front steps and through the house to the pantry. But for that, at least, Macon finally thought of a solution. At the foot of the old coal chute in the basement he set a plastic trash can, with a square cut out of the bottom. Then he poured the remainder of a sack of kibble into the trash can, which magically became a continuous feeder like the cat's. Next time he bought dog food, he could just drive around to the side of the house and send it rattling down the coal chute.

The only hitch was, Edward turned out to be scared of the basement. Every morning he went to the pantry where his breakfast used to be served, and he sat on his fat little haunches and whimpered. Macon had to carry him bodily down the basement stairs, staggering slightly while Edward scrabbled in his arms. Since the whole idea had been to spare Macon's trick back, he felt he'd defeated his purpose. Still, he kept trying.

Also with his back in mind, he tied the clothes basket to Ethan's old skateboard and he dropped a drawstring bag down the laundry chute at the end of a rope. This meant he never had to carry the laundry either up or down the stairs, or even across the basement. Sometimes, though—laboriously scooting the wheeled basket from the clothesline to the laundry chute, stuffing clean sheets into the bag, running upstairs to haul them in by the long, stiff rope— Macon felt a twinge of embarrassment. Was it possible that this might be sort of silly?

Well, everything was silly, when you got right down to it.

The neighborhood must have learned by now that Sarah had left him. People started telephoning on ordinary weeknights and inviting him to take "potluck" with them. Macon thought at first they meant one of those arrangements where everybody brings a different pot of something and if you're lucky you end up with a balanced meal. He arrived at Bob and Sue Carney's with a bowl of macaroni and cheese. Since Sue was serving spaghetti, he didn't feel he'd been all that lucky. She set his macaroni at one end of the table and no one ate it but Delilah, the three-year-old. She had several helpings, though.

Macon hadn't expected to find the children at the table. He saw he was somebody different now, some kind of bachelor uncle who was assumed to need a glimpse of family life from time to time. But the fact was, he had never much liked other people's children. And gatherings of any sort depressed him. Physical contact with people not related to him—an arm around his shoulder, a hand on his sleeve—made him draw inward like a snail. "You know, Macon," Sue Carney said, leaning across the table to pat his wrist, "whenever you get the urge, you're welcome to drop in on us. Don't wait for an invitation."

"That's nice of you, Sue," he said. He wondered why it was that outsiders' skin felt so unreal—almost waxy, as if there were an invisible extra layer between him and them. As soon as possible, he moved his wrist.

"If you could live any way you wanted," Sarah had once told him, "I suppose you'd end up on a desert island with no other human beings."

"Why! That's not true at all," he'd said. "I'd have you, and Ethan, and my sister and brothers . . ."

"But no people. I mean, people there just by chance, people you didn't know."

"Well, no, I guess not," he'd said. "Would you?"

But of course she would—back then. Back before Ethan died. She'd always been a social person. When there was nothing else to do she'd stroll happily through a shopping mall—Macon's notion of hell, with all those strangers' shoulders brushing his. Sarah thought crowds were exciting. She liked to meet new people. She was fond of parties, even cocktail parties. You'd have to be crazy to like cocktail parties, Macon thought—those scenes of confusion she used to drag him to, where he was made to feel guilty if he managed by some fluke to get involved in a conversation of any depth. "Circulate. Circulate," Sarah would hiss, passing behind him with her drink.

That had changed during this past year. Sarah didn't like crowds anymore. She never went near a mall, hadn't made him go to any parties. They attended only quiet little dinners and she herself had not given a dinner since Ethan died. He'd asked her once, "Shouldn't we have the Smiths and Millards over? They've had us so often."

Sarah said, "Yes. You're right. Pretty soon." And then did nothing about it.

He and she had met at a party. They'd been seventeen years old. It was one of those mixer things, combining their two schools. Even at that age Macon had disliked parties, but he was secretly longing to fall in love and so he had braved this mixer but then stood off in a corner looking unconcerned, he hoped, and sipping his ginger ale. It was 1958. The rest of the world was in button-down shirts, but Macon wore a black turtleneck sweater, black slacks, and sandals. (He was passing through his poet stage.) And Sarah, a bubbly girl with a tumble of copper-brown curls and a round face, large blue eyes, a plump lower lip—she wore something pink, he remembered, that made her skin look radiant. She was ringed by admiring boys. She was short and tidily made, and there was something plucky about the way her little tan calves were so firmly braced, as if she were determined that this looming flock of basketball stars and football stars would not bowl her over. Macon gave up on her at once. No, not even that—he didn't even consider her, not for a single second, but gazed beyond her to other, more attainable girls. So it had to be Sarah who made the first move. She came over to him and asked what he was acting so stuck-up about. "Stuck-up!" he said. "I'm not stuck-up."

"You sure do look it."

"No, I'm just . . . bored," he told her.

"Well, so do you want to dance, or not?"

They danced. He was so unprepared that it passed in a blur. He enjoyed it only later, back home, where he could think it over in a calmer state of mind. And thinking it over, he saw that if he hadn't looked stuck-up she never would have noticed him. He was the only boy who had not openly pursued her. He would be wise not to pursue her in the future; not to seem too eager, not to show his feelings. With Sarah you had to keep your dignity, he sensed.

Lord knows, though, keeping his dignity wasn't easy. Macon lived with his grandparents, and they believed that no one under eighteen ought to have a driver's license. (Never mind if the state of Maryland felt otherwise.) So Grandfather Leary drove Macon and Sarah on their dates. His car was a long black Buick with a velvety gray backseat on which Macon sat all by himself, for his grandfather considered it unseemly for the two of them to sit there together. "I am not your hired chauffeur," he said, "and besides, the backseat has connotations." (Much of Macon's youth was ruled by connotations.) So Macon sat alone in back and Sarah sat up front with Grandfather Leary. Her cloud of hair, seen against the glare of oncoming headlights, reminded Macon of a burning bush. He would lean forward, clear his throat, and ask, "Um, did you finish your term paper?"

Sarah would say, "Pardon?"

"Term paper," Grandfather Leary would tell her. "Boy wants to know if you finished it."

"Oh. Yes, I finished it."

"She finished it," Grandfather Leary relayed to Macon.

"I do have ears, Grandfather."

"You want to get out and walk? Because I don't have to stand for any mouthing off. I could be home with my loved ones, not motoring around in the dark."

"Sorry, Grandfather."

Macon's only hope was silence. He sat back, still and aloof, knowing that when Sarah looked she'd see nothing but a gleam of blond hair and a blank face—the rest darkness, his black turtleneck blending into the shadows. It worked. "What do you *think* about all the time?" she asked in his ear as they two-stepped around her school gym. He only quirked a corner of his mouth, as if amused, and didn't answer.

Things weren't much different when he got his license. Things weren't much different when he went away to college, though he did give up his black turtlenecks and turn into a Princeton man, crisply, casually attired in white shirts and khakis. Separated from Sarah, he felt a constant hollowness, but in his letters he talked only about his studies. Sarah, home at Goucher, wrote back, *Don't you miss me a little? I can't go anywhere we've been for fear I'll see you looking so mysterious across the room.* She signed her letters *I love you* and he signed his *Fondly.* At night he dreamed she lay next to him, her curls making a whispery sound against his pillow, although all they'd done in real life was a lengthy amount of kissing. He wasn't sure, to tell the truth, that he could manage much more without . . . how did they put it in those days? Losing his cool. Sometimes, he was almost angry with Sarah. He felt he'd been backed into a false position. He was forced to present this impassive front if he wanted her to love him. Oh, so much was expected of men!

She wrote she wasn't dating other people. Neither was Macon, but of course he didn't say so. He came home in the summer and worked at his grandfather's factory; Sarah worked on a tan at the neighborhood pool. Halfway through that summer, she said she wondered why he'd never asked to sleep with her. Macon thought about that and then said, levelly, that in fact he'd like to ask her now. They went to her parents' house; her parents were vacationing in Rehoboth. They climbed the stairs to her little bedroom, all white ruffles and hot sunlight baking the smell of fresh paint. "Did you bring a whatchamacallit?" Sarah asked, and Macon, unwilling to admit that he hardly knew what one looked like, barked, "No, I didn't bring a whatchamacallit, who do you think I am?"—a senseless question, if you stopped to examine it, but Sarah took it to mean that he was shocked by her, that he thought her too forward, and she said, "Well, excuse me for living!" and ran down the stairs and out of the house. It took him half an hour to find her, and longer than that to make her stop crying. Really, he said, he'd only been thinking of her welfare: In his experience, whatchamacallits weren't all that safe. He tried to sound knowledgeable and immune to passions of the moment. He suggested she visit a doctor he knew—it happened to be the doctor who treated his grandmother's Female Complaint. Sarah dried her tears and borrowed Macon's pen to write the doctor's name on the back of a chewing gum wrapper. But wouldn't the doctor refuse her? she asked. Wouldn't he say she ought to be at least engaged? Well, all right, Macon said, they would get engaged. Sarah said that would be lovely.

Their engagement lasted three years, all through college. Grandfather Leary felt the wedding should be delayed even further, till Macon was firmly settled in his place of employment; but since his place of employment would be Leary Metals, which manufactured cork-lined caps for soft drink bottles, Macon couldn't see himself concentrating on that even briefly. Besides, the rush to and from Sarah's bedroom on her mother's Red Cross days had begun to tell on them both.

So they married the spring they graduated from college, and Macon went to work at the factory while Sarah taught English at a private school. It was seven years before Ethan was born. By that time, Sarah was no longer calling Macon "mysterious." When he was quiet now it seemed to annoy her. Macon sensed this, but there was nothing he could do about it. In some odd way, he was locked inside the standoffish self he'd assumed when he and she first met. He was frozen there. It was like that old warning of his grandmother's: Don't cross your eyes, they might get stuck that way. No matter how he tried to change his manner, Sarah continued to deal with him as if he were someone unnaturally cool-headed, someone more even in temperament than she but perhaps not quite as feeling.

He had once come upon a questionnaire that she'd filled out in a ladies' magazine—one of those "How Happy Is Your Marriage?" things—and where it said, *I believe I love my spouse more than he/she loves me*, Sarah had checked *True*. The unsettling part was that after Macon gave his automatic little snort of denial, he had wondered if it might be true after all. Somehow, his role had sunk all the way through to the heart. Even internally, by now, he was a fairly chilly man, and if you didn't count his son (who was easy,

easy; a child is no test at all), there was not one person in his life whom he really agonized over.

When he thought about this now, it was a relief to remind himself that he did miss Sarah, after all. But then his relief seemed unfeeling too, and he groaned and shook his head and tugged his hair in great handfuls.

. . .

Some woman phoned and said, "Macon?" He could tell at once it wasn't Sarah. Sarah's voice was light and breathy; this one was rough, tough, wiry. "It's Muriel," she said.

"Muriel," he said.

"Muriel Pritchett."

"Ah, yes," he said, but he still had no clue who she was.

"From the vet's?" she asked. "Who got on so good with your dog?"

"Oh, the vet's!"

He saw her, if dimly. He saw her saying her own name, the long *u* sound and the *p* drawing up her dark red mouth.

"I was just wondering how Edward was."

Macon glanced over at Edward. The two of them were in the study, where Macon had managed to type half a page. Edward lay flat on his stomach with his legs straight out behind him—short, pudgy legs like the drumsticks of a dressed Long Island duckling. "He looks all right to me," Macon said.

"I mean, is he biting?"

"Well, not lately, but he's developed this new symptom. He gets angry if I leave the house. He starts barking and showing his teeth."

"I still think he ought to be trained."

"Oh, you know, he's four and a half and I suppose—"

"That's not too old! I could do it in no time. Tell you what, maybe I could just come around and discuss it. You and me could have a drink or something and talk about what his problems are."

"Well, I really don't think—"

"Or you could come to *my* place. I'd fix you supper."

Macon wondered how it would help Edward to be dragged to supper at some stranger's house.

"Macon? What do you say?" she asked.

"Oh, why, um . . . I think for now I'll just try to manage on my own."

"Well, I can understand that," she said. "Believe me. I've been through that stage. So what I'll do is, I'll wait for you to get in touch. You do still have my card, don't you?"

Macon said he did, although he had no idea where it had got to.

"I don't want to be pushy!" she said.

"No, well . . ." Macon said. Then he hung up and went back to his guidebook.

He was still on the introduction, and it was already the end of August. How would he meet his deadline? The back of the desk chair hit his spine in just the wrong place. The s key kept sticking. The typewriter tapped out audible words. "Inimitable," it said. His typing sounded just like Sarah saying "inimitable." "You in your inimitable way . . ." she told him. He gave a quick shake of his head. *Generally food in England is not as jarring as in other foreign countries. Nice cooked vegetables, things in white sauce, pudding for dessert . . . I don't know why some travelers complain about English food.*

. . .

In September, he decided to alter his system of dressing. If he wore sweat suits at home—the zipper-free kind, nothing to scratch or bind him—he could go from one shower to the next without changing clothes. The sweat suit would serve as both pajamas and day wear.

He bought a couple of them, medium gray. The first night he wore one to bed he enjoyed the feel of it, and he liked not having to dress the next morning. In fact, it occurred to him that he might as well wear the same outfit two days in a row; skip his shower on alternate evenings. Talk about saving energy! In the morning all he had to do was shave. He wondered if he ought to grow a beard.

Around noon of the second day, though, he started feeling a little low. He was sitting at his typewriter and something made him notice his posture—stooped and sloppy. He blamed the sweat suit. He rose and went to the full-length mirror in the hall. His reflection reminded him of a patient in a mental hospital. Part of the trouble, perhaps, was his shoes—regular black tie shoes intended for dressier clothes. Should he buy sneakers? But he would hate to be mistaken for a jogger. He noticed that without a belt around his waist, he tended to let his stomach stick out. He stood up straighter. That evening when it was time to wash the first sweat suit, he used extra-hot water to shrink out some of the bagginess.

He felt much worse in the morning. It had been a warm night and he woke up sticky and cross. He couldn't face the thought of popcorn for breakfast. He laundered a load of sheets and then, in the midst of hanging them, found himself standing motionless with his head bowed, both wrists dangling over the clothesline as if he himself had been pinned there. "Buck up," he said aloud. His voice sounded creaky, out of practice.

This was his day for grocery shopping—Tuesday, when the supermarket was least crowded with other human beings. But somehow, he couldn't bring himself to get going. He dreaded all that business with the address books, the three tabbed books he shopped with. (One held data from *Consumer Reports*—the top-rated brand of bread, for instance, listed under B. In another he noted prices, and in the third he filed his coupons.) He kept having to stop and riffle through them, muttering prices under his breath, comparing house brands to cents-off name brands. Oh, everything seemed so complicated. Why bother? Why eat at all, in fact?

On the other hand, he needed milk. And Edward was low on dog food, and Helen was completely out of cat food.

He did something he'd never done before. He telephoned The Market Basket, a small, expensive grocery that delivered. And he didn't order just emergency rations. No, he called in the whole week's list. "Shall we bring this to the front or the back?" the clerk asked in her tinselly voice.

"The back," Macon said. "No, wait. Bring the perishables to the back, but put the dog food next to the coal chute."

"Coal chute," the clerk repeated, apparently writing it down.

"The coal chute at the side of the house. But not the cat food; that goes in back with the perishables."

"Well, wait now—"

"And the upstairs items at the front of the house."

"What upstairs items?"

"Toothpaste, Ivory soap, dog biscuits . . ."

"I thought you said the dog biscuits went to the coal chute."

"Not the dog biscuits, the dog *food*! It's the food that goes to the coal chute, dammit."

"Now, look here," the clerk said. "There's no call to be rude."

"Well, I'm sorry," Macon told her, "but I just want the simplest thing, it seems to me: one puny box of Milkbone biscuits up beside my bed. If I give Edward my buttered popcorn it upsets his stomach. Otherwise I wouldn't mind; it's not as if I'm hoarding it all for myself or something, but he has this sensitivity to fats and I'm the only one in the house, it's me who has to clean up if he gets sick. I'm the only one to do it; I'm all alone; it's just me; it seems everybody's just . . . fled from me, I don't know, I've lost them, I'm left standing here saying, 'Where'd they go? Where is everybody? Oh, God, what did I do that was so bad?' "

His voice was not behaving right and he hung up. He stood over the telephone rubbing his forehead. Had he given her his name? Or not. He couldn't remember. Please, please, let him not have given her his name.

He was falling apart; that much was obvious. He would have to get a grip on himself. First thing: out of this sweat suit. It was some kind of jinx. He clapped his hands together briskly, and then he climbed the stairs. In the bathroom, he yanked off the sweat suit and dropped it into the tub. Yesterday's hung from the shower curtain rod, still damp. There wasn't a chance it would be dry by tonight. What a mistake! He felt like a fool. He'd come within an inch, within a hairsbreadth of turning into one of those pathetic creatures you see on the loose from time to time—unwashed, unshaven, shapeless, talking to themselves, padding along in their institutional garb.

Neatly dressed now in a white shirt and khakis, he gathered the damp sweat suit and carried it down to the basement. It would make good winter pajamas, at least. He put it in the dryer, wedged the exhaust tube in the window again, and set the dials. Better to consume a little energy than to fall into despair over a soggy sweat suit.

At the top of the basement stairs, Edward was complaining. He was hungry, but not brave enough to descend the stairs on his own. When he caught sight of Macon he lay flat, with his nose poking over the topmost step, and put on a hopeful expression. "Coward," Macon told him. He scooped Edward up in both arms and turned to lumber back down. Edward's teeth started chattering—a tickety-tick like rice in a cup. It occurred to Macon that Edward might know something he didn't. Was the basement haunted, or what? It had been weeks now, and Edward was still so frightened that sometimes, set in front of his food, he just stood there dismally and made a puddle without bothering to lift his leg. "You're being very silly, Edward," Macon told him.

Just then, an eerie howl rose from . . . where? From the basement's very air, it seemed. It continued steadily; it grew. Edward, who must have been expecting this all along, kicked off instantly with his sturdy, clawed hind legs against Macon's diaphragm. Macon felt the wind knocked out of him. Edward whomped into the wall of damp body bags on the clothesline, rebounded, and landed in the center of Macon's stomach. Macon set one foot blindly in the wheeled basket and his legs went out from under him. He stepped down hard into empty space.

He was lying on his back, on the clammy cement floor, with his left leg doubled beneath him. The sound that had set all this in motion paused for one split second and then resumed. It was clear now that it came from the dryer's exhaust tube. "Shoot," Macon said to Edward, who lay panting on top of him. "Wouldn't you think that idiot cat would know the dryer was running?"

He could see how it must have happened. Attempting to enter from outside, she'd been met by a whistling wind, but she had stubbornly continued into the tube. He pictured her eyes pressed into slits, her ears flattened back by a lint-filled gale. Wailing and protesting, she had nonetheless clung to her course. What persistence!

Macon shook Edward off and rolled over on his stomach. Even so small a movement caused him agony. He felt a lump of nausea beginning in his throat, but he rolled once more, dragging his leg behind him. With his teeth set, he reached for the door of the dryer and pulled it open. The sweat suit slowly stopped revolving. The cat stopped howling. Macon watched her bumbling, knobby shape inching backward through the tube. Just as she reached her exit, the entire tube fell out of the window and into the laundry sink, but Helen didn't fall with it. He hoped she was all right. He watched until she scurried past the other window, looking just slightly rumpled. Then he drew a breath and began the long, hard trip up the stairs for help.

f i v e

O h, I've erred and I have stumbled," Macon's sister sang in the kitchen, "I've been sinful and unwise . . ."

She had a tremulous soprano that sounded like an old lady's, although she was younger than Macon. You could imagine such a voice in church, some country kind of church where the women still wore flat straw hats.

I'm just a lucky pilgrim
On the road to Paradise.

Macon was lying on the daybed in his grandparents' sun porch. His left leg, encased in plaster from mid-thigh to instep, was not painful so much as absent. There was a constant dull, cottony numbness that made him want to pinch his own shin. Not that he could, of course. He was sealed away from himself. The hardest blow felt like a knock on the wall from a neighboring room.

Still, he felt a kind of contentment. He lay listening to his sister fix breakfast, idly scratching the cat who had made herself a nest in the blankets. "I've had trials, I've had sorrows," Rose trilled merrily, "I've had grief and sacrifice . . ." Once she got the coffee started, she would come help him across the living room to the downstairs bathroom. He still found it difficult to navigate, especially on polished floors. Nowadays he marveled at all those people on crutches whom he used to take for granted. He saw them as a flock of stalky wading birds, dazzlingly competent with their sprightly hops and debonair pivots. How did they do it?

His own crutches, so new their rubber tips were not yet scuffed, leaned against the wall. His bathrobe hung over a chair. Beneath the window was a folding card table with a wood-grained cardboard top and rickety legs. His grandparents had been dead for years, but the table remained set up as if for one of their eternal bridge games. Macon knew that on its underside was a yellowed label reading ATLAS MFG. CO. with a steel engraving of six plump, humorless men in high-collared suits standing upon a board laid across the very same table. FURNISHINGS OF DECEPTIVE DELICACY, the caption said. Macon associated the phrase with his grandmother: deceptive delicacy. Lying on the sun porch floor as a boy, he had studied her fragile legs, from which her anklebones jutted out like doorknobs. Her solid, black, chunky-heeled shoes were planted squarely a foot apart, never tapping or fidgeting.

He heard his brother Porter upstairs, whistling along with Rose's song. He knew it was Porter because Charles never whistled. There was the sound of a shower running. His sister looked through the sun porch door, with Edward peering around her and panting at Macon as if he were laughing.

"Macon? Are you awake?" Rose asked.

"I've *been* awake for hours," he told her, for there was something vague about her that caused her brothers to act put-upon and needy whenever she chanced to focus on them. She was pretty in a sober, prim way, with beige hair folded unobtrusively at the back of her neck where it wouldn't be a bother. Her figure was a very young girl's, but her clothes were spinsterly and concealing.

She wrapped him in his bathrobe and helped him stand up. Now his leg actively hurt. It seemed the pain was a matter of gravity. A throbbing ache sank slowly down the length of the bone. With Rose supporting him on one side and a crutch on the other, he hobbled out of the sun porch, through the living room with its shabby, curlicued furniture. The dog kept getting underfoot. "Maybe I could stop and rest a moment," Macon said when they passed the couch.

"It's only a little farther."

They entered the pantry. Rose opened the bathroom door and helped him inside. "Call me when you're ready," she said, closing the door after him. Macon sagged against the sink.

At breakfast, Porter was cheerily talkative while the others ate in silence. Porter was the best-looking of all the Learys—more tightly knit than Macon, his hair a brighter shade of blond. He gave an impression of vitality and direction that his brothers lacked. "Got a lot to do today," he said between mouthfuls. "That meeting with Herrin, interviews for Dave's old job, Cates flying in from Atlanta . . ."

Charles just sipped his coffee. While Porter was already dressed, Charles still wore his pajamas. He was a soft, sweet-faced man who never seemed to move; any time you looked at him he'd be watching you with his sorrowful eyes that slanted downward at the outer corners.

Rose brought the coffeepot from the stove. "Last night, Edward woke me twice asking to go out," she said. "Do you think he has some sort of kidney problem?"

"It's the adjustment," Macon said. "Adjustment to change. I wonder how he knows not to wake *me*."

Porter said, "Maybe we could rig up some sort of system. One of those little round pet doors or something."

"Edward's kind of portly for a pet door," Macon said.

"Besides," Rose said, "the yard's not fenced. We can't let him out on his own if he's not fenced in."

"A litterbox, then," Porter suggested.

"Litterbox! For a dog?"

"Why not? If it were big enough."

Macon said, "Use a bathtub. The one in the basement. No one goes there anymore."

"But who would clean it?"

"Ah."

They all looked down at Edward, who was lying at Rose's feet. He rolled his eyes at them.

"How come you have him, anyway?" Porter asked Macon.

"He was Ethan's."

"Oh. I see," Porter said. He gave a little cough. "Animals!" he said brightly. "Ever considered what they must think of us? I mean, here we come back from the grocery store with the most amazing haul—chicken, pork, half a cow. We leave at nine and we're back at ten, evidently having caught an entire herd of beasts. They must think we're the greatest hunters on earth!"

Macon leaned back in his chair with his coffee mug cupped in both hands. The sun was warming the breakfast table, and the kitchen smelled of toast. He almost wondered whether, by some devious, subconscious means, he had engineered this injury—every elaborate step leading up to it—just so he could settle down safe among the people he'd started out with.

. . .

Charles and Porter left for the factory, and Rose went upstairs and ran the vacuum cleaner. Macon, who was supposed to be typing his guidebook, struggled back to the sun porch and collapsed. Since he'd come home he'd been sleeping too much. The urge to sleep was like a great black cannonball rolling around inside his skull, making his head heavy and droopy.

On the wall at the end of the room hung a portrait of the four Leary children: Charles, Porter, Macon, and Rose, clustered in an armchair. Their grandfather had commissioned that portrait several years before they came to live with him. They were still in California with their mother—a giddy young war widow. From time to time she sent snapshots, but Grandfather Leary found those inadequate. By their very nature, he told her in his letters, photos lied. They showed what a person looked like over a fraction of a second—not over long, slow minutes, which was what you'd take to study someone in real life. In that case, said Alicia, didn't paintings lie also? They showed hours instead of minutes. It wasn't Grandfather Leary she said this to, but the artist, an elderly Californian whose name Grandfather Leary had somehow got hold of. If the artist had had a reply, Macon couldn't remember what it was.

He could remember sitting for the portrait, though, and now when he looked at it he had a very clear picture of his mother standing just outside the gilded frame in a pink kimono, watching the painting take shape while she toweled her hair dry. She had fluffy, short, brittle hair whose color she "helped along," as she put it. Her face was a type no longer seen — it wasn't just unfashionable, it had vanished altogether. How did women mold their basic forms to suit the times? Were there no more of those round chins, round foreheads, and bruised, baroque little mouths so popular in the forties?

The artist, it was obvious, found her very attractive. He kept pausing in his work to say he wished she were the subject. Alicia gave a breathless laugh and shooed away his words with one hand. Probably later she had gone out with him a few times. She was always taking up with new men, and they were always the most exciting men in the world, to hear her tell it. If they were artists, why, she had to give a party and get all her friends to buy their paintings. If they flew small planes on weekends, she had to start pilot's lessons. If they were political, there she was on street corners thrusting petitions on passersby. Her children were too young to worry about the men themselves, if there was any reason to worry. No, it was her enthusiasm that disturbed them. Her enthusiasm came in spurts, a violent zigzag of hobbies, friends, boyfriends, causes. She always seemed about to fall over the brink of something. She was always going too far. Her voice had an edge to it, as if at any moment it might break. The faster she talked and the brighter her eyes grew, the more fixedly her children stared at her, as if willing her to follow their example of steadiness and dependability. "Oh, what is it with you?" she would ask them. "Why are you such sticks?" And she would give up on them and flounce off to meet her crowd. Rose, the baby, used to wait for her return in the hall, sucking her thumb and stroking an old fur stole that Alicia never wore anymore.

Sometimes Alicia's enthusiasm turned to her children—an unsettling experience. She took them all to the circus and bought them cotton candy that none of them enjoyed. (They liked to keep themselves tidy.) She yanked them out of school and enrolled them briefly in an experimental learning community where no one wore clothes. The four of them, chilled and miserable, sat hunched in a row in the common room with their hands pressed flat between their bare knees. She dressed as a witch and went trick-or-treating with them, the most mortifying Halloween of their lives, for she got carried away as usual and cackled, croaked, scuttled up to strangers and shook her ragged broom in their faces. She started making mother-daughter outfits for herself and Rose, in strawberry pink with puffed sleeves, but stopped when the sewing machine pierced her finger and made her cry. (She was always getting hurt. It may have been because she rushed so.) Then she turned to something else, and something else, and something else. She believed in change as if it were a religion. Feeling sad? Find a new man! Creditors after you, rent due, children running fevers? Move to a new apartment! During one year, they moved so often that every day after school, Macon had to stand deliberating a while before setting out for home.

In 1950, she decided to marry an engineer who traveled around the world building bridges. "Portugal. Panama. Brazil," she told the children. "We'll finally get to see our planet." They gazed at her stonily. If they had met this man before, they had no recollection of it. Alicia said, "Aren't you excited?" Later—it may have been after he took them all out to dinner—she said she was sending them to live with their grandparents instead. "Baltimore's more suitable for children, really," she said. Did they protest? Macon couldn't remember. He recalled his childhood as a glassed-in place with grown-ups rushing past, talking at him, making changes, while he himself stayed mute. At any rate, one hot night in June Alicia put them on a plane to Baltimore. They were met by their grandparents, two thin, severe, distinguished people in dark clothes. The children approved of them at once.

After that, they saw Alicia only rarely. She would come breez-ing into town with an armload of flimsy gifts from tropical coun-tries. Her print dresses struck the children as flashy; her makeup was too vivid, like a foreigner's. She seemed to find her children comical — their navy-and-white school uniforms, their perfect pos-ture. "My God! How stodgy you've grown!" she would cry, evi-dently forgetting she'd thought them stodgy all along. She said they took after their father. They sensed this wasn't meant as a compli-ment. (When they asked what their father had been like, she looked down at her own chin and said, "Oh, Alicia, grow up.") Later, when her sons married, she seemed to see even more resem-blance, for at one time or another she'd apologized to all three daughters-in-law for what they must have to put up with. Like some naughty, gleeful fairy, Macon imagined, she darted in and out of their lives leaving a trail of irresponsible remarks, apparently never considering they might be passed on. "I don't see how you stay mar-ried to the man," she'd said to Sarah. She herself was now on her fourth husband, a rock-garden architect with a white goatee.

It was true the children in the portrait seemed unrelated to her. They lacked her blue-and-gold coloring; their hair had an ashy cast and their eyes were a steely gray. They all had that distinct center groove from nose to upper lip. And never in a million years would Alicia have worn an expression so guarded and suspicious.

Uncomfortably arranged-looking, they gazed out at the viewer. The two older boys, plump Charles and trim Porter, perched on ei-ther arm of the chair in white shirts with wide, flat, open collars. Rose and Macon sat on the seat in matching playsuits. Rose ap-peared to be in Macon's lap, although actually she'd been settled between his knees, and Macon had the indrawn tenseness of some-one placed in a physically close situation he wasn't accustomed to. His hair, like the others', slanted silkily across his forehead. His mouth was thin, almost colorless, and firmed a bit, as if he'd de-cided to take a stand on something. The set of that mouth echoed now in Macon's mind. He glanced at it, glanced away, glanced back. It was Ethan's mouth. Macon had spent twelve years imagining

Ethan as a sort of exchange student, a visitor from the outside world, and here it turned out he'd been a Leary all along. What a peculiar thing to recognize at this late date.

He sat up sharply and reached for his trousers, which Rose had cut short across the left thigh and hemmed with tiny, even stitches.

. . .

No one else in the world had the slightest idea where he was. Not Julian, not Sarah, not anyone. Macon liked knowing that. He said as much to Rose. "It's nice to be so unconnected," he told her. "I wish things could stay that way a while."

"Why can't they?"

"Oh, well, you know, someone will call here, Sarah or someone—"

"Maybe we could just not answer the phone."

"What, let it go on ringing?"

"Why not?"

"Not answer it *any* time?"

"Most who call me are neighbors," Rose said. "They'll pop over in person if they don't get an answer. And you know the boys: Neither one of them likes dealing with telephones."

"That's true," Macon said.

Julian would come knocking on his door, planning to harangue him for letting his deadline slip past. He'd have to give up. Then Sarah would come for a soup ladle or something, and when he didn't answer she would ask the neighbors and they'd say he hadn't shown his face in some time. She would try to get in touch with his family and the telephone would ring and ring, and then she would start to worry. *What's happened?* she would wonder. *How could I have left him on his own?*

Lately, Macon had noticed he'd begun to view Sarah as a form of enemy. He'd stopped missing her and started plotting her remorsefulness. It surprised him to see how quickly he'd made the transition. Was this what two decades of marriage amounted to? He liked to imagine her self-reproaches. He composed and recomposed her apologies. He hadn't had such thoughts since he was a child, dreaming of how his mother would weep at his funeral.

In the daytime, working at the dining room table, he would hear the telephone and he'd pause, fingers at rest on the typewriter keys. One ring, two rings. Three rings. Rose would walk in with a jar of silver polish. She didn't even seem to hear. "What if that's some kind of emergency?" he would ask. Rose would say, "Hmm? Who would call *us* for an emergency?" and then she would take the silver from the buffet and spread it at the other end of the table.

There had always been some family member requiring Rose's care. Their grandmother had been bedridden for years before she died, and then their grandfather got so senile, and first Charles and later Porter had failed in their marriages and come back home. So she had enough right here to fill her time. Or she made it enough; for surely it couldn't be necessary to polish every piece of silver every week. Shut in the house with her all day, Macon noticed how painstakingly she planned the menus; how often she reorganized the utensil drawer; how she ironed even her brothers' socks, first separating them from the clever plastic grips she used to keep them mated in the washing machine. For Macon's lunch, she cooked a real meal and served it on regular place mats. She set out cut-glass dishes of pickles and olives that had to be returned to their bottles later on. She dolloped homemade mayonnaise into a tiny bowl.

Macon wondered if it ever occurred to her that she lived an odd sort of life—unemployed, unmarried, supported by her brothers. But what job would she be suited for? he asked himself. Although he could picture her, come to think of it, as the mainstay of some musty, antique law firm or accounting firm. Nominally a secretary, she would actually run the whole business, arranging everything just so on her employer's desk every morning and allowing no one below her or above her to overlook a single detail. Macon could use a secretary like that. Recalling the gum-chewing redhead in Julian's disastrous office, he sighed and wished the world had more Roses.

He zipped a page from his typewriter and set it face down on a stack of others. He had finished with his introduction—general instructions like A *subway is not an underground train* and *Don't say restroom, say toilet*—and he'd finished the chapter called "Trying to Eat in England." Rose had mailed those off for him yesterday. That was his new stratagem: sending his book piece by piece from this undisclosed location. "There's no return address on this," Rose told him. "There's not meant to be," Macon said. Rose had nodded solemnly. She was the only one in the family who viewed his guidebooks as real writing. She kept a row of them in her bedroom bookcase, alphabetized by country.

In midafternoon, Rose stopped work to watch her favorite soap opera. This was something Macon didn't understand. How could she waste her time on such trash? She said it was because there was a wonderfully evil woman in it. "There are enough evil people in real life," Macon told her.

"Yes, but not wonderfully evil."

"Well, that's for sure."

"This one, you see, is so obvious. You know exactly whom to mistrust."

While she watched, she talked aloud to the characters. Macon could hear her in the dining room. "It isn't *you* he's after, sweetie," she said, and "Just you wait. Ha!"—not at all her usual style of speech. A commercial broke in, but Rose stayed transfixed where she was. Macon, meanwhile, worked on "Trying to Sleep in England," typing away in a dogged, uninspired rhythm.

When the doorbell rang, Rose didn't respond. Edward went mad, barking and scratching at the door and running back to Macon and racing again to the door. "Rose?" Macon called. She said nothing. Finally he stood up, assembled himself on his crutches, and went as quietly as possible to the hall.

Well, it wasn't Sarah. A glance through the lace curtain told him that much. He opened the door and peered out. "Yes?" he said.

It was Garner Bolt, a neighbor from home—a scrawny little gray man who had made his fortune in cleaning supplies. When he saw Macon, every line in his pert, pointed face turned upward. "There you are!" he said. It was hard to hear him over Edward, who went on barking frantically.

"Why, Garner," Macon said.

"We worried you had died."

"You did?"

Macon grabbed at Edward's collar, but missed.

"Saw the papers piling up on your lawn, mail inside your screen door, didn't know what to think."

"Well, I meant to send my sister for those," Macon said. "I broke my leg, you see."

"Now, how did you do that?"

"It's a long story."

He gave up blocking the door. "Come on in," he told Garner.

Garner took off his cap, which had a Sherwin-Williams Paint sign across the front. His jacket was part of some long-ago suit, a worn shiny brown, and his overalls were faded to white at the knees. He stepped inside, skirting the dog, and shut the door behind him. Edward's barks turned to whimpers. "My car is full of your mail," Garner said. "Brenda said I ought to bring it to your sister and ask if she knew of your whereabouts. Also I promised your friend."

"What friend?"

"Lady in pedal pushers."

"I don't know any lady in pedal pushers," Macon said. He hadn't realized pedal pushers still existed, even.

"Saw her standing on your porch, rattling your doorknob. Calling out, 'Macon? You in there?' Skinny little lady with hair. Looked to be in her twenties or so."

"Well, I can't imagine who it was."

"Squinching in and shading her eyes."

"Who could it be?"

"Tripping down the porch steps in her great tall pointy high heels."

"The dog lady," Macon said. "Jesus."

"Kind of young, ain't she?"

"I don't even know her!"

"Going round the back of the house to call out, 'Macon? Macon?'"

"I barely met her!"

"It was her that told me about the windle."

"Windle?"

"Windle to the basement, all broke out. Fall sets in and it'll turn your furnace on. Waste all kinds of energy."

"Oh. Well. Yes, I suppose it would," Macon said.

"We thought you might've been burglarized or something."

Macon led the way to the dining room. "See, what happened," he said, "I broke my leg and I came to live at my family's till I could manage for myself again."

"We didn't see no ambulance though or nothing."

"Well, I called my sister."

"Sister's a doctor?"

"Just to come and take me to the emergency room."

"When Brenda broke her hip on the missing step," Garner said, "she called the ambulance."

"Well, I called my sister."

"Brenda called the ambulance."

They seemed to be stuck.

"I guess I ought to notify the post office about my mail," Macon said finally. He lowered himself into his chair.

Garner pulled out another chair and sat down with his cap in his hands. He said, "I could just keep on bringing it."

"No, I'll have Rose notify them. Lord, all these bills must be coming due and so forth—"

"I could bring it just as easy."

"Thanks anyway."

"Why don't I bring it."

"To tell the truth," Macon said, "I'm not so sure I'll be going back there."

This hadn't occurred to him before. He placed his crutches together delicately, like a pair of chopsticks, and laid them on the floor beside his chair. "I might stay on here with my family," he said.

"And give up that fine little house?"

"It's kind of big for just one person."

Garner frowned down at his cap. He put it on his head, changed his mind, and took it off again. "Look," he said. "Back when me and Brenda were newlyweds we were awful together. Just awful. Couldn't neither one of us stand the other, I'll never know how we lasted."

"We aren't newlyweds, though," Macon said. "We've been married twenty years."

"Brenda and me did not speak to each other for very nearly every bit of nineteen and thirty-five," Garner said. "January to August, nineteen and thirty-five. New Year's Day till my summer vacation. Not a single blessed word."

Macon's attention was caught. "What," he said, "not even 'Pass the salt'? 'Open the window'?"

"Not even that."

"Well, how did you manage your daily life?"

"Mostly, she stayed over to her sister's."

"Oh, then."

"The morning my vacation began, I felt so miserable I like to died. Thought to myself, 'What am I doing, anyhow?' Called long distance to Ocean City and booked a room for two. In those days long distance was some big deal, let me tell you. Took all these operators and so forth and it cost a mint. Then I packed some clothes for me and some clothes for Brenda and went on over to her sister's house. Her sister says, 'What do *you* want?' She was the type that likes to see dissension. I walk right past her. Find Brenda in the living room, mending hose. Open my suitcase: 'Look at here. Your sundress for dining in a seafood restaurant,' I tell her. 'Two pairs of shorts. Two blouses. Your swimsuit.' She don't even look at me. 'Your bathrobe,' I say. 'Your nightgown you wore on our honeymoon.' Acts like I'm not even there. 'Brenda,' I tell her. I say, 'Brenda, I am nineteen years old and I'll never be nineteen again. I'll never be *alive* again. I mean this is the only life I get to go through, Brenda, so far as I know, and I've spent this great large chunk of it sitting alone in an empty apartment too proud to make up, too scared you'd say no, but even if you did say no it can't be worse than what I got now. I'm the loneliest man in the world,

Brenda, so please come to Ocean City with me.' And Brenda, she lays down her mending and says, 'Well, since you ask, but it looks to me like you forgot my bathing cap.' And off we went."

He sat back triumphantly in his chair. "So," he said.

"So," Macon said.

"So you get my point."

"What point?"

"You have to let her know you need her."

"See, Garner, I think we've gone beyond little things like letting her know I—"

"Don't take this personally, Macon, but I got to level with you: There's times when you've been sort of frustrating. I'm not talking about myself, mind; *I* understand. It's just some of the others in the neighborhood, they've been put off a little. Take during your tragedy. I mean people like to offer help at occasions like that— send flowers and visit at the viewing hour and bring casseroles for after the service. Only you didn't even have a service. Held a cremation, Lord God, somewheres off in Virginia without a word to anyone and come home directly. Peg Everett tells you she's put you in her prayers and Sarah says, 'Oh, bless you, Peg,' but what do *you* say? You ask Peg if her son might care to take Ethan's bike off your hands."

Macon groaned. "Yes," he said, "I never know how to behave at these times."

"Then you mow your lawn like nothing has happened."

"The grass did keep on growing, Garner."

"We was all dying to do it for you."

"Well, thanks," Macon said, "but I enjoyed the work."

"See what I mean?"

Macon said, "Now, wait. Just to insert some logic into this discussion—"

"That's *exactly* what I mean!"

"You started out talking about Sarah. You've switched to how I disappoint the neighbors."

"What's the difference? You might not know this, Macon, but you come across as a person that charges ahead on your own somewhat. Just look at the way you walk! The way you, like, *lunge*, lope on down the street with your head running clear in front of your body. If a fellow wants to stop you and, I don't know, offer his con-dolences, he'd be liable to get plowed down. Now, I know you care, and you know you care, but how does it look to the others? I ask you! No wonder she up and left."

"Garner, I appreciate your thoughts on this," Macon said, "but Sarah's fully aware that I care. I'm not as tongue-tied as you like to make out. And this isn't one of those open-shut, can-this-marriage-be-saved deals, either. I mean, you're just plain goddamned *wrong*, Garner."

"Well," Garner said. He looked down at his cap, and after a mo-ment he jammed it abruptly on his head. "I guess I'll fetch your mail in, then," he said.

"Right. Thanks."

Garner rose to his feet and shuffled out. His leaving alerted Ed-ward, who started barking all over again. There was an empty spell during which Macon looked down at his cast and listened to the soap opera from the living room. Meanwhile Edward whined at the door and paced back and forth, clicking his toenails. Then Garner returned. "Mostly catalogs," he said, flinging his load on the table. He brought with him the smell of fresh air and dry leaves. "Brenda said we might as well not bother with the newspapers; just throw them out."

"Oh, yes, of course," Macon said.

He stood up and they shook hands. Garner's fingers were crisp and intricately shaped, like crumpled paper. "Thanks for stopping by," Macon told him.

"Any time," Garner said, looking elsewhere.

Macon said, "I didn't mean, you know—I hope I didn't sound short-tempered."

"Naw," Garner said. He lifted an arm and let it drop. "Shoot. Don't think a thing about it." Then he turned to leave.

As soon as he did, Macon thought of a flood of other things he should have mentioned. It wasn't all his fault, he wanted to say. Sarah had a little to do with it too. What Sarah needed was a rock, he wanted to say; someone who wouldn't crumble. Otherwise, why had she picked him to marry? But he held his peace and watched Garner walk out. There was something pitiable about the two sharp cords that ran down the back of Garner's neck, cupping a little ditch of mapped brown skin between them.

. . .

When his brothers came home from work, the house took on a relaxed, relieved atmosphere. Rose drew the living room curtains and lit a few soft lamps. Charles and Porter changed into sweaters. Macon started mixing his special salad dressing. He believed that if you pulverized the spices first with a marble mortar and pestle, it made all the difference. The others agreed that no one else's dressing tasted as good as Macon's. "Since you've been gone," Charles told him, "we've had to buy that bottled stuff from the grocery store." He made it sound as if Macon had been gone a few weeks or so—as if his entire marriage had been just a brief trip elsewhere.

For supper they had Rose's pot roast, a salad with Macon's dressing, and baked potatoes. Baked potatoes had always been their favorite food. They had learned to fix them as children, and even after they were big enough to cook a balanced meal they used to exist solely on baked potatoes whenever Alicia left them to their own devices. There was something about the smell of a roasting Idaho that was so cozy, and also, well, *conservative*, was the way Macon put it to himself. He thought back on years and years of winter evenings: the kitchen windows black outside, the corners furry with gathering darkness, the four of them seated at the chipped enamel table meticulously filling scooped-out potato skins with butter. You let the butter melt in the skins while you mashed and seasoned the floury insides; the skins were saved till last. It was almost a ritual. He recalled that once, during one of their mother's longer absences, her friend Eliza had served them what she called potato boats—restuffed, not a bit like the genuine article. The children, with pinched, fastidious expressions, had emptied the stuffing and proceeded as usual with the skins, pretending to overlook her mistake. The skins should be crisp. They should not be salted. The pepper should be freshly ground. Paprika was acceptable, but only if it was American. Hungarian paprika had too distinctive a taste. Personally, Macon could do without paprika altogether.

While they ate, Porter discussed what to do with his children. Tomorrow was his weekly visitation night, when he would drive over to Washington, where his children lived with their mother. "The thing of it is," he said, "eating out in restaurants is so artificial. It doesn't seem like real food. And anyway, they all three have different tastes. They always argue over where to go. Someone's on a diet, someone's turned vegetarian, someone can't stand food that crunches. And I end up shouting, 'Oh, for God's sake, we're going to Such-and-Such and that's that!' So we go and everybody sulks throughout the meal."

"Maybe you should just not visit," Charles said reasonably. (He had never had children of his own.)

"Well, of course I want to visit, Charles. I just wish we had some different program. You know what would be ideal? If we could all do something with tools together. I mean like the old days before the divorce, when Danny helped me drain the hot water heater or Susan sat on a board I was sawing. If I could just drop by their house, say, and June and her husband could go to a movie or something, then the kids and I would clean the gutters, weatherstrip the windows, wrap the hot water pipes . . . Well, that husband of hers is no use at all, you can bet he lets his hot water pipes sit around naked. I'd bring my own tools, even. We'd have a fine time! Susan could fix us cocoa. Then at the end of the evening I'd pack up my tools and off I'd go, leaving the house in perfect repair. Why, June ought to jump at the chance."

"Then why not suggest it," Macon said.

"Nah. She'd never go for it. She's so impractical. I said to her last week, I said, 'You know that front porch step is loose? Springing up from its nails every time you walk on it wrong.' She said, 'Oh, Lord, yes, it's *been* that way,' as if Providence had decreed it. As if nothing could be done about it. They've got leaves in the gutter from way last winter but leaves are natural, after all; why go against nature. She's so impractical."

Porter himself was the most practical man Macon had ever known. He was the only Leary who understood money. His talent with money was what kept the family firm solvent—if just barely. It wasn't a very wealthy business. Grandfather Leary had founded it in the early part of the century as a tinware factory, and turned to bottle caps in 1915. The Bottle Cap King, he called himself, and was called in his obituary, but in fact most bottle caps were manufactured by Crown Cork and always had been; Grandfather Leary ran a distant second or third. His only son, the Bottle Cap Prince, had barely assumed his place in the firm before quitting to volunteer for World War II—a far more damaging enthusiasm, it turned out, than any of Alicia's. After he was killed the business limped along, never quite succeeding and never quite failing, till Porter bounced in straight from college and took over the money end. Money to Porter was something almost chemical—a volatile substance that reacted in various interesting ways when combined with other substances. He wasn't what you'd call mercenary; he didn't want the money for its own sake but for its intriguing possibilities, and in fact when his wife divorced him he handed over most of his property without a word of complaint.

It was Porter who ran the company, pumping in money and ideas. Charles, more mechanical, dealt with the production end. Macon had done a little of everything when he worked there, and had wasted away with boredom doing it, for there wasn't really enough to keep a third man busy. It was only for symmetry's sake that Porter kept urging him to return. "Tell you what, Macon," he said now, "why not hitch a ride down with us tomorrow and look over your old stomping ground?"

"No, thanks," Macon told him.

"Plenty of room for your crutches in back."

"Maybe some other time."

They followed Rose around while she washed the dishes. She didn't like them to help because she had her own method, she said. She moved soundlessly through the old-fashioned kitchen, replacing dishes in the high wooden cabinets. Charles took the dog out; Macon couldn't manage his crutches in the spongy backyard. And Porter pulled the kitchen shades, meanwhile lecturing Rose on how the white surfaces reflected the warmth back into the room now that the nights were cooler. Rose said, "Yes, Porter, I know all that," and lifted the salad bowl to the light and examined it a moment before she put it away.

They watched the news, dutifully, and then they went out to the sun porch and sat at their grandparents' card table. They played something called Vaccination—a card game they'd invented as children, which had grown so convoluted over the years that no one else had the patience to learn it. In fact, more than one outsider had accused them of altering the rules to suit the circumstances. "Now, just a minute," Sarah had said, back when she'd still had hopes of figuring it out. "I thought you said aces were high."

"They are."

"So that means—"

"But not when they're drawn from the deck."

"Aha! Then why was the one that Rose drew counted high?"

"Well, she did draw it after a deuce, Sarah."

"Aces drawn after a deuce are high?"

"No, aces drawn after a number that's been drawn two times in a row just before that."

Sarah had folded her fan of cards and laid them face down— the last of the wives to give up.

Macon was in quarantine and had to donate all his cards to Rose. Rose moved her chair over next to his and played off his points while he sat back, scratching the cat behind her ears. Opposite him, in the tiny dark windowpanes, he saw their reflections— hollow-eyed and severely cheekboned, more interesting versions of themselves.

The telephone in the living room gave a nipped squeak and then a full ring. Nobody seemed to notice. Rose laid a king on Porter's queen and Porter said, "Stinker." The telephone rang again and then again. In the middle of the fourth ring, it fell silent. "Hypodermic," Rose told Porter, and she topped the king with an ace.

"You're a real stinker, Rose."

In the portrait on the end wall, the Leary children gazed out with their veiled eyes. It occurred to Macon that they were sitting in much the same positions here this evening: Charles and Porter on either side of him, Rose perched in the foreground. Was there any real change? He felt a jolt of something very close to panic. Here he still was! The same as ever! *What have I gone and done?* he wondered, and he swallowed thickly and looked at his own empty hands.

H elp! Help! Call off your dog!"

Macon stopped typing and lifted his head. The voice came from somewhere out front, rising above a string of sharp, excited yelps. But Edward was taking a walk with Porter. This must be some other dog.

"Call him off, dammit!"

Macon rose, propping himself on his crutches, and made his way to the window. Sure enough, it was Edward. He seemed to have treed somebody in the giant magnolia to the right of the walk. He was barking so hard that he kept popping off the ground perfectly level, all four feet at once, like one of those pull toys that bounce straight up in the air when you squeeze a rubber bulb.

"Edward! Stop that!" Macon shouted.

Edward didn't stop. He might not even have heard. Macon stubbed out to the hall, opened the front door, and said, "Come here this instant!"

Edward barely skipped a beat.

It was a Saturday morning in early October, pale gray and cool. Macon felt the coolness creeping up his cut-off pants leg as he crossed the porch. When he dropped one crutch and took hold of the iron railing to descend the steps, he found the metal beaded with moisture.

He hopped over to the magnolia, leaned down precariously, and grabbed the leash that Edward was trailing. Without much effort, he reeled it in; Edward was already losing interest. Macon peered into the inky depths of the magnolia. "Who *is* that?" he asked.

"This is your employer, Macon."

"Julian?"

Julian lowered himself from one of the magnolia's weak, sprawling branches. He had a line of dirt across the front of his slacks. His white-blond hair, usually so neat it made him look like a shirt ad, struck out at several angles. "Macon," he said. "I really hate a man with an obnoxious dog. I don't hate just the dog. I hate the man who owns him."

"Well, I'm sorry about this. I thought he was off on a walk."

"You send him on walks by himself?"

"No, no . . ."

"A dog who takes solitary strolls," Julian said. "Only Macon Leary would have one." He brushed off the sleeves of his suede blazer. Then he said, "What happened to your leg?"

"I broke it."

"Well, I see that, but how?"

"It's kind of hard to explain," Macon told him.

They started toward the house, with Edward trotting docilely alongside. Julian supported Macon as they climbed the steps. He was an athletic-looking man with a casual, sauntering style—a boater. You could tell he was a boater by his nose, which was raw across the tip even this late in the year. No one so startlingly blond, so vividly flushed in the face, should expose himself to sunburn, Macon always told him. But that was Julian for you: reckless. A dashing sailor, a speedy driver, a frequenter of singles bars, he was the kind of man who would make a purchase without consulting *Consumer Reports*. He never seemed to have a moment's self-doubt and was proceeding into the house now as jauntily as if he'd been invited, first retrieving Macon's other crutch and then holding the door open and waving him ahead.

"How'd you find me, anyway?" Macon asked.

"Why, are you hiding?"

"No, of course not."

Julian surveyed the entrance hall, which all at once struck Macon as slightly dowdy. The satin lampshade on the table had dozens of long vertical rents; it seemed to be rotting off its frame.

"Your neighbor told me where you were," Julian said finally.

"Oh, Garner."

"I stopped by your house when I couldn't reach you by phone. Do you know how late you're running with this guidebook?"

"Well, you can see I've had an accident," Macon said.

"Everybody's held up, waiting for the manuscript. I keep telling them I expect it momentarily, but—"

"Any moment," Macon said.

"Huh?"

"You expect it any moment."

"Yes, and all I've seen so far is two chapters mailed in with no explanation."

Julian led the way to the living room as he spoke. He selected the most comfortable chair and sat down. "Where's Sarah?" he asked.

"Who?"

"Your wife, Macon."

"Oh. Um, she and I are . . ."

Macon should have practiced saying it out loud. The word "separated" was too bald; it was something that happened to other people. He crossed to the couch and made a great business of settling himself and arranging his crutches at his side. Then he said, "She's got this apartment downtown."

"You've *split*?"

Macon nodded.

"Jesus."

Edward nosed Macon's palm bossily, demanding a pat. Macon was grateful to have something to do.

"Well, Jesus, Macon, what went wrong?" Julian asked.

"Nothing!" Macon told him. His voice was a little too loud. He lowered it. "I mean, that's not something I can answer," he said.

"Oh. Excuse me."

"No, I mean . . . there *is* no answer. It turns out these things can happen for no particular reason."

"Well, you've been under a strain, you two," Julian said. "Shoot, with what happened and all . . . She'll be back, once she's gotten over it. Or not gotten *over* it of course but, you know . . ."

"Maybe so," Macon said. He felt embarrassed for Julian, who kept jiggling one Docksider. He said, "What did you think of those first two chapters?"

Julian opened his mouth to answer, but he was interrupted by the dog. Edward had flown to the hall and was barking furiously. There was a clang that Macon recognized as the sound of the front door swinging open and hitting the radiator. "Hush, now," he heard Rose tell Edward. She crossed the hall and looked into the living room.

Julian got to his feet. Macon said, "Julian Edge, this is my sister Rose. And this," he said as Charles arrived behind her, "is my brother Charles."

Neither Rose nor Charles could shake hands; they were carrying the groceries. They stood in the center of the room, hugging brown paper bags, while Julian went into what Macon thought of as his Macon Leary act. "Macon Leary with a sister! And a brother, too. Who'd have guessed it? That Macon Leary had a family just never entered my mind, somehow."

Rose gave him a polite, puzzled smile. She wasn't looking her best. She wore a long black coat that drew all the color from her face. And Charles, rumpled and out of breath, was having trouble with one of his bags. He kept trying to get a better grip on it. "Here, let me help you," Julian said. He took the bag and then peered into it. Macon was afraid he'd go off on some tangent about Macon Leary's groceries, but he didn't. He told Rose, "Yes, I do see a family resemblance."

"You're Macon's publisher," Rose said. "I remember from the address label."

"Address label?"

"I'm the one who mailed you Macon's chapters."

"Oh, yes."

"I'm supposed to send you some more, but first I have to buy nine-by-twelve envelopes. All we've got left is ten-by-thirteen. It's terrible when things don't fit precisely. They get all out of alignment."

"Ah," Julian said. He looked at her for a moment.

Macon said, "We wouldn't want to keep you, Rose."

"Oh! No," she said. She smiled at Julian, hoisted her groceries higher, and left the room. Charles retrieved his bag from Julian and slogged after her.

"The Macon Leary Nine-by-Twelve Envelope Crisis," Julian said, sitting back down.

Macon said, "Oh, Julian, drop it."

"Sorry," Julian said, sounding surprised.

There was a pause. Then Julian said, "Really I had no idea, Macon, I mean, if you'd let me know what was going on in your life . . ."

He was jiggling a Docksider again. He always seemed uneasy when he couldn't do his Macon Leary act. After Ethan died he'd avoided Macon for weeks; he'd sent a tree-sized bouquet to the house but never again mentioned Ethan's name.

"Look," he said now. "If you want another, I don't know, another month—"

Macon said, "Oh, nonsense, what's a missing wife or two, right? Ha, ha! Here, let me get what I've typed and you can check it."

"Well, if you say so," Julian said.

"After this there's only the conclusion," Macon said. He was calling over his shoulder as he made his way to the dining room, where his latest chapter lay stacked on the buffet. "The conclusion's nothing, a cinch. I'll crib from the old one, mostly."

He returned with the manuscript and handed it to Julian. Then he sat on the couch again, and Julian started reading. Meanwhile,

Macon heard Porter come in the back way, where he was greeted by explosive barks from Edward. "Monster," Porter said. "Do you know how long I've been looking for you?" The phone rang over and over, unanswered. Julian looked at Macon and raised his eyebrows but made no comment.

Macon and Julian had met some dozen years ago, when Macon was still at the bottle-cap factory. He'd been casting about for other occupations at the time. He'd begun to believe he might like to work on a newspaper. But he'd had no training, not a single journalism course. So he started the only way he could think of: He contributed a freelance article to a neighborhood weekly. His subject was a crafts fair over in Washington. *Getting there is difficult,* he wrote, *because the freeway is so blank you start feeling all lost and sad. And once you've arrived, it's worse. The streets are not like ours and don't even run at right angles.* He went on to evaluate some food he'd sampled at an outdoor booth, but found it contained a spice he wasn't used to, *something sort of cold and yellow I would almost describe as foreign,* and settled instead for a hot dog from a vendor across the street who wasn't even part of the fair. *The hot dog I can recommend,* he wrote, *though it made me a little regretful because Sarah, my wife, uses the same kind of chili sauce and I thought of home the minute I smelled it.* He also recommended the patchwork quilts, one of which had a starburst pattern like the quilt in his grandmother's room. He suggested that his readers leave the fair no later than three thirty, *since you'll be driving into Baltimore right past Lexington Market and will want to pick up your crabs before it closes.*

His article was published beneath a headline reading CRAFTS FAIR DELIGHTS, INSTRUCTS. There was a subhead under that. *Or,* it read, *I Feel So Broke-Up, I Want to Go Home.* Until he saw the subhead, Macon hadn't realized what tone he'd given his piece. Then he felt silly.

But Julian Edge thought it was perfect. Julian phoned him. "You the fellow who wrote that hot dog thing in the *Watchbird*?"

"Well, yes."

"Ha!"

"Well, I don't see what's so funny," Macon said stiffly.

"Who said it was funny? It's perfect. I've got a proposition for you."

They met at the Old Bay Restaurant, where Macon's grandparents used to take the four children on their birthdays. "I can personally guarantee the crab soup," Macon said. "They haven't done a thing to it since I was nine." Julian said, "Ha!" again and rocked back in his chair. He was wearing a polo shirt and white duck trousers, and his nose was a bright shade of pink. It was summer, or maybe spring. At any rate, his boat was in the water.

"Now, here's my plan," he said over the soup. "I own this little company called the Businessman's Press. Well, little: I say little. Actually we sell coast to coast. Nothing fancy, but useful, you know? Appointment pads, expense account booklets, compound interest charts, currency conversion wheels . . . And now I want to put out a guidebook for commercial travelers. Just the U.S., to begin with; maybe other countries later. We'd call it something catchy, I don't know: *Reluctant Tourist* . . . And you're the fellow to write it."

"Me?"

"I knew the minute I read your hot dog piece."

"But I hate to travel."

"I kind of guessed that," Julian said. "So do businessmen. I mean, these folks are not running around the country for the hell of it, Macon. They'd rather be home in their living rooms. So you'll be helping them pretend that's where they are."

Then he pulled a square of paper from his breast pocket and said, "What do you think?"

It was a steel engraving of an overstuffed chair. Attached to the chair's back were giant, feathered wings such as you would see on seraphim in antique Bibles. Macon blinked.

"Your logo," Julian explained. "Get it?"

"Um . . ."

"While armchair travelers dream of going places," Julian said, "traveling armchairs dream of staying put. I thought we'd use this on the cover."

"Ah!" Macon said brightly. Then he said, "But would I actually have to travel myself?"

"Well, yes."

"Oh."

"But just briefly. I'm not looking for anything encyclopedic, I'm looking for the opposite of encyclopedic. And think of the pay."

"It pays?"

"It pays a bundle."

Well, not a bundle, exactly. Still, it did make a comfortable living. It sold briskly at airport newsstands, train stations, and office supply shops. His guide to France did even better. That was part of a major promotion by an international car-rental agency—slipcased with *The Businessman's Foreign Phrase Book*, which gave the German, French, and Spanish for "We anticipate an upswing in cross-border funds." Macon, of course, was not the author of the phrase book. His only foreign language was Latin.

Now Julian restacked the pages he'd been reading. "Fine," he said. "I think we can send this through as is. What's left of the conclusion?"

"Not much."

"After this I want to start on the U.S. again."

"So soon?"

"It's been three years, Macon."

"Well, but . . ." Macon said. He gestured toward his leg. "You can see I'd have trouble traveling."

"When does your cast come off?"

"Not till the first of November at the earliest."

"So? A few weeks!"

"But it really seems to me I just did the U.S.," Macon said. A kind of fatigue fell over him. These endlessly recurring trips, Boston and Atlanta and Chicago . . . He let his head drop back on the couch.

Julian said, "Things are changing every minute, Macon. Change! It's what keeps us in the black. How far do you think we'd get selling out-of-date guidebooks?"

Macon thought of the crumbling old *Tips for the Continent* in his grandfather's library. Travelers were advised to invert a wine-glass on their hotel beds, testing the sheets for damp. Ladies should seal the corks of their perfume bottles with melted candlewax before packing. Something about that book implied that tourists were all in it together, equally anxious and defenseless. Macon might almost have enjoyed a trip in those days.

Julian was preparing to go now. He stood up, and with some difficulty Macon did too. Then Edward, getting wind of a leavetaking, rushed into the living room and started barking. "Sorry!" Macon shouted above the racket. "Edward, stop it! I figure that's his sheepherding instinct," he explained to Julian. "He hates to see anyone straying from the flock."

They moved toward the front hall, wading through a blur of dancing, yelping dog. When they reached the door, Edward blocked it. Luckily, he was still trailing his leash, so Macon gave one crutch to Julian and bent to grasp it. The instant Edward felt the tug, he turned and snarled at Macon. "Whoa!" Julian said, for Edward when he snarled was truly ugly. His fangs seemed to lengthen. He snapped at his leash with an audible click. Then he snapped at Macon's hand. Macon felt Edward's hot breath and the oddly intimate dampness of his teeth. His hand was not so much bitten as struck— slammed into with a jolt such as you'd get from an electric fence. He stepped back and dropped the leash. His other crutch clattered to the floor. The front hall seemed to be full of crutches; there was some splintery, spiky feeling to the air.

"Whoa, there!" Julian said. He spoke into a sudden silence. The dog sat back now, panting and shamefaced. "Macon? Did he get you?" Julian asked.

Macon looked down at his hand. There were four red puncture marks in the fleshy part—two in front, two in back—but no blood at all and very little pain. "I'm all right," he said.

Julian gave him his crutches, keeping one eye on Edward. "I wouldn't have a dog like that," he said. "I'd shoot him."   .

"He was just trying to protect me," Macon said.

"I'd call the S.P.C.A."

"Why don't you go now, Julian, while he's calm."

"Or the what's-it, dogcatcher. Tell them you want him done away with."

"Just go, Julian."

Julian said, "Well, fine." He opened the door and slid through it sideways, glancing back at Edward. "That is not a well dog," he said before he vanished.

Macon hobbled to the rear of the house and Edward followed, snuffling a bit and staying close to the ground. In the kitchen, Rose stood on a stepstool in front of a towering glass-fronted cupboard, accepting the groceries that Charles and Porter handed up to her. "Now I need the *n*'s, anything starting with *n*," she was saying.

"How about these noodles?" Porter asked. "*N* for noodles? *P* for pasta?"

"*E* for elbow macaroni. You might have passed those up earlier, Porter."

"Rose?" Macon said. "It seems Edward's given me a little sort of nip."

She turned, and Charles and Porter stopped work to examine the hand he held out. It was hurting him by now—a deep, stinging pain. "Oh, Macon!" Rose cried. She came down off the stepstool. "How did it happen?"

"It was an accident, that's all. But I think I need an antiseptic."

"You need a tetanus shot, too," Charles told him.

"You need to get rid of that dog," Porter said.

They looked at Edward. He grinned up at them nervously.

"He didn't mean any harm," Macon said.

"Takes off your hand at the elbow and he means no harm? You should get rid of him, I tell you."

"See, I can't," Macon said.

"Why not?"

"Well, see . . ."

They waited.

"You know I don't mind the cat," Rose said. "But Edward is so disruptive, Macon. Every day he gets more and more out of control."

"Maybe you could give him to someone who wants a guard dog," Charles said.

"A service station," Rose suggested. She took a roll of gauze from a drawer.

"Oh, never," Macon said. He sat where she pointed, in a chair at the kitchen table. He propped his crutches in the corner. "Edward alone in some Exxon? He'd be wretched."

Rose swabbed Mercurochrome on his hand. It looked bruised; each puncture mark was puffing and turning blue.

"He's used to sleeping with me," Macon told her. "He's never been alone in his life."

Besides, Edward wasn't a bad dog at heart—only a little unruly. He was sympathetic and he cared about Macon and plodded after him wherever he went. There was a furrowed W on his forehead that gave him a look of concern. His large, pointed, velvety ears seemed more expressive than other dogs' ears; when he was happy they stuck straight out at either side of his head like airplane wings. His smell was unexpectedly pleasant—the sweetish smell a favorite sweater takes on when it's been folded away in a drawer unwashed.

And he'd been Ethan's.

Once upon a time Ethan had brushed him, bathed him, wrestled on the floor with him; and when Edward stopped to paw at one ear Ethan would ask, with the soberest courtesy, "Oh, may I scratch that for you?" The two of them watched daily at the window for the afternoon paper, and the instant it arrived Ethan sent Edward bounding out to fetch it—hind legs meeting front legs, heels kicking up joyfully. Edward would pause after he got the paper in his mouth and look around him, as if hoping to be noticed, and then he'd swagger back all bustling and self-important and pause again at the front hall mirror to admire the figure he cut. "Conceited," Ethan would say fondly. Ethan picked up a tennis ball to throw and Edward grew so excited that he wagged his whole hind end. Ethan took Edward outside with a soccer ball and when Edward got carried away—tearing about and shouldering the ball into a hedge and growling ferociously—Ethan's laugh rang out so high and clear, such a buoyant sound floating through the air on a summer evening.

"I just can't," Macon said.

There was a silence.

Rose wrapped gauze around his hand, so gently he hardly felt it. She tucked the end under and reached for a roll of adhesive tape. Then she said, "Maybe we could send him to obedience school."

"Obedience school is for minor things—walking to heel and things," Porter told her. "What we have here is major."

"It is not!" Macon said. "It's really nothing at all. Why, the woman at the Meow-Bow got on wonderfully with him."

"Meow-Bow?"

"Where I boarded him when I went to England. She was just crazy about him. She wanted me to let her train him."

"So call her, why don't you."

"Maybe I will," Macon said.

He wouldn't, of course. The woman had struck him as bizarre. But there was no sense going into that now.

. . .

On Sunday morning Edward tore the screen door, trying to get at an elderly neighbor who'd stopped by to borrow a wrench. On Sunday afternoon he sprang at Porter to keep him from leaving on an errand. Porter had to creep out the rear when Edward wasn't watching. "This is undignified," Porter told Macon. "When are you going to call the Kit-Kat or whatever it is?"

Macon explained that on Sundays the Meow-Bow would surely be closed.

Monday morning, when Edward went for a walk with Rose, he lunged at a passing jogger and yanked Rose off her feet. She came home with a scraped knee. She said, "Have you called the Meow-Bow yet?"

"Not quite," Macon said.

"Macon," Rose said. Her voice was very quiet. "Tell me something."

"What's that, Rose?"

"Can you explain why you're letting things go on this way?"

No, he couldn't, and that was the truth. It was getting so he was baffling even to himself. He felt infuriated by Edward's misdeeds, but somehow he viewed them as visitations of fate. There was nothing he could do about them. When Edward approached him later with a mangled belt of Porter's trailing from his mouth, all Macon said was, "Oh, Edward . . ."

He was sitting on the couch at the time, having been snagged by an especially outrageous moment in Rose's soap opera. Rose looked over at him. Her expression was odd. It wasn't disapproving; it was more like . . . He cast about for the word. Resigned. That was it. She looked at him the way she would look at, say, some hopeless wreck of a man wandering drugged on a downtown street. After all, she seemed to be thinking, there was probably not much that you could do for such a person.

.   .   .

"Meow-Bow Animal Hospital."

"Is, ah, Muriel there, please?"

"Hold on a minute."

He waited, braced against a cabinet. (He was using the pantry telephone.) He heard two women discussing Fluffball Cohen's rabies shot. Then Muriel picked up the receiver. "Hello?"

"Yes, this is Macon Leary. I don't know if you remember me or—"

"Oh, Macon! Hi there! How's Edward doing?"

"Well, he's getting worse."

She tsk-tsked.

"He's been attacking right and left. Snarling, biting, chewing things—"

"Did your neighbor tell you I came looking for you?"

"What? Yes, he did."

"I was right on your street, running an errand. I make a little extra money running errands. George, it's called. Don't you think that's cute?"

"Excuse me?"

"George. It's the name of my company. I stuck a flyer under your door. *Let George do it*, it says, and then it lists all the prices: meeting planes, chauffeuring, courier service, shopping . . . Gift shopping's most expensive because for that I have to use my own taste. Didn't you get my flyer? I really stopped by just to visit, though. But your neighbor said you hadn't been around."

"No, I broke my leg," Macon said.

"Oh, that's too bad."

"And I couldn't manage alone of course, so—"

"You should have called George."

"George who?"

"George my company! The one I was just telling you about."

"Oh, yes."

"Then you wouldn't have had to leave that nice house. I liked your house. Is that where you lived when you were married, too?"

"Well, yes."

"I'm surprised she agreed to give it up."

"The point is," Macon said, "I'm really at the end of my rope with Edward here, and I was wondering if you might be able to help me."

"Sure I can help!"

"Oh, that's wonderful," Macon said.

"I can do anything," Muriel told him. "Search and alert, search and rescue, bombs, narcotics—"

"Narcotics?"

"Guard training, attack training, poison-proofing, kennelosis—"

"Wait, I don't even know what some of those things are," Macon said.

"I can even teach split personality."

"What's split personality?"

"Where your dog is, like, nice to you but kills all others."

"You know, I think I may be over my head here," Macon said.

"No, no! Don't say that!"

"But this is just the simplest problem. His only fault is, he wants to protect me."

"You can take protection too far," Muriel told him.

Macon tried a little joke. " 'It's a jungle out there,' he's saying. That's what he's trying to say. 'I know better than you do, Macon.' "

"Oh?" Muriel said. "You let him call you by your first name?"

"Well—"

"He needs to learn respect," she said. "Five or six times a week I'll come out, for however long it takes. I'll start with the basics; you always do that: sitting, heeling . . . My charge is five dollars a lesson. You're getting a bargain. Most I charge ten."

Macon tightened his hold on the receiver. "Then why not ten for me?" he asked.

"Oh, no! You're a friend."

He felt confused. He gave her his address and arranged a time with the nagging sense that something was slipping out of his control. "But look," he said, "about the fee, now—"

"See you tomorrow!" she said. She hung up.

At supper that night when he told the others, he thought they did a kind of double take. Porter said, "You actually called?" Macon said, "Yes, why not?"—acting very offhand—and so the others took their cue and dropped the subject at once.

W hen I was a little girl," Muriel said, "I didn't like dogs at all or any other kinds of animals either. I thought they could read my mind. My folks gave me a puppy for my birthday and he would, like, cock his head, you know how they do? Cock his head and fix me with these bright round eyes and I said, 'Ooh! Get him away from me! You know I can't stand to be stared at.' "

She had a voice that wandered too far in all directions. It screeched upward; then it dropped to a raspy growl. "They had to take him back. Had to give him to a neighbor boy and buy me a whole different present, a beauty-parlor permanent which is what I'd set my heart on all along."

She and Macon were standing in the entrance hall. She still had her coat on—a bulky-shouldered, three-quarter length, nubby black affair of a type last seen in the 1940s. Edward sat in front of her as he'd been ordered. He had met her at the door with his usual display, leaping and snarling, but she'd more or less walked right through him and pointed at his rump and told him to sit. He'd gaped at her. She had reached over and poked his rear end down with a long, sharp index finger.

"Now you kind of cluck your tongue," she'd told Macon, demonstrating. "They get to know a cluck means praise. And when I hold my hand out—see? That means he has to stay."

Edward stayed, but a yelp erupted from him every few seconds, reminding Macon of the periodic bloops from a percolator. Muriel hadn't seemed to hear. She'd started discussing her lesson plan and then for no apparent reason had veered to her autobiography. But shouldn't Edward be allowed to get up now? How long did she expect him to sit there?

"I guess you're wondering why I'd want a permanent when this hair of mine is so frizzy," she said. "Old mop! But I'll be honest, this is not natural. My natural hair is real straight and lanky. Times I've just despaired of it. It was blond when I was a baby, can you believe that? Blond as a fairy-tale princess. People told my mother I'd look like Shirley Temple if she would just curl my hair, and so she did, she rolled my hair on orange juice tins. I had blue eyes, too, and they stayed that way for a long long time, a whole lot longer than most babies' do. People thought I'd look that way forever and they talked about me going into the movies. Seriously! My mother arranged for tap-dance school when I wasn't much more than a toddler. No one ever dreamed my hair would turn on me."

Edward moaned. Muriel looked past Macon, into the glass of a picture that hung behind him. She cupped a hand beneath the ends of her hair, as if testing its weight. "Think what it must feel like," she said, "waking up one morning and finding you've gone dark. It near about killed my mother, I can tell you. Ordinary dull old Muriel, muddy brown eyes and hair as black as dirt."

Macon sensed he was supposed to offer some argument, but he was too anxious about Edward. "Oh, well . . ." he said. Then he said, "Shouldn't we be letting him up now?"

"Up? Oh, the dog. In a minute," she said. "So anyway. The reason it's so frizzy is, I got this thing called a body perm. You ever heard of those? They're supposed to just add body, but something went wrong. You think *this* is bad. If I was to take a brush to it, my hair would spring straight out from my head. I mean absolutely straight out. Kind of like a fright wig, isn't that what you call it? So I can't even brush it. I get up in the morning and there I am, ready to go. Lord, I hate to think of the tangles."

"Maybe you could just comb it," Macon suggested.

"Hard to drag a comb *through* it. All the little teeth would break off."

"Maybe one of those thick-toothed combs that black people use."

"I know what you mean but I'd feel silly buying one."

"What for?" Macon asked. "They're just hanging there in supermarkets. It wouldn't have to be a big deal. Buy milk and bread or something and an Afro comb, no one will even think twice."

"Well, I suppose you're right," she said, but now that she'd got him involved it seemed she'd lost interest in the problem herself. She snapped her fingers over Edward's head. "Okay!" she said. Edward jumped up, barking. "That was very good," she told him.

In fact, it was so good that Macon felt a little cross. Things couldn't be that easy, he wanted to say. Edward had improved too quickly, the way a toothache will improve the moment you step into a dentist's waiting room.

Muriel slipped her purse off her shoulder and set it on the hall table. Out came a long blue leash attached to a choke chain. "He's supposed to wear this all the time," she said. "Every minute till he's trained. That way you can yank him back whenever he does something wrong. The leash is six dollars even, and the chain is two ninety-five. With tax it comes to, let's see, nine forty. You can pay me at the end of the lesson."

She slipped the choke chain over Edward's head. Then she paused to examine a fingernail. "If I break another nail I'm going to scream," she said. She took a step back and pointed to Edward's rump. After a brief hesitation, he sat. Seated, he looked noble, Macon thought—chesty and solemn, nothing like his usual self. But when Muriel snapped her fingers, he jumped up as unruly as ever.

"Now you try," Muriel told Macon.

Macon accepted the leash and pointed to Edward's rump. Edward stood fast. Macon frowned and pointed more sternly. He felt foolish. Edward knew, if this woman didn't, how little authority Macon had.

"Poke him down," Muriel said.

This was going to be awkward. He propped a crutch against the radiator and bent stiffly to jab Edward with one finger. Edward sat. Macon clucked. Then he straightened and backed away, holding out his palm, but instead of staying, Edward rose and followed him. Muriel hissed between her teeth. Edward shrank down again. "He doesn't take you seriously," Muriel said.

"Well, I know that," Macon snapped.

His broken leg was starting to ache.

"In fact I didn't have so much as a kitten the whole entire time I was growing up," Muriel said. Was she just going to leave Edward sitting there? "Then a couple of years ago I saw this ad in the paper, *Make extra money in your off hours. Work as little or as much as you like.* Place was a dog-training firm that went around to people's houses. Doggie, Do, it was called. Don't you just hate that name? Reminds me of dog-do. But anyhow, I answered the ad. 'To be honest I don't like animals,' I said, but Mr. Quarles, the owner, he told me that was just as well. He told me it was people who got all mushy about them that had the most trouble."

"Well, that makes sense," Macon said, glancing at Edward. He had heard that dogs developed backaches if they were made to sit too long.

"I was just about his best pupil, it turns out. Seems I had a way with animals. So then I got a job at the Meow-Bow. Before that I worked at the Rapid-Eze Copy Center and believe me, I was looking for a change. Who's the lady?"

"Lady?"

"The lady I just saw walking through the dining room."

"That's Rose."

"Is she your ex-wife? Or what."

"She's my sister."

"Oh, your sister!"

"This house belongs to her," Macon said.

"I don't live with anybody either," Muriel told him.

Macon blinked. Hadn't he just said he lived with his sister?

"Sometimes late at night when I get desperate for someone to talk to I call the time signal," Muriel said. " 'At the tone the time will be eleven . . . forty-eight. And fifty seconds.' " Her voice took on a fruity fullness. " 'At the tone the time will be eleven . . . forty-nine. Exactly.' You can release him now."

"Pardon?"

"Release your dog."

Macon snapped his fingers and Edward jumped up, yapping.

"How about you?" Muriel asked. "What do you do for a living?"

Macon said, "I write tour guides."

"Tour guides! Lucky."

"What's lucky about it?"

"Why, you must get to travel all kinds of places!"

"Oh, well, travel," Macon said.

"I'd love to travel."

"It's just red tape, mostly," Macon said.

"I've never even been on an airplane, you realize that?"

"It's red tape in motion. Ticket lines, custom lines . . . Should Edward be barking that way?"

Muriel gave Edward a slit-eyed look and he quieted.

"If I could go anywhere I'd go to Paris," she said.

"Paris is terrible. Everybody's impolite."

"I'd walk along the Seine, like they say in the song. 'You will find your love in Paris,' " she sang scratchily, " 'if you walk along the —' I just think it sounds so romantic."

"Well, it's not," Macon said.

"I bet you don't know where to look, is all. Take me with you next time! I could show you the good parts."

Macon cleared his throat. "Actually, I have a very limited expense account," he told her. "I never even took my wife, or, um, my . . . wife."

"I was only teasing," she told him.

"Oh."

"You think I meant it?"

"Oh, no."

She grew suddenly brisk. "That will be fourteen forty, including the leash and the choke chain." Then while Macon was fumbling through his wallet she said, "You have to practice what he's learned, and no one else can practice for you. I'll come back tomorrow for the second lesson. Will eight in the morning be too early? I've got to be at the Meow-Bow at nine."

"Eight will be fine," Macon told her. He counted out fourteen dollars and all the change he had loose in his pocket — thirty-six cents.

"You can pay me the other four cents tomorrow," she said.

Then she made Edward sit and she handed the leash to Macon. "Release him when I'm gone," she said.

Macon held out his palm and stared hard into Edward's eyes, begging him to stay. Edward stayed, but he moaned when he saw Muriel leave. When Macon snapped his fingers, Edward jumped up and attacked the front door.

. . .

All that afternoon and evening, Macon and Edward practiced. Edward learned to plop his rump down at the slightest motion of a finger. He stayed there, complaining and rolling his eyes, while Macon clucked approvingly. By suppertime, a cluck was part of the family language. Charles clucked over Rose's pork chops. Porter clucked when Macon dealt him a good hand of cards.

"Imagine a flamenco dancer with galloping consumption," Rose told Charles and Porter. "That's Edward's trainer. She talks nonstop, I don't know when she comes up for air. When she talked about her lesson plan she kept saying 'simplistic' for 'simple.' "

"I thought you were going to stay out of sight," Macon told Rose.

"Well? Did you ever see me?"

"Muriel did."

"I guess so! The way she was always peering around your back and snooping."

There were constant slamming sounds from the living room, because Edward's new leash kept catching on the rocking chair and dragging it behind him. During the course of the evening he chewed a pencil to splinters, stole a pork-chop bone from the garbage bin, and threw up on the sun porch rug; but now that he could sit on command, everyone felt more hopeful.

. . .

"When I was in high school I made nothing but A's," Muriel said. "You're surprised at that, aren't you. You think I'm kind of like, not an intellect. I know what you're thinking! You're surprised."

"No, I'm not," Macon said, although he was, actually.

"I made A's because I caught on to the trick," Muriel told him. "You think it's not a trick? There's a trick to everything; that's how you get through life."

They were in front of the house—both of them in raincoats, for it was a damp, drippy morning. Muriel wore truncated black suede boots with witchy toes and needle heels. Her legs rose out of them like toothpicks. The leash trailed from her fingers. Supposedly, she was teaching Edward to walk right. Instead she went on talking about her schooldays.

"Some of my teachers told me I should go to college," she said. "This one in particular, well she wasn't a teacher but a librarian. I worked in the library for her, shelving books and things; she said, 'Muriel, why don't you go on to Towson State?' But I don't know . . . and now I tell my sister, 'You be thinking of college, hear? Don't drop out like I dropped out.' I've got this little sister? Claire? *Her* hair never turned. She's blond as an angel. Here's what's funny, though: she couldn't care less. Braids her hair back any old how to keep it out of her eyes. Wears raggy jeans and forgets to shave her legs. Doesn't it always work that way? My folks believe she's wonderful. She's the good one and I'm the bad one. It's not her fault, though; I don't blame Claire. People just get fixed in these certain frames of other people's opinions, don't you find that's true? Claire was always Mary in the Nativity Scene at Christmas. Boys in her grade school were always proposing, but there I was in high school and no one proposed to *me*, I can tell you. Aren't high school boys just so frustrating? I mean they'd invite me out and all, like to drive-in movies and things, and they'd act so tense and secret, sneaking one arm around my shoulder inch by inch like they thought I wouldn't notice and then dropping a hand down, you know how they do, lower and lower while all the time staring straight ahead at the movie like it was the most fascinating spectacle they'd ever seen in their lives. You just had to feel sorry for them. But then Monday morning there they were like nothing had taken place, real boisterous and horsing around with their friends and nudging each other when I walked past but not so much as saying hello to me. You think that didn't hurt my feelings? Not one boy in all that time treated me like a steady girlfriend. They'd ask me out on Saturday night and expect me to be so nice to them, but you think they ever ate lunch with me next Monday in the school cafeteria, or walked me from class to class?"

She glanced down at Edward. Abruptly, she slapped her hip; her black vinyl raincoat made a buckling sound. "That's the 'heel' command," she told Macon. She started walking. Edward followed uncertainly. Macon stayed behind. It had been hard enough getting down the front porch steps.

"He's supposed to match his pace to anything," she called back. "Slow, fast, anything I do." She speeded up. When Edward crossed in front of her, she walked right into him. When he dawdled, she yanked his leash. She tip-tapped briskly eastward, her coat a stiff, swaying triangle beneath the smaller triangle of her hair blowing back. Macon waited, ankle-deep in wet leaves.

On the return trip, Edward kept close to Muriel's left side. "I think he's got the hang of it," she called. She arrived in front of Macon and offered him the leash. "Now you."

He attempted to slap his hip—which was difficult, on crutches. Then he set off. He was agonizingly slow and Edward kept pulling ahead. "Yank that leash!" Muriel said, clicking along behind. "He knows what he's supposed to do. Contrary thing."

Edward fell into step, finally, although he gazed off in a bored, lofty way. "Don't forget to cluck," Muriel said. "Every little minute, you have to praise him." Her heels made a scraping sound behind them. "Once I worked with this dog that had never in her life been housebroken. Two years old and not one bit housebroken and the owners were losing their minds. First I can't figure it out; then it comes to me. That dog thought she wasn't supposed to piddle *any-*place, not indoors or outdoors, either one. See, no one had ever praised her when she did it right. Did you ever hear of such a thing? I had to catch her peeing outdoors which wasn't easy, believe me, because she was all the time ashamed and trying to hide it, and then I praised her to bits and after a while she caught on."

They reached the corner. "Now, when you stop, he has to sit," she said.

"But how will I practice?" Macon asked.

"What do you mean?"

"I'm on these crutches."

"So? It's good exercise for your leg," she said. She didn't ask how the leg had been broken. Come to think of it, there was something impervious about her, in spite of all her interest in his private life. She said, "Practice lots, ten minutes a session."

"Ten minutes!"

"Now let's start back."

She led the way, her angular, sashaying walk broken by the jolt of her sharp heels. Macon and Edward followed. When they reached the house, she asked what time it was. "Eight fifty," Macon said severely. He mistrusted women who wore no watches.

"I have to get going. That will be five dollars, please, and the four cents you owe me from yesterday."

He gave her the money and she stuffed it in her raincoat pocket. "Next time, I'll stay longer and talk," she said. "That's a promise." She trilled her fingers at him, and then she clicked off toward a car that was parked down the street—an aged, gray, boat-like sedan polished to a high shine. When she slid in and slammed the door behind her, there was a sound like falling beer cans. The engine twanged and rattled before it took hold. Macon shook his head, and he and Edward returned to the house.

· · ·

Between Wednesday and Thursday, Macon spent what seemed a lifetime struggling up and down Dempsey Road beside Edward. His armpits developed a permanent ache. There was a vertical seam of pain in his thigh. This made no sense; it should have been in the shin. He wondered if something had gone wrong—if the break had been set improperly, for instance, so that some unusual strain was being placed upon the thighbone. Maybe he'd have to go back to the hospital and get his leg rebroken, probably under general anesthesia with all its horrifying complications; and then he'd spend months in traction and perhaps walk the rest of his life with a limp. He imagined himself tilting across intersections with a grotesque, lopsided gait. Sarah, driving past, would screech to a halt. "Macon?" She would roll down her window. "Macon, what *happened?*"

He would raise one arm and let it flop and totter away from her. Or tell her, "I'm surprised you care enough to inquire."

No, just totter away.

Most likely these little spells of self-pity (an emotion he despised ordinarily) were caused by sheer physical exhaustion. How had he got himself into this? Slapping his haunch was the first problem; then summoning his balance to jerk the leash when Edward fell out of step, and staying constantly alert for any squirrel or pedestrian. "Sss!" he kept saying, and "Cluck-cluck!" and "Sss!" again. He supposed passersby must think he was crazy. Edward loped beside him, occasionally yawning, looking everywhere for bikers. Bikers were his special delight. Whenever he saw one, the hair between his shoulders stood on end and he lunged forward. Macon felt like a man on a tightrope that was suddenly set swinging.

At this uneven, lurching pace, he saw much more than he would have otherwise. He had a lengthy view of every bush and desiccated flower bed. He memorized eruptions in the sidewalk that might trip him. It was an old people's street, and not in the best of repair. The neighbors spent their days telephoning back and forth among themselves, checking to see that no one had suffered a stroke alone on the stairs or a heart attack in the bathroom, a broken hip, blocked windpipe, dizzy spell over the stove with every burner alight. Some would set out for a walk and find themselves hours later in the middle of the street, wondering where they'd been headed. Some would start fixing a bite to eat at noon, a soft-boiled egg or a cup of tea, and by sundown would still be puttering in their kitchen, fumbling for the salt and forgetting how the toaster worked. Macon knew all this through his sister, who was called upon by neighbors in distress. "Rose, dear! Rose, dear!" they would quaver, and they'd stumble into her yard waving an overdue bill, an alarming letter, a bottle of pills with a childproof top.

In the evening, taking Edward for his last walk, Macon glanced in windows and saw people slumped in flowered armchairs, lit blue and shivery by their TV sets. The Orioles were winning the second game of the World Series, but these people seemed to be staring at their own thoughts instead. Macon imagined they were somehow dragging him down, causing him to walk heavily, to slouch, to grow short of breath. Even the dog seemed plodding and discouraged.

And when he returned to the house, the others were suffering one of their fits of indecisiveness. Was it better to lower the thermostat at night, or not? Wouldn't the furnace have to work harder if it were lowered? Hadn't Porter read that someplace? They debated back and forth, settling it and then beginning again. Why! Macon thought. They were not so very different from their neighbors. They were growing old themselves. He'd been putting in his own two bits (by all means, lower the thermostat), but now his voice trailed off, and he said no more.

.   .   .

That night, he dreamed he was parked near Lake Roland in his grandfather's '57 Buick. He was sitting in the dark and some girl was sitting next to him. He didn't know her, but the bitter smell of her perfume seemed familiar, and the rustle of her skirt when she moved closer. He turned and looked at her. It was Muriel. He drew a breath to ask what she was doing here, but she put a finger to his lips and stopped him. She moved closer still. She took his keys from him and set them on the dashboard. Gazing steadily into his face, she unbuckled his belt and slipped a cool, knowing hand down inside his trousers.

He woke astonished and embarrassed, and sat bolt upright in his bed.

. . .

"Everybody always asks me, 'What is *your* dog like?'" Muriel said. "'I bet he's a model of good behavior,' they tell me. But you want to hear something funny? I don't own a dog. In fact, the one time I had one around, he ran off. That was Norman's dog, Spook. My ex-husband's. First night we were married, Spook ran off to Norman's mom's. I think he hated me."

"Oh, surely not," Macon said.

"He hated me. I could tell."

They were outdoors again, preparing to put Edward through his paces. By now, Macon had adjusted to the rhythm of these lessons. He waited, gripping Edward's leash. Muriel said, "It was just like one of those Walt Disney movies. You know: where the dog walks all the way to the Yukon or something. Except Spook only walked to Timonium. Me and Norman had him downtown in our apartment, and Spook took off and traveled the whole however many miles it was back to Norman's mom's house in Timonium. His mom calls up: 'When did you drop Spook off?' 'What're you talking about?' Norman asks her."

She changed her voice to match each character. Macon heard the thin whine of Norman's mother, the stammering boyishness of Norman himself. He remembered last night's dream and felt embarrassed all over again. He looked at her directly, hoping for flaws, and found them in abundance—a long, narrow nose, and sallow skin, and two freckled knobs of collarbone that promised an unluxurious body.

"Seems his mom woke up in the morning," she was saying, "and there was Spook, sitting on the doorstep. But that was the first we realized he was missing. Norman goes, 'I don't know what got into him. He never ran off before.' And gives me this doubtful kind of look. I could tell he wondered if it might be my fault. Maybe he thought it was an omen or something. We were awful young to get married. I can see that now. I was seventeen. He was eighteen—an only child. His mother's pet. Widowed mother. He had this fresh pink face like a girl's and the shortest hair of any boy in my school and he buttoned his shirt collars all the way to the neck. Moved in from Parkville the end of junior year. Caught sight of me in my strapless sundress and goggled at me all through every class; other boys teased him but he didn't pay any mind. He was just so . . . innocent, you know? He made me feel like I had powers. There he was following me around the halls with his arms full of books and I'd say, 'Norman? You want to eat lunch with me?' and he'd blush and say, 'Oh, why, uh, you serious?' He didn't even know how to drive, but I told him if he got his license I'd go out with him. 'We could ride to someplace quiet and talk and be alone,' I'd say, 'you know what I mean?' Oh, I was bad. I don't know what was wrong with me, back then. He got his license in no time flat and came for me in his mother's Chevy, which incidentally she happened to have purchased from my father, who was a salesman for Ruggles Chevrolet. We found that out at the wedding. Got married the fall of senior year, he was just dying to marry me so what could I say? and at the wedding my daddy goes to Norman's mom, 'Why, I believe I sold you a car not long ago,' but she was too busy crying to take much notice. That woman carried on like marriage was a fate worse than death. Then when Spook runs off to her house she tells us, 'I suppose I'd best keep him, it's clear as day he don't like it there with you-all.' With *me*, is what she meant. She held it against me I took her son away. She claimed I ruined his chances; she wanted him to get his diploma. But I never kept him from getting his diploma. He was the one who said he might as well drop out; said why bother staying in school when he could make a fine living on floors."

"On what?" Macon asked.

"Floors. Sanding floors. His uncle was Pritchett Refinishing. Norman went into the business as soon as we got married and his mom was always talking about the waste. She said he could have been an accountant or something, but I don't know who she thought she was kidding. He never mentioned accounting to *me*."

She pulled a dog hair off her coat sleeve, examined it, and flicked it away. "So let's see him," she said.

"Pardon?"

"Let's see him heel."

Macon slapped his hip and started off, with Edward lagging just a bit behind. When Macon stopped, Edward stopped too and sat down. Macon was pleasantly surprised, but Muriel said, "He's not sitting."

"What? What do you call it, then?"

"He's keeping his rear end about two inches off the ground. Trying to see what he can get away with."

"Oh, Edward," Macon said sadly.

He pivoted and returned. "Well, you'll have to work on that," Muriel said. "But meantime, we'll go on to the down-stay. Let's try it in the house."

Macon worried they'd meet up with Rose, but she was nowhere to be seen. The front hall smelled of radiator dust. The clock in the living room was striking the half hour.

"This is where we start on Edward's real problem," Muriel said. "Getting him to lie down and stay, so he won't all the time be jumping at the door."

She showed him the command: two taps of the foot. Her boot made a crisp sound. When Edward didn't respond, she bent and pulled his forepaws out from under him. Then she let him up and went through it again, several times over. Edward made no progress. When she tapped her foot, he panted and looked elsewhere. "Stubborn," Muriel told him. "You're just as stubborn as they come." She said to Macon, "A lot of dogs will act like this. They hate to lie down; I don't know why. Now you."

Macon tapped his foot. Edward seemed fascinated by something off to his left.

"Grab his paws," Muriel said.

"On crutches?"

"Sure."

Macon sighed and propped his crutches in the corner. He lowered himself to the floor with his cat in front of him, took Edward's paws and forced him down. Edward rumbled threateningly, but in the end he submitted. To get up again, Macon had to hold onto the lamp table. "This is really very difficult," he said, but Muriel said, "Listen, I've taught a man with no legs at all."

"You have?" Macon said. He pictured a legless man dragging along the sidewalk with some vicious breed of dog, Muriel standing by unconcerned and checking her manicure. "I don't suppose *you* ever broke a leg," he accused her. "Getting around is harder than it looks."

"I broke an arm once," Muriel said.

"An arm is no comparison."

"I did it training dogs, in fact. Got knocked off a porch by a Doberman pinscher."

"A Doberman!"

"Came to to find him standing over me, showing all his teeth. Well, I thought of what they said at Doggie, Do: Only one of you can be boss. So I tell him, 'Absolutely not.' Those were the first words that came to me—what my mother used to say when she wasn't going to let me get away with something. 'Absolutely not,' I tell him and my right arm is broken so I hold out my left, hold out my palm and stare into his eyes—they can't stand for you to meet their eyes—and get to my feet real slow. And durned if that dog doesn't settle right back on his haunches."

"Good Lord," Macon said.

"I've had a cocker spaniel fly directly at my throat. Meanest thing you ever saw. Had a German shepherd take my ankle in his teeth. Then he let it go."

She lifted a foot and rotated it. Her ankle was about the thickness of a pencil.

"Have you ever met with a failure?" Macon asked her. "Some dog you just gave up on?"

"Not a one," she said. "And Edward's not about to be the first."

But Edward seemed to think otherwise. Muriel worked with him another half hour, and although he would stay once he was down, he flatly refused to lie down on his own. Each time, he had to be forced. "Never mind," Muriel said. "This is the way most of them do. I bet tomorrow he'll be just as stubborn, so I'm going to skip a day. You keep practicing, and I'll be back this same time Saturday."

Then she told Edward to stay, and she accepted her money and slipped out the door. Observing Edward's erect, resisting posture, Macon felt discouraged. Why hire a trainer at all, if she left him to do the training? "Oh, I don't know, I don't know," he said. Edward gave a sigh and walked off, although he hadn't been released.

. . .

All that afternoon and evening, Edward refused to lie down. Macon wheedled, threatened, cajoled; Edward muttered ominously and stood firm. Rose and the boys edged around the two of them, politely averting their eyes as if they'd stumbled on some private quarrel.

Then the next morning, Edward charged the mailman. Macon managed to grab the leash, but it raised some doubts in his mind. What did all this sitting and heeling have to do with Edward's real problem? "I should just ship you off to the pound," he told Edward. He tapped his foot twice. Edward did not lie down.

In the afternoon, Macon called the Meow-Bow. "May I speak to Muriel, please?" he asked. He couldn't think of her last name.

"Muriel's not working today," a girl told him.

"Oh, I see."

"Her little boy is sick."

He hadn't known she had a little boy. He felt some inner click of adjustment; she was a slightly different person from the one he'd imagined. "Well," he said, "this is Macon Leary. I guess I'll talk to her tomorrow."

"Oh, Mr. Leary. You want to call her at home?"

"No, that's all right."

"I can give you her number if you want to call her at home."

"I'll just talk to her tomorrow. Thank you."

. . .

Rose had an errand downtown, so she agreed to drop him off at the Businessman's Press. He wanted to deliver the rest of his guidebook. Stretched across the backseat with his crutches, he gazed at the passing scenery: antique office buildings, tasteful restaurants, health food stores and florists' shops, all peculiarly hard-edged and vivid in the light of a brilliant October afternoon. Rose perched behind the wheel and drove at a steady, slow pace that was almost hypnotic. She wore a little round basin-shaped hat with ribbons down the back. It made her look prim and Sunday schoolish.

One of the qualities that all four Leary children shared was a total inability to find their way around. It was a kind of dyslexia, Macon believed—a geographic dyslexia. None of them ever stepped outside without obsessively noting all available landmarks, clinging to a fixed and desperate mental map of the neighborhood. Back home, Macon had kept a stack of index cards giving detailed directions to the houses of his friends—even friends he'd known for decades. And it used to be that whenever Ethan met a new boy, Macon's first anxious question was, "Where exactly does he live, do you know?" Ethan had had a tendency to form inconvenient alliances. He couldn't just hang out with the boy next door; oh, no, it had to be someone who lived way beyond the Beltway. What did Ethan care? *He* had no trouble navigating. This was because he'd lived all his life in one house, was Macon's theory; while a person who'd been moved around a great deal never acquired a fixed point of reference but wandered forever in a fog—adrift upon the planet, helpless, praying that just by luck he might stumble across his destination.

At any rate, Rose and Macon got lost. Rose knew where she wanted to go—a shop that sold a special furniture oil—and Macon had visited Julian's office a hundred times; but even so, they drove in circles till Macon noticed a familiar steeple. "Stop! Turn left," he said. Rose pulled up where he directed. Macon struggled out. "Will you be all right?" he asked Rose. "Do you think you can find your way back to pick me up?"

"I hope so."

"Look for the steeple, remember."

She nodded and drove away.

Macon swung up three granite steps to the brick mansion that housed the Businessman's Press. The door was made of polished, golden wood. The floor inside was tiled with tiny black and white hexagons, just uneven enough to give purchase to Macon's crutches.

This wasn't an ordinary office. The secretary typed in a back room while Julian, who couldn't stand being alone, sat out front. He was talking on a red telephone, lounging behind a desk that was laden with a clutter of advertisements, pamphlets, unpaid bills, unanswered letters, empty Chinese carryout cartons, and Perrier bottles. The walls were covered with sailing charts. The bookshelves held few books but a great many antique brass mariners' instruments that probably didn't even work anymore. Anybody with eyes could see that Julian's heart was not in the Businessman's Press but out on the Chesapeake Bay someplace. This was to Macon's advantage, he figured. Surely no one else would have continued backing his series, with its staggering expenses and its constant need for updating.

"Rita's bringing croissants," Julian said into the phone. "Joe is making his quiche." Then he caught sight of Macon. "Macon!" he said. "Stefanie, I'll get back to you." He hung up. "How's the leg? Here, have a seat."

He dumped a stack of yachting magazines off a chair. Macon sat down and handed over his folder. "Here's the rest of the material on England," he said.

"Well, finally!"

"This edition as I see it is going to run about ten or twelve pages longer than the last one," Macon said. "It's adding the business *women* that does it—listing which hotels offer elevator escorts, which ones serve drinks in the lobbies . . . I think I ought to be paid more."

"I'll talk it over with Marvin," Julian said, flipping through the manuscript.

Macon sighed. Julian spent money like water but Marvin was more cautious.

"So now you're on the U.S. again," Julian said.

"Well, if you say so."

"I hope it's not going to take you long."

"I can only go so fast," Macon said. "The U.S. has more cities."

"Yes, I realize that. In fact I might print this edition in sections: northeast, mid-Atlantic, and so forth; I don't know . . ." But then he changed the subject. (He had a rather skittery mind.) "Did I tell you my new idea? Doctor friend of mine is looking into it: *Accidental Tourist in Poor Health*. A list of American-trained doctors and dentists in every foreign capital, plus maybe some suggestions for basic medical supplies: aspirin, Merck Manual—"

"Oh, not a Merck Manual away from home!" Macon said. "Every hangnail could be cancer, when you're reading a Merck Manual."

"Well, I'll make a note of that," Julian said (without so much as lifting a pencil). "Aren't you going to ask me to autograph your cast? It's so white."

"I like it white," Macon said. "I polish it with shoe polish."

"I didn't realize you could do that."

"I use the liquid kind. It's the brand with a nurse's face on the label, if you ever need to know."

"*Accidental Tourist on Crutches*," Julian said, and he rocked back happily in his chair.

Macon could tell he was about to start his Macon Leary act. He got hastily to his feet and said, "Well, I guess I'll be going."

"So soon? Why don't we have a drink?"

"No, thanks, I can't. My sister's picking me up as soon as she gets done with her errand."

"Ah," Julian said. "What kind of errand?"

Macon looked at him suspiciously.

"Well? Dry cleaner's? Shoe repair?"

"Just an ordinary errand, Julian. Nothing special."

"Hardware store? Pharmacy?"

"No."

"So what is it?"

"Uh . . . she had to buy Furniture Food."

Julian's chair rocked so far back, Macon thought he was going to tip over. He wished he would, in fact. "Macon, do me a favor," Julian said. "Couldn't you just once invite me to a family dinner?"

"We're really not much for socializing," Macon told him.

"It wouldn't have to be fancy. Just whatever you eat normally. What *do* you eat normally? Or I'll bring the meal myself. You could lock the dog up . . . what's his name again?"

"Edward."

"Edward. Ha! And I'll come spend the evening."

"Oh, well," Macon said vaguely. He arranged himself on his crutches.

"Why don't I step outside and wait with you."

"I'd really rather you didn't," Macon said.

He couldn't bear for Julian to see his sister's little basin hat.

He pegged out to the curb and stood there, gazing in the direction Rose should be coming from. He supposed she was lost again. The cold was already creeping through the stretched-out sock he wore over his cast.

The trouble was, he decided, Julian had never had anything happen to him. His ruddy, cheerful face was unscarred by anything but sunburn; his only interest was a ridiculously inefficient form of transportation. His brief marriage had ended amicably. He had no children. Macon didn't want to sound prejudiced, but he couldn't help feeling that people who had no children had never truly grown up. They weren't entirely . . . real, he felt.

Unexpectedly, he pictured Muriel after the Doberman had knocked her off the porch. Her arm hung lifeless; he knew the leaden look a broken limb takes on. But Muriel ignored it; she didn't even glance at it. Smudged and disheveled and battered, she held her other hand up. "Absolutely not," she said.

.   .   .

She arrived the next morning with a gauzy bouffant scarf swelling over her hair, her hands thrust deep in her coat pockets. Edward danced around her. She pointed to his rump. He sat, and she bent to pick up his leash.

"How's your little boy?" Macon asked her.

She looked over at him. "What?" she said.

"Wasn't he sick?"

"Who told you that?"

"Someone at the vet's, when I phoned."

She went on looking at him.

"What was it? The flu?" he asked.

"Oh, yes, probably," she said after a moment. "Some little stomach thing."

"It's that time of year, I guess."

"How come you phoned?" she asked him.

"I wanted to know why Edward wouldn't lie down."

She turned her gaze toward Edward. She wound the leash around her hand and considered him.

"I tap my foot but he never obeys me," Macon said. "Something's wrong."

"I told you he'd be stubborn about it."

"Yes, but I've been practicing two days now and he's not making any—"

"What do you expect? You think I'm magical or something? Why blame me?"

"Oh, I'm not blaming—"

"You most certainly are. You tell me something's wrong, you call me on the phone—"

"I just wanted to—"

"You think it's weird I didn't mention Alexander, don't you?"

"Alexander?"

"You think I'm some kind of unnatural mother."

"What? No, wait a minute—"

"You're not going to give me another thought, are you, now you know I've got a kid. You're like, 'Oh, forget it, no point getting involved in *that*,' and then you wonder why I didn't tell you about him right off. Well, isn't it obvious? Don't you see what happens when I do?"

Macon wasn't quite following her logic, perhaps because he was distracted by Edward. The shriller Muriel's voice grew, the stiffer Edward's hair stood up on the back of his neck. A bad sign. A very bad sign. Edward's lip was slowly curling. Gradually, at first almost soundlessly, he began a low growl.

Muriel glanced at him and stopped speaking. She didn't seem alarmed. She merely tapped her foot twice. But Edward not only failed to lie down; he rose from his sitting position. Now he had a distinct, electrified hump between his shoulders. He seemed to have altered his basic shape. His ears were flattened against his skull.

"Down," Muriel said levelly.

With a bellow, Edward sprang straight at her face. Every tooth was bare and gleaming. His lips were drawn back in a horrible grimace and flecks of white foam flew from his mouth. Muriel instantly raised the leash. She jerked it upward with both fists and lifted Edward completely off the floor. He stopped barking. He started making gargling sounds.

"He's choking," Macon said.

Edward's throat gave an odd sort of click.

"Stop it. It's enough! You're choking him!"

Still, she let him hang. Now Edward's eyes rolled back in their sockets. Macon grabbed at Muriel's shoulder but found himself with a handful of coat, bobbled and irregular like something alive. He shook it, anyhow. Muriel lowered Edward to the floor. He landed in a boneless heap, his legs crumpling beneath him and his head flopping over. Macon crouched at his side. "Edward? Edward? Oh, God, he's dead!"

Edward raised his head and feebly licked his lips.

"See that? When they lick their lips it's a sign they're giving in," Muriel said cheerfully. "Doggie, Do taught me that."

Macon stood up. He was shaking.

"When they lick their lips it's good but when they put a foot on top of your foot it's bad," Muriel said. "Sounds like a secret language, just about, doesn't it?"

"Don't you ever, ever do that again," Macon told her.

"Huh?"

"In fact, don't even bother coming again."

There was a startled silence.

"Well, fine," Muriel said, tightening her scarf. "If that's the way you feel, just fine and dandy." She stepped neatly around Edward and opened the front door. "You want a dog you can't handle? Fine with me."

"I'd rather a barking dog than a damaged, timid dog," Macon said.

"You want a dog that bites all your friends? Scars neighbor kids for life? Gets you into lawsuits? You want a dog that hates the whole world? Evil, nasty, *angry* dog? That kills the whole world?"

She slipped out the screen door and closed it behind her. Then she looked through the screen directly into Macon's eyes. "Why, yes, I guess you do," she said.

From the hall floor, Edward gave a moan and watched her walk away.

Now the days were shorter and colder, and the trees emptied oceans of leaves on the lawn but remained, somehow, as full as ever, so you'd finish raking and look upward to see a great wash of orange and yellow just waiting to cover the grass again the minute your back was turned. Charles and Porter drove over to Macon's house and raked there as well, and lit the pilot light in the furnace and repaired the basement window. They reported that everything seemed fine. Macon heard the news without much interest. Next week he'd be out of his cast, but no one asked when he was moving back home.

Each morning he and Edward practiced heeling. They would trudge the length of the block, with Edward matching Macon's gait so perfectly that he looked crippled himself. When they met passersby now he muttered but he didn't attack. "See there?" Macon wanted to tell someone. Bikers were another issue, but Macon had confidence they would solve that problem too, eventually.

He would make Edward sit and then he'd draw back, holding out a palm. Edward waited. Oh, he wasn't such a bad dog! Macon wished he could change the gestures of command—the palm, the pointed finger, all vestiges of that heartless trainer—but he supposed it was too late. He tapped his foot. Edward growled. "Dear one," Macon said, dropping heavily beside him. "Won't you please consider lying down?" Edward looked away. Macon stroked the soft wide space between his ears. "Ah, well, maybe tomorrow," he said.

His family was not so hopeful. "What about when you start traveling again?" Rose said. "You're not leaving him with me. I wouldn't know how to handle him."

Macon told her they would get to that when they got to it.

It was hard for him to imagine resuming his travels. Sometimes he wished he could stay in his cast forever. In fact, he wished it covered him from head to foot. People would thump faintly on his chest. They'd peer through his eyeholes. "Macon? You in there?" Maybe he was, maybe he wasn't. No one would ever know.

One evening just after supper, Julian stopped by with a stack of papers. Macon had to slam Edward into the pantry before he opened the door. "Here you are!" Julian said, strolling past him. He wore corduroys and looked rugged and healthy. "I've been phoning you for three days straight. That dog sounds awfully close by, don't you think?"

"He's in the pantry," Macon said.

"Well, I've brought some materials, Macon—mostly on New York. We've got a lot of suggestions for New York."

Macon groaned. Julian set his papers on the couch and looked around him. "Where are the others?" he asked.

"Oh, here and there," Macon said vaguely, but just then Rose appeared, and Charles was close behind.

"I hope I'm not interfering with supper," Julian told them.

"No, no," Rose said.

"We've finished," Macon said triumphantly.

Julian's face fell. "Really?" he said. "What time do you eat, anyhow?"

Macon didn't answer that. (They ate at five-thirty. Julian would laugh.)

Rose said, "But we haven't had our coffee. Wouldn't you like some coffee?"

"I'd love some."

"It seems a little silly," Macon said, "if you haven't eaten."

"Well, yes," Julian said, "I suppose it does, Macon, to someone like you. But for me, home-brewed coffee is a real treat. All the people in my apartment building eat out, and there's nothing in any of the kitchens but a couple cans of peanuts and some diet soda."

"What kind of place *is* that?" Rose asked.

"It's the Calvert Arms—a singles building. Everybody's single."

"Oh! What an interesting idea."

"Well, not really," Julian said gloomily. "Not after a while. I started out enjoying it but now I think it's getting me down. Sometimes I wish for the good old-fashioned way of doing things, with children and families and old people like normal buildings have."

"Well, of course you do," Rose told him. "I'm going to get you some nice hot coffee."

She left, and the others sat down. "So. Are you three all there is?" Julian asked.

Macon refused to answer, but Charles said, "Oh, no, there's Porter too."

"Porter? Where is Porter?"

"Um, we're not too sure."

"*Missing?*"

"He went to a hardware store and we think he got lost."

"A little while before supper."

"Supper. You mean today."

"He's just running an errand," Macon said. "Not lost in any permanent sense."

"Where was the store?"

"Someplace on Howard Street," Charles said. "Rose needed hinges."

"He got lost on Howard Street."

Macon stood up. "I'll go help Rose," he said.

Rose was setting their grandmother's clear glass coffee mugs on a silver tray. "I hope he doesn't take sugar," she said. "The sugarbowl is empty and Edward's in the pantry where I keep the bag."

"I wouldn't worry about it."

"Maybe you could go to the pantry and get it for me."

"Oh, just give him his coffee straight and tell him to take it or leave it."

"Why, Macon! This is your employer!"

"He's only here because he hopes we'll do something eccentric," Macon told her. "He has this one-sided notion of us. I just pray none of us says anything unconventional around him, are you listening?"

"What would we say?" Rose asked. "We're the most conventional people I know."

This was perfectly true, and yet in some odd way it wasn't. Macon couldn't explain it. He sighed and followed her out of the kitchen.

In the living room, Charles was doggedly debating whether they should answer the phone in case it rang, in case it might be Porter, in case he needed them to consult a map. "Chances are, though, he wouldn't bother calling," he decided, "because he knows we wouldn't answer. Or he thinks we wouldn't answer. Or I don't know, maybe he figures we would answer even so, because we're worried."

"Do you always give this much thought to your phone calls?" Julian asked.

Macon said, "Have some coffee, Julian. Try it black."

"Why, thank you," Julian said. He accepted a mug and studied the inscription that arched across it. "CENTURY OF PROGRESS 1933," he read off. He grinned and raised the mug in a toast. "To progress," he said.

"Progress," Rose and Charles echoed. Macon scowled.

Julian said, "What do you do for a living, Charles?"

"I make bottle caps."

"Bottle caps! Is that a fact!"

"Oh, well, it's no big thing," Charles said. "I mean it's not half as exciting as it sounds, really."

"And Rose? Do you work?"

"Yes, I do," Rose said, in the brave, forthright style of someone being interviewed. "I work at home; I keep house for the boys. Also I take care of a lot of the neighbors. They're mostly old and they need me to read their prescriptions and repair their plumbing and such."

"You repair their plumbing?" Julian asked.

The telephone rang. The others stiffened.

"What do you think?" Rose asked Macon.

"Um . . ."

"But he knows we wouldn't answer," Charles told them.

"Yes, he'd surely call a neighbor instead."

"On the other hand . . ." Charles said.

"On the other hand," Macon said.

It was Julian's face that decided him—Julian's pleased, perked expression. Macon reached over to the end table and picked up the receiver. "Leary," he said.

"Macon?"

It was Sarah.

Macon shot a glance at the others and turned his back to them. "Yes," he said.

"Well, finally," she said. Her voice seemed oddly flat and concrete. All at once he saw her clearly: She wore one of his cast-off shirts and she sat hugging her bare knees. "I've been trying to get in touch with you at home," she said. "Then it occurred to me you might be having supper with your family."

"Is something wrong?" he asked.

He was nearly whispering. Maybe Rose understood, from that, who it was, for she suddenly began an animated conversation with the others. Sarah said, "What? I can't hear you."

"Is everything all right?"

"Who's that talking?"

"Julian's here."

"Oh, Julian! Give him my love. How's Sukie?"

"Sukie?"

"His boat, Macon."

"It's fine," he said. Or should he have said "she"? For all he knew, *Sukie* was at the bottom of the Chesapeake.

"I called because I thought we should talk," Sarah said. "I was hoping we could meet for supper some night."

"Oh. Well. Yes, we could do that," Macon said.

"Would tomorrow be all right?"

"Certainly."

"What restaurant?"

"Well, why not the Old Bay," Macon said.

"The Old Bay. Of course," Sarah said. She either sighed or laughed, he wasn't sure which.

"It's only because you could walk there," he told her. "That's the only reason I suggested it."

"Yes, well, let's see. You like to eat early; shall we say six o'clock?"

"Six will be fine," he said.

When he hung up, he found Rose embarked on a discussion of the English language. She pretended not to notice he had rejoined them. It was shocking, she was saying, how sloppy everyday speech had become. How the world seemed bound and determined to say "*the* hoi polloi," a clear redundancy in view of the fact that "hoi" was an article. How "chauvinist" had come to be a shorthand term for "male chauvinist," its original meaning sadly lost to common knowledge. It was incredible, Charles chimed in, that a female movie star traveled "incognito" when any fool should know she was "incognita" instead. Julian appeared to share their indignation. It was more incredible still, he said, how everyone slung around the word "incredible" when really there was very little on earth that truly defied credibility. "Credence," Macon corrected him, but Rose rushed in as if Macon hadn't spoken. "Oh, I know just what you mean," she told Julian. "Words are getting devalued, isn't that right?" She tugged handfuls of her gray tube skirt over her knees in a childlike gesture. You would think she had never been warned that outsiders were not to be trusted.

. . .

To enter the Old Bay Restaurant, Macon had to climb a set of steps. Before he broke his leg he hadn't even noticed those steps existed—let alone that they were made of smooth, unblemished marble, so that his crutches kept threatening to slide out from under him. Then he had to fight the heavy front door, hurrying a bit because Rose had taken a wrong turn driving him down and it was already five after six.

The foyer was dark as night. The dining room beyond was only slightly brighter, lit by netted candles on the tables. Macon peered into the gloom. "I'm meeting someone," he told the hostess. "Is she here yet?"

"Not as I know of, hon."

She led him past a tankful of sluggish lobsters, past two old ladies in churchy hats sipping pale pink drinks, past a whole field of empty tables. It was too early for anyone else to be eating; all the other customers were still in the bar. The tables stood very close together, their linens brushing the floor, and Macon had visions of catching a crutch on a tablecloth and dragging the whole thing after him, candle included. The maroon floral carpet would burst into flames. His grandfather's favorite restaurant—his great-grandfather's too, quite possibly—would be reduced to a heap of charred metal crab pots. "Miss! Slow down!" he called, but the hostess strode on, muscular and athletic in her off-the-shoulder square-dance dress and sturdy white crepe-soled shoes.

She put him in a corner, which was lucky because it gave him a place to lean his crutches. But just as he was matching them up and preparing to set them aside, she said, "I'll take those for you, darlin'."

"Oh, they'll be fine here."

"I need to check them up front, sweetheart. It's a rule."

"You have a rule about crutches?"

"They might trip the other customers, honeybunch."

This was unlikely, since the two other customers were clear across the room, but Macon handed his crutches over. Come to think of it, he might be better off without them. Then Sarah wouldn't get the impression (at least at first glance) that he'd fallen apart in her absence.

As soon as he was alone he tugged each shirt cuff till a quarter-inch of white showed. He was wearing his gray tweed suit coat with gray flannel trousers—an old pair of trousers, so it hadn't mattered if he cut one leg off. Charles had fetched them from home and Rose had hemmed them, and she'd also trimmed his hair. Porter had lent him his best striped tie. They had all been so discreetly helpful that Macon had felt sad, for some reason.

The hostess reappeared in the doorway, followed by Sarah. Macon had an instant of stunned recognition; it was something like accidentally glimpsing his own reflection in a mirror. Her halo of curls, the way her coat fell around her in soft folds, her firm, springy walk in trim pumps with wineglass heels—how had he forgotten all that?

He half stood. Would she kiss him? Or just, God forbid, coolly shake hands. But no, she did neither; she did something much worse. She came around the table and pressed her cheek to his briefly, as if they were mere acquaintances meeting at a cocktail party.

"Hello, Macon," she said.

He waved her speechlessly into the chair across from his. He sat again, with some effort.

"What happened to your leg?" she asked.

"I had a kind of . . . fall."

"Is it broken?"

He nodded.

"And what did you do to your hand?"

He held it up to examine. "Well, it's a sort of dog bite. But it's nearly healed by now."

"I meant the other one."

The other one had a band of gauze around the knuckles. "Oh, that," he said. "It's just a scrape. I've been helping Rose build a cat door."

She studied him.

"But I'm all right!" he told her. "In fact the cast is almost comfortable. Almost familiar! I'm wondering if I broke a leg once before in some previous incarnation."

Their waitress asked, "Can I bring you something from the bar?"

She was standing over them, pad and pencil poised. Sarah started flipping hastily through the menu, so Macon said, "A dry sherry, please." Then he and the waitress turned back to Sarah. "Oh, my," Sarah said. "Let me see. Well, how about a Rob Roy. Yes, a Rob Roy would be nice, with extra cherries."

That was something else he'd forgotten—how she loved to order complicated drinks in restaurants. He felt the corners of his mouth twitching upward.

"So," Sarah said when the waitress had gone. "Why would Rose be building a cat door? I thought they didn't have any pets."

"No, this is for our cat. Helen. Helen and I have been staying there."

"What for?"

"Well, because of my leg."

Sarah said nothing.

"I mean, can you see me managing those steps at home?" Macon asked her. "Taking Edward for walks? Lugging the trash cans out?"

But she was busy shucking off her coat. Beneath it she wore a gathered wool dress in an indeterminate color. (The candlelight turned everything to shades of sepia, like an old-fashioned photograph.) Macon had time to wonder if he'd given her the wrong idea. It sounded, perhaps, as if he were complaining—as if he were reproaching her for leaving him alone.

"But really," he said, "I've been getting along wonderfully."

"Good," Sarah said, and she smiled at him and went back to her menu.

Their drinks were set before them on little cardboard disks embossed with crabs. The waitress said, "Ready to order, dearies?"

"Well," Sarah said, "I think I'll have the hot antipasto and the beef Pierre."

The waitress, looking startled, peered over Sarah's shoulder at the menu. (Sarah had never seemed to realize what the Old Bay Restaurant was all about.) "Here," Sarah said, pointing, "and here."

"If you say so," the waitress said, writing it down.

"I'll just have the, you know," Macon said. "Crab soup, shrimp salad platter . . ." He handed back his menu. "Sarah, do you want wine?"

"No, thank you."

When they were alone again, she said, "How long have you been at your family's?"

"Since September," Macon said.

"September! Your leg's been broken all that time?"

He nodded and took a sip of his drink. "Tomorrow I get the cast off," he said.

"And is Edward over there too?"

He nodded again.

"Was it Edward who bit your hand?"

"Well, yes."

He wondered if she'd act like the others, urge him to call the S.P.C.A.; but instead she meditatively plucked a cherry off the plastic sword from her drink. "I guess he's been upset," she said.

"Yes, he has, in fact," Macon said. "He's not himself at all."

"Poor Edward."

"He's getting kind of out of control, to tell the truth."

"He always did have a sensitivity to change," Sarah said.

Macon took heart. "Actually, he's been attacking right and left," he told her. "I had to hire a special trainer. But she was too harsh; let's face it, she was brutal. She nearly strangled him when he tried to bite her."

"Ridiculous," Sarah said. "He was only frightened. When Edward's frightened he attacks; that's just the way he is. There's no point scaring him more."

Macon felt a sudden rush of love.

Oh, he'd raged at her and hated her and entirely forgotten her, at different times. He'd had moments when he imagined he'd never cared for her to begin with; only went after her because everybody else had. But the fact was, she was his best friend. The two of them had been through things that no one else in the world knew of. She was embedded in his life. It was much too late to root her out.

"What he wants," she was saying, "is a sense of routine. That's all he needs: reassurance."

"Sarah," he said, "it's been awful living apart."

She looked at him. Some trick of light made her eyes appear a darker blue, almost black.

"Hasn't it?" he said.

She lowered her glass. She said, "I asked you here for a reason, Macon."

He could tell it was something he didn't want to hear.

She said, "We need to spell out the details of our separation."

"We've been separated; what's to spell out?" he asked.

"I meant in a legal way."

"Legal. I see."

"Now, according to the state of Maryland—"

"I think you ought to come home."

Their first course arrived, placed before them by a hand that, as far as Macon was concerned, was not attached to a body. Condiment bottles were shifted needlessly; a metal stand full of sugar packets was moved a half-inch over. "Anything else?" the waitress asked.

"No!" Macon said. "Thank you."

She left.

He said, "Sarah?"

"It's not possible," she told him.

She was sliding a single pearl up and down the chain at her throat. He had given her that pearl when they were courting. Was there any significance in her wearing it this evening? Or maybe she cared so little now, it hadn't even occurred to her to leave it off. Yes, that was more likely.

"Listen," he said. "Don't say no before you hear me out. Have you ever considered we might have another baby?"

He had shocked her, he saw; she drew in a breath. (He had shocked himself.)

"Why not?" he asked her. "We're not too old."

"Oh, Macon."

"This time, it would be easy," he said. "It wouldn't take us seven years again; I bet you'd get pregnant in no time!" He leaned toward her, straining to make her see it: Sarah blossoming in that luscious pink maternity smock she used to wear. But oddly enough, what flashed across his mind instead was the memory of those first seven years—their disappointment each month. It had seemed to Macon back then (though of course it was pure superstition) that their failures were a sign of something deeper, some essential incompatibility. They had missed connections in the most basic and literal sense. When she finally got pregnant, he had felt not only relieved but guilty, as if they had succeeded in putting something over on someone.

He pushed these thoughts back down. "I realize," he said, "that it wouldn't be Ethan. I realize we can't replace him. But—"

"No," Sarah said.

Her eyes were very steady. He knew that look. She'd never change her mind.

Macon started on his soup. It was the best crab soup in Baltimore, but unfortunately the spices had a tendency to make his nose run. He hoped Sarah wouldn't think he was crying.

"I'm sorry," she said more gently. "But it would never work."

He said, "All right, forget that. It was crazy, right? Crazy notion. By the time that baby was twenty we'd be . . . Aren't you going to eat?"

She glanced down at her plate. Then she picked up a fork.

"Suppose I did this," Macon said. "Suppose I packed a suitcase with your clothes and knocked on your door and said, 'Come on, we're going to Ocean City. We've wasted long enough.'"

She stared, an artichoke heart raised halfway to her mouth.

"Ocean City?" she said. "You hate Ocean City!"

"Yes, but I meant—"

"You always said it was way too crowded."

"Yes, but—"

"And what clothes could you be talking about? They're all in my apartment."

"It was only a manner of speaking," Macon said.

"Really, Macon," she told him. "You don't even communicate when you communicate."

"Oh, *communicate*," he said. (His least favorite word.) "All I'm saying is, I think we ought to start over."

"I am starting over," she said. She returned the artichoke heart to her plate. "I'm doing everything I can to start over," she said, "but that doesn't mean I want to live the same life twice. I'm trying to branch off in new directions. I'm taking some courses. I'm even dating, a little."

"Dating?"

"I've been going out with this physician."

There was a pause.

Macon said, "Why not just call him a doctor."

Sarah briefly closed her eyes.

"Look," she said. "I know this is hard for you. It's hard for both of us. But we really didn't have much left, don't you see? Look who you turned to when you broke your leg: your sister Rose! You didn't even let me know, and you do have my telephone number."

"If I'd turned to you instead," he said, "would you have come?"

"Well . . . but at least you could have asked. But no, you called on your family. You're closer to them than you ever were to me."

"That's not true," Macon said. "Or rather, it's true but it's not the point. I mean, in one sense, of course we're closer; we're blood relations."

"Playing that ridiculous card game no one else can fathom," Sarah said. "Plotting your little household projects, Rose with her crescent wrench and her soldering gun. Cruising hardware stores like other people cruise boutiques."

"*As* other people cruise boutiques," Macon said. And then regretted it.

"Picking apart people's English," Sarah said. "Hauling forth the dictionary at every opportunity. Quibbling over *method*. The kind of family that always fastens their seatbelts."

"For God's sake, Sarah, what's wrong with fastening your seatbelt?"

"They always go to one restaurant, the one their grandparents went to before them, and even there they have to rearrange the silver and set things up so they're sitting around the table the same way they sit at home. They dither and deliberate, can't so much as close a curtain without this group discussion back and forth, to and fro, all the pros and cons. 'Well, if we leave it open it will be so hot but if we close it things will get musty . . .' They have to have their six glasses of water every day. Their precious baked potatoes every night. They don't believe in ballpoint pens or electric typewriters or automatic transmissions. They don't believe in hello and good-bye."

"Hello? Good-bye?" Macon said.

"Just watch yourself some time! People walk in and you just, oh, register it with your eyes; people leave and you just look away quickly. You don't admit to comings and goings. And the best house in the world might come on the market, but you can't buy it because you've ordered these address labels for the old house, a thousand five hundred gummed labels, and you have to use them up before you move."

"That wasn't me, it was Charles," Macon said.

"Yes, but it could have been you. And his wife divorced him for it, and I don't blame her."

"And now you're about to do the same damn thing," Macon said. "Ruin twenty years of marriage over whether I fasten my seatbelt."

"They were ruined long ago, believe me," Sarah said.

Macon laid down his spoon. He forced himself to take a deep breath.

"Sarah," he said. "We're getting away from the point."

After a silence, Sarah said, "Yes, I guess we are."

"It's what happened to Ethan that ruined us," Macon told her.

She set an elbow on the table and covered her eyes.

"But it wouldn't have to," he said. "Why, some people, a thing like this brings them closer together. How come we're letting it part us?"

The waitress said, "Is everything all right?"

Sarah sat up straighter and started rummaging through her purse.

"Yes, certainly," Macon said.

The waitress was carrying a tray with their main dishes. She cast a doubtful look at Sarah's antipasto. "Isn't she going to eat that, or what?" she asked Macon.

"No, I guess, um, maybe not."

"Didn't she like it?"

"She liked it fine. Take it away."

The waitress bustled around the table in an offended silence. Sarah put aside her purse. She looked down at her meal, which was something brown and gluey.

"You're welcome to half my shrimp salad," Macon told her when the waitress had gone.

She shook her head. Her eyes were deep with tears, but they hadn't spilled over.

"Macon," she said, "ever since Ethan died I've had to admit that people are basically bad. Evil, Macon. So evil they would take a twelve-year-old boy and shoot him through the skull for no reason. I read a paper now and I despair; I've given up watching the news on TV. There's so much wickedness, children setting other children on fire and grown men throwing babies out second-story windows, rape and torture and terrorism, old people beaten and robbed, men in our very own government willing to blow up the world, indifference and greed and instant anger on every street corner. I look at my students and they're so ordinary, but they're exactly like the boy who killed Ethan. If it hadn't said beneath that boy's picture what he'd been arrested for, wouldn't you think he was just anyone? Someone who'd made the basketball team or won a college scholarship? You can't believe in a soul. Last spring, Macon, I didn't tell you this, I was cutting back our hedge and I saw the bird feeder had been stolen out of the crape myrtle tree. Someone will even steal food from little birds! And I just, I don't know, went kind of crazy and attacked the crape myrtle. Cut it all up, ripped off the branches, slashed it with my pruning shears . . ."

Tears were running down her face now. She leaned across the table and said, "There are times when I haven't been sure I could— I don't want to sound melodramatic but—Macon, I haven't been sure I could live in this kind of a world anymore."

Macon felt he had to be terribly careful. He had to choose exactly the right words. He cleared his throat and said, "Yes, um, I see what you mean but . . ." He cleared his throat again. "It's true," he said, "what you say about human beings. I'm not trying to argue. But tell me this, Sarah: Why would that cause you to leave me?"

She crumpled up her napkin and dabbed at her nose. She said, "Because I *knew* you wouldn't try to argue. You've believed all along they were evil."

"Well, so—"

"This whole last year I felt myself retreating. Withdrawing. I could feel myself shrinking. I stayed away from crowds, I didn't go to parties, I didn't ask our friends in. When you and I went to the beach in the summer I lay on my blanket with all those people around me, their squawking radios and their gossip and their quarrels, and I thought, 'Ugh, they're so depressing. They're so unlikable. So vile, really.' I felt myself shrinking away from them. Just like you do, Macon—just *as* you do; sorry. Just as you have always done. I felt I was turning into a Leary."

Macon tried for a lighter tone. He said, "Well, there are worse disasters than that, I guess."

She didn't smile. She said, "I can't afford it."

"Afford?"

"I'm forty-two years old. I don't have enough time left to waste it holing up in my shell. So I've taken action. I've cut myself loose. I live in this apartment you'd hate, all clutter. I've made a whole bunch of new friends, and you wouldn't like them much either, I guess. I'm studying with a sculptor. I always did want to be an artist, only teaching seemed more sensible. That's how you would think: sensible. You're so quick to be sensible, Macon, that you've given up on just about everything."

"What have I given up on?"

She refolded the napkin and blotted her eyes. An appealing blur of mascara shadowed the skin beneath them. She said, "Remember Betty Grand?"

"No."

"Betty Grand, she went to my school. You used to like her before you met me."

"I never liked anyone on earth before I met you," Macon said.

"You liked Betty Grand, Macon. You told me so when we first went out. You asked me if I knew her. You said you used to think she was pretty and you'd invited her to a ball game but she turned you down. You told me you'd changed your mind about her being pretty. Her gums showed any time she smiled, you said."

Macon still didn't remember, but he said, "Well? So?"

"Everything that might touch you or upset you or disrupt you, you've given up without a murmur and done without, said you never wanted it anyhow."

"I suppose I would have done better if I'd gone on pining for Betty Grand all my life."

"Well, you would have shown some feeling, at least."

"I do show feeling, Sarah. I'm sitting here with you, am I not? You don't see me giving up on *you*."

She chose not to hear this. "And when Ethan died," she said, "you peeled every single Wacky Pack sticker off his bedroom door. You emptied his closet and his bureau as if you couldn't be rid of him soon enough. You kept offering people his junk in the basement, stilts and sleds and skateboards, and you couldn't understand why they didn't accept them. 'I hate to see stuff there useless,' you said. Macon, I know you loved him but I can't help thinking you didn't love him as much as I did, you're not so torn apart by his going. I know you mourned him but there's something so what-do-you-call, so muffled about the way you experience things, I mean love or grief or anything; it's like you're trying to slip through life unchanged. Don't you see why I had to get out?"

"Sarah, I'm not muffled. I . . . endure. I'm trying to endure. I'm standing fast, I'm holding steady."

"If you really think that," Sarah said, "then you're fooling yourself. You're not holding steady; you're ossified. You're encased. You're like something in a capsule. You're a dried-up kernel of a man that nothing real penetrates. Oh, Macon, it's not by chance you write those silly books telling people how to take trips without a jolt. That traveling armchair isn't just your logo; it's you."

"No, it's not," Macon said. "It's not!"

Sarah pulled her coat on, making a sloppy job of it. One corner of her collar was tucked inside. "So anyway," she said. "This is what I wanted to tell you: I'm having John Albright send you a letter."

"Who's John Albright?"

"He's an attorney."

"Oh," Macon said.

It was at least a full minute before he thought to say, "I guess you must mean a lawyer."

Sarah collected her purse, stood up, and walked out.

.   .   .

Macon made his way conscientiously through his shrimp salad. He ate his cole slaw for the vitamin C. Then he finished every last one of his potato chips, although he knew his tongue would feel shriveled the following morning.

Once when Ethan was little, not more than two or three, he had run out into the street after a ball. Macon had been too far away to stop him. All he could do was shout, "No!" and then watch, frozen with horror, as a pickup truck came barreling around the curve. In that instant, he released his claim. In one split second he adjusted to a future that held no Ethan—an immeasurably bleaker place but also, by way of compensation, plainer and simpler, free of the problems a small child trails along with him, the endless demands and the mess and the contests for his mother's attention. Then the truck stopped short and Ethan retrieved his ball, and Macon's knees went weak with relief. But he remembered forever after how quickly he had adjusted. He wondered, sometimes, if that first adjustment had somehow stuck, making what happened to Ethan later less of a shock than it might have been. But if people didn't adjust, how could they bear to go on?

He called for his bill and paid it. "Was there something wrong?"

the waitress asked. "Did your friend not like her meal? She could always have sent it back, hon. We always let you send it back."

"I know that," Macon said.

"Maybe it was too spicy for her."

"It was fine," he said. "Could I have my crutches, please?"

She went off to get them, shaking her head.

He would have to locate a taxi. He'd made no arrangements for Rose to pick him up. Secretly, he'd been hoping to go home with Sarah. Now that hope seemed pathetic. He looked around the dining room and saw that most of the tables were filled, and that every person had someone else to eat with. Only Macon sat alone. He kept very erect and dignified but inside, he knew, he was crumbling. And when the waitress brought him his crutches and he stood to leave, it seemed appropriate that he had to walk nearly doubled, his chin sunk low on his chest and his elbows jutting out awkwardly like the wings of a baby bird. People stared at him as he passed. Some snickered. Was his foolishness so obvious? He passed the two churchy old ladies and one of them tugged at his sleeve. "Sir? Sir?"

He came to a stop.

"I suspect they may have given you my crutches," she said.

He looked down at the crutches. They were, of course, not his. They were diminutive—hardly more than child-sized. Any other time he would have grasped the situation right off, but today it had somehow escaped him. Any other time he would have swung into action—called for the manager, pointed out the restaurant's lack of concern for the handicapped. Today he only stood hanging his head, waiting for someone to help him.

nine

Back when Grandfather Leary's mind first began to wander, no one had guessed what was happening. He was such an upright, firm old man. He was all sharp edges. Definite. "Listen," he told Macon, "by June the twelfth I'll need my passport from the safe deposit box. I'm setting sail for Lassaque."

"Lassaque, Grandfather?"

"If I like it I may just stay there."

"But where is Lassaque?"

"It's an island off the coast of Bolivia."

"Ah," Macon said. And then, "Well, wait a minute . . ."

"It interests me because the Lassaquans have no written language. In fact if you bring any reading matter they confiscate it. They say it's black magic."

"But I don't think Bolivia *has* a coast," Macon said.

"They don't even allow, say, a checkbook with your name on it. Before you go ashore you have to soak the label off your deodorant. You have to get your money changed into little colored wafers."

"Grandfather, is this a joke?"

"A joke! Look it up if you don't believe me." Grandfather Leary checked his steel pocket watch, then wound it with an assured, back-and-forth motion. "An intriguing effect of their illiteracy," he said, "is their reverence for the elderly. This is because the Lassaquans' knowledge doesn't come from books but from living; so they hang on every word from those who have lived the longest."

"I see," Macon said, for now he thought he did see. "We hang on *your* words, too," he said.

"That may be so," his grandfather told him, "but I still intend to see Lassaque before it's corrupted."

Macon was silent a moment. Then he went over to the bookcase and selected a volume from his grandfather's set of faded brown encyclopedias. "Give it here," his grandfather said, holding out both hands. He took the book greedily and started riffling through the pages. A smell of mold floated up. "Laski," he muttered, "Lassalle, Lassaw . . ." He lowered the book and frowned. "I don't . . ." he said. He returned to the book. "Lassalle, Lassaw . . ."

He looked confused, almost frightened. His face all at once collapsed—a phenomenon that had startled Macon on several occasions lately. "I don't understand," he whispered to Macon. "I don't understand."

"Well," Macon said, "maybe it was a dream. Maybe it was one of those dreams that seem real."

"Macon, this was no dream. I *know* the place. I've bought my ticket. I'm sailing June the twelfth."

Macon felt a strange coldness creeping down his back.

Then his grandfather became an inventor—spoke of various projects he was tinkering with, he said, in his basement. He would sit in his red leather armchair, his suit and white shirt immaculate, his black dress shoes polished to a glare, his carefully kept hands folded in his lap, and he would announce that he'd just finished welding together a motorcycle that would pull a plow. He would earnestly discuss crankshafts and cotter pins, while Macon—though terribly distressed—had to fight down a bubble of laughter at the thought of some leather-booted Hell's Angel grinding away at a wheatfield. "If I could just get the kinks ironed out," his grandfather said, "I'd have my fortune made. We'll all be rich." For he seemed to believe he was poor again, struggling to earn his way in the world. His motorized radio that followed you from room to room, his floating telephone, his car that came when you called it— wouldn't there be some application for those? Wouldn't the right person pay an arm and a leg?

Having sat out on the porch for one entire June morning, studiously pinching the creases of his trousers, he announced that he had perfected a new type of hybrid: flowers that closed in the presence of tears. "Florists will be mobbing me," he said. "Think of the dramatic effect at funerals!" He was working next on a cross between basil and tomatoes. He said the spaghetti-sauce companies would make him a wealthy man.

By then, all three of his grandsons had left home and his wife had died; so Rose alone took care of him. Her brothers began to worry about her. They took to dropping by more and more often. Then Rose said, "You don't have to do this, you know."

They said, "What? Do what? What are you talking about?" And other such things.

"If you're coming so often on account of Grandfather, it's not necessary. I'm managing fine, and so is he. He's very happy."

"Happy!"

"I honestly believe," Rose said, "that he's having the richest and most . . . colorful, really, time of his life. I'll bet even when he was young, he never enjoyed himself this much."

They saw what she meant. Macon felt almost envious, once he thought about it. And later, when that period was over, he was sorry it had been so short. For their grandfather soon passed to pointless, disconnected mumbles, and then to a staring silence, and at last he died.

Early Wednesday morning, Macon dreamed Grandfather Leary woke him and asked where the center punch was. "What are you talking about?" Macon said. "I never had your center punch."

"Oh, Macon," his grandfather said sadly, "can't you tell that I'm not saying what I mean?"

"What do you mean, then?"

"You've lost the center of your *life*, Macon."

"Yes, I know that," Macon said, and it seemed that Ethan stood just slightly to the left, his bright head nearly level with the old man's.

But his grandfather said, "No, no," and made an impatient, shaking-off gesture and went over to the bureau. (In this dream, Macon was not in the sun porch but upstairs in his boyhood bedroom, with the bureau whose cut-glass knobs Rose had stolen long ago to use as dishes for her dolls.) "It's Sarah I mean," his grandfather said, picking up a hairbrush. "Where is Sarah?"

"She's left me, Grandfather."

"Why, Sarah's the best of all of us!" his grandfather said. "You want to sit in this old house and rot, boy? It's time we started digging out! How long are we going to stay fixed here?"

Macon opened his eyes. It wasn't morning yet. The sun porch was fuzzy as blotting paper.

There was still a sense of his grandfather in the air. His little shaking-off gesture was one that Macon had forgotten entirely; it had reappeared on its own. But Grandfather Leary would never have said in real life what he'd said in the dream. He had liked Sarah well enough, but he seemed to view wives as extraneous, and he'd attended each of his grandsons' weddings with a resigned and tolerant expression. He wouldn't have thought of any woman as a "center." Except, perhaps Macon thought suddenly, his own wife, Grandmother Leary. After whose death—why, yes, immediately after—his mind had first begun to wander.

Macon lay awake till dawn. It was a relief to hear the first stirrings overhead. Then he got up and shaved and dressed and sent Edward out for the paper. By the time Rose came downstairs, he had started the coffee perking. This seemed to make her anxious. "Did you use the morning beans or the evening beans?" she asked.

"The morning beans," he assured her. "Everything's under control."

She moved around the kitchen raising shades, setting the table, opening a carton of eggs. "So today's the day you get your cast off," she said.

"Looks that way."

"And this afternoon's your New York trip."

"Oh, well . . ." he said vaguely, and then he asked if she wanted a bacon coupon he'd spotted in the paper.

She persisted: "Isn't it this afternoon you're going?"

"Well, yes."

The fact of the matter was, he was leaving for New York without having made any arrangements for Edward. The old place wouldn't accept him, the new place had that Muriel woman . . . and in Macon's opinion, Edward was best off at home with the family. Rose, no doubt, would disagree. He held his breath, but Rose started humming "Clementine" and breaking eggs into a skillet.

At nine o'clock, in an office down on St. Paul Street, the doctor removed Macon's cast with a tiny, purring electric saw. Macon's leg emerged dead-white and wrinkled and ugly. When he stood up, his ankle wobbled. He still had a limp. Also, he'd forgotten to bring different trousers and he was forced to parade back through the other patients in his one-legged summer khakis, exposing his repulsive-looking shin. He wondered if he'd ever return to his old, unbroken self.

Driving him home, Rose finally thought to ask where he planned to board Edward. "Why, I'm leaving him with you," Macon said, acting surprised.

"With me? Oh, Macon, you know how out of hand he gets."

"What could happen in such a short time? I'll be home by to-morrow night. If worst comes to worst you could lock him in the pantry; toss him some kibble now and then till I get back."

"I don't like this at all," Rose said.

"It's visitors that set him off. It's not as if you're expecting any visitors."

"Oh, no," she said, and then she let the subject drop, thank heaven. He'd been fearing more of a battle.

He took a shower, and he dressed in his traveling suit. Then he had an early lunch. Just before noon Rose drove him down to the railroad station, since he didn't yet trust his clutch foot. When he stepped from the car, his leg threatened to buckle. "Wait!" he said to Rose, who was handing his bag out after him. "Do you suppose I'm up to this?"

"I'm sure you are," she said, without giving it anywhere near enough thought. She pulled the passenger door shut, waved at him, and drove off.

In the period since Macon's last train trip, something wonderful had happened to the railroad station. A skylight in shades of watery blue arched gently overhead. Pale globe lamps hung from brass hooks. The carpenters' partitions that had divided the waiting room for so long had disappeared, revealing polished wooden benches. Macon stood bewildered at the brand-new, gleaming ticket window. Maybe, he thought, travel was not so bad. Maybe he'd got it all wrong. He felt a little sprig of hopefulness beginning.

But immediately afterward, limping toward his gate, he was overcome by the lost feeling that always plagued him on these trips. He envisioned himself as a stark Figure 1 in a throng of 2's and 3's. Look at that group at the Information counter, those confident young people with their knapsacks and sleeping bags. Look at the family occupying one entire bench, their four little daughters so dressed up, so stiff in new plaid coats and ribboned hats, you just knew they'd be met by grandparents at the other end of the line. Even those sitting alone—the old woman with the corsage, the blonde with her expensive leather luggage—gave the impression of belonging to someone.

He sat down on a bench. A southbound train was announced and half the crowd went off to catch it, followed by the inevitable breathless, disheveled woman galloping through some time later with far too many bags and parcels. Arriving passengers began to straggle up the stairs. They wore the dazed expressions of people who had been elsewhere till just this instant. A woman was greeted by a man holding a baby; he kissed her and passed her the baby at once, as if it were a package he'd been finding unusually heavy. A young girl in jeans, reaching the top of the stairs, caught sight of another girl in jeans and threw her arms around her and started crying. Macon watched, pretending not to, inventing explanations. (She was home for their mother's funeral? Her elopement hadn't worked out?)

Now his own train was called, so he picked up his bag and

limped behind the family with all the daughters. At the bottom of the stairs a gust of cold, fresh air hit him. Wind always seemed to be howling down these platforms, no matter what the weather elsewhere. The smallest of the daughters had to have her coat buttoned. The train came into view, slowly assembling itself around a pinpoint of yellow light.

Most of the cars were full, it turned out. Macon gave up trying to find a completely empty seat and settled next to a plump young man with a briefcase. Just to be on the safe side, he unpacked *Miss MacIntosh*.

The train lurched forward and then changed its mind and then lurched forward again and took off. Macon imagined he could feel little scabs of rust on the tracks; it wasn't a very smooth ride. He watched the sights of home rush toward him and disappear—a tumble of row houses, faded vacant lots, laundry hanging rigid in the cold.

"Gum?" his seatmate asked.

Macon said, "No, thanks," and quickly opened his book.

When they'd been traveling an hour or so, he felt his lids grow heavy. He let his head fall back. He thought he was only resting his eyes, but he must have gone to sleep. The next thing he knew, the conductor was announcing Philadelphia. Macon jerked and sat up straight and caught his book just before it slid off his lap.

His seatmate was doing some kind of paperwork, using his briefcase as a desk. A businessman, obviously—one of the people Macon wrote his guides for. Funny, Macon never pictured his readers. What did businessmen do, exactly? This one was jotting notes on index cards, referring now and then to a booklet full of graphs. One graph showed little black trucks marching across the page—four trucks, seven trucks, three and a half trucks. Macon thought the half-truck looked deformed and pitiable.

Just before they arrived, he used the restroom at the rear of the car—not ideal, but more homey than anything he'd find in New York. He went back to his seat and packed *Miss MacIntosh*. "Going to be cold there," his seatmate told him.

"I imagine so," Macon said.

"Weather report says cold and windy."

Macon didn't answer.

He believed in traveling without an overcoat—just one more thing to carry—but he wore a thermal undershirt and long johns. Cold was the least of his worries.

In New York the passengers scattered instantly. Macon thought of a seed pod bursting open. He refused to be rushed and made his way methodically through the crowd, up a set of clanking, dark stairs, and through another crowd that seemed more extreme than the one he had left down below. Goodness, where did these women get their clothes? One wore a bushy fur tepee and leopardskin boots. One wore an olive-drab coverall exactly like an auto mechanic's except that it was made of leather. Macon took a firmer grip on his bag and pushed through the door to the street, where car horns blasted insistently and the air smelled gray and sharp, like the interior of a dead chimney. In his opinion, New York was a foreign city. He was forever taken aback by its pervasive atmosphere of purposefulness—the tight focus of its drivers, the brisk intensity of its pedestrians drilling their way through all obstacles without a glance to either side.

He hailed a cab, slid across the worn, slippery seat, and gave the address of his hotel. The driver started talking at once about his daughter. "I mean she's thirteen years old," he said, nosing out into traffic, "and got three sets of holes in her ears and an earring in each hole, and now she wants to get another set punched up toward the top. Thirteen years old!" He either had or had not heard the address. At any rate, he was driving along. "I wasn't even in favor of the first set of holes," he said. "I told her, 'What; you don't read Ann Landers?' Ann Landers says piercing your ears is mutilating your body. Was it Ann Landers? I think it was Ann Landers. You might as well wear a ring through your nose like the Africans, right? I told my daughter that. She says, 'So? What's wrong with a ring through my nose? Maybe that's what I'll get next.' I wouldn't put it past her, either. I would not put it past her. Now this fourth set goes through cartilage and most of these ear-piercing places won't do that; so you see how crazy it is. Cartilage is a whole different ball game. It's not your earlobe, all spongy."

Macon had the feeling he wasn't fully visible. He was listening to a man who was talking to himself, who may have been talking before he got in and might possibly go on talking after he got out. Or was he present in this cab at all? Such thoughts often attacked while he was traveling. In desperation, he said, "Um—"

The driver stopped speaking, surprisingly enough. The back of his neck took on an alert look. Macon had to continue. He said, "Tell her something scary."

"Like what?"

"Like . . . tell her you know a girl whose ears dropped off."

"She'd never go for that."

"Make it scientific. Say if you puncture cartilage, it will wither right away."

"Hmm," the driver said. He honked his horn at a produce truck.

" 'Imagine how you'd feel,' tell her, 'having to wear the same hairstyle forever. Covering up your withered ears.' "

"Think she'd believe me?"

"Why not?" Macon asked. And then, after a pause, "In fact, it may be true. Do you suppose I could have read it someplace?"

"Well, now, maybe you did," the driver said. "There's this sort of familiar ring to it."

"I might even have seen a photograph," Macon said. "Somebody's ears, shriveled. All shrunken."

"Wrinkly, like," the driver agreed.

Macon said, "Like two dried apricots."

"Christ! I'll tell her."

The taxi stopped in front of Macon's hotel. Macon paid the fare and said, as he slid out, "I hope it works."

"Sure it will," the driver said, "till next time. Till she wants a nose ring or something."

"Noses are cartilage too, remember! Noses can wither too!"

The driver waved and pulled into traffic again.

After Macon had claimed his room, he took a subway to the

Buford Hotel. An electronics salesman had written to suggest it; the Buford rented small apartments, by the day or the week, to business-men. The manager, a Mr. Aggers, turned out to be a short, round man who walked with a limp exactly like Macon's. Macon thought they must look very odd together, crossing the lobby to the elevators. "Most of our apartments are owned by corporations," Mr. Aggers said. He pressed the "Up" button. "Companies who send their men to the city regularly will often find it cheaper to buy their own places. Then those weeks the apartments are empty, they look to me to find other tenants, help defray the costs."

Macon made a note of this in the margin of his guidebook. Us-ing an infinitesimal script, he also noted the decor of the lobby, which reminded him of some old-fashioned men's club. On the massive, claw-footed table between the two elevators stood a yard-high naked lady in brass, trailing brass draperies and standing on brass clouds, holding aloft a small, dusty light bulb with a frayed electric cord dangling from it. The elevator, when it arrived, had dim floral carpeting and paneled walls.

"May I ask," Mr. Aggers said, "whether you personally write the Accidental Tourist series?"

"Yes, I do," Macon told him.

"Well!" Mr. Aggers said. "This is a real honor, then. We keep your books in the lobby for our guests. But I don't know, I somehow pictured you looking a little different."

"How did you think I would look?" Macon asked.

"Well, maybe not quite so tall. Maybe a bit, well, heavier. More . . . upholstered."

"I see," Macon said.

The elevator had stopped by now but it took its time sliding open. Then Mr. Aggers led Macon down a hall. A woman with a laundry cart stood aside to let them pass. "Here we are," Mr. Aggers said. He unlocked a door and turned on a light.

Macon walked into an apartment that could have come straight from the 1950s. There was a square sofa with metallic threads in its fabric, a chrome-trimmed dinette set, and in the bedroom a double bed whose headboard was quilted in cream-colored vinyl. He tested the mattress. He took off his shoes, lay down, and thought a while. Mr. Aggers stood above him with his fingers laced. "Hmm," Macon said. He sat up and put his shoes back on. Then he went into the bathroom, where the toilet bore a white strip reading SANITIZED. "I've never understood these things," he said. "Why should it reassure me to know they've glued a paper band across my toilet seat?" Mr. Aggers made a helpless gesture with both hands. Macon drew aside a shower curtain printed with pink and blue fish, and he inspected the tub. It looked clean enough, although there was a rust stain leading down from the faucet.

In the kitchenette he found a single saucepan, two faded plastic plates and mugs, and an entire shelf of highball glasses. "Usually our guests don't cook much," Mr. Aggers explained, "but they might have their associates in for drinks." Macon nodded. He was faced with a familiar problem, here: the narrow line between "comfortable" and "tacky." In fact, sometimes comfortable *was* tacky. He opened the refrigerator, a little undercounter affair. The ice trays in the freezing compartment were exactly the same kind of trays—scummy aqua plastic, heavily scratched—that Rose had back in Baltimore.

"You have to admit it's well stocked," Mr. Aggers said. "See? An apron in the kitchen drawer. My wife's idea. Protects their suits."

"Yes, very nice," Macon said.

"It's just like home away from home; that's how I like to think of it."

"Oh, well, home," Macon said. "Nothing's *home*, really."

"Why? What's missing?" Mr. Aggers asked. He had very pale, fine-grained skin that took on a shine when he was anxious. "What more would you like to see added?"

"To tell the truth," Macon said, "I've always thought a hotel ought to offer optional small animals."

"Animals?"

"I mean a cat to sleep on your bed at night, or a dog of some kind to act pleased when you come in. You ever notice how a hotel room feels so lifeless?"

"Yes, but—well, I don't see how I could—there are surely

health regulations or something ... complications, paperwork, feeding all those different ... and allergies, of course, many guests have—"

"Oh, I understand, I understand," Macon said. In the margin of his guidebook he was noting the number of wastebaskets: four. Excellent. "No," he said, "it doesn't seem that people ever take me up on that."

"Will you recommend us anyway?"

"Certainly," Macon said, and he closed his guidebook and asked for a list of the rates.

. . .

The rest of the afternoon he spent in hotels that he'd covered before. He visited managers in their offices, took brief guided tours to see that nothing had slid into ruin, and listened to talk of rising costs and remodeling plans and new, improved conference settings. Then he returned to his room and switched on the evening news. The world was doing poorly; but watching this unfamiliar TV set, propping his aching leg and braced in this chair that seemed designed for someone else's body, Macon had the feeling that none of the wars and famines he saw were real. They were more like, oh, staged. He turned off the set and went downstairs to hail a cab.

At Julian's suggestion, he was dining on the very top of an impossibly tall building. (Julian had a fondness for restaurants with gimmicks, Macon had noticed. He wasn't happy unless a place revolved, or floated, or could be reached only by catwalk.) "Imagine," Julian had said, "the effect on your out-of-town client. Yes, he'd have to be from out of town; I don't suppose a native New Yorker ..." Macon had snorted. Now the cabdriver snorted, too. "Cup of coffee there will cost you five bucks," he told Macon.

"It figures."

"You're better off at one of those little Frenchy places."

"That's for tomorrow. *In*-town clients."

The taxi coasted down streets that grew darker and more silent, leading away from the crowds. Macon peered out of his window.

He saw a lone man huddled in a doorway, wrapped in a long coat. Wisps of steam drifted up from manhole covers. All the shops were locked behind iron grilles.

At the end of the darkest street of all, the taxi stopped. The driver gave another snort, and Macon paid his fare and stepped out. He wasn't prepared for the wind, which rushed up against him like a great flat sheet of something. He hurried across the sidewalk, or was propelled, while his trousers twisted and flapped about his legs. Just before entering the building, he thought to look up. He looked up and up and up, and finally he saw a faint white pinnacle dwindling into a deep, black, starless sky eerily far away. He thought of once long ago when Ethan, visiting the zoo as a toddler, had paused in front of an elephant and raised his face in astonishment and fallen over backwards.

Inside, everything was streaky pink marble and acres of texture-less carpeting. An elevator the size of a room stood open, half filled with people, and Macon stepped in and took his place between two women in silks and diamonds. Their perfume was almost visible. He imagined he could see it rippling the air.

Have chewing gum handy, he wrote in his guidebook as the elevator shot upward. His ears were popping. There was a dense, unresonant stillness that made the women's voices sound tinny. He tucked his guidebook in his pocket and glanced at the numbers flashing overhead. They progressed by tens: forty, fifty, sixty . . . One of the men said they'd have to bring Harold sometime—remember Harold when he got so scared on the ski lift?—and everyone laughed.

The elevator gave a sort of lilt and the door slid open without a sound. A girl in a white trouser suit directed them down a corridor, into a spacious darkness flickering with candles. Great black windows encircled the room from floor to ceiling, but Macon was taken to a table without a view. Lone diners, he supposed, were an embarrassment here. He might be the first they'd ever had. The array of silver at his single place could easily serve a family of four.

His waiter, far better dressed than Macon, handed him a menu and asked what he wanted to drink. "Dry sherry, please," Macon said. The minute the waiter left, Macon folded his menu in two and sat on it. Then he looked around at his neighbors. Everyone seemed to be celebrating something. A man and a pregnant woman held hands and smiled across the moony glow of their candle. A boisterous group to his left toasted the same man over and over.

The waiter returned, balancing a sherry neatly on a tray. "Very good," Macon said. "And now perhaps a menu."

"Menu? Didn't I give you one?"

"There could have been an oversight," he said, not exactly lying.

A second menu was brought and opened with a flourish before him. Macon sipped his sherry and considered the prices. Astronomical. He decided, as usual, to eat what he thought his readers might eat—not the quenelles or the sweetbreads but the steak, medium rare. After he'd given his order, he rose and slid his chair in and took his sherry over to a window.

All of a sudden he thought he had died.

He saw the city spread below like a glittering golden ocean, the streets tiny ribbons of light, the planet curving away at the edges, the sky a purple hollow extending to infinity. It wasn't the height; it was the distance. It was his vast, lonely distance from everyone who mattered. Ethan, with his bouncy walk—how would he ever know that his father had come to be trapped in this spire in the heavens? How would Sarah know, lazily tanning herself in the sunshine? For he did believe the sun could be shining wherever she was at this moment; she was so removed from him. He thought of his sister and brothers going about their business, playing their evening card game, unaware of how far behind he'd left them. He was too far gone to return. He would never, ever get back. He had somehow traveled to a point completely isolated from everyone else in the universe, and nothing was real but his own angular hand clenched around the sherry glass.

He dropped the glass, causing a meaningless little flurry of voices, and he spun around and ran lopsidedly across the room and out the door. But there was that endless corridor, and he couldn't manage the trip. He took a right turn instead. He passed a telephone alcove and stumbled into a restroom—yes, a men's room, luckily. More marble, mirrors, white enamel. He thought he was going to throw up, but when he entered one of the cubicles the sick feeling left his stomach and floated to his head. He noticed how light his brain felt. He stood above the hotel pressing his temples. It occurred to him to wonder how many feet of pipe a toilet at this altitude required.

He heard someone else come in, coughing. A cubicle door slammed shut. He opened his own door a crack and looked out. The impersonal lushness of the room made him think of science-fiction movies.

Well, this difficulty probably happened here often, didn't it? Or maybe not this difficulty exactly but others like it—people with a fear of heights, say, going into a panic, having to call upon . . . whom? The waiter? The girl who met the elevator?

He ventured cautiously out of the cubicle, then out of the restroom altogether, and he nearly bumped into a woman in the telephone alcove. She wore yards and yards of pale chiffon. She was just hanging up the phone, and she gathered her skirts around her and moved languidly, gracefully toward the dining room. *Excuse me, ma'am, I wonder if you would be so kind as to, um* . . . But the only request that came to mind rose up from his earliest childhood: *Carry me!*

The woman's little sequined evening purse was the last of her to go, trailed behind her in one white hand as she disappeared into the darkness of the restaurant.

He stepped over to the telephone and lifted the receiver. It was cool to the touch; she hadn't talked long. He fumbled through his pockets, found coins and dropped them in. But there was no one he could contact. He didn't know a soul in all New York. Instead he called home, miraculously summoning up his credit card number. He worried his family would let the phone ring—it was a habit, by now—but Charles answered. "Leary."

"Charles?"

"Macon!" Charles said, unusually animated.

"Charles, I'm up on top of this building and a sort of . . . silly thing has happened. Listen: You've got to get me out of here."

"*You* out! What are you talking about? You've got to get *me* out!"

"Pardon?"

"I'm shut in the pantry; your dog has me cornered."

"Oh. Well, I'm sorry, but . . . Charles, it's like some kind of illness. I don't think I can manage the elevator and I doubt I could manage a stairway either and—"

"Macon, do you hear that barking? That's Edward. Edward has me treed, I tell you, and you have to come home this instant."

"But I'm in New York! I'm up on top of this building and I can't get down!"

"Every time I open the door he comes roaring over and I slam the door and he attacks it, he must have clawed halfway through it by now."

Macon made himself take a deep breath. He said, "Charles, could I speak to Rose?"

"She's out."

"Oh."

"How do you think I got into this?" Charles asked. "Julian came to take her to dinner and—"

"Julian?"

"Isn't that his name?"

"Julian my *boss*?"

"Yes, and Edward went into one of his fits; so Rose said, 'Quick, shut him in the pantry.' So I grabbed his leash and he turned on me and nearly took my hand off. So I shut myself in the pantry instead and Rose must have left by then so—"

"Isn't Porter there?"

"It's his visitation night."

Macon imagined how safe the pantry must feel, with Rose's jams lined up in alphabetical order and the black dial telephone so ancient that the number on its face was still the old Tuxedo exchange. What he wouldn't give to be there!

Now he had a new symptom. His chest had developed a flutter that bore no resemblance to a normal heartbeat.

"If you don't get me out of this I'm going to call for the police to come shoot him," Charles said.

"No! Don't do that!"

"I can't just sit here waiting for him to break through."

"He won't break through. You could open the door and walk right past him. Believe me, Charles. Please. I'm up on top of this building and—"

"Maybe you don't know that I'm prone to claustrophobia," Charles said.

One possibility, Macon decided, was to tell the restaurant people he was having a coronary. A coronary was so respectable. They would send for an ambulance and he would be, yes, carried—just what he needed. Or he wouldn't have to be carried but only touched, a mere human touch upon his arm, a hand on his shoulder, something to put him back in connection with the rest of the world. He hadn't felt another person's touch in so long.

"I'll tell them about the key in the mailbox so they won't have to break down the door," Charles said.

"What? Who?"

"The police, and I'll tell them to—Macon, I'm sorry but you knew that dog would have to be done away with sooner or later."

"Don't do it!" Macon shouted.

A man emerging from the restroom glanced in his direction.

Macon lowered his voice and said, "He was Ethan's."

"Does that mean he's allowed to tear my throat out?"

"Listen. Let's not be hasty. Let's think this through. Now, I'm going to . . . I'm going to telephone Sarah. I'm going to ask her to come over and take charge of Edward. Are you listening, Charles?"

"But what if he attacks her too?" Charles asked.

"He won't, believe me. Now, don't do anything till she comes, you understand? Don't do anything hasty."

"Well . . ." Charles said doubtfully.

Macon hung up and took his wallet from his pocket. He rummaged through the business cards and torn-off snippets of paper, some of them yellow with age, that he kept in the secret compartment. When he found Sarah's number he punched it in with a trembling finger and held his breath. *Sarah,* he would say, *I'm up on top of this building and—*

She didn't answer.

That possibility hadn't occurred to him. He listened to her phone ring. What now? What on earth now?

Finally he hung up. He sifted despairingly through the other numbers in his wallet—dentist, pharmacist, animal trainer . . .

Animal trainer?

He thought at first of someone from a circus—a brawny man in satin tights. Then he saw the name: Muriel Pritchett. The card was handwritten, even hand-cut, crookedly snipped from a larger piece of paper.

He called her. She answered at once. "*Hel*-lo," roughly, like a weary barmaid.

"Muriel? It's Macon Leary," he told her.

"Oh! How you doing?"

"I'm fine. Or, rather . . . See, the trouble is, Edward's got my brother cornered in the pantry, overreacting. Charles I mean, he always overreacts, and here I am on top of this building in New York and I'm having this kind of, um, disturbance, you know? I was looking down at the city and it was miles away, miles. I can't describe to you how—"

"Let's make sure I've got this right," Muriel said. "Edward's in your pantry—"

Macon collected himself. He said, "Edward's *outside* the pantry, barking. My brother's inside. He says he's going to call the police and tell them to come shoot Edward."

"Well, what a dumb fool idea."

"Yes!" Macon said. "So I thought if you could go over and get the key from the mailbox, it's lying on the bottom of the mailbox—"

"I'll go right away."

"Oh, wonderful."

"So good-bye for now, Macon."

"Well, but also—" he said.

She waited.

"See, I'm up on top of this building," he said, "and I don't know what it is but something has scared the hell out of me."

"Oh, Lord, I'd be scared too after I went and saw *Towering Inferno*."

"No, no, it's nothing like that, fire or heights—"

"Did you see *Towering Inferno*? Boy, after that you couldn't get me past jumping level in any building. I think people who go up in skyscrapers are just plain brave. I mean if you think about it, Macon, you *have* to be brave to be standing where you are right now."

"Oh, well, not so brave as all that," Macon said.

"No, I'm serious."

"You're making too much out of it. It's nothing, really."

"You just say that because you don't realize what you went through before you stepped into the elevator. See, underneath you said, 'Okay, I'll trust it.' That's what everyone does; I bet it's what they do on airplanes, too. 'This is dangerous as all get-out but what the hay,' they say, 'let's fling ourselves out on thin air and trust it.' Why, you ought to be walking around that building so amazed and proud of yourself!"

Macon gave a small, dry laugh and gripped the receiver more tightly.

"Now here's what I'm going to do," she said. "I'm going to go get Edward and take him to the Meow-Bow. It doesn't sound to me like your brother is much use with him. Then when you get back from your trip, we need to talk about his training. I mean, things just can't go on this way, Macon."

"No, they can't. You're right. They can't," Macon said.

"I mean this is ridiculous."

"You're absolutely right."

"See you, then. Bye."

"Well, wait!" he said.

But she was gone.

After he hung up, he turned and saw the latest arrivals just heading toward him from the elevator. First came three men, and then three women in long gowns. Behind them was a couple who couldn't be past their teens. The boy's wrist bones stuck out of the sleeves of his suit. The girl's dress was clumsy and touching, her small chin obscured by a monstrous orchid.

Halfway down the corridor, the boy and girl stopped to gaze around them. They looked at the ceiling, and then at the floor. Then they looked at each other. The boy said, "Hoo!" and grabbed both the girl's hands, and they stood there a moment, laughing, before they went into the restaurant.

Macon followed them. He felt soothed and tired and terribly hungry. It was good to find the waiter just setting his food in place when he sank back into his seat.

I'll be honest," Muriel said, "My baby was not exactly planned for. I mean we weren't exactly even married yet, if you want to know the truth. If you want to know the truth the baby was the reason we got married in the first place, but I did tell Norman he didn't have to go through with it if he didn't want to. It's not like I pushed him into it or anything."

She looked past Macon at Edward, who lay prone on the front hall rug. He'd had to be forced into position, but at least he was staying put.

"Notice I let him move around some, as long as he stays down," she said. "Now I'm going to turn my back, and you watch how he does."

She wandered into the living room. She lifted a vase from a table and examined its underside. "So anyhow," she said, "we went ahead and got married, with everybody acting like it was the world's biggest tragedy. My folks really never got over it. My mom said, 'Well, I always knew this was going to happen. Back when you were hanging out with Dana Scully and them, one or another of them no-count boys always honking out front for you, didn't I tell you this was going to happen?' We had a little bitty wedding at my folks' church, and we didn't take a honeymoon trip but went straight to our apartment and next day Norman started work at his uncle's. He just settled right into being married—shopping with me for groceries and picking out curtains and such. Oh, you know, sometimes I get to thinking what kids we were. It was almost like playing house! It was pretend! The candles I lit at suppertime, flowers on the table, Norman calling me 'hon' and bringing his plate to the sink for me to wash. And then all at once it turned serious. Here I've got this little boy now, this great big seven-year-old boy with his clompy leather shoes, and it wasn't playing house after all. It was for real, all along, and we just didn't know it."

She sat on the couch and raised one foot in front of her. She turned it admiringly this way and that. Her stockings bagged at the ankle.

"What is Edward up to?" she asked.

Macon said, "He's still lying down."

"Pretty soon he'll do that for three hours straight."

"Three *hours*?"

"Easy."

"Isn't that sort of cruel?"

"I thought you promised not to talk like that," she told him.

"Right. Sorry," Macon said.

"Maybe tomorrow he'll lie down on his own."

"You think so?"

"If you practice. If you don't give in. If you don't go all softhearted."

Then she stood up and came over to Macon. She patted his arm. "But never mind," she told him, "I think soft-hearted men are sweet."

Macon backed away. He just missed stepping on Edward.

. . .

It was getting close to Thanksgiving, and the Learys were debating as usual about Thanksgiving dinner. The fact was, none of them cared for turkey. Still, Rose said, it didn't seem right to serve anything else. It would just feel wrong. Her brothers pointed out that she'd have to wake up at five a.m. to put a turkey in the oven. But it was she who'd be doing it, Rose said. It wouldn't be troubling *them* any.

Then it began to seem she had had an ulterior motive, for as soon as they settled on turkey she announced that she might just invite Julian Edge. Poor Julian, she said, had no close family nearby, and he and his neighbors gathered forlornly at holidays, each bringing his or her specialty. Thanksgiving dinner last year had been a vegetarian pasta casserole and goat cheese on grape leaves and kiwi tarts. The least she could do was offer him a normal family dinner.

"What!" Macon said, acting surprised and disapproving, but unfortunately, it wasn't that much of a surprise. Oh, Julian was up to something, all right. But what could it be? Whenever Rose came down the stairs in her best dress and two spots of rouge, whenever she asked Macon to shut Edward in the pantry because Julian would be stopping by to take her this place or that—well, Macon had a very strong urge to let Edward accidentally break loose. He made a point of meeting Julian at the door, eyeing him for a long, silent moment before calling Rose. But Julian behaved; no glint of irony betrayed him. He was respectful with Rose, almost shy, and hovered clumsily when he ushered her out the door. Or was that the irony? His Rose Leary act. Macon didn't like the looks of this.

Then it turned out that Porter's children would be coming for Thanksgiving too. They usually came at Christmas instead, but wanted to trade off this year due to some complication with their grandparents on their stepfather's side. So really, Rose said, wasn't it good they were having turkey? Children were such traditionalists. She set to work baking pumpkin pies. "We gather together," she sang, "to ask the Lord's blessing . . ." Macon looked up from the sheaf of stolen menus he was spreading across the kitchen table. There was a note of gaiety in her voice that made him uneasy. He wondered if she had any mistaken ideas about Julian—if, for in-

stance, she hoped for some kind of romance. But Rose was so plain
and sensible in her long white apron. She reminded him of Emily
Dickinson; hadn't Emily Dickinson also baked for her nieces and
nephews? Surely there was no need for concern.

.   .   .

"My son's name is Alexander," Muriel said. "Did I tell you that?
I named him Alexander because I thought it sounded high-class.
He was never an easy baby. For starters something went wrong
while I was carrying him and they had to do a Caesarean and take
him out early and I got all these complications and can't ever have
any more children. And then Alexander was so teeny he didn't even
look like a human, more like a big-headed newborn kitten, and he
had to stay in an incubator forever, just about, and nearly died.
Norman said, 'When's it going to look like other babies?' He always
called Alexander 'it.' I adjusted better; I mean pretty soon it seemed
to me that that was what a baby *ought* to look like, and I hung
around the hospital nursery but Norman wouldn't go near him, he
said it made him too nervous."

Edward whimpered. He was just barely lying down—his
haunches braced, his claws digging into the carpet. But Muriel
gave no sign she had noticed.

"Maybe you and Alexander should get together some time," she
told Macon.

"Oh, I, ah . . ." Macon said.

"He doesn't have enough men in his life."

"Well, but—"

"He's supposed to see men a lot; it's supposed to show him how
to act. Maybe the three of us could go to a movie. Don't you ever
go to movies?"

"No, I don't," Macon said truthfully. "I haven't been to a movie
in months. I really don't care for movies. They make everything
seem so close up."

"Or just out to a McDonald's, maybe."

"I don't think so," Macon said.

. . .

Porter's children arrived the evening before Thanksgiving, traveling by car because Danny, the oldest, had just got his driver's license. That worried Porter considerably. He paced the floor from the first moment they could be expected. "I don't know where June's brain is," he said. "Letting a sixteen-year-old boy drive all the way from Washington the first week he has his license! With his two little sisters in the car! I don't know how her mind works."

To make it worse, the children were almost an hour late. When Porter finally saw their headlights, he rushed out the door and down the steps well ahead of the others. "What kept you?" he cried.

Danny unfurled himself from the car with exaggerated nonchalance, yawning and stretching, and shook Porter's hand as a kind of afterthought while turning to study his tires. He was as tall as Porter now but very thin, with his mother's dark coloring. Behind him came Susan, fourteen—just a few months older than Ethan would have been. It was lucky she was so different from Ethan, with her cap of black curls and her rosy cheeks. This evening she wore jeans and hiking boots and one of those thick down jackets that made young people look so bulky and graceless. Then last came Liberty. What a name, Macon always thought. It was an invention of her mother's—a flighty woman who had run away from Porter with a hippie stereo salesman eight and a half years ago and discovered immediately afterward that she was two months pregnant. Ironically, Liberty was the one who looked most like Porter. She had fair, straight hair and a chiseled face and she was dressed in a little tailored coat. "Danny got lost," she said severely. "What a dummy." She kissed Porter and her aunt and uncles, but Susan wandered past them in a way that let everyone know she had outgrown all that.

"Oh, isn't this nice?" Rose said. "Aren't we going to have a wonderful Thanksgiving?" She stood on the sidewalk wrapping her hand in her apron, perhaps to stop herself from reaching out to Danny as he slouched toward the house. It was dusk, and Ma-

con, happening to glance around, saw the grown-ups as pale gray
wraiths—four middle-aged unmarried relatives yearning after the
young folks.

For supper they had carry-out pizza, intended to please the
children, but Macon kept smelling turkey. He thought at first it was
his imagination. Then he noticed Danny sniffing the air. "Turkey?
Already?" Danny asked his aunt.

"I'm trying this new method," she said. "It's supposed to save
energy. You set your oven extremely low and cook your meat all
night."

"Weird."

After supper they watched TV—the children never
seemed to warm to cards—and then they went to bed. But in the
middle of the night, Macon woke with a start and gave serious
thought to that turkey. She was cooking it till tomorrow? At an extremely low temperature? What temperature was that, exactly?

He was sleeping in his old room, now that his leg had mended.
Eventually he nudged the cat off his chest and got up. He made
his way downstairs in the dark, and he crossed the icy kitchen
linoleum and turned on the little light above the stove. One hundred and forty degrees, the oven dial read. "Certain death," he told
Edward, who had tagged along behind him. Then Charles walked
in, wearing large, floppy pajamas. He peered at the dial and sighed.
"Not only that," he said, "but this is a *stuffed* turkey."

"Wonderful."

"Two quarts of stuffing. I heard her say so."

"Two quarts of teeming, swarming bacteria."

"Unless there's something to this method we don't understand."

"We'll ask her in the morning," Macon said, and they went
back to bed.

In the morning, Macon came down to find Rose serving pancakes to the children. He said, "Rose, what exactly is it you're doing
to this turkey?"

"I told you: slow heat. Jam, Danny, or syrup?"

"Is that *it*?" Macon asked.

"You're dripping," Rose said to Liberty. "What, Macon? See, I read an article about slow-cooked beef and I thought, well, if it works with beef it must work with turkey too so I—"

"It might work with beef but it will murder us with turkey," Macon told her.

"But at the end I'm going to raise the temperature!"

"You'd have to raise it mighty high. You'd have to autoclave the thing."

"You'd have to expose it to a nuclear flash," Danny said cheerfully.

Rose said, "Well, you're both just plain wrong. Who's the cook here, anyhow? I say it's going to be delicious."

Maybe it was, but it certainly didn't look it. By dinnertime the breast had caved in and the skin was all dry and dull. Rose entered the dining room holding the turkey high as if in triumph, but the only people who looked impressed were those who didn't know its history—Julian and Mrs. Barrett, one of Rose's old people. Julian said, "Ah!" and Mrs. Barrett beamed. "I just wish my neighbors could see this," Julian said. He wore a brass-buttoned navy blazer, and he seemed to have polished his face.

"Well, there may be a little problem here," Macon said.

Rose set the turkey down and glared at him.

"Of course, the rest of the meal is excellent," he said. "Why, we could fill up on the vegetables alone! In fact I think I'll do that. But the turkey . . ."

"It's pure poison," Danny finished for him.

Julian said, "Come again?" but Mrs. Barrett just smiled harder.

"We think it may have been cooked at a slightly inadequate temperature," Macon explained.

"It was not!" Rose said. "It's perfectly good."

"Maybe you'd rather just stick to the side dishes," Macon told Mrs. Barrett. He was worried she might be deaf.

But she must have heard, for she said, "Why, perhaps I will," never losing her smile. "I don't have much of an appetite anyhow," she said.

"And I'm a vegetarian," Susan said.

"So am I," Danny said suddenly.

"Oh, Macon, how could you do this?" Rose asked. "My lovely turkey! All that work!"

"I think it looks delicious," Julian said.

"Yes," Porter told him, "but you don't know about the other times."

"Other times?"

"Those were just bad luck," Rose said.

"Why, of course!" Porter said. "Or economy. You don't like to throw things away; I can understand that! Pork that's been sitting too long or chicken salad left out all night . . ."

Rose sat down. Tears were glazing her eyes. "Oh," she said, "you're all so mean! You don't fool me for an instant; I know why you're doing this. You want to make me look bad in front of Julian."

"Julian?"

Julian seemed distressed. He took a handkerchief from his breast pocket but then went on holding it.

"You want to drive him off! You three wasted your chances and now you want me to waste mine, but I won't do it. I can see what's what. Just listen to any song on the radio; look at any soap opera. *Love* is what it's all about. On soap operas everything revolves around love. A new person comes to town and right away the question is, who's he going to love? Who's going to love him back? Who'll lose her mind with jealousy? Who's going to ruin her life? And you want to make me miss it!"

"Well, goodness," Macon said, trying to sort this out.

"You know perfectly well there's nothing wrong with that turkey. You just don't want me to stop cooking for you and taking care of this house, you don't want Julian to fall in love with me."

"Do what?"

But she scraped her chair back and ran from the room. Julian sat there with his mouth open.

"Don't you dare laugh," Macon told him.

Julian just went on gaping.

"Don't even consider it."

Julian swallowed. He said, "Do you think I ought to go after her?"

"No," Macon said.

"But she seems so—"

"She's fine! She's perfectly fine."

"Oh."

"Now, who wants a baked potato?"

There was a kind of murmur around the table; everyone looked unhappy. "That poor, dear girl," Mrs. Barrett said. "I feel just awful."

"Me too," Susan said.

"Julian?" Macon asked, clanging a spoon. "Potato?"

"I'll take the turkey," Julian said firmly.

At that moment, Macon almost liked the man.

. . .

"It was having the baby that broke our marriage up," Muriel said. "When you think about it, that's funny. First we got married on account of the baby and then we got divorced on account of the baby, and in between, the baby was what we argued about. Norman couldn't understand why I was all the time at the hospital visiting Alexander. 'It doesn't know you're there, so why go?' he said. I'd go early in the morning and just hang around, the nurses were as nice as could be about it, and I'd stay till night. Norman said, 'Muriel, won't we ever get our ordinary life back?' Well, you can see his point, I guess. It's like I only had room in my mind for Alexander. And he was in the hospital for months, for really months; there was everything in this world wrong with him. You should have seen our medical bills. We only had partial insurance and there were these bills running up, thousands and thousands of dollars. Finally I took a job at the hospital. I asked if I could work in the nursery but they said no, so I got a kind of, more like a maid's job, cleaning patients' rooms and so forth. Emptying trash cans, wet-mopping floors . . ."

She and Macon were walking along Dempsey Road with Edward, hoping to run into a biker. Muriel held the leash. If a biker came, she said, and Edward lunged or gave so much as the smallest yip, she was going to yank him so hard he wouldn't know what hit him. She warned Macon of that before they started out. She said he'd better not object because this was for Edward's own good. Macon hoped he'd be able to remember that when the time came.

It was the Friday after Thanksgiving and there'd been a light snow earlier, but the air didn't have a real bite to it yet and the sidewalks were merely damp. The sky seemed to begin about two feet above their heads.

"This one patient, Mrs. Brimm, she took a liking to me," Muriel said. "She said I was the only person who ever bothered talking to her. I'd come in and tell her about Alexander. I'd tell her what the doctors said, how they didn't give him much of a chance and some had even wondered if we *wanted* a chance, what with all that might be wrong with him. I'd tell her about me and Norman and the way he was acting, and she said it sounded exactly like a story in a magazine. When they let her go home she wanted me to come with her, take a job looking out for her, but I couldn't on account of Alexander."

A biker appeared at the end of the street, a girl with a Baskin-Robbins uniform bunching below her jacket. Edward perked his ears up. "Now, act like we expect no trouble," Muriel told Macon. "Just go along, go along, don't even look in Edward's direction."

The girl skimmed toward them—a little slip of a person with a tiny, serious face. When she passed, she gave off a definite smell of chocolate ice cream. Edward sniffed the breeze but marched on.

"Oh, Edward, that was wonderful!" Macon told him.

Muriel just clucked. She seemed to take his good behavior for granted.

"So anyhow," she said. "They finally did let Alexander come home. But he was still no bigger than a minute. All wrinkles like a little old man. Cried like a kitten would cry. Struggled for every breath. And *Norman* was no help. I think he was jealous. He got this kind of stubborn look whenever I had to do something, go warm a bottle or something. He'd say, 'Where you off to? Don't you want to watch the end of this program?' I'd be hanging over the crib watching Alexander fight for air, and Norman would call, 'Muriel? Commercial's just about over!' Then next thing I knew, there was his mother standing on my doorstep saying it wasn't his baby anyhow."

"What? Well, of all things!" Macon said.

"Can you believe it? Standing on my doorstep looking so pleased with herself. 'Not his baby!' I said. 'Whose then?' 'Well, that I couldn't say,' she said, 'and I doubt if you could either. But I can tell you this much: If you don't give my son a divorce and re-lease all financial claims on him, I will personally produce Dana Scully and his friends in a court of law and they will swear you're a known tramp and that baby could be any one of theirs. Clearly it's not Norman's; Norman was a *darling* baby.' Well. I waited till Norman got home from work and I said, 'Do you know what your mother told me?' Then I saw by his face that he did. I saw she must have been talking behind my back for who knows how long, putting these suspicions in his head. I said, 'Norman?' He just stut-tered around. I said 'Norman, she's lying, it's not true, I wasn't go-ing with those boys when I met you! That's all in the past!' He said, 'I don't know what to think.' I said, 'Please!' He said, 'I don't know.' He went out to the kitchen and started fixing this screen I'd been nagging him about, window screen halfway out of its frame even though supper was already on the table. I'd made him this special supper. I followed after him. I said, 'Norman. Dana and them are from way, way back. That baby couldn't be theirs.' He pushed up on one side of the screen and it wouldn't go, and he pushed up on the other side and it cut his hand, and all at once he started crying and wrenched the whole thing out of the window and threw it as far as he could. And next day his mother came to help him pack his clothes and he left me."

"Good Lord," Macon said. He felt shocked, as if he'd known Norman personally.

"So I thought about what to do. I knew I couldn't go back to my folks. Finally I phoned Mrs. Brimm and asked if she still wanted me to come take care of her, and she said yes, she did; the woman she had wasn't any use at all. So I said I would do it for room and board if I could bring the baby and she said yes, that would be fine. She had this little row house downtown and there was an extra bedroom where me and Alexander could sleep. And that's how I managed to keep us going."

They were several blocks from home now, but she didn't suggest turning back. She held the leash loosely and Edward strutted next to her, matching her pace. "I was lucky, wasn't I," she said. "If it wasn't for Mrs. Brimm I don't know what I'd have done. And it's not like it was all that much work. Just keeping the house straight, fixing her a bite to eat, helping her around. She was crippled up with arthritis but just as spunky! It's not like I really had to nurse her."

She slowed and then came to a stop. Edward, with a martyred sigh, sat down at her left heel. "When you think about it, it's funny," she said. "All that time Alexander was in the hospital seemed so awful, seemed it would go on forever, but now when I look back, I almost miss it. I mean there was something cozy about it, now that I recall. I think about those nurses gossiping at the nurses' station and those rows of little babies sleeping. It was winter and sometimes I'd stand at a window and look out and I'd feel happy to be warm and safe. I'd look down at the emergency room entrance and watch the ambulances coming in. You ever wonder what a Martian might think if he happened to land near an emergency room? He'd see an ambulance whizzing in and everybody running out to meet it, tearing the doors open, grabbing up the stretcher, scurrying along with it. 'Why,' he'd say, 'what a helpful planet, what kind and helpful creatures.' He'd never guess we're not always that way; that we had to, oh, put aside our natural selves to do it. 'What a helpful race of beings,' a Martian would say. Don't you think so?"

She looked up at Macon then. Macon experienced a sudden twist in his chest. He felt there was something he needed to do, some kind of connection he wanted to make, and when she raised her face he bent and kissed her chapped, harsh lips even though that wasn't the connection he'd intended. Her fist with the leash in it was caught between them like a stone. There was something insistent about her — pressing. Macon drew back. "Well . . ." he said.

She went on looking up at him.

"Sorry," he said.

Then they turned around and walked Edward home.

. . .

Danny spent the holiday practicing his parallel parking, tirelessly wheeling his mother's car back and forth in front of the house. And Liberty baked cookies with Rose. But Susan had nothing to do, Rose said, and since Macon was planning a trip to Philadelphia, wouldn't he consider taking her along? "It's only hotels and restaurants," Macon said. "And I'm cramming it into one day, leaving at crack of dawn and coming back late at night — "

"She'll be company for you," Rose told him.

However, Susan went to sleep when the train was hardly out of Baltimore, and she stayed asleep for the entire ride, sunk into her jacket like a little puffed-up bird roosting on a branch. Macon sat next to her with a rock magazine he'd found rolled up in one of her pockets. He saw that the Police were experiencing personality conflicts, that David Bowie worried about mental illness, that Billy Idol's black shirt appeared to have been ripped halfway off his body. Evidently these people led very difficult lives; he had no idea who they were. He rolled the magazine up again and replaced it in Susan's pocket.

If Ethan were alive, would he be sitting where Susan was? He hadn't traveled with Macon as a rule. The overseas trips were too expensive, the domestic trips too dull. Once he'd gone with Macon to New York, and he'd developed stomach pains that resembled appendicitis. Macon could still recall his frantic search for a doctor, his own stomach clenching in sympathy, and his relief when they were told it was nothing but too many breakfasts. He hadn't taken

Ethan anywhere else after that. Only to Bethany Beach every summer, and that was not so much a trip as a kind of relocation of home base, with Sarah sunbathing and Ethan joining other Baltimore boys, also relocated, and Macon happily tightening all the doorknobs in their rented cottage or unsticking the windows or—one blissful year—solving a knotty problem he'd discovered in the plumbing.

In Philadelphia, Susan came grumpily awake and staggered off the train ahead of him. She complained about the railroad station. "It's way too big," she said. "The loudspeakers echo so you can't hear what they're saying. Baltimore's station is better."

"Yes, you're absolutely right," Macon said.

They went for breakfast to a café he knew well, which unfortunately seemed to have fallen upon hard times. Little chips of ceiling plaster kept dropping into his coffee. He crossed the name out of his guidebook. Next they went to a place that a reader had suggested, and Susan had walnut waffles. She said they were excellent. "Are you going to quote me on this?" she asked. "Will you put my name in your book and say I recommended the waffles?"

"It's not that kind of a book," he told her.

"Call me your companion. That's what restaurant critics do. 'My companion, Susan Leary, pronounced the waffles remarkable.' "

Macon laughed and signaled for their bill.

After their fourth breakfast, they started on hotels. Susan found these less enjoyable, though Macon kept trying to involve her. He told a manager, "My companion here is the expert on bathrooms." But Susan just opened a medicine cabinet, yawned, and said, "All they have is Camay."

"What's wrong with that?"

"When Mama came back from her honeymoon she brought us perfumed designer soap from her hotel. One bar for me and one for Danny, in little plastic boxes and drainage racks."

"*I* think Camay is fine," Macon told the manager, who was looking worried.

Late in the afternoon Susan started feeling peckish again; so they had two more breakfasts. Then they went to Independence Hall. (Macon felt they should do something educational.) "You can tell your civics teacher," he said. She rolled her eyes and said, "Social studies."

"Whatever."

The weather was cold, and the interior of the hall was chilly and bleak. Macon noticed Susan gaping vacantly at the guide, who wasn't making his spiel very exciting; so he leaned over and whispered, "Imagine. George Washington sat in that very chair."

"I'm not really into George Washington, Uncle Macon."

"Human beings can only go 'into' houses, cars, and coffins, Susan."

"Huh?"

"Never mind."

They followed the crowd upstairs, through other rooms, but Susan had plainly exhausted her supply of good humor. "If it weren't for what was decided in this building," Macon told her, "you and I might very well be living under a dictatorship."

"We are anyhow," she said.

"Pardon?"

"You really think that you and me have any power?"

"You and I, honey."

"It's just free speech, that's all we've got. We can say whatever we like, then the government goes on and does exactly what it pleases. You call that democracy? It's like we're on a ship, headed someplace terrible, and somebody else is steering and the passengers can't jump off."

"Why don't we go get some supper," Macon said. He was feeling a little depressed.

He took her to an old-fashioned inn a few streets over. It wasn't even dark yet, and they were the first customers. A woman in a Colonial gown told them they'd have to wait a few minutes. She led them into a small, snug room with a fireplace, and a waitress offered them their choice of buttered rum or hot spiked cider. "I'll have buttered rum," Susan said, shucking off her jacket.

Macon said, "Uh, Susan."

She glared at him.

"Oh, well, make that two," he told the waitress. He supposed a little toddy couldn't do much harm.

But it must have been an exceptionally strong toddy—either that, or Susan had an exceptionally weak head for alcohol. At any rate, after two small sips she leaned toward him in an unbalanced way. "This is sort of fun!" she said. "You know, Uncle Macon, I like you much better than I thought I did."

"Why, thank you."

"I used to think you were kind of finicky. Ethan used to make us laugh, pointing to your artichoke plate."

"My artichoke plate."

She pressed her fingertips to her mouth. "I'm sorry," she said.

"For what?"

"I didn't mean to talk about him."

"You can talk about him."

"I don't want to," she said.

She gazed off across the room. Macon, following her eyes, found only a harpsichord. He looked back at her and saw her chin trembling.

It had never occurred to him that Ethan's cousins missed him too.

After a minute, Susan picked her mug up and took several large swallows. She wiped her nose with the back of her hand. "Hot," she explained. It was true she seemed to have recovered herself.

Macon said, "What was funny about my artichoke plate?"

"Oh, nothing."

"I won't be hurt. Was it funny?"

"Well, it looked like geometry class. Every leaf laid out in such a perfect circle when you'd finished."

"I see."

"He was laughing *with* you, not at you," Susan said, peering anxiously into his face.

"Well, since I wasn't laughing myself, that statement seems inaccurate. But if you mean he wasn't laughing unkindly, I believe you."

She sighed and drank some more of her rum.

"Nobody talks about him," Macon said. "None of you mentions his name."

"We do when you're not around," Susan said.

"You do?"

"We talk about what he'd think, you know. Like when Danny got his license, or when I had a date for the Halloween Ball. I mean we used to make so much fun of the grown-ups. And Ethan was the funniest one; he could always get us to laugh. Then here we are, growing up ourselves. We wonder what Ethan would think of us, if he could come back and see us. We wonder if he'd laugh at *us*. Or if he'd feel . . . left out. Like we moved on and left him behind."

The woman in the Colonial gown came to show them to their table. Macon brought his drink; Susan had already finished hers. She was a bit unsteady on her feet. When their waitress asked them if they'd like a wine list, Susan gave Macon a bright-eyed look but Macon said, "No," very firmly. "I think we ought to start with soup," he said. He had some idea soup was sobering.

But Susan talked in a reckless, headlong way all through the soup course, and the main course, and the two desserts she hadn't been able to decide between, and the strong black coffee that he pressed upon her afterward. She talked about a boy she liked who either liked her back or else preferred someone named Sissy Pace. She talked about the Halloween Ball where this really juvenile eighth-grader had thrown up all over the stereo. She said that when Danny was eighteen, the three of them were moving to their own apartment because now that their mother was expecting (which Macon hadn't known), she wouldn't even realize they were gone. "That's not true," Macon told her. "Your mother would feel terrible if you left." Susan propped her cheek on her fist in a sort of slipshod manner and said that she wasn't born yesterday. Her hair had grown wilder through the evening, giving her an electrified appearance. Macon found it difficult to stuff her into her jacket, and he had to hold her up more or less by the back of her collar while they were waiting for a taxi.

In the railroad station she got a confused, squinty look, and once they were on the train she fell asleep with her head against the window. In Baltimore, when he woke her, she said, "You don't think he's mad at us, do you, Uncle Macon?"

"Who's that?"

"You think he's mad we're starting to forget him?"

"Oh, no, honey. I'm sure he's not."

She slept in the car all the way from the station, and he drove very gently so as not to wake her. When they got home, Rose said it looked as if he'd worn the poor child right down to a frazzle.

. . .

"You want your dog to mind you in every situation," Muriel said. "Even out in public. You want to leave him outside a public place and come back to find him waiting. That's what we'll work on this morning. We'll start with him waiting right on your own front porch. Then next lesson we'll go on to shops and things."

She picked up the leash and they stepped out the door. It was raining, but the porch roof kept them dry. Macon said, "Hold on a minute, I want to show you something."

"What's that?"

He tapped his foot twice. Edward looked uncomfortable; he gazed off toward the street and gave a sort of cough. Then slowly, slowly, one forepaw crumpled. Then the other. He lowered himself by degrees until he was lying down.

"Well! Good dog!" Muriel said. She clucked her tongue.

Edward flattened his ears back for a pat.

"I worked on him most of yesterday," Macon said. "It was Sunday and I had nothing to do. And then my brother's kids were getting ready to leave and Edward was growling the way he usually does; so I tapped my foot and down he went."

"I'm proud of both of you."

She told Edward, "Stay," holding out a hand. She backed into the house again. "Now, Macon, you come in too."

They closed the front door. Muriel tweaked the lace curtain and peered out. "Well, he's staying so far," she announced.

She turned her back to the door. She checked her fingernails and said, "Tsk!" Tiny beads of rain trickled down her raincoat, and her hair—reacting to the damp—stood out in corkscrews. "Someday I'm going to get me a professional manicure," she said.

Macon tried to see around her; he wasn't sure that Edward would stay put.

"Have you ever been to a manicurist?" she asked.

"Me? Goodness, no."

"Well, some men go."

"Not me."

"I'd like just once to get everything done professional. Nails, skin . . . My girlfriend goes to this place where they vacuum your skin. They just vacuum all your pores, she says. I'd like to go there sometime. And I'd like to have my colors done. What colors look good on me? What don't? What brings out the best in me?"

She looked up at him. All at once, Macon got the feeling she had not been talking about colors at all but something else. It seemed she used words as a sort of background music. He took a step away from her. She said, "You didn't have to apologize, the other day."

"Apologize?"

Although he knew exactly what she was referring to.

She seemed to guess that. She didn't explain herself.

"Um, I don't remember if I ever made this clear," Macon said, "but I'm not even legally divorced yet."

"So?"

"I'm just, what do you call. Separated."

"Well? So?"

He wanted to say, *Muriel, forgive me, but since my son died, sex has . . . turned.* (As milk turns; that was how he thought of it. As milk will alter its basic nature and turn sour.) *I really don't think of it anymore. I honestly don't. I can't imagine anymore what all that fuss was about. Now it seems pathetic.*

But what he said was, "I'm worried the mailman's going to come."

She looked at him for a moment longer, and then she opened the door for Edward.

. . .

Rose was knitting Julian a pullover sweater for Christmas. "Already?" Macon asked. "We've barely got past Thanksgiving."

"Yes, but this is a really hard pattern and I want to do it right."

Macon watched her needles flashing. "Actually," he said, "have you ever noticed that Julian wears cardigans?"

"Yes, I guess he does," she said.

But she went on knitting her pullover.

It was a heathery gray wool, what he believed they called Ragg wool. Macon and both his brothers had sweaters that color. But Julian wore crayon colors or navy blue. Julian dressed like a golfer. "He tends toward the V-necked look," Macon said to Rose.

"That doesn't mean he wouldn't wear a crew neck if he had one."

"Look," Macon said. "I guess what I'm getting at—"

Rose's needles clicked serenely.

"He's really kind of a playboy," he said. "I don't know if you realize that. And besides, he's younger."

"Two years," she said.

"But he's got a younger, I don't know, style of living. Singles and apartments and so on."

"He says he's tired of all that."

"Oh, Lord."

"He says he likes homeyness. He appreciates my cooking. He can't believe I'm knitting him a sweater."

"No, I guess not," Macon said grimly.

"Don't try to spoil this, Macon."

"Sweetheart, I only want to protect you. It's wrong, you know, what you said at Thanksgiving. Love is *not* what it's all about. There are other things to consider besides, all kinds of other issues."

"He ate my turkey and did not get sick. Two big helpings," Rose said.

Macon groaned and tore at a handful of his hair.

. . .

"First we try him on a real quiet street," Muriel said. "Someplace public, but not too busy. Some out-of-the-way little store or something."

She was driving her long gray boat of a car. Macon sat in front beside her, and Edward sat in back, his ears out horizontal with joy. Edward was always happy to be invited for a car ride, though very soon he'd turn cranky. ("How much *longer*?" you could almost hear him whine.) It was lucky they weren't going far.

"I got this car on account of its big old trunk," Muriel said. She slung it dashingly around a corner. "I needed it for my errand business. Guess how much it cost?"

"Um . . ."

"Only two hundred dollars. That's because it needed work, but I took it to this boy down the street from where I live. I said, 'Here's the deal. You fix my car up, I let you have the use of it three nights a week and all day Sunday.' Wasn't that a good idea?"

"Very inventive," Macon said.

"I've *had* to be inventive. It's been scrape and scrounge, nail and knuckle, ever since Norman left me," she said. She had pulled into a space in front of a little shopping center, but she made no move to get out of the car. "I've lain awake, oh, many a night, thinking up ways to earn money. It was bad enough when room and board came free, but after Mrs. Brimm died it was worse; her house passed on to her son and I had to pay him rent. Her son's an old skinflint. Always wanting to jack up the price. I said, 'How's about this? You leave the rent where it is and I won't trouble you with maintenance. I'll tend to it all myself,' I said. 'Think of the headaches you'll save.' So he agreed and now you should see what I have to deal with, things go wrong and *I* can't fix them and so we just live with them. Leaky roof, stopped-up sink, faucet dripping hot water so my gas bill's out of this world, but at least I've kept the rent down. And I've got about fifty jobs, if you count them all up. You could say I'm lucky; I'm good at spotting a chance. Like those lessons at Doggie, Do, or another time a course in massage at the Y. The massage turned out to be a dud, seems you have to have a license and all like that, but I will say Doggie, Do paid off. And also I'm trying to start this research service; that's on account of all I picked up helping the school librarian. Wrote out these little pink cards I passed around at Towson State: We-Search Research. Xeroxed these flyers and mailed them to every Maryland name in the *Writer's Directory. Men and Women of Letters!* I said. *Do you want a long slow illness that will effectively kill off a character without unsightly disfigurement?* So far no one's answered but I'm still hoping. Twice now I've paid for an entire Ocean City vacation just by going up and down the beach offering folks these box lunches me and Alexander fixed in our motel room every morning. We lug them in Alexander's red wagon; I call out, 'Cold drinks! Sandwiches! Step right up!' And this is not even counting the regular jobs, like the Meow-Bow or before that the Rapid-Eze. Tiresome old Rapid-Eze; they did let me bring Alexander but it was nothing but copying documents and tedious things like that, canceled checks and invoices, little chits of things. I've never been so disinterested."

Macon stirred and said, "Don't you mean uninterested?"

"Exactly. Wouldn't you be? Copies of letters, copies of exams, copies of articles on how to shop for a mortgage. Knitting instructions, crochet instructions, all rolling out of the machine real slow and stately like they're such a big deal. Finally I quit. When I got my training at Doggie, Do I said, 'I quit. I've had it!' Why don't we try the grocery."

Macon felt confused for a second. Then he said, "Oh. All right."

"You go into the grocery, put Edward on a down-stay outside. I'll wait here in the car and see if he behaves."

"All right."

He climbed from the car and opened the back door for Edward. He led him over to the grocery. He tapped his foot twice. Edward looked distressed, but he lay down. Was this humane, when the sidewalk was still so wet? Reluctantly, Macon stepped into the store. It had the old-fashioned smell of brown paper bags. When he looked back out, Edward's expression was heartbreaking. He wore a puzzled, anxious smile and he was watching the door intently.

Macon cruised an aisle full of fruits and vegetables. He picked up an apple and considered it and set it down again. Then he went back outside. Edward was still in place. Muriel had emerged from her car and was leaning against the fender, making faces into a brown plastic compact. "Give him lots of praise!" she called, snapping the compact shut. Macon clucked and patted Edward's head.

They went next door to the drugstore. "This time we'll both go in," Muriel said.

"Is that safe?"

"We'll have to try it sooner or later."

They strolled the length of the hair care aisle, all the way back to cosmetics, where Muriel stopped to try on a lipstick. Macon imagined Edward yawning and getting up and leaving. Muriel said, "Too pink." She took a tissue from her purse and rubbed the pink off. Her own lipstick stayed on, as if it were not merely a 1940s color but a 1940s formula—the glossless, cakey substance that used to cling to pillowcases, napkins, and the rims of coffee cups. She said, "What are you doing for dinner tomorrow night?"

"For—?"

"Come and eat at my house."

He blinked.

"Come on. We'll have fun."

"Um . . ."

"Just for dinner, you and me and Alexander. Say six o'clock. Number Sixteen Singleton Street. Know where that is?"

"Oh, well, I don't believe I'm free then," Macon said.

"Think it over a while," she told him.

They went outside. Edward was still there but he was standing up, bristling in the direction of a Chesapeake Bay retriever almost a full block away. "Shoot," Muriel said. "Just when I thought we were getting someplace." She made him lie down again. Then she released him and the three of them walked on. Macon was wondering how soon he could decently say that he had thought it over and now remembered he definitely had an invitation elsewhere. They rounded a corner. "Oh, look, a thrift shop!" Muriel said. "My biggest weakness." She tapped her foot at Edward. "This time, I'll go in," she said. "I want to see what they have. You step back a bit and watch he doesn't stand up like before."

She went inside the thrift shop while Macon waited, skulking around the parking meters. Edward knew he was there, though. He kept turning his head and giving Macon beseeching looks.

Macon saw Muriel at the front of the shop, picking up and setting down little gilded cups without saucers, chipped green glass florists' vases, ugly tin brooches as big as ashtrays. Then he saw her dimly in the back where the clothes were. She drifted into sight and out again like a fish in dark water. She appeared all at once in the doorway, holding up a hat. "Macon? What do you think?" she called. It was a dusty beige turban with a jewel pinned to its center, a great false topaz like an eye.

"Very interesting," Macon said. He was starting to feel the cold.

Muriel vanished again, and Edward sighed and settled his chin on his paws.

A teenaged girl walked past—a gypsy kind of girl with layers of flouncy skirts and a purple satin knapsack plastered all over with Grateful Dead emblems. Edward tensed. He watched every step she took; he rearranged his position to watch after her as she left. But he said nothing, and Macon—tensed himself—felt relieved but also a little let down. He'd been prepared to leap into action. All at once the silence seemed unusually deep; no other people passed. He experienced one of those hallucinations of sound that he sometimes got on planes or trains. He heard Muriel's voice, gritty and thin, rattling along. "At the tone the time will be . . ." she said, and then she sang, "You will find your love in . . ." and then she shouted, "Cold drinks! Sandwiches! Step right up!" It seemed she had webbed his mind with her stories, wound him in slender steely threads from her life—her Shirley Temple childhood, unsavory girlhood, Norman flinging the screen out the window, Alexander mewing like a newborn kitten, Muriel wheeling on Doberman pinschers and scattering her salmon-pink business cards and galloping down the beach, all spiky limbs and flying hair, hauling a little red wagon full of lunches.

Then she stepped out of the thrift shop. "It was way too expensive," she told Macon. "Good dog," she said, and she snapped her fingers to let Edward up. "Now one more test." She was heading back toward her car. "We want to try both of us going in again. We'll do it down at the doctor's."

"What doctor's?"

"Dr. Snell's. I've got to pick up Alexander; I want to return him to school after I drop you off."

"Will that take long?"

"Oh, no."

They drove south, with the engine knocking in a way that Macon hadn't noticed the first time. In front of a building on Cold Spring Lane, Muriel parked and got out. Macon and Edward followed her. "Now, I don't know if he's ready or not," she said. "But all the better if he's not; gives Edward practice."

"I thought you said this wouldn't take long."

She didn't seem to hear him.

They left Edward on the stoop and went into the waiting room. The receptionist was a gray-haired woman with sequined glasses dangling from a chain of fake scarabs. Muriel asked her, "Is Alexander through yet?"

"Any minute, hon."

Muriel found a magazine and sat down but Macon remained standing. He raised one of the slats of the venetian blind to check on Edward. A man in a nearby chair glanced over at him suspiciously. Macon felt like someone from a gangster movie—one of those shady characters who twitches back a curtain to make sure the coast is clear. He dropped the blind. Muriel was reading an article called "Put on the New Sultry, Shadowed Eyes!" There were pictures of different models looking malevolent.

"How old did you say Alexander was?" Macon asked.

She glanced up. Her own eyes, untouched by cosmetics, were disquietingly naked compared to those in the magazine.

"He's seven," she said.

Seven.

Seven was when Ethan had learned to ride a bicycle.

Macon was visited by one of those memories that dent the skin, that strain the muscles. He felt the seat of Ethan's bike pressing into his hand—the curled-under edge at the rear that you hold onto when you're trying to keep a bicycle upright. He felt the sidewalk slapping against his soles as he ran. He felt himself let go, slow to a walk, stop with his hands on his hips to call out, "You've got her now! You've got her!" And Ethan rode away from him, strong and proud and straight-backed, his hair picking up the light till he passed beneath an oak tree.

Macon sat down next to Muriel. She looked over and said, "Have you thought?"

"Hmm?"

"Have you given any thought to coming to dinner?"

"Oh," he said. And then he said, "Well, I could come. If it's only for dinner."

"What else would it be for?" she asked. She smiled at him and tossed her hair back.

The receptionist said, "*Here* he is."

She was talking about a small, white, sickly boy with a shaved-looking skull. He didn't appear to have quite enough skin for his face; his skin was stretched, his mouth was stretched to an unattractive width, and every bone and blade of cartilage made its presence known. His eyes were light blue and lashless, bulging slightly, rimmed with pink, magnified behind large, watery spectacles whose clear frames had an unfortunate pinkish cast themselves. He wore a carefully coordinated shirt-and-slacks set such as only a mother would choose.

"How'd it go?" Muriel asked him.

"Okay."

"Sweetie, this is Macon. Can you say hi? I've been training his dog."

Macon stood up and held out his hand. After a moment, Alexander responded. His fingers felt like a collection of wilted stringbeans. He took his hand away again and told his mother, "You have to make another appointment."

"Sure thing."

She went over to the receptionist, leaving Macon and Alexander standing there. Macon felt there was nothing on earth he could talk about with this child. He brushed a leaf off his sleeve. He pulled his cuffs down. He said, "You're pretty young to be at the doctor's without your mother."

Alexander didn't answer, but Muriel—waiting for the receptionist to flip through her calendar—turned and answered for him. "He's used to it," she said, "because he's had to go so often. He's got these allergies."

"I see," Macon said.

Yes, he was just the type for allergies.

"He's allergic to shellfish, milk, fruits of all kinds, wheat, eggs, and most vegetables," Muriel said. She accepted a card from the receptionist and dropped it into her purse. She said as they were walking out, "He's allergic to dust and pollen and paint, and there's some belief he's allergic to air. Whenever he's outside a long time he gets these bumps on any uncovered parts of his body."

She clucked at Edward and snapped her fingers. Edward jumped up, barking. "Don't pat him," she told Alexander. "You don't know what dog fur will do to you."

They got into her car. Macon sat in back so Alexander could take the front seat, as far from Edward as possible. They had to drive with all the windows down so Alexander wouldn't start wheezing. Over the rush of wind, Muriel called, "He's subject to asthma, eczema, and nosebleeds. He has to get these shots all the time. If a bee ever stings him and he hasn't had his shots he could be dead in half an hour."

Alexander turned his head slowly and gazed at Macon. His expression was prim and censorious.

When they drew up in front of the house, Muriel said, "Well, let's see now. I'm on full time at the Meow-Bow tomorrow . . ." She ran a hand through her hair, which was scratchy, rough, disorganized. "So I guess I won't see you till dinner," she said.

Macon couldn't think of any way to tell her this, but the fact was he would never be able to make that dinner. He missed his wife. He missed his son. They were the only people who seemed real to him. There was no point looking for substitutes.

M

uriel Pritchett was how she was listed. Brave and cocky: no timorous initials for Muriel. Macon circled the number. He figured now was the time to call. It was nine in the evening. Alexander would have gone to bed. He lifted the receiver.

But what would he say?

Best to be straightforward, of course, much less hurtful; hadn't Grandmother Leary always told them so? *Muriel, last year my son died and I don't seem to . . . Muriel, this has nothing to do with you personally but really I have no . . .*

Muriel, I can't. I just can't.

It seemed his voice had rusted over. He held the receiver to his ear but great, sharp clots of rust were sticking in his throat.

He had never actually said out loud that Ethan was dead. He hadn't needed to; it was in the papers (page three, page five), and then friends had told other friends, and Sarah got on the phone . . . So somehow, he had never spoken the words. How would he do it now? Or maybe he could make Muriel do it. *Finish the sentence, please: I did have a son but he—.* "He what?" she would ask. "He went to live with your wife? He ran away? He died?" Macon would nod. "But *how* did he die? Was it cancer? Was it a car wreck? Was it a nineteen-year-old with a pistol in a Burger Bonanza restaurant?"

He hung up.

He went to ask Rose for notepaper and she gave him some from her desk. He took it to the dining room table, sat down, and uncapped his fountain pen. *Dear Muriel,* he wrote. And stared at the page a while.

Funny sort of name.

Who would think of calling a little newborn baby Muriel?

He examined his pen. It was a Parker, a swirly tortoiseshell lacquer with a complicated gold nib that he liked the looks of. He examined Rose's stationery. Cream colored. Deckle edged. Deckle! What an odd word.

Well.

Dear Muriel.

I am very sorry, he wrote, *but I won't be able to have dinner with you after all. Something has come up.* He signed it, *Regretfully, Macon.*

Grandmother Leary would not have approved.

He sealed the envelope and tucked it in his shirt pocket. Then he went to the kitchen where Rose kept a giant city map thumbtacked to the wall.

Driving through the labyrinth of littered, cracked, dark streets in the south of the city, Macon wondered how Muriel could feel safe living here. There were too many murky alleys and stairwells full of rubbish and doorways lined with tattered shreds of posters. The gridded shops with their ineptly lettered signs offered services that had a sleazy ring to them: CHECKS CASHED NO QUESTIONS, TINY BUBBA'S INCOME TAX, SAME DAY AUTO RECOLORING. Even this late on a cold November night, clusters of people lurked in the shadows — young men drinking out of brown paper bags, middle-aged women arguing under a movie marquee that read CLOSED.

He turned onto Singleton and found a block of row houses that gave a sense of having been skimped on. The roofs were flat, the windows flush and lacking depth. There was nothing to spare, no excess material for overhangs or decorative moldings, no generosity. Most were covered in formstone, but the bricks of Number 16 had been painted a rubbery maroon. An orange bugproof bulb glowed dimly above the front stoop.

He got out of the car and climbed the steps. He opened the screen door, which was made of pitted aluminum. It clattered in a cheap way and the hinges shrieked. He winced. He took the letter from his pocket and bent down.

"I've got a double-barreled shotgun," Muriel said from inside the house, "and I'm aiming it exactly where your head is."

He straightened sharply. His heart started pounding. (Her voice sounded level and accurate—like her shotgun, he imagined.) He said, "It's Macon."

"Macon?"

The latch clicked and the inner door opened several inches. He saw a sliver of Muriel in a dark-colored robe. She said, "Macon! What are you doing here?"

He gave her the letter.

She took it and opened it, using both hands. (There wasn't a trace of a shotgun.) She read it and looked up at him.

He saw he had done it all wrong.

"Last year," he said, "I lost . . . I experienced a . . . loss, yes, I lost my . . ."

She went on looking into his face.

"I lost my son," Macon said. "He was just . . . he went to a hamburger joint and then . . . someone came, a holdup man, and shot him. I can't go to dinner with people! I can't talk to their little boys! You have to stop asking me. I don't mean to hurt your feelings but I'm just not up to this, do you hear?"

She took one of his wrists very gently and she drew him into the house, still not fully opening the door, so that he had a sense of slipping through something, of narrowly evading something. She closed the door behind him. She put her arms around him and hugged him.

"Every day I tell myself it's time to be getting over this," he said into the space above her head. "I know that people expect it of me.

They used to offer their sympathy but now they don't; they don't even mention his name. They think it's time my life moved on. But if anything, I'm getting worse. The first year was like a bad dream— I was clear to his bedroom door in the morning before I remembered he wasn't there to be wakened. But this second year is real. I've stopped going to his door. I've sometimes let a whole day pass by without thinking about him. That absence is more terrible than the first, in a way. And you'd suppose I would turn to Sarah but no, we only do each other harm. I believe that Sarah thinks I could have prevented what happened, somehow—she's so used to my arranging her life. I wonder if all this has only brought out the truth about us—how far apart we are. I'm afraid we got married *because* we were far apart. And now I'm far from everyone; I don't have any friends anymore and everyone looks trivial and foolish and not related to me."

She drew him through a living room where shadows loomed above a single beaded lamp, and a magazine lay face down on a lumpy couch. She led him up a stairway and across a hall and into a bedroom with an iron bedstead and a varnished orange bureau.

"No," he said, "wait. This is not what I want."

"Just sleep," she told him. "Lie down and sleep."

That seemed reasonable.

She removed his duffel coat and hung it on a hook in a closet curtained with a length of flowered sheeting. She knelt and untied his shoes. He stepped out of them obediently. She rose to unbutton his shirt and he stood passive with his hands at his sides. She hung his trousers over a chair back. He dropped onto the bed in his underwear and she covered him with a thin, withered quilt that smelled of bacon grease.

Next he heard her moving through the rest of the house, snapping off lights, running water, murmuring something in another room. She returned to the bedroom and stood in front of the bureau. Earrings clinked into a dish. Her robe was old, shattered silk, the color of sherry. It tied at the waist with a twisted cord and the elbows were clumsily darned. She switched off the lamp. Then she came over to the bed and lifted the quilt and slid under it. He wasn't surprised when she pressed against him. "I just want to sleep," he told her. But there were those folds of silk. He felt how cool and fluid the silk was. He put a hand on her hip and felt the two layers of her, cool over warm. He said, "Will you take this off?"

She shook her head. "I'm bashful," she whispered, but immediately afterward, as if to deny that, she put her mouth on his mouth and wound herself around him.

.   .   .

In the night he heard a child cough, and he swam up protestingly through layers of dreams to answer. But he was in a room with one tall blue window, and the child was not Ethan. He turned over and found Muriel. She sighed in her sleep and lifted his hand and placed it upon her stomach. The robe had fallen open; he felt smooth skin, and then a corrugated ridge of flesh jutting across her abdomen. The Caesarean, he thought. And it seemed to him, as he sank back into his dreams, that she had as good as spoken aloud. *About your son,* she seemed to be saying: *Just put your hand here. I'm scarred, too. We're all scarred. You are not the only one.*

t w e l v e

I don't understand you," Rose told Macon. "First you say yes, you'll be here all afternoon, and then you say you won't. How can I plan when you're so disorganized?"

She was folding linen napkins and stacking them on the table, preparing her annual tea for the old people. Macon said, "Sorry, Rose, I didn't think it would matter that much."

"Last night you said you'd want supper and then you weren't here to eat it. Three separate mornings these past two weeks I go to call you for breakfast and I find you haven't slept in your bed. Don't you think I worry? Anything might have happened."

"Well, I said I was sorry."

Rose smoothed the stack of napkins.

"Time creeps up on me," he told her. "You know how it is. I mean I don't intend to go out at all, to begin with, but then I think, 'Oh, maybe for a little while,' and next thing I know it's so late, much too late to be driving, and I think to myself, 'Well . . .' "

Rose turned away quickly and went over to the buffet. She started counting spoons. "I'm not asking about your private life," she said.

"I thought in a sense you were."

"I just need to know how much food to cook, that's all."

"I wouldn't blame you for being curious," he said.

"I just need to know how many breakfasts to fix."

"You think I don't notice you three? Whenever she's here giving Edward his lesson, everyone starts coming out of the woodwork. Edging through the living room—'Just looking for the pliers! Don't mind me!' Sweeping the entire front porch the minute we take Edward out for a walk."

"Could I help it if the porch was dirty?"

"Well, I'll tell you what," he said. "Tomorrow night I'll definitely be here for supper. That's a promise. You can count on it."

"I'm not asking you to stay if you don't want to," she told him.

"Of course I want to! It's just this evening I'll be out," he said, "but not late, I'm sure of that. Why, I bet I'll be home before ten!"

Although even as he spoke, he heard how false and shallow he sounded, and he saw how Rose lowered her eyes.

.   .   .

He bought a large combination pizza and drove downtown with it. The smell made him so hungry that he kept snitching bits off the top at every stoplight—coins of pepperoni, crescents of mushroom. His fingers got all sticky and he couldn't find his handkerchief. Pretty soon the steering wheel was sticky too. Humming to himself, he drove past tire stores, liquor stores, discount shoe stores, the Hot-Tonight Novelty Company. He took a shortcut through an alley and jounced between a double row of backyards—tiny rectangles crammed with swing sets and rusted auto parts and stunted, frozen bushes. He turned onto Singleton and drew up behind a pickup truck full of moldy rolls of carpet.

The next-door neighbor's twin daughters were perched on their front stoop—flashy sixteen-year-olds in jeans as tight as sausage casings. It was too cold to sit outside, but that never stopped them. "Hey there, Macon," they sing-songed.

"How are you, girls."

"You going to see Muriel?"

"I thought I might."

He climbed Muriel's steps, holding the pizza level, and knocked on the door. Debbie and Dorrie continued to watch him. He flashed them a broad smile. They sometimes baby-sat with Alexander; he had to be nice to them. Half the neighborhood sat with Alexander, it seemed. He still felt confused by Muriel's network of arrangements.

It was Alexander who opened the door. "Pizza man!" Macon told him.

"Mama's on the phone," Alexander said flatly. He turned away and wandered back to the couch, adjusting his glasses on his nose. Evidently he was watching TV.

"Extra-large combination, no anchovies," Macon said.

"I'm allergic to pizza."

"What part of it?"

"Huh?"

"What part are you allergic to? The pepperoni? Sausage? Mushrooms? We could take those off."

"All of it," Alexander said.

"You can't be allergic to all of it."

"Well, I am."

Macon went on into the kitchen. Muriel stood with her back to him, talking on the phone with her mother. He could tell it was her mother because of Muriel's high, sad, querulous tone. "Aren't you going to ask how Alexander is? Don't you want to know about his rash? I ask after *your* health, why don't you ask about ours?"

He stepped up behind her soundlessly. "You didn't even ask what happened with his eye doctor," she said, "and here I was so worried about it. I swear sometimes you'd think he wasn't your grandson! That time I sprained my ankle falling off my shoes and called to see if you'd look after him, what did you say? Said, 'Now let me get this straight. You want me to come all the way down to your house.' You'd think Alexander was nothing to do with you!"

Macon presented himself in front of her, holding out the pizza.

"Ta-da!" he whispered. She looked up at him and gave that perky smile of hers—an ornate, Victorian V.

"Ma," she said, "I'm going now! Macon's here!"

It had been a long, long time since anyone made such an event of his arrival.

. . .

He went to Julian's office on a Monday afternoon and handed over what he'd done on the U.S. guidebook. "That wraps up the Northeast," he said. "I guess next I'll start on the South."

"Well, good," Julian told him. He was bent over behind his desk, rummaging through a drawer. "Excellent. Like to show you something, Macon. Now, where in hell—ah."

He straightened, with his face flushed. He gave Macon a tiny blue velvet box. "Your sister's Christmas present," he said.

Macon raised the lid. Inside, on a bed of white satin, was a diamond ring. He looked at Julian.

"What is it?" he asked.

"What *is* it?"

"I mean, is this a . . . what you would call, dinner ring? Or is it meant to be, rather . . ."

"It's an engagement ring, Macon."

"Engagement?"

"I want to marry her."

"You want to marry Rose?"

"What's so odd about that?"

"Well, I—" Macon said.

"If she'll agree to it, that is."

"What, you haven't asked her yet?"

"I'll ask her at Christmas, when I give her the ring. I want to do this properly. Old-fashioned. Do you think she'll have me?"

"Well, I really couldn't say," Macon said. Unfortunately, he was sure she would, but he'd be damned if he'd tell Julian that.

"She's got to," Julian said. "I am thirty-six years old, Macon, but I tell you, I feel like a schoolboy about that woman. She's every-

thing those girls in my apartment building are not. She's so . . .
true. Want to know something? I've never even slept with her."

"Well, I don't care to hear about that," Macon said hastily.

"I want us to have a real wedding night," Julian told him. "I
want to do everything right. I want to join a real family. God, Macon, isn't it amazing how two separate lives can link up together? I
mean two *differentnesses*? What do you think of the ring?"

Macon said, "It's okay." He looked down at it. Then he said,
"It's very nice, Julian," and he closed the box gently and handed
it back.

. . .

"Now, this is not your ordinary airplane," Macon told Muriel.
"I wouldn't want you to get the wrong idea. This is what they call a
commuter plane. It's something a businessman would take, say, to
hop to the nearest city for a day and make a few sales and hop back
again."

The plane he was referring to—a little fifteen-seater that resembled a mosquito or a gnat—stood just outside the door of the commuter's waiting room. A girl in a parka was loading it with baggage.
A boy was checking something on the wings. This appeared to be
an airline run by teenagers. Even the pilot was a teenager, it
seemed to Macon. He entered the waiting room, carrying a clipboard. He read off a list of names. "Marshall? Noble? Albright?"
One by one the passengers stepped forward—just eight or ten of
them. To each the pilot said, "Hey, how you doing." He let his eyes
rest longest on Muriel. Either he found her the most attractive or
else he was struck by her outfit. She wore her highest heels, black
stockings spattered with black net roses, and a flippy little fuchsia
dress under a short fat coat that she referred to as her "fun fur." Her
hair was caught all to one side in a great bloom of frizz, and there
was a silvery dust of some kind on her eyelids. Macon knew she'd
overdone it, but at the same time he liked her considering this such
an occasion.

The pilot propped open the door and they followed him outside, across a stretch of concrete, and up two rickety steps into the plane. Macon had to bend almost double as he walked down the aisle. They threaded between two rows of single seats, each seat as spindly as a folding chair. They found spaces across from each other and settled in. Other passengers struggled through, puffing and bumping into things. Last came the copilot, who had round, soft, baby cheeks and carried a can of Diet Pepsi. He slammed the door shut behind him and went up front to the controls. Not so much as a curtain hid the cockpit. Macon could lean out into the aisle and see the banks of knobs and gauges, the pilot positioning his headset, the copilot taking a final swig and setting his empty can on the floor.

"Now, on a bigger plane," Macon called to Muriel as the engines roared up, "you'd hardly feel the takeoff. But here you'd better brace yourself."

Muriel nodded, wide-eyed, gripping the seat ahead of her. "What's that light that's blinking in front of the pilot?" she asked.

"I don't know."

"What's that little needle that keeps sweeping round and round?"

"I don't know."

He felt he'd disappointed her. "I'm used to jets, not these toys," he told her. She nodded again, accepting that. It occurred to Macon that he was really a very worldly and well-traveled man.

The plane started taxiing. Every pebble on the runway jolted it; every jolt sent a series of creaks through the framework. They gathered speed. The crew, suddenly grave and professional, made complicated adjustments to their instruments. The wheels left the ground. "Oh!" Muriel said, and she turned to Macon with her face all lit up.

"We're off," he told her.

"I'm flying!"

They rose—with some effort, Macon felt—over the fields surrounding the airport, over a stand of trees and a grid of houses. Above-ground swimming pools dotted backyards here and there like pale blue thumbtacks. Muriel pressed so close to her window that she left a circle of mist on the glass. "Oh, look!" she said to Macon, and then she said something else that he couldn't hear. The engines on this plane were loud and harsh, and the Pepsi can was rolling around with a clattering sound, and also the pilot was bellowing to the copilot, saying something about his refrigerator. "So I wake up in the middle of the night," he was shouting, "damn thing's thudding and thumping—"

Muriel said, "Wouldn't Alexander enjoy this!"

Macon hadn't seen Alexander enjoying anything yet, but he said dutifully, "We'll have to bring him sometime."

"We'll have to take just lots of trips! France and Spain and Switzerland . . ."

"Well," Macon said, "there's the little matter of money."

"Just America, then. California, Florida . . ."

California and Florida took money too, Macon should have said (and Florida wasn't even given space in his guidebook), but for the moment, he was borne along by her vision of things. "Look!" she said, and she pointed to something. Macon leaned across the aisle to see what she meant. The airplane flew so low that it might have been following road signs; he had an intimate view of farmlands, woodlands, roofs of houses. It came to him very suddenly that every little roof concealed actual lives. Well, of course he'd known that, but all at once it took his breath away. He saw how real those lives were to the people who lived them—how intense and private and absorbing. He stared past Muriel with his mouth open. Whatever she had wanted him to look at must be long past by now, but still he went on gazing out her window.

· · ·

Porter and the others were talking money. Or Porter was talking money and the others were half listening. Porter was planning ahead for income taxes. He was interested in something called a chicken straddle. "The way it works," he said, "you invest in baby chicks right now, before the end of the year. Deduct the cost of feed and such. Then sell the grown hens in January and collect the profit."

Rose wrinkled her forehead. She said, "But chickens are so prone to colds. Or would you call it distemper. And December and January aren't usually all that warm here."

"They wouldn't be here in Baltimore, Rose. God knows where they'd be. I mean these are not chickens you actually see; they're a way to manage our taxes."

"Well, I don't know," Charles said. "I hate to get involved in things someone else would be handling. It's someone else's word those chickens even exist."

"You people have no imagination," Porter said.

The four of them stood around the card table in the sun porch, helping Rose with her Christmas present for Liberty. She had constructed an addition to Liberty's dollhouse—a garage with a guest apartment above it. The garage was convincingly untidy. Miniature wood chips littered the floor around a stack of twig-sized fire logs, and a coil of green wire made a perfect garden hose. Now they were working on the upstairs. Rose was stuffing an armchair cushion no bigger than an aspirin. Charles was cutting a sheet of wallpaper from a sample book. Porter was drilling holes for the curtain rods. There was hardly elbow room; so Macon, who had just come in with Edward, stood back and merely watched.

"Besides," Charles said, "chickens are really not, I don't know, very classy animals. I would hate to go round saying I'm a chicken magnate."

"You don't even have to mention the fact," Porter said.

"*Beef* magnate, now; that I wouldn't mind. Beef has more of a ring to it."

"They're not offering a straddle for beef, Charles."

Macon picked up some color photos that sat beside the wallpaper book. The top photo showed a window in a room he didn't recognize—a white-framed window with louvered shutters closed across its lower half. The next was a group portrait. Four people—

blurry, out of focus—stood in a line in front of the couch. The woman wore an apron, the men wore black suits. There was something artificial about their posture. They were lined up too precisely; none of them touched the others. "Who *are* these people?" Macon asked.

Rose glanced over. "That's the family from Liberty's dollhouse," she said.

"Oh."

"Her mother sent me those pictures."

"It's a family with nothing but grown-ups?" he asked.

"One's a boy; you just can't tell. And one's a grandpa or a butler; June says Liberty switches him back and forth."

Macon laid the photos aside without looking at the rest of them. He knelt to pat Edward. "A cattle straddle," Charles was saying thoughtfully. Macon suddenly wished he were at Muriel's. He wrapped his arms around Edward and imagined he smelled her sharp perfume deep in Edward's fur.

. . .

Oh, above all else he was an orderly man. He was happiest with a regular scheme of things. He tended to eat the same meals over and over and to wear the same clothes; to drop off his cleaning on a certain set day and to pay all his bills on another. The teller who helped him on his first trip to a bank was the teller he went to forever after, even if she proved not to be efficient, even if the next teller's line was shorter. There was no room in his life for anyone as unpredictable as Muriel. Or as extreme. Or as . . . well, unlikable, sometimes.

Her youthfulness was not appealing but unsettling. She barely remembered Vietnam and had no idea where she'd been when Kennedy was shot. She made him anxious about his own age, which had not previously troubled him. He realized how stiffly he walked after he had been sitting in one position too long; how he favored his back, always expecting it to go out on him again; how once was plenty whenever they made love.

And she talked so much—almost ceaselessly; while Macon was the kind of man to whom silence was better than music. ("Listen! They're playing my song," he used to say when Sarah switched the radio off.) She talked about blushers, straighteners, cellulite, hemlines, winter skin. She was interested in the appearance of things, only the appearance: in lipstick shades and nail wrapping and facial masques and split ends. Once, on one of her more attractive days, he told her she was looking very nice, and she grew so flustered that she stumbled over a curb. She asked if that was because she had tied her hair back; and was it the hair itself or the ribbon; or rather the color of the ribbon, which she'd feared might be just a little too bright and set off the tone of her complexion wrong. And didn't he think her hair was hopeless, kerblamming out the way it did in the slightest bit of humidity? Till he was sorry he had ever brought it up. Well, not sorry, exactly, but tired. Exhausted.

Yet she could raise her chin sometimes and pierce his mind like a blade. Certain images of her at certain random, insignificant moments would flash before him: Muriel at her kitchen table, ankles twined around her chair rungs, filling out a contest form for an all-expense-paid tour of Hollywood. Muriel telling her mirror, "I look like the wrath of God"—a kind of ritual of leavetaking. Muriel doing the dishes in her big pink rubber gloves with the crimson fingernails, raising a soapy plate and trailing it airily over to the rinse water and belting out one of her favorite songs—"War is Hell on the Home Front Too" or "I Wonder if God Likes Country Music." (Certainly *she* liked country music—long, complaining ballads about the rocky road of life, the cold gray walls of prison, the sleazy, greasy heart of a two-faced man.) And Muriel at the hospital window, as he'd never actually seen her, holding a mop and gazing down at the injured coming in.

Then he knew that what mattered was the pattern of her life; that although he did not love her he loved the surprise of her, and also the surprise of himself when he was with her. In the foreign country that was Singleton Street he was an entirely different person. This person had never been suspected of narrowness, never been accused of chilliness; in fact, was mocked for his soft heart. And was anything but orderly.

. . .

"Why don't you come to my folks' house for Christmas dinner?" she asked him.

Macon was in her kitchen at the time. He was crouched beneath the sink, turning off a valve. For a moment he didn't answer; then he emerged and said, "Your folks?"

"For Christmas dinner."

"Oh, well, I don't know," he said.

"Come on, Macon, please say yes! I want you to meet them. Ma thinks I'm making you up. 'You made him up,' she says. You know how she is."

Yes, Macon did know, at least from second hand, and he could just imagine what that dinner would be like. Booby-trapped. Full of hidden digs and hurt feelings. The fact was, he just didn't want to get involved.

So instead of answering, he turned his attention to Alexander. He was trying to teach Alexander how to fix a faucet. "Now," he said, "you see I shut the valve off. What did I do that for?"

All he got was a glassy pale stare. This was Macon's idea, not Alexander's. Alexander had been hauled away from the TV like a sack of stones, plunked on a kitchen chair, and instructed to watch closely. "Oh," Muriel said, "I'm not sure about this. He's not so very strong."

"You don't have to be Tarzan to fix a kitchen faucet, Muriel."

"Well, no, but I don't know . . ."

Sometimes Macon wondered if Alexander's ailments were all in Muriel's head.

"Why did I shut off the valve, Alexander?" he asked.

Alexander said, "Why."

"You tell me."

"You tell *me*."

"No, you," Macon said firmly.

There was a bad moment or two in which it seemed that

Alexander might keep up that stare of his forever. He sat C-shaped in his chair, chin on one hand, eyes expressionless. The shins emerging from his trousers were thin as Tinkertoys, and his brown school shoes seemed very large and heavy. Finally he said, "So the water won't whoosh all over."

"Right."

Macon was careful not to make too much of his victory.

"Now, this leak is not from the spout, but from the handle," he said. "So you want to take the handle apart and replace the packing. First you unscrew the top screw. Let's see you do it."

"Me?"

Macon nodded and offered him the screwdriver.

"I don't want to," Alexander said.

"Let him just watch," Muriel suggested.

"If he just watched he won't know how to fix the one in the bathtub, and I'm going to ask him to manage that without me."

Alexander took the screwdriver, in one of those small, stingy gestures of his that occupied a minimum of space. He inched off the chair and came over to the sink. Macon pulled another chair up close and Alexander climbed onto it. Then there was the problem of fitting the screwdriver into the slot of the screw. It took him forever. He had tiny fingers, each tipped with a little pink pad above painfully bitten nails. He concentrated, his glasses slipping down on his nose. Always a mouth-breather, he was biting his tongue now and panting slightly.

"Wonderful," Macon said when the screwdriver finally connected.

At each infinitesimal turn, though, it slipped and had to be repositioned. Macon's stomach muscles felt tight. Muriel, for once, was silent, and her silence was strained and anxious.

Then, "Ah!" Macon said. The screw had loosened enough so that Alexander could twist it by hand. He managed that part fairly easily. He even removed the faucet without being told. "Very good," Macon said. "I believe you may have natural talents."

Muriel relaxed. Leaning back against the counter, she said, "My folks have their Christmas dinner in the daytime. I mean it's not at noon but it's not at night either, it's more like midafternoon, or this year it's really late afternoon because I've got the morning shift at the Meow-Bow and—"

"Look at this," Macon told Alexander. "See that gunk? That's old, rotted packing. So take it away. Right. Now here's the new packing. You wind it around, wind even a little more than you need. Let's see you wind it around."

Alexander wrapped the thread. His fingers turned white with the effort. Muriel said, "Usually we have a goose. My daddy brings a goose from the Eastern Shore. Or don't you care for goose. Would you rather just a turkey? A duck? What are you used to eating, Macon?"

Macon said, "Oh, well . . ." and was saved by Alexander. Alexander turned, having reassembled the faucet without any help, and said, "Now what?"

"Now make sure the screw is well in."

Alexander resumed his struggles with the screwdriver. Muriel said, "Maybe you'd rather a good hunk of beef. I know some men are like that. They think poultry is kind of pansy. Is that how you think too? You can tell me! I won't mind! My folks won't mind!"

"Oh, um, Muriel . . ."

"Now what," Alexander ordered.

"Why, now we turn the water back on and see what kind of job you've done."

Macon crouched beneath the sink and showed him where the valve was. Alexander reached past him and twisted it, grunting. Wasn't it odd, Macon thought, how little boys all had that same slightly green smell, like a cedar closet. He rose and turned on the faucet. No leak. "Look at that!" he told Alexander. "You've solved the problem."

Alexander fought to hold a grin back.

"Will you know how to do it the next time?"

He nodded.

"Now when you're grown," Macon said, "you can fix the faucets for your wife."

Alexander's face squinched up with amusement at the thought.

" 'Step back, dearie,' you can say. 'Just let me see to this.' "

Alexander said, "Tssh!"—his face like a little drawstring purse.

" 'Let a real *man* take care of this,' you can tell her."

"Tssh! Tssh!"

"Macon? Are you coming to my folks', or aren't you?" Muriel asked.

It seemed unreasonable to say he wasn't. Somehow or other, he had got himself involved already.

thirteen

Muriel's parents lived out in Timonium, in a development called Foxhunt Acres. Muriel had to show Macon the way. It was the coldest Christmas Day either of them could remember, but they drove with the windows slightly open so that Alexander, riding in back, would not be bothered by the dog hair. The radio was tuned to Muriel's favorite station. Connie Francis was singing "Baby's First Christmas."

"You warm enough?" Muriel asked Alexander. "You doing okay?"

Alexander must have nodded.

"You feel like you're wheezing at all?"

"Nope."

"No, ma'am," she corrected him.

Sarah used to do that, too, Macon remembered—give their son a crash course in manners anytime they set out to visit her mother.

Muriel said, "Once I was riding Alexander uptown on some errands for George? My company? And I had these two cats in the car just the day before? And I didn't think a thing about it, clean forgot to vacuum like I usually do, and all at once I turn around and Alexander's stretched across the seat, flat out."

"I wasn't flat *out*," Alexander said.

"You were just as good as."

"I was only laying down so I wouldn't need so much air."

"See there?" Muriel said to Macon.

They were traveling up York Road now, past body shops and fast food outlets all closed and bleak. Macon had never seen this road so empty. He overtook a van and then a taxicab; nothing else. Swags of Christmas greens hung stiffly above a used car lot.

"He can get shots, though," Muriel said.

"Shots?"

"He can get shots to keep him from wheezing."

"Then why doesn't he?"

"Well, if Edward was to move in I guess that's what we'd do."

"Edward?"

"I mean if, you know. If you moved in on a permanent basis and Edward came too."

"Oh," Macon said.

Brenda Lee was singing "I'm Gonna Lasso Santa Claus." Muriel hummed along, tipping her head perkily left and right to keep time.

"Would you ever think of doing that?" she asked him finally.

"Doing what?" he said, pretending not to know.

"Would you ever think of moving in with us?"

"Oh, um . . ."

"Or we could move in with you," she said. "Either way you preferred."

"With me? But my sister and my—"

"I'm talking about *your* house."

"Oh. My house."

His house swam up before him—small and dim and abandoned, hunkered beneath the oak trees like a woodchopper's cottage in a fairy tale. Muriel glanced at his face and then said, quickly, "I could understand if you didn't want to go back there."

"It's not that," he said. He cleared his throat. He said, "It's just that I haven't given it much thought."

"Oh, I understand!"

"Not yet, at least."

"You don't have to explain!"

She pointed out where to turn, and they started down a winding road. The eating places grew sparser and shabbier. There were scratchy little trees, frozen fields, a whole village of different-sized mailboxes bristling at the end of a driveway.

Every time the car jounced, something rattled on the backseat. That was Macon's Christmas present to Alexander—a kit full of tools that were undersized but real, with solid wooden handles. Macon had hunted those tools down one by one. He had rearranged them in their compartments a dozen times at least, like a miser counting his money.

They passed a segment of rickrack fence that was dissolving back into the ground. Muriel said, "What is *your* family doing today?"

"Oh, nothing much."

"Having a big Christmas dinner?"

"No, Rose has gone to Julian's. Charles and Porter are, I don't know, I think they said something about caulking the second-floor bathtub."

"Oh, the poor things! They should have come with us to my folks'."

Macon smiled, picturing that.

He turned where she directed, into a meadow dotted with houses. All were built to the same general plan—brick with half-stories of aluminum siding above. The streets were named for trees that weren't there, Birch Lane and Elm Court and Apple Blossom Way. Muriel had him make a right onto Apple Blossom Way. He pulled up behind a station wagon. A girl burst out of the house—a chunky, pretty teenager in blue jeans and a long yellow ponytail. "Claire!" Alexander shouted, bouncing in his seat.

"That's my sister," Muriel told Macon.

"Ah."

"Do you think she's good-looking?"

"Yes, she's very good-looking."

Claire had the car door open by now and was hoisting Alexander into her arms. "How's my fellow?" she was asking. "What did Santa Claus bring you?" She was so unlike Muriel that you'd never guess they were sisters. Her face was almost square, and her skin was golden, and by present-day standards she was probably ten pounds overweight. After she'd set Alexander down, she stuffed her hands awkwardly into the back pockets of her jeans. "So anyhow," she told Macon and Muriel. "Merry Christmas, and all that."

"Look," Muriel said, flashing a wristwatch. "See what Macon gave me."

"What'd you give him?"

"A key tag from a thrift shop. Antique."

"Oh."

With her house key attached, Muriel had neglected to say.

Macon unloaded things from the trunk—Muriel's presents for her family, along with his hostess gift—and Alexander took his tool-box from the backseat. They followed Claire across the yard. Muriel was anxiously feeling her hair as she walked. "You ought to see what Daddy gave Ma," Claire told her. "Gave her a microwave oven. Ma says she's scared to death of it. 'I just know I'll get radiation,' she says. We're worried she won't use it."

The door was held open for them by a small, skinny, gray woman in an aqua pantsuit. "Ma, this is Macon," Muriel said. "Macon, this is my mother."

Mrs. Dugan studied him, pursing her lips. Lines radiated from the corners of her mouth like cat whiskers. "Pleased to meet you," she said finally.

"Merry Christmas, Mrs. Dugan," Macon said. He handed her his gift—a bottle of cranberry liqueur with a ribbon tied around it. She studied that, too.

"Just put the rest of those things under the tree," Muriel told Macon. "Ma, aren't you going to say hello to your grandson?"

Mrs. Dugan glanced briefly at Alexander. He must not have expected anything more; he was already wandering over to the Christmas tree. Unrelated objects sat beneath it—a smoke detector, an electric drill, a makeup mirror encircled with light bulbs. Macon laid Muriel's packages next to them, and then he removed his coat and draped it across the arm of a white satin couch. Fully a third of the couch was occupied by the microwave oven, still jauntily decorated with a large red bow. "Look at my new microwave," Mrs. Dugan said. "If that's not just the weirdest durn thing I ever laid eyes on." She cleared a crumple of gift wrap off an armchair and waved Macon into it.

"Something certainly smells good," he said.

"Goose," she told him. "Boyd went and shot me a goose."

She sat down next to the oven. Claire was on the floor with Alexander, helping him open a package. Muriel, still in her coat, scanned a row of books on a shelf. "Ma—" she said. "No, never mind, I found it." She came over to Macon with a photo album, the modern kind with clear plastic pages. "Look here," she said, perching on the arm of his chair. "Pictures of me when I was little."

"Why not take off your coat and stay a while," Mrs. Dugan told her.

"Me at six months. Me in my stroller. Me and my first birthday cake."

They were color photos, shiny, the reds a little too blue. (Macon's own baby pictures were black-and-white, which was all that was generally available back then.) Each showed her to be a chubby, giggling blonde, usually with her hair fixed in some coquettish style—tied in a sprig at the top of her head, or in double ponytails so highly placed they looked like puppy ears. At first the stages of her life passed slowly—it took her three full pages to learn to walk—but then they speeded up. "Me at two. Me at five. Me when I was seven and a half." The chubby blonde turned thin and dark and sober and then vanished altogether, replaced by the infant Claire. Muriel said, "Oh, well," and snapped the album shut just midway through. "Wait," Macon told her. He had an urge to see her at her worst, at her most outlandish, hanging out with motorcycle gangs. But when he took the album away from her and flipped to the very last pages, they were blank.

Mr. Dugan wandered in—a fair, freckled man in a plaid flannel shirt—and gave Macon a callused hand to shake and then wandered out again, mumbling something about the basement. "He's fretting over the pipes," Mrs. Dugan explained. "Last night it got down below zero, did you know that? He's worried the pipes'll freeze."

"Oh, could I help?" Macon asked, perking up.

"Now, you just sit right where you are, Mr. Leary."

"Macon," he said.

"Macon. And you can call me Mother Dugan."

"Um . . ."

"Muriel tells me you're separated, Macon."

"Well, yes, I am."

"Do you think it's going to take?"

"Pardon?"

"I mean you're not just leading this child around Robin Hood's barn now, are you?"

"Ma, quit that," Muriel said.

"Well, I wouldn't have to ask, Muriel, if you had ever showed the least bit of common sense on your own. I mean face it, you don't have such a great track record."

"She's just worried for me," Muriel told Macon.

"Well, of course," he said.

"This girl was not but thirteen years old," Mrs. Dugan said, "when all at once it seemed boys of the very slipperiest character just came crawling out of the woodwork. I haven't had a good night's sleep since."

"Well, I don't know why not," Muriel told her. "That was years and years ago."

"Seemed every time we turned around, off she'd gone to the Surf'n'Turf or the Torch Club or the Hi-Times Lounge on Highway Forty."

"Ma, will you please open up you and Daddy's Christmas present?"

"Oh, did you bring us a present?"

Muriel rose to fetch it from under the tree, where Claire sat with Alexander. She was helping him set up some little cardboard figures. "This one goes on the green. This one goes on the blue," she said. Alexander jittered next to her, impatient to take over.

"Claire was the one who picked that game for him," Mrs. Dugan said, accepting the package Muriel handed her. "I thought it was too advanced, myself."

"It is not," Muriel said (although she hadn't even glanced at it). She returned to Macon's chair. "Alexander's just as smart as a tack. He'll catch on in no time."

"Nobody said he wasn't smart, Muriel. You don't have to take offense at every little thing a person says."

"Will you just open your present?"

But Mrs. Dugan proceeded at her own pace. She took off the ribbon and laid it in a box on the coffee table. "Your daddy has a bit of cash for your Christmas," she told Muriel. "Remind him before you go." She examined the wrapping. "Will you look at that! Teeny little Rudolph the Red-nosed Reindeers all over it. Real aluminum foil for their noses. I don't know why you couldn't just use tissue like I do."

"I wanted it to be special," Muriel told her.

Mrs. Dugan took off the paper, folded it, and laid it aside. Her gift was something in a gilded frame. "Well, isn't that nice," she said finally. She turned it toward Macon. It was a picture of Muriel and Alexander—a studio portrait in dreamy pastels, the lighting so even that it seemed to be coming from no particular place at all. Muriel was seated and Alexander stood beside her, one hand resting delicately upon her shoulder. Neither of them smiled. They looked wary and uncertain, and very much alone.

Macon said, "It's beautiful."

Mrs. Dugan only grunted and leaned forward to lay the photo beside the box of ribbons.

. . .

Dinner was an industrious affair, with everyone working away at the food—goose, cranberry relish, two kinds of potatoes, and three kinds of vegetables. Mr. Dugan remained spookily quiet, although Macon offered him several openers about the basement plumbing. Muriel devoted herself to Alexander. "There's bread in that stuffing, Alexander. Put it back this instant. You want your allergy to start up? I wouldn't trust that relish, either."

"Oh, for Lord's sake, let him be," Mrs. Dugan said.

"You wouldn't say that if it was you he kept awake at night with itchy rashes."

"Half the time I believe you bring on those rashes yourself with all your talk," Mrs. Dugan said.

"That just shows how much you know about it."

Macon had a sudden feeling of dislocation. What would Sarah say if she could see him here? He imagined her amused, ironic expression. Rose and his brothers would just look baffled. Julian would say, "Ha! *Accidental Tourist in Timonium.*"

Mrs. Dugan brought out three different pies, and Claire scurried around with the coffeepot. Over her jeans now she wore an embroidered dirndl skirt—her gift from Muriel, purchased last week at Value Village. Her layers of clothing reminded Macon of some native costume. "What about the liqueur?" she asked her mother. "Shall I set out Macon's liqueur?"

"Maybe he wants you to call him Mr. Leary, hon."

"No, please, Macon's fine," he said.

He supposed there'd been a lot of discussion about his age. Oh, no doubt about it: He was too old, he was too tall, he was too dressed up in his suit and tie.

Mrs. Dugan said the liqueur was just about the best thing she'd ever drunk. Macon himself found it similar to the fluoride mixture his dentist coated his teeth with; he'd envisioned something different. Mr. Dugan said, "Well, these sweet-tasting, pretty-colored drinks are all very well for the ladies, but personally I favor a little sipping whiskey, don't you, Macon?" and he rose and brought back a fifth of Jack Daniel's and two shot glasses. The mere weight of the bottle in his hand seemed to loosen his tongue. "So!" he said, sitting down. "What you driving these days, Macon?"

"Driving? Oh, um, a Toyota."

Mr. Dugan frowned. Claire giggled. "Daddy hates and despises foreign cars," she told Macon.

"What is it, you don't believe in buying American?" Mr. Dugan asked him.

"Well, as a matter of fact—"

As a matter of fact his wife drove a Ford, he'd been going to say, but he changed his mind. He took the glass that Mr. Dugan held out to him. "I did once have a Rambler," he said.

"You want to try a Chevy, Macon. Want to come to the show-room sometime and let me show you a Chevy. What's your preference? Family-size? Compact?"

"Well, compact, I guess, but—"

"I'll tell you one thing: There is no way on earth you're going to get me to sell you a *sub*compact. No sir, you can beg and you can whine, you can get down on bended knee, I won't sell you one of those deathtraps folks are so set on buying nowadays. I tell my customers, I say, 'You think I got no principles? You're looking here before you at a man of principle,' I tell them, and I say, 'You want a subcompact you better go to Ed Mackenzie there. He'll sell you one without a thought. What does he care? But I'm a man of principle.' Why Muriel here near about lost her life in one of them things."

"Oh, Daddy, I did not," Muriel said.

"Came a lot closer than *I'd* like to get."

"I walked away without a scratch."

"Car looked like a little stove-in sardine can."

"Worst thing I got was a run in my stocking."

"Muriel was taking a lift from Dr. Kane at the Meow-Bow," Mr. Dugan told Macon, "one day when her car was out of whack, and some durn fool woman driver swung directly into their path. See, she was hanging a left when—"

"Let me tell it," Mrs. Dugan said. She leaned toward Macon, gripping the wineglass that held her liqueur. "I was just coming in from the grocery store, carrying these few odds and ends I needed for Claire's school lunches. That child eats more than some grown men I know. Phone rings. I drop everything and go to answer. Man says, 'Mrs. Dugan?' I say, 'Yes.' Man says, 'Mrs. Dugan, this is the

Baltimore City Police and I'm calling about your daughter Muriel.' I think, 'Oh, my God.' Right away my heart starts up and I have to find someplace to sit. Still have my coat on, rain scarf tied around my head so I couldn't even hear all that good but I never thought to take it off, that's how flustered I was. It was one of those hard rainy days like someone is purposely heaving buckets of water at you. I think, 'Oh, my God, now what has Muriel gone and—' "

"Lillian, you are getting way off the subject here," Mr. Dugan said.

"How can you say that? I'm telling him about Muriel's accident."

"He don't want to hear every little oh-my-God, he wants to know why he can't have a subcompact. Lady hangs a left smack in front of Dr. Kane's little car," Mr. Dugan told Macon, "and he has no choice but to ram her. He had the right of way. Want to know what happened? His little car is totaled. Little bitty Pinto. Lady's big old Chrysler barely dents its fender. Now tell me you still want a subcompact."

"But I didn't—"

"And the other thing is that Dr. Kane never, ever offered her another ride home, even after he got a new car," Mrs. Dugan said.

"Well, I don't exactly live in his neighborhood, Ma."

"He's a bachelor," Mrs. Dugan told Macon. "Have you met him? Real good-looking, Muriel says. First day on the job she says, 'Guess what, Ma.' Calls me on the phone. 'Guess what, my boss is single and he's real good-looking, a professional man, the other girls tell me he isn't even engaged.' Then he offers her that one lift home and they go and have an accident and he never offers again. Even when she lets him know she don't have her car some days, he never offers again."

"He does live clear up in Towson," Muriel said.

"I believe he thinks you're bad luck."

"He lives up in Towson and I live down on Singleton Street! What do you expect?"

"Next he got a Mercedes sports car," Claire put in.

"Well, sports cars," Mr. Dugan said. "We don't even talk about those."

Alexander said, "Can I be excused now?"

"I really had high hopes for Dr. Kane," Mrs. Dugan said sadly.

"Oh, quit it, Ma."

"You did, too! You said you did!"

"Why don't you just hush up and drink your drink."

Mrs. Dugan shook her head, but she took another sip of liqueur.

.   .   .

They left in the early evening, when the last light had faded and the air seemed crystallized with cold. Claire stood in the doorway singing out, "Come back soon! Thanks for the skirt! Merry Christmas!" Mrs. Dugan shivered next to her, a sweater draped over her shoulders. Mr. Dugan merely lifted an arm and disappeared — presumably to check on the basement again.

Traffic was heavier now. Headlights glowed like little white smudges. The radio — having given up on Christmas for another year — played "I Cut My Fingers on the Pieces of Your Broken Heart," and the toolbox rattled companionably in the backseat.

"Macon? Are you mad?" Muriel asked.

"Mad?"

"Are you mad at me?"

"Why, no."

She glanced back at Alexander and said no more.

It was night when they reached Singleton Street. The Butler twins, bundled into identical lavender jackets, stood talking with two boys on the curb. Macon parked and opened the back door for Alexander, who had fallen asleep with his chin on his chest. He gathered him up and carried him into the house. In the living room, Muriel set down her own burdens — the toolbox, Alexander's new game, and a pie Mrs. Dugan had pressed on them — and followed Macon up the stairs. Macon walked sideways to keep Alexander's feet from banging into the wall. They went into the smaller of the bedrooms and he laid Alexander on the bed. "I know what you must be thinking," Muriel said. She took Alexander's shoes off. "You're thinking, 'Oh, now I see, this Muriel was just on the lookout for anybody in trousers.' Aren't you."

Macon didn't answer. (He worried they'd wake Alexander.)

"I know what you're thinking!"

She tucked Alexander in. Turned off the light. They started back downstairs. "But that's not the way it was; I swear it," she said. "Oh, of course since he was single the possibility did cross my mind. Who would I be kidding if I said it didn't? I'm all alone, raising a kid. Scrounging for money. Of course it crossed my mind!"

"Well, of course," Macon said mildly.

"But it wasn't like she made it sound," Muriel told him.

She clattered after him across the living room. When he sat on the couch she sat next to him, still in her coat. "Are you going to stay?" she asked.

"If you're not too sleepy."

Instead of answering, she tipped her head back against the couch. "I meant are you giving up on me. I meant did you want to stop seeing me."

"Why would I want to stop seeing you?"

"After how bad she made me look."

"You didn't look bad."

"Oh, no?"

When she was tired, her skin seemed to tighten over her bones. She pressed her fingertips to her eyelids.

"Last Christmas," Macon said, "was the first one we had without Ethan. It was very hard to get through."

He often found himself talking with her about Ethan. It felt good to say his name out loud.

"We didn't know how to have a childless Christmas anymore," he said. "I thought, 'Well, after all, we managed before we had him, didn't we?' But in fact I couldn't remember how. It seemed to me we'd *always* had him; it's so unthinkable once you've got children that they ever didn't exist. I've noticed: I look back to when I was a boy, and it seems to me that Ethan was somehow there even then;

just not yet visible, or something. So anyway. I decided what I
should do was get Sarah a whole flood of presents, and I went out to
Hutzler's the day before Christmas and bought all this junk—closet
organizers and such. And Sarah: She went to the other extreme.
She didn't buy anything. So there we were, each of us feeling we'd
done it all wrong, acted inappropriately, but also that the other had
done wrong; I don't know. It was a terrible Christmas."

He smoothed Muriel's hair off her forehead. "This one was better," he said.

She opened her eyes and studied him a moment. Then she
slipped her hand in her pocket, came up with something and held
it toward him—palming it, like a secret. "For you," she said.

"For me?"

"I'd like you to have it."

It was a snapshot stolen from her family album: Muriel as a toddler, clambering out of a wading pool.

She meant, he supposed, to give him the best of her. And so she
had. But the best of her was not that child's Shirley Temple hairdo.
It was her fierceness—her spiky, pugnacious fierceness as she
fought her way toward the camera with her chin set awry and her
eyes bright slits of determination. He thanked her. He said he
would keep it forever.

f o u r t e e n

Y ou would have to say that he was living with her now. He began to spend all his time at her house, to contribute toward her rent and her groceries. He kept his shaving things in her bathroom and squeezed his clothes among the dresses in her closet. But there wasn't one particular point at which he made the shift. No, this was a matter of day by day. First there was that long Christmas vacation when Alexander was home alone; so why shouldn't Macon stay on with him once he'd spent the night there? And why not fetch his typewriter and work at the kitchen table? And then why not remain for supper, and after that for bed?

Though if you needed to put a date on it, you might say he truly moved in the afternoon he moved Edward in. He'd just got back from a business trip—an exhausting blitz of five southern cities, not one of which was any warmer than Baltimore—and he stopped by Rose's house to check the animals. The cat was fine, Rose said. (She had to speak above Edward's yelps; he was frantic with joy and relief.) The cat had probably not noticed Macon was missing. But Edward, well . . . "He spends a lot of time sitting in the hall," she said, "staring at the door. He keeps his head cocked and he waits for you to come back."

That did it. He brought Edward with him when he returned to Singleton Street.

"What do you think?" he asked Muriel. "Could we keep him just a day or two? See if Alexander can take it, without any shots?"

"I can take it!" Alexander said. "It's cats that get to me; not dogs."

Muriel looked doubtful, but she said they could give it a try.

Meanwhile, Edward darted madly all over the house snuffling into corners and under furniture. Then he sat in front of Muriel and grinned up at her. He reminded Macon of a schoolboy with a crush on his teacher; all his fantasies were realized, here he was at last.

For the first few hours they tried to keep him in a separate part of the house, which of course was hopeless. He had to follow Macon wherever he went, and also he developed an immediate interest in Alexander. Lacking a ball, he kept dropping small objects at Alexander's feet and then stepping back to look expectantly into his face. "He wants to play fetch," Macon explained. Alexander picked up a matchbook and tossed it, angling his arm behind him in a prissy way. While Edward went tearing after it, Macon made a mental note to buy a ball first thing in the morning and teach Alexander how to throw.

Alexander watched TV and Edward snoozed on the couch beside him, curled like a little blond cashew nut with a squinty, blissful expression on his face. Alexander hugged him and buried his face in Edward's ruff. "Watch it," Macon told him. He had no idea what to do if Alexander started wheezing. But Alexander didn't wheeze. By bedtime he just had a stuffy nose, and he usually had that anyhow.

. . .

Macon liked to believe that Alexander didn't know he and Muriel slept together. "Well, that's just plain ridiculous," Muriel said. "Where does he imagine you spend the night—on the living room couch?"

"Maybe," he said. "I'm sure he has some explanation. Or maybe he doesn't. All I'm saying is, we shouldn't hit him in the face with it. Let him think what he wants to think."

So every morning, Macon rose and dressed before Alexander woke. He started fixing breakfast and then roused him. "Seven o'clock! Time to get up! Go call your mother, will you?" In the past, he learned, Muriel had often stayed in bed while Alexander woke up on his own and got ready for school. Sometimes he left the house while she was still asleep. Macon thought that was shocking. Now he made a full breakfast, and he insisted that Muriel sit at the table with them. Muriel claimed breakfast made her sick to her stomach. Alexander said it made him sick, too, but Macon said that was just too bad. "Ninety-eight percent of all A students eat eggs in the morning," he said (making it up as he went along). "Ninety-nine percent drink milk." He untied his apron and sat down. "Are you listening, Alexander?"

"I'll throw up if I drink milk."

"That's all in your head."

"Tell him, Mama!"

"He throws up," Muriel said gloomily. She sat hunched at the table in her long silk robe, resting her chin on one hand. "It's something to do with enzymes," she said. She yawned. Her hair, growing out of its permanent at last, hung down her back in even ripples like the crimps on a bobby pin.

Alexander walked to school with Buddy and Sissy Ebbetts, two tough-looking older children from across the street. Muriel either went back to bed or dressed and left for one or another of her jobs, depending on what day it was. Then Macon did the breakfast dishes and took Edward out. They didn't go far; it was much too cold. The few people they encountered walked rapidly, with jerky steps, like characters in a silent film. They knew Macon by sight now and would allow their eyes to flick over his face as they passed—a gesture like a nod—but they didn't speak. Edward ignored them. Other dogs could come up and sniff him and he wouldn't even break stride. Mr. Marcusi, unloading crates outside Marcusi's Grocery, would pause to say, "Well, hey there, stubby. Hey there, tub of lard."

Edward, smugly oblivious, marched on. "Weirdest animal I ever saw," Mr. Marcusi called after Macon. "Looks like something that was badly drawn." Macon always laughed.

He was beginning to feel easier here. Singleton Street still unnerved him with its poverty and its ugliness, but it no longer seemed so dangerous. He saw that the hoodlums in front of the Cheery Moments Carry-Out were pathetically young and shabby— their lips chapped, their sparse whiskers ineptly shaved, an uncertain, unformed look around their eyes. He saw that once the men had gone off to work, the women emerged full of good intentions and swept their front walks, picked up the beer cans and potato chip bags, even rolled back their coat sleeves and scrubbed their stoops on the coldest days of the year. Children raced past like so many scraps of paper blowing in the wind—mittens mismatched, noses running—and some woman would brace herself on her broom to call, "You there! I see you! Don't think I don't know you're skipping school!" For this street was always backsliding, Macon saw, always falling behind, but was caught just in time by these women with their carrying voices and their pushy jaws.

Returning to Muriel's house, he would warm himself with a cup of coffee. He would set his typewriter on the kitchen table and sit down with his notes and brochures. The window next to the table had large, cloudy panes that rattled whenever the wind blew. Something about the rattling sound reminded him of train travel. *The airport in Atlanta must have ten miles of corridors*, he typed, and then a gust shook the panes and he had an eerie sensation of movement, as if the cracked linoleum floor were skating out from under him.

He would telephone hotels, motels, Departments of Commerce, and his travel agent, arranging future trips. He would note these arrangements in the datebook that Julian gave him every Christmas—a Businessman's Press product, spiral-bound. In the back were various handy reference charts that he liked to thumb through. The birthstone for January was a garnet; for February, an amethyst. One square mile equaled 2.59 square kilometers. The proper gift for a first anniversary was paper. He would ponder these facts dreamily. It seemed to him that the world was full of equations; that there must be an answer for everything, if only you knew how to set forth the questions.

Then it was lunchtime, and he would put away his work and make himself a sandwich or heat a can of soup, let Edward have a quick run in the tiny backyard. After that he liked to putter around the house a bit. There was so much that needed fixing! And all of it somebody else's, not his concern, so he could approach it lightheartedly. He whistled while he probed the depth of a crack. He hummed as he toured the basement, shaking his head at the disarray. Upstairs he found a three-legged bureau leaning on a can of tomatoes, and he told Edward, "Scandalous!" in a tone of satisfaction.

It occurred to him—as he oiled a hinge, as he tightened a doorknob—that the house reflected amazingly little of Muriel. She must have lived here six or seven years by now, but still the place had an air of transience. Her belongings seemed hastily placed, superimposed, not really much to do with her. This was a disappointment, for Macon was conscious while he worked of his intense curiosity about her inner workings. Sanding a drawer, he cast a guilty eye upon its contents but found only fringed shawls and yellowed net gloves from the forties—clues to other people's lives, not hers.

But what was it he wanted to know? She was an open book, would tell him anything—more than he felt comfortable with. Nor did she attempt to hide her true nature, which was certainly far from perfect. It emerged that she had a nasty temper, a shrewish tongue, and a tendency to fall into spells of self-disgust from which no one could rouse her for hours. She was inconsistent with Alexander to the point of pure craziness—one minute overprotective, the next minute callous and offhand. She was obviously intelligent, but she counteracted that with the most global case of superstition Macon had ever witnessed. Hardly a day passed when she didn't tell him some dream in exhaustive detail and then sift through it for omens. (A dream of white ships on a purple sea came true the very next morning, she claimed, when a door-to-door salesman showed up in a purple sweater patterned with little white boats. "The very same purple! Same shape of ship!" Macon only wondered what kind of salesman would wear such clothing.) She believed in horoscopes and tarot cards and Ouija boards. Her magic number was seventeen. In a previous incarnation she'd been a fashion designer, and she swore she could recall at least one of her deaths. ("We think she's passed on," they told the doctor as he entered, and the doctor unwound his muffler.) She was religious in a blurry, nondenominational way and had no doubt whatsoever that God was looking after her personally—ironic, it seemed to Macon, in view of how she'd had to fight for every little thing she wanted.

He knew all this and yet, finding a folded sheet of paper on the counter, he opened it and devoured her lurching scrawl as if she were a stranger. *Pretzels. Pantyhose. Dentist*, he read. *Pick up Mrs. Arnold's laundry.*

No, not that. Not that.

Then it was three o'clock and Alexander was home from school, letting himself in with a key that he wore on a shoelace around his neck. "Macon?" he'd call tentatively. "Is that you out there?" He was scared of burglars. Macon said, "It's me." Edward leapt up and went running for his ball. "How was your day?" Macon always asked.

"Oh, okay."

But Macon had the feeling that school never went very well for Alexander. He came out of it with his face more pinched than ever, his glasses thick with fingerprints. He reminded Macon of a homework paper that had been erased and rewritten too many times. His clothes, on the other hand, were as neat as when he'd left in the morning. Oh, those clothes! Spotless polo shirts with a restrained brown pinstripe, matching brown trousers gathered bulkily around his waist with a heavy leather belt. Shiny brown shoes. Blinding white socks. Didn't he ever play? Didn't kids have recess anymore?

Macon gave him a snack: milk and cookies. (Alexander drank milk in the afternoons without complaint.) Then he helped him with his schoolwork. It was the simplest sort—arithmetic sums and reading questions. "Why did Joe need the dime? Where was Joe's daddy?"

"Umm . . ." Alexander said. Blue veins pulsed in his temples.

He was not a stupid child but he was limited, Macon felt. Limited. Even his walk was constricted. Even his smile never dared to venture beyond two invisible boundaries in the center of his face. Not that he was smiling now. He was wrinkling his forehead, raising his eyes fearfully to Macon.

"Take your time," Macon told him. "There's no hurry."

"But I can't! I don't know! I don't know!"

"You remember Joe," Macon said patiently.

"I don't think I do!"

Sometimes Macon stuck with it, sometimes he simply dropped it. After all, Alexander had managed without him up till now, hadn't he? There was a peculiar kind of luxury here: Alexander was not his own child. Macon felt linked to him in all sorts of complicated ways, but not in that inseparable, inevitable way that he'd been linked to Ethan. He could still draw back from Alexander; he could still give up on him. "Oh, well," he could say, "talk it over with your teacher tomorrow." And then his thoughts could wander off again.

The difference was, he realized, that he was not held responsible here. It was a great relief to know that.

When Muriel came home she brought fresh air and bustle and excitement. "Is it ever cold! Is it ever windy! Radio says three below zero tonight. Edward, down, this minute. Who wants lemon pie for dessert? Here's what happened: I had to go shopping for Mrs. Quick. First I had to buy linens for her daughter who's getting married, then I had to take them back because they were all the wrong color, her daughter didn't want pastel but white and told her mother plain as day, she said . . . and then I had to pick up pastries for the bridesmaids' party and when Mrs. Quick sees the lemon pie she says, 'Oh, no, not lemon! Not that tacky lemon that always tastes like Kool-Aid!' I'm like, 'Mrs. Quick, you don't have any business telling me what is tacky. This is a fresh-baked, lemon meringue pie without a trace of artificial . . .' So anyway, to make a long story short, she said to take it home to my little boy. 'Well, for your information I'm certain he can't eat it,' I say. 'Chances are he's allergic.' But I took it."

She ranged around the kitchen putting together a supper—BLT's, usually, and vegetables from a can. Sometimes things were not where she expected (Macon's doing—he couldn't resist reorganizing), but she adapted cheerfully. While the bacon sputtered in the skillet she usually phoned her mother and went over all she'd just told Macon and Alexander. "But the daughter wanted white and . . . 'oh, not that tacky lemon pie!' she says . . ."

If Mrs. Dugan couldn't come to the phone (which was often the case), Muriel talked to Claire instead. Evidently Claire was having troubles at home. "Tell them!" Muriel counseled her. "Just tell them! Tell them you won't stand for it." Cradling the receiver against her shoulder, she opened a drawer and took out knives and forks. "Why should they have to know every little thing you do? It doesn't *matter* that you're not up to anything, Claire. Tell them, 'I'm seventeen years old and it's none of your affair anymore if I'm up to anything or not. I'm just about a grown woman,' tell them."

But later, if Mrs. Dugan finally came to the phone, Muriel herself sounded like a child. "Ma? What kept you? You can't say a couple of words to your daughter just because your favorite song is playing on the radio? 'Lara's Theme' is more important than flesh and blood?"

Even after Muriel hung up, she seldom really focused on dinner. Her girlfriend might drop by and stay to watch them eat—a fat young woman named Bernice who worked for the Gas and Electric Company. Or neighbors would knock on the kitchen door and walk right in. "Muriel, do you happen to have a coupon for support hose? Young and slim as *you* are, I know you wouldn't need it yourself." "Muriel, Saturday morning I got to go to the clinic for my teeth, any chance of you giving me a lift?" Muriel was an oddity on this street—a woman with a car of her own—and they knew by heart her elaborate arrangement with the boy who did her repairs.

Sundays, when Dominick had the car all day, nobody troubled her; but as soon as Monday rolled around they'd be lining up with their requests. "Doctor wants me to come in and show him my . . ." "I promised I'd take my kids to the . . ."

If Muriel couldn't do it, they never thought to ask Macon instead. Macon was still an outsider; they shot him quick glances but pretended not to notice he was listening. Even Bernice was bashful with him, and she avoided using his name.

By the time the lottery number was announced on TV, everyone would have left. That was what mattered here, Macon had discovered: the television schedule. The news could be missed but the lottery drawing could not; nor could "Evening Magazine" or any of the action shows that followed. Alexander watched these shows but Muriel didn't, although she claimed to. She sat on the couch in front of the set and talked, or painted her nails, or read some article or other. "Look here! 'How to Increase Your Bustline.' "

"You don't want to increase your bustline," Macon told her.

" 'Thicker, More Luxurious Eyelashes in Just Sixty Days.' "

"You don't want thicker eyelashes."

He felt content with everything exactly the way it was. He seemed to be suspended, his life on hold.

And later, taking Edward for his final outing, he liked the feeling of the neighborhood at night. This far downtown the sky was too pale for stars; it was pearly and opaque. The buildings were muffled dark shapes. Faint sounds threaded out of them—music, rifle shots, the whinnying of horses. Macon looked up at Alexander's window and saw Muriel unfolding a blanket, as delicate and distinct as a silhouette cut from black paper.

.   .   .

One Wednesday there was a heavy snowstorm, starting in the morning and continuing through the day. Snow fell in clumps like white woolen mittens. It wiped out the dirty tatters of snow from earlier storms; it softened the street's harsh angles and hid the trash cans under cottony domes. Even the women who swept their stoops hourly could not keep pace with it, and toward evening they gave up and went inside. All night the city glowed lilac. It was absolutely silent.

The next morning, Macon woke late. Muriel's side of the bed was empty, but her radio was still playing. A tired-sounding announcer was reading out cancellations. Schools were closed, factories were closed, Meals on Wheels was not running. Macon was impressed by the number of activities that people had been planning for just this one day—the luncheons and lectures and protest meetings. What energy, what spirit! He felt almost proud, though he hadn't been going to attend any of these affairs himself.

Then he realized he was hearing voices downstairs. Alexander must be awake, and here he was trapped in Muriel's bedroom.

He dressed stealthily, making sure the coast was clear before crossing the hall to the bathroom. He tried not to creak the floorboards as he descended the stairs. The living room was unnaturally bright, reflecting the snow outside. The couch was opened, a mass of sheets and blankets; Claire had slept over the last few nights. Macon followed the voices into the kitchen. He found Alexander eating pancakes, Claire at the stove making more, Muriel curled in her usual morning gloom above her coffee cup. Just inside the back door Bernice stood dripping snow, swathed in various enormous plaids. "So anyhow," Claire was telling Bernice, "Ma says, 'Claire, who was that boy you drove up with?' I said, 'That was no boy, that was Josie Tapp with her new punk haircut,' and Ma says, 'Expect me to believe a cock-and-bull story like that!' So I say, 'I've had enough of this! Grillings! Curfews! Suspicions!' And I leave and catch a bus down here."

"They're just worried you'll turn out like Muriel did," Bernice told her.

"But Josie Tapp! I mean God Almighty!"

There was a general shifting motion in Macon's direction. Claire said, "Hey there, Macon. Want some pancakes?"

"Just a glass of milk, thanks."

"They're nice and hot."

"Macon thinks sugar on an empty stomach causes ulcers," Muriel said. She wrapped both hands around her cup.

Bernice said, "Well, *I'm* not saying no," and she crossed the kitchen to pull out a chair. Her boots left pads of snow with each step. Edward toddled after her, licking them up. "You and me ought to build a snowman," Bernice told Alexander. "Snow must be four feet deep out there."

"Have the streets been cleared?" Macon asked.

"Are you kidding?"

"They couldn't even get through with the newspaper," Alexander told him. "Edward's about to lose his mind wondering where it's got to."

"And there's cars abandoned all over the city. Radio says nobody's going anywhere at all."

But Bernice had hardly spoken when Edward wheeled toward the back door and started barking. A figure loomed outside. "Who's that?" Bernice asked.

Muriel tapped her foot at Edward. He lay down but kept on barking, and Macon opened the door. He found himself face to face with his brother Charles—unusually rugged-looking in a visored cap with earflaps. "Charles?" Macon said. "What are you doing here?"

Charles stepped in, bringing with him the fresh, expectant smell of new snow. Edward's yelps changed to welcoming whines. "I came to pick you up," Charles said. "Couldn't reach you on the phone."

"Pick me up for what?"

"Your neighbor Garner Bolt called and said pipes or something have burst in your house, water all over everything. I've been trying to get you since early morning but your line was always busy."

"That was me," Claire said, setting down a platter of pancakes. "I took the receiver off the hook so my folks wouldn't call me up and nag me."

"This is Muriel's sister, Claire," Macon said, "and that's Alexander and that's Bernice Tilghman. My brother Charles."

Charles looked confused.

Come to think of it, this wasn't an easy group to sort out. Claire was her usual mingled self—rosebud bathrobe over faded jeans, fringed moccasin boots that laced to her knees. Bernice could have been a lumberjack. Alexander was neat and polished, while Muriel in her slinky silk robe was barely decent. Also, the kitchen was so small that there seemed to be more people than there actually were. And Claire was waving her spatula, spangling the air with drops of grease. "Pancakes?" she asked Charles. "Orange juice? Coffee?"

"No, thank you," Charles said. "I really have to be—"

"I bet you want milk," Muriel said. She got to her feet, fortunately remembering to clutch her robe together. "I bet you don't want sugar on an empty stomach."

"No, really I—"

"It won't be any trouble!" She was taking the carton from the refrigerator. "How'd you get here, anyways?"

"I drove."

"I thought the streets were blocked."

"They weren't so bad," Charles said, accepting a glass of milk. "*Finding* the place was the hard part." He told Macon, "I looked it up on the map but evidently I was mizzled."

"Mizzled?" Muriel asked.

"He was misled," Macon explained. "What did Garner say, exactly, Charles?"

"He said he saw water running down the inside of your living room window. He looked in and saw the ceiling dripping. Could have been that way for weeks, he said; you know that cold spell we had over Christmas."

"Doesn't sound good," Macon said.

He went to the closet for his coat. When he came back, Muriel was saying, "Now that you don't have an empty stomach, Charles, won't you try some of Claire's pancakes?"

"I've had a half a dozen," Bernice told him. "They don't call me Big-Ass Bernice for nothing."

Charles said, "Uh, well—" and gave Macon a helpless look.

"We have to be going," Macon told the others. "Charles, are you parked in back?"

"No, in front. Then I went around back because I couldn't get the doorbell to work."

There was a reserved, disapproving note in Charles's voice when he said this, but Macon just said airily, "Oh, yes! Place is a wreck." He led the way toward the front of the house. He felt like someone demonstrating how well he got on with the natives.

They pushed open the door with some difficulty and floundered down steps so deeply buried that both men more or less fell the length of them, trusting that they would be cushioned. The sunlight sparked and flashed. They waded toward the street, Macon's shoes quickly filling with snow—a refreshing sharpness that almost instantly turned painful.

"I guess we'd better take both cars," he told Charles.

"How come?"

"Well, you don't want to have to drive all the way back down here."

"But if we take just one, then one of us can drive and one can push if we get stuck."

"Let's take mine, then."

"But mine's already cleared and dug out."

"But with mine I could drop you off home and save you the trip back down."

"But that leaves my car stranded on Singleton Street."

"We could get it to you after they plow."

"And *my* car has its engine warmed!" Charles said.

Was this how they had sounded, all these years? Macon gave a short laugh, but Charles waited intently for his answer. "Fine, we'll take yours," Macon told him. They climbed into Charles's VW.

It was true there were a lot of abandoned cars. They sat in no particular pattern, featureless white mounds turned this way and that, so the street resembled a river of drifting boats. Charles dodged expertly between them. He kept a slow, steady speed and talked about Rose's wedding. "We told her April was too iffy. Better wait, we told her, if she's so set on an outdoor service. But

Rose said no, she'll take her chances. She's sure the weather will be perfect."

A snow-covered jeep in front of them, the only moving vehicle they'd yet encountered, suddenly slurred to one side. Charles passed it smoothly in a long, shallow arc. Macon said, "Where will they live, anyhow?"

"Why, at Julian's, I suppose."

"In a singles building?"

"No, he's got another place now, an apartment near the Belvedere."

"I see," Macon said. But he had trouble picturing Rose in an apartment—or anywhere, for that matter, if it wasn't her grand-parents' house with its egg-and-dart moldings and heavily draped windows.

All through the city people were digging out—tunneling toward their parked cars, scraping off their windshields, shoveling sidewalks. There was something holidaylike about them; they waved to each other and called back and forth. One man, having cleared not only his walk but a section of the street as well, was do-ing a little soft-shoe dance on the wet concrete, and when Charles and Macon drove through he stopped to shout, "What are you, crazy? Traveling around in this?"

"I must say you're remarkably calm in view of the situation," Charles told Macon.

"What situation?"

"Your house, I mean. Water pouring through the ceiling for who knows how long."

"Oh, that," Macon said. Yes, at one time he'd have been very upset about that.

By now they were high on North Charles Street, which the plows had already cleared. Macon was struck by the spaciousness here—the buildings set far apart, wide lawns sloping between them. He had never noticed that before. He sat forward to gaze at the side streets. They were still completely white. And just a few blocks over, when Charles turned into Macon's neighborhood, they saw a young girl on skis.

His house looked the same as ever, though slightly dingy in comparison with the snow. They sat in the car a moment studying it, and then Macon said, "Well, here goes, I guess," and they climbed out. They could see where Garner Bolt had waded through the yard; they saw the scalloping of footprints where he'd stepped closer to peer in a window. But the sidewalk bore no tracks at all, and Macon found it difficult in his smooth-soled shoes.

The instant he unlocked the door, they heard the water. The living room was filled with a cool, steady, dripping sound, like a greenhouse after the plants have been sprayed. Charles, who was the first to enter, said, "Oh, my God." Macon stopped dead in the hallway behind him.

Apparently an upstairs pipe (in that cold little bathroom off Ethan's old room, Macon would bet) had frozen and burst, heaven only knew how long ago, and the water had run and run until it saturated the ceiling and started coming through the plaster. All over the room it was raining. Chunks of plaster had fallen on the furniture, turning it white and splotchy. The floorboards were mottled. The rug, when Macon stepped on it, squelched beneath his feet. He marveled at the thoroughness of the destruction; not a detail had been overlooked. Every ashtray was full of wet flakes and every magazine was sodden. There was a gray smell rising from the upholstery.

"What are you going to *do*?" Charles breathed.

Macon pulled himself together. "Why, turn off the water main, of course," he said.

"But your living room!"

Macon didn't answer. His living room was . . . appropriate, was what he wanted to say. Even more appropriate if it had been washed away entirely. (He imagined the house under twelve feet of water, uncannily clear, like a castle at the bottom of a goldfish bowl.)

He went down to the basement and shut off the valve, and then he checked the laundry sink. It was dry. Ordinarily he let the tap run all winter long, a slender stream to keep the pipes from freezing, but this year he hadn't thought of it and neither had his brothers, evidently, when they came to light the furnace.

"Oh, this is terrible, just terrible," Charles was saying when Macon came back upstairs. But he was in the kitchen now, where there wasn't any problem. He was opening and shutting cabinet doors. "Terrible. Terrible."

Macon had no idea what he was going on about. He said, "Just let me find my boots and we can leave."

"Leave?"

He thought his boots must be in his closet. He went upstairs to the bedroom. Everything here was so dreary—the naked mattress with its body bag, the dusty mirror, the brittle yellow newspaper folded on the nightstand. He bent to root through the objects on the closet floor. There were his boots, all right, along with some wire hangers and a little booklet of some sort. *A Gardener's Diary, 1976.* He flipped through it. *First lawn-mowing of the spring,* Sarah had written in her compact script. *Forsythia still in bloom.* Macon closed the diary and smoothed the cover and laid it aside.

Boots in hand, he went back downstairs. Charles had returned to the living room; he was wringing out cushions. "Never mind those," Macon said. "They'll just get wet again."

"Will your insurance cover this?"

"I suppose so."

"What would they call it? Flood damage? Weather damage?"

"I don't know. Let's get going."

"You should phone our contractor, Macon. Remember the man who took care of our porch?"

"Nobody lives here anyhow," Macon said.

Charles straightened, still holding a cushion. "What's that supposed to mean?" he asked.

"Mean?"

"Are you saying you'll just let this stay?"

"Probably," Macon told him.

"All soaked and ruined? Nothing done?"

"Oh, well," Macon said, waving a hand. "Come along, Charles."

But Charles hung back, still gazing around the living room. "Terrible. Even the curtains are dripping. Sarah will feel just terrible."

"I doubt she'll give it a thought," Macon said.

He paused on the porch to pull his boots on. They were old and stiff, the kind with metal clasps. He tucked his wet trouser cuffs inside them and then led the way to the street.

Once they were settled in the car, Charles didn't start the engine but sat there, key in hand, and looked soberly at Macon. "I think it's time we had a talk," he said.

"What about?"

"I'd like to know what you think you're up to with this Muriel person."

"Is that what you call her? 'This Muriel person'?"

"No one else will tell you," Charles said. "They say it's none of their business. But I can't just stand by and watch, Macon. I have to say what I think. How old are you—forty-two? Forty-three now? And she is . . . but more than that, she's not your type of woman."

"You don't even know her!"

"I know her type."

"I have to be getting home now, Charles."

Charles looked down at his key. Then he started the car and pulled into the street, but he didn't drop the subject. "She's some kind of symptom, Macon! You're not yourself these days and this Muriel person's a symptom. Everybody says so."

"I'm more myself than I've been my whole life long," Macon told him.

"What kind of remark is that? It doesn't even make sense!"

"And who is 'everybody,' anyway?"

"Why, Porter, Rose, me . . ."

"All such experts."

"We're just worried for you, Macon."

"Could we switch to some other topic?"

"I had to tell you what I thought," Charles said.

"Well, fine. You've told me."

But Charles didn't look satisfied.

The car wallowed back through the slush, with ribbons of bright water trickling down the windshield from the roof. Then out on the main road, it picked up speed. "Hate to think what all that salt is doing to your underbody," Macon said.

Charles said, "I never told you this before, but it's my opinion sex is overrated."

Macon looked at him.

"Oh, when I was in my teens I was as interested as anyone," Charles said. "I mean it occupied my thoughts for every waking moment and all that. But that was just the *idea* of sex, you know? Somehow, the real thing was less . . . I don't mean I'm opposed to it, but it's just not all I expected. For one thing, it's rather messy. And then the weather is such a problem."

"Weather," Macon said.

"When it's cold you hate to take your clothes off. When it's hot you're both so sticky. And in Baltimore, it does always seem to be either too cold or too hot."

"Maybe you ought to consider a change of climate," Macon said. He was beginning to enjoy himself. "Do you suppose anyone's done a survey? City by city? Maybe the Businessman's Press could put out some sort of pamphlet."

"And besides it often leads to children," Charles said. "I never really cared much for children. They strike me as disruptive."

"Well, if that's why you brought this up, forget it," Macon said. "Muriel can't have any more."

Charles gave a little cough. "That's good to hear," he said, "but it's not why I brought it up. I believe what I was trying to say is, I just don't think sex is important enough to ruin your life for."

"So? Who's ruining his life?"

"Macon, face it. She's not worth it."

"How can you possibly know that?"

"Can you tell me one unique thing about her?" Charles asked. "I mean one really special quality, Macon, not something sloppy like 'She appreciates me' or 'She listens . . .' "

She looks out hospital windows and imagines how the Martians would see us, Macon wanted to say. But Charles wouldn't understand that, so instead he said, "I'm not such a bargain myself, in case you haven't noticed. I'm kind of, you could say, damaged merchandise. Somebody ought to warn *her* away from *me*, when you get right down to it."

"That's not true. That's not true at all. As a matter of fact, I imagine her people are congratulating her on her catch."

"Her catch!"

"Someone to support her. Anyone," Charles said. "She'd be lucky to find anyone. Why, she doesn't even speak proper English! She lives in that slummy house, she dresses like some kind of bag lady, she's got that little boy who appears to have hookworm or something—"

"Charles, just shut the hell up," Macon said.

Charles closed his mouth.

They had reached Muriel's neighborhood by now. They were driving past the stationery factory with its tangled wire fence like old bedsprings. Charles took a wrong turn. "Let's see, now," he said, "where do I . . ."

Macon didn't offer to help.

"Am I heading in the right direction? Or not. Somehow I don't seem to . . ."

They were two short blocks from Singleton Street, but Macon hoped Charles would drive in circles forever. "Lots of luck," he said, and he opened the door and hopped out.

"Macon?"

Macon waved and ducked down an alley.

Freedom! Sunlight glinting off blinding white drifts, and children riding sleds and TV trays. Cleared parking spaces guarded with lawn chairs. Throngs of hopeful boys with shovels. And then Muriel's house with its walk still deep in snow, its small rooms smelling of pancakes, its cozy mix of women lounging about in the kitchen. They were drinking cocoa now. Bernice was braiding Claire's hair. Alexander was painting a picture. Muriel kissed Macon hello and squealed at his cold cheeks. "Come in and get warm! Have some cocoa! Look at Alexander's picture," she said. "Don't you love it? Isn't he something? He's a regular da Vinci."

"Leonardo," Macon said.

"What?"

"Not da Vinci. For God's sake. It's Leonardo," he told her. Then he stamped upstairs to change out of his clammy trousers.

fifteen

I'm sorry I'm so fat," Macon's seatmate said.

Macon said, "Oh, er, ah—"

"I know I'm using more than my share of space," the man told him. "Do you think I'm not aware of that? Every trip I take, I have to ask the stewardess for a seatbelt extender. I have to balance my lunch on my knees because the tray can't unfold in front of me. Really I ought to purchase two seats but I'm not a wealthy man. I ought to purchase two tickets and not spread all over my fellow passengers."

"Oh, you're not spreading all over me," Macon said.

This was because he was very nearly sitting in the aisle, with his knees jutting out to the side so that every passing stewardess ruffled the pages of *Miss MacIntosh*. But he couldn't help feeling touched by the man's great, shiny, despairing face, which was as round as a baby's. "Name's Lucas Loomis," the man said, holding out a hand. When Macon shook it, he was reminded of risen bread dough.

"Macon Leary," Macon told him.

"The stupid thing is," Lucas Loomis said, "I travel for a living."

"Do you."

"I demonstrate software to computer stores. I'm sitting in an airplane seat six days out of seven sometimes."

"Well, none of us finds them all that roomy," Macon said.

"What do you do, Mr. Leary?"

"I write guidebooks," Macon said.

"Is that so? What kind?"

"Oh, guides for businessmen. People just like you, I guess."

"*Accidental Tourist*," Mr. Loomis said instantly.

"Why, yes."

"Really? Am I right? Well, what do you know," Mr. Loomis said. "Look at this." He took hold of his own lapels, which sat so far in front of him that his arms seemed too short to reach them. "Gray suit," he told Macon. "Just what you recommend. Appropriate for all occasions." He pointed to the bag at his feet. "See my luggage? Carry-on. Change of underwear, clean shirt, packet of detergent powder."

"Well, good," Macon said. This had never happened to him before.

"You're my hero!" Mr. Loomis told him. "You've improved my trips a hundred percent. You're the one who told me about those springy items that turn into clotheslines."

"Oh, well, you could have run across those in any drugstore," Macon said.

"I've stopped relying on hotel laundries; I hardly need to venture into the streets anymore. I tell my wife, I say, you just ask her, I tell her often, I say, 'Going with the *Accidental Tourist* is like going in a capsule, a cocoon. Don't forget to pack my *Accidental Tourist*!' I tell her."

"Well, this is very nice to hear," Macon said.

"Times I've flown clear to Oregon and hardly knew I'd left Baltimore."

"Excellent."

There was a pause.

"Although," Macon said, "lately I've been wondering."

Mr. Loomis had to turn his entire body to look at him, like someone encased in a hooded parka.

"I mean," Macon said, "I've been out along the West Coast. Updating my U.S. edition. And of course I've covered the West Coast before, Los Angeles and all that; Lord, yes, I knew the place as a child; but this was the first I'd seen of San Francisco. My publisher wanted me to add it in. Have you been to San Francisco?"

"That's where we just now got on the plane," Mr. Loomis reminded him.

"San Francisco is certainly, um, beautiful," Macon said.

Mr. Loomis thought that over.

"Well, so is Baltimore too, of course," Macon said hastily. "Oh, no place on earth like Baltimore! But San Francisco, well, I mean it struck me as, I don't know . . ."

"I was born and raised in Baltimore, myself," Mr. Loomis said. "Wouldn't live anywhere else for the world."

"No, of course not," Macon said. "I just meant—"

"Couldn't pay me to leave it."

"No, me either."

"You a Baltimore man?"

"Yes, certainly."

"No place like it."

"Certainly isn't," Macon said.

But a picture came to his mind of San Francisco floating on mist like the Emerald City, viewed from one of those streets so high and steep that you really could hang your head over and hear the wind blow.

.   .   .

He'd left Baltimore on a sleety day with ice coating the airport runways, and he hadn't been gone all that long; but when he returned it was spring. The sun was shining and the trees were tipped with green. It was still fairly cool but he drove with his windows down. The breeze smelled exactly like Vouvray—flowery with a hint of mothballs underneath.

On Singleton Street, crocuses were poking through the hard squares of dirt in front of basement windows. Rugs and bedspreads flapped in backyards. A whole cache of babies had surfaced. They cruised imperiously in their strollers, propelled by their mothers or by pairs of grandmothers. Old people sat out on the sidewalk in beach chairs and wheelchairs, and groups of men stood about on corners, their hands in their pockets and their posture elaborately casual—the unemployed, Macon imagined, emerging from the darkened living rooms where they'd spent the winter watching TV. He caught snatches of their conversation:

"What's going down, man?"

"Nothing much."

"What you been up to?"

"Not a whole lot."

He parked in front of Muriel's house, where Dominick Saddler was working on Muriel's car. The hood was open and Dominick was deep in its innards; all Macon saw was his jeans and his gigantic, ragged sneakers, a band of bare flesh showing above his cowhide belt. On either side of him stood the Butler twins, talking away a mile a minute. "So she says to us we're grounded—"

"Can't go out with no one till Friday—"

"Takes away our fake i.d.'s—"

"Won't let us answer the phone—"

"We march upstairs and slam our bedroom door, like, just a little slam to let her know what we think of her—"

"And up she comes with a screwdriver and takes our door off its hinges!"

"Hmm," Dominick said.

Macon rested his bag on the hood and peered down into the engine. "Car acting up again?" he asked.

The Butler twins said, "Hey there, Macon," and Dominick straightened and wiped his forehead with the back of his hand. He was a dark, good-looking boy whose bulging muscles made Macon feel inadequate. "Damn thing keeps stalling out," he said.

"How'd Muriel get to work?"

"Had to take the bus."

Macon was hoping to hear she'd stayed home.

He climbed the steps and unlocked the front door. Just inside, Edward greeted him, squeaking and doing back flips and trying to hold still long enough to be petted. Macon walked through the rest of the house. Clearly, everyone had left in a hurry. The sofa was opened out. (Claire must have had another fight with her folks.) The kitchen table was littered with dishes and no one had put the cream away. Macon did that. Then he took his bag upstairs. Muriel's bed was unmade and her robe was slung across a chair. There was a snarl of hair in the pin tray on her bureau. He picked it up between thumb and index finger and dropped it into the waste-basket. It occurred to him (not for the first time) that the world was divided sharply down the middle: Some lived careful lives and some lived careless lives, and everything that happened could be explained by the difference between them. But he could not have said, not in a million years, why he was so moved by the sight of Muriel's thin quilt trailing across the floor where she must have dragged it when she rose in the morning.

It wasn't quite time for Alexander to come home from school, so he thought he would walk the dog. He put Edward on his leash and let himself out the front door. When he passed the Butler twins again they said, "Hey, there, Macon," singsong as ever, while Dominick cursed and reached for a wrench.

The men standing on the corner were discussing a rumor of jobs in Texas. Someone's brother-in-law had found work there. Macon passed with his head lowered, feeling uncomfortably privi-leged. He skirted a welcome mat that had been scrubbed and set out to dry on the pavement. The women here took spring clean-ing seriously, he saw. They shook their dust mops out of upstairs windows; they sat on their sills to polish the panes with crumpled sheets of newspapers. They staggered between houses with borrowed vacuum cleaners, rug machines, and gallon jugs of upholstery shampoo. Macon rounded the block and started home, having paused to let Edward pee against a maple sapling.

Just as he was approaching Singleton Street, whom should he see but Alexander scurrying up ahead. There was no mistaking that stiff little figure with the clumsy backpack. "Wait!" Alexander was crying. "Wait for me!" The Ebbetts children, some distance away, turned and called something back. Macon couldn't hear what they said but he knew the tone, all right—that high, mocking chant. "Nyah-nyah-nyah-NYAH-nyah!" Alexander started running, stumbling over his own shoes. Behind him came another group, two older boys and a girl with red hair, and they began jeering too. Alexander wheeled and looked at them. His face was somehow smaller than usual. "Go," Macon told Edward, and he dropped the leash. Edward didn't need any urging. His ears had perked at the sound of Alexander's voice, and now he hurtled after him. The three older children scattered as he flew through them, barking. He drew up short in front of Alexander, and Alexander knelt to hug his neck.

When Macon arrived, he said, "Are you all right?"

Alexander nodded and got to his feet.

"What was that all about?" Macon asked him.

Alexander said, "Nothing."

But when they started walking again, he slipped his hand into Macon's.

Those cool little fingers were so distinct, so particular, so full of character. Macon tightened his grip and felt a pleasant kind of sorrow sweeping through him. Oh, his life had regained all its old perils. He was forced to worry once again about nuclear war and the future of the planet. He often had the same secret, guilty thought that had come to him after Ethan was born: *From this time on I can never be completely happy.*

Not that he was before, of course.

. . .

Macon's U.S. edition was going to be five separate pamphlets now, divided geographically, slipcased together so you had to buy all five even if you needed only one. Macon thought this was immoral. He said so when Julian stopped by for the West Coast material. "What's immoral about it?" Julian asked. He wasn't really paying attention; Macon could see that. He was filing mental notes on Muriel's household, no doubt the real purpose of this unannounced, unnecessary visit. Even though he'd already collected his material, he was wandering around the living room in an abstracted way, first examining a framed school photo of Alexander and then a beaded moccasin that Claire had left on the couch. It was Saturday and the others were in the kitchen, but Macon had no intention of letting Julian meet them.

"It's always immoral to force a person to buy something he doesn't want," Macon said. "If he only wants the Midwest, he shouldn't have to buy New England too, for heaven's sake."

Julian said, "Is that your friend I hear out there? Is it Muriel?"

"Yes, I suppose it is," Macon said.

"Aren't you going to introduce us?"

"She's busy."

"I'd really like to meet her."

"Why? Hasn't Rose given you a full report?"

"Macon," Julian said, "I'm soon going to be a relative of yours."

"Ah, God."

"It's only natural I'm interested in knowing her."

Macon said nothing.

"Besides," Julian told him, "I want to invite her to the wedding."

"You do?"

"So can I talk to her?"

"Oh. Well. I guess so."

Macon led the way to the kitchen. He felt he'd made a mistake—that having acted so thorny, he'd caused this meeting to seem more important than it was. But Julian, as it happened, was breezy and offhand. "Hello, ladies," he said.

They looked up—Muriel, Claire, and Bernice, seated around a sheaf of notebook paper. Macon reeled their names off rapidly but got stuck on Julian's. "Julian, ah, Edge, my . . ."

"Future brother-in-law," Julian said.

"My boss."

"I've come to invite you to the wedding, Muriel. Also your little boy, if—where's your little boy?"

"He's out walking the dog," Muriel said. "But he's not too good in churches."

"This'll be a garden wedding."

"Well, maybe, then, I don't know . . ."

Muriel was wearing what she called her "paratrooper look"— a coverall from Sunny's Surplus—and her hair was concealed beneath a wildly patterned silk turban. A ballpoint pen mark slashed across one cheekbone. "We're entering this contest," she told Julian. "Write a country-music song and win a trip for two to Nashville. We're working on it all together. We're going to call it 'Happier Days.' "

"Hasn't that already been written?"

"Oh, I hope not. You know how they always have these photographs of couples in magazines? 'Mick Jagger and Bianca in happier days.' 'Richard Burton and Liz Taylor, in—' "

"Yes, I get it."

"So this man is talking about his ex-wife. 'I knew her in another time and place . . .' "

She sang it right out, in her thin scratchy voice that gave a sense of distance, like a used-up phonograph record:

When we kissed in the rain,
When we shared every pain,
When we both enjoyed happier days.

"Very catchy," Julian said, "but I don't know about 'shared every pain.' "

"What's wrong with it?"

"I mean, in happier days they had pain?"

"He's right," Bernice told Muriel.

"Rain, brain, drain," Julian reflected. " 'When our lives were more sane,' 'When we used to raise Cain . . .' "

"Let it be, why don't you," Macon told him.

" 'When I hadn't met Jane,' 'When she didn't know Wayne . . .' "

"Wait!" Bernice said, scribbling furiously.

"I may have tapped some hidden talent here," Julian told Macon.

"I'll see you to the door," Macon said.

" 'When our love had no stain,' 'When she wasn't insane . . .' " Julian said, trailing Macon through the living room. "Don't forget the wedding!" he called back. He told Macon, "If she wins, you could cover Nashville free for your next U.S. edition."

"I think she's planning on taking Bernice," Macon told him.

" 'When we guzzled champagne . . .' " Julian mused.

"I'll be in touch," Macon said, "as soon as I start on the Canada guide."

"Canada! Aren't you coming to the wedding?"

"Well, that too, of course," Macon said, opening the door.

"Wait a minute, Macon. What's your hurry? Wait, I want to show you something."

Julian set down the West Coast material to search his pockets. He pulled out a shiny, colored advertisement. "Hawaii," he said.

"Well, I certainly see no point in covering—"

"Not for you; for me! For our honeymoon. I'm taking Rose."

"Oh, I see."

"Look," Julian said. He unfolded the ad. It turned out to be a map—one of those useless maps that Macon detested, with out-sized, whimsical drawings of pineapples, palm trees, and hula dancers crowding the apple-green islands. "I got this from The Travel People Incorporated. Have you heard of them? Are they reliable? They suggested a hotel over here on . . ." He drew a forefinger across the page, hunting down the hotel.

"I know nothing at all about Hawaii," Macon said.

"Somewhere here . . ." Julian said. Then he gave up, perhaps just at that moment hearing what Macon had told him, and re-folded the map. "She may be exactly what you need," he said.

"Pardon?"

"This Muriel person."

"Why does everyone call her—"

"She's not so bad! I don't think your family understands how you're feeling."

"No, they don't. They really don't," Macon said. He was surprised that it was Julian, of all people, who saw that.

Although Julian's parting words were, " 'When we stuffed on chow mein . . .' "

Macon shut the door firmly behind him.

.   .   .

He decided to buy Alexander some different clothes. "How would you like some blue jeans?" he asked. "How would you like some work shirts? How would you like a cowboy belt with 'Budweiser Beer' on the buckle?"

"You serious?"

"Would you wear that kind of thing?"

"Yes! I would! I promise!"

"Then let's go shopping."

"Is Mama coming?"

"We'll surprise her."

Alexander put on his spring jacket—a navy polyester blazer that Muriel had just paid a small fortune for. Macon didn't know if she would approve of jeans, which was why he'd waited till she was off buying curtains for a woman in Guilford.

The store he drove to was a Western-wear place where he used to take Ethan. It hadn't changed a bit. Its wooden floorboards creaked, its aisles smelled of leather and new denim. He steered Alexander to the boys' department, where he spun a rack of shirts. How many times had he done this before? It wasn't even painful. Only disorienting, in a way, to see that everything continued no matter what. The student jeans were still stacked according to waist and inseam. The horsey tie pins were still arrayed behind glass. Ethan was dead and gone but Macon was still holding up shirts and asking, "This one? This one? This one?"

"What I'd really like is T-shirts," Alexander said.

"T-shirts. Ah."

"The kind with a sort of stretched-out neck. And jeans with raggedy bottoms."

"Well, that you have to do for yourself," Macon said. "You have to break them in."

"I don't want to look new."

"Tell you what. Everything we buy, we'll wash about twenty times before you wear it."

"But nothing *pre*washed," Alexander said.

"No, no."

"Only nerds wear prewashed."

"Right."

Alexander chose several T-shirts, purposely too big, along with an assortment of jeans because he wasn't sure of his size. Then he went off to try everything on. "Shall I come with you?" Macon asked.

"I can do it myself."

"Oh. All right."

That was familiar, too.

Alexander disappeared into one of the stalls and Macon went on a tour of the men's department. He tried on a leather cowboy hat but took it off immediately. Then he went back to the stall. "Alexander?"

"Huh?"

"How's it going?"

"Okay."

In the space below the door, Macon saw Alexander's shoes and his trouser cuffs. Evidently he hadn't got around to putting on the jeans yet.

Someone said, "Macon?"

He turned and found a woman in a trim blond pageboy, her wrap skirt printed with little blue whales. "Yes," he said.

"Laurel Canfield. Scott's mother, remember?"

"Of course," Macon said, shaking her hand. Now he caught sight of Scott, who had been in Ethan's class at school—an unexpectedly tall, gawky boy lurking at his mother's elbow with an armload of athletic socks. "Why, Scott. Nice to see you," Macon said.

Scott flushed and said nothing. Laurel Canfield said, "It's nice to see *you*. Are you doing your spring shopping?"

"Oh, well, ah—"

He looked toward the stall. Now Alexander's trousers were slumped around his ankles. "I'm helping the son of a friend," he explained.

"We've just been buying out the sock department."

"Yes, I see you have."

"Seems every other week I find Scott's run through his socks again; you know how they are at this age—"

She stopped herself. She looked horrified. She said, "Or, rather . . ."

"Yes, certainly!" Macon said. "Amazing, isn't it?" He felt so embarrassed for her that he was pleased, at first, to see another familiar face behind her. Then he realized whose it was. There stood his mother-in-law. "Why!" he said. Was she still Mother Sidey? *Mrs.* Sidey? Who, for God's sake?

Luckily, it turned out that Laurel Canfield knew her too. "Paula Sidey," she said. "I haven't seen you since last year's Hunt Cup."

"Yes, I've been away," Mrs. Sidey told her, and then she dropped her lids somewhat, as if drawing a curtain, before saying, "Macon."

"How are you?" Macon said.

She was flawlessly groomed, industriously tended—a blue-haired woman in tailored slacks and a turtleneck. He used to worry that Sarah would age the same way, develop the same brittle carapace, but now he found himself admiring Mrs. Sidey's resolve. "You're looking well," he told her.

"Thank you," she said, touching her hairdo. "I suppose you're here for your spring wardrobe."

"Oh, Macon's helping a friend!" Laurel Canfield caroled. She was so chirpy, all of a sudden, that Macon suspected she'd just now recalled Mrs. Sidey's relationship to him. She looked toward Alexander's stall. Alexander was in his socks now. One sock rose and vanished, stepping into a flood of blue denim. "Isn't shopping for boys so difficult?" she said.

"I wouldn't know," Mrs. Sidey said. "I never had one. I'm here for the denim skirts."

"Oh, the skirts, well, I notice they're offering a—"

"What friend are you helping to buy for?" Mrs. Sidey asked Macon.

Macon didn't know what to tell her. He looked toward the stall. If only Alexander would just stay hidden forever, he thought. How to explain this scrawny little waif, this poor excuse of a child who could never hold a candle to the real child?

Contrary as always, Alexander chose that moment to step forth.

He wore an oversized T-shirt that slipped a bit off one shoulder, as if he'd just emerged from some rough-and-tumble game. His jeans were comfortably baggy. His face, Macon saw, had somehow filled out in the past few weeks without anybody's noticing; and his hair—which Macon had started cutting at home—had lost that shaved prickliness and grown thick and floppy.

"I look *wonderful!*" Alexander said.

Macon turned to the women and said, "Actually, I find shopping for boys is a pleasure."

s i x t e e n

There is no sound more peaceful than rain on the roof, if you're safe asleep in someone else's house. Macon heard the soft pattering; he heard Muriel get up to close a window. She crossed his vision like the gleam of headlights crossing a ceiling, white and slim and watery in a large plain slip from Goodwill Industries. She shut the window and the stillness dropped over him and he went back to sleep.

But in the morning his first thought was, *Oh, no! Rain! On Rose's wedding day!*

He got up, careful not to wake Muriel, and looked out. The sky was bright but flat, the color of oyster shells—not a good sign. The scrawny little dogwood in back was dripping from every twig and bud. Next door, Mr. Butler's ancient heap of scrap lumber had grown several shades darker.

Macon went downstairs, tiptoeing through the living room where Claire lay snoring in a tangle of blankets. He fixed a pot of coffee and then called Rose on the kitchen phone. She answered instantly, wide awake. "Are you moving the wedding indoors?" he asked her.

"We've got too many guests to move it indoors."

"Why? How many are coming?"

"Everyone we've ever known."

"Good grief, Rose."

"Never mind, it will clear."

"But the grass is all wet!"

"Wear galoshes," she told him. She hung up.

Since she'd met Julian she'd grown so airy, Macon thought. So flippant. Lacking in depth.

She was right about the weather, though. By afternoon there was a weak, pale sun. Muriel decided to wear the short-sleeved dress she'd planned on, but maybe with a shawl tossed over her shoulders. She wanted Alexander to put on a suit—he did have one, complete with waistcoat. He protested, though, and so did Macon. "Jeans and a good white shirt. That's plenty," Macon told her.

"Well, if you're sure."

Lately, she'd been deferring to him about Alexander. She had finally given in on the question of sneakers and she'd stopped policing his diet. Contrary to her predictions, Alexander's arches did not fall flat and he was not overtaken by raging eczema. At worst, he suffered a mild skin rash now and then.

The wedding was set for three o'clock. Around two thirty they started out, proceeding self-consciously toward Macon's car. It was a Saturday and no one else in the neighborhood was so dressed up. Mr. Butler was standing on a ladder with a hammer and a sack of nails. Rafe Daggett was taking his van apart. The Indian woman was hosing down a glowing threadbare carpet that she'd spread across the sidewalk, and then she turned off the water and lifted the hem of her sari and stamped around so the carpet radiated little bursts of droplets. Every passing car, it seemed, labored under a top-heavy burden of mattresses and patio furniture, reminding Macon of those ants who scuttle back to their nests with loads four times their own size.

"I think I'm supposed to be the best man," Macon told Muriel after he'd started driving.

"You didn't mention that!"

"And Charles is giving her away."

"It's a real wedding, then," Muriel said. "Not just two people standing up together."

"That's what Rose said she wanted."

"I wouldn't do it like that at all," Muriel said. She glanced toward the rear and said, "Alexander, quit kicking my seat. You're about to drive me crazy. No," she said, facing forward, "if I was to marry, know what I'd do? Never tell a soul. Act like I'd been married for years. Slip off somewheres to a justice of the peace and come back like nothing had happened and make out like I'd been married all along."

"This is Rose's first time, though," Macon told her.

"Yes, but even so, people can say, 'It sure *took* you long enough.' I can hear my mother now; that's what she'd say for certain. 'Sure *took* you long enough. I thought you'd never get around to it,' is what she'd say. If I was ever to marry."

Macon braked for a traffic light.

"If I was ever to decide to marry," Muriel said.

He glanced over at her and was struck by how pretty she looked, with the color high in her cheeks and the splashy shawl flung around her shoulders. Her spike-heeled shoes had narrow, shiny ankle straps. He never could figure out why ankle straps were so seductive.

The first person they saw when they arrived was Macon's mother. For some reason it hadn't occurred to Macon that Alicia would be invited to her daughter's wedding, and when she opened the front door it took him a second to place her. She was looking so different, for one thing. She had dyed her hair a dark tomato red. She wore a long white caftan trimmed with vibrant bands of satin, and when she reached up to hug him a whole culvert of metal bangles clattered and slid down her left arm. "Macon, dear!" she said. She smelled of bruised gardenias. "And who may this be?" she asked, peering past him.

"Oh, um, I'd like you to meet Muriel Pritchett. And Alexander, her son."

"Really?"

A politely inquisitive look remained on her face. Evidently no one had filled her in. (Or else she hadn't bothered to listen.) "Well, since I seem to be the maître d'," she said, "I'll show you out back where the bride and groom are."

"Rose is not in hiding?"

"No, she says she doesn't see the logic in missing her own wedding," Alicia said, leading them toward the rear of the house. "Muriel, have you known Macon long?"

"Oh, kind of."

"He's very stuffy," Alicia said confidingly. "All my children are. They get it from the Leary side."

"I think he's nice," Muriel said.

"Oh, *nice*, yes. All very well and good," Alicia said, throwing Macon a look he couldn't read. She had linked arms with Muriel; she was always so physical. The trim on her caftan nearly matched Muriel's shawl. Macon had a sudden appalling thought: Maybe in his middle age he was starting to choose his mother's style of person, as if concluding that Alicia—silly, vain, annoying woman—might have the right answers after all. But no. He put the thought away from him. And Muriel slipped free of Alicia's arm. "Alexander? Coming?" she asked.

They stepped through the double doors of the sun porch. The backyard was full of pastels—Rose's old ladies in pale dresses, daffodils set everywhere in buckets, forsythia in full bloom along the alley. Dr. Grauer, Rose's minister, stepped forward and shook Macon's hand. "Aha! The best man," he said, and behind him came Julian in black—not his color. His nose was peeling. It must be boating season again. He put a gold ring in Macon's palm and said, "Like for you to have this." For a moment Macon imagined he was really meant to *have* it. Then he said, "Oh, yes, the ring," and dropped it in his pocket.

"I can't believe I'm finally getting a son-in-law," Alicia told Julian. "All I've ever had is daughter-in-laws."

"Daughters," Macon said automatically.

"No, daughter-in-laws."

"*Daughters*-in-law, Mother."

"And didn't manage to keep them long, either," Alicia said.

When Macon was small, he used to worry that his mother was teaching him the wrong names for things. "They call this corduroy," she'd said, buttoning his new coat, and he had thought, *But do they really?* Funny word, in fact, corduroy. Very suspicious. How could he be sure that other people weren't speaking a whole different language out there? He'd examined his mother distrustfully— her foolish fluff of curls and her flickery, unsteady eyes.

Now here came Porter's children, the three of them sticking close together; and behind them June, their mother. Wasn't it unusual to invite your brother's ex-wife to your wedding? Particularly when she was big as a barn with another man's baby. But she seemed to be enjoying herself. She pecked Macon on the cheek and cocked her head appraisingly at Muriel. "Kids, this is Alexander," Macon said. He was hoping against hope that they'd all just fall in together somehow and be friends, which of course didn't happen. Porter's children eyed Alexander sullenly and said nothing. Alexander knotted his fists in his pockets. June told Julian, "Your bride is looking just radiant," and Julian said, "Yes, isn't she," but when Macon located Rose he thought she looked tense and frayed, as most brides do if people would only admit it. She wore a white dress, mid-calf length but very simple, and a little puff of lace or net or something on her head. She was talking to their hardware man. And yes, there was the girl who cashed their checks at the Mercantile Bank, and over next to Charles was the family dentist. Macon thought of *Mary Poppins*—those late-night adventures he used to read to Ethan, where all the tradespeople showed up behaving nothing like their daytime selves.

"I'm not sure if there's been any research on this," Charles was telling the dentist, "but have you ever tried polishing your teeth with a T-shirt after flossing?"

"Er . . ."

"A plain cotton T-shirt. One hundred percent cotton. I think you're going to be impressed when I have my next checkup. See, my theory is—"

Muriel and June were discussing Caesareans. Julian was asking Alicia if she'd ever sailed the Intracoastal Waterway. Mrs. Barrett was telling the mailman that Leary Metals used to make the handsomest stamped tin ceilings in Baltimore.

And Sarah was talking to Macon about the weather.

"Yes, I worried when it rained last night," Macon said. Or he said something; something or other . . .

He was looking at Sarah. Really he was consuming her: her burnished curls and her round, sweet face, and the dusting of powder on the down along her jawline.

"How have you been, Macon?" she asked him.

"I've been all right."

"Are you pleased about the wedding?"

"Well," he said, "I am if Rose is, I guess. Though I can't help feeling . . . well, Julian. You know."

"Yes, I know. But there's more to him than you think. He might be a very good choice."

When she stood in this kind of sunlight her eyes were so clear that it seemed you could see to the backs of them. He knew that from long ago. They might have been his own eyes; they were so familiar. He said, "How have *you* been?"

"I've been fine."

"Well. Good."

"I know that you're living with someone," she told him in a steady voice.

"Ah, yes, actually I . . . yes, I am."

She knew who it was, too, because she looked past him then at Muriel and Alexander. But all she said was, "Rose told me when she invited me."

He said, "How about you?"

"Me?"

"Are you living with anyone?"

"Not really."

Rose came over and touched their arms, which was unlike her. "We're ready now," she said. She told Macon, "Sarah's my matron of honor, did I happen to mention that?"

"No, you didn't," Macon said.

Then he and Sarah followed her to a spot beneath a tulip tree, where Julian and Dr. Grauer were waiting. There was some kind of makeshift altar there—some little table or something covered with a cloth; Macon didn't pay much attention. He stood beside the minister and fingered the ring in his pocket. Sarah stood across from him, looking gravely into his face.

It all felt so natural.

seventeen

Muriel said, "I never told you this, but a while before I met you I was dating somebody else."

"Oh? Who was that?" Macon asked.

"He was a customer at the Rapid-Eze Copy Center. He brought me his divorce papers to copy and we started having this conversation and ended up going out together. His divorce was awful. Really messy. His wife had been two-timing him. He said he didn't think he could ever trust a woman again. It was months before he would spend the night, even; he didn't like going to sleep when a woman was in the same room. But bit by bit I changed all that. He relaxed. He got to be a whole different man. Moved in with me and took over the bills, paid off all I still owed. Alexander's doctor. We started talking about getting married. Then he met an airline stewardess and eloped with her within the week."

"I see," Macon said.

"It was like I had, you know, cured him, just so he could elope with another woman."

"Well," he said.

"You wouldn't do anything like that, would you, Macon?"

"Who, me?"

"Would you elope with someone else? Would you see someone else behind my back?"

"Oh, Muriel, of course not," he told her.

"Would you leave me and go home to your wife?"

"What are you talking about?"

"Would you?"

"Don't be silly," he said.

She cocked her head and considered him. Her eyes were alert and bright and knowing, like the eyes of some small animal.

It was a rainy Tuesday morning and Edward, who was squeamish about rain, insisted he didn't need to go out, but Macon took him anyway. While he was waiting in the backyard beneath his umbrella, he saw a young couple walking down the alley. They caught his attention because they walked so slowly, as if they didn't realize they were getting wet. The boy was tall and frail, in ragged jeans and a soft white shirt. The girl wore a flat straw hat with ribbons down the back and a longish limp cotton dress. They swung hands, looking only at each other. They came upon a tricycle and they separated to walk around it; only instead of simply walking the girl did a little sort of dance step, spinning her skirt out, and the boy spun too and laughed and took her hand again.

Edward finally, finally peed, and Macon followed him back into the house. He set his umbrella in the kitchen sink and squatted to dry Edward off with an old beach towel. He rubbed briskly at first, and then more slowly. Then he stopped but remained on the floor, the towel bunched in his hands, the tin-can smell of wet dog rising all around him.

When he'd asked Sarah whether she was living with anyone, and Sarah had said, "Not really," what exactly had she meant by that?

. . .

The rain stopped and they put Edward on his leash and went out shopping. Muriel needed bedroom slippers with feathers on them. "Red. High-heeled. Pointy-toed," she said.

"Goodness. Whatever for?" Macon asked her.

"I want to clop around the house in them on Sunday mornings. Can't you just see it? I wish I smoked cigarettes. I wish Alexander wasn't allergic to smoke."

Yes, he could see it, as a matter of fact. "In your black-and-gold kimono," he said.

"Exactly."

"But I don't believe they sell those feathered slippers anymore."

"In thrift shops they do."

"Oh. Right."

Lately, Macon had begun to like thrift shops himself. In the usual sea of plastic he had found, so far, a folding boxwood carpenter's rule, an ingenious wheeled cookie cutter that left no waste space between cookies, and a miniature brass level for Alexander's toolbox.

The air outside was warm and watery. Mrs. Butler was propping up the squashed geraniums that flopped in the white-washed tire in her yard. Mrs. Patel—out of her luminous sari for once, clumsy and unromantic in tight, bulgy Calvin Klein jeans—was sweeping the puddles off her front steps. And Mrs. Saddler stood in front of the hardware store waiting for it to open. "I don't guess you'd have seen Dominick," she said to Muriel.

"Not lately."

"Last night he never came home," Mrs. Saddler said. "That boy just worries the daylights out of me. He's not what you would call bad," she told Macon, "but he's worrisome, know what I mean? When he's at home he's so much at home, those big noisy boots all over the place, but then when he's away he's so much away. You wouldn't believe how the house feels; just empty. Just echoing."

"He'll be back," Muriel said. "Tonight's his turn to have the car."

"Oh, and when he's out with the car it's worst of all," Mrs. Saddler said. "Then every siren I hear, I wonder if it's Dommie. I know how he screeches round corners! I know those fast girls he goes out with!"

They left her still standing there, distractedly fingering her coin purse, although the hardware-store owner had unlocked his door by now and was cranking down his awnings.

Outside a shop called Re-Runs, they ordered Edward to stay. He obeyed, looking put upon, while they went in. Muriel sifted through stacks of curled, brittle shoes that had hardened into the shapes of other people's feet. She shucked off her own shoes and stepped into a pair of silver evening sandals. "What do you think?" she asked Macon.

"I thought you were looking for slippers."

"But what do you think of these?"

"I can live without them," he said.

He was feeling bored because Re-Runs carried nothing but clothes.

Muriel abandoned the shoes and they went next door to Garage Sale Incorporated. Macon tried to invent a need for a rusty metal Rolodex file he found in a heap of tire chains. Could he use it for his guidebooks in some way? And make it tax-deductible. Muriel picked up a tan vinyl suitcase with rounded edges; it reminded Macon of a partly sucked caramel. "Should I get this?" she asked.

"I thought you wanted slippers."

"But for travel."

"Since when do you travel?"

"I know where you're going next," she said. She came closer to him, both hands clutching the suitcase handle. She looked like a very young girl at a bus stop, say, or out hitching a ride on the highway. "I wanted to ask if I could come with you."

"To Canada."

"I mean the next place after that. France."

He set down the Rolodex. (Mention of France always depressed him.)

"Julian *said*!" she reminded him. "He said it's getting to be time to go to France again."

"You know I can't afford to bring you."

Muriel replaced the suitcase and they left the shop. "But just this once," she said, hurrying along beside him. "It wouldn't cost much!"

Macon retrieved Edward's leash and motioned him up. "It

would cost a mint," he said, "not to mention that you'd have to miss work."

"No, I wouldn't. I've quit."

He looked over at her. "Quit?"

"Well, at the Meow-Bow. Then things like George and the dog training I'll just rearrange; if I was to travel I could just—"

"You quit the Meow-Bow?"

"So what?"

He couldn't explain the sudden weight that fell on him.

"It's not like it really paid much," Muriel said. "And you do buy most of the groceries now and help me with the rent and all; it's not like I needed the money. Besides, it took so much time! Time I could spend with you and Alexander! Why, I was coming home nights literally dead with exhaustion, Macon."

They passed Methylene's Beauty Salon, an insurance agency, a paint-stripping shop. Edward gave an interested glance at a large, jowly tomcat basking on the hood of a pickup.

"Figuratively," Macon said.

"Huh?"

"You were *figuratively* dead with exhaustion. Jesus, Muriel, you're so imprecise. You're so sloppy. And how could you quit your job like that? How could you just assume like that? You never even warned me!"

"Oh, don't make such a big deal about it," Muriel said.

They arrived at her favorite shop—a nameless little hole in the wall with a tumble of dusty hats in the window. Muriel started through the door but Macon stayed where he was. "Aren't you coming in?" she asked him.

"I'll wait here."

"But it's the place with all the gadgets!"

He said nothing. She sighed and disappeared.

Seeing her go was like shucking off a great, dragging burden.

He squatted to scratch behind Edward's ears, and then he rose and studied a sun-bleached election poster as if it held some fascinating coded message. Two black women passed him, pulling wire carts full of laundry. "It was just as warm as this selfsame day I'm speaking to you but she wore a very very fur coat . . ."

"May-con."

He turned toward the door of the shop.

"Oh, Maay-con!"

He saw a mitten, one of those children's mittens designed to look like a puppet. The palm was a red felt mouth that widened to squeak, "Macon, *please* don't be angry with Muriel."

Macon groaned.

"Come into this nice store with her," the puppet urged.

"Muriel, I think Edward's getting restless now."

"There's lots of things to buy here! Pliers and wrenches and T-squares . . . There's a silent hammer."

"What?"

"A hammer that doesn't make a sound. You can pound in nails in the dead of night."

"Listen—" Macon said.

"There's a magnifying glass all cracked and broken, and when you look at broken things through the lens you'd swear they'd turned whole again."

"Really, Muriel."

"I'm not Muriel! I'm Mitchell Mitten! Macon, don't you know Muriel can always take care of herself?" the puppet asked him. "Don't you know she could find another job tomorrow, if she wanted? So come inside! Come along! There's a pocket-knife here with its own whetstone blade."

"Oh, for Lord's sake," Macon said.

But he gave a grudging little laugh.

And went on inside.

. . .

Over the next few days she kept bringing up France again and again. She sent him an anonymous letter pasted together from magazine print: *Don't FoRget tO BUY plANe Ticket for MuRiel.*

(And the telltale magazine—with little blocks clipped out of its pages—still lay on the kitchen table.) She asked him to get her her keys from her purse and when he opened her purse he found photographs, two slick colored squares on thin paper showing Muriel's eyes at half mast. Passport photos, plainly. She must have meant for him to see them; she was watching him so intently. But all he did was drop her keys in her palm without comment.

He had to admire her. Had he ever known such a fighter? He went grocery shopping with her unusually late one evening, and just as they were crossing a shadowed area a boy stepped forth from a doorway. "Give over all what you have in your purse," he told Muriel. Macon was caught off guard; the boy was hardly more than a child. He froze, hugging the sack of groceries. But Muriel said, "The hell I will!" and swung her purse around by its strap and clipped the boy in the jaw. He lifted a hand to his face. "You get on home this instant or you'll be sorry you were ever born," Muriel told him. He slunk away, looking back at her with a puzzled expression.

When Macon had caught his breath again, he told Muriel she was a fool. "He might have had a gun, for all you knew," he said. "Anything might have happened! Kids show less mercy than grownups; you can see that any day in the papers."

"Well, it turned out fine, didn't it?" Muriel asked. "What are you so mad at?"

He wasn't sure. He supposed he might be mad at himself. He had done nothing to protect her, nothing strong or chivalrous. He hadn't thought as fast as she had or thought at all, in fact. While Muriel . . . why, Muriel hadn't even seemed surprised. She might have strolled down that street expecting a neighbor here, a stray dog there, a holdup just beyond—all equally part of life. He felt awed by her, and diminished. Muriel just walked on, humming "Great Speckled Bird" as if nothing particular had happened.

· · ·

"I don't think Alexander's getting a proper education," he said to her one evening.

"Oh, he's okay."

"I asked him to figure what change they'd give back when we bought the milk today, and he didn't have the faintest idea. He didn't even know he'd have to subtract."

"Well, he's only in second grade," Muriel said.

"I think he ought to switch to a private school."

"Private schools cost money."

"So? I'll pay."

She stopped flipping the bacon and looked over at him. "What are you saying?" she asked.

"Pardon?"

"What are you saying, Macon? Are you saying you're committed?"

Macon cleared his throat. He said, "Committed."

"Alexander's got ten more years of school ahead of him. Are you saying you'll be around for all ten years?"

"Um . . ."

"I can't just put him in a school and take him out again with every passing whim of yours."

He was silent.

"Just tell me this much," she said. "Do you picture us getting married sometime? I mean when your divorce comes through?"

He said, "Oh, well, marriage, Muriel . . ."

"You don't, do you. You don't know *what* you want. One minute you like me and the next you don't. One minute you're ashamed to be seen with me and the next you think I'm the best thing that ever happened to you."

He stared at her. He had never guessed that she read him so clearly.

"You think you can just drift along like this, day by day, no plans," she said. "Maybe tomorrow you'll be here, maybe you won't. Maybe you'll just go on back to Sarah. Oh yes! I saw you at Rose's wedding. Don't think I didn't see how you and Sarah looked at each other."

Macon said, "All I'm saying is—"

"All *I'm* saying," Muriel told him, "is take care what you promise my son. Don't go making him promises you don't intend to keep."

"But I just want him to learn to subtract!" he said.

She didn't answer, and so the last word rang in the air for moments afterward. Subtract. A flat, sharp, empty sound that dampened Macon's spirits.

At supper she was too quiet; even Alexander was quiet, and excused himself the minute he'd finished his BLT. Macon, though, hung around the kitchen. Muriel was running a sinkful of water. He said, "Shall I dry?" Without any sort of warning, she whirled and flung a wet sponge in his face. Macon said, "Muriel?"

"Just get out!" she shouted, tears spiking her lashes, and she turned away again and plunged her hands into water so hot that it steamed. Macon retreated. He went into the living room where Alexander was watching TV, and Alexander moved over on the couch to give him space. He didn't say anything, but Macon could tell he'd heard from the way he tensed at each clatter in the kitchen. After a while the clatters died down. Macon and Alexander looked at each other. There was a silence; a single murmuring voice. Macon rose and returned to the kitchen, walking more quietly than usual and keeping a weather eye out, the way a cat creeps back after it's been dumped from someone's lap.

Muriel was talking on the phone with her mother. Her voice was gay and chirpy but just a shade thicker than usual, as if she were recovering from a cold. "So anyhow," she said, "I asked what kind of trouble her dog is giving her and the lady's like, 'Oh, no trouble,' so I ask her, 'Well, what's his problem, then?' and the lady's like, 'No real problem.' I say, 'Ma'am. You must have called me here for some reason.' She says, 'Oh. Well. That.' She says, 'Actually,' she says, 'I was wondering about when he makes.' I say, 'Makes?' She says, 'Yes, when he makes number one. He makes like little girl dogs do, he doesn't lift his leg.' I say to her, 'Now let me see if I've got this straight. You have called me here to teach your dog to lift his leg when he tinkles.' "

Her free hand kept flying out while she talked, as if she imagined her mother could see her. Macon came up behind her and put his arms around her, and she leaned back against him. "Oh, there's never a dull moment, I tell you," she said into the phone.

That night he dreamed he was traveling in a foreign country, only it seemed to be a medley of all the countries he'd ever been to and even some he hadn't. The sterile vast spaces of Charles de Gaulle airport chittered with those tiny birds he'd seen inside the terminal at Brussels; and when he stepped outdoors he was in Julian's green map of Hawaii with native dancers, oversized, swaying near the dots that marked various tourist attractions. Meanwhile his own voice, neutral and monotonous, murmured steadily: *In Germany the commercial traveler must be punctual for all appointments, in Switzerland he should be five minutes early, in Italy delays of several hours are not uncommon* . . .

He woke. It was pitch dark, but through the open window he heard distant laughter, a strain of music, faint cheers as if some sort of game were going on. He squinted at the clock radio: three thirty. Who would be playing a game at this hour? And on this street—this worn, sad street where nothing went right for anyone, where the men had dead-end jobs or none at all and the women were running to fat and the children were turning out badly. But another cheer went up, and someone sang a line from a song. Macon found himself smiling. He turned toward Muriel and closed his eyes; he slept dreamlessly the rest of the night.

. . .

The mailman rang the doorbell and presented a long, tube-shaped package addressed to Macon. "What's this?" Macon asked. He returned to the living room, frowning down at the label. Muriel was reading a paperback book called *Beauty Tips from the Stars.* She glanced up and said, "Why not open it and find out."

"Oh? Is this some of your doing?"

She only turned a page.

Another plea for the France trip, he supposed. He pulled off the tape on one end and shook the package till a cylinder of glossy paper slid out. When he unrolled it, he found a full-color photo of two puppies in a basket, with DR. MACK'S PETVITES above it and a calendar for January below it.

"I don't understand," he said to Muriel.

She turned another page.

"Why would you send me a calendar for a year that's half gone?"

"Maybe there's something written on it," she told him.

He flipped through February, March, April. Nothing there. May. Then June: a scribble of red ink across a Saturday, "*Wedding,*" he read out. "Wedding? Whose wedding?"

"Ours?" she asked him.

"Oh, Muriel . . ."

"You'll be separated a year then, Macon. You'll be able to get your divorce."

"But, Muriel—"

"I always did want to have a June wedding."

"Muriel, please, I'm not ready for this! I don't think I ever will be. I mean I don't think marriage ought to be as common as it is; I really believe it ought to be the exception to the rule; oh, perfect couples could marry, maybe, but who's a perfect couple?"

"You and Sarah, I suppose," Muriel said.

The name brought Sarah's calm face, round as a daisy.

"No, no . . ." he said weakly.

"You're so selfish!" Muriel shouted. "You're so self-centered! You've got all these fancy reasons for never doing a single thing I want!"

Then she flung down her book and ran upstairs.

Macon heard the cautious, mouselike sounds of Alexander as he tiptoed around the kitchen fixing himself a snack.

. . .

Muriel's sister Claire arrived on the doorstep with a suitcase spilling clothes and her eyes pink with tears. "I'm never speaking to

Ma again," she told them. She pushed past them into the house. "You want to know what happened? Well, I've been dating this guy, see: Claude McEwen. Only I didn't let on to Ma, you know how she's scared I'll turn out like Muriel did, and so last night when he came for me I jumped into his car and she happened to catch sight of me from the window, noticed he had a bumper sticker reading EDGEWOOD. That's because he used to go to a high school called Edgewood Prep in Delaware, but Ma thought it was Edgewood Arsenal and therefore he must be an Army man. So anyhow, this morning I get up and there she is fit to be tied, says, 'I know what you've been up to! Out all hours last night with the General!' and I say, 'Who? The what?' but there's never any stopping her once she gets started. She tells me I'm grounded for life and can't ever see the General again or she'll have him hauled up for court-martial and all his stars ripped off his uniform, so quick as a wink I packed up my clothes . . ."

Macon, listening absently while Edward sighed at his feet, had a sudden view of his life as rich and full and astonishing. He would have liked to show it off to someone. He wanted to sweep out an arm and say, "See?"

But the person he would have liked to show it to was Sarah.

. . .

Rose and Julian were back from their honeymoon; they were giving a family supper and Macon and Muriel were invited. Macon bought a bottle of very good wine as a hostess gift. He set the bottle on the counter, and Muriel came along and said, "What's this?"

"It's wine for Rose and Julian."

"Thirty-six dollars and ninety-nine cents!" she said, examining the sticker.

"Yes, well, it's French."

"I didn't know a wine *could* cost thirty-six ninety-nine."

"I figured since, you know, this'll be our first visit to their apartment . . ."

"You sure do think a lot of your family," Muriel said.

"Yes, of course."

"You never bought *me* any wine."

"I didn't know you wanted any; you told me it makes your teeth feel rough."

She didn't argue with that.

Later that day he happened to notice that the bottle had been moved. And was opened. And was half emptied. The cork lay beside it, still impaled on the corkscrew. A cloudy little juice glass gave off the smell of grapes. Macon called, "Muriel?"

"What," she answered from the living room.

He went to the living room doorway. She was watching a ball game with Alexander. He said, "Muriel, have you been drinking that wine I bought?"

"Yes."

He said, "Why, Muriel?"

"Oh, I just had this irresistible urge to try it out," she said.

Then she looked at him with slitted eyes, tilting her chin. He felt she was challenging him to take some action, but he said nothing. He picked up his car keys and went out to buy another bottle.

. . .

Macon felt shy about attending this dinner, as if Rose had turned into a stranger. He took longer than usual dressing, unable to decide between two shirts, and Muriel seemed to be having some trouble too. She kept putting on outfits and taking them off; brightly colored fabrics began to mount on the bed and on the floor all around it. "Oh, Lord, I wish I was just a totally nother person," she sighed. Macon, concentrating on tying his tie, said nothing. Her baby photo grinned out at him from the frame of the mirror. He happened to notice the date on the border: AUG 60. Nineteen sixty.

When Muriel was two years old, Macon and Sarah were already engaged to be married.

Downstairs, Dominick Saddler was sitting on the couch with Alexander. "Now this here is your paste wax," he was saying. He held up a can. "You never want to polish a car with anything but paste wax. And here we have a diaper. Diapers make real good rags because they don't shed hardly no lint. I generally buy a dozen at a time from Sears and Roebuck. And chamois skins: well, you know chamois skins. So what you do is, you get yourself these here supplies and a case of good beer and a girl, and you head on out to Loch Raven. Then you park in the sun and you take off your shirt and you and the girl start to polishing. Ain't no sweeter way that I know of to use up a spring afternoon."

Dominick's version of a bedtime story, Macon supposed. He was baby-sitting tonight. (The Butler twins had dates, and Claire was out with the General. As everybody referred to him now.) In payment, Muriel's car would be Dominick's to use for a week; mere money would never have persuaded him. He slouched next to Alexander with the diaper spread over one knee, muscles bulging under a T-shirt that read WEEKEND WARRIOR. A Greek sailor cap was tipped back on his head with a Judas Priest button pinned above the visor. Alexander looked enthralled.

Muriel came tapping down the stairs; she arrived craning her neck to see if her slip showed. "Is this outfit okay?" she asked Macon.

"It's very nice," he said, which was true, although it was also totally unlike her. Evidently, she had decided to take Rose for her model. She had pulled her hair back in a low bun and she wore a slim gray dress with shoulder pads. Only her spike-heeled sandals seemed her own; probably she didn't possess any shoes so sensible as Rose's schoolgirl flats. "I want you to tell me if there's anything not right," she said to Macon. "Anything you think is tacky."

"Not a thing," Macon assured her.

She kissed Alexander, leaving a dark red mark on his cheek. She made one last survey in the mirror beside the front door, meanwhile calling, "Don't let him stay up too late now, Dommie; don't let him watch anything scary on TV—"

Macon said, "*Muriel.*"

"I look like the wrath of God."

The Leary children had been raised to believe that when an invitation involved a meal, the guests should arrive exactly on time. Never mind that they often caught their hostess in curlers; they went on doing what they were taught. So Macon pressed the buzzer in the lobby at precisely six twenty-seven, and Porter and Charles joined them in front of the elevator. They both told Muriel it was nice to see her. Then they rode upward in a gloomy silence, eyes fixed on the numbers over the door. Charles carried a potted jade tree, Porter another bottle of wine.

"Isn't this exciting?" Muriel said. "We're their first invited guests."

"At home now we'd be watching the CBS Evening News," Charles told her.

Muriel couldn't seem to think of any answer to that.

By six thirty sharp they were ringing the doorbell, standing in a hushed corridor carpeted in off-white. Rose opened the door and called, "They're here!" and set her face lightly against each of theirs. She wore Grandmother Leary's lace-trimmed company apron and she smelled of lavender soap, the same as always.

But there was a strip of peeling sunburn across the bridge of her nose.

Julian, natty and casual in a navy turtleneck and white slacks (when it wasn't yet Memorial Day), fixed the drinks while Rose retreated to the kitchen. This was one of those ultra-modern apartments where the rooms all swam into each other, so they could see her flitting back and forth. Julian passed around snapshots of Hawaii. Either he had used inferior film or else Hawaii was a very different place from Baltimore, because some of the colors were wrong. The trees appeared to be blue. In most of the photos Rose stood in front of flower beds or flowering shrubs, wearing a white sleeveless dress Macon had never seen before, hugging her arms and smiling too broadly so that she looked older than she was. "I tell Rose you'd think she went on our honeymoon by herself," Julian said. "I'm the one who took the pictures because Rose never did learn how to work my camera."

"She didn't?" Macon asked.

6767

67

7267

"It was one of those German models with all the buttons."

"She couldn't figure out the buttons?"

"I tell her, 'People will think I wasn't even there.' "

"Why, Rose could have taken that camera apart and put it together twice over," Macon said.

"No, this was one of those German models with—"

"It wasn't very logically constructed," Rose called from the kitchen.

"Ah," Macon said, sitting back.

She entered the room with a tray and placed it on the glass coffee table. Then she knelt and began to spread pâté on little crackers. There was some change in the way she moved, Macon noticed. She was more graceful, but also more self-conscious. She offered the pâté first to Muriel, then to each of her brothers, last to Julian. "In Hawaii I started learning to sail," she said. She pronounced the two *i*'s in "Hawaii" separately; Macon thought it sounded affected. "Now I'm going to practice out on the Bay."

"She's trying to find her sea legs," Julian said. "She tends to feel motion-sick."

Macon bit into his cracker. The pâté was something familiar. It was rough in texture but delicate in taste; there was a kind of melting flavor that he believed came from adding a great amount of butter. The recipe was Sarah's. He sat very still, not chewing. He was flooded by a subtle blend of tarragon and cream and home.

"Oh, I know just what you're going through," Muriel said to Rose. "All I have to do is look at a boat and I get nauseous."

Macon swallowed and gazed down at the carpet between his feet. He waited for someone to correct her, but nobody did. That was even worse.

.   .   .

In bed she said, "You wouldn't ever leave me, would you? Would you ever think of leaving me? You won't be like the others, will you? Will you promise not to leave me?"

"Yes, yes," he said, floating in and out of dreams.

"You do take me seriously, don't you? Don't you?"

"Oh, Muriel, for pity's sake . . ." he said.

But later, when she turned in her sleep and moved away from him, his feet followed hers of their own accord to the other side of the bed.

eighteen

Macon was sitting in a hotel room in Winnipeg, Manitoba, when the phone rang. Actually it took him a second to realize it was the phone. He happened to be having a very good time with a mysterious object he'd just discovered—an ivory-painted metal cylinder affixed to the wall above the bed. He'd never noticed such a thing before, although he'd stayed in this hotel on two previous trips. When he touched the cylinder to see what it was, it rotated, disappearing into the wall, while from within the wall a light bulb swung out already lit. At the same moment, the phone rang. Macon experienced an instant of confusion during which he imagined it was the cylinder that was ringing. Then he saw the telephone on the nightstand. Still he was confused. No one had his number, so far as he knew.

He picked up the receiver and said, "Yes?"

"Macon."

His heart lurched. He said, "Sarah?"

"Have I caught you at a bad time?"

"No, no . . . How did you know where I was?"

"Well, Julian thought you'd be in either Toronto or Winnipeg by now," she said, "so I looked in your last guidebook, and I knew the hotels where you discussed night noises were the ones where you stayed yourself, so . . ."

"Is anything wrong?" he asked.

"No, I just needed a favor. Would it be all right with you if I moved back into our house?"

"Um—"

"Just as a place to stay," she said hastily. "Just for a little while. My lease runs out at the end of the month and I can't find a new apartment."

"But the house is a mess," he told her.

"Oh, I'll take care of that."

"No, I mean something happened to it over the winter, pipes burst or something, ceiling came down—"

"Yes, I know."

"You do?"

"Your brothers told me."

"My brothers?"

"I went to ask them your whereabouts when they wouldn't answer their phone. And Rose said she'd been over to the house herself and—"

"You went to Rose's, too?"

"No, Rose was at your brothers'."

"Oh."

"She's living there for a while."

"I see," he said. Then he said, "She's what?"

"Well, June has had her baby," Sarah said, "so she asked Porter to keep the children a while."

"But what does that have to do with Rose?" he said. "Does Rose imagine Porter can't open a tin of soup for them? And how come June sent them away?"

"Oh, you know June, she always was kind of a birdbrain."

She sounded like her old self, when she said that. Up till now there'd been something careful about her voice, something wary and ready to retreat, but now a certain chuckly, confiding quality emerged. Macon leaned back against his pillow.

"She told the children she needs time to bond," Sarah said.

"Time to what?"

"She and her husband need to bond with the baby."

"Good grief," Macon said.

"When Rose heard that, she told Porter she was coming home. Anyhow she didn't think the boys were eating right, Porter and Charles; and also there's a crack in the side of the house and she wanted to get it patched before it spreads."

"What kind of crack?" Macon asked.

"Some little crack in the masonry; I don't know. When the rain comes from a certain direction water seeps in above the kitchen ceiling, Rose says, and Porter and Charles were planning to fix it but they couldn't agree on the best way to do it."

Macon slipped out of his shoes and hoisted his feet up onto the bed. He said, "So is Julian living alone now, or what?"

"Yes, but she brings him casseroles," Sarah said. Then she said, "Have you thought about it, Macon?"

His heart gave another lurch. He said, "Have I thought about what?"

"About my using the house."

"Oh. Well. It's fine with me, but I don't believe you realize the extent of the damage."

"But we'd have to fix that anyway, if we were to sell it. So here's what I was thinking: I could pay for the repairs myself—anything the insurance doesn't cover—with what I'd ordinarily use for rent. Does that seem fair to you?"

"Yes, of course," Macon said.

"And maybe I'll get someone to clean the upholstery," she said.

"Yes."

"And the rugs."

"Yes."

After all these years, he knew when she was leading up to something. He recognized that distracted tone that meant she was bracing herself for what she really wanted to say.

"Incidentally," she said, "the papers came through from the lawyer."

"Ah."

"The final arrangements. You know. Things I have to sign."

"Yes."

"It was kind of a shock."

He said nothing.

"I mean, of course I knew that they were coming; it's been nearly a year; in fact he called ahead and told me they were coming, but when I saw them in black and white they just seemed so brisk. They didn't take into account the feelings of the thing. I guess I wasn't expecting that."

Macon had a sense of some danger approaching, something he couldn't handle. He said, "Ah! Yes! Certainly! That seems a natural reaction. So anyway, good luck with the house, Sarah."

He hung up quickly.

. . .

His seatmate on the flight to Edmonton was a woman who was scared of flying. He knew that before the plane had left the ground, before he'd looked in her direction. He was gazing out the window, keeping to himself as usual, and he heard her swallowing repeatedly. She kept tightening and releasing her grasp on the armrests and he could feel that, too. Finally he turned to see who this was. A pair of pouched eyes met his. A very old, baggy woman in a flowered dress was staring at him intently, had perhaps been willing him to turn. "Do you think this plane is safe," she said flatly, not exactly asking.

"It's perfectly safe," he told her.

"Then why have all these signs about. Oxygen. Life vests. Emergency exits. They're clearly expecting the worst."

"That's just federal regulations," Macon said.

Then he started thinking about the word "federal." In Canada, would it apply? He frowned at the seat ahead of him, considering. Finally he said, "*Government* regulations." When he checked the old woman's expression to see if this made any better sense to her, he discovered that she must have been staring at him all this time.

Her face lunged toward him, gray and desperate. He began to worry about her. "Would you like a glass of sherry?" he asked.

"They don't give us sherry till we're airborne. By then it's much too late."

"Just a minute," he said.

He bent to unzip his bag, and from his shaving kit he took a plastic travel flask. This was something he always packed, in case of sleepless nights. He had never used it, though—not because he'd never had a sleepless night but because he'd gone on saving it for some occasion even worse than whatever the current one was, something that never quite arrived. Like his other emergency supplies (the matchbook-sized sewing kit, the tiny white Lomotil tablet), this flask was being hoarded for the *real* emergency. In fact, its metal lid had grown rusty inside, as he discovered when he unscrewed it. "I'm afraid this may have . . . turned a bit, or whatever sherry does," he told the old woman. She didn't answer but continued staring into his eyes. He poured the sherry into the lid, which was meant to double as a cup. Meanwhile the plane gave a creak and started moving down the runway. The old woman drank off the sherry and handed him the cup. He understood that she was not returning it for good. He refilled it. She drank that more slowly and then let her head tip back against her seat.

"Better?" he asked her.

"My name is Mrs. Daniel Bunn," she told him.

He thought it was her way of saying she was herself again—her formal, dignified self. "How do you do," he said. "I'm Macon Leary."

"I know it's foolish, Mr. Leary," she said, "but a drink does give the illusion one is doing something to cope, does it not."

"Absolutely," Macon said.

He wasn't convinced, though, that she was coping all that well. As the plane gathered speed, her free hand tightened on the armrest. Her other hand—the one closest to him, clutching the cup—grew white around the nails. All at once the cup popped up in the air, squeezed out of her grip. Macon caught it nimbly and said,

"Whoa there!" and screwed it onto the flask. Then he replaced the flask in his bag. "Once we're off the ground—" he said.

But a glance at her face stopped him. She was swallowing again. The plane was beginning to rise now—the nose was lifting off—and she was pressed back against her seat. She seemed flattened. "Mrs. Bunn?" Macon said. He was scared she was having a heart attack.

Instead of answering, she turned toward him and crumpled onto his shoulder. He put an arm around her. "Never mind," he said. "Goodness. You'll be all right. Never mind."

The plane continued slanting backward. When the landing gear retracted (groaning), Macon felt the shudder through Mrs. Bunn's body. Her hair smelled like freshly ironed tea cloths. Her back was large and boneless, a mounded shape like the back of a whale.

He was impressed that someone so old still wanted so fiercely to live.

Then the plane leveled off and she pulled herself together—straightening and drawing away from him, brushing at the teardrops that lay in the folds beneath her eyes. She was full of folds, wide and plain and sagging, but valiantly wore two pearl buttons in her long, spongy earlobes and maintained a coat of brave red lipstick on a mouth so wrinkled that it didn't even have a clear outline.

He asked, "Are you all right?"

"Yes, and I apologize a thousand times," she said. And she patted the brooch at her throat.

When the drink cart came he ordered her another sherry, which he insisted on paying for, and he ordered one for himself as well, even though he didn't plan to drink it. He thought it might be needed for Mrs. Bunn. He was right, as things turned out, because their flight was unusually rough. The seatbelt sign stayed lit the whole way, and the plane bounced and grated as if rolling over gravel. Every now and then it dropped sharply and Mrs. Bunn winced, but she went on taking tiny sips of sherry. "This is nothing," Macon told her. "I've been in much worse than this." He told her how to give with the bumps. "It's like traveling on a boat," he said. "Or on wheels, on roller skates. You keep your knees loose. You bend. Do you understand what I'm saying? You go along with it. You ride it out."

Mrs. Bunn said she'd certainly try.

Not only was the air unsteady, but also little things kept going wrong inside the plane. The drink cart raced away from the stewardess every time she let go of it. Mrs. Bunn's tray fell into her lap twice without warning. At each new mishap Macon laughed and said, "Ah, me," and shook his head. "Oh, not again," he said. Mrs. Bunn's eyes remained fixed on his face, as if Macon were her only hope. Once there was a bang and she jumped; the door to the cockpit had flung itself open for no good reason. "What? What?" she said, but Macon pointed out that now she could see for herself how unconcerned the pilot was. They were close enough to the front so she could even hear what the pilot was talking about; he was shouting some question to the copilot, asking why any ten-year-old girl with half a grain of sense would wear a metal nightbrace in a sauna room. "You call that a worried man?" Macon asked Mrs. Bunn. "You think a man about to bail out of his plane would be discussing orthodontia?"

"Bail out!" Mrs. Bunn said. "Oh, my, I never thought of that!"

Macon laughed again.

He was reminded of a trip he'd taken alone as a boy, touring colleges. Heady with his new independence, he had lied to the man sitting next to him and said he came from Kenya, where his father led safaris. In the same way he was lying now, presenting himself to Mrs. Bunn as this merry, tolerant person.

But after they had landed (with Mrs. Bunn hardly flinching, bolstered by all those sherries), and she had gone off with her grown daughter, a very small child ran headlong into Macon's kneecap. This child was followed by another and another, all more or less the same size—some kind of nursery school, Macon supposed, visiting the airport on a field trip—and each child, as if powerless to veer from the course the first had set, careened off Macon's knees and said, "Oops!" The call ran down the line like little bird cries — "Oops!" "Oops!" "Oops!" — while behind the children, a harassed-looking woman clapped a hand to her cheek. "Sorry," she said to Macon, and he said, "No harm done."

Only later, when he passed a mirror and noticed the grin on his face, did he realize that, in fact, he might not have been lying to Mrs. Bunn after all.

. . .

"The plumber says it won't be hard to fix," Sarah told him. "He says it *looks* bad but really just one pipe is cracked."

"Well, good," Macon said.

He was not as surprised this time by her call, of course, but he did feel there was something disconcerting about it — standing in an Edmonton hotel room on a weekday afternoon, listening to Sarah's voice at the other end of the line.

"I went over there this morning and straightened up a little," she said. "Everything's so disorganized."

"Disorganized?"

"Why are some of the sheets sewn in half? And the popcorn popper's in the bedroom. Were you eating popcorn in the bedroom?"

"I guess I must have been," he said.

He was near an open window, and he could look out upon a strangely beautiful landscape: an expanse of mathematical flatness, with straight-edged buildings rising in the distance like a child's toy blocks on a rug. It was difficult, in these surroundings, to remember why he'd had a popcorn popper in the bedroom.

"So how's the weather there?" Sarah asked.

"Kind of gray."

"Here it's sunny. Sunny and humid."

"Well, it's certainly not humid here," he told her. "The air's so dry that rain disappears before it hits the ground."

"Really? Then how can you tell it's raining?"

"You can see it above the plains," he said. "It looks like stripes that just fade away about halfway down from the sky."

"I wish I were there to watch it with you," Sarah said.

Macon swallowed.

Gazing out of the window, he all at once recalled Ethan as an infant. Ethan used to cry unless he was tightly wrapped in a blanket; the pediatrician had explained that new babies have a fear of flying apart. Macon had not been able to imagine that at the time, but now he had no trouble. He could picture himself separating, falling into pieces, his head floating away with terrifying swiftness in the eerie green air of Alberta.

. . .

In Vancouver she asked if the rain vanished there as well. "No," he said.

"No?"

"No, it rains in Vancouver."

It was raining this minute—a gentle night rain. He could hear it but not see it, except for the cone of illuminated drops spilling beneath a street lamp just outside his hotel room. You could almost suppose it was the lamp itself that was raining.

"Well, I've moved back into the house," she said. "Mostly I just stay upstairs. The cat and I: We camp in the bedroom. Creep downstairs for meals."

"What cat is that?" he asked.

"Helen."

"Oh, yes."

"I went and picked her up at Rose's. I needed company. You wouldn't believe how lonely it is."

Yes, he would believe it, he could have said. But didn't.

So here they were in the same old positions, he could have said: He had won her attention only by withdrawing. He wasn't surprised when she said, "Macon? Do you . . . What's her name? The person you live with?"

"Muriel," he said.

Which she knew before she asked, he suspected.

"Do you plan on staying with Muriel forever?"

"I really couldn't say," he said.

He was noticing how oddly the name hung in this starchy, old-fashioned hotel room. Muriel. Such a peculiar sound. So unfamiliar, suddenly.

. . .

On the flight back, his seatmate was an attractive young woman in a tailored suit. She spread the contents of her briefcase on her folding tray, and she riffled through computer printout sheets with her perfectly manicured hands. Then she asked Macon if he had a pen she might borrow. This struck him as amusing—her true colors shining out from beneath her businesslike exterior. However, his only pen was a fountain pen that he didn't like lending, so he said no. She seemed relieved; she cheerfully repacked all she'd taken from her briefcase. "I could have sworn I swiped a ballpoint from my last hotel," she said, "but maybe that was the one before this one; you know how they all run together in your mind."

"You must do a lot of traveling," Macon said politely.

"Do I? Some mornings when I wake up I have to check my hotel stationery just to find out what city I'm in."

"That's terrible."

"Oh, I like it," she said, bending to slip her briefcase under her seat. "It's the only time I can relax anymore. When I come home I'm all nervous, can't sit still. I prefer to be a . . . moving target, you could say."

Macon thought of something he'd once read about heroin: how it's not a pleasure, really, but it so completely alters the users' body chemistry that they're forced to go on once they've started.

He turned down drinks and dinner, and so did his seatmate; she rolled her suit jacket expertly into a pillow and went to sleep. Macon got out *Miss MacIntosh* and stared at a single page for a while. The top line began with *brows bristling, her hair streaked with white*. He studied the words so long that he almost wondered if they *were* words; the whole English language seemed chunky and brittle. "Ladies and gentlemen," the loudspeaker said, "we will be starting our descent . . ." and the word "descent" struck him as an invention, some new euphemism concocted by the airlines.

After they landed in Baltimore, he took a shuttle bus to the parking lot and retrieved his car. It was late evening here and the sky was pale and radiant above the city. As he drove he continued to see the words from *Miss MacIntosh*. He continued to hear the stewardess's gliding voice: *complimentary beverages* and *the captain has asked us* and *trays in an upright position*. He considered switching on the radio but he didn't know what station it was set to. Maybe it was Muriel's country music station. This possibility made him feel weary; he felt he wouldn't have the strength to press the buttons, and so he drove in silence.

He came to Singleton Street and flicked his signal on but didn't turn. After a while the signal clicked off on its own. He rode on through the city, up Charles Street, into his old neighborhood. He parked and cut the engine and sat looking at the house. The downstairs windows were dark. The upstairs windows were softly glowing. Evidently, he had come home.

nineteen

Macon and Sarah needed to buy a new couch. They set aside a Saturday for it—actually just half a Saturday, because Sarah had a class to attend in the afternoon. At breakfast, she flipped through an interior decorating book so they could get a head start on their decision. "I'm beginning to think along the lines of something flowered," she told Macon. "We've never had a flowered couch before. Or would that be too frilly?"

"Well, I don't know. I wonder about winter," Macon said.

"Winter?"

"I mean right now in the middle of June a flowered couch looks fine, but it might seem out of place in December."

"So you prefer something in a solid," Sarah said.

"Well, I don't know."

"Or maybe stripes."

"I'm not sure."

"I know you don't like plaids."

"No."

"How do you feel about tweeds?"

"Tweeds," Macon said, considering.

Sarah handed over the book and started loading the dishwasher.

Macon studied pictures of angular modern couches, cozy chintz-covered couches, and period reproduction couches covered in complex fabrics. He took the book to the living room and squinted at the spot where the couch would be sitting. The old one, which had turned out to be too waterlogged to salvage, had been carted away, along with both armchairs. Now there was just a long blank wall, with the freshly plastered ceiling glaring above it. Macon observed that a room without furniture had a utilitarian feeling, as if it were merely a container. Or a vehicle. Yes, a vehicle: He had a sense of himself speeding through the universe as he stood there.

While Sarah got dressed, Macon took the dog out. It was a warm, golden morning. Neighbors were trimming their grass and weeding their flower beds. They nodded as Macon walked past. He had not been back long enough for them to feel at ease yet; there was something a little too formal about their greetings. Or maybe he was imagining that. He made an effort to remind them of how many years he had lived here: "I've always liked those tulips of yours!" and "Still got that nice hand mower, I see!" Edward marched beside him with a busybody waggle of his hind end.

In movies and such, people who made important changes in their lives accomplished them and were done with it. They walked out and never returned; or they married and lived happily ever after. In real life, things weren't so clean-cut. Macon, for instance, had had to go down to Muriel's and retrieve his dog, once he'd decided to move back home. He had had to collect his clothing and pack up his typewriter while Muriel watched in silence with her accusing, reproaching eyes. Then there were all kinds of other belongings that he discovered too late he'd forgotten—clothes that had been in the wash at the time, and his favorite dictionary, and the extra-large pottery mug he liked to drink his coffee from. But of course he couldn't go back for them. He had to abandon them— messy, trailing strings of himself cluttering his leavetaking.

By the time he and Edward returned from their outing, Sarah was waiting in the front yard. She wore a yellow dress that made her tan glow; she looked very pretty. "I was just wondering about the azaleas," she told Macon. "Weren't we supposed to feed them in the spring?"

"Well, probably," Macon said, "but they seem all right to me."

"In April, I think," she said. "Or maybe May. No one was here to do it."

Macon veered away from that. He preferred to pretend that their lives had been going on as usual. "Never mind, Rose has whole sacks of fertilizer," he said. "We'll pick up some from her while we're out."

"No one was here to seed the lawn, either."

"The lawn looks fine," he said, more forcefully than he'd meant to.

They shut Edward in the house and climbed into Macon's car. Sarah had brought along a newspaper because there were several furniture ads. "Modern Housewares," she read off. "But that's all the way down on Pratt Street."

"Might as well give it a try," Macon said. Pratt was one of the few streets he knew how to find.

After they left their neighborhood, with its trees arching over-head, the car grew hotter and Macon rolled his window down. Sarah lifted her face to the sunlight. "Be a good day to go to the pool," she said.

"Well, if we have time. I was thinking of asking you to lunch."

"Oh, where?"

"Anywhere you like. Your choice."

"Aren't you nice," she said.

Macon drove past two unshaven men talking on a corner. Sarah locked her door. Macon thought of what the men would be saying: "What's coming down, man?" "Not all that much."

The sidewalks grew more crowded. Women lugged string-handled shopping bags, an old man dragged a grocery cart, and a girl in a faded dress leaned her head against a bus stop sign.

At Modern Homewares, huge paper banners covered the plate

glass windows. SPECIAL FOR FATHER'S DAY! they read. Sarah hadn't mentioned that this was a Father's Day sale. Macon made a point of mentioning it himself, to show it didn't bother him. Taking her arm as they entered, he said, "Isn't that typical. Father's Day! They'll capitalize on anything."

Sarah looked away from him and said, "All they seem to have is beds."

"I suppose it began with reclining chairs," Macon said. "A Barcalounger for Dad, and next thing you know it's a whole dinette set."

"Could we see your couches," Sarah told a salesman firmly.

The couches were all of the straight-back, Danish sort, which was fine with Macon. He didn't really care. Sarah said, "What do you think? Legs? Or flush with the floor."

"It's all the same to me," he said. He sat down heavily on something covered in leather.

Sarah chose a long, low couch that opened into a queen-sized bed. "Macon? What do you say?" she asked. "Do you like what you're sitting on better?"

"No, no," he said.

"Well, what do you think of this one?"

"It's fine."

"Don't you have any opinion?"

"I just gave you my opinion, Sarah."

Sarah sighed and asked the salesman if he offered same-day delivery.

They'd been so efficient about picking out the couch that time remained for other errands as well. First they drove to Hutzler's and bought queen-sized sheets. Then they checked the furniture department for armchairs; there was a Father's Day sale there, too. "Maybe we're on a roll," Sarah told Macon. But they weren't as lucky with the armchairs; nothing looked just right. Not to Macon, at least. He gave up trying and stood watching a kiddie show on a row of television sets.

After Hutzler's they went to get fertilizer from Rose, but Macon braked on the way and said, "Wait! There's my bank." It had come upon him unexpectedly—the branch where he rented a safe deposit box. "I need my passport for the France trip,' he told Sarah. "Might as well pick it up while I'm here."

Sarah said she'd just wait in the car.

He had to stand in line; two elderly women were ahead of him. They were checking out their jewels for Saturday night, he liked to imagine. Or clipping their coupons—whatever coupons were. While he stood there he kept feeling the presence of someone behind him. For some reason he didn't want to turn and find out who it was. He just kept staring ahead, every now and then glancing at his watch in a businesslike way. This person breathed very gently and smelled like flowers—bitter, real-life flowers, not the kind in perfume bottles. But when he finally squared his shoulders and looked around, he found only another stranger waiting for her jewels.

It wasn't true that Muriel had watched in silence as he packed. Actually, she had spoken. She had said, "Macon? Are you really doing this? Do you mean to tell me you can just use a person up and then move on? You think I'm some kind of . . . bottle of something you don't have any further need for? Is that how you see me, Macon?"

His turn for the vault had arrived, and he followed a girl in a miniskirt across a carpeted area, into the windowless cubicle lined with drawers. "I won't need to take my box to the other room," he told the girl. "I just want to get one thing."

She gave him his card to sign and accepted his key. After she had unlocked his box she stood back, scrutinizing her nails, while he rummaged through various papers for his passport. Then he turned to tell her he was finished, but all at once he was so moved by her tact in looking elsewhere, by the delicacy that people could come up with on their own (for surely it wouldn't have been written into the bank's instructions) . . . Well, he must be going soft in the head. It was the weather or something; it was the season or something; he had not been sleeping well. He said, "Thank you very much," and took back his key and left.

At his grandfather's house, Rose was out front pruning the

hedge. Her gardening smock was an enormous gray workshirt inherited from Charles. When she saw their car pull up she straightened and waved. Then she went on pruning while they consulted her about fertilizers. "For azaleas and what else do you have, andromeda, acid-loving plants . . ." she mused.

Sarah said, "Where are the children today?"

"Children?"

"Your nephew and nieces."

"Oh, they went home to their mother."

Sarah said, "I just assumed, since you hadn't moved back with Julian . . ."

"Well, not yet, of course," Rose said.

Macon, anxious to guard her privacy, murmured, "No, of course not," practically at the same moment, but Sarah said, "Why? What's keeping you?"

"Oh, Sarah, you wouldn't believe what a state I found the boys in when I came back here," Rose said. "They were living in their pajamas so as not to have too much laundry. They were eating gorp for their suppers."

"I'm not even going to ask what gorp is," Sarah said.

"It's a mixture of wheat germ and nuts and dried—"

"But what about your apartment, Rose? What about Julian?"

"Oh, you know, I kept losing that apartment every time I turned around," Rose said vaguely. "I'd head one block east to the grocery store and then turn west to get back again and I'd always be wrong; always. The apartment building would have worked over to the east somehow; *I* don't know how."

There was a silence. Finally Macon said, "Well, if you could get us some of that fertilizer, Rose . . ."

"Certainly," she said. And she went off to the toolshed.

. . .

They had lunch at the Old Bay Restaurant—Sarah's idea. Macon said, "Are you sure?" and Sarah said, "Why wouldn't I be?"

"But you always tell me it's boring," Macon said.

"There are worse things than boring, I've decided."

He didn't think that was much of a recommendation, but he went along with it.

The restaurant was full, even though it was barely noon, and they had to wait a few minutes to be seated. Macon stood by the hostess's podium trying to adjust to the dimness. He surveyed the other diners and found something odd about them. They were not the usual Old Bay crowd—middle aged, one face much like the next—but an assortment of particular and unusual individuals. He saw a priest offering a toast to a woman in a tennis dress, and a smartly suited woman with a young man in an orange gauze robe, and two cheerful schoolgirls loading all their potato chips onto the plate of a small boy. From where he stood Macon couldn't hear what any of these people were saying; he had to guess. "Maybe the woman wants to join a convent," he told Sarah, "and the priest is trying to discourage her."

"Pardon?"

"He's pointing out that sorting her husband's socks can be equally whatever-he'd-call-it, equally holy. And the young man in gauze, well . . ."

"The young man in gauze is Ashley Demming," Sarah said. "You know Ashley. Peter and Lindy Demming's son. My, he's aged poor Lindy twenty years in the last six months, hasn't he? I don't think they're ever going to get over this."

"Ah, well," Macon said.

Then they were shown to a table.

Sarah ordered something called a White Lady and Macon ordered a sherry. With their meal they had a bottle of wine. Macon wasn't used to drinking in the daytime; he grew a little fuzzy. So did Sarah, evidently, for she drifted off in the middle of a sentence about upholstery fabrics. She touched his hand, which was lying on the tablecloth. "We ought to do this more often," she said.

"Yes, we ought to."

"You know what I missed most when we were separated? The little, habitual things. The Saturday errands. Going to Eddie's for

287

coffee beans. Even things that used to seem tiresome, like the way you'd take forever in the hardware store."

When he folded her hand into a fist it was round, like a bird. It had no sharp angles.

"I'm not sure if you know this," she said, "but for a while I was seeing another man."

"Well, fine; whatever; eat your salad," he told her.

"No, I want to say it, Macon. He was just getting over the death of his wife, and I was getting over things too so of course . . . Well, we started out very slowly, we started as friends, but then he began talking about getting married someday. After we'd given ourselves some time, he meant. In fact I think he really loved me. He took it hard when I told him you'd moved back."

She looked straight at Macon when she said that, her eyes a sudden blue flash. He nodded.

"But there were these things I had trouble with," she said. "I mean good things; qualities I'd always wished for. He was a very dashing driver, for instance. Not unsafe; just dashing. At first, I liked that. Then bit by bit it began to feel wrong. 'Double-check your rearview mirror!' I wanted to tell him. 'Fasten your seatbelt! Inch past stop signs the way my husband does!' He never examined a restaurant bill before he paid it—shoot, he didn't even take his credit card receipt when he walked away from a table—and I thought of all the times I sat stewing while you totted up every little item. I thought, 'Why do I miss that? It's perverse!' "

Like "eck cetera," Macon thought.

Like Muriel saying, "eck cetera." And Macon wincing.

And the emptiness now, the thinness when he heard it pronounced correctly.

He stroked the dimpled peaks that were Sarah's knuckles.

"Macon, I think that after a certain age people just don't have a choice," Sarah said. "You're who I'm with. It's too late for me to change. I've used up too much of my life now."

You mean to tell me you can just use a person up and then move on? Muriel had asked.

Evidently so, was the answer. For even if he had stayed with Muriel, then wouldn't Sarah have been left behind?

"After a certain age," he told Sarah, "it seems to me you can only choose what to lose."

"What?" she said.

"I mean there's going to be something you have to give up, whichever way you cut it."

"Well, of course," she said.

He supposed she'd always known that.

They finished their meal but they didn't order coffee because they were running late. Sarah had her class; she was studying with a sculptor on Saturdays. Macon called for the bill and paid it, self-consciously totaling it first. Then they stepped out into the sunshine. "What a pretty day," Sarah said. "It makes me want to play hooky."

"Why don't you?" Macon asked. If she didn't go to class, he wouldn't have to work on his guidebook.

But she said, "I can't disappoint Mr. Armistead."

They drove home, and she changed into a sweat suit and set off again. Macon carried in the fertilizer, which Rose had poured into a bucket. It was something shredded that had no smell — or only a harsh, chemical smell, nothing like the truckloads of manure the men used to bring for his grandmother's camellias. He set it on the pantry floor and then he took the dog out. Then he made himself a cup of coffee to clear his head. He drank it at the kitchen sink, staring into the yard. The cat rubbed against his ankles and purred. The clock over the stove ticked steadily. There was no other sound.

When the telephone rang, he was glad. He let it ring twice before he answered so as not to seem overeager. Then he picked up the receiver and said, "Hello?"

"Mr. Leary?"

"Yes!"

"This is Mrs. Morton calling, at Merkle Appliance Store. Are you aware that the maintenance policy on your hot water heater expires at the end of the month?"

"No, I hadn't realized," Macon said.

"You had a two-year policy at a cost of thirty-nine eighty-eight. Now to renew it for another two years the cost of course would be slightly higher since your hot water heater is older."

"Well, that makes sense," Macon said. "Gosh! How old *is* that thing by now?"

"Let's see. You purchased it three years ago this July."

"Well, I'd certainly like to keep the maintenance policy."

"Wonderful. I'll send you a new contract then, Mr. Leary, and thank you for—"

"And would that still include replacement of the tank?" Macon asked.

"Oh, yes. Every part is covered."

"And they'd still do the yearly checkups."

"Why, yes."

"I've always liked that. A lot of the other stores don't offer it; I remember from when I was shopping around."

"So I'll send you the contract, Mr.—"

"But I would have to arrange for the checkup myself, as I recall."

"Yes, the customer schedules the checkup."

"Maybe I'll just schedule it now. Could I do that?"

"That's a whole different department, Mr. Leary. I'll mail you out the contract and you can read all about it. Bye bye."

She hung up.

Macon hung up too.

He thought a while.

He had an urge to go on talking; anyone would do. But he couldn't think what number to dial. Finally he called the time lady. She answered before the first ring was completed. (*She* had no worries about seeming overeager.) "At the tone," she said, "the time will be one . . . forty-nine. And ten seconds." What a voice. So melodious, so well modulated. "At the tone the time will be one . . . forty-nine. And twenty seconds."

He listened for over a minute, and then the call was cut off.

The line clicked and the dial tone started. This made him feel rebuffed, although he knew he was being foolish. He bent to pat the cat. The cat allowed it briefly before walking away.

There was nothing to do but sit down at his typewriter.

He was behind schedule with this guidebook. Next week he was supposed to start on France, and he still hadn't finished the conclusion to the Canada book. He blamed it on the season. Who could sit alone indoors when everything outside was blooming? *Travelers should be forewarned*, he typed, but then he fell to admiring a spray of white azaleas that trembled on the ledge of his open window. A bee crawled among the blossoms, buzzing. He hadn't known the bees were out yet. Did Muriel know? Would she recall what a single bee could do to Alexander?

. . . *should be forewarned*, he read over, but his concentration was shot now.

She was so careless, so unthinking; how could he have put up with her? That unsanitary habit she had of licking her finger before she turned a magazine page; her tendency to use the word "enormity" as if it referred to size. There wasn't a chance in this world that she'd remember about bee stings.

He reached for the phone on his desk and dialed her number. "Muriel?"

"What," she said flatly.

"This is Macon."

"Yes, I know."

He paused. He said, "Um, it's bee season, Muriel."

"So?"

"I wasn't sure you were aware. I mean summer just creeps up, *I* know how summer creeps up, and I was wondering if you'd thought about Alexander's shots."

"Don't you believe I can manage that much for myself?" she screeched.

"Oh. Well."

"What do you think I am, some sort of ninny? Don't you think I know the simplest dumbest thing?"

"Well, I wasn't sure, you see, that—"

"A fine one you are! Ditch that child without a word of farewell and then call me up on the telephone to see if I'm raising him right!"

"I just wanted to—"

"Criticize, criticize! Tell me Oodles of Noodles is not a balanced meal and then go off and desert him and then have the nerve to call me up and tell me I'm not a good mother!"

"No, wait, Muriel—"

"Dominick is dead," she said.

"What?"

"Not that you would care. He died."

Macon noticed how the sounds in the room had stopped. "Dominick Saddler?" he asked.

"It was his night to take my car and he went to a party in Cockeysville and coming home he crashed into a guardrail."

"Oh, no."

"The girl he had with him didn't get so much as a scratch."

"But Dominick . . ." Macon said, because he didn't believe it yet.

"But Dominick died instantly."

"Oh, my Lord."

He saw Dominick on the couch with Alexander, holding aloft a can of paste wax.

"Want to hear something awful? My car will be just fine," Muriel said. "Straighten the front end and it'll run good as ever."

Macon rested his head in his hand.

"I have to go now and sit with Mrs. Saddler in the funeral home," she said.

"Is there something I can do?"

"No," she said, and then spitefully, "How could *you* be any help?"

"I could stay with Alexander, maybe."

"Alexander's got people of our own to stay with him," she said.

The doorbell rang, and Edward started barking. Macon heard him in the front hall.

"Well, I'll say good-bye now," Muriel said. "Sounds like you have company."

"Never mind that."

"I'll let you get back to your *life*," she said. "So long."

He kept the receiver to his ear for a moment, but she had hung up.

He went out to the hall and tapped his foot at Edward. "Down!" he said. Edward lay down, the hump on his back still bristling. Macon opened the door and found a boy with a clipboard.

"Modern Housewares," the boy told him.

"Oh. The couch."

While the couch was being unloaded, Macon shut Edward in the kitchen. Then he returned to the hall and watched the couch lumbering toward him, borne by the first boy and another, just slightly older, who had an eagle tattooed on his forearm. Macon thought of Dominick Saddler's muscular, corded arms grappling beneath the hood of Muriel's car. The first boy spat as he approached the house, but Macon saw how young and benign his face was. "Aw, man," the second one said, stumbling over the doorstep.

Macon said, "That's all right," and gave them each a five-dollar bill when they'd placed the couch where he directed.

After they'd gone he sat down on the couch, which still had some sort of cellophane covering. He rubbed his hands on his knees. Edward barked in the kitchen. Helen padded in softly, stopped still, eyed the couch, and continued through the room with an offended air. Macon went on sitting.

When Ethan died, the police had asked Macon to identify the body. But Sarah, they suggested, might prefer to wait outside. Yes, Sarah had said; she would. She had taken a seat on a molded beige chair in the hallway. Then she'd looked up at Macon and said, "Can you do this?"

"Yes," he'd told her, evenly. He had felt he was barely breathing; he was keeping himself very level, with most of the air emptied out of his lungs.

He had followed a man into a room. It was not as bad as it could have been because someone had folded a wad of toweling under the back of Ethan's head to hide the damage. Also it wasn't Ethan. Not the real Ethan. Odd how clear it suddenly became, once a person had died, that the body was the very least of him. This was simply an untenanted shell, although it bore a distant resemblance to Ethan—the same groove down the upper lip, same cowlick over the forehead. Macon had a sensation like pressing against a blank wall, willing with all his being something that could never happen: *Please, please come back inside.* But finally he said, "Yes. That is my son."

He'd returned to Sarah and given her a nod. Sarah had risen and put her arms around him. Later, when they were alone in their motel, she'd asked him what he had seen. "Not really much of anything, sweetheart," he had told her. She kept at him. Was Ethan . . . well, hurt-looking? Scared? He said, "No, he was nothing." He said, "Let me get you some tea."

"I don't want tea, I want to hear!" she'd said. "What are you hiding?" He had the impression she was blaming him for something. Over the next few weeks it seemed she grew to hold him responsible, like a bearer of bad tidings—the only one who could say for a fact that Ethan had truly died. She made several references to Macon's chilliness, to his appalling calm that night in the hospital morgue. Twice she expressed some doubt as to whether, in fact, he was really capable of distinguishing Ethan from some similar boy. In fact, that may not have been Ethan at all. It may have been somebody else who had died. She should have ascertained for herself. She was the mother, after all; she knew her child far better; what did Macon know?

Macon said, "Sarah. Listen. I will tell you as much as I can. He was very pale and still. You wouldn't believe how still. He didn't have any expression. His eyes were closed. There was nothing bloody or gruesome, just a sense of . . . futility. I mean I wondered what the purpose had been. His arms were down by his sides and I thought about last spring when he started lifting weights. I thought, 'Is this what it comes to? Lift weights and take vitamins and build yourself up and then—nothing?' "

He hadn't been prepared for Sarah's response. "So what are you saying?" she asked him. "We die in the end, so why bother living in the first place? Is that what you're saying?"

"No—" he said.

"It all comes down to a question of economy?" she asked.

"No, Sarah. Wait," he had said.

Thinking back on that conversation now, he began to believe that people could, in fact, be used up—could use each other up, could be of no further help to each other and maybe even do harm to each other. He began to think that who you are when you're with somebody may matter more than whether you love her.

Lord knows how long he sat there.

Edward had been barking in the kitchen all this time, but now he went into a frenzy. Somebody must have knocked. Macon rose and went to the front of the house, where he found Julian standing on the porch with a file folder. "Oh. It's you," Macon said.

"What's all that barking I hear?"

"Don't worry, he's shut in the kitchen. Come on in."

He held the screen door open and Julian stepped inside. "Thought I'd bring you the material for Paris," Julian said.

"I see," Macon said. But he suspected he was really here for some other reason. Probably hoping to hurry the Canada book. "Well, I was just this minute touching up my conclusion," he said, leading the way to the living room. And then, hastily, "Few details here and there I'm not entirely happy with; maybe a little while yet . . ."

Julian didn't seem to be listening. He sat down on the cellophane that covered the couch. He tossed the folder aside and said, "Have you seen Rose lately?"

"Yes, we were over there just this morning."

"Do you think she's not coming back?"

Macon hadn't expected him to be so direct. In fact, Rose's situation had begun to look like one of those permanent irregularities that couples never refer to. "Oh, well," he told Julian, "you know how it is. She's worried about the boys. They're eating glop or something."

"Those are not boys, Macon. They're men in their forties."

Macon stroked his chin.

"I'm afraid she's left me," Julian said.

"Oh, now, you can't be sure of that."

"And not even for a decent reason!" Julian said. "Or for any reason. I mean our marriage was working out fine; that much I can swear to. But she'd worn herself a groove or something in that house of hers, and she couldn't help swerving back into it. At least, I can't think of any other explanation."

"Well, it sounds about right," Macon told him.

"I went to see her two days ago," Julian said, "but she was out. I was standing in the yard wondering where she'd got to when who should drive past but Rose in person, with her car stuffed full of old ladies. All the windows packed with these little old faces and feathered hats. I shouted after her, I said, 'Rose! Wait!' but she didn't hear me and she drove on by. Then just at the last minute she caught sight of me, I guess, and she turned and stared, and I got the funniest feeling, like the car was driving *her*—like she was just gliding past helpless and couldn't do a thing but send me one long look before she disappeared."

Macon said, "Why don't you give her a job, Julian."

"Job?"

"Why don't you show her that office of yours. That filing system you never get sorted, that secretary chewing her gum and forgetting whose appointment is when. Don't you think Rose could take all that in hand?"

"Well, sure, but—"

"Call her up and tell her your business is going to pieces. Ask if she could just come in and get things organized, get things under control. Put it that way. Use those words. *Get things under control,* tell her. Then sit back and wait."

Julian thought that over.

"But of course, what do I know," Macon said.

"No, you're right."

"Now let's see your folder."

"You're absolutely right," Julian said.

"Look at this!" Macon said. He held up the topmost letter. "Why do you bother me with this? *I just wanted to appraise you folks of a wonderful little hotel in* . . . A man who says he wants to 'appraise' us, do you really suppose he'd know a good hotel when he saw one?"

"Macon," Julian said.

"The whole damn language has been slaughtered," Macon said.

"Macon, I know you feel I'm crass and brash."

This took Macon a moment to answer, only partly because he first heard it as "crash and brass." "Oh," he said. "Why, no, Julian, not at—"

"But I just want to say this, Macon. I care about that sister of yours more than anything else in the world. It's not just Rose, it's the whole way she lives, that house and those turkey dinners and those evening card games. And I care about you, too, Macon. Why, you're my best friend! At least, I hope so."

"Oh, why, ah—" Macon said.

Julian rose and shook his hand, mangling all the bones inside, and clapped him on the shoulder and left.

. . .

Sarah came home at five-thirty. She found Macon standing at the kitchen sink with yet another cup of coffee. "Did the couch get here?" she asked him.

"All safe and sound."

"Oh, good! Let's see it."

She went into the living room, leaving tracks of gray dust that Macon supposed was clay or granite. There was dust in her hair, even. She squinted at the couch and said, "What do you think?"

"Seems fine to me," he said.

"Honestly, Macon. I don't know what's come over you; you used to be downright finicky."

"It's fine, Sarah. It looks very nice."

She stripped off the cellophane and stood back, arms full of crackling light. "We ought to see how it opens out," she said.

While she was stuffing the cellophane into the wastebasket, Macon pulled at the canvas strap that turned the couch into a bed. It made him think of Muriel's house. The strap's familiar graininess reminded him of all the times Muriel's sister had slept over, and when the mattress slid forth he saw the gleam of Claire's tangled golden hair.

"Maybe we should put on the sheets, now that we've got it open," Sarah said. She brought the sack of linens from the front hall. With Macon positioned at the other side of the couch, she floated a sheet about the mattress and then bustled up and down, tucking it in. Macon helped, but he wasn't as fast as Sarah. The clay dust or whatever it was had worked itself into the seams of her knuckles, he saw. There was something appealing about her small, brown, creased hands against the white percale. He said, "Let's give the bed a trial run."

Sarah didn't understand at first. She looked up from unfolding the second sheet and said, "Trial run?"

But she allowed him to take the sheet away and slip her sweat shirt over her head.

Making love to Sarah was comfortable and soothing. After all their years together, her body was so well known to him that he couldn't always tell the difference between what he was feeling and what she was feeling. But wasn't it sad that they hadn't the slightest uneasiness about anyone walking in on them? They were so alone. He nestled his face in her warm, dusty neck and wondered if she shared that feeling as well—if she sensed all the empty air in the house. But he would never ask.

.   .   .

While Sarah took a shower, he shaved. They were supposed to go to Bob and Sue Carney's for supper. When he came out of the bathroom Sarah was standing in front of the bureau, screwing on little gold earrings. (She was the only woman Macon knew of who didn't have pierced ears.) He thought Renoir could have painted her: Sarah in her slip with her head cocked slightly, plump tanned arms upraised. "I'm really not in the mood to go out," she said.

"Me neither," Macon said, opening his closet door.

"I'd be just as content to stay home with a book."

He pulled a shirt off a hanger.

"Macon," she said.

"Hmm."

"You never asked me if I slept with anyone while we were separated."

Macon paused, halfway into one sleeve.

"Don't you want to know?" she asked him.

"No," he said.

He put on the shirt and buttoned the cuffs.

"I would think you'd wonder."

"Well, I don't," he said.

"The trouble with you is, Macon—"

It was astonishing, the instantaneous flare of anger he felt. "Sarah," he said, "don't even start. By God, if that doesn't sum up every single thing that's wrong with being married. 'The trouble with you is, Macon—' and, 'I know you better than you know yourself, Macon—'"

"The trouble with you is," she continued steadily, "you think people should stay in their own sealed packages. You don't believe in opening up. You don't believe in trading back and forth."

"I certainly don't," Macon said, buttoning his shirt front.

"You know what you remind me of? The telegram Harpo Marx sent his brothers: *No message. Harpo.*"

That made him grin. Sarah said, "You *would* think it was funny."

"Well? Isn't it?"

"It isn't at all! It's sad! It's infuriating! It would be infuriating to go to your door and sign for that telegram and tear it open and find no message!"

He took a tie from the rack in his closet.

"For your information," she said, "I didn't sleep with anyone the whole entire time."

He felt like she'd won some kind of contest. He pretended he hadn't heard her.

. . .

Bob and Sue had invited just neighbors—the Bidwells and a new young couple Macon hadn't met before. Macon stuck mainly to the new couple because with them, he had no history. When they asked if he had children, he said, "No." He asked if they had any children.

"No," Brad Frederick said.

"Ah."

Brad's wife was in transit between girlhood and womanhood. She wore her stiff navy blue dress and large white shoes as if they belonged to her mother. Brad himself was still a boy. When they all went out back to watch the barbecue, Brad found a Frisbee in the bushes and flung it to little Delilah Carney. His white polo shirt pulled loose from his trousers. Dominick Saddler came to Macon's mind like a deep, hard punch. He remembered how, after his grandfather died, the sight of any old person could make his eyes fill with tears. Lord, if he wasn't careful he could end up feeling sorry for the whole human race. "Throw that thing here," he said briskly to Delilah, and he set aside his sherry and held out a hand for the Frisbee. Before long they had a real game going—all the guests joining in except Brad's wife, who was still too close to childhood to risk getting stuck there on a visit back.

At supper, Sue Carney seated Macon at her right. She put a hand on his and said it was wonderful that he and Sarah had worked things out. "Well, thank you," Macon said. "Gosh you make a really good salad, Sue."

"We all have our ups and downs," she said. For a second he thought she meant her salads weren't consistently successful. "I'll be honest," she told him, "there've been times when I have wondered if Bob and I would make it. There's times I feel we're just hanging in there, you know what I mean? Times I say, 'Hi, honey, how was your day?' but inside I'm feeling like a Gold Star mother."

Macon turned the stem of his glass and tried to think what step he'd missed in her logic.

"Like someone who's suffered a loss in a war," she said, "and then forever afterward she has to go on supporting the war; she has to support it louder than anyone else, because otherwise she'd be admitting the loss was for no purpose."

"Um . . ."

"But that's just a passing mood," she said.

"Well, naturally," Macon said.

. . .

He and Sarah walked home through air as heavy as water. It was eleven o'clock and the teenagers who had eleven o'clock curfews were just returning. These were the youngest ones, most of them too young to drive, and so they were chauffeured by grown-ups. They jumped out of cars shouting, "See you! Thanks! Call me tomorrow, hear?" Keys jingled. Front doors blinked open and blinked shut again. The cars moved on.

Sarah's skirt had the same whispery sound as the Tuckers' lawn sprinkler, which was still revolving slowly in a patch of ivy.

When they reached the house, Macon let Edward out for one last run. He tried to get the cat to come in, but she stayed hunched on the kitchen window ledge glaring down at him, owlish and stubborn; so he let her be. He moved through the rooms turning off lights. By the time he came upstairs Sarah was already in bed, propped against the headboard with a glass of club soda. "Have some," she said, holding out the glass. But he said no, he was tired; and he undressed and slid under the covers.

The tinkling of Sarah's ice cubes took on some meaning in his mind. It seemed that with every tinkle, he fell deeper. Finally he opened a door and traveled down an aisle and stepped into the witness stand. They asked him the simplest of questions. "What color were the wheels?" "Who brought the bread?" "Were the shutters closed or open?" He honestly couldn't remember. He tried but he couldn't remember. They took him to the scene of the crime, a winding road like something in a fairy tale. "Tell us all you know," they said. He didn't know a thing. By now it was clear from their faces that he wasn't merely a witness; they suspected him. So he racked his brain, but still he came up empty. "You have to see my side of this!" he cried. "I put it all out of my mind; I worked to put it out! Now I can't bring it back."

"Not even to defend yourself?" they asked.

He opened his eyes. The room was dark, and Sarah breathed softly next to him. The clock radio said it was midnight. The midnight-curfew group was just returning. Hoots and laughter rang out, tires scraped a curb, and a fanbelt whinnied as someone struggled to park. Then gradually the neighborhood fell silent. It would stay that way, Macon knew, till time for the one-o'clock group. He would first hear faint strands of their music and then more laughter, car doors slamming, house doors slamming. Porch lights would switch off all along the street, gradually dimming the ceiling as he watched. In the end, he would be the only one left awake.

twenty

The plane to New York was a little bird of a thing, but the plane to Paris was a monster, more like a building. Inside, great crowds were cramming coats and bags into overhead compartments, stuffing suitcases under seats, arguing, calling for stewardesses. Babies were crying and mothers were snapping at children. Steerage could not have been worse than this, Macon felt.

He took his place next to a window and was joined almost immediately by an elderly couple speaking French. The man sat next to Macon and gave him a deep, unsmiling nod. Then he said something to his wife, who passed him a canvas bag. He unzipped it and sorted through its contents. Playing cards, an entire tin of Band-aids, a stapler, a hammer, a lightbulb . . . Macon was fascinated. He kept sliding his eyes to the right to try and see more. When a wooden mousetrap tumbled out, he began to wonder if the man might be some sort of lunatic; but of course even a mousetrap could be explained, given a little thought. Yes, what he was witnessing, Macon decided, was just one answer to the traveler's eternal choice: Which was better? Take all you own, and struggle to carry it? Or travel light, and spend half your trip combing the shops for what you've left behind? Either way had its drawbacks.

He glanced up the aisle, where more passengers were arriving. A Japanese man festooned with cameras, a nun, a young girl in braids. A woman with a little red vanity kit, her hair a dark tent, her face a thin triangle.

Muriel.

First he felt a kind of flush sweep through him—that flood of warmth that comes when someone familiar steps forth from a mass of strangers. And then: *Oh, my God*, he thought, and he actually looked around for some means of escape.

She walked toward him in a graceful, picky way, watching her feet, and then when she was next to him she raised her eyes and he saw that she'd known all along he was there. She wore a white suit that turned her into one of those black-white-and-red women he used to admire on movie screens as a child.

"I'm going to France," she told him.

"But you can't!" he said.

The French couple peered at him curiously, the wife sitting slightly forward so as to see him better.

More passengers arrived behind Muriel. They muttered and craned around her, trying to edge past. She stood in the aisle and said, "I'm going to walk along the Seine."

The wife made a little O with her mouth.

Then Muriel noticed the people behind her and moved on.

Macon wasn't even sure it was possible to walk along the Seine. As soon as the aisle was cleared he half stood and peered over the back of his seat, but she had vanished. The French couple turned to him, eyes expectant. Macon settled down again.

Sarah would find out about this. She would just somehow know. She had always said he had no feelings and this would confirm it—that he could tell her good-bye so fondly and then fly off to Paris with Muriel.

Well, it was none of his doing and he'd be damned if he'd assume the blame.

By the time it was dark they were airborne, and some kind of order had emerged inside the plane. It was one of those flights as fully programmed as a day in kindergarten. Safety film, drinks, headphones, dinner, movie. Macon turned down all he was offered and studied Julian's file folder instead. Most of the material was ridiculous. Sam'n'Joe's Hotel, indeed! He wondered if Julian had made it up to tease him.

A woman passed wearing white and he glanced at her surreptitiously, but it was no one he knew.

Just before the end of the movie, he got out his shaving kit and went to use one of the lavatories near the rear. Unfortunately other people had had the same idea. Both doors were locked, and he was forced to wait in the aisle. He felt someone arrive at his side. He looked and there was Muriel.

He said, "Muriel, what in—"

"You don't own this plane!" she told him.

Heads turned.

"And you don't own Paris, either," she said.

She was standing very close to him, face to face. She gave off a scent that barely eluded him; it was not just her perfume, no, but her house; yes, that was it—the smell inside her closet, the tantalizing unsettling smell of other people's belongings. Macon pressed his left temple. He said, "I don't understand any of this. I don't see how you knew which flight to take, even."

"I called your travel agent."

"Becky? You called Becky? What must she have thought?"

"She thought I was your editorial assistant."

"And how could you afford the fare?"

"Oh, some I borrowed from Bernice and then some from my sister, she had this money she earned at . . . and I did everything economy-style, I took a train to New York instead of a plane—"

"Well, *that* wasn't smart," Macon said. "It probably cost you the same, in the long run, or maybe even more."

"No, what I did was—"

"But the point is, why, Muriel? Why are you doing this?"

She lifted her chin. (Her chin could get so sharp, sometimes.) "Because I felt like it," she said.

"You felt like spending five days alone in a Paris hotel? That's what it will be, Muriel."

"You need to have me around," she said.

"Need you!"

"You were falling to pieces before you had me."

A latch clicked and a man stepped out of one of the lavatories. Macon stepped inside and locked the door quickly behind him.

He wished he could just vanish. If there had been a window, he believed he would have pried it open and jumped—not because he wanted to commit any act so definite as suicide but because he wanted to erase it all; oh, Lord, just go back and erase all the untidy, unthinking things he'd been responsible for in his life.

If she had read even one of his guidebooks, she'd have known not to travel in white.

When he emerged, she was gone. He went back to his seat. The French couple drew in their knees to let him slide past; they were transfixed by the movie screen, where a blonde wearing nothing but a bath towel was pounding on a front door. Macon got out *Miss MacIntosh* just for something to pin his mind to. It didn't work, though. Words flowed across his vision in a thin, transparent stream, meaningless. He was conscious only of Muriel somewhere behind him. He felt wired to her. He caught himself wondering what she made of this—the darkened plane, the invisible ocean beneath her, the murmur of half-real voices all around her. When he turned off his reading light and shut his eyes, he imagined he could sense that she was still awake. It was a feeling in the air—something alert, tense, almost vibrating.

. . .

By morning he was resolved. He used a different lavatory, toward the front. For once he was glad to be in such a large crowd. When they landed he was almost the first one off, and he cleared Immigration quickly and darted through the airport. The airport was Charles de Gaulle, with its space-age pods of seats. Muriel would be thoroughly lost. He exchanged his money in haste. Muriel must still be at Baggage Claims. He knew she would carry lots of baggage.

There was no question of waiting for a bus. He hailed a cab and sped off, feeling wonderfully lightweight all of a sudden. The tangle of silvery highways struck him as actually pleasant. The city of Paris, when he entered, was as wide and pale and luminous as a cool gray stare, and he admired the haze that hung over it. His cab raced down misty boulevards, turned onto a cobbled street, lurched to a stop. Macon sifted through his envelopes of money.

Not till he was entering his hotel did he recall that his travel agent knew exactly where he was staying.

It wasn't a very luxurious hotel—a small brown place where mechanical things tended to go wrong, as Macon had discovered on past visits. This time, according to a sign in the lobby, one of the two elevators was not marching. The bellman led him into the other, then up to the third floor and down a carpeted corridor. He flung open a door, loudly exclaiming in French as if overcome by such magnificence. (A bed, a bureau, a chair, an antique TV.) Macon burrowed into one of his envelopes. "Thank you," he said, offering his tip.

Once he was alone, he unpacked and he hung up his suit coat, then he went to the window. He stood looking out over the rooftops; the dust on the glass made them seem removed in time, part of some other age.

How would she manage alone in such an unaccustomed place?

He thought of the way she navigated a row of thrift shops—the way she cruised a street, deft and purposeful, greeting passersby by name. And the errands she took the neighbors on: chauffeuring Mr. Manion to the reflexologist who dissolved his kidney stones by massaging his toes; Mr. Runkle to the astrologer who told him when he'd win the million-dollar lottery; Mrs. Carpaccio to a certain tiny grocery near Johns Hopkins where the sausages hung from the ceiling like strips of flypaper. The places Muriel knew!

But she didn't know Paris. And she was entirely on her own. She didn't even have a credit card, probably carried very little money, might not have known to change what she did carry into francs. Might be wandering helpless, penniless, unable to speak a word of the language.

By the time he heard her knock, he was so relieved that he rushed to open the door.

"Your room is bigger than mine is," she said. She walked past him to the window. "I have a better view, though. Just think, we're really in Paris! The bus driver said it might rain but *I* told him I didn't care. Rain or shine, it's Paris."

"How did you know what bus to take?" he asked her.

"I brought along your guidebook."

She patted her pocket.

"Want to go to Chez Billy for breakfast?" she asked. "That's what your book recommends."

"No, I don't. I can't," he said. "You'd better leave, Muriel."

"Oh. Okay," she said. She left.

Sometimes she would do that. She'd press in till he felt trapped, then suddenly draw back. It was like a tug of war where the other person all at once drops the rope, Macon thought. You fall flat on the ground; you're so unprepared. You're so empty-feeling.

.   .   .

He decided to call Sarah. At home it was barely dawn, but it seemed important to get in touch with her. He went over to the phone on the bureau and picked up the receiver. It was dead. He pressed the button a few times. Typical. He dropped his key in his pocket and went down to the lobby.

The lobby telephone was housed in an ancient wooden booth, very genteel. There was a red leather bench to sit on. Macon hunched over and listened to the ringing at the other end, far away. "Hello?" Sarah said.

"Sarah?"

"Who is this?"

"It's Macon."

"Macon?"

She took a moment to absorb that. "Macon, where are you?" she asked. "What's the matter?"

"Nothing's the matter. I just felt like talking to you."

"What? What time is it?"

"I know it's early and I'm sorry I woke you but I wanted to hear your voice."

"There's some kind of static on the line," she said.

"It's clear at this end."

"You sound so thin."

"That's because it's an overseas call," he said. "How's the weather there?"

"How's who?"

"The weather! Is it sunny?"

"I don't know. All the shades are down. I don't think it's even light yet."

"Will you be gardening today?"

"What?"

"Gardening!"

"Well, I hadn't thought. It depends on whether it's sunny, I guess."

"I wish I were there," he said. "I could help you."

"You hate to garden!"

"Yes, but . . ."

"Macon, are you all right?"

"Yes, I'm fine," he said.

"How was the flight over?"

"Oh, the flight, well, goodness! Well, I don't know; I guess I was so busy reading that I didn't really notice," he said.

"Reading?" she said. Then she said, "Maybe you've got jet lag."

"Yes, maybe I do," he told her.

. . .

Fried eggs, scrambled eggs, poached eggs, omelets. He walked blindly down the sidewalk, scribbling in the margins of his guidebook. He did not go near Chez Billy. *It's puzzling*, he wrote, *how the French are so tender in preparing their food but so rough in serving it*. In the window of a restaurant, a black cat closed her eyes at him. She seemed to be gloating. She was so much at home, so sure of her place.

Displays of crushed velvet, scattered with solid gold chains and watches no thicker than poker chips. Women dressed as if for the stage: elaborate hairdos, brilliant makeup, strangely shaped trousers that had nothing to do with the human anatomy. Old ladies in little-girl ruffles and white tights and Mary Janes. Macon descended the steps to the Métro; he ostentatiously dropped his canceled ticket into a tiny receptacle marked PAPIERS. Then he turned to glare at all the others who flung their tickets on the floor, and as he turned he thought he saw Muriel, her white face glimmering in the crowd, but he must have been mistaken.

In the evening he returned to his hotel—footsore, leg muscles aching—and collapsed on his bed. Not two minutes later he heard a knock. He groaned and rose to open the door. Muriel stood there with her arms full of clothes. "Look," she said, pushing past him. "See what-all I bought." She dumped the clothes on the bed. She held them up one by one: a shiny black cape, a pair of brown jodhpurs, a bouffant red net evening dress sprinkled with different-sized disks of glass like the reflectors on bicycles. "Have you lost your senses?" Macon asked. "What must all this have cost?"

"Nothing! Or next to nothing," she said. "I found a place that's like the granddaddy of all garage sales. A whole city of garage sales! This French girl was telling me about it where I went to have my breakfast. I complimented her hat and she told me where she got it. I took a subway train to find it; your book's really helpful about the subways; and sure enough there's everything there. Tools and gadgets too, Macon. Old car batteries, fuse boxes . . . and if you say something's too expensive, they'll bring the price down till it's cheap enough. I saw this leather coat I would have killed for but that never did get cheap enough; the man wanted thirty-five francs."

"Thirty-five francs!" Macon said. "I don't know how you could get any cheaper than that. Thirty-five francs is four dollars or so."

"Oh, really? I thought francs and dollars were about the same."

"Lord, no."

"Well, then these things were *super* bargains," Muriel said. "Maybe I'll try again tomorrow."

"But how will you get all this stuff on the plane?"

"Oh, I'll figure out some way. Now let me take it back to my room so we can go eat."

He stiffened. He said, "No, I can't."

"What harm would it do to eat supper with me, Macon? I'm someone from home! You've run into me in Paris! Can't we have a bite together?"

When she put it that way, it seemed so simple.

They went to the Burger King on the Champs-Elysées; Macon wanted to recheck the place anyhow. He ordered two 'Wop-paires.' "Careful," he warned Muriel, "these are not the Whoppers you're used to. You'll want to scrape the extra pickle and onion off." But Muriel, after trying hers, said she liked it the way it was. She sat next to him on a hard little seat and licked her fingers. Her shoulders touched his. He was amazed, all at once, that she really was here.

"Who's looking after Alexander?" he asked her.

"Oh, different people."

"What different people? I hope you haven't just parked him, Muriel. You know how insecure a child that age can—"

"Relax. He's fine. Claire has him in the daytime and then Bernice comes in and cooks supper and any time Claire has a date with the General the twins will keep him or if the twins can't do it then the General says Alexander can . . ."

Singleton Street rose up in front of Macon's eyes, all its color and confusion.

After supper Muriel suggested they take a walk, but Macon said he was tired. He was exhausted, in fact. They returned to their hotel. In the elevator Muriel asked, "Can I come to your room a while? My TV set only gets snow."

"We'd better say good night," he told her.

"Can't I just come in and keep you company?"

"No, Muriel."

"We wouldn't have to *do* anything," she said.

The elevator stopped at his floor. He said, "Muriel. Don't you understand my position? I've been married to her forever. Longer than you've been alive, almost. I can't change now. Don't you see?"

She just stood in her corner of the elevator with her eyes on his face. All her makeup had worn off and she looked young and sad and defenseless.

"Good night," he said.

He got out, and the elevator door slid shut.

He went to bed immediately but couldn't sleep after all, and ended up switching on the TV. They were showing an American western, dubbed. Rangy cowboys spoke a fluid, intricate French. Disaster followed disaster—tornadoes, Indians, droughts, stampedes. The hero stuck in there, though. Macon had long ago noticed that all adventure movies had the same moral: Perseverance pays. Just once he'd like to see a hero like himself—not a quitter, but a man who did face facts and give up gracefully when pushing onward was foolish.

He rose and switched the set off again. He tossed and turned a long time before he slept.

. . .

Large hotels, small hotels, dingy hotels with their wallpaper flaking, streamlined hotels with king-sized American beds and Formica-topped American bureaus. Dim café windows with the proprietors displayed like mannequins, clasping their hands behind their backs and rocking from heel to toe. *Don't fall for* prix fixe. *It's like a mother saying, "Eat, eat"—all those courses forced on you . . .*

In the late afternoon Macon headed wearily back to his own hotel. He was crossing the final intersection when he saw Muriel up ahead. Her arms were full of parcels, her hair was flying out, and her spike-heeled shoes were clipping along. "Muriel!" he called. She turned and he ran to catch up with her.

"Oh, Macon, I've had the nicest day," she said. "I met these people from Dijon and we ended up eating lunch together and they told me about . . . Here, can you take some of these? I think I overbought."

He accepted several of her parcels—crumpled, used-looking bags stuffed with fabrics. He helped her carry them into the hotel and up to her room, which seemed even smaller than it was because of the piles of clothing everywhere. She dumped her burdens on the bed and said, "Let me show you, now, where is it . . ."

"What's this?" Macon asked. He was referring to an oddly shaped soft drink bottle on the bureau.

"Oh, I found that in the fridge," she said. "They have this little fridge in the bathroom, Macon, and it's just full of soft drinks, and wine and liquor too."

"Muriel, don't you know those cost an arm and a leg? They'll put it on your bill, don't you know that? Now, that fridge is called a mini-bar, and here's what you use it for: In the morning, when they wheel in the continental breakfast, they bring a pitcher of hot milk for some strange reason and you just take that pitcher and stick it in the mini-bar so later you can have a glass of milk. Otherwise, Lord knows how you'd get your calcium in this country. And don't eat the rolls; you know that, don't you? Don't start your day with carbohydrates, especially under the strain of travel. You're better off taking the trouble to go to some café for eggs."

"Eggs, ugh," Muriel said. She was stepping out of her skirt and trying on another—one she'd just bought, with long fringes at the hem. "I *like* the rolls," she said. "And I like the soft drinks, too."

"Well, I don't know how you can say that," he said. He picked up the bottle. "Just look at the brand name: Pschitt. If that's not the most suspicious-sounding . . . and there's another kind called Yukkie, Yukkery, something like that—"

"That's my favorite. I already finished those off," Muriel said. She was pinning her hair on top of her head. "Where we having dinner tonight?"

"Well, I don't know. I guess it's time to try someplace fancy."

"Oh, goody!"

He moved what appeared to be an antique satin bedjacket and sat down to watch her put her lipstick on.

. . .

They went to a restaurant lit with candles, although it wasn't quite dark yet, and were seated next to a tall, curtained window. The only other customers were American—four American business types, plainly enjoying themselves over four large platters of snails. (Sometimes Macon wondered if there really was any call for his books.)

"Now, what do I want?" Muriel said, studying the menu. "If I ask them what something is in English, do you think they'll be able to tell me?"

"Oh, you don't have to bother doing that," Macon said. "Just order Salade Niçoise."

"Order what?"

"I thought you said you'd read my guide. Salade Niçoise. It's the one safe dish. I've been all through France eating nothing but, day in and day out."

"Well, that sounds kind of monotonous," Muriel said.

"No, no. Some places put green beans in it, some don't. And at least it's low-cholesterol, which is more than you can say for—"

"I think I'll just ask the waiter," Muriel told him. She laid her menu aside. "Do you suppose they call them French windows in France?"

"What? I wouldn't have the slightest idea," he said. He looked toward the window, which was paned with deep, greenish glass. Outside, in an overgrown courtyard, a pitted stone cherub was cavorting in a fountain.

The waiter spoke more English than Macon had expected. He directed Muriel toward a cream of sorrel soup and a special kind of fish. Macon decided to go for the soup as well, rather than sit idle while Muriel had hers. "There," Muriel said. "Wasn't he nice?"

"That was a rare exception," Macon said.

She batted at the hem of her skirt. "Durn fringe! I keep thinking something's crawling up my leg," she said. "Where you going tomorrow, Macon?"

"Out of Paris altogether. Tomorrow I start on the other cities."

"You're leaving me here alone?"

"This is high-speed travel, Muriel. Not fun. I'm waking up at crack of dawn."

"Take me anyway."

"I can't."

"I haven't been sleeping so good," she said. "I get bad dreams."

"Well, then you certainly don't want to go gallivanting off to more new places."

"Last night I dreamed about Dominick," she said. She leaned toward him across the table, two spots of color high on her cheekbones. "I dreamed he was mad at me."

"Mad?"

"He wouldn't talk to me. Wouldn't look at me. Kept kicking something on the sidewalk. Turned out he was mad because I wouldn't let him use the car anymore. I said, 'Dommie, you're dead. You *can't* use the car. I'd let you if I could, believe me.' "

"Well, don't worry about it," Macon said. "It was just a travel dream."

"I'm scared it means he's mad for real. Off wherever he's at."

"He's not," Macon told her. "He wouldn't be mad."

"I'm scared he is."

"He's happy as a lark."

"You really think so?"

"Sure! He's up there in some kind of motor heaven, polishing a car all his own. And it's always spring and the sun is always shining and there's always some blonde in a halter top to help him with the buffing."

"You really think that might be true?" Muriel asked.

"Yes, I do," he said. And the funny thing was that he did, just at that moment. He had a vivid image of Dominick in a sunlit meadow, a chamois skin in his hand and a big, pleased, cocky grin on his face.

. . .

She said at the end of the evening that she wished he would come to her room—couldn't he? to guard against bad dreams?—

and he said no and told her good night. And then he felt how she drew at him, pulling deep strings from inside him, when the elevator creaked away with her.

In his sleep he conceived a plan to take her along tomorrow. What harm would it do? It was only a day trip. Over and over in his scattered, fitful sleep he picked up his phone and dialed her room. It was a surprise when he woke in the morning, to find he hadn't invited her yet.

He sat up and reached for the phone and remembered only then—with the numb receiver pressed to his ear—that the phone was out of order and he'd forgotten to report it. He wondered if it were something he could repair himself, a cord unplugged or something. He rose and peered behind the bureau. He stooped to hunt for a jack of some kind.

And his back went out.

No doubt about it—that little twang! in a muscle to the left of his spine. The pain was so sharp it snagged his breath. Then it faded. Maybe it was gone for good. He straightened, a minimal movement. But it was enough to bring the pain zinging in again.

He lowered himself to the bed inch by inch. The hard part was getting his feet up, but he set his face and accomplished that too. Then he lay pondering what to do next.

Once he had had this happen and the pain had vanished in five minutes and not returned. It had been only a freaky thing like a foot cramp.

But then, once he'd stayed flat in bed for two weeks and crept around like a very old man for another month after that.

He lay rearranging his agenda in his mind. If he canceled one trip, postponed another . . . Yes, possibly what he'd planned for the next three days could be squeezed into two instead. If only he were able to get around by tomorrow.

He must have gone back to sleep. He didn't know for how long. He woke to a knock and thought it was breakfast, though he'd left instructions for none to be brought today. But then he heard Muriel. "Macon? You in there?" She was hoping he hadn't left Paris yet; she was here to beg again to go with him. He knew that as clearly as if she'd announced it. He was grateful now for the spasm that gripped him as he turned away from her voice. Somehow that short sleep had cleared his head, and he saw that he'd come perilously close to falling in with her again. *Falling in:* That was the way he put it to himself. What luck that his back had stopped him. Another minute—another few seconds—and he might have been lost.

He dropped into sleep so suddenly that he didn't even hear her walk away.

When he woke again it was much later, he felt, although he didn't want to go through the contortions necessary to look at his watch. A wheeled cart was passing his room and he heard voices— hotel employees, probably—laughing in the corridor. They must be so comfortable here; they must all know each other so well. There was a knock on his door, then a jingle of keys. A small, pale chambermaid poked her face in and said, *"Pardon, monsieur."* She started to retreat but then stopped and asked him something in French, and he gestured toward his back and winced. "Ah," she said, entering, and she said something else very rapidly. (She would be telling him about *her* back.) He said, "If you would just help me up, please," for he had decided he had no choice but to go call Julian. She seemed to understand what he meant and came over to the bed. He turned onto his stomach and then struggled up on one arm—the only way he could manage to rise without excruciating pain. The chambermaid took his other arm and braced herself beneath his weight as he stood. She was much shorter than he, and pretty in a fragile, meek way. He was conscious of his unshaven face and his rumpled pajamas. "My jacket," he told her, and they proceeded haltingly to the chair where his suit jacket hung. She draped it around his shoulders. Then he said, "Downstairs? To the telephone?" She looked over at the phone on the bureau, but he made a negative movement with the flat of his hand—a gesture that cost him. He grimaced. She clucked her tongue and led him out into the corridor.

Walking was not particularly difficult; he felt hardly a twinge. But the elevator jerked agonizingly and there was no way he could predict it. The chambermaid uttered soft sounds of sympathy. When they arrived in the lobby she led him to the telephone booth and started to seat him, but he said, "No, no, standing's easier. Thanks." She backed out and left him there. He saw her talking to the clerk at the desk, shaking her head in pity; the clerk shook his head, too.

Macon worried Julian wouldn't be in his office yet, and he didn't know his home number. But the phone was answered on the very first ring. "Businessman's Press." A woman's voice, confusingly familiar, threading beneath the hiss of long distance.

"Um—" he said. "This is Macon Leary. To whom am I—"

"Oh, Macon."

"Rose?"

"Yes, it's me."

"What are *you* doing there?"

"I work here now."

"Oh, I see."

"I'm putting things in order. You wouldn't believe the state this place is in."

"Rose, my back has gone out on me," Macon said.

"Oh, no, of all times! Are you still in Paris?"

"Yes, but I was just about to start my day trips and there are all these plans I have to change—appointments, travel reservations—and no telephone in my room. So I was wondering if Julian could do it from his end. Maybe he could get the reservations from Becky and—"

"I'll take care of it myself," Rose said. "Don't you bother with a thing."

"I don't know when I'm going to get to the other cities, tell him. I don't have any idea when I'll be—"

"We'll work it out. Have you seen a doctor?"

"Doctors don't help. Just bed rest."

"Well, rest then, Macon."

He gave her the name of his hotel, and she repeated it briskly and then told him to get on back to bed.

When he emerged from the phone booth the chambermaid

had a bellboy there to help him, and between the two of them he made it to his room without much trouble. They were very solicitous. They seemed anxious about leaving him alone, but he assured them he would be all right.

All that afternoon he lay in bed, rising twice to go to the bathroom and once to get some milk from the mini-bar. He wasn't really hungry. He watched the brown flowers on the wallpaper; he thought he had never known a hotel room so intimately. The side of the bureau next to the bed had a streak in the woodgrain that looked like a bony man in a hat.

At suppertime he took a small bottle of wine from the mini-bar and inched himself into the armchair to drink it. Even the motion of raising the bottle to his lips caused him pain, but he thought the wine would help him sleep. While he was sitting there the chambermaid knocked and let herself in. She asked him, evidently, whether he wanted anything to eat, but he thanked her and said no. She must have been on her way home; she carried a battered little pocketbook.

Later there was another knock, after he had dragged himself back to bed, and Muriel said, "Macon? Macon?" He kept absolutely silent. She went away.

The air grew fuzzy and then dark. The man on the side of the bureau faded. Footsteps crossed the floor above him.

He had often wondered how many people died in hotels. The law of averages said some would, right? And some who had no close relatives—say one of his readers, a salesman without a family— well, what was done about such people? Was there some kind of potters' field for unknown travelers?

He could lie in only two positions—on his left side or on his back—and switching from one to the other meant waking up, consciously deciding to undertake the ordeal, plotting his strategy. Then he returned to a fretful, semi-consciousness.

He dreamed he was seated on an airplane next to a woman dressed all in gray, a very narrow, starched, thin-lipped woman, and he tried to hold perfectly still because he sensed she disapproved of movement. It was a rule of hers; he knew that somehow. But he grew more and more uncomfortable, and so he decided to confront her. He said, "Ma'am?" She turned her eyes on him, mild, mournful eyes under finely arched brows. "Miss MacIntosh!" he said. He woke in a spasm of pain. He felt as if a tiny, cruel hand had snatched up part of his back and wrung it out.

. . .

When the waiter brought his breakfast in the morning, the chambermaid came along. She must keep grueling hours, Macon thought. But he was glad to see her. She and the waiter fussed over him, mixing his hot milk and coffee, and the waiter helped him into the bathroom while the chambermaid changed his sheets. He thanked them over and over; *"Merci,"* he said clumsily. He wished he knew the French for "I don't know why you're being so kind." After they left he ate all of his rolls, which the chambermaid had thoughtfully buttered and spread with strawberry jam. Then he turned on the TV for company and got back in bed.

He was sorry about the TV when he heard the knock on the door, because he thought it was Muriel and she would hear. But it seemed early for Muriel to be awake. And then a key turned in the lock, and in walked Sarah.

He said, "Sarah?"

She wore a beige suit, and she carried two pieces of matched luggage, and she brought a kind of breeze of efficiency with her. "Now, everything's taken care of," she told him. "I'm going to make your day trips for you." She set down her suitcases, kissed his forehead, and picked up a glass from his breakfast table. As she went off to the bathroom she said, "We've rescheduled the other cities and I start on them tomorrow."

"But how did you get here so soon?" he asked.

She came out of the bathroom; the glass was full of water. "You have Rose to thank for that," she said, switching off the TV. "Rose is just a wizard. She's revamped that entire office. Here's a pill from Dr. Levitt."

"You know I don't take pills," he said.

"This time you do," she told him. She helped him rise up on one elbow. "You're going to sleep as much as you can, so your back has a chance to heal. Swallow."

The pill was tiny and very bitter. He could taste it even after he'd lain down again.

"Is the pain bad?" she asked him.

"Kind of."

"How've you been getting your meals?"

"Well, breakfast comes anyway, of course. That's about it."

"I'll ask about room service," she told him, picking up the phone. "Since I'll be gone so . . . What's the matter with the telephone?"

"It's dead."

"I'll go tell the desk. Can I bring you anything while I'm out?"

"No, thank you."

When she left, he almost wondered if he'd imagined her. Except that her suitcases sat next to his bed, sleek and creamy—the same ones she kept on the closet shelf at home.

He thought about Muriel, about what would happen if she were to knock now. Then he thought about two nights ago, or was it three, when she had strolled in with all her purchases. He wondered if she'd left any traces. A belt lost under the bed, a glass disk fallen off her cocktail dress? He began to worry about it seriously. It seemed to him almost inevitable; of course she'd left something. The only question was, what. And where.

Groaning, he rolled over and pushed himself upright. He struggled off the bed and then sagged to his knees to peer beneath it. There didn't seem to be anything there. He got to his feet and tilted over the armchair to feel around the edges of the cushion. Nothing there either. Actually she hadn't gone anywhere near the armchair, to his recollection; nor had she gone to the bureau, but even so he slid out the drawers one by one to make sure. His own belongings— just a handful—occupied one drawer. The others were empty, but the second one down had a sprinkling of pink face powder. It wasn't Muriel's, of course, but it looked like hers. He decided to get rid of it. He tottered into the bathroom, dampened a towel, and came back to swab the drawer clean. Then he saw that the towel had developed a large pink smear, as if a woman wearing too much makeup had wiped her face with it. He folded the towel so the smear was concealed and laid it in the back of the drawer. No, too incriminating. He took it out again and hid it beneath the armchair cushion. That didn't seem right either. Finally he went into the bathroom and washed the towel by hand, scrubbing it with a bar of soap till the spot was completely gone. The pain in his back was constant, and beads of sweat stood out on his forehead. At some point he decided he was acting very peculiar; in fact it must be the pill; and he dropped the wet towel in a heap on the floor and crawled back into bed. He fell asleep at once. It wasn't a normal sleep; it was a kind of burial.

He knew Sarah came in but he couldn't wake up to greet her. And he knew she left again. He heard someone knock, he heard lunch being brought, he heard the chambermaid whisper, "*Monsieur?*" He remained in his stupor. The pain was muffled but still present—just covered up, he thought; the pill worked like those inferior room sprays in advertisements, the ones that only mask offending odors. Then Sarah came back for the second time and he opened his eyes. She was standing over the bed with a glass of water. "How do you feel?" she asked him.

"Okay," he said.

"Here's your next pill."

"Sarah, those things are deadly."

"They help, don't they?"

"They knock me out," he said. But he took the pill.

She sat down on the edge of the mattress, careful not to jar him. She still wore her suit and looked freshly groomed, although she must be bushed by now. "Macon," she said quietly.

"Hmm."

"I saw that woman friend of yours."

He tensed. His back seized up.

"She saw me, too," she said. "She seemed very surprised."

"Sarah, this is not the way it looks," he told her.

"What is it then, Macon? I'd like to hear."

"She came over on her own. I didn't even know till just before the plane took off, I swear it! She followed me. I told her I didn't want her along. I told her it was no use."

She kept looking at him. "You didn't know till just before the plane took off," she said.

"I swear it," he said.

He wished he hadn't taken the pill. He felt he wasn't in full possession of his faculties.

"Do you believe me?" he asked her.

"Yes, I believe you," she said, and then she got up and started uncovering his lunch dishes.

. . .

He spent the afternoon in another stupor, but he was aware of the chambermaid's checking on him twice, and he was almost fully awake when Sarah came in with a bag of groceries. "I thought I'd make you supper myself," she told him. "Fresh fruit and things; you always complain you don't get enough fresh fruit when you travel."

"That's very nice of you, Sarah."

He worked himself around till he was half sitting, propped against a pillow. Sarah was unwrapping cheeses. "The phone's fixed," she said. "You'll be able to call for your meals and all while I'm out. Then I was thinking: After I've finished the trips, if your back is better, maybe we could do a little sightseeing on our own. Take some time for ourselves, since we're here. Visit a few museums and such."

"Fine," he said.

"Have a second honeymoon, sort of."

"Wonderful."

He watched her set the cheeses on a flattened paper bag. "We'll change your plane ticket for a later date," she said. "You're reserved to leave tomorrow morning; no chance you could manage that. I left my own ticket open-ended. Julian said I should. Did I tell you where Julian is living?"

"No, where?"

"He's moved in with Rose and your brothers."

"He's what?"

"I took Edward over to Rose's to stay while I was gone, and there was Julian. He sleeps in Rose's bedroom; he's started playing Vaccination every night after supper."

"Well, I'll be damned," Macon said.

"Have some cheese."

He accepted a slice, changing position as little as possible.

"Funny, sometimes Rose reminds me of a flounder," Sarah said. "Not in looks, of course . . . She's lain on the ocean floor so long, one eye has moved to the other side of her head."

He stopped chewing and stared at her. She was pouring two glasses of cloudy brown liquid. "Apple cider," she told him. "I figured you shouldn't drink wine with those pills."

"Oh. Right," he said.

She passed him a glass. "A toast to our second honeymoon," she said.

"Our second honeymoon," he echoed.

"Twenty-one more years together."

"Twenty-one!" he said. It sounded like such a lot.

"Or would you say twenty."

"No, it's twenty-one, all right. We were married in nineteen—"

"I mean because we skipped this past year."

"Oh," he said. "No, it would still be twenty-one."

"You think so?"

"I consider last year just another stage in our marriage," he said. "Don't worry: It's twenty-one."

She clinked her glass against his.

Their main dish was a potted meat that she spread on French bread, and their dessert was fruit. She washed the fruit in the bathroom, returning with handfuls of peaches and strawberries; and meanwhile she kept up a cozy patter that made him feel he was home again. "Did I mention we had a letter from the Averys? They might be passing through Baltimore later this summer. Oh, and the termite man came."

"Ah."

"He couldn't find anything wrong, he said."

"Well, that's a relief."

"And I've almost finished my sculpture and Mr. Armistead says it's the best thing I've done."

"Good for you," Macon said.

"Oh," she said, folding the last paper bag, "I know you don't think my sculptures are important, but—"

"Who says I don't?" he asked.

"I know you think I'm just this middle-aged lady playing artist—"

"Who says?"

"Oh, I know what you think! You don't have to pretend with me."

Macon started to slump against his pillow, but was brought up short by a muscle spasm.

She cut a peach into sections, and then she sat on the bed and passed him one of the sections. She said, "Macon. Just tell me this. Was the little boy the attraction?"

"Huh?"

"Was the fact that she had a child what attracted you to that woman?"

He said, "Sarah, I swear to you, I had no idea she was planning to follow me over here."

"Yes, I realize that," she said, "but I was wondering about the child question."

"What child question?"

"I was remembering the time you said we should have another baby."

"Oh, well, that was just—I don't know what that was," he said. He handed her back the peach; he wasn't hungry anymore.

"I was thinking maybe you were right," Sarah said.

"What? No, Sarah; Lord, that was a terrible idea."

"Oh, I know it's scary," she told him. "I admit I'd be scared to have another."

"Exactly," Macon said. "We're too old."

"No, I'm talking about the, you know, the world we'd be bringing him into. So much evil and danger. I admit it: I'd be frantic any time we let him out on the street."

Macon saw Singleton Street in his mind, small and distant like Julian's little green map of Hawaii and full of gaily drawn people scrubbing their stoops, tinkering with their cars, splashing under fire hydrants.

"Oh, well, you're right," he said. "Though really it's kind of . . . heartening, isn't it? How most human beings do try. How they try to be as responsible and kind as they can manage."

"Are you saying yes, we can have a baby?" Sarah asked.

Macon swallowed. He said, "Well, no. It seems to me we're past the time for that, Sarah."

"So," she said, "her little boy wasn't the reason."

"Look, it's over with. Can't we close the lid on it? I don't cross-examine *you*, do I?"

"But I don't have someone following me to Paris!" she said.

"And what if you did? Do you think I'd hold you to blame if someone just climbed on a plane without your knowing?"

"Before it left the ground," she said.

"Pardon? Well, I should hope so!"

"Before it left the ground, you saw her. You could have walked up to her and said, 'No. Get off. Go this minute. I want nothing more to do with you and I never want to see you again.' "

"You think I own the airline, Sarah?"

"You could have stopped her if you'd really wanted," Sarah said. "You could have taken steps."

And then she rose and began to clear away their supper.

.   .   .

She gave him his next pill, but he let it stay in his fist for a while because he didn't want to risk moving. He lay with his eyes closed, listening to Sarah undress. She ran water in the bathroom, slipped the chain on the door, turned off the lights. When she got into bed it stabbed his back, even though she settled carefully, but he gave no sign. He heard her breathing soften almost at once. She must have been exhausted.

He reflected that he had not taken steps very often in his life, come to think of it. Really never. His marriage, his two jobs, his time with Muriel, his return to Sarah—all seemed to have simply befallen him. He couldn't think of a single major act he had managed of his own accord.

Was it too late now to begin?

Was there any way he could learn to do things differently?

He opened his hand and let the pill fall among the bedclothes. It was going to be a restless, uncomfortable night, but anything was better than floating off on that stupor again.

.   .   .

In the morning, he negotiated the journey out of bed and into the bathroom. He shaved and dressed, spending long minutes on each task. Creeping around laboriously, he packed his bag. The heaviest thing he packed was *Miss MacIntosh, My Darling*, and after thinking that over a while, he took it out again and set it on the bureau.

Sarah said, "Macon?"

"Sarah. I'm glad you're awake," he said.

"What are you doing?"

"I'm packing to leave."

She sat up. Her face was creased down one side.

"But what about your back?" she asked. "And I've got all those appointments! And we were going to take a second honeymoon!"

"Sweetheart," he said. He lowered himself cautiously till he was sitting on the bed. He picked up her hand. It stayed lifeless while she watched his face.

"You're going back to that woman," she said.

"Yes, I am," he said.

"Why, Macon?"

"I just decided, Sarah. I thought about it most of last night. It wasn't easy. It's not the easy way out, believe me."

She sat staring at him. She wore no expression.

"Well, I don't want to miss the plane," he said.

He inched to a standing position and hobbled into the bathroom for his shaving kit.

"You know what this is? It's all due to that pill!" Sarah called after him. "You said yourself it knocks you out!"

"I didn't take the pill."

There was a silence.

She said, "Macon? Are you just trying to get even with me for the time I left you?"

He returned with the shaving kit and said, "No, sweetheart."

"I suppose you realize what your life is going to be like," she said. She climbed out of bed. She stood next to him in her nightgown, hugging her bare arms. "You'll be one of those mismatched couples no one invites to parties. No one will know what to make of you. People will wonder whenever they meet you, 'My God, what does he see in her? Why choose someone so inappropriate? It's grotesque, how does he put up with her?' And her friends will no doubt be asking the same about you."

"That's probably true," Macon said. He felt a mild stirring of interest; he saw now how such couples evolved. They were not, as he'd always supposed, the result of some ludicrous lack of perception, but had come together for reasons that the rest of the world would never guess.

He zipped his overnight bag.

"I'm sorry, Sarah. I didn't want to decide this," he said.

He put his arm around her painfully, and after a pause she let her head rest against his shoulder. It struck him that even this moment was just another stage in their marriage. There would probably be still other stages in their thirtieth year, fortieth year—forever, no matter what separate paths they chose to travel.

.　.　.

He didn't take the elevator; he felt he couldn't bear the willy-nilliness of it. He went down the stairs instead. He managed the front door by backing through it, stiffly.

Out on the street he found the usual bustle of a weekday morning—shopgirls hurrying past, men with briefcases. No taxis in sight. He set off for the next block, where his chances were better. Walking was fairly easy but carrying his bag was torture. Lightweight though it was, it twisted his back out of line. He tried it in his left hand, then his right. And after all, what was inside it? Pajamas, a change of underwear, emergency supplies he never used . . . He stepped over to a building, a bank or office building with a low stone curb running around its base. He set the bag on the curb and hurried on.

Up ahead he saw a taxi with a boy just stepping out of it, but he discovered too late that hailing it was going to be a problem. Raising either arm was impossible. So he was forced to run in an absurd, scuttling fashion while shouting bits of French he'd never said aloud before: "*Attendez! Attendez, monsieur!*"

The taxi was already moving off and the boy was just slipping his wallet back into his jeans, but then he looked up and saw Macon. He acted fast; he spun and called out something and the taxi braked. "*Merci beaucoup*," Macon panted and the boy, who had a sweet, pure face and shaggy yellow hair, opened the taxi door for him and gently assisted him in. "Oof!" Macon said, seized by a spasm. The boy shut the door and then, to Macon's surprise, lifted a hand in a formal good-bye. The taxi moved off. Macon told the driver where he was going and sank back into his seat. He patted his inside pocket, checking passport, plane ticket. He unfolded his handkerchief and wiped his forehead.

Evidently his sense of direction had failed him, as usual. The driver was making a U-turn, heading back where Macon had just come from. They passed the boy once again. He had a jaunty, stiff-legged way of walking that seemed familiar.

If Ethan hadn't died, Macon thought, wouldn't he have grown into such a person?

He would have turned to give the boy another look, except that he couldn't manage the movement.

The taxi bounced over the cobblestones. The driver whistled a tune between his teeth. Macon found that bracing himself on one arm protected his back somewhat from the jolts. Every now and then, though, a pothole caught him off guard.

And if dead people aged, wouldn't it be a comfort? To think of Ethan growing up in heaven—fourteen years old now instead of twelve—eased the grief a little. Oh, it was their immunity to time that made the dead so heartbreaking. (Look at the husband who dies young, the wife aging on without him; how sad to imagine the husband coming back to find her so changed.) Macon gazed out the cab window, considering the notion in his mind. He felt a kind of inner rush, a racing forward. The real adventure, he thought, is the flow of time; it's as much adventure as anyone could wish. And if he pictured Ethan still part of that flow—in some other place, however unreachable—he believed he might be able to bear it after all.

The taxi passed Macon's hotel—brown and tidy, strangely home-like. A man was just emerging with a small anxious dog on his arm. And there on the curb stood Muriel, surrounded by suitcases and string-handled shopping bags and cardboard cartons overflowing with red velvet. She was frantically waving down taxis—first one ahead, then Macon's own. "*Arrêtez!*" Macon cried to the driver. The taxi lurched to a halt. A sudden flash of sunlight hit the windshield, and spangles flew across the glass. The spangles were old water spots, or maybe the markings of leaves, but for a moment Macon thought they were something else. They were so bright and festive, for a moment he thought they were confetti.

Ladder of Years

BALTIMORE WOMAN DISAPPEARS
DURING FAMILY VACATION

Delaware State Police announced early today that Cordelia F. Grinstead, 40, wife of a Roland Park physician, has been reported missing while on holiday with her family in Bethany Beach.

Mrs. Grinstead was last seen around noon this past Monday, walking south along the stretch of sand between Bethany and Sea Colony.

Witnesses of her departure—her husband, Dr. Samuel Grinstead, 55, and her three children, Susan, 21, Ramsay, 19, and Carroll, 15—were unable to recall any suspicious characters in the vicinity. They reported that to the best of their recollection she simply strolled away. Her failure to return was not remarked until late afternoon.

A slender, small-boned woman with curly fair or light-brown hair, Mrs. Grinstead stands 5'2" or possibly 5'5" and weighs either 90 or 110 pounds. Her eyes are blue or gray or perhaps green, and her nose is mildly sunburned in addition to being freckled.

Presumably she was carrying a large straw tote trimmed with a pink bow, but family members could not agree upon her clothing. In all probability it was something pink or blue, her husband suggested, either frilled or lacy or "looking kind of baby-doll."

Authorities do not suspect drowning, since Mrs. Grinstead avoided swimming whenever possible and professed a distinct aversion to water. In fact, her sister, Eliza Felson, 52, has alleged to reporters that the missing woman "may have been a cat in her most recent incarnation."

Anyone with knowledge of Mrs. Grinstead's whereabouts is urged to contact the Delaware State Police at once.

I

This all started on a Saturday morning in May, one of those warm spring days that smell like clean linen. Delia had gone to the supermarket to shop for the week's meals. She was standing in the produce section, languidly choosing a bunch of celery. Grocery stores always made her reflective. Why was it, she was wondering, that celery was not called "corduroy plant"? That would be much more colorful. And garlic bulbs should be "moneybags," because their shape reminded her of the sacks of gold coins in folktales.

A customer on her right was sorting through the green onions. It was early enough so the store was nearly empty, and yet this person seemed to be edging in on her a bit. Once or twice the fabric of his shirt sleeve brushed her dress sleeve. Also, he was really no more than stirring those onions around. He would lift one rubber-banded clump and then drop it and alight on another. His fingers were very long and agile, almost spidery. His cuffs were yellow oxford cloth.

He said, "Would you know if these are called scallions?"

"Well, sometimes," Delia said. She seized the nearest bunch of celery and stepped toward the plastic bags.

"Or would they be shallots?"

"No, they're scallions," she told him.

Needlessly, he steadied the roll of bags overhead while she peeled one off. (He towered a good foot above her.) She dropped the celery into the bag and reached toward the cup of twist ties, but he had already plucked one out for her. "What are shallots, anyway?" he asked.

She would have feared that he was trying to pick her up, except that when she turned she saw he was surely ten years her junior, and very good-looking besides. He had straight, dark-yellow hair and milky blue eyes that made him seem dreamy and peaceful. He was smiling down at her, standing a little closer than strangers ordinarily stand.

"Um . . . ," she said, flustered.

"Shallots," he reminded her.

"Shallots are fatter," she said. She set the celery in her grocery cart. "I believe they're above the parsley," she called over her shoulder, but she found him next to her, keeping step with her as she wheeled her cart toward the citrus fruits. He wore blue jeans, very faded, and soft moccasins that couldn't be heard above "King of the Road" on the public sound system.

"I also need lemons," he told her.

She slid another glance at him.

"Look," he said suddenly. He lowered his voice. "Could I ask you a big favor?"

"Um . . ."

"My ex-wife is up ahead in potatoes. Or not ex I guess but . . . estranged, let's say, and she's got her boyfriend with her. Could you just pretend we're together? Just till I can duck out of here?"

"Well, of course," Delia said.

And without even taking a deep breath first, she plunged happily back into the old high-school atmosphere of romantic intrigue and deception. She narrowed her eyes and lifted her chin and said, "We'll show *her*!" and sailed past the fruits and made a U-turn into root vegetables. "Which one is she?" she murmured through ventriloquist lips.

"Tan shirt," he whispered. Then he startled her with a sudden burst of laughter. "Ha, ha!" he told her too loudly. "Aren't you clever to say so!"

But "tan shirt" was nowhere near an adequate description. The woman who turned at the sound of his voice wore an ecru raw-silk tunic over black silk trousers as slim as two pencils. Her hair was absolutely black, cut shorter on one side, and her face was a perfect oval. "Why, Adrian," she said. Whoever was with her—some man or other—turned too, still gripping a potato. A dark, thick man with rough skin like stucco and eyebrows that met in the middle. Not up to the woman's standard at all; but how many people were?

Delia's companion said, "Rosemary. I didn't see you. So don't forget," he told Delia, not breaking his stride. He set a hand on her cart to steer it into aisle 3. "You promised me you'd make your marvelous blancmange tonight."

"Oh, yes, my . . . blancmange," Delia echoed faintly. Whatever blancmange might be, it sounded the way she felt just then: pale and plain-faced and skinny, with her freckles and her frizzy brown curls and her ruffled pink round-collared dress.

They had bypassed the dairy case and the juice aisle, where Delia had planned to pick up several items, but she didn't point that out because this Adrian person was still talking. "Your blancmange and then your, uh, what, your meat and vegetables and da-da-da . . ."

The way he let his voice die reminded her of those popular songs that end with the singers just absentmindedly drifting away from the microphone. "Is she looking at us?" he whispered. "Check it out. Don't make it obvious."

Delia glanced over, pretending to be struck by a display of converted rice. Both the wife and the boyfriend had their backs to her, but there was something artificial in their posture. No one could find russet potatoes so mesmerizing. "Well, she's *mentally* looking," Delia murmured. She turned to see her grocery cart rapidly filling with pasta. Egg noodles, rotini, linguine—Adrian flung in boxes at random. "Excuse me . . . ," she said.

"Oh, sorry," he told her. He stuffed his hands in his pockets and loped off. Delia followed, pushing her cart very slowly in case he meant for them to separate now. But at the end of the aisle, he paused and considered a row of tinned ravioli until she caught up with him. "The boyfriend's name is Skipper," he said. "He's her accountant."

"Accountant!" Delia said. He didn't fit the image.

"Half a dozen times, at least, he's come to our house. Sat in our actual living room, going over her taxes. Rosemary owns this catering firm. The Guilty Party, it's called. Ha. 'Sinfully Delicious Foods for Every Occasion.' Then next thing I know, she's moved in with him. She claimed she only needed a few weeks by herself, but when she phoned to say so, I could hear him coaching her in the background."

"Oh, that's terrible," Delia said.

A woman with a baby in her cart reached between them for a can of macaroni and cheese. Delia stepped back to give her room.

"If it's not too much trouble," Adrian said when the woman had moved away, "I'll just tag along while you finish your shopping. It would look sort of fishy if I left right now, all alone. I hope you don't mind."

Mind? This was the most interesting thing that had happened to her in years. "Not a bit," she told him. She wheeled her cart into aisle 4. Adrian strolled alongside her.

"I'm Adrian Bly-Brice, by the way," he said. "I guess I ought to know *your* name."

"I'm Delia Grinstead," she told him. She plucked a bottle of mint flakes from the spice rack.

"I don't believe I've ever run into a Delia before."

"Well, it's Cordelia, really. My father named me that."

"And are you one?"

"Am I one what?"

"Are you your father's Cordelia?"

"I don't know," she said. "He's dead."

"Oh, I'm sorry."

"He died this past winter," she said.

Ridiculously, tears filled her eyes. This whole conversation had taken a wrong turn somewhere. She squared her shoulders and pushed her cart on down the aisle, veering around an elderly couple conferring over salt substitutes. "Anyhow," she said, "it got shortened to Delia right away. Like in the song."

"What song?"

"Oh, the . . . you know, the one about Delia's gone, one more round . . . My father used to sing me to sleep with that."

"I never heard it," Adrian said.

The tune on the loudspeaker now was "By the Time I Get to Phoenix," competing with her father's gruff voice muttering "Delia's Gone" in her mind. "Anyhow!" she said again, more brightly.

They started up the next aisle: cereals on the left, popcorn and sweets on the right. Delia needed cornflakes, but cornflakes were such a *family* item, she decided against them. (What ingredients were required for blancmange?) Adrian gazed idly at sacks of butterscotch drops and rum balls. His skin had that slight tawniness that you occasionally see in fair-haired men, and it seemed almost without texture. He must not have to shave more than two or three times a week.

"I myself was named for an uncle," he said. "Rich Uncle Adrian Brice. Probably all for nothing, though. He's mad I changed my name when I married."

"You changed your name when you married?"

"I used to be Adrian Brice the Second, but then I married Rosemary Bly and we both became Bly-Brice."

"Oh, so there's a hyphen," Delia said. She hadn't realized.

"It was entirely her idea, believe me."

As if summoned up by his words, Rosemary appeared at the other end of the aisle. She tossed something into the red plastic tote basket hanging from Skipper's fist. Women like Rosemary never purchased their groceries by the cartload.

"If we went to the movie, though, we'd miss the concert," Adrian said instantly, "and you know how I've looked forward to the concert."

"I forgot," Delia said. "The concert! They'll be playing . . ."

But she couldn't think of a single composer. (And maybe he had meant some other kind of concert—a rock show, for instance. He was young enough.) Rosemary watched without a flicker of expression as Delia and Adrian approached. Delia was the first to lower her eyes. "We'll just save the movie for tomorrow," Adrian was saying. He guided her cart to the left a bit. All at once Delia felt woefully small—not dainty and petite, but squat, humble, insignificant. She didn't stand much taller than Adrian's armpit. She increased her speed, anxious to leave this image of herself behind. "They do have a Sunday matinee, don't they?" Adrian was asking.

"Of course they do," she told him, a little too emphatically. "We could go to the two o'clock showing, right after our champagne brunch."

By now she was tearing down the next aisle. Adrian had to lengthen his stride to keep up. They narrowly missed hitting a man whose cart was stacked with gigantic Pampers boxes.

In aisle 7 they zipped through the gourmet section—anchovy paste, smoked oysters—and arrived at baby foods, where Delia collected herself enough to remember she needed strained spinach. She slowed to study the rows of little jars. "Not those!" Adrian hissed. They raced on, leaving behind aisle 7 and careening into 8. "Sorry," he said. "I just thought if Rosemary saw you buying baby food . . ."

If she saw her buying baby food, she'd think Delia was just a housewife with an infant waiting at home. Ironically, though, Delia had long passed the infant stage. To suspect her of having a child that young was to flatter her. All she needed the spinach for was her mint pea soup. But she didn't bother explaining that and instead selected a can of chicken broth. "Oh," Adrian said, traveling past her, "consommé! I meant to buy some."

He dropped a tin in her cart—a fancy brand with a sleek white label. Then he wandered on, hands jammed flat in his rear pockets. Come to think of it, he reminded Delia of her first real boyfriend—in fact, her only boyfriend, not counting her husband. Will Britt had possessed this same angularity, which had seemed graceful at some moments and ungainly at others; and he had cocked his elbows behind him in just this way, like knobby, sharp wings, and his ears had stuck out a bit too. It was a relief to find that Adrian's ears stuck out. She distrusted men who were too handsome.

At the end of the aisle they looked in both directions. No telling where Rosemary might pop up next, with that carefree, untrammeled tote basket. But the coast was clear, and Delia nosed her cart toward paper goods. "What," Adrian said, "you want to buy *more?*"

Yes, she did. She had barely passed the halfway mark. But she saw his point. The longer they hung around, the greater his chances of another confrontation. "We'll leave," she decided. She started for the nearest checkout counter, but Adrian, lacing his fingers through the grid of the cart, drew it toward the express lanes. "One, two, three . . ." She counted her purchases aloud. "We can't go there! I've got sixteen, seventeen . . ."

He pulled the cart into the fifteen-item lane, behind an old woman buying nothing but a sack of dog chow. He started dumping noodle boxes onto the counter. Ah, well. Delia rummaged through her bag for her checkbook. The old woman in front of them, meanwhile, was depositing bits of small change in the cashier's palm. She handed over a penny and then, after a search, another penny. A third penny had a piece of lint stuck to it, and she plucked that away painstakingly. Adrian gave an exasperated sigh. "I forgot cat food," Delia told him. She hadn't a hope in this world that he would volunteer to go back for it; she just thought a flow of talk might settle him down some. "Seeing that dog chow reminded me, we're almost out," she said. "Oh, never mind. I'll send Ramsay for it later."

The old woman was hunting a fourth penny. She was positive, she said, that she had another one somewhere.

"Ramsay!" Adrian repeated to himself. He sighed again—or no, this time he was laughing. "I bet you live in Roland Park," he told Delia.

"Well, yes, I do."

"I knew it! Everybody in Roland Park has a last name for a first name."

"So?" she said, stung. "What's wrong with that?"

"Oh, nothing."

"It isn't even true," she said. "Why, I know lots of people who—"

"Don't take offense! I live in Roland Park myself," he said. "It's just pure luck I wasn't named . . . oh, Bennington, or McKinney; McKinney was my mother's maiden name. I bet your *husband's* mother's . . . and if we decide against the blancmange tonight we can always have it tomorrow night, don't you think?"

She felt dislocated for a second, until she understood that Rosemary must be in earshot again. Sure enough: a tote basket, still loaded, arrived on the counter behind her own groceries. By now the old woman had moved away, tottering under her burden of dog chow, and the cashier was asking them, "Plastic bags, or paper?"

"Plastic, please," Adrian said.

Delia opened her mouth to object (she generally chose paper, herself), but she didn't want to contradict Adrian in front of his wife.

Adrian said, "Delia, I don't believe you've met my . . ."

Delia turned around, already plastering a pleasantly surprised smile on her face.

"My, ah, Rosemary," Adrian said, "and her, ah, Skipper. This is Delia Grinstead."

Rosemary wasn't smiling at all, which made Delia feel foolish, but Skipper gave her an amiable nod. He kept his arms folded across his chest—short, muscular arms, heavily furred, bulging from the sleeves of his polo shirt. "Any relation to *Dr.* Grinstead?" he asked her.

"Yes! He's my . . . he was my . . . he's my husband," she said. How to explain the existence of a husband, in the present situation?

But Skipper seemed to take this in stride. He told Rosemary, "Dr. Grinstead's my mother's GP. Been treating her forever. Right?" he asked Delia.

"Right," she agreed, not having the faintest idea. Rosemary, meanwhile, went on studying her coolly. She carried her head at a deliberate tilt, accentuating the asymmetrical hairdo with its dramatic downward slant toward her chin. It was none of Delia's business, of course, but privately she thought Adrian deserved somebody more likable. She thought even Skipper deserved somebody more likable. She wished she had worn high heels this morning, and a dressier dress.

"Dr. Grinstead is just about the last man in Baltimore who makes house calls," Skipper was telling Rosemary.

"Well, only if it's absolutely essential," Delia said. A reflex: she never gave up trying to protect her husband from his patients.

Behind her, the scanner said *peep . . . peep . . . peep*, registering her groceries. The music had stopped playing several minutes back, as Delia just now noticed, and the murmuring of shoppers elsewhere in the store sounded hushed and ominous.

"That'll be thirty-three forty," the cashier announced.

Delia turned to fill in her check and found Adrian handing over the money. "Oh!" she said, preparing to argue. But then she grew conscious of Rosemary listening.

Adrian flashed her a wide, sweet smile and accepted his change. "Good seeing you," he told the other couple. He walked on out, pushing the cart, with Delia trailing behind.

It had been raining off and on for days, but this morning had dawned clear and the parking lot had a rinsed, fresh, soft look under a film of lemony sunlight. Adrian halted the cart at the curb and lifted out two of the grocery bags, leaving the third for Delia. Next came the problem of whose car to head for. He was already starting toward his own, which was evidently parked somewhere near the dry cleaner's, when she stopped him. "Wait," she said. "I'm right here."

"But what if they see us? We can't leave in two different cars!"

"Well, I do have a *life* to get back to," Delia snapped. This whole business had gone far enough, it occurred to her. She was missing her baby-food spinach and her cornflakes and untold other items on account of a total stranger. She flung open the trunk of her Plymouth.

"Oh, all right," Adrian said. "What we'll do is load these groceries very, very slowly, and by that time they'll have driven away. They didn't have so much to ring up: two steaks, two potatoes, a head of lettuce, and a box of after-dinner mints. That won't take long."

Delia was astonished at his powers of observation. She watched him arrange his bags in her trunk, after which he consumed a good half minute repositioning a small box of something. Orzo, it was—a most peculiar, tiny-sized pasta that she'd often noticed on the shelf but never bought. She had thought it resembled rice, in which case why not serve rice instead, which was surely more nutritious? She handed him the bag she was holding, and he settled that with elaborate care between the first two. "Are they coming out yet?" he asked.

"No," she said, looking past him toward the store. "Listen, I owe you some money."

"My treat."

"No, really, I have to pay you back. Only I planned to write a check and I don't have any cash. Would you accept a check? I could show you my driver's license," she said.

He laughed.

"I'm serious," she told him. "If you don't mind taking a—"

Then she caught sight of Skipper and Rosemary emerging from the supermarket. Skipper hugged a single brown paper bag. Rosemary carried nothing but a purse the size of a sandwich, on a glittery golden chain.

"Is it them?" Adrian asked.

"It's them."

He bent inside her trunk and started rearranging groceries again. "Tell me when they're gone," he said.

The couple crossed to a low red sports car. Rosemary was at least Skipper's height if not taller, and she had the slouching, indifferent gait of a runway model. If she had walked into a wall, her hipbones would have hit first.

"Are they looking our way?" Adrian asked.

"I don't think they see us."

Skipper opened the passenger door, and Rosemary folded herself out of sight. He handed in the sack of groceries and shut the door, strode to the driver's side, slid in and started the engine. Only then did he shut his own door. With a tightly knit, snarling sound, the little car spun around and buzzed off.

"They're gone," Delia said.

Adrian closed the trunk lid. He seemed older now. For the first time, Delia saw the fragile lines etched at the corners of his mouth.

"Well," he said sadly.

It seemed crass to mention money again, but she had to say, "About the check . . ."

"Please. I owe *you*," he said. "I owe you more than that. Thanks for going along with me on this."

"It was nothing," she told him. "I just wish there'd been, oh, somebody really appropriate."

"Appropriate?"

"Somebody . . . *you* know," she said. "As glamorous as your wife."

"What are you talking about?" he asked. "Why, you're very pretty! You have such a little face, like a flower."

She felt herself blushing. He must have thought she was fishing for compliments. "Anyhow, I'm glad I could help out," she said. She backed away from him and opened her car door. "Bye, now!"

"Goodbye," he said. "Thanks again."

As if he had been her host, he went on standing there while she maneuvered out of the parking slot. Naturally she made a mess of it, knowing he was watching. She cut her wheel too sharply, and the power-steering belt gave an embarrassing screech. But finally the car was free and she rolled away. Her rearview mirror showed Adrian lifting a palm in farewell, holding it steady until she turned south at the light.

Halfway home, she had a sudden realization: she should have given him the groceries he had picked out. Good heavens—all that pasta, those little grains of orzo, and now she remembered his consommé too. Consommé madrilene: she wasn't even sure how to pronounce it. She was driving away with property that belonged to someone else, and it was shameful how pleased she felt, and how lucky, and how rich.

2

The trouble with plastic bags was, those convenient handles tempted you to carry too many at once. Delia had forgotten that. She remembered halfway across her front yard, when the crooks of her fingers began to ache. She hadn't been able to bring the car around to the rear because someone's station wagon was blocking the driveway. Nailed to the trunk of the largest oak was a rusty metal sign directing patients to park on the street, but people tended to ignore it.

She circled the front porch and picked her way through the scribble of spent forsythia bushes at the side. This was a large house but shabby, its brown shingles streaked with mildew and its shutters snaggletoothed where the louvers had fallen out over the years. Delia had never lived anywhere else. Neither had her father, for that matter. Her mother, an import from the Eastern Shore, had died of kidney failure before Delia could remember, leaving her in the care of her father and her two older sisters. Delia had played hopscotch on the parquet squares in the hall while her father doctored his patients in the glassed-in porch off the kitchen, and she had married his assistant beneath the sprawling brass chandelier that reminded her to this day of a daddy longlegs. Even after the wedding she had not moved away but simply installed her husband among her sweet-sixteen bedroom furniture, and once her children were born it was not uncommon for a patient to wander out of the waiting room calling, "Delia? Where are you, darlin'? Just wanted to see how those precious little babies were getting along."

The cat was perched on the back stoop, meowing at her reproachfully. His short gray fur was flattened here and there by drops of water. "Didn't I tell you?" Delia scolded as she let him in. "Didn't I warn you the grass would still be wet?" Her shoes were soaked just from crossing the lawn, the thin soles cold and papery-feeling. She stepped out of them as soon as she entered the kitchen. "Well, hi there!" she said to her son. He sat slumped over the table in his pajamas, buttering a piece of toast. She placed her bags on the counter and said, "Fancy finding you awake so early!"

"It's not like I had any choice," he told her glumly.

He was her youngest child and the one who most resembled her, she had always thought (with his hair the light-brown color and frazzled texture of binder's twine, his freckled white face shadowed violet beneath the eyes), but last month he had turned fifteen, and all at once she saw more of Sam in him. He had shot up to nearly six feet, and his pointy chin had suddenly squared, and his hands had grown muscular and disconcertingly competent-looking. Even the way he held his butter knife suggested some new authority.

His voice was Sam's too: deep but fine-grained, not subject to the cracks and creaks his brother had gone through. "I hope you bought cornflakes," he told her.

"Why, no, I—"

"Aw, Mom!"

"But wait till you hear why I didn't," she said. "The funniest thing, Carroll! This real adventure. I was standing in the produce section, minding my own business—"

"There's not one decent thing in this house to eat."

"Well, you don't usually want breakfast on a Saturday."

He scowled at her. "Try telling Ramsay that," he said.

"Ramsay?"

"He's the one who woke me. Came stumbling into the room in broad daylight, out all night with his lady friend. No way could I get back to sleep after that."

Delia turned her attention to the grocery bags. (She knew where this conversation was headed.) She started rummaging through them as if the cornflakes might emerge after all. "But let me tell you my adventure," she said over her shoulder. "Out of the blue, this man is standing next to me. . . . Good-looking? He looked like my very first sweetheart, Will Britt. I don't believe I ever mentioned Will to you."

"Mom," Carroll said. "When are you going to let me move across the hall?"

"Oh, Carroll."

"Nobody else I know has to room with their brother."

"Now, now. Plenty of people in this world have to room with whole families," she told him.

"Not with their boozehead college-boy brother, though. Not when there's another room, perfectly empty, right across the hall."

Delia set down the box of orzo and faced him squarely. She noticed that he needed a haircut, but this was not the moment to point that out. "Carroll, I'm sorry," she said, "but I am just not ready."

"Aunt Eliza's ready! Why aren't you? Aunt Liza was Grandpa's daughter too, and she says of course I should have his room. She doesn't understand what's stopping me."

"Oh, listen to us!" Delia said gaily. "Spoiling such a pretty day with disagreements! Where's your father? Is he seeing a patient?"

Carroll didn't answer. He had dropped his toast to his plate, and now he sat tipping his chair back defiantly, no doubt adding more dents to the linoleum. Delia sighed.

"Sweetie," she said, "I do know how you feel. And pretty soon you can have the room, I promise. But not just yet! Not right now! Right now it still smells of his pipe tobacco."

"It won't once I'm living there," Carroll said.

"But that's what I'm afraid of."

"Shoot, I'll take up smoking, then."

She waved his words away with a dutiful laugh. "Anyhow," she said. "Is your father with a patient?"

"Naw."

"Where is he?"

"He's out running."

"He's what?"

Carroll picked up his toast again and chomped down on it noisily.

"He's doing *what*?"

"He's running, Mom."

"Well, didn't you at least offer to go with him?"

"He's only running around the Gilman track, for gosh sakes."

"I asked you children; I begged you not to let him go alone. What if something happens and no one's around to help?"

"Fat chance, on the Gilman track," Carroll said.

"He shouldn't be running anyway. He ought to be walking."

"Running's good for him," Carroll said. "Look. He's not worried. His doctor's not worried. So what's your problem, Mom?"

Delia could have come up with so many responses to that; all she did was press a hand to her forehead.

These were the facts she had neglected to tell that young man in the supermarket: She was a sad, tired, anxious, forty-year-old woman who hadn't had a champagne brunch in decades. And her husband was even older, by a good fifteen years, and just this past February he had suffered a bout of severe chest pain. Angina, they said in the emergency room. And now she was terrified any time he went anywhere alone, and she hated to let him drive, and she kept finding excuses not to make love for fear it would kill him, and at night while he slept she lay awake, tensing every muscle between each of his long, slow breaths.

And not only were her children past infancy; they were huge. They were great, galumphing, unmannerly, supercilious creatures—Susie a Goucher junior consumed by a baffling enthusiasm for various outdoor sports; Ramsay a Hopkins freshman on the brink of flunking out, thanks to the twenty-eight-year-old single-parent girlfriend he had somehow acquired. (And both of them, Susie and Ramsay both, were miffed beyond belief that the family finances forced them to live at home.) And Delia's baby, her sweet, winsome Carroll, had been replaced by this rude adolescent, flinching from his mother's hugs and criticizing her clothes and rolling his eyes disgustedly at every word she uttered.

Like now, for instance. Determined to start afresh, she perked all her features upward and asked, "Any calls while I was gone?" and he said, "Why would I answer the *grown-ups'* line," not bothering to add a question mark.

Because the grown-ups buy the celery for your favorite mint pea soup, she could have told him, but years of dealing with teenagers had turned her into a pacifist, and she merely padded out of the kitchen in her stocking feet and crossed the hall to the study, where Sam kept the answering machine.

The study was what they called it, and books did line the floor-to-ceiling shelves, but mainly this was a TV room now. The velvet draperies were kept permanently drawn, coloring the air the dusty dark red of an old-time movie house. Soft-drink cans and empty pretzel bags and stacks of rented videotapes littered the coffee table, and Susie lounged on the couch, watching Saturday-morning cartoons with her boyfriend, Driscoll Avery. The two of them had been dating so long that they looked like brother and sister, with their smooth beige coloring and stocky, waistless figures and identical baggy sweat suits. Driscoll barely blinked when Delia entered. Susie didn't even do that much; just flipped a channel on the remote control.

"Morning, you two," Delia said. "Any calls?"

Susie shrugged and flipped another channel. Driscoll yawned out loud. Just for that, Delia didn't excuse herself when she walked in front of them to the answering machine. She bent to press the Message button, but nothing happened. Electronic devices were always double-crossing her. "How do I—?" she said, and then an old man's splintery voice filled the room. "Dr. Grinstead, can you get back to me right away? It's Grayson Knowles, and I told the pharmacist about those pills, but he asked if—"

Whatever the pharmacist had asked was submerged by a flood of Bugs Bunny music. Susie must have raised the volume on the TV. *Beep*, the machine said, and then Delia's sister came on. "Dee, it's Eliza. I need an address. Could you please call me at work?"

"What's she doing at work on a Saturday?" Delia asked, but nobody answered.

Beep. "This is Myrtle Allingham," an old woman stated forthrightly.

"Oh, God," Susie told Driscoll.

"Marshall and I were wondering if you-all would like to take supper with us Sunday evening. Nothing fancy! Just us folks! And do tell young Miss Susie she should bring that darlin' Driscoll. Say seven o'clock?"

Beep beep beep beep beep. The end.

"We went *last* time," Susie said, slouching lower on the couch. "Count us out."

"Well, I don't know," Driscoll said. "That crab dip she served was not half bad."

"We aren't going, Driscoll, so forget it."

"She's lonesome, is all," Delia said. "Stuck at home with her hip, no way to get around—"

Something banged overhead.

"What's that?" she asked.

More bangs. Or clanks, really. *Clank! Clank!* at measured intervals, as if on purpose.

"Plumber?" Driscoll said tentatively.

"What plumber?"

"Plumber upstairs in the bathroom?"

"I never called for a plumber."

"Dr. Grinstead did, maybe?"

Delia gave Susie a look. Susie met it blandly.

"I don't know what's come over that man," Delia said. "He's been re—what's the word?—rejuvenating, resuscitating . . ." Fully aware that neither one of them was listening, she walked on out of the room, still talking. ". . . renovating, I mean: renovating this house to a fare-thee-well. If it's about that place in the ceiling, then really you'd think . . ."

She climbed the stairs, halfway up encountering the cat, who was hurrying down in a scattered, ungraceful fashion. Vernon detested loud noises. "Hello?" Delia called. She poked her head into the bathroom off the hall. A ponytailed man in coveralls crouched beside the claw-footed tub, studying its pipes. "Well, hello," she said.

He twisted around to look at her. "Oh. Hey," he said.

"What seems to be the trouble?"

"Can't say just yet," he said. He turned back to the pipes.

She waited a moment, in case he wanted to add something, but she could tell he was one of those repairmen who think only the husband worth talking to.

In her bedroom, she sat down on Sam's side of the bed, picked up the telephone, and dialed Eliza's work number. "Pratt Library," a woman said.

"Eliza Felson, please."

"Just a minute."

Delia propped a pillow against the headboard, and then she swung her feet up onto the frilled pink spread. The plumber had progressed to the bathroom between her room and her father's. She couldn't see him, but she could hear him banging around. What information could you hope to gain from whacking pipes?

"I'm sorry," the woman said, "but we can't seem to locate Miss Felson. Are you sure she's working today?"

"She must be; she told me to call her there, and she isn't here at home."

"I'm sorry."

"Well, thanks anyway."

She hung up. The plumber was whistling "Clementine." While Delia was dialing Mrs. Allingham, he ambled into the bedroom, still whistling, and she demurely smoothed her skirt around her knees. He squatted in front of the miniature door that opened onto the pipes in the wall. *Thou art lost and gone forever,* he whistled; Delia mentally supplied the words. One tug at the door's wooden knob, and it came off in his hand. She could have told him it would. She watched with some satisfaction as he muttered a curse beneath his breath and fished a pair of pliers from his belt loop.

Seven rings. Eight. She wasn't discouraged. Mrs. Allingham walked with a limp, and it took her ages to get to the phone.

Nine rings. "Hello?"

"Mrs. Allingham, it's Delia."

"Delia, dear! How *are* you?"

"I'm fine, how are you?"

"Oh, we're fine, doing just fine. Enjoying this nice spring weather! Nearly forgot what sunshine looks like, till today."

"Yes, me too," Delia said. She was overtaken suddenly by a swell of something like homesickness; Mrs. Allingham's chipper, slightly rasping voice was so reminiscent of all the women on this street where she had grown up. "Mrs. Allingham," she said, "Sam and I would love to come for supper tomorrow night, but we can't bring the children, I'm afraid."

"Oh!" Mrs. Allingham said.

"It's just that they're so busy these days. You know how it is."

"Yes, of course," Mrs. Allingham said faintly.

"But another time, maybe! They always enjoy your company."

"Yes, well, and we enjoy theirs too."

"So we'll see you at seven tomorrow," Delia said briskly, for she could hear Sam downstairs and she had a million things to do. "Goodbye till then."

By now the plumber had the little door prized open and was peering into the bowels of the wall, but she knew better than to ask him what he'd found.

In the kitchen, Sam stood propped against a counter, taking off his mud-caked running shoes. He was telling Carroll, ". . . sort of a toboggan effect when you hit those cedar chips . . ."

"Sam, how could you go off alone like that?" Delia asked. "You knew I'd worry!"

"Hello, Dee," he said.

His T-shirt was translucent with sweat, his sharp-boned face glistened, and his glasses were fogged. His hair—that shade that could be either blond or gray, it had faded so imperceptibly—lay in damp spikes on his forehead. "Look at you," Delia scolded. "You got overheated. You went running all alone and got overheated to boot when the doctor told you a dozen times—"

"Whose car is that in the driveway?"

"Car?"

"Station wagon parked in the driveway."

"Well, doesn't it belong to a patient? No, I guess not."

"Plumber," Carroll said from behind a glass of orange juice.

"Oh, good," Sam said. "The plumber's here."

He set his shoes on the doormat and started out of the kitchen, no doubt happily anticipating one of those laconic, man-to-man discussions of valves and joints and gaskets. "Sam, wait," Delia said, for she had a pang of guilt nagging at the back of her mind. "Before I forget—"

He turned, already wary.

"Mr. Knowles phoned—something to do with his pills," she said.

"I thought he got that straightened out."

"And also, um, Mrs. Allingham. She wanted to know if we could come for—"

He groaned. "No," he said, "we can't."

"But you haven't even heard yet! A light Sunday supper, she said, and I told her—"

"*I'm* sure not going," Carroll broke in.

"No, I told her that; I told her you kids were tied up. But you and I, Sam, just for—"

"We can't make it," Sam said flatly.

"But I've already accepted."

He had been on the point of turning away again, but now he stopped and looked at her.

"I know I should have checked with you first, but by accident somehow I just went ahead and accepted."

"Well, then," he said, "you'll have to call her back and unaccept."

"But, Sam!"

He left.

She looked over at Carroll. "How can he be so mean?" she asked, but Carroll just raised one eyebrow in that urbane new way she suspected him of practicing in the mirror.

Sometimes she felt like a tiny gnat, whirring around her family's edges.

The linoleum was slick and chilly beneath her feet, and she would have gone back upstairs for her slippers except that Sam and the plumber were upstairs. Instead, she turned to her grocery bags and unpacked several more boxes of pasta. Maybe she could tell Mrs. Allingham that Sam had been taken ill. That was always risky, though, when you lived in the same block and could so easily be observed, hale and hearty, stepping out to collect your morning paper or whatever. She sighed and shut a cabinet door. "When did this start happening to me?" she asked Carroll.

"Huh?"

"When did sweet and cute turn into silly and inefficient?"

He didn't seem to have an opinion.

Her sister appeared in the doorway, rolling up her shirt sleeves. "Morning, all!" she announced.

"Eliza?"

There were days when Eliza seemed almost gnomish, and this was one of them. She wore her gardening clothes—a pith helmet that all but obscured her straight black Dutch-boy bob, a khaki shirt and stubby brown trousers, and boys' brown oxfords with thick, thick soles intended to make her seem taller. (She was the shortest of the three Felson sisters.) Her horn-rimmed glasses overwhelmed her small, blunt, sallow face. "I figured I'd transplant some of those herbs before the ground dried out," she told Delia.

"But I thought you were at work."

"Work? It's Saturday."

"You called from work, I thought."

Eliza looked over at Carroll. He raised that eyebrow again.

"You called and left a message on the machine," Delia said, "asking me to find an address."

"That was ten days ago, at least. I needed Jenny Coop's address, remember?"

"Then why did I just get it off the answering machine?"

"Mom," Carroll said. "You must have been playing back *old* calls."

"Well, how is that possible?"

"You didn't have the machine turned on in the first place, see, and then when you pressed the Message button—"

"Oh, Lord," Delia said. "Mrs. Allingham."

"Is there coffee?" Eliza asked her.

"Not that I know of. Oh, Lord . . ."

She went over to the wall phone and dialed Mrs. Allingham's number. "I'm snug in bed," Eliza was telling Carroll, "thinking, *Goody, Saturday morning, I can sleep till noon*—when who should come crawling through that door in the back of my closet but another one of your father's blasted repairmen."

"Mrs. Allingham?" Delia said into the phone. "This is Delia again. Mrs. Allingham, I feel like such a dummy but it seems I got my calls mixed up and it was *last* week you invited us for. And of course last week we went, and a lovely time we had too; did I write you a thank-you note? I meant to write you a thank-you note. But *this* week we're not coming; I mean I realize now that you didn't invite us for—"

"But, Delia, darlin', we'd be happy to have you this week! We'd be happy to have you any old time, and I've already sent Marshall off to the Gourmet To Go with a shopping list."

"Oh, I'm so sorry," Delia said, but then the coffee grinder started up—a deafening racket—and she shouted, "Anyhow! We'll have to invite you to our place, very soon! Goodbye!"

She replaced the receiver and glared at Eliza.

"If only coffee tasted as good as it smells," Eliza said serenely when the grinder stopped.

Sam and the plumber were descending the stairs. Delia could hear the plumber's elasticized East Baltimore vowels; he was waxing lyrical about water. "It's the most amazing substance," he was saying. "It'll burst out one place and run twenty-five feet along the underside of a pipe and commence to dripping another place, where you least expect to see it. It'll lie in wait, it'll bide its time, it'll search out some little cranny you would never think to look."

Delia placed her hands on her hips and stood waiting. The instant the two men stepped through the door, she said, "I certainly hope you're satisfied, Sam Grinstead."

"Hmm?"

"I called back poor Mrs. Allingham and canceled supper."

"Oh, good," Sam said absently.

"I broke our promise. I ducked out of our commitment. I probably hurt her feelings for all time," Delia told him.

But Sam wasn't listening. He was following the plumber's forefinger as it pointed upward to a line of blistered plaster. And Eliza was measuring coffee, so the only one who paid any heed was Carroll. He sent Delia a look of utter contempt.

Delia turned sheepishly to her grocery bags. From the depths of one she drew the celery, pale green and pearly and precisely ribbed. She gazed at it for a long, thoughtful moment. "Aren't you clever to say so!" she heard Adrian exclaim once again, and she held the words close; she hugged them to her breast as she turned back to give her son a beatific smile.

3

"Aren't you clever to say so," he had said, and, "Why, you're very pretty!" and, "You have such a little face, like a flower." Had he meant that she had such a flowerlike face, which incidentally was little? Or had its littleness been his sole point? She preferred the first interpretation, although the second, she supposed, was more likely.

Also, he had praised her marvelous blancmange. Of course the blancmange did not really exist, but still she felt a lilt of pride, remembering that he had found it marvelous.

She studied her face in the mirror when nobody else was around. Yes, maybe it did resemble a flower. If he had been referring to those flowers that seem freckled. She had always wanted to look more dramatic, more mysterious—more adult, in fact. It had struck her as unfair that she should be wrinkling around the eyes without ever losing the prim-featured, artless, triangular face of her childhood. But evidently Adrian had considered that attractive.

Unless he had been speaking out of kindness.

She checked for his name in the phone book, but he must have had an unlisted number. She kept watch for him on the streets and in the local shops. Twice in the next three days she drove back to the super-market, on both occasions wearing the dress with the smocked, gathered front that made her seem less flat-chested. But Adrian never appeared.

And if he had, what would she have done? It wasn't that she'd fallen in love with him or anything like that. Why, she didn't even know what kind of person he was! And she certainly didn't want (as she put it to herself) "something to start up." Ever since she was seventeen, she had centered her life on Sam Grinstead. She had not so much as glanced at any other man from the moment she first met him. Even in her day-dreams, she wasn't the type to be unfaithful.

Still, whenever she imagined running into Adrian, she was conscious all at once of the light, quick way she naturally moved, and the outline of her body within the folds of her dress. She couldn't remember when she had last been so aware of herself from outside, from a distance.

At home, four workmen were installing air-conditioning—another of Sam's sudden renovations. They were slicing through floors and walls; they were running huge, roaring machines; they were lugging in metal ducts and bales of what looked like gray cotton candy. Delia could lie in bed at night and gaze straight upward through a new rectangle in the ceiling to the stark bones of the attic. She pictured bats and barn swallows swooping down on her while she slept. She fancied she could hear the house groaning in distress—such a modest, mild house, so unprepared for change.

But Sam was jubilant. Oh, he could hardly fit in his patients between visits from repairmen. Electricians, plasterers, and painters streamed through his office with estimates for the many improvements he planned. A carpenter arrived for the shutters, and a man with a spray for the mildewed shingles. Twenty-two years Sam had lived here; had he felt so critical of his surroundings all along?

He had first walked into her father's waiting room on a Monday morning in July, some three weeks after her high-school graduation. Delia had been sitting in her usual place at the desk, even though it was not her usual time (she worked afternoons, mostly), because she was so eager to meet him. She and her sisters had talked of nothing else since Dr. Felson had announced his hiring. Was this person married? they had asked, and how old was he? and what did he look like? (No, he was not married, their father said, and he was, oh, thirty-two, thirty-three, and he looked fine. Fine? Well, normal; perfectly all right, their father said impatiently, for to him what counted most was whether the man could ease his workload some—take over house calls and the morning office hours.) So Delia rose early that summer day and put on her prettiest sundress, the one with the sweetheart neckline. Then she seated herself behind the spinet desk, where she ostentatiously set to work transcribing her father's notes. At nine o'clock exactly, young Dr. Grinstead stepped through the outside door, carrying a starched white coat folded over his forearm. Sunlight flashed off his clear-rimmed, serious glasses and glazed his sifted-looking blond hair, and Delia could still recall the pang of pure desire that had caused her insides to lurch as if she had leaned out over a canyon.

Sam didn't even remember that meeting. He claimed he'd first seen her when he came to dinner. It was true there had been such a dinner, on the evening of that same day. Eliza had cooked a roast and Linda had baked a cake (both advertising their housewifely skills), while Delia, the baby, still two months short of her eighteenth birthday and supposedly not even in the running, sat across from Sam and her father in the living room and sipped a grown-up glass of sherry. The sherry had tasted like liquefied raisins and flowed directly to that powerful new root of longing that branched deeper minute by minute. But Sam claimed that when he first walked in, all three girls had been seated on the couch. Like the king's three daughters in a fairy tale, he said, they'd been lined up according to age, the oldest farthest left, and like the woodcutter's honest son, he had chosen the youngest and prettiest, the shy little one on the right who didn't think she stood a chance.

Well, let him believe what he wanted. In any case, it had *ended* like a fairy tale.

Except that real life continues past the end, and here they were with air-conditioning men destroying the attic, and the cat hiding under the bed, and Delia reading a paperback romance on the love seat in Sam's waiting room—the house's only refuge, since the office and the waiting room were air-conditioned already. Her head was propped on one arm of the love seat, and her feet, in fluffy pink slippers, rested on the other. Above her hung her father's framed Norman Rockwell print of the kindly old doctor setting his stethoscope to the chest of a little girl's doll. And behind the flimsy partition that rose not quite all the way to the ceiling, Sam was explaining Mrs. Harper's elbow trouble. Her joints were wearing out, he said. There was a stupefied silence; even the electric saw fell silent. Then, "Oh, no!" Mrs. Harper gasped. "Oh, my! Oh, my heavens above! This comes as such a shock!"

A shock? Mrs. Harper was ninety-two years old. What did she expect?

Delia would have asked. But Sam said, gently, "Yes, well, I suppose . . ." and something else, which Delia couldn't catch, for the saw just then started up again as if all at once recalling its assignment.

She turned a page. The heroine was touring the hero's vast estate, admiring its magnificent grounds and its tasteful "appointments," whatever those might be. So many of these books had wealthy heroes, Delia had noticed. It didn't matter about the women; sometimes they were rich and sometimes they were poor, but the men came complete with castles and a staff of devoted servants. Never again would the women they married need to give a thought to the grinding gears of daily life—the leaky basement, the faulty oven, the missing car keys. It sounded wonderful.

"Delia, dear heart!" Mrs. Harper cried, staggering out of the office. She was a stylish, silk-clad skeleton of a woman with clawlike hands, which she stretched toward Delia beseechingly. "Your husband tells me my joints have just ground themselves down to nubbins!"

"Now, now," Sam protested behind her. "I didn't say that exactly, Mrs. Harper."

Delia sat up guiltily and smoothed her skirt. She grew aware of the bunny ears on her slippers and the temptress on the cover of her book. "I'm so sorry, Mrs. Harper," she said. "Should I schedule another appointment?"

"No, he says I have to go to a specialist. A man I don't know from Adam!"

"Get her Peterson's phone number, would you, Dee?" Sam asked.

She rose and went over to the desk, scuffing along in her slippers. (Mrs. Harper herself wore sharp-toed high heels, which she kept planted on the rug in a herringbone pattern to show off her trim ankles.) Delia flipped through Rolodex cards arranged not by name but by specialty— allergy, arthritis. . . . Nowadays, this office served most often as a sort of clearinghouse. Her father used to deliver babies and even performed the more elementary surgeries once upon a time, but now it was largely a matter of bee shots in the spring, flu shots in the fall; and as for childbirth, why, these patients were long past the age. They were hand-me-downs from her father, most of them. (Or even, Sam joked, from her grandfather, who had opened this office in 1902, when Roland Park was still country and no one batted an eye at running a practice out of a residence.)

She copied Dr. Peterson's number onto a card and passed it to Mrs. Harper, who examined it suspiciously before tucking it into her bag. "I trust this person is not some mere snip of a boy," she told Sam.

"He's thirty if he's a day," Sam assured her.

"Thirty! My grandson is older than that! Oh, please, can't I go on seeing you instead?" But already knowing his answer, she turned without a pause toward Delia. "This husband of yours is a saint," she said. "He's just too good to exist on this earth. I hope you realize that."

"Oh, yes."

"You make sure you appreciate him, hear?"

"Yes, Mrs. Harper."

Delia watched Sam escort the old woman to the door, and then she dropped back onto the love seat and picked up her book. "Beatrice," the hero was saying, "I want you more than life itself," and his voice was rough and desperate—uncontrolled, was the way the author put it: *uncontrolled, and it sent a thrill down her slender spine within the clinging ivory satin of her negligee.*

Maybe, instead of running into Adrian, she could just sit still and let him track her down. Maybe he was even now dwelling on his image of her and cruising the streets in search of her. Or he had looked up her address, perhaps; for he did know her last name. He was parked down the block at this very moment, hoping to catch a glimpse of her.

She took to stepping into the yard several times a day. She seized any excuse to arrange herself on the front-porch swing. Never an outdoor person, and most certainly not a gardener, she spent half an hour posed in goatskin gloves among Eliza's medicinal herbs. And after someone telephoned but merely breathed and said nothing when she answered, she jumped up at every new call like a teenager. "I'll get it! I'll get it!" When there weren't any calls, she made a teenager's bargains with Fate: *I won't think about it, and then the phone will ring. I'll go out of the room; I'll pretend I'm busy and the phone will ring for sure.* Shepherding her family into the car for a Sunday visit to Sam's mother, she moved fluidly, sensuously, like an actress or a dancer conscious every minute of being watched.

But if someone really had been watching, think of what he would see: the ragged disarray of Delia's home life. Ramsay, short and stone-faced and sullen, kicking a tire in disgust; Carroll and Susie bickering over who would get a window seat; Sam settling himself behind the wheel, pushing his glasses higher on his nose, wearing an unaccustomed knit shirt that made him look weak-armed and fussy. And at the end of their trip, the Iron Mama (as Delia called her)—sturdy, plain Eleanor Grinstead, who patched her own roof and mowed her own lawn and had reared her one son single-handed in that spotless Calvert Street row house where she waited now, lips clamped tight, to hear what new piece of tomfoolery her daughter-in-law had contrived.

No, not a one of them would bear up beneath the celestial blue gaze of Adrian Bly-Brice.

The oldest of the air-conditioning men, the one named Lysander, asked what those hay-bunch things were doing, hanging from the attic rafters. "Those are my sister's herbs," Delia said. She hoped to let it rest at that, but her sister happened to be right there in the kitchen with her, stringing beans for supper, and she told him, "Yes, I burn them in little pots around the house."

"You set fire to them?" Lysander asked.

"Each one does something different," Eliza explained. "One prevents bad dreams and another promotes a focused mind and another clears the atmosphere after interpersonal strife."

Lysander looked over at Delia, raising his gray toothbrush eyebrows.

"So anyhow," Delia said hastily. "Is this job about wrapped up, do you think?"

"This one here? Oh, no," he said. He plodded toward the sink; he had come down to refill his thermos. Waiting for the water to run cold, he said, "We got several more days, at the least."

"Several days!" Delia squawked. She cleared her throat. "But the noisy part: will that be over soon? Even the cat is getting a headache."

"Now, how would you know that?" he asked.

"Oh, Delia can read a cat's mind," Eliza told him. "She's got all of us trained in cat etiquette: what kind of voice to use with them and how to do your eyes when you look at them and—"

"Eliza, I need those beans *now*," Delia broke in.

Too late, though: Lysander snorted as he set his thermos under the faucet. "Me, I'll take a dog any day," he said. "Cats are too sneaky for my taste."

"Oh, well, I like dogs too, of course," Delia said. (In fact, she was slightly afraid of dogs.) "It's just that dogs are so . . . sudden. You know?"

"But honest," Lysander said. It sounded like an accusation. "Okay if I swipe a few ice cubes?"

"Go right ahead," Delia told him.

He stood there helplessly, clasping the neck of his thermos, until she realized that he meant for her to get them. He would be one of those men who didn't know where their wives kept the spoons. She dried her hands on her apron and went to fetch the bin from the freezer.

"Last place we worked?" he said. "Putting in a new heat pump? Guy next door owned one of them attack dogs. Dog trained to attack. Lady we was working for warned us all about him."

He kept a staunch grip on his thermos while Delia tried to fit an ice cube in. It wouldn't go. She hit it with the flat of her hand (Lysander not even flinching) and, "Eek!" she cried, for the ice cube flew up in the air and then skittered across the floor. Lysander stared down at it dolefully.

"Just let me at this little devil," Delia told him, and she snatched the thermos from him and slammed it into the sink. She ran water over a second ice cube. "Aha!" she crowed, pounding it in. She started working on a third.

Lysander said, "So we're hauling in stuff from the truck one day, come to see the attack dog rounding the side of the house. Big old bristle-necked dog like a wolf, growling real deep in his throat. Lord, I thought I would die. Then out steps the lady we worked for like she had just been waiting for this. Says, 'Come along,' and takes hold of his collar, calm-natured as you please. Walks him into the yard next door and, 'Mr. What's-it?' she calls. 'I'm about to shoot your dog dead unless you come out this minute and retrieve him.' With her voice just as clear, just as cool. That was some kind of woman, believe me."

Why was he telling this story? Was it meant to show Delia up? She dispatched the third ice cube with as little commotion as possible. For some reason, she imagined that the woman had resembled Rosemary Bly-Brice. Maybe she *was* Rosemary Bly-Brice. She wore an expression of tolerant detachment; she bent in a graceful S-curve; she hooked a single finger through the dog's spiked collar. Unexpectedly, Delia felt a rush of admiration, as if her entrancement with Adrian extended to his wife as well.

She turned off the faucet, picked up the thermos, and offered it to Lysander. "Why, looky there," Lysander said. Water was dripping rapidly from the bottom of the thermos. "Why, you've gone and broke it," he said.

Delia didn't apologize. She went on offering the thermos, wishing he would just take it and leave. In the supermarket, she recalled at that instant, she had made some reference to Ramsay, and Adrian had assumed she meant her husband. No wonder he hadn't come by yet! He'd been looking for Ramsay Grinstead, who wasn't in the phone book. Sooner or later, though, he would realize his mistake. She began smiling at the thought, and she continued holding the thermos out until Eliza, clucking, rose to fetch the mop.

In the dark the phone rang twice, and Delia woke with a start. She was reviewing her children's whereabouts even before her eyes were fully open. All three were safe in bed, she decided, but her heart went on racing anyhow.

"Hello?" Sam said. "Yes, this is Dr. Grinstead. Oh. Mr. Maxwell."

Delia sighed and rolled over. Mr. Maxwell was married to the Dowager Queen of Hypochondria.

"How long has she been experiencing this?" Sam asked. "I see. Well, that doesn't sound serious. Yes, I'm sure it *is* uncomfortable, but I doubt very much if—"

A miniature babbling sound issued from the receiver.

"Of course she does," Sam said. "I understand. All right, Mr. Maxwell—if you think it's that important, I'll come take a look."

"Oh, Sam!" Delia hissed, sitting up.

He ignored her. "See you in a few minutes, then," he was telling Mr. Maxwell.

As soon as he had replaced the receiver, Delia said, "Sam Grinstead, you are such a patsy. You know it's going to be nothing. Why can't he take her to the emergency room, if she's so sick?"

"Well, neither one of them drives anymore," Sam said mildly. He swung his feet to the floor and reached for his trousers, which lay folded over the back of the rocker. As always, he'd worn tomorrow's underwear to bed and placed tomorrow's clothes conveniently at hand.

Delia pressed a palm to her heart, which was only now settling down. Was this anything like what Sam had felt with his chest pains? She kept trying to imagine. Think of him operating a car at such a time—humming along toward a meeting and then noticing his symptoms and smoothly, composedly (she pictured) turning his wheel toward Sinai Hospital. Arranging his own admission and asking a nurse to phone Delia and break the news by degrees. ("Your husband wants you to know he'll be a tad bit later getting home than planned.") And Delia, meanwhile, had been reading *Lucinda's Lover* by the fire, without a qualm.

She switched on her lamp and climbed out of bed. Two-fifteen, the alarm clock said. Squinting against the light, Sam reached for his glasses and put them on to look at her. "Where are *you* off to?" he asked. The glasses made his face seem crisper, less vague around the eyes, as if they had corrected Delia's vision rather than his.

She drew her ruffled housecoat over her nightgown and zipped the front before she answered. "I'm coming with you," she said.

"Pardon?"

"I'll take you in my car."

"Why on earth would you do that?"

"I just want to, that's why," she said. She tied her sash very tight, in hopes her housecoat would pass for streetwear. As she stepped into her flats, she could feel him staring at her, but all she said was, "Ready?" She collected her keys from the bureau.

"Delia, are you doubting my ability to drive my own car anymore?" Sam asked.

"Oh, no! What a thought!" she told him. "But I'm awake, why not come with you? Besides, it's such a nice spring night."

He didn't look convinced, but he offered no more arguments when she led the way downstairs.

It was not a nice spring night at all. It was cool and breezy, and she wished for a sweater as soon as they stepped out the back door. Towering, luminous clouds scudded across an inky sky. But she headed toward her car at a leisurely pace, resisting the urge to hunch her shoulders against the chill. The streetlights were so bright that she could see her shadow, elongated like a stick figure in a child's drawing.

"This makes me think of Daddy," she said. She had to speak up, since Sam had walked over to his Buick to retrieve his black bag. She hoped he didn't hear the shiver in her voice. "All the house calls I used to make with Daddy, just the two of us! Seems like old times."

She slid behind her steering wheel and reached across to unlock the passenger door. The air inside the car felt refrigerated. It even smelled refrigerated—dank and stale.

"Of course, Daddy never let me drive him," she said when Sam had got in. Then she worried this would give him second thoughts, and so she added, laughing slightly, "You know how prejudiced he was! Women drivers, he always said . . ." She started the engine and turned on her lights, illuminating the double doors of the garage and the tattered net of the basketball hoop overhead. "But whenever I was still up, he'd say I could come with him. Oh, I tagged along many a night! Eliza just never was interested, and Linda was so, you know, at odds with him all the time, but I was ready at a moment's notice. I just loved to go."

Sam had heard all this before, of course. He merely settled his bag between his feet while she backed the car out of the driveway.

Once they were on Roland Avenue, she said, "In fact I ought to come with you more often, now the kids are growing up. Don't you think?" She was aware that she was chattering, but she said, "It might be kind of fun! And it's not as if you go out every night, or even every week anymore."

"Delia, I give you my word I am still capable of making the odd house call without a baby-sitter," Sam told her.

"Baby-sitter!"

"I'm strong as an ox. Stop fretting."

"I'm not fretting! I just thought it would be romantic, something the two of us could do together!" she said.

This wasn't the whole truth, but as soon as she said it she started to believe it, and so she felt a bit hurt. Sam merely sat back and gazed out the side window.

There was almost no traffic at this hour, and the avenue seemed very flat and empty, shimmering pallidly beneath the streetlights as if veiled by yellow chiffon. The newly leafed trees, lit from below, had a tumbled, upside-down look. Here and there a second-floor window glowed cozily, and Delia sent it a wistful glance as they passed.

In front of the Maxwells' house, she parked. She turned off the headlights but left the engine and the heater on. "Aren't you coming in?" Sam asked.

"I'll wait in the car."

"You'll freeze!"

"I'm not dressed for company."

"Come in, Dee. The Maxwells don't care how you're dressed."

He was right, she supposed. (And the heater hadn't even started heating yet.) She took the keys from the ignition and slid out of the car to follow him up the front walk, toward the broad, columned house where those two lone Maxwells must rattle around like dice in a cup. All the windows were blazing, and the inner door stood open. Mr. Maxwell waited just inside, a stooped, bulky figure fumbling to unhook the screen as they crossed the porch.

"Dr. Grinstead!" he said. "Thank you so much for coming. And Delia too. Hello, dear."

He wore food-stained trousers belted just beneath his armpits, and a frayed gray cardigan over a T-shirt. (He used to be such a natty dresser.) Without a pause, he turned to lead Sam toward the carpeted stairs. "It breaks my heart to see her this way," he said as they started the climb. "I'd suffer in her stead, if I could."

Delia watched after them from the foyer, and when they were out of sight she sat down on one of the two antique chairs that flanked a highboy. She sat cautiously; for all she knew, the chairs were purely for show.

Overhead the voices murmured—Mrs. Maxwell's thin and complaining, Sam's a rumble. The grandfather clock facing Delia ticked so slowly that it seemed each tick might be its last. For lack of anything better to do (she had thoughtlessly left her purse at home), she fanned her keys across her lap and sorted through them.

How many hours had she sat like this in her childhood? Perched on a chair or a bottom step, scratching at the insect bites on her bare knees or leafing through a magazine some grown-up had thrust upon her before leading her father up the stairs. And overhead that same murmur, the words never quite distinguishable. When her father spoke, all others fell silent, and she had felt proud and flattered to hear how people revered him.

The stairs creaked, and she looked up. It was Mr. Maxwell, descending by himself. "Dr. Grinstead's just examining her," he said. He inched down, clinging to the banister, and when he reached the foyer he settled with a wheeze onto the other antique chair. Because the highboy stood between them, all she saw of him was his outstretched trouser legs and his leather slippers, backless, exposing maroon silk socks with transparent heels. "He says he thinks it's a touch of indigestion, but I told him, I said, at our age . . . well, you can't be too careful, I told him."

"I'm sure she'll be all right," Delia said.

"I just thank heaven for Dr. Grinstead. A lot of those younger fellows wouldn't come out like this."

"None of them would," Delia couldn't resist saying.

"Oh, some, maybe."

"None. Believe me."

Mr. Maxwell sat forward to look at her. She found his veiny, florid face peering around the highboy.

"That Sam is just too nice for his own good," she told him. "Did you know he has angina? Angina, at age fifty-five! What could that mean for his future? If it were up to me, he'd be home in bed this very minute."

"Well, luckily it's *not* up to you," Mr. Maxwell said a bit peevishly. He sat back again and there was a pause, during which she heard Mrs. Maxwell say something opinionated that sounded like "Nee-nee. Nee-nee."

"We were Dr. Grinstead's first house call—did he ever mention that?" Mr. Maxwell asked. "Yessir: very first house call. Your dad said, 'Think you'll like this boy.' I admit we were a mite apprehensive, having relied on your dad all those years."

Sam was speaking more briskly now. He must be finishing up.

"I asked Dr. Grinstead when he came to us," Mr. Maxwell said dreamily. "I said, 'Well, young man?' He'd only been on the job a couple days by then. I said, 'Well?' Said, 'Which one of those Felson girls do you plan to set about marrying?' Pretty smart of me, eh?"

Delia laughed politely and rearranged her keys.

" 'Oh,' he said; said, 'I guess I've got my eye on the youngest.' Said, 'The oldest is too short and the middle one's too plump, but the youngest,' he said, 'is just right.' So. See there? I knew before you did."

"Yes, I guess you did," Delia said, and then Sam started down the stairs, the instruments in his black bag cheerily jingling. Mr. Maxwell rose at once, but Delia stayed seated and kept her gaze fixed on her keys. They seemed uncannily distinct—dull-finished, ill-assorted, incised with brand names as clipped and choppy as words from another language.

"Just what I . . . ," Sam was saying, and, "Nothing but a touch of . . . ," and, "Left some medication on the . . ." Then he and Mr. Maxwell were shaking hands, and he said, "Dee?" and she stood up without a word and stepped through the door that Mr. Maxwell held open.

Outside, the grass had grown white with dew and the air itself seemed white, as if dawn were not far off. Delia climbed into the car and started the engine before Sam was completely settled. "You have to feel for those folks," he said, shutting his door. "Aging all alone like that, they must dwell on every symptom."

Delia swung out into the street and drove slightly above the speed limit, concentrating, not speaking. They were nearly home before she said, "Mr. Maxwell told me they were your very first house call."

"Really?"

"The second day you worked here."

"I'd forgotten."

"He said he asked which of the Felson girls you planned to marry and you said the youngest."

"Hmm," Sam said, unzipping his bag. He checked something inside and told her, "Delia, remind me tomorrow morning to pick up more—"

" 'The oldest is too short and the middle one's too plump,' you said, 'but the youngest one is just right.' "

Sam laughed.

"Did you say that?" she asked him.

"Oh, sweetie, how would I remember after all these years?"

She pulled into their driveway and turned the engine off. Sam opened his door, but then, noticing she had not moved, he looked over at her. The little ceiling bulb cast sharp hollows in his face.

"You did say it," she told him. "I recognize the fairy-tale sound of it."

"So? Maybe I did," he said. "Gosh, Dee, I wasn't weighing every word. I might have *said* 'too short' and 'too plump,' but what I probably meant was 'too unconventional' and 'too Francophile.' "

"That's not it," Delia said.

"Why, Linda spent half the evening speaking French, remember? And when your dad made her switch to English, she still had an accent."

"You don't even know what I'm objecting to, do you?" Delia asked.

"Well, no," Sam said. "I don't."

She got out of the car and walked toward the back steps. Sam went to replace his bag in the Buick; she heard the clunk of his trunk lid.

"And Eliza!" he said as he followed her to the house. "She kept asking my opinion of homeopathic medicine."

"You arrived here that very first day planning to marry one of the Felson girls," Delia told him.

She had unlocked the door now, but instead of entering she turned to face him. He was looking down at her, with his forehead creased.

"Why, I suppose it must naturally have crossed my mind," he said. "I'd completed all my training by then. I'd reached the marrying age, so to speak. The marrying stage of life."

"But then why not a nurse, or a fellow student, or some girl your mother knew?"

"My mother?" he said. He blinked.

"You had your eye on Daddy's practice, that's why," she told him. "You thought, 'I'll just marry one of Dr. Felson's daughters and inherit all his patients and his nice old comfortable house.'"

"Well, sweetheart, I probably did think that. Probably I did. But I never would have married someone I didn't love. Is that what you believe? You believe I didn't marry for love?"

"I don't know what to believe," she told him.

Then she spun around and walked back down the steps.

"Dee?" Sam called.

She passed her car without slowing. Most women would have *driven* away, but she preferred to walk. The soles of her flats gritted against the asphalt driveway in a purposeful rhythm, reminding her of some tune she could almost name but not quite. Part of her was listening for Sam (she had a sense of perking one ear backward, like a cat), but another part was glad to be rid of him and pleased to have her view of him confirmed. *Look at that, he won't even deign to come after me.* She reached the street, turned right, and kept going. Her frail-edged shadow preceded her and then drew back and then fell behind as she traveled from streetlight to streetlight. No longer did she feel the cold. She seemed warmed from inside by her anger.

Now she understood why Sam had forgotten his actual first glimpse of her. He had prepared to meet the Felson girls as a boxed set, that was why. It had not figured in his plans to encounter an isolated sample ahead of time. What *had* figured was the social occasion that evening, with marriageable maidens one, two, and three on display on the living-room couch. She could envision that scene herself now. All it took was the proper perspective to bring it back entire: the itchy red plush cushions, the clothlike texture of her frosted sherry glass, and the fidgeting, encroaching, irritating plumpness of the middle sister, next to her.

On a branch overhead, the neighborhood's silly mockingbird was imitating a burglar alarm. "Doy! Doy! Doy!" he sang in his most lyrical voice, until he was silenced by a billow of rock music approaching from the south. Teenagers, evidently—a whole carload. Delia heard their hoots and cheers growing steadily louder. It occurred to her that even Roland Park was not absolutely safe at this hour. Also, her housecoat wouldn't fool a soul. She was running around in her nightclothes, basically. She took a sudden right turn onto a smaller, darker street and walked close to a boxwood hedge, whose shadow swallowed hers.

Sam would be back in bed now, his trousers draped over the rocking chair. And the children didn't know she was missing. With their jumbled, separate schedules, they might not know for days.

What kind of a life was she leading, if every single one of last week's telephone messages could as easily be this week's?

She walked faster, hearing the carload of music fade away behind her. She reached Bouton Road, crossed over, and turned left, and one split second later, *whomp!* she collided with someone. She ran smack against a stretch of tallness and boniness, overlaid by warm flannel. "Oh!" she said, and she recoiled violently, heart pounding, while somehow a dog became involved as well, one of those shaggy hunting-type dogs shouting around her knees.

"Butch! Down!" the man commanded. "Are you all right?" he asked Delia.

Delia said, "Adrian?"

In the half-dark he had no color, but still she recognized his narrow, distinctly cheekboned face. She saw that his mouth was wider and fuller, more sculptured, than she had been imagining, and she wondered how she could have forgotten something so important. "Adrian, it's me. Delia," she said. The dog was still barking. She said, "Delia Grinstead? From the supermarket?"

"Why, Delia," Adrian said. "My rescuer!" He laughed, and the dog grew quiet. "What are *you* doing here?"

She said, "Oh, just . . . ," and then she laughed too, glancing down at her housecoat and smoothing it with her palms. "Just couldn't sleep," she said.

She was relieved to find that he was not so well dressed himself. He wore a dark-hued robe of some kind and pale pajamas. On his feet were jogging shoes, laces trailing, no socks. "Do you live nearby?" she asked him.

"Right here," he said, and he waved toward a matted screen of barberry bushes. Behind it Delia glimpsed a porch light and a section of white clapboard. "I got up to let Butch here take a pee," he said. "It's his new hobby: waking me in the dead of night and claiming he needs to go out."

At the sound of his name, Butch sat down on his haunches and grinned up at her. Delia leaned over to give his muzzle a timid pat. His breath warmed and dampened her fingers. "I ran off with your groceries that day," she said, ostensibly to the dog. "I felt terrible about it."

"Groceries?" Adrian asked.

"Your orzo and your rotini . . ." She straightened and met his eyes. "I considered hunting up your address and bringing them over."

"Oh. Well . . . orzo? Well, never mind," he told her. "I'm just grateful you helped me out like that. You must have thought I was kind of weird, right?"

"No, not at all! I enjoyed it," she said.

"You know how sometimes you just want to, say, keep up appearances in front of someone."

"Certainly," she said. "I ought to start a business: Appearances, Incorporated."

"Rent-a-Date," Adrian suggested. "Impostors To Go."

"With blondes to pose as second wives, and football stars to take jilted girls to proms—"

"And beautiful women in black to weep at funerals," Adrian said.

"Oh, why *don't* they have such things?" Delia asked. "There's just nothing like that . . . what? Like that fury, that prideful sort of fury you feel when you've been hurt or insulted or taken for granted—"

Well. She stopped herself. Adrian was watching her with such peculiar intentness, she worried all at once that she had curlers in her hair. She nearly raised a hand to check, till she remembered she hadn't worn curlers since high school. "Goodness. I should get home," she said.

"Wait!" Adrian said. "Would you like . . . could I offer you some coffee?"

"Coffee?"

"Or tea? Or cocoa? Or a drink?"

"Well," she said, "I guess cocoa, maybe. Cocoa might be nice. I mean caffeine at this hour would probably . . . But are you sure it's not too much trouble?"

"No trouble at all," he told her. "Come on inside."

He led her to a gap in the barberry bushes. A flagstone path curved toward the house, which was one of those lace-trimmed Victorian cottages young couples nowadays found so charming. The front door was paned with lozenges of glass in sugared-almond colors impossible to see through. Delia felt a sudden pinch of uneasiness. Why, she didn't know a thing about this man! And no one else on earth had any inkling where she was.

"Usually if I'm up at this hour I'm up for good," Adrian was saying, "so I fix myself a pot of—"

"What a lovely porch!" Delia exclaimed. "Maybe we could have our cocoa out here."

"Here?"

He paused on the topmost step and looked around him. It was a depressing porch, really. The floorboards were battleship gray, and the furniture was painted a harsh bright shade of green. "Don't you think you'd be cold?" he asked.

"Not a bit," she told him, although now that she had stopped walking, it did seem cold. She stuffed both fists in the pockets of her housecoat.

He gazed down at her a moment. Then he said, "Ah. I see," and the corners of his mouth quirked upward with amusement.

"But if *you're* cold . . . ," she said, flushing.

"I understand," he said. "You can't be too careful."

"Oh, it's not that! Heavens!"

"I don't blame you in the least. We'll have our cocoa out here."

"Really," she said, "why don't I come in?"

"No, you wait here. I'll bring it out."

"Please," she said. "Please let me come in."

And because she saw that the argument would otherwise go on forever, she took one hand from her pocket and laid it on his wrist. "I want to," she said.

She wanted to come in, she meant. That was what she honestly meant, but the moment the words were out of her mouth she saw that they implied something more, and she dropped her hand and stepped back. "Or maybe . . . ," she said. "Yes, the . . . porch, why don't we have our cocoa on the . . ." And she felt behind her for a chair and sat down. The icy, uncushioned seat took her breath away for an instant, as if she had heard a piece of startling news, or glimpsed some possibility that had never crossed her mind before.

4

"I told Eliza when she picked us up at the airport," Linda said. "I told her, 'Well, one good thing: now that Dad's gone I won't have to share a room with you, Eliza.' Considering how she snores."

Delia said, "Yes, but—"

" 'And the twins won't have to bunk with Susie,' I said. I figured I could fit both of them in Dad's big bed with me. Then I get to the house, and guess what."

"I did plan at first for you to stay there," Delia said, "but it seemed so . . . when I walked in to put the sheets on, it seemed so . . ."

"Fine, I'll put the sheets on myself," Linda said. "I'll tell you this much: I am surely not sleeping with Eliza when there's a whole extra room going empty."

They were standing in the doorway of their father's room at that moment, gazing in on its heartbreaking neatness, the dim air laden with dust motes, the candlewick bedspread unnaturally straight on the mattress. Linda, still in her traveling clothes, had not yet lost that aura of focus and efficiency that travel gives some people. She surveyed the room without a trace of sentiment, as far as Delia could see. "You've certainly wasted no time making changes elsewhere," she said. "Air-conditioning vents every place you look, nursery men tearing out the shrubs, I don't know *what* all."

"Oh, well, that's—"

"I suppose it's what Sam Grinstead has been waiting for," Linda said. "He's finally got the house in his clutches."

Delia didn't argue. Linda sent her a quizzical glance before crossing to their father's bureau. Leaning into the mirror above it, she raked her fingers through her short brown pageboy. Then she removed her pocketbook, which she wore bandolier style, with the strap slanted over her chest—just one more of her European ways. You would never take her for American. (You would never guess she lived in Michigan, divorced from the French-literature professor who had not, after all, swooped her off to his native Paris as she'd hoped.) Her full, soft face was powdered white, her only other makeup a bloom of sticky scarlet on her lips, and although her clothes were unexceptional, she wore them with authority—those dowdy brown medium-heeled pumps, for instance, defiantly teamed with a navy suit. "But why are we standing around? No telling what Marie-Claire and Thérèse have got into," she said, and the *r*'s in her children's names were very nearly gargled. When she whisked past Delia toward the stairs, she smelled of airplane.

In the kitchen, they found Eliza making lemonade for the twins. This fall the twins would be nine years old—a long-limbed, sproutlike stage—and although they had their mother's blocky brown haircut, they resembled the professor in every other way. Their eyes were almost black, mournfully downturned; their mouths were the color of plums. They were assisting each other up a bank of glass-fronted cabinets, the first pulling the second after her once she'd reached the counter, and for mobility's sake they had tucked their old-fashioned, European-schoolgirl dresses into their underpants, which made them look all the leggier.

"As soon as your cousin Susie shows up, she'll take you to the pool," Eliza was saying. She stood at the drainboard, reaming lemons. "She promised she'd do it first thing, but I guess she must be off someplace with her boyfriend."

The mention of a boyfriend diverted them for a second. "Driscoll?" Marie-Claire asked, pausing in her climb. "Does Susie still date Driscoll?"

"She does indeed."

"Do they go to dances together? Do they kiss good night?"

"Now, that I wouldn't know," Eliza said tartly, and she bent to take a pitcher from a cupboard.

The twins had reached their goal: a jar of peppermints on the top shelf. Inch by inch, Thérèse maneuvered it through the partially opened door. (Thérèse was the uneven-featured twin, her face less balanced, less symmetrical, which made her appear slightly anxious. There was one in every set, Delia had noticed.) For a moment the jar seemed suspended, but then it arrived safely in Marie-Claire's outstretched hands. "Do Ramsay and Carroll have sweethearts too?" she asked.

"Well, Ramsay does, I'm sorry to say."

"How come you're sorry?" Thérèse asked, and Marie-Claire said, "What's wrong with her?"—the two of them so alert for scandal that Delia laughed aloud. Thérèse wheeled and said, "Are you sorry too, Aunt Delia? Do you forbid her to darken your door? Is she coming to the beach with us?"

"No, she's not," Delia said, answering only the easiest question. "The beach is just a family trip."

They were leaving for a week at the beach early the following morning, a Sunday. It had come to be an annual event. In mid-June, as soon as the schools closed, Linda arrived from Michigan and they all took off for a cottage they rented on the Delaware shore. Already the front porch was heaped with rubber rafts and badminton rackets; the freezer was stuffed with casseroles; and Sam's patients were thronging in for last-minute consultations in hopes of avoiding any contact with his backup.

"Delia, could you get the sugar?" Eliza asked. She was running water into the pitcher. "And girls, I'd like five tumblers from that cabinet to your right."

While Delia was measuring sugar, she secretly checked the clock on the wall above her. Ten minutes till four. She glanced at the twins and cleared her throat. "If Susie isn't back by the time you finish your lemonade, maybe I could take you to the pool," she said.

Linda said, "You?" and the twins said, in a single voice, "You *hate* to swim!"

"Oh, well, I wouldn't actually go in. I'd just drive you over, and then Susie could pick you up later."

Eliza clinked ice into the tumblers. Linda took a seat at the head of the table, and the twins claimed the chairs on either side of her. When Delia placed the pitcher of lemonade in front of them, Marie-Claire cried, "Ick! It's full of shreddy things!"

"Those are good for you," Linda said as she started pouring.

"And big seeds besides!"

"They won't hurt you."

"That's what *she* says," Thérèse told Marie-Claire in an ominous tone. "Really they'll take root in your stomach and grow lemon trees out your ears."

"Oh, honestly, Thérèse," Linda said.

Ignoring her, the twins gazed significantly across the table at each other. Finally Marie-Claire said, "I guess we're not thirsty after all."

"We'll just go change into our swimsuits," Thérèse added.

They scooted their chairs back and raced out of the kitchen.

"Ah, me," Linda sighed. "Sorry, Lize."

"That's all right," Eliza said stiffly.

There were times when Delia realized, for an instant, that Eliza was what they used to call an old maid. She looked so forlorn in her eccentric weekend outfit of safari suit and clunky shoes; she pulled out a chair with her head down, her chopped black hair falling forward to hide her expression, and she seated herself and folded her small hands resolutely on the table.

"Well, *I'm* thirsty!" Delia said loudly, and she sat down too and reached for one of the tumblers. From the hall she heard a series of thumps—the twins' suitcase, no doubt, being hauled up the stairs. Apparently they still planned to room with Susie, if the creaks that began overhead were any indication.

Outside the open window, a workman's bearded face popped into view. He looked at the women, blinked, and disappeared. Delia and Linda saw him, but Eliza, who had her back to him, did not. "What is he up to, anyhow?" Linda asked.

Eliza said, "He? Who?"

"The workman," Delia explained.

"No, not the workman," Linda said. "I meant Sam. Why is he having all the shrubs torn out?"

"Well, they're old and straggly, he says."

"Can't he just cut them back or something? And central air-conditioning! This house is not the type for air-conditioning."

"I'm sure we'll appreciate it once the weather heats up," Eliza said. "Have some lemonade, Linda."

Linda took a tumbler, but she didn't drink from it. "I'd just like to know where he found the money," she said darkly. "Plus: this house is in *our* three names, not his. We're the ones Dad left it to."

Delia glanced toward the window. (She suspected the workman of lurking beneath it, absorbed as all workmen seemed to be in other people's private lives.) "Goodness!" she said. "We'd better get to the pool. Anybody want anything from Eddie's?"

"Eddie's?" Eliza asked.

"I might stop for some fruit on my way home."

"Delia, have you forgotten Sam's mother is coming to dinner? And you still have the Medicare bills to see to! Why don't I take the twins, instead, and then go to Eddie's after."

"No! Please!" Delia said. "I mean, I have plenty of time. And besides, I need to choose the fruit myself because I'm not sure what I—"

She was offering too many explanations—always a mistake. Linda didn't notice, but Eliza could read her mind, Delia sometimes thought, and she was watching Delia consideringly. "Anyhow," Delia said. "I'll see you both in a while. Okay?" And she stood up. Already she heard the twins racketing down the stairs. "Hand me my purse, will you?" she asked. Eliza was still watching her, but she reached for Delia's purse on the counter and passed it over.

In the hall, the twins were quarreling over a pair of goggles they must have liberated from the beach equipment. They wore identical skinny knit swimsuits in different colors—one red, one blue—and a red-and-blue flip-flop apiece on their long, pale, knobby feet. Neither one had a towel, but the towels were upstairs and so Delia didn't remind them. "Let's go," she told them. "I'm parked out front." From the kitchen, Linda called, "You do what the lifeguard tells you, girls, hear?"

Delia followed them across the porch, avoiding the shaft of a beach umbrella. Beside the steps, a young man in a red bandanna was hacking at the roots of an azalea bush. He straightened, wiped his face on his forearm, and gave them a grin. "Wisht I was going swimming," he said.

"Come with us, then," Thérèse said, but Marie-Claire told her, "Dope, you can see he's not wearing his bathing suit." They skipped ahead of Delia down the walk, chanting a routine that she remembered from her childhood:

"Well, that's life."

"*What's* life?"

"Fifteen cents a copy."

"But I only have a dime."

"Well, that's life."

"*What's* life?"

"Fifteen cents a . . ."

The weather was perfect, sunny and not too warm, but Delia's car had been sitting at the curb collecting heat all day. Both girls squealed as they slid across the back seat. "Could you turn on the air-conditioning?" they asked Delia.

"I don't have air-conditioning."

"Don't have air-conditioning!"

"Just open your windows," she told them, rolling down her own. She started the engine and pulled into the street. The steering wheel was almost too hot to touch.

You could tell it was a weekend, because so many joggers were out. And people were at work in their yards, running their mowers or their hedge trimmers, filling the air with a visible green dust that made Thérèse (the allergic one) sneeze. At Wyndhurst the traffic light changed to amber, but Delia didn't stop. She had a sense of time slipping away from her. She took the long downhill slope at a good ten miles above the speed limit, and screeched left on Lawndale and parked in the first available space. The twins were in a hurry themselves; they tore ahead of her to the gate, and even before she paid for them they had disappeared among the other swimmers.

Driving back up the hill, she kept plucking at the front of her blouse and blowing toward the damp frizz sticking to her forehead. If only she could stop by home and freshen up a bit! But she would never manage to escape her sisters a second time. She turned south, not so much as glancing northward to Eddie's. She traveled through a blessedly cool corridor of shade trees, and when she reached Bouton Road she parked beneath a maple. Before she got out, she blotted her face on a tissue from her purse. Then she walked through Adrian's front yard and climbed the porch steps and rang the doorbell.

By now the dog knew her well enough so he merely roused himself from the mat to nose her skirt. "Hi, Butch," she said. She dabbed at his muzzle ineptly, at the same time backing off a bit. The front door opened, and Adrian said, "Finally!"

"I'm sorry," she told him, stepping inside. "I couldn't get away till Linda came, and wouldn't you know her plane was late, and then of course I had to make sure that she and the children were . . ."

She was talking too much, but she couldn't seem to stop herself. These first few minutes were always so awkward. Adrian took her purse from her and set it on a chair, and she fell silent. Then he bent and kissed her. She supposed she must taste of salt. They had not been kissing for very long—at least not like this, so seriously. They had started with the breeziest peck on the cheek, pretending to be just friends; then day by day more parts of them became involved—their lips, their open mouths, their arms around each other, their bodies pressing closer until Delia (it was always Delia) drew back with a little laugh and a "Well!" and some adjustment of her clothes. "Well! Did you get much work done?" she asked now. He was looking down at her, smiling. He wore khakis and a faded blue chambray shirt that matched his eyes. Over these past few weeks of sunshine his hair had turned almost golden, so that it seemed to give off a light of its own as he stood in the dark hallway—one more detail to make her spin away abruptly and walk on into the house as if she had some business to attend to.

Adrian's house always struck her as only marginally inhabited, which was odd because until three months ago his wife had lived here too. Why, then, did the rooms have this feeling of long-term indifference and neglect? The living room, viewed from the hall, never enticed her inside. Its walls were bare except for a single bland still life above the mantel, and instead of a couch, three chairs stood at offended-looking angles to each other. The tabletops bore only what was useful—a lamp, a telephone; none of the decorative this-and-thats that would have taken the chill off.

"I finished printing out the Adwater piece," Adrian was saying. "I thought you might look it over and tell me what you think."

He was leading her up the narrow stairway and across the hall, into an area that must once have been called the conservatory or the sunroom. Now it was his office. Cloudy windows lined three walls, their sills piled high with papers. Along the fourth wall ran a built-in desk that held various pieces of computer equipment. This was where Adrian produced his newsletter. Subscribers from thirty-four states paid actual money for *Hurry Up, Please*, a quarterly devoted to the subject of time travel. Its cover was a glossy sky blue, its logo an arched wooden mantel clock on spoked wheels. Each issue contained an assortment of science fiction and nonfiction, as well as reviews of time-machine novels and time-machine movies, and even an occasional cartoon or joke. In fact, was this whole publication a joke, or was it for real? Reading the letters to the editor, Delia often wondered. Many of the subscribers seemed to believe in earnest. At least a few claimed to speak from personal experience. And she detected an almost anthropological tone to the article Adrian handed her now—an essay by one Charles L. Adwater, Ph.D., proposing that the quality known as "charisma" was merely the superior grace and dash found in visitors from the future who are sojourning in the present. *Consider*, Dr. Adwater wrote, *how easily you and I would navigate the 1940s, which today seems a rather naive period, by and large, and one in which a denizen of our own decade could hope to make a considerable impact with relatively little effort.*

"Would you say the 1940s seems, or the 1940s seem?" Adrian asked. "Either one has arguments for and against it."

Delia didn't answer. She paced the room as she read, chewing her lower lip, squinting at draft-quality print as dotty and sparse as the scabs on an old brier scratch. "Well . . . ," she said, and pretending absent-mindedness, she wandered out to the hall while she flipped to the second page.

Adrian followed. "In my opinion, Adwater's style is kind of stuffy," he was saying, "but I can't suggest too many changes because he's one of the biggest names in the field."

How would you make a name for yourself in the time-travel field? Delia was intrigued, but only briefly. Her visit to Adrian's office was a ruse, in fact, as even Adrian must know. It was being upstairs that mattered: roaming the second floor, the *bedroom* floor, and peeking through each doorway. Adrian slept in a drab little dressing room; he had moved there after Rosemary left him, so Delia felt free to stroll into the master bedroom while flipping to page three. She went over to stand near a bureau—just trying to get more reading light from the window above it, she could argue. Behind her, Adrian straightened her collar. His fingers made a whispery sound. "Why do you always wear a necklace?" he asked, very close to her ear.

"Hmm?" she said in a small voice. She turned another page, blindly.

"You always wear a string of pearls, or a cameo, or today this heart-shaped locket. Always something snug around your throat, and these little round innocent collars."

"It's only habit," she said, but her thoughts were racing. Did he mean that she looked silly, unsuited to her age?

He had never asked how old she was, and although she wouldn't have lied to him, she didn't feel any need to volunteer the truth. When he'd told her that he himself was thirty-two, she had said, "Thirty-two! Young enough to be my son!"—a deliberate exaggeration, calculated to make him laugh. She had not mentioned the ages of her children, even. Nor had he inquired, for like most childless people, he seemed ignorant of the enormous space that children occupy in a life.

Also, he had a slightly skewed image of her husband. She could tell from some of his remarks that he was picturing Sam as beefy and athletic (because he jogged) and perhaps possessed of a jealous disposition. And Delia had not set him straight.

All it would take was bringing the two men together once—inviting Adrian for supper, say, as a neighbor left wifeless and forced to cook for himself—and the situation would lose all its potential for drama. Sam would start referring to "your pal Bly-Brice," in that sardonic way of his; the children would roll their eyes if she talked to him too long on the phone. But Delia made no move to arrange such a meeting. She had not so much as spoken his name to anyone in her family. And when Adrian's hands left her collar to settle on both her shoulders and draw her closer, she didn't resist but tipped her head back to rest it against his chest. "You're such a little person," he said. She heard the rumble of his voice within his rib cage. "You're so little and dainty and delicate."

Compared with his wife, she supposed he meant; and the notion pulled her upright. She walked away from him, briskly realigning pages. She circled the bed (Rosemary's bed! covered with a rather seedy sateen quilt) and approached the closet. "What I want to know," she said over her shoulder, "is can you really make a living this way? Because a magazine like yours is kind of specialized, isn't it?"

"Oh, I'm not so much as breaking even," Adrian told her offhandedly. "Pretty soon I'll have to fold, I guess. Switch to something new. But I'm used to that. Before this, I published a bulletin for rotisserie-baseball owners."

The closet was filled with Rosemary's clothes—tops, then dresses, then pants, so there was an orderly progression from short to long; and they hung evenly spaced, not bunched together as in Delia's closet. According to Adrian, Rosemary had abandoned every single one of her possessions when she left. All she took was the black silk jumpsuit she was wearing and a slim black purse tucked under her arm. Why did Delia find that so alluring? This was not the first time she had stood mesmerized in front of Rosemary's closet.

"And before that," Adrian said, "I had a quarterly for M*A*S*H fans." He was behind her again. He reached out one finger to stroke the point of her bent elbow.

Delia said, "How've you been supporting yourself all this time?"

"Well, Rosemary had a bit of an inheritance."

She closed the closet door. She said, "Did you know that before you married her?"

"Why do you ask?"

"Lately I've been wondering if Sam married me for my father's practice," she said.

She shouldn't have told him. Adrian would look at her and think, *Yes, she is rather homely, and her elbows are chapped besides.*

But he smiled and said, "If it were me, I'd have married you for your freckles."

She went over to Rosemary's side of the bed. She knew it was Rosemary's because a blown-glass perfume bottle sat next to the lamp. First she laid Dr. Adwater's article on the nightstand, and then, as if it were the logical next step, she opened the little drawer underneath. She gazed into a clutter of manicure scissors, emery boards, and nail polish bottles.

How fitting, the name Rosemary! Rosemary was such a sophisticated herb, so sharp-tasting, almost chemical. Put too much in a recipe, and you'd swear you were eating a petroleum product. There was nothing plain about it, nothing mild or dull. Nothing freckled.

Adrian came up behind her. He turned her to face him and wrapped his arms around her, and this time she didn't move away but set her hands at his waist and strained upward to meet his kisses. He kissed her mouth, her eyelids, her mouth once more. He whispered, "Lie down with me, Delia."

Then the phone rang.

He didn't seem to hear it; he never heard it. And he never answered it. He said it was his mother-in-law, who liked him better than she liked her own daughter and was always trying to get them back together. "How do you know it's not Rosemary?" Delia once asked, and Adrian, shrugging, said, "The telephone isn't Rosemary's instrument of choice." Now he didn't flinch, didn't even tense. Delia would have felt it if he had. He kissed the curve where her neck met her shoulder, and she began to notice the bed pressing the backs of her knees. But the phone continued to ring. Ten rings, eleven. Subconsciously, she must be counting. The realization enabled her, somehow, to pull away, although she felt that she was dragging her limbs through water. "Oh, my," she said, out of breath, and she made a great business of tucking her blouse more securely into her skirt. "I really should be . . . did I leave my purse downstairs?"

He was out of breath too. He didn't speak. She said, "Yes, I remember! On the chair. I have to hurry; Sam's mother is coming to dinner."

Meanwhile she was clattering down the stairs. The extension phone in the living room was on its fourteenth ring. Its fifteenth. She reached the front hall and seized her purse and turned at the door to say, "You know we're leaving tomorrow for—"

"You never stay," he said. "You're always rushing off as soon as you get here."

"Oh, well, I—"

"What are you afraid of?"

I'm afraid of getting undressed in front of someone thirty-two years old, she did not say. She smiled up at him, falsely. She said, "I'll see you after the beach, I guess."

"Can't you ever manage a solid block of time? A whole night? Can't you tell them you're visiting one of your girlfriends?"

"I don't have a girlfriend," she said.

She really didn't, come to think of it. When she married Sam she had switched generations and left everyone behind, all her old high-school classmates. "Although it's true there's Bootsy Fisher," she said. (Whom Sam called Bootsy Officious: the thought rose out of nowhere.) "Her kids and mine used to carpool."

"Can't you say you're at Bootsy's?"

"Oh, no, I don't see how I—"

And then, because she guessed from the way his mouth seemed to soften that he was about to kiss her again, she gave him a fluttery wave and hurried out the door, nearly tripping over Butch on the mat.

Funny, she thought, as she settled herself in her car, how often lately her high-school days came to mind. It must be this dizzy, damp, rumpled feeling as she rushed home from secret meetings; her telltale flushed cheeks, the used and smushed look of her lips when she risked a glance in the rearview mirror. At a stop sign she made sure that all her buttons were buttoned, and she patted her locket into place between her collar-bones. Once again she heard Adrian say, "Why do you always wear a necklace?" And then, "Lie down with me, Delia," and just as in her high-school days, she felt stirred even more by the memory than by the event itself. If she hadn't already been seated, her legs might have buckled.

Maybe she *could* say she was visiting Bootsy. Not for a whole night, of course, but for an evening. Certainly no one in her family would bother checking up on her.

She parked in the driveway, which was clear now of all cars except for Sam's. Smoke billowed from the yard on the other side of the house. He must be firing up the grill for dinner.

She followed the trail of smoke to the little flagstone rectangle beneath the office windows. Yes, there he was, peering at the grill's thermometer with his glasses raised. He still wore his shirt and tie and his suit trousers, minus his white coat. He looked so professional that Delia felt a flash of anxiety. Didn't he know everything? But when he straightened, lowering his glasses, all he said was, "Hi, Dee. Where've you been?"

"Oh, I was . . . running a few errands," she said.

She was amazed that he didn't ask why, then, she had returned empty-handed. He just nodded and tapped the thermometer with his index finger.

Climbing the steps to the kitchen door, she felt like a woman emerging from a deep, thick daytime sleep. She walked past Eliza and drifted toward the hall. "Are you going to grill the vegetables too? Or put them in the oven?" Eliza called after her.

There wouldn't be space for them on the grill. They would have to go in the oven, and she meant to say as much to Eliza but forgot, lost the words, and merely floated into the study. It was unoccupied, thank heaven. She didn't believe she could have waited till she reached the phone upstairs. She lifted the receiver, dialed Adrian's number, let his phone ring twice, and then hung up—her way of letting him know that this was not his mother-in-law. She redialed, and he answered half-way through the first ring. "Is that you?" he asked. His voice sounded urgent, intense. She sank onto a footstool and gripped the receiver more tightly.

"Yes," she whispered.

"Come back here, Delia."

"I wish I could."

"Come back and stay with me."

"I want to. I do want to," she said.

Sam's mother said, "Delia?"

Delia slammed the phone down and jumped to her feet. "Eleanor!" she cried. She thrust her hands in the folds of her skirt to hide their tremor. "I was just—I was just—"

"Sorry to barge in," Eleanor said, "but nobody answered the door." She advanced to kiss the air near Delia's ear. She smelled of soap; she was an unperfumed, unfrilled woman, sensibly clad in a drip-dry shirtdress and Nikes, with a handsome face and clipped white monkish hair. "Didn't mean to interrupt your conversation."

"No, I was just winding it up," Delia told her.

"It appears that someone has left some articles on your front porch."

"Articles?"

Delia had a fleeting vision of Dr. Adwater's article on charisma.

"Badminton sets and rafts and such, scattered all about where anyone might stumble on them."

Eleanor was the kind of guest who felt it her duty to point out alarming flaws in the household. How long had their toilet been making that noise? Did they know they had a tree limb about to come down? Delia always countered by pretending that she was a guest herself. "Imagine that!" she said. "Let me take you to Sam. He's out by the grill."

"Now, I thought you weren't going to any fuss," Eleanor told her, leading the way from the study. Instead of a purse, she had one of those belt packs, glow-in-the-dark chartreuse nylon, riding in front of her stomach like some sort of add-on pregnancy. It caused her to walk slightly swaybacked, although ordinarily her posture was perfect.

"I'm only serving grilled chicken," Delia said as they crossed the hall. "Nothing complicated."

"Tinned soup would have been plenty," Eleanor said. She eyed a browning apple core centered on the newel post. "Particularly in view of all you need to do for your beach trip."

Did she mean this as a reproach? Every year, Sam suggested inviting his mother along to the beach, and every year Delia talked him out of it, which was why they always held this placatory family dinner the night before they left. It wasn't that Delia disliked his mother. She knew that Eleanor was admirable. She knew that she herself would never have coped so magnificently in Eleanor's circumstances—widowed early, forced to take a secretarial job to support herself and her young son. (And to hear Sam tell it, his father had not been much use anyhow—a weak and ineffectual, watery sort of man.) The trouble was, in Eleanor's presence Delia felt so inadequate. She felt so frivolous and spendthrift and disorganized. Their vacation was the one time she could hope to shake off that feeling.

Besides, she couldn't imagine the Iron Mama lolling on a beach towel.

"Did Linda get here?" Eleanor was asking as they entered the kitchen. "Are the twins just huge? Where are they all?"

It was Eliza, standing at the sink, who answered. "The twins are at the pool," she said. "Linda just left with Susie to fetch them home. How're you doing, Eleanor?"

"Oh, couldn't be better. Is that asparagus I see? Delia, my word, do you know what asparagus *costs*?"

"I found some on sale," Delia lied. "I'm going to roast it in the oven in this new way, really simple. No fuss," she added craftily.

"Well, if your idea of simple is asparagus and roast squab!"

"Chicken, actually."

"Just an old withered carrot would have been good enough for me," Eleanor said.

She headed for the back door, with Delia meekly shadowing her.

In the side yard, Sam was tinkering with the grill knobs. "Looks about the right temperature," he told Delia. "Hello, Mother. Good to see you."

"What's going on with the shrubbery, son?" Eleanor asked, looking past him.

"We're having it taken out," he said. "Putting in a whole new bunch of plantings."

"Why, that must cost a fortune! Couldn't you just work with what you had, for gracious sake?"

"We wanted totally new," Sam told her. (*We?* Delia thought.) "We're tired of working with what we had. Dee, believe I'm ready to start cooking."

As Delia walked toward the house, she heard Eleanor say, "Well, I don't know, son. This life of yours seems mighty rich for *my* blood, what with asparagus for dinner and grilled pheasant."

"Chicken!" Delia called back.

Eliza must have heard too, for she was grinning to herself when Delia opened the screen door. "You bring it to him," Delia told her. "I can't stand another minute."

"Oh, now, you take her too much to heart," Eliza said as she went over to the refrigerator. Eliza seemed to find Eleanor merely amusing. But then, Eliza wasn't Eleanor's daughter-in-law. She didn't have Eleanor held up before her daily as a paragon of thrift, with her professional-quality tool chest and her twelve-column budget book and her thrice-used, washed-and-dried sandwich bags.

Did it ever occur to Sam that Delia and his father might well have been kindred spirits?

She gathered up the silverware, ten of everything, and went into the

dining room. Here the sounds from the yard were muted, and she could
let her mind return to Adrian. She traveled around the table, doling out
knives and forks and remembering the rustle of Adrian's fingers on her
collar, his warm breath when he kissed her. But she could no longer
truly feel the kiss, she discovered. Eleanor's interruption must have startled all feeling out of her, as in the old days when the telephone rang
while she and Sam were making love and she had lost her place, so to
speak, and not been able to fall back into it afterward.

She returned to the kitchen and found Eliza pondering in front of
the glassware cupboard. "Which do we want?" Eliza asked her. "Iced
tea or wine?"

"Wine," Delia answered promptly.

From the side yard, Eleanor's confident voice came sailing: "Have
you checked the price of asparagus lately?"

"Pretty steep, is it," Sam said equably.

"Sky-high," Eleanor told him. "But that's what we're having for
dinner tonight: asparagus and grilled peacock."

Eliza was the only one who laughed.

Supper was late, for one reason or another. First Linda and Susie took
forever bringing the twins from the pool, and then Ramsay didn't appear
till seven although he'd promised faithfully to be home by six, and when
he did show up he had his girlfriend in tow and her wan and silent six-
year-old daughter. This enthralled the twins, of course, but Delia was
furious. It had been understood that tonight would be strictly family.
However, she didn't have quite what it took to face Ramsay down in
public. Seething inwardly, she scrunched two extra, mismatched place
settings in among the others before she called everyone to the table.

Velma, the girlfriend, was a tiny, elfin woman with a cap of glassy
hair and a pert little figure set off by trim white shorts. Delia could see
what her appeal was, sort of. For one thing, when she entered the dining
room she went straight to one of the orphan place settings, as if she were
accustomed to existing on the edges of events. And for another, she was
so inexhaustibly vivacious that even Carroll—surly Carroll—brightened
in her presence, and Sam made a point of giving her the largest piece
of chicken. ("Got to put some meat on your bones," he said—not his
type of remark at all.) Then she endeared herself to Linda by marveling
at the twins' names. "I'm crazy about things that sound French—I guess

you can tell from me naming my daughter Rosalie," she said. "Shoot, I'd like to *go* to France. The furtherest I've been is Hagerstown a few times for hair shows."

Velma was a beautician. She worked in one of those unisex places, which was how she and Ramsay had met. He had come in for a haircut and invited her on the spot to a tea at the house of his freshman adviser. Now he sat proudly next to her, one arm resting on the back of her chair, and beamed around the table at his family. Short though he was (he took after Delia's father), he seemed manly and imposing alongside Velma.

"Although last fall I did attend a color conference in Pittsburgh," Velma was recalling. "I stayed overnight and left Rosalie with my mother."

Rosalie, perched behind the other odd plate, raised her enormous, liquid eyes and gave Velma a look that struck Delia as despairing.

"Everybody in our whole entire shop has been trained to do your colors," Velma went on. Was she speaking to Eleanor, of all people? Eleanor nodded encouragingly, wearing her most gracious expression.

"Some people ought to wear cool colors and some people ought to wear warm," Velma told her, "and they should never, ever cross over, though you'd be shocked at how many try."

"Would that be determined by temperament, dear?" Eleanor asked.

"Ma'am?"

But Eleanor was sidetracked just then by the plate that Sam was filling for her. "Oh, mercy, Sam," she said, "not such a great big helping!"

"I thought you asked for a breast."

"Well, I did, but just a little one. That one's way too big for me."

He forked another and held it up. "This okay?"

"Oh, that's huge!"

"Well, there's nothing smaller, Mother."

"Can't you just cut it in half? I could never manage to eat all that."

He put it back on the platter to cut it.

"This one lady," Velma told the others, "she was wearing pink when she came in and I'm like, 'Lady, you are so, so wrong. You should be all in cools,' I tell her, 'with the tone of skin you got.' She says, 'Oh, but that's why I head for warm.' Says, 'I go for what's my opposite.' I could not believe her. I really could not believe her."

"Sam, dear, that's about six times as much asparagus as I can possibly handle," Eleanor said.

"It's three spears, Mother. How can I give you a sixth of that?"

"I just want a half a spear, if it isn't too much trouble."

"You, now," Velma told Eliza, "you would look stunning in magenta. With your coal-black hair? That tan color doesn't do a thing for you."

"However, I'm partial to tan," Eliza said in her declarative way.

"And Susie, I bet you had your colors done already. Right? That aqua's real becoming."

"It was the only thing not in the laundry," Susie said. But she was fighting down a pleased expression around the mouth.

"I dress Rosalie in nothing *but* aqua, just about. She turns washed out in any other color."

"Sam, I hate to be a nuisance," Eleanor said, "but I'm going to send my plate back to you so you can take a teensy little bit of that potato salad off and give it to someone else."

"Well, why not just keep it, Mother."

"But it's much too large a helping, dear."

"Then eat what you can and leave the rest, why don't you."

"Now, you know how I hate to waste food."

"Oh, just force yourself to choke the damn stuff down, then, Mother!"

"Goodness," Eleanor said.

The telephone rang.

Delia said, "Carroll, would you answer that? If it's a patient, tell them we're eating."

Not that she imagined a patient could be so easily dissuaded.

Carroll slouched off to the kitchen, muttering something about the grown-ups' phone, and Delia took a bite of her drumstick. It was dry and stringy as old bark from being kept warm in the oven too long.

"For you, Mom," Carroll said, poking his head through the door.

"Well, see who it is and ask if I can call back."

"He says it's about a time machine."

"Oh!"

Sam said, "Time machine?"

"I'll just be a minute," Delia said, setting aside her napkin.

"Someone wants to sell you a *time* machine?" Sam asked her.

"No! Not that I know of. Or, I don't know . . ." She sank back in her seat. "Tell him we don't need a thing," she told Carroll.

Carroll withdrew his head.

It seemed to Delia that her one bite of chicken was stuck halfway down her throat. She picked up the basket of rolls and said, "Thérèse? Marie-Claire? Take one and pass them on, please."

When Carroll returned to the table, she didn't so much as glance at him. She sent the butter plate after the rolls, and only then looked up to face Eliza's steady gaze.

It was Eliza she had to watch out for. Eliza was uncanny sometimes.

"This china belonged to your great-grandmother," Linda was telling the twins. "Cynthia Ramsay, her name was. She was a famous Baltimore beauty, and the whole town wondered why she ever said yes to that short, stumpy nobody, Isaiah Felson. But he was a doctor, you see, and he promised that if she married him she would never get TB. See, just about her whole family had died of TB. So sure enough, she married him and moved out to Roland Park and stayed healthy as a horse all her days and bore two healthy children besides, one of them your grandpa. You remember your grandpa."

"He wouldn't let us roller-skate in the house."

"Right. Anyhow, your great-grandmother ordered her wedding china all the way from Europe, these very plates you are eating from tonight."

"Except for Rosalie," Marie-Claire said.

"What, sweet?"

"*Rosalie's* plate is not wedding china."

"No, Rosalie's comes from Kmart," Linda said, and she passed the butter to Eleanor, not noticing how Rosalie's eyes started growing even more liquid.

"Heavens, no butter for *me*, dear," Eleanor said.

Why had he phoned her? Delia wondered. How unlike him. He must have had something crucial to tell her. She should have taken the call.

She would go to the kitchen for water or something and call him back.

Grabbing the water pitcher, she stood up, and just then the doorbell rang. She froze. Her first, heart-pounding thought was that this was Adrian. He had come to take her away; he would no longer listen to reason. A whole scenario played itself out rapidly in her mind—her family's bewilderment as she allowed herself to be led from the house, her journey through the night with him (in a horse-drawn carriage, it seemed), and their blissful life together in a sunlit, whitewashed room on some Mediterranean shore. Meanwhile Sam was saying, "I've told them and told them . . . ," and he rose and strode out to the hall, apparently assuming that this was a patient. Well, maybe it was. Delia remained on her feet, straining to hear. One of the twins said, "*Rosalie's* napkin is plain old paper," and Delia had an urge to bat her voice away physically.

It was a woman. An elderly, querulous woman, saying something unintelligible. So. A patient after all. Delia felt more relieved than she would have expected. She said, "Well! Anybody want anything from the kitchen?" But before she could turn to go, Sam was ushering in his visitor.

Easily past seventy, doughy and wrinkled beneath her heap of dyed black curls and her plastering of red rouge and dark-red lipstick, the woman advanced on absurdly small, open-toed shoes that barely poked forth from the hem of her shapeless black dress. She was clutching a drawstring purse in both fat, ringed hands, and diamond teardrops swung from her long earlobes. All of this Delia somehow took in while at the same time registering Sam's astonished face just beyond the woman's shoulder. "Dee?" he said. "This person's saying—"

The woman asked, "Are you Mrs. Delia Grinstead?"

"Well, yes."

"I want you to leave my daughter's husband alone."

Around the table there was a sort of snapping to attention. Delia sensed it, even though she forced her eyes to remain on the woman. She said, "I can't imagine what you're talking about."

"You know who I mean! My son-in-law, Adrian Bly-Brice. Or don't you even keep track? Have you collected so many paramours you can't tell one from another?"

Somebody snickered. Ramsay. Delia felt slightly affronted by this, but she made herself focus on the issue at hand. She said, "Mrs., um, really I . . ."

She hated how little-girlish her voice came out.

"That is a happy marriage you're destroying," the old woman told her. She was stationed now at the far end of the table, just behind Sam's empty chair. She glared at Delia from underneath lashes so thickly beaded with mascara that they shaded her face like awnings. "They may have their ups and downs, like any other young couple," she said, "but they're trying to work things out, I tell you! They're dating again, has he mentioned that? Twice they've gone to dinner at the restaurant where they got engaged. They're thinking it might help if they started a baby. But every time I look out of my house, what do I find? Your car, parked across the street. You at his front door kissing him, all over him, can't get enough of him, going up the stairs with him to paw him at his bedroom window for all the neighbors to gawk at."

Adrian's mother-in-law lived across the street from him?

Delia felt burning hot. She sensed the others' thunderstruck expressions.

Sam said, quietly, "Delia, do you know anything about this?"

"No! Nothing!" she cried. "She's making it up! She's confused me with somebody else!"

"Then what's this?" the old woman asked, and she started tweaking at her purse. The drawstring was held tight by some sort of sliding clasp, and it took her whole minutes, it seemed, to work it loose, while everybody watched in riveted silence. Delia realized she had not released a breath in some time. She was prepared for absolutely anything to emerge from that purse—something steamy and lurid and reeking of sex, although what would that be, precisely? But all the old woman brought forth in the end was a photograph. "See? See?" she demanded, and she held it up and swung slowly from left to right.

It was a Polaroid snapshot, so underexposed that it amounted to no more than a square of mangled darkness. But not till Ramsay snickered once again did Delia understand that she was safe.

"Now, there," Sam was saying, "don't you worry, I'm sure your daughter is *very* happily married. . . ." In the most chivalrous fashion, he was turning the old woman toward the door. "May I see you to your car?" he asked.

"Oh. Well . . . yes, maybe . . . yes, maybe so," she said. She was still fumbling with her purse, but she let him guide her out. She walked beneath the shelter of his arm in a dazed, uncertain manner that filled Delia with sudden pity.

"Who was *that*?" Marie-Claire asked distinctly.

Ramsay said, "Oh, just somebody for your aunt Delia; you know what a siren she is," and everybody stirred and chuckled.

It was perverse of her, she knew, but for one split second Delia actually considered confessing, just to show them. She didn't, of course. She smiled around the table and sat back down and placed the water pitcher on her left. "Who's for more chicken?" she asked, and she looked brazenly into Eliza's measuring eyes.

It was Susie's night to do the dishes, and Eleanor said she would help. She wouldn't think of letting Delia lift a finger, she said, after that extravagant meal. So Delia backed out of the kitchen, pretending reluctance, but instead of heading toward the porch with the others, she sped up the stairs and into her bedroom. She shut the door behind her, sat on the edge of the bed, and picked up the phone.

He answered almost instantly. She had braced herself to go through that whole two-ring rigmarole, but right away he said, "Hello?"

"Adrian?"

"Oh, God, Delia, did she come?"

"She came."

"I tried to warn you. I called your house, and even after your husband answered I went ahead and—"

"My husband answered? When?"

"Wasn't that your husband?"

"Oh, Carroll. My son. At suppertime, you mean."

"Yes, and I was hoping you would . . . That was your son?"

"Yes, my younger son. Carroll."

"But he was so old."

"Old? He's not old!"

"He sounded like a grown man."

"Well, he isn't," Delia said curtly. "Adrian, why did you stand there kissing me in doors and windows when you knew your mother-in-law lived across the street?"

"So she did what she said she would, did she?"

"She came and told my family I had a 'paramour,' if that's what you mean."

"Lord, Delia, what did they say?"

"I think they just thought she was crazy or something, but . . . Adrian. She claimed you were happily married."

"Of course she did. You know she would want to believe that."

"She claimed you and Rosemary have started dating; you've gone out together twice to the restaurant where you got engaged."

"Well, that much is true."

"It is?"

"Just to talk things over; sure. We do have a lot in common, after all. A lot of shared history."

"I see."

"But it wasn't how you imagine. We met for dinner! Just to eat dinner!"

"And you're thinking of starting a baby."

"Is that what she told you?"

"Yes."

"Well, naturally it came up."

"Naturally?" Delia cried.

"I mean, Rosemary isn't getting any younger."

"No, that's right, she must be all of thirty," Delia said with some bitterness. She twined the telephone cord between her fingers. The connection was the kind with a rushing sound in the background, like long distance.

"Well, probably she's not the maternal type, though, anyhow," Adrian said cheerfully. "Weird, isn't it? The very thing that attracts you to someone can end up putting you off. When Rosemary and I first met, she was so . . . cool, I guess you'd say, so cool-mannered I was bewitched, but now I see she might be too cool to be a good mother."

"How about me?" Delia asked him.

"You?"

"What is it about *me* that attracts you but puts you off?"

"Oh, why, nothing, Delia. Why do you ask?"

"Nothing attracts you?"

"Oh! Well, maybe . . . well, when we met, you acted so fresh and sweet and childish, I mean childlike, you know? But then when we reached the point where most people would, for example, um, get more involved, you were *still* so damn sweet and childlike. Turning all flustered, saying you should leave: you'd think we were teenagers or something."

"I see," Delia said.

Adrian said, "Delia. Just how old is your son, anyway?"

"Ancient," she told him. But it was herself she was referring to.

She hung up and walked out of the room.

Downstairs, she heard water running in the kitchen, and dishes clattering, and Eleanor saying, "Susie, dear, you're not planning to *discard* that, surely." Delia crossed the hall to stand at the screen door, gazing out toward the porch. She saw no sign of the boys, who had not stayed to talk after dinner in years; no sign of Velma or Rosalie. But Sam and Linda sat sniping at each other in the swing. "Some of those azaleas were planted by our grandfather," Linda said, "not that that would be any concern of yours," and Sam said, "Or yours either, unless you plan to start sharing a little of the burden here," and Eliza, rocking in the cane rocker, said, "Oh, just quit it, both of you." The twins were twirling on the front walk beneath the pole lamp, with grass blades stuck to their skin and white moths flickering above them. They had reached that high-pitched, overwrought state that seizes children outdoors on summer evenings, and they were chanting at breakneck speed:

"*What's* life?"

"Fifteen cents a copy."

"But I only have a dime."

"Well, that's life."

"*What's* life?"

"Fifteen cents a copy."

"But I only have a dime."

5

It rained during their first evening at the beach, and their cottage roof turned out to have a leak. This was not a very fancy cottage, not an oceanfront, resort-style cottage, but a dumpy little house on the inland side of Highway 1. Delia could imagine an ordinary Delaware feed-store clerk living there until about a week ago. The kitchen sink was skirted in chintz, the living-room floor was blue linoleum squiggled to suggest a hooked rug, and all the beds sagged toward the middle and creaked at the slightest movement. Still, Sam said, they shouldn't have to endure a puddle in the upstairs hall. He phoned the rental agent at once, using the after-hours emergency number, and insisted that the problem be seen to the first thing the following morning.

"What," Linda asked him, "do you have to have your crew of workmen even on vacation?"

And Eliza said, "Let's just mop it up and forget it. It surely won't rain again while we're here, because if it does I'm going to sue God."

Delia herself said nothing. She really couldn't gather the strength.

In their own house back in Baltimore, workmen would be using the week to sand down the floors and refinish them. This meant that Delia had had to bring the cat along. (He wouldn't tolerate boarding—had nearly pined away the one time they had tried it.) Sam claimed they were sure to be evicted, since pets were expressly forbidden, but Delia told him that was impossible. How would anyone ever guess Vernon was there? For he'd been so incensed by the car trip that the instant he was set down in the cottage, he streaked to the back of a kitchen cabinet. Delia knew enough to leave him tactfully alone, but the twins wouldn't rest, and after supper they hovered at the cabinet door with a plate of leftovers, trying to coax him out. "Here, Vernon! *Nice* Vernon." His only response was that disheartening, numb silence cats seem to radiate when they're determined to keep to themselves. "Oh," Marie-Claire wailed, "what'll we do? He's going to starve to death!"

"Good riddance," Sam told her. "It's only live pets that we're not allowed."

Sam had been out of sorts all day, it seemed to Delia.

So that first evening, when they should have been taking a stroll on the beach or walking into town for ice cream, the grown-ups sat in the kerosene-smelling, poorly lighted living room, reading tattered magazines left behind by earlier tenants and listening to the pecking of the rain against the windows. The twins were still in the kitchen, badgering Vernon. Susie and the boys had borrowed the Plymouth and driven to Ocean City, which made Delia anxious because she always pictured Ocean City as a gigantic arena of bumper cars manned by drunken college students. But she tried to keep her mind on *American Deck and Patio.*

"If tomorrow isn't sunny," Linda said, "maybe we could take a little day trip out past Salisbury. I want the twins to get some sense of their heritage."

"Oh, Linda, not that damn cemetery again," Eliza said.

"Well, fine, then. Just lend me a car and I'll take them myself. That's what happened last year, as I recall."

"Yes, and last year both twins came back bored to tears and cranky. What do they care for a bunch of dead Carrolls and Webers?"

"They had a wonderful time! And I'd like to find Great-Uncle Roscoe's place too, if I can."

"Well, good hunting, is all I can say. I'm sure it's a parking lot by now, and anyhow, Mother never got along with Uncle Roscoe."

"Eliza, why do you have to run me down at every turn?" Linda demanded. "Why is it that every little thing I propose you have to mock and denigrate?"

"Now, ladies," Sam said absently, leafing through *Offshore Angler*.

Linda turned on him. She said, "Don't you 'Now, ladies' *me*, Sam Grinstead."

"Sorry," Sam murmured.

"Mr. Voice of Reason, here!"

"My mistake."

She rose in a huff and went off to check the twins. Eliza closed her *Yachting World* and stared bleakly at the cover.

Linda and Eliza were in their Day Two Mode, was how Delia always thought of it—that edgy, prickly stage after the first flush of Linda's arrival had faded. Once, Delia had asked Eliza why she and Linda weren't closer, and Eliza had said, "Oh, people who've shared an unhappy childhood rarely *are* close, I've found." Delia was surprised. Their childhood had been unhappy? Hers had been idyllic. But she refrained from saying so.

Linda returned with the twins, who were still fretting over Vernon, and Sam set aside his magazine and suggested a game of rummy. "Did you bring the cards?" he asked Delia.

She had not. She realized it the instant he asked, but made a show of rooting through the shopping bag on the coffee table. Jigsaw puzzles, Monopoly, and a Parcheesi board emerged, but no cards. "Um . . . ," she said.

"Oh, well," Sam said, "we'll play Parcheesi, then." His tone was weightily patient, which seemed worse than shouting.

At the bottom of the bag, Delia came across her current library book. *Captive of Clarion Castle*, it was called. She had started it last week and found it slow, but anything was preferable to deck plans. When Sam asked, "Are you playing too, Delia?" she said, "I think I'll go read in bed."

"Now? It's not even nine o'clock."

"Well, I'm tired," she told him. She said good night to the others and walked out with the front of her book concealed, although no one made any attempt to see the title.

Upstairs, a new ribbon of water meandered from the sodden bath mat alongside the chimney. She ignored it and proceeded to the room she was sharing with Sam. It was small and musty-smelling, with one, uncurtained window. For privacy's sake she changed into her nightgown in the dark, and then she washed up in the bathroom across the hall. Back in the bedroom, she switched on the lamp and aimed its weak yellow beam in the direction of her pillow. Then she slid under the covers, wriggled her toes luxuriously, and opened her book.

The heroine of this book was a woman named Eleanora, which unfortunately brought Eleanor to Delia's mind. Eleanora's long raven tresses and "piquant" face kept giving way to Eleanor's no-nonsense haircut and Iron Mama jawline; and when Kendall, the hero, crushed her to him, Delia saw Eleanor's judging gaze directed past his broad shoulder. Kendall was Eleanora's future brother-in-law, the younger brother of her aristocratic, suave fiancé. Impetuously, Kendall kidnapped Eleanora the first time he laid eyes on her, which happened to be about fifteen minutes before her wedding. "I will never love you! Never!" Eleanora cried, pummeling his chest with her tiny fists, but Kendall seized her wrists and waited, masterful and confident, until she subsided.

Delia closed the book, leaving one finger inside as a marker. She stared down at the couple embracing on the cover.

Not once, from the moment they met, had Adrian truly pursued her. It had all been a matter of happenstance. Happenstance had led him to ask her to pose as his girlfriend (Who else was remotely eligible? The woman with the baby? The old lady at the checkout counter?), and happenstance had brought them together again a few nights later. In addition, his every act had betrayed that he was still in love with his wife. He loved her so much that he couldn't face her on his own in the supermarket; he couldn't sleep in their bedroom after she left. But Delia, like some self-deluded teenage ninny, had chosen not to see.

And she had overlooked other clues as well—clues that revealed the very nature of his character. For instance, his behavior at that first encounter: his rearrangement of her shopping plans, his condescending reference to Roland Park names, his trendy groceries. He was not a *bad* person, surely, but his mind was on his own concerns. And he was just the least bit shallow.

In romance novels, this realization would have made her turn thankfully to the man who had been waiting in the wings all along. But in real life, when she heard Sam's step on the stairs she closed her eyes and pretended to be asleep. She felt him standing over her, and then he slipped her book from her hands and switched off the lamp and left the room.

By morning the rain had stopped and the sun was out, shining all the brighter in the washed-clean air. The whole family set off for the ocean shortly before noon—the grown-ups in Sam's Buick, the younger ones in the Plymouth with Ramsay at the wheel. Scattered puddles hissed beneath their tires as they drove across Highway 1 and threaded past the higher-priced cottages, closer to the water. When the road dead-ended, they parked and fed two meters with quarters and unloaded the day's supplies—the thermos jugs and blankets, towels, Styrofoam coolers, rafts, and beach bags. Delia carried a stack of towels, along with her straw tote stuffed so full of emergency provisions that the handles dug a furrow in her bare shoulder. She was wearing her pink gingham swimsuit with the eyelet-edged skirt, and navy canvas espadrilles, but no robe or cover-up, because she didn't care *what* Sam said, she wanted to get at least a hint of a tan.

"Watch it, girls," Linda told the twins as they lugged a cooler between them up the wooden walkway. "You're letting the bottom drag."

"It's Thérèse's fault—she's making me do all the work!"

"Am not."

"Are so."

"Didn't I tell you to take something lighter?" Linda asked them. "Didn't I offer you the blankets, or the—"

But then they crested the low, sandy rise, and there was the ocean, reminding them what they had come all this way for. Oh, every year it seemed Delia forgot. That vast, slaty, limitless sweep, that fertile, rotting, dog's-breath smell, that continual to-and-fro shushing that had been going on forever while she'd been elsewhere, stewing over trivia! She paused, letting her eyes take rest in the dapples of yellow sunlight that skated the water, and then Carroll's armload of rafts crashed into her from behind, and he said, "Geez, Mom."

"Oh, excuse me," she said. She started down the wooden steps to the beach.

There were advantages to coming so early in the season. True, the water had not had time to warm up yet, but also the beach was less crowded. Blankets were spread at civilized intervals, with space between.

Only a few children splashed at the edge of the breakers, and Delia could easily count the heads that bobbed farther out.

She and Eliza unfolded a blanket and arranged themselves on it, while Sam worked an umbrella pole into the sand. Susie and the boys, however, walked a good twenty feet beyond before stopping to set up their own station. They had been keeping apart for several years now; it no longer hurt Delia's feelings. But she did always notice.

"Now, you two are not stirring from here," Linda told the twins, "until I get every inch of you covered with sunblock." She held them close, one after the other, and slathered lotion on their skinny arms and legs. As soon as she let go of them, off they raced to the young people's blanket.

Susie's radio was playing "Under the Boardwalk," which had always seemed to Delia a very lonesome song. In fact, "Under the Boardwalk" was rising from other radios as well, on other blankets, so that the Atlantic Ocean seemed to have acquired its own melancholy background music.

"Believe I'll go for a jog," Sam told Delia.

"Oh, Sam. You're on vacation!"

"So?"

He shucked off his beach robe and adjusted the leather band of his watch. (The watch was evidently part of his new exercise routine; in just what way, Delia wasn't sure.) Then he walked down to the surf, turned, and started loping northward, a lanky figure in beige trunks and gigantic white sneakers.

"At least here they have all these lifeguards who've been trained in CPR," Delia told her sisters. She folded Sam's robe and packed it away in her tote.

"Oh, he'll be fine," Eliza said. "The doctors told him to jog."

"Not to overdo, though!"

"To me he looks just the same as always," Linda said. "If you consider that a good thing." She was shading her forehead to gaze after him. "I never would have known he'd had a heart attack."

"It wasn't a heart attack! It was chest pains."

"Whatever," Linda said carelessly.

She was wearing a one-piece swimsuit held up by a center cord that encircled her neck. It made her breasts appear to droop at either side like a pair of weary eyes. Eliza, who scorned the notion of a whole separate outfit for one week of swimming per year, wore denim shorts and a black knit tank top rolled up beneath her bra.

Delia took off her shoes and dropped them into her tote. Then she lay down flat on her back, with the sun's mild warmth soaking into her skin. Gradually sounds grew fainter, like remembered sounds—the voices of other sunbathers nearby, the high, sad cries of the seagulls, the music from the radios (Paul McCartney now, singing "Uncle Albert"), and under everything, so she almost stopped hearing it, the ocean's rush, as constant and unvaried as the ocean inside a seashell.

She and Sam had come to this beach on their honeymoon. They had stayed at an inn downtown that no longer existed, and every morning, lying out here side by side with their bare, fuzzed arms just touching, they had reached such a state that, eventually, they had to rise and rush back to their room. Once even that had seemed too far, and they'd plunged into the ocean instead, out past the breakers, and she could still remember the layers of contrast—his warm, bony legs brushing hers beneath the cool, silky water—and the fishy scent of his wet face when they kissed. But the summer after that they had the baby with them (little Susie, two months old and fussy, fussy, fussy) and in later years the boys, and they had seldom managed even to stretch out on their blanket together, let alone steal back to their cottage. Eliza started coming too, and Linda before she married, and their father because he never could have kept house on his own; and Delia spent her days ankle-deep in the surf tending children, making sure they didn't drown, admiring each new skill they mastered. "Watch this, Mom." "No, watch *this*!" They used to think she was so important in their lives.

Someone's feet passed in the sand with a sound like rubbing velvet, and she opened her eyes and sat up. For a moment she felt light-headed. "Your face is burning," Eliza told her. "Better put some lotion on." She herself was sitting sensibly in the shade of the umbrella. Linda was down in the surf, braced for an incoming wave with both plump arms outflung and her hands posed as liltingly as bird wings, and the twins had returned from the other blanket and were filling buckets near Delia. Damp sand caked Marie-Claire's knees and made two circles on the empty-looking seat of Thérèse's swimsuit.

"Did Sam get back from jogging?" Delia asked Eliza.

"Not yet. Want to go for a dip?"

Delia didn't dignify that with an answer. (As everyone in her family well knew, the temperature had to be blistering, the ocean flat as glass, and not a sea nettle sighted all day before she would venture in.) Instead, she reached for her tote bag. Delving past espadrilles, Sam's robe, and her billfold, she came up with *Captive of Clarion Castle*. Eliza humphed when she saw the cover. "Guess I'll leave you to your *literature*," she told Delia. She got to her feet and set off, dusting the back of her shorts in a businesslike manner.

"Aunt Eliza, can we come too?" Marie-Claire shrilled.

"Wait for us, Aunt Liza!"

When they ran after her, they looked as skittery and high-bottomed as two little hermit crabs.

Eleanora was beginning to notice that Kendall was not the monster she had imagined. He brought trays of food to her locked tower room and let it be known he had cooked all the dishes himself. Eleanora pretended to be unimpressed, but later, after he left, she reflected on the incongruity of someone so brawny and virile stirring pots at a stove.

"Whew!" Sam said. He was back. Sweat trickled down the ridged bones of his chest, and he had the drawn, strained, gasping look that always distressed Delia after his runs. "Sam," she said, setting aside her book, "you're going to kill yourself! Sit here and rest."

"No, I have to wind down gradually," he told her. He started walking in circles around the blanket, stopping every now and then to bend over and grip his kneecaps. Drops of sweat fell from his forehead to the sand. "What have we got to drink?" he asked her.

"Lemonade, Pepsi, iced tea—"

"Iced tea sounds good."

She stood to fill a paper cup and hand it to him. He was no longer breathing so hard, at least. He drained the cup in a single draft and set it on the lid of the cooler. "Your nose is burning," he told her.

"I want to get a *little* tan."

"Melanoma is what you're going to get."

"Well, maybe after lunch I'll put on some—"

But he had already picked up Linda's bottle of sunblock. "Hold still," he said, unscrewing the cap. He started smoothing lotion across her face. It smelled like bruised peaches, an artificial, trashy smell that made her wrinkle her nose. "Turn around and I'll do your back," he told her.

Obediently, she turned. She faced inland now, where the roofs of cottages hulked beyond the sand fence. A flock of tiny dark birds crossed the blue sky in the distance, keeping a perfectly triangular formation so that they seemed connected by invisible wires. They swung around and caught the sun, and suddenly they were white, in fact almost silver, like a veil of sequins; and then they swung again, and once more they were plain black specks. Sam smoothed lotion over Delia's shoulders. It went on warm but cooled in the breeze, tingling slightly.

"Delia," he said.

"Hmm?"

"I was wondering about the old woman who came by the house Saturday night."

She grew still beneath his palm, but she felt that every one of her nerves was thrumming like a twanged string.

"I know she was, maybe, peculiar," he said. "But she had an actual photograph, and she seemed to think it really did show you and that who's-it, that what's-his-name . . ."

She had already turned toward him to deny it when he said, "That Adrian Fried Rice."

"Bly-Brice," she said.

For he had twisted the name on purpose. He always did that. The maid of honor at their wedding, Missy Pringle, he had kept referring to as Prissy Mingle. It was just like him to be so belittling! So contemptuous of her friends, with that ironic glint to his voice! Her entire marriage unrolled itself before her: ancient hurts and humiliations and resentments, theoretically forgotten but just waiting to revive at moments such as this.

"His name is Adrian, Bly, Brice," she told him.

"I see," Sam said. His face had a sheeted look.

"But that woman got it all wrong. He's nothing but an acquaintance."

"I see."

In silence, he replaced the bottle of sunblock.

"You don't believe me."

"I never said that."

"No, but you implied it."

"I surely can't be blamed for what you imagine I might have implied," Sam said. "Of course he's just an acquaintance. You're not exactly the type to have an affair. But I'm wondering how it seems to outsiders, Dee. You know?"

"No, I don't know," she said, between set teeth. "And my name is not *Dee*."

"All right," he said. "Delia. Now, why don't you just calm down."

And he leveled the air between them with both palms, in that patronizing gesture she always found so infuriating, and turned away from her and walked toward the water.

Every quarrel they had ever had, he had walked off before it was resolved. He would get her all riled up and then loftily remove himself, giving the impression that he, at least, could behave like an adult. Adult? Old man was more the case. Who else would wade into the surf in his sneakers? Who else would pat water so fastidiously on his chest and upper arms before ducking under? And check his watch, for Lord's sake, when he rose? To Delia it seemed he was timing the waves, engaging in some precise and picky ritual that filled her with irritation.

She snatched her tote bag from the blanket, spun on one bare heel, and stamped off down the beach.

More people had arrived without her noticing. Only a slender path wound among the umbrellas and canvas chairs and mesh playpens, and so after a few yards she changed course till she was marching alongside the ocean, on wet, packed sand that cooled the soles of her feet.

This part of the beach belonged to the walkers. They walked in twos, mostly: young couples, old couples, almost always holding hands or at least matching their strides. From time to time small children cut in front of them. Delia pictured a map of the entire East Coast from Nova Scotia to Florida—an irregular strip of beige sand dotted with tiny humans, a wash of blue Atlantic next to it even more sparsely dotted. She herself was a dot in motion, heading south. She would keep going till she fell off the bottom of the continent, she decided. By and by Sam would think to ask, "Have you seen Delia?" "Why, no, where could she have got to?" the others would say, but she would keep on the move, like someone running between raindrops, and they would never, ever find her.

Already, though, something was slowing her down. The first of the Sea Colony condominiums towered ahead—ugly Sea Colony with its impassive monochrome high-rises, like a settlement from an alien galaxy. She could have made her way past, but that mysterious, Star Wars hum that the buildings always emitted chilled her so that she stopped short. In her childhood, this had been grassy marshland, with a few plain-faced cottages scattered about. In her childhood, she was almost certain, she and her father had flown homemade kites right where that complex of orange plastic pyramids now shaded a modernistic sundeck. For an instant she could feel her father's blunt fingers closing over hers on the kite string. She brushed a hand across her eyes. Then she turned and started walking back.

A lifeguard slouched on his chair, surveying the bathers inscrutably from behind his dark glasses. A lardy young boy on a raft landed in the foam at Delia's feet. She stepped around him and, looking ahead, spotted her family's green-and-white umbrella and her children on their blanket just beyond. They were sitting up now, and Sam stood some distance away, still shiny after his swim. From here it didn't seem that anyone was speaking, for the children faced the horizon and Sam was studying his watch.

Just that abruptly, Delia veered inland. She left the ocean behind and picked her way around sand tunnels and forts and collections of toys. When she had traversed the wooden walkway to the road, she stopped to dust her feet off and dig her espadrilles from her tote. Sam's beach robe lay beneath them—a wad of navy broadcloth—and after a moment's consideration, she shook it out and put it on. Her shoulders were so burned by now that they seemed to give off heat.

If she had thought to get the car keys from Ramsay, she could have driven. She wasn't looking forward to that trek to the cottage. In fact, she could return for the keys right now. But then some of the others might want to come with her, and so she decided against it.

Already the ocean seemed far away and long ago, a mere whisper on this sunny paved road with its silent cottages and empty, baking automobiles and motionless rows of swimsuits on clotheslines. She cut through someone's backyard—mostly sand—and circled an enclosure of garbage cans that smelled of crab and buzzed with glittery blue flies. Then she was facing Highway 1. Traffic whizzed by so fast that she had to wait several minutes before she could cross.

On the other side of the highway, her footsteps were the loudest sound around—her stiff straw soles clopping out a rhythm. Perhaps because she'd been thinking of her father, the rhythm seemed to keep time with the song he used to sing when she was small. She stalked past screened porches, with her shoes beating out "Delia's Gone"—asking where she'd been so long, saying her lover couldn't sleep, saying all around his bed at night he kept hearing little Delia's bare feet. She especially liked that last line; she always had. Except, wasn't the other Delia dead? Yes, obviously: there was mention in the very first verse of little Delia dead and gone. But she preferred to believe the woman had simply walked out. It was more satisfying that way.

Her face felt sticky, and her shoulder hurt where the handles of her tote bag chafed her sunburn. She switched the tote to her other side. She was almost there now, anyhow. She was planning on a tall iced tea as soon as she stepped through the door, and after that a cool bath and a little private visit with her cat. It was time to lure Vernon from under her bed, where he had taken up residence at some point during the night. In fact, maybe she ought to do that first.

She smiled at a woman carrying a suitcase out of the cottage next to theirs. "Lovely beach weather!" the woman called. "Hate to leave it!"

"It's perfect," Delia said, and she rounded a van parked in the driveway and climbed her own steps.

Inside, the dimness turned her momentarily blind. She peered up the stairwell and called, "Vernon?"

"What."

She gasped.

"Somebody page me?" a man's voice asked.

He lumbered down the stairs—a chubby young man with a clipboard, dressed in jeans and a red plaid shirt. His moon-shaped face, with its round pink cheeks and nubbin nose and buttonhole mouth, reassured her somewhat, but even so she could barely draw breath to ask, "Who . . . ?"

"I'm Vernon, didn't you holler my name? I'm here about the roof."

"Oh," she said. She gave a shaky laugh and clutched her tote bag to her chest. "I was just calling my cat," she told him.

"Well, I haven't seen no cat about. Sorry if I scared you."

"You didn't scare me!"

He squinted at her doubtfully. The satiny skin beneath his eyes glistened with sweat, which made him look earnest and boyish. "Anyhow," he said. "Seems I'll need to replace that flashing up top round the chimney. I won't be doing it today, though; I got to get on back. So if those folks at the realtor's phone, tell them I'll be in touch, okay?"

"Okay," Delia said.

He waved his clipboard amiably and headed past her out the door. On the steps, he turned and asked, "How you like my vehicle?"

"Vehicle?"

"Ain't it something?"

It was, in fact. She wondered how she could have missed it. Big as a house trailer, painted a metallic bronze with a desert landscape lighting up one side, it occupied the whole driveway. "Got a microwave," Vernon was saying, "got a dinky little 'frigerator—"

"You mean it's for living in?"

"Sure, what else?"

"I thought vans would just have rows and rows of seats."

"Ain't you ever been inside a RV before? Shoot, come on and I'll show you."

"Oh, I don't know if I—"

"Come on! This'll knock your socks off."

"Well, maybe I *will* take a peek," Delia said, and she followed him, still hugging her tote bag. One section of the desert scene proved to be a sliding panel. Vernon slid it open and stood back to let her see inside. When she poked her head in she found gold shag carpeting halfway up the walls, and built-in cabinets, and a platform bed at the rear with storage drawers underneath. Two high-backed seats faced the windshield—the only sign that this was, after all, a means of transportation.

"Gosh," Delia said.

"Climb in. Get a load of my entertainment center."

"You have an entertainment center?"

"State of the art," he told her. He climbed in himself, causing the van to tilt beneath his weight, and then turned to offer a hand as big as a baseball glove. She accepted it and clambered inside. The oily, exciting smell of new carpet reminded her of airports and travel.

"Ta-daah!" Vernon said. He flung open a cabinet. "What it is," he said, "in the bottom of this here TV is a slot for a videotape, see? Integrated VCR. Evenings, I just swivel it out and watch the latest hit movies from the bed."

"You stay here all the time?"

"Just about," he said. "Well, more or less. Well, for now I do." Then he sent her a look, with his head ducked. "I'll tell you the honest truth," he said. "This van belongs to my brother."

He seemed to think the news would disappoint her deeply. He fixed her with a worried blue gaze and waited, scarcely breathing, until she said, "Oh, really?"

"I guess I kind of gave the impression it was mine," he said. "But see, my brother's off on this fishing trip, him and his wife. Left his van at our mom's house in Nanticoke Landing. Told her to watch over it and not let nobody drive it. Me is who he meant. But he's due back this afternoon and so yesterday I got to thinking. 'Well, durn,' I got to thinking. 'Here's this fully equipped RV, been setting in Mom's yard all week and I have not so much as tried that little microwave.' So last night I stayed in it, and this morning I took it out to make my estimates. Mom said she don't even want to know about it. Said not to drag her into it.

But what can he do to me, right? What's he going to do to me—haul me off to jail?"

"Maybe he won't find out," Delia said.

"Oh, he'll find out, all right. Be just like him to have wrote down the mileage before he left," Vernon told her gloomily.

"You could always say you thought the battery needed charging."

"Battery. Sure."

"Does he live here? In the van, I mean?"

"Naw."

"Well, I would," Delia said. She bent to raise the seat of an upholstered bench. Just as she had expected, there was storage space underneath. She glimpsed woolens of some kind—blankets or jackets. "I would make it my year-round home," she said. "Really! Who needs a big old house and all those extra rooms?"

"Yeah, but my brother's got three kids," Vernon said.

"Have you ever seen those under-cabinet coffeemakers?" Delia asked him.

"Huh?"

She was inspecting the kitchen area now. It was a model of miniaturization, with a sink the size of a salad bowl and a two-burner stovetop. A dented metal percolator stood on one of the burners. "They have these coffeepots," she told Vernon, "that you permanently install beneath the overhang of a cabinet. So you don't waste any space."

"Is that a fact."

"Actually, there's a whole line of under-cabinet equipment. Toaster ovens, can openers . . . electric can opener you install beneath the—"

"I believe my brother just uses the hand-cranked kind," Vernon said.

"Well, if this were mine, I'd have everything under-cabinet."

"Hand-cranked don't take no space at all, to speak of."

"I'd have nothing rattling around," Delia said, "nothing interfering, so at a moment's notice I could hop behind the wheel and go. Travel with my house on my back, like a snail. Stop when I got tired. Park in whatever campground caught my fancy."

"Well, but campgrounds," Vernon said. "Mostly you'd need to reserve ahead, for a campground."

"And next morning I'd say, 'Okay! That's it for this place!' And move on."

"The rates are kind of steep too, if the campground's halfway decent," Vernon said. "Durn. Is that the time?"

He was looking at the clock above the sink. Delia was glad to see that the clock, at least, was attached to the wall. In her opinion, there was far too much loose and adrift here—not just the percolator but sloppily refolded newspapers and videotapes out of their boxes and cast-off pieces of clothing. "What I can't fathom," she said, "is how you manage to drive with these things sliding all over. Wouldn't you have flying objects every time you hit a speed bump?"

"Not as I've noticed," Vernon said. "But remember this ain't my property. And speaking of which, my brother's due back in like a couple of hours so I reckon I better be going."

"I wish I could come too," Delia said.

"Yeah. Right. Well, look, it's been great talking with you—"

"Maybe I could just ride along for a little tiny part of the way," Delia said.

"When—now?"

"Just to see how it handles on the road."

"Well, it . . . handles fine on the road," Vernon said. "But I'm going inland, you know? I'm nowhere near any beaches. Going down Three eighty past Ashford, *way* past Ashford, over to—"

"I'll just ride to, um, Ashford," Delia said.

She knew she was making him nervous. He stood staring at her, his eyebrows crinkled and his mouth slightly open, his clipboard dangling forgotten from one hand. Never mind: any moment now she would let him off the hook. She would give a little coming-to-her-senses laugh and tell him that on second thought, she couldn't possibly ride to Ashford. She did have a family after all, and already they must be wondering where she was.

And yet here stood this van, this beautiful, completely stocked, entirely self-sufficient van that you could travel in forever, unentangled with anyone else. Oh, couldn't she offer to buy it? How much did such things cost? Or steal it, even—shove Vernon out the door and zoom off, careening west on little back roads where no one could ever track her.

But: "Well," she said regretfully, "I do have a family."

"Family in Ashford? Oh, in that case," Vernon said.

It took her a minute to understand. His eyebrows smoothed themselves out, and he leaned past her to slide the door shut. Then he flung his clipboard on the bench and said, "Long as you've got transportation back, then . . ."

Speechless, Delia made her way to the front. She sat in the passenger seat and perched her tote bag on her knees. Next to her, Vernon was settling behind the wheel. When he switched on the ignition, the van roared to life so suddenly that she fancied it had been jittering with impatience all this time.

"Hear that?" Vernon asked her.

She nodded. She supposed it must be the engine's vibration that caused her teeth to start chattering.

Traveling down Highway 1 toward the Maryland border, past giant beach-furniture stores and brand-new "Victorian" developments and the jumbled cafés and apartments of Fenwick Island, Delia kept telling herself that she could still get back on her own. It would mean a long walk, was all (which stretched longer moment by moment). And when they entered Ocean City, with its honky-tonk razzle-dazzle—well, Ocean City had buses, she happened to know. She could take a bus to its northernmost edge and *then* walk back. So she rode quietly, beginning to feel almost relaxed, while Vernon hunched over the wheel and steered with his forearms. He was one of those drivers who talked to traffic. "Not to pressure you or anything, fella," he said when a car ahead of him stalled, and he clucked at four teenage boys crossing the street with their surfboards. "Aren't *you*-all hotshots," he told them. Delia gazed after them. The tallest boy wore ticking-striped shorts exactly like a pair Carroll owned—that voluminous new fashion that billowed to mid-knee.

When her family discovered she was gone, they would be baffled. Flummoxed. If she stayed away long enough, they would wonder if she'd met with an accident. "Or could she have left on purpose?" Sam would at last ask the children. "Did one of you say something? Did *I* say something? Was I mistaken to believe she wasn't the type for an affair?"

An airy sense of exhilaration filled her chest. She felt so lightweight, all at once.

Then after they had had time to get really concerned, she would phone. Find a booth before night fell and, "It's me," she would announce. "Just took a little jaunt to the country; could one of you come pick me up?" No harm done.

So when Vernon turned onto Highway 50 and started inland (talking now about the "differential," whatever that was), she still said nothing to stop him. The percolator clanked on the stovetop; they rattled across a bridge she'd never seen before and entered a bleached, pale country entirely unfamiliar to her. She merely stared out the window. They passed yellowing, papery houses set in the middle of careful lawns that appeared to have been hand clipped, blade by blade. They flickered through leafy woodlands. "One place he flubbed up is not opting for a CB," Vernon said, referring evidently to his brother, but Delia was just then picturing how Sam's lips always formed a straight line when he was angry. And it occurred to her that what he might tell the children was, "Well, at least we can get things done right, now she's gone."

"Besides which you will notice there's no stereo," Vernon said. "That's my brother for you: he don't care much for music. I say there's something lacking in a man who don't like music."

Maybe Eleanor would step in (speaking of doing things right). Oh, Eleanor would take over gladly—plan all the menus a year in advance and set up one of her Iron Mama budgets.

"I guess you think that's awful," Vernon said. "To pick fault with my own brother."

Delia said, "No, no . . ."

Here and there, now, gaunt old dignified farmhouses stood at the end of long driveways, with crops growing all around them and lightning rods bristling on their rooftops. Imagine living in such a place! It would be so wholesome. Delia saw herself feeding chickens, flinging corn or wheat or whatever from her capacious country apron. First she'd have to marry a farmer, though. You always had to begin by finding some man to set things in motion, it seemed.

"But I'll be honest," Vernon was saying. "Me and him never have been what you'd call close. He is three years older than me and never lets me forget it. Keeps yammering about head of the family, when fact is he hardly lays eyes on our family from one month to the next. *I'm* the one takes Mom grocery shopping. *I'm* the one runs her hither and yon for her bingo nights and her covered-dish suppers and what all."

Why did everyone maintain that men were uncommunicative? In Delia's experience, they talked a blue streak, especially repairmen. And Sam was no exception. Sam communicated all too well, if you asked Delia.

She let her eyes follow a trailer park as they passed it. Each trailer was anchored by awnings and cinder-block steps and sometimes a screened extension. Whole menageries of plaster animals filled the little yards.

"Now, you take this fishing trip: know who's tending his kids? Me and Mom. Course mostly it's Mom, but time I come home from work nights, she is so wore out the rest is up to me. But don't expect Vincent to thank me. No, sir. And if he gets wind I drove his van, he'll have my head."

In her tote bag Delia had five hundred dollars of vacation money, split between her billfold and a deceptive little vinyl cosmetic kit. She could stay away overnight, if she really wanted to alarm them—take a room in some motel or even a picturesque inn. However, all she had on was her swimsuit. Oh, Lord. Her scrunchy-skirted swimsuit and her espadrilles and Sam's beach robe. But supposing she kept the robe tightly closed . . . Viewed in a certain way, it was not all that different from a dress. The sleeves were three-quarter length; the hem covered her knees. And hotels around here must be used to tourists, in their skimpy tourist outfits.

They were approaching the edge of a town now. Vernon slowed for a traffic light. He was talking about his brother's wife, Eunice. "I feel kind of sorry for her, if you really want to know," he said. "Picture being married to Vincent!"

"What town is this?" Delia asked him.

"This? Why, Salisbury."

The light changed, and he resumed driving. Delia was thinking that maybe she could just get out here. Maybe at the next red light. But the lights from then on were green, and also they had reached a residential section, very middle class and staid. And then beyond were unappealing malls, and messy commercial establishments, and somehow nothing struck her as very inviting.

"It's my belief he hits her," Vernon was saying. "Or at least, like, sort of pushes her. Anyways I know they fight a lot, because half the time when they come over she won't look him in the face."

They were riding through open country again, and Delia was beginning to fear she had missed her last chance. It was such *empty* country, so cardboard flat and desolate. She gripped her door handle and gazed at a naked dirt field in which violently uprooted trees lay every which way, their roots and branches clawing air. Unexpectedly Vernon braked, then took a sharp left onto a narrow paved road. "Three eighty," he informed her. He didn't seem to notice the clattering of the percolator behind them. "But this fishing trip they're on is supposed to be a second honeymoon."

"Honeymoon!" Delia said. She was looking at a pasture filled with rusted-out cars. Around the next curve lay a ramshackle barn halfway returned to the earth—the ridgepole almost U-shaped, the warped gray boards slumping into waist-high weeds. Every minute, she saw, she was traveling farther from civilization.

"Well, how Eunice put it to my mom," Vernon said, "she put it that her and Vincent were going off on the boat by themselves, just the two of them together."

Delia thought that a trip alone on a fishing boat would strain the best of marriages, but all she said was, "Well, I wish them luck."

"That's what I told Mom," Vernon said. He swerved around an antique tractor, whose driver was wearing what looked like a duster. "I told Mom, I said, 'Lots of luck, when her husband is Vincent the Dweeb.'"

"She should give up on him," Delia said, forgetting it was none of her business. "Especially if he hits her."

"Oh, I'm pretty sure he hits her."

Was that a brick building in the distance? Yes, and a grove of dark trees that cooled and relieved Delia's eyes, and beyond them a sparkling white steeple. She knew there must be guest accommodations here. She gathered up her tote bag and smoothed her robe around her knees.

"One time Eunice dropped by the house with a puffy place on her cheekbone," Vernon said. "And when Mom asked where she got it she said, 'I walked into a wall,' which if it had been me I could have come up with a lot better story than that."

"She should leave him," Delia said, but her mind was on the town ahead. They were passing the outskirts now—small white houses, a diner, a collection of men talking in front of a service station. "There's no point trying to mend a marriage that's got to the point of violence," she told Vernon.

Now they had reached the brick building, which turned out to be a school. DOROTHY G. UNDERWOOD HIGH SCHOOL. A street leading off just past that ended, evidently, in a park, for Delia glimpsed distant greenery and a statue of some kind. And now they were nearing the church that the steeple belonged to. Vernon was saying, "Well, I don't know; maybe you're right. Like I was telling Mom the other day, I told her—"

"I believe I'll get out here," Delia said.

"What?" he said. He slowed.

"Here is where I think I'll get out."

He brought the van to a stop and looked at the church. Two ladies in straw hats were weeding a patch of geraniums at the foot of the announcement board. "But I thought you were going to Ashford," he said. "*This* is not Ashford."

"Well, still," she said, looping the handles of her tote bag over her shoulder. She opened the passenger door and said, "Thanks for the ride."

"I hope I didn't say nothing to upset you," Vernon told her.

"No! Honest! I just think I'll—"

"Was it Eunice?"

"Eunice?"

"Vincent hitting her and all? I won't talk about it no more if it upsets you."

"No, really, I enjoyed our talk," she told him. And she hopped to the ground and sent him a brilliant smile as she closed the door. She started walking briskly in the direction they had come from, and when she reached the street where she had seen the statue she turned down it, not even slowing, as if she had some specific destination in mind.

Behind her, she heard the van shift gears and roar off again. Then a deep silence fell, like the silence after some shocking remark. It seemed this town felt as stunned as Delia by what she had gone and done.

6

What kind of trees lined this street? Beeches, she believed, judging by the high, arched corridor they formed. But she had never been very good at identifying trees.

Identifying the town itself, though, was easy. First she passed an imposing old house with a sign in one ground-floor window: MIKE POTTS—"BAY BOROUGH'S FRIENDLIEST INSURANCE AGENT." Then the Bay Borough Federal Savings Bank. And she was traveling down Bay Street, as she discovered when she reached the first intersection. But would the bay in question be the Chesapeake? She was fairly sure she had not come so far west. Also, this didn't have the feel of a waterside town. It smelled only of asphalt.

She found her explanation in the square. There, where scanty blades of grass struggled with plantain beneath more trees, a plaque at the base of the single bronze statue proclaimed:

ON THIS SPOT, IN AUGUST 1863,
GEORGE PENDLE BAY,
A UNION SOLDIER ENCAMPED OVERNIGHT WITH HIS COMPANY,
DREAMED THAT A MIGHTY ANGEL APPEARED TO HIM AND SAID,
"YE ARE SITTING IN THE BARBER'S CHAIR OF INFINITY,"

WHICH HE INTERPRETED AS INSTRUCTION
TO ABSENT HIMSELF FROM THE REMAINDER OF THE WAR
AND STAY ON TO FOUND THIS TOWNSHIP.

Delia blinked and took a step backward. Mr. Bay, a round-faced man in a bulging suit, did happen to be sitting, but his chair was the ordinary, non-barber kind, as near as she could make out, with a skirt of twisted bronze fringe. He gripped the chair's arms in a manner that squashed his fingertips; evidently he had been a nail biter. This struck Delia as comical. She gave a snuffle of laughter and then glanced over her shoulder, fearing someone had heard. But the square was empty, its four green benches uninhabited. Around the perimeter, cars cruised past, one or two at a time, and people walked in and out of the low brick and clapboard buildings, but nobody seemed to notice her.

Still, she was conscious all at once of her outfit. It wasn't so much the beach robe as the swimsuit underneath, the *feeling* of it, crumpled and bunchy and saggy. She'd give anything for some underwear. So she crossed the little square and gazed toward the row of storefronts on the other side of the street.

Clearly, modern times had overtaken the town. Buildings that must have been standing for a century—the bricks worn down like old pencil erasers, the clapboards gently rubbed to gray wood—now held the Wild Applause Video Shop, Tricia's House of Hair, and a Potpourri Palace. One place that seemed unchanged, though, was the dime store on the corner, with its curlicued red-and-gilt sign and a window full of flags and bunting.

She had been taught to buy only top-quality underwear, however else she might economize, but this was an emergency. She crossed the street and entered the dime-store smells of caramel and cheap cosmetics and old wooden floors. Apparently the notion of consolidated checkout lanes had not caught on here. At each and every counter, a clerk stood by a cash register. A floss-haired girl rang up a coloring book for a child; an elderly woman bagged a younger woman's cookie sheets. The lingerie department was staffed by a man, oddly enough; so Delia made her selections in haste and handed them over without quite raising her eyes. A plain white nylon bra, white cotton underpants. The underpants came three to a pack. Other styles could be purchased singly, but it was the pack of three that her fingers alighted on. *Just in case I'm away for more than one night*, she caught herself thinking. Then, as she counted out her money, she thought, *But I can always use them at home, of course, too. This doesn't mean a thing.*

Now she had her underclothes but no place to get into them, for she didn't see a rest room in the dime store. She went back outside, tucking her parcel into her tote, and looked up the street. Next door was Debbi's Dress Shoppe. Nineteen-forties mannequins with painted-on hair sported the latest fashions—broad-shouldered business suits or linen sheaths shaped like upside-down triangles. Not Delia's style at all, but at least she would find a changing booth here. She breezed in, trying to look purposeful, and snatched the nearest dress off a rack and hurried toward a row of compartments at the rear. "May I help you?" a woman called after her, but Delia said, "Oh, thanks, I'm only . . ." and disappeared behind a curtain.

The underwear fit, thank heaven. (She did her best to silence the rustling of the bag.) It was a relief to feel *contained* again. She folded her swimsuit into her tote. Then she reached for Sam's robe, but the sight of it gave her pause. It seemed so obviously a beach robe, all at once. She looked toward the dress she'd snatched up—a gray knit of some sort. Way too long, she could tell at a glance, but still she slipped it off its hanger and drew it over her head. The acrid smell of new fabric engulfed her. She smoothed down the skirt, zipped the side zipper, and turned to confront her reflection.

She had assumed she would resemble a child playing dress-up, for the hem nearly brushed her ankles. What she found, though, was someone entirely unexpected: a somber, serious-minded woman in a slender column of pearl gray. She might be a librarian or a secretary, one of those managerial executive secretaries who actually run the whole office from behind the scenes. "You'll find it in the Jones file, Mr. Smith," she imagined herself saying curtly. "And don't forget you're lunching with the mayor today; you'll want to take along the materials on the—"

"How're we doing in there?" the saleswoman called.

"Oh, fine."

"Can I bring you anything else to try?"

"No," Delia said. "This is perfect."

She stuffed Sam's robe into her tote and emerged from the booth to ask, "Could you just take the tags off, please? I think I'll wear it home."

The saleswoman—an overtanned blond in a geometric black-and-white print—directed a dubious frown toward the hemline. "We do offer alterations," she said. "Would you like that shortened a bit?"

"No, thanks," Delia told her in a starchy, secretarial voice.

The saleswoman adjusted seamlessly. "Well, it certainly becomes you," she said.

Delia raised her left arm, and the woman reached for her scissors and snipped off the tags that dangled from the zipper pull.

Seventy-nine ninety-five, the dress cost, not including tax. But Delia paid without a moment's hesitation and strode out of the shop.

The momentum of her exit carried her some distance, past the dime store again and across an intersection to a row of smaller shops—a copy center, a travel agent, a florist. She noticed she walked differently now, not with her usual bouncy gait but more levelly, because of her slim skirt. *Here is the secretary, Miss X, speeding back to her office after lunch. Preparing to type up her notes for the board of directors.*

Just as a game, she started choosing her office, the same way she used to choose her house when riding through a posh neighborhood. NICHOLS & TRIMBLE FAMILY DENTISTS. But there she might have to clean teeth or something. VALUE VISION OPTICIANS. But did opticians use secretaries? EZEKIEL POMFRET, ATTORNEY. Possibly defunct, from the expressionless look of the lowered window shade. And none of these places bore a HELP WANTED sign. Not that that made any practical difference.

At the next intersection, she took a left. She passed a pet supply and an antique store, so called (its window full of Fiesta ware and aqua plastic ashtrays shaped like boomerangs). A pharmacy. Two frame houses. A mom-and-pop grocery. Then another frame house, set so close to the street that its porch floor seemed an extension of the sidewalk. Propped in the dusty front window stood a cardboard notice, ROOM FOR RENT, bracketed by limp gauze curtains.

Room for rent.

This would be, of course, a "boardinghouse." The word summoned a picture of the secretary tidying the covers on her spinsterly white bed; her fellow boarders shuffling down the hall in their carpet slippers; her ancient landlady, dressed in black, setting the dining-room table—the "board"—for tomorrow's breakfast. In the time it took Delia to cross the porch and ring the bell, she became so well entrenched that she hardly felt the need to introduce herself to the woman who appeared at the door.

"Well, hi!" the woman said. "Can I help you?"

She didn't fit Delia's vision of a landlady. She was plump and fortyish, heavily rouged, wearing a towering dessert tray of lavish golden curls and a hot-pink pantsuit. Still, she seemed to be the one in charge, so Delia said, "I'm inquiring about the room."

"Room?"

"The room for rent," Delia reminded her.

"Oh, the room," the woman said. "Well. I was hoping to rent to a man."

Was that even legal, nowadays? Delia didn't know what to say next.

"Up to last April," the woman told her, opening the baggy screen door, "I just always had men. It just always seemed to work that way. I only rent out two rooms, you know, and so I had these two men, Mr. Lamb who travels weekdays and Larry Watts who was separated. But when Larry got back with his wife last April, why, I rented his room to a woman. And did I ever regret it!"

She turned, leaving the door to Delia, and started up a flight of stairs. Uncertainly, Delia followed. She had an impression of a house that had long ago been abandoned. Ovals of lighter wallpaper showed where pictures must once have hung, and the floorboards of the upstairs hall revealed the ghost of a rug.

"Katie O'Connell, her name was," the woman said. Even so short a climb had winded her. She patted her wide pink bosom with little spanking sounds. "A Delaware girl, I believe. She came to town to work for Zeke Pomfret—Zeke had just had his dear old Miss Percy *die* on him —and so Katie needed a place to stay and I said, 'Fine,' not having the slightest inkling: 'Fine,' I told her, thinking this would be no different from renting to a man. But, oh, it was, 'Where's this, where's that, where's my fresh towels daily, where's my little bar of soap . . . ?' I am not a bed-and-breakfast, mind you. I hope you don't think I'm a bed-and-breakfast."

"Of course not," Delia said.

"I'm only renting out rooms, you know? I bought this place three years ago. Fixer-upper, they called it. I bought it after I passed my real estate exam, thought I'd fix it up and sell it, but the way the market's been doing I just never have found the money for that, and so I'm living here myself and renting out two of the rooms. But there's no meals involved; I hope you're not looking for meals. This Katie, she was, 'Oh, let me just keep this quart of milk in your fridge,' and not two shakes later she was cooking in my kitchen. Why, *I* don't even cook in my kitchen! This is a bare-bones operation."

Proving it, she opened the door to the right of the stairs. Delia followed her into a long, narrow room, its outside wall slanting inward under the eaves, a window at each end. A metal cot extended from beneath the front window, and a low, orange-brown bureau sat against the inside wall. There was a smell like a hornet's nest—a dry, sharp, moldering smell that came, perhaps, from the brittle-looking tan wallpaper traced with mottled roses.

"Now, Katie had drapes on these windows," the woman said, "but she took them when she left. Left last Thursday with Larry Watts; we think they went to Hawaii."

"The . . . Larry Watts who was separated?" Delia asked in confusion.

"Oh, I didn't realize you knew him. Yes, once I put it all together, I recalled he did come back for his raincoat—raincoat he'd left in the downstairs closet. That must be how they met. Next thing anyone knows, he's flown the coop, leaving that little wife of his for the second time in two years. Not to mention Zeke Pomfret needing to hunt up a whole new girl now, so soon after losing poor Miss Percy."

She flung open a door at the rear, exposing a shallow closet. Three hangers tinkled faintly. "Bathroom's off the hall, full bath with tub and shower," she said, "and you wouldn't have to share it but on weekends, when Mr. Lamb gets back from his sales trips. I stay downstairs, myself. Rent is forty-two dollars a week. You want it?"

Forty-two dollars was less than a single night in most hotels. And a hotel would not be anything like so satisfyingly Spartan. Delia said, "You mean it's all right I'm not a man?"

The woman shrugged. "No one *else* has come along," she said.

Delia walked over to the cot, which was made up with white sheets and a white woolen blanket washed bald. When she tested the mattress with one palm, it sounded the same tinny note as the hangers.

She said, "Definitely I want it."

"Well, great. I'm Belle Flint, by the way."

"I'm Delia Grinstead," Delia said, and then she wondered if she should have used an alias. But Belle seemed reassuringly uninterested. She was fluffing her curls now in the mirror over the bureau. "So," Delia said, "would I have to . . . sign a contract?"

"Contract?"

"I mean . . ."

It must be painfully apparent that she had never arranged for her own housing before. "I mean a . . . lease or something?" she asked.

"Lord, no, just pay in advance, every Saturday morning," Belle said, baring her front teeth to the mirror. "Let's see. Today's Monday. . . . Pay me thirty dollars; that'll cover this week. You plan on staying here long?"

"Oh, maybe," Delia said, deliberately vague, and she started making a to-do over digging through her tote. Belle was tilting her chin now to study the cushion of flesh beneath it. Her entire face was a cushion; she resembled one of those lush, soft flowers, a peony or a big floppy iris.

"Well, here," Delia told her, "ten, twenty . . . ," and only then did Belle turn away from the mirror. If she was surprised to receive cash, she didn't show it. She folded the bills and tucked them into her breast pocket.

"I guess you'll want to go fetch your belongings," she said, "and meantime I'll put your key on the bureau, just in case I'm out when you get back. I'm showing a house at four-thirty. You won't be bringing a lot of *stuff*, I hope."

"No, I—"

"Because this room doesn't have much storage space, and I hate for things to spill over. That's how all that happened with Larry Watts and Katie: his raincoat spilled into the downstairs closet, and so naturally he forgot it when he moved."

"I'm bringing very little," Delia said.

She would wait to come back till, say, five o'clock, when Belle was sure to be out. That way Belle wouldn't see she was really bringing nothing. It was now . . . Surreptitiously, she checked her watch. Three forty-five. Belle was clattering out of the room in her wedge-heeled sandals. "Rules are, the first floor is mine," she said, pausing in the hall, "and that includes the kitchen. Café across the street is pretty good: Rick-Rack's. There's a laundromat on East Street, and Mrs. Auburn comes Fridays to clean the rooms. We never lock the front door, but that key to your room does work, if you're the nervous type. You got all that?"

"Yes, thanks."

"And I don't suppose you'll have guests," Belle said. She gave Delia a sudden appraising look. "Men guests, that is."

"Oh! No, I won't."

"Your private life is your private life, but that forty-two dollars covers utilities for one. Sheets and towels for one, too."

"I don't even know anybody to invite," Delia assured her.

"You're not a local girl, huh?"

"Well, no."

"Me neither. Till I came here with a fella, I never heard of Bay Borough," Belle said cheerfully. "The fella didn't work out, but I stayed on anyhow."

Delia knew she should volunteer some information in exchange, but all she said was, "I guess I'll wash up before I go get my things."

"Help yourself," Belle said with a wave. And she went clomping down the stairs.

Delia waited a polite half second before stepping into the bathroom. She hadn't peed since ten o'clock that morning.

The bathroom wallpaper—seahorses breathing silver bubbles—curled at the seams, and the fixtures were old and rust-stained, but everything looked clean. First Delia used the toilet, and then she patted her face with cool water and let it air-dry. (The one towel belonged to the other boarder, she assumed.) She avoided her face in the mirror; she preferred to hang on to the image she'd seen in the changing booth. She did glance down at her dress, though, checking it for neatness, for secretarial properness. And just before walking out, she slipped her wedding ring off her finger and dropped it into her tote.

Then she made a brief return trip to her room. She didn't go inside but merely stood in the doorway, claiming it—reveling in its starkness, now that she had it completely to herself.

Clop-clop back up the street, eyes front, as if she knew where she was headed. Well, she did, more or less. Already the little town held pockets of familiar sights: the faded red soft-drink machine outside the Gobble-Up Grocery, the chipped Fiesta ware in Bob's Antiques, the stacked bags of kibble for overweight dogs in Pet Heaven. She took a right at the corner, and the green square in the distance seemed as comfortable, as well known and faintly boring, as if she had spent her childhood at the foot of Mr. Bay's fringed chair.

Ezekiel Pomfret still had his shade pulled down, but when Delia tried the door it yielded. A steep flight of stairs climbed straight ahead. A ground-floor door to the right bore, on its cloudy, pebbled glass, Ezekiel Pomfret's name once again and WILLS & ESTATES—DOMESTIC-CRIMINAL LAW. That door, too, opened when Delia tried it. She stepped into a walnut-lined room with a reception desk in the center. No one sat at the desk, she was pleased to see. No one was visible anywhere, but behind another door, this one ornately paneled, she heard a man's voice. It stopped and started, interspersed by silence, so she knew he must be talking on the phone.

She crossed to the desk, which was bare except for a telephone and a typewriter. She lifted a corner of the typewriter's gray rubber hood. Manual; not even electric. (She had worried she would find a computer.) She gave a small, testing spin to the swivel chair behind it.

Good afternoon, she would say. *I'm here to ask if* . . .

No, not *ask*. *Ask* was too tentative.

She reached up to pat her hair, which felt as crumbly as dry sand on the beach. (The beach! No: shoo that thought away.) She smoothed her skirt around her hips and made sure that the trim on her tote—a flashy pink bow, ridiculous—was hidden beneath her arm.

It just seemed so fateful, Mr. Pomfret, it seemed almost like a direct command, that I should learn about poor Miss Percy exactly at the moment when . . .

The voice behind the door gathered energy and volume. Mr. Pomfret must be winding up his conversation.

Like having something accidentally break my fall, does that make any sense? Like I've been falling, falling all day and then was snagged by a random hook, or caught by an outjutting ledge, and this is where I happened to land, so I was wondering whether . . .

Slam of receiver, squeak of caster wheels, heavy tread on carpet. The paneled door swung open, and a big-bellied middle-aged man in a seersucker suit surveyed her over his half-glasses. "I *thought* I heard someone," he said.

"Mr. Pomfret, I'm Delia Grinstead," she told him. "I've come to be your secretary."

At four-fifteen she returned to the dime store and bought one cotton nightgown, white, and two pairs of nylon panty hose. At four twenty-five she crossed the square to Bassett Bros. Shoe Store and bought a large black leather handbag. The bag cost fifty-seven dollars. When she first saw the price she considered settling for vinyl, but then she decided that only genuine leather would pass muster with Miss Grinstead.

Miss Grinstead was Delia—the new Delia; for after one grimacing, acidic "Ms.," that was how Mr. Pomfret had addressed her throughout their interview. It seemed apt that she should accept this compromise—the unmarried title, the married surname. Certainly the aproned, complacent sound of "Mrs." no longer applied, and yet she couldn't go back to being giggly young Miss Felson. Besides, her Social Security card said Grinstead. She had drawn it from her wallet and read off the number to Mr. Pomfret (not having had enough use of it, all these years, to know it by heart). She had told him she was relocating after burying her mother. A whole unspoken history insinuated itself in the air between them: the puttery female household, the daughter's nunnish devotion. She said she had worked in a doctor's office her entire adult life. "Twenty-two years," she told Mr. Pomfret, "and I felt so sad to leave, but I simply couldn't stay on in Baltimore with all those memories." She seemed to have been infected with Miss Grinstead's manner of speaking. She would never herself have used "simply" in casual conversation, and the word "memories" in that context had a certain mealymouthed tone that was unlike her.

If references had been called for, she was prepared to say that her employer had recently died as well. (She was killing off people right and left today.) But Mr. Pomfret didn't mention references. His sole concern was the nature of her past duties. Had she typed, had she filed, taken shorthand? She answered truthfully, but it felt like lies. "I typed all the bills and correspondence and the doctor's charts," she said. Sam's worn face rose up before her, along with his mended white coat and the paisley tie that he called his "paramecium tie." She sat straighter in her chair. "I filed and manned the phone and kept the appointment book, but unfortunately I do not take shorthand."

"Well, no matter," Mr. Pomfret said. "Neither did Miss Percy or Miss What's-her-name. I've always dreamed of having a secretary with shorthand, but I guess it's not meant to be."

There was an uncomfortable moment when he asked for her address, since she had no idea what it was. But when she mentioned Belle Flint he said, "Oh, yes, on George Street." He added, as he made a notation, "Belle's a real fun gal." That was the advantage to a small town, Delia supposed. Or the disadvantage, depending on how you looked at it.

He said she should start tomorrow; her hours were nine to five. Sorry the pay was just minimum wage, he said (sliding his eyes over subtly to gauge her reaction). Also, she was expected to brew the coffee; he hoped that wasn't a problem.

Of course it wasn't, Delia said brusquely, and she rose and terminated the interview. Her impression of Mr. Pomfret was that he was a man without any grain to him, someone benign but not especially interesting, and that was fine with her. In fact, she didn't much like him, and that was fine too. For the impersonal new life she seemed to be manufacturing for herself, Mr. Pomfret was ideal.

Her watch said twenty minutes till five, and she hadn't eaten since breakfast. Before heading back to her room, therefore, she walked to the café that Belle had recommended. It turned out to be not directly across from Belle's but a few doors farther west, next to a hardware. Still, she could see the boardinghouse from the window; so she sat in the booth that offered the best view and kept watch against Belle's return. Maybe she should have purchased a suitcase, just so she could move in openly. But it was foolish to spend money on appearances. Already her five hundred dollars had dwindled to . . . what? Mentally she tallied it up and then winced. When the waitress arrived, she confined her order to a bowl of vegetable soup and a glass of milk.

Rick-Rack's was the kind of place where she might have eaten in high school—a diner, basically, linoleum floored and tile walled, with six or eight booths and a row of stools along a Formica counter. One little redhead served the whole room, and a blue-black young man, gigantically muscled and shaven skulled, did the cooking. He was grilling a cheese sandwich for the only other customer, a boy about Ramsay's age. The smell of fried food gave Delia hunger pangs even as she was spooning her soup, but she reminded herself that soup provided more vitamins for the money, and she declined the homemade pie for dessert. She paid at the register. The cook, after wiping his hands on his apron, rang up her total without comment. Next time she'd bring something to read, she decided. She had felt awkward, munching her saltines and staring fixedly out the window.

No sign of Belle back at the house. Delia unlatched the front door and felt a thin, bare silence all around her. She climbed the stairs, thinking, *Here comes the executive secretary, returning from her lone meal to the solitude of her room.* It wasn't a complaint, though. It was a boast. An exultation.

When she opened her own door the hornet's-nest smell seemed stronger, perhaps because of the afternoon heat that had penetrated the eaves. She set her belongings on the bureau and went to raise both windows. The rear window offered a view of the tiny backyard and an alley. The front window showed the porch overhang and the buildings across the street. Delia leaned her forehead against the screen and picked out the café (B. J. "RICK" RACKLEY, PROP.) and the hardware store and a brown shingled house with the bars of a crib or a playpen visible in one upstairs window. The only sounds were soothing sounds—occasional cars swishing past and footsteps on the sidewalk.

Belle had left an old-fashioned, spindly key on the bureau, and Delia fitted it into the door and turned the lock. Then she took the tags off her new handbag, dropped her wallet inside, and hung the bag from a hook in the closet. She stowed her other purchases in the bureau. (The drawers stuck and slid out crookedly; they were cheaply made, like the house itself.) She hung Sam's beach robe on a hanger. She placed her cosmetic kit in a drawer. Her tote, with its remaining litter of sun lotions and swimsuit and rubber bands and such, she boosted onto the closet shelf. Then she closed the closet door and went over to the cot and sat down.

So.

She was settled.

She could look around the room and detect not the slightest hint that anybody lived here.

It was twilight before Belle returned. Delia heard the clunk of a car door out front, then loud heels on the porch. But neither woman called out a greeting. In fact, Delia, who had been staring into space for who knows how long, rose from the cot as soundlessly as possible, and tiptoed when she went over to collect some things from the bureau, and took care not to creak any floorboards when she crossed the hall to the bathroom.

While she waited for the shower to run warm, she brushed her teeth and undressed, putting her underwear to soak in the sink. A second towel and washcloth now hung on the other towel bar, she saw. She took the washcloth with her and stepped behind the shower curtain, which was crackly with age and slightly mildewed.

Grime and sweat and sunblock streamed off her, uncovering a whole new layer of skin. The soles of her feet, which felt ironed flat from all that walking, seemed to be drinking up water. She lifted her face to the spray and let her hair get wet. Finally, regretfully, she shut off the faucets and stepped out to towel herself dry. The new nightgown drifted airily over her scorched shoulders.

She chose not to leave her toothbrush in the holder above the sink. Instead, she returned it to her cosmetic kit and carried everything back to her room. Her wrung-out underclothes she draped on one of the hangers in the closet. This meant she would have to keep the closet door open during the night—a blot on the room's sterility. Better that, though, than letting her laundry clutter the bathroom. She approved of Belle's house rules; she did not intend to "spill over."

She turned the bedcovers back and lay down, drawing up just the top sheet. The breeze from the window chilled her damp head, but not so much that she needed a blanket.

Outside, children were playing. It wasn't even completely dark yet. She lay on her back with her eyes open, keeping her mind as blank as the ceiling above her. Once, though, perhaps hours later, a single thought did present itself. *Oh, God,* she thought, *how am I going to get out of this?* But immediately afterward she closed her eyes, and that was how she fell asleep.

7

Baltimore Woman Disappears, Delia read, and she felt a sudden thud in her stomach, as if she'd been punched. *Baltimore Woman Disappears During Family Vacation.*

She had been checking the Baltimore newspapers daily, morning and evening. There was nothing in either paper Tuesday, nothing Wednesday, nothing Thursday morning. But the Thursday evening edition, which arrived in the vending box near the square in time for Delia's lunch hour, carried a notice in the Metro section. *Delaware State Police announced early today . . .*

She folded the paper open to the article, glancing around as she did so. On the park bench opposite hers, a young woman was handing her toddler bits of something to feed the pigeons, piece by piece. On the bench to her right, a very old man was leafing through a magazine. No one seemed aware of Delia's presence.

Mrs. Grinstead was last seen around noon this past Monday, walking south along the stretch of sand between . . .

Probably the police had some rule that people were not considered missing till a certain amount of time had passed. That must be why there'd been no announcement earlier. (Searching each paper before this, Delia had felt relieved and wounded, both. Did no one realize she was gone? Or maybe she *wasn't* gone; this whole experience had been so dreamlike. Maybe she was still moving through her previous life the same as always, and the Delia here in Bay Borough had somehow just split off from the original.)

It hurt to read her physical description: *fair or light-brown hair . . . eyes are blue or gray or perhaps green . . .* For heaven's sake, hadn't anyone in her family ever looked at her? And how could Sam have made her clothing sound so silly? *Kind of baby-doll*, indeed! She refolded the paper with a snap and then darted another glance around her. The toddler was throwing a tantrum now, a silent little stomping dance, because he'd run out of pigeon food. The old man was licking a finger to turn a page. Delia hated when he did that. Every lunch hour he came here with a magazine and licked his way clear through it, and Delia could only hope that no one else was planning to read it after him.

Like a commuter who always chooses the same seat on the train, like a guest who always settles in the same chair in the living room, Delia had managed in just three days to establish a routine for herself. Breakfast at Rick-Rack's, over the morning paper. Lunch in the square—yogurt and fresh fruit purchased earlier from the Gobble-Up Grocery. Always on the southeast park bench, always with the evening paper. Then some kind of shopping task to fill the hour: Tuesday, a pair of low-heeled black shoes because her espadrilles were blistering her heels. Wednesday, a gooseneck reading lamp. Today she had planned to look for one of those immersion coils so she could brew herself a cup of tea first thing every morning. But now, with this newspaper item, she didn't know. She felt so exposed, all at once. She just wanted to scuttle back to the office.

She dropped her lunch leavings into a wire trash basket and buried the newspaper underneath them. As a rule she left the paper on the bench for others, but not today.

The mother was trying to stuff the toddler into his stroller. The toddler was resisting, refusing to bend in the middle. The old man had finished his magazine and was fussily fitting his glasses into their case. None of the three looked at Delia when she walked past them. Or maybe they were pretending, even the toddler; maybe they'd been instructed not to alarm her. No. She gave her shoulders a shake. *Get ahold of yourself.* It wasn't as if she'd committed any crime. She decided to go on with her routine—drop by the dime store as she'd planned.

Funny how life contrived to build up layers of *things* around a person.

Already she had that goosenecked lamp, because the overhead bulb had proved inadequate for reading in bed; and she kept a stack of paper cups and a box of tea bags on her closet shelf, making do till now with hot water from the bathroom faucet; and it was becoming clear she needed a second dress. Last night, the first really warm night of summer, she had thought, *I should buy a fan.* Then she had told herself, *Stop. Stop while you're ahead.*

She walked into the dime store and paused. Housewares, maybe? The old woman presiding over the cookie sheets and saucepans stood idle, twiddling her beads; so Delia approached her. "Would you have one of those immersion coils?" she asked. "Those things you put in a cup to heat up water?"

"Well, I know what you mean," the old woman said. "I can see it just as plain as the nose on your face. Electric, right?"

"Right," Delia said.

"My grandson took one to college with him, but would you believe it? He didn't read the directions. Tried to heat a bowl of soup when the directions said only water. Stink? He said you couldn't imagine the stink! But I don't have any here. Maybe try the hardware department."

"Thanks," Delia said crisply, and she moved away.

Sure enough, she found it in Hardware, hanging on a rack among the extension cords and three-prong adapters. She paid in exact change. The clerk—a gray-haired man in a bow tie—winked when he handed her the bag. "Have a nice day, young lady," he said. He probably thought he was flattering her. Delia didn't bother smiling.

She had noticed that Miss Grinstead was not a very friendly person. The people involved in her daily routine remained two-dimensional to her, like the drawings in those children's books about the different occupations. She hadn't developed the easy, bantering relationships Delia was accustomed to.

Leaving the dime store, she crossed Bay Street and passed the row of little shops. The clock in the optician's window said 1:45. She always tried her best to fill her whole lunch hour, one o'clock to two o'clock, but so far had not succeeded.

And what would she do in wintertime, when it grew too cold to eat in the square? For she was looking that far ahead now, it seemed—this Miss Grinstead with her endless, unmarked, unchanging string of days.

But in Bay Borough it was always summer. That was the only season she could picture here.

She opened Mr. Pomfret's outside door, then the pebble-paned inner door. He was already back from his own lunch, talking on his office phone as usual. *Wurlitzer, wurlitzer,* it sounded like from here. Delia shut her handbag in the bottom desk drawer, smoothed her skirt beneath her, and seated herself in the swivel chair. She had left a letter half finished, and now she resumed typing, keeping her back very straight and her hands almost level as she had been taught in high school.

Authorities do not suspect drowning, the paper had said. It hadn't occurred to her they might. *Since Mrs. Grinstead professed a*—how had they put it?—*professed an aversion to water.* Or something of the sort. Made her sound like a woman who never bathed. She slammed the carriage return more violently than was necessary. And that business about Eliza saying she'd been a cat! People must think the both of them were lunatics.

This typewriter had a stiffer action than the one in Sam's office. Her first day at work, she'd broken two fingernails. After that she had filed all her nails down blunt, which was more appropriate anyhow to Miss Grinstead's general style. Besides, it had used up twenty minutes of an evening. She was devoting a lot of thought these days to how to use up her evenings.

"Well, let's do that! We'll have to get together and do that!" Mr. Pomfret was saying, suddenly louder and heartier. Delia typed the closing ("Esquire," he called himself) and rolled the letter out of the carriage. Mr. Pomfret burst through the door. "Miss Grinstead, when Mr. Miller shows up I'll need you in here taking notes," he said. "We're going to send a . . . What's that you've got?"

"Letter to Gerald Elliott?" Delia reminded him.

"Elliott! I met with Elliott back in . . ."

She checked the date at the top of the page. "May," she said. "May fourteenth."

"Damn."

It had come to light that Delia's immediate predecessor had stowed her more irksome chores in the filing cabinet under *Ongoing.* Anything red-inked by Mr. Pomfret had conveniently vanished. (And a great deal had been red-inked, since Katie O'Connell couldn't spell and apparently did not believe in paragraphs.) Mr. Pomfret had turned purple when Delia brought him the evidence, but Delia was secretly pleased. This way she looked so capable herself—so efficient, so take-charge. (She felt a bit like a grade-school tattletale.) Also, the retyping job amounted to a low-key training course. She would be sorry when she finished.

"Mr. Miller is due at two-thirty," Mr. Pomfret told her. He was leaning over her desk to sign the letter. "I want you to write down word for word everything he specifies."

"Yes, Mr. Pomfret."

He straightened, capping his pen, and gave her a sudden sharp look over his lizardy lower lids. Sometimes Delia carried her secretary act a bit too far, she suspected. She flashed him an insincere smile and gathered up the letter. His signature was large and sweeping, smeared on the curves. He used one of those expensive German fountain pens that leaked.

"And we'll want coffee, so you might as well fix it ahead," he told her.

"Yes, Mr.—. Certainly," she said.

She went into his office for the carafe, then took it to the sink in the powder room. When she came back he was seated at the credenza, short thighs twisted sideways, tapping once again at his computer. For he did have a computer. He had bought it sometime just recently and fallen under its spell, which might explain his failure to notice Katie O'Connell's filing methods. Theoretically, he was going to learn the machine's mysterious ways and then teach Delia, but after her first morning Delia knew she had nothing to fear. The computer would sit forever in its temporary position while Mr. Pomfret wrestled happily with questions of "backups" and "macros." Right now he was recording every dinner party he and his wife had ever hosted—guest list, menu, wines, and even seating arrangements—so their variables could be rotated into infinity. Delia gave the screen a scornful glance and circled it widely, heading for the coffeemaker at the other end of the credenza.

Water, filter, French roast. This coffeemaker was top-of-the-line: it ground its own beans. She supposed it came from one of those catalogs that weighed down the office mail. Whenever Mr. Pomfret spotted an item he liked, he had Delia place an order. ("Yes, Mr. Pomfret . . .") She called 1-800 numbers clear across the country, requesting a bedside clock that talked, a pocket-sized electronic dictionary, a black leather map case for the glove compartment. Her employer's greed, like his huge belly, made Delia feel trim and virtuous. She didn't at all mind placing the orders. She enjoyed everything about this job, especially its dryness. No one received word of inoperable cancer in a lawyer's office. No one told Delia how it felt to be going blind. No one claimed to remember Delia's babyhood.

She pressed a button on the coffeemaker, and it started grinding. "Help!" Mr. Pomfret shouted over the din. He was goggling at his computer screen, where the lines of text shivered and shimmied. For some reason, it never occurred to him that this always happened when the grinder was running. Delia left the office, closing the door discreetly behind her.

She typed another letter, this one enumerating the corporate bylaws of an accounting firm. ("Buy-laws," Katie O'Connell had spelled it.) *Pursuant to our discussion*, she typed, and *fiscal liability*, and *consent of those not in attendance*. She sacrificed speed for accuracy, as befitted Miss Grinstead, and corrected her rare mistakes with Wite-Out fluid on original and carbon both.

Mr. Miller arrived—a big, handsome, olive-skinned man with a narrow band of black hair. Delia followed him into Mr. Pomfret's office to serve their coffee and then perched on a chair, pen and pad ready. She had worried she couldn't write fast enough, but there wasn't much to write. The question was how often Mr. Miller's ex-wife could see their son, and the answer, according to Mr. Miller, was "Never," which Mr. Pomfret amended to once a week and alternate holidays, hours to be arranged at client's convenience. Then the conversation drifted to computers, and when it didn't drift back again, Delia cleared her throat and asked, "Will that be all?"

Mr. Pomfret said, "Hmm? Oh. Yes, thank you, Miss Grinstead." As she left, she heard him tell Mr. Miller, "We'll see to that right away. I'll have my girl mail it out this afternoon."

Delia settled in her swivel chair, rolled paper into the carriage, and started typing. You could have balanced a glass of water on the back of each of her hands.

The only other appointment was at four—a woman with some stock certificates belonging to her late mother—but Delia's services were not required for that. She addressed a number of envelopes and folded and inserted the letters Mr. Pomfret had signed. She sealed the flaps, licked stamps. She answered a call from a Mrs. Darnell, who made an appointment for Monday. Mr. Pomfret walked past her, cramming his arms into his suit coat. "Good night, Miss Grinstead," he said.

"Good night, Mr. Pomfret."

She sorted her carbons and filed them. She returned what was left of the Ongoing file to its drawer. She answered a call from a man who was disappointed to find Mr. Pomfret gone but would try him at home. She cleaned the coffeemaker. At five o'clock exactly she lowered all the shades, gathered the letters and her handbag, and left the office.

Mr. Pomfret had given her her own key, and she already knew the crotchets of the pebble-paned door—the way you had to push it inward a bit before it would lock.

Outside, the sun was still shining and the air felt warm and heavy after the air-conditioning. Delia walked at a leisurely pace, letting others pass her—men in business suits hurrying home from work, women rushing by with plastic bags from the Food King. She dropped her letters into the mailbox on the corner, but instead of turning left there, she continued north to the library—the next stop in her routine.

By now she had a sense of the town's layout. It was a perfect grid, with the square mathematically centered between three streets north and south of it, two streets east and west. Look west as you crossed an intersection, and you'd see pasture, sometimes even a cow. (In the mornings, when Delia woke, she heard distant roosters crowing.) The sidewalks were crumpled and given over in spots to grass, breaking off entirely when a tree stood in the way. The streets farther from the square had a tendency to slant into scabby asphalt mixed with weeds at the edges, like country highways.

On Border Street, the town's northern boundary, the Bay Borough Public Library crouched between a church and an Exxon station. It was hardly more than a cottage, but the instant Delia stepped inside she always felt its seriousness, its officialness. A smell of aged paper and glue hung above the four tables with their wooden chairs, the librarian's high varnished counter, the bookcases chockablock with elderly books. No CDs or videotapes here, no spin racks of paperback novels; just plain, sturdy volumes in buckram bindings with their Dewey decimal numbers handwritten on the spines in white ink. It was a matter of finances, Delia supposed. Nothing seemed to have been added in the last decade. Bestsellers were nowhere to be seen, but there was plenty of Jane Austen, and Edith Wharton, and various solemn works of history and biography. The children's corner gave off a glassy shine from all the layers of Scotch tape holding the tattered picture books together.

Closing time was five-thirty, which meant that the librarian was busy with her last-minute shelving. Delia could place yesterday's book on the counter without any chitchat; she could hunt down a book for today unobserved, since at this hour all the tables were empty. But what to choose? She wished this place carried romances. Dickens or Dostoyevsky she would never finish in one evening (she had an arrangement with herself where she read a book an evening). George Eliot, Faulkner, Fitzgerald . . .

She settled on *The Great Gatsby*, which she dimly remembered from sophomore English. She took it to the counter, and the librarian (a cocoa-colored woman in her fifties) stopped her shelving to come wait on her. "Oh, *Gatsby*!" she said. Delia merely said, "Mmhmm," and handed over her card.

The card had her new address on it: 14 George Street. A dash in the space for her telephone number. She had never been unreachable by phone before.

Tucking the book in her handbag, she left the library and headed south. The Pinchpenny Thrift Shop had changed its window display, she noticed. Now a navy knit dress hung alongside a shell-pink tuxedo. Would it be tacky to buy her second dress from a thrift shop? In a town this size, no doubt everyone could name the previous owner.

But after all, what did she care? She made a mental note to come try on the dress tomorrow during lunch hour.

Taking a right onto George Street, she met up with the mother and toddler who fed the pigeons in the square. The mother smiled at her, and before Delia thought, she smiled back. Immediately afterward, though, she averted her eyes.

Next stop was Rick-Rack's Café. She glanced over at the boarding-house as she passed. No cars were parked in front, she was glad to see. With luck, Belle would be out all evening. She seemed to lead a very busy life.

Rick-Rack's smelled of crab cakes, but whoever had ordered them had already eaten and gone. The little redheaded waitress was filling salt shakers. The cook was scraping down his griddle. "Well, hey!" he said, turning as Delia walked in.

"Hello," she said, smiling. (She had nothing against simple courtesy, as long as it went no further.) She settled in her usual booth. By the time the waitress came over, she was already deep in her library book, and all she said was, "Milk and the chicken pot pie, please." Then she went on reading.

Last night she'd had soup and whole-wheat toast; the night before that, tuna salad. Her plan was to alternate soup nights with protein nights.

Just inexpensive proteins, though. She couldn't afford the crab cakes, at least not till she got her first salary check.

Paying for her new shoes on Tuesday, she had wished she could use the credit card she was carrying in her wallet. If only a credit-card trail were not so easily traced! And then a peculiar thought had struck her. *Most untraceable of all*, she had thought, *would be dying*.

But of course she hadn't meant that the way it sounded.

The print in her library book was so large, she worried she had chosen something that wouldn't last the evening. She forced her eyes to travel more slowly, and when her meal arrived she stopped reading altogether. She kept the book open, though, next to her plate, in case somebody approached.

The waitress set out scalloped paper place mats for the supper crowd. The cook stirred something on the burner. Two creases traversed the base of his skull; his smooth black scalp seemed overlaid with a pattern of embroidery knots. He had made the pot pie from scratch, Delia suspected. The crust shattered beneath her fork. And the potatoes accompanying it seemed hand mashed, not all gluey and machine mashed.

She wondered whether her family had thought to thaw the casseroles she'd packed.

"If he do come," the cook was telling the waitress, "you got to keep him occupied. Because *I* ain't going to."

"You have to be around some, though," the waitress said.

"I ain't saying I won't be around. I say I won't keep him occupied."

The waitress looked toward Delia before Delia could look away. She had those bachelor's-button eyes you often see in redheads, and a round-chinned, innocent face. "My dad is planning a visit," she told Delia.

"Ah," Delia said, reaching for her book.

"He wasn't all that thrilled when me and Rick here got married."

The waitress and the cook were married? Delia was afraid that if she started reading now, they would think she disapproved too; so she marked her place on the page with one finger and said, "I'm sure he'll accept it eventually."

"Oh, he's accepted it, all right! Or says he has. But now whenever Rick sees him, he always gets to remembering how ugly Daddy acted at the start."

"I can't stand to be around the man," Rick said sadly.

"Daddy walks into a room and Rick is like, *whap!* and his mouth slams shut."

"Then Teensy here feels the pressure and goes to talking a mile a minute, nothing but pure silliness."

Delia knew what that was like. When her sister Linda was married to the Frenchman, whom their father had detested . . .

But she couldn't tell them that. She was sitting in this booth alone, utterly alone, without the conversational padding of father, sisters, husband, children. She was a person without a past. She took a breath to speak and then had nothing to say. It was Teensy who finally broke the silence. "Well," Teensy said, "at least we've got ourselves a few days to prepare for this." And she went off to wait on a couple who had just entered.

When Delia walked out of the café, she felt she was surrounded by a lighter kind of air than usual—thinner, more transparent—and she crossed the street with a floating gait. Just inside Belle's front door she found an array of letters scattered beneath the mail slot, but she didn't pick them up, didn't even check the names on the envelopes, because she knew for a fact that none of them was hers.

Upstairs, she went about her coming-home routine: putting away her things, showering, doing her laundry. Meanwhile she kept an ear out for Belle's return, because she would have moved more quietly with someone else in the house. But she could tell she had the place to herself.

When every last task was completed, she climbed into bed with her library book. If there had been a chair she would have sat up to read, but this was her only choice. She wondered whether Mr. Lamb's room was any better equipped. She supposed she could request a chair from Belle. That would mean a conversation, though, and Delia was avoiding conversation as much as possible. Heaven forbid they should get to be two cozy, chatty lady friends, exchanging news of their workdays every evening.

She propped her pillow against the metal rail at the head of the cot and leaned back. For this first little bit, the light from outdoors was enough to read by—a slant of warm gold that made her feel pleasantly lazy. She could hear a baby crying in the house across the street. A woman far away called, "Robbie! Kenny!" in that bell-like, two-note tune that mothers everywhere fetch their children home with. Delia read on, turning pages with a restful sound. She was interested in Gatsby's story but not what you would call carried away. It would serve to pass the evening, was all.

The light grew dimmer, and she switched on the gooseneck lamp that craned over her shoulder from the windowsill. Now the children across the street, released from the supper table, were playing something argumentative outdoors. Delia heard them for a while but gradually forgot to listen, and when she thought of them again she realized they must have gone in to bed. Night had fallen, and moths were thumping against the screen. Down in the street, a car door closed; heels clopped across the porch; Belle entered the house and went directly to the front room, where she started talking on the phone. "You know it's got great resale value," Delia heard, before forgetting to listen to that as well. Later she stopped reading for a moment and heard only silence, inside and out, except for the distant traffic on 380. It was cooler now, and she felt grateful for the lamp's small circle of warmth.

She came to the end of her book, but she kept rereading the final sentence till her eyes blurred over with tears. Then she placed the book on the floor and reached up to switch the lamp off so she could sit weeping in the dark—the very last step in her daily routine.

She wept without a thought in her head, heaving silent sobs that racked her chest and contorted her mouth. Every few minutes she blew her nose on the strip of toilet paper she kept under her pillow. When she felt completely drained, she gave a deep, shuddering sigh and said aloud, "Ah, well." Then she blew her nose one last time and lay down to sleep.

It amazed her that she always slept so soundly.

The toddler wanted the pigeons to eat from his fingers. He squatted in their midst, his bulky corduroy bottom just inches from the ground, and held a crouton toward them. But the pigeons strutted around him with shrewd, evasive glances, and when it dawned on him that they would never come closer he suddenly toppled backward, not giving the slightest warning, and pedaled the air in a fury. Delia smiled, but only behind the shield of her newspaper.

Today there was no further mention of her disappearance. She wondered if the authorities had forgotten her that quickly.

She folded the Metro section and laid it on the bench beside her. She reached for the cup of yogurt at her left and then noticed, out of the corner of her eye, the woman who stood watching her from several yards away.

Her heart gave a lurch. She said, "Eliza?"

Eliza moved forward abruptly, as if she had just this second deter-mined something.

There was no one beside her. No one behind her.

No one.

She was wearing a dress—a tailored tan shirtwaist that dated from the time when they still had a Stewart's department store. Eliza almost never wore dresses. This must be a special occasion, Delia thought, and then she thought, *Why, I am the occasion.* She rose, fumbling with her yogurt cup. "Hello, Eliza," she said.

"Hello, Delia."

They stood awkwardly facing each other, Eliza gripping a boxy leather purse in both hands, until Delia recollected the old man on the east bench. He appeared to be intent on his magazine, but that didn't fool her in the least. "Would you like to take a walk?" she asked Eliza.

"We could," Eliza said stiffly.

She was probably angry. Well, of course she was angry. Bundling her lunch things into the trash basket, Delia felt like a little girl hiding some mischief. She sensed she was blushing, too. Hateful thin-skinned complexion, always giving her away. She slung the strap of her handbag over her shoulder and set off across the square, with Eliza lagging a step behind as if to accentuate Delia's willfulness, her lack of consideration. When they reached the street, Delia stopped and turned to face her. "I guess you think I shouldn't have done this," she said.

"I didn't say that. I'm waiting to hear your reasons."

Delia started walking again. If she had known Eliza would pop up this way, she would have invented some reasons ahead of time. It was ridiculous not to have any.

"Mr. Sudler thought you were a battered wife," Eliza said.

"Who?"

"The roofer. Vernon Sudler."

"Oh, Vernon," Delia said. Yes, of course: he would have seen the newspaper.

They crossed the street and headed north. Delia had planned to visit the thrift shop, but now she didn't know where she was going.

"He phoned us in Baltimore," Eliza said. "He asked for—"

"Baltimore! What were you doing in Baltimore?"

"Why, we packed up and drove there after you left. Surely you didn't think we'd stay at the beach."

Actually, Delia *had* thought that. But she could see now it would have looked strange: everybody slathering on the suntan lotion as usual, industriously blowing air into their rafts while the policemen gave their bloodhounds a sniff of Delia's slippers.

"We thought at first you'd gone to Baltimore yourself," Eliza was saying. "You can imagine the fuss with the floor refinishers when all of us walked in. And when we didn't find you there . . . Well, thank goodness Mr. Sudler called. He called the house last night, inquiring how to get in touch with me personally, and as luck would have it I was the one who answered. So he said he could swear you hadn't been kidnapped, but he hesitated to tell the police because he believed you'd had good cause to run away. He said you got out of his van at a church that counsels battered women."

"I did?"

Delia stopped in front of the florist's shop.

"You saw their signboard and asked him to let you out, he said."

"Signboard?"

"And also there'd been some discussion, he said, something you two were discussing that made him wonder later if . . . But he wouldn't tell me your whereabouts, in case your husband was dangerous. 'Dangerous!' I said. 'Why, Sam Grinstead is the kindest man alive!' I said. But Mr. Sudler was very fixed in his mind. He said, 'I only called to tell you she's all right, and I want to say too I didn't know at the time that she was running away. She just begged me for a ride to this certain town,' he said, 'and claimed that she had family there, so I didn't see the harm.' Then he said not to tell Sam, but of course I did tell Sam; I could hardly keep it a secret. I told Sam I would come talk to you first and find out how things stood."

She waited. She was going to make Delia ask. All right. "And what did Sam say back?" Delia asked.

"He said well *naturally* I should come. He agreed completely."

"Oh."

Another wait.

"And he quite understood that I couldn't divulge which town it was till we'd talked."

"I see," Delia said.

Then she said, "But how did *you* know the town?"

"Why, because you told Mr. Sudler you had family there."

"Family. Um . . ."

"Our mother's family! In Bay Borough."

"Mother's family lives in Bay Borough?"

"Well, they used to. Maybe some still do, but nobody I would have heard of. You knew that. Bay Borough? Where Aunt Henny lived? And Great-Uncle Roscoe had his chicken farm just west of?"

"That was in Bay Borough?"

"Where else!"

"I never realized," Delia said.

"I can't imagine why not. Shoot, there's even a Weber Street—Grandmother Carroll's maiden name. I crossed it coming in from Three eighty. And a Carroll Street just south of here, if I remember correctly. Isn't there a Carroll Street?"

"Well, yes," Delia said, "but I thought that was the other Carrolls. The Declaration of Independence Carrolls."

"No, dear heart, it's our Carrolls," Eliza said comfortably. Proving her point had evidently put her in a better mood.

They started walking again, passing the dentists' office and the optician's. "In fact, I believe we're related to the man who started this town," Eliza said. "But only by marriage."

"The man : . . You mean George Bay?"

"Right."

"George Bay the deserter?"

"Well, you're a fine one to talk, might I mention."

Delia flinched.

"So I drove on over this morning," Eliza said, "and inquired anywhere I thought you might be staying. Turns out there's only one inn, not counting that sleazy little motel on Union Street. And when I didn't find you there I figured I'd keep an eye on the square, because it looked to be the kind of square that everybody in town passes through at one time of day or another."

They were abreast of Mr. Pomfret's office now. If he had returned from lunch he could glance out the front window and see her walking by. Miss Grinstead with a companion! Acting sociable! She hoped he was still in the Bay Arms Restaurant with his cronies. At George Street she steered Eliza left. They passed Pet Heaven, where a boy was arranging chew toys next to the sacks of kibble.

"Delia," Eliza said, "Mr. Sudler had it wrong, didn't he? I mean, is there some . . . problem you want to tell me about?"

"Oh, no," Delia said.

"Ah." Eliza suddenly looked almost pretty. "See there? I told him so!" she cried. "I told him I was positive you just needed a little breather. You know what the police said? When we called them, this one policeman said, 'Folks,' he said, 'I'll wager any amount she is perfectly safe and healthy.' Said, 'The most surprising number of women seem to take it into their heads to walk out during family vacations.' Did you know that? Isn't that odd?"

"Hmm," Delia said. Her feet felt very burdensome. She could just barely drag them along.

"I guess he'd had lots of experience, working in Bethany Beach and all."

"Yes, I guess he had," Delia said.

"So should we collect your things, Dee?"

"My things," Delia said. She stopped short.

"I'm parked down next to the square. Do you have any luggage?"

Something hard rose up in Delia's throat—a kind of stubbornness, only fiercer. She was taken aback by the force of it. "No!" she said. She swallowed. "I mean, no, I'm not going with you."

"Pardon?"

"I want . . . I need . . . I have a place now, I mean a job, a position, and a place to stay. See? There's where I live," Delia said, gesturing toward Belle's. The gauze curtains in the downstairs windows looked like bandages, she noticed.

"You have a house?" Eliza asked incredulously.

"Well, a room. Come see! Come inside!"

She took Eliza's elbow and drew her toward the porch. Eliza hung back, her arm as rigid as a chicken wing. "A real estate agent owns it," Delia told her as she opened the door. "A *woman* real estate agent, very nice. The rent is extremely reasonable."

"I should think so," Eliza said, gazing about.

"I work for a lawyer just around the corner. He's the only lawyer in town and he handles everything, wills, estates . . . and I have total charge of his office. I bet you didn't think I could do that, did you? You probably thought it was just because I was Daddy's daughter that I worked in the office at home, but now I'm finding . . ."

They were climbing the stairs, Delia in front. She wished Belle would hang some pictures. Either that or put up new wallpaper. "Basically this whole floor is mine," she said, "because the other boarder travels during the week. So I have a private bathroom, see?" She waved toward it. She unlocked the door to her room and walked in. "All mine," she said, setting her handbag on the bureau.

Eliza advanced slowly.

"Isn't it perfect?" Delia asked. "I know it might seem a bit bare, but—"

"Delia, are you telling me you plan to live here?"

"I do live here!"

"But . . . forever?"

"Yes, why not?" Delia said.

She kept feeling the urge to swallow again, but she didn't give in to it. "Sit down," she told Eliza. "Could I offer you some tea?"

"Oh, I . . . no, thanks." Eliza took a tighter grip on her purse. She seemed out of place in these surroundings—somebody from home, with that humble, faded look that home people always have. "Let me make sure I'm understanding this," she said.

"I could heat up the water in no time. Just have a seat on the bed."

"You are telling me you're leaving us forever," Eliza said, not moving. "You plan to stay on permanently in Bay Borough. You're leaving your husband, and you're leaving all three of your children, one of whom is still in high school."

"In high school, yes, and fifteen years old, and able to manage without me fine and dandy," Delia said. To her horror, she felt tears beginning to warm her eyelids. "Better than with me, in fact," she continued firmly. "How are the kids, by the way?"

"They're bewildered; what would you expect?" Eliza said.

"But are they doing all right otherwise?"

"Do you care?" Eliza asked her.

"Of course I care!"

Eliza moved away. Delia thought she planned to relent and take a seat, but no, she went to gaze out the front window. "Sam, as you might imagine, is just dumbfounded," she announced, with her back to Delia.

"Yes, he must wish now he'd chosen Daughter One or Two instead," Delia said.

Eliza wheeled around. She said, "Delia, what is the *matter* with you? Have you totally lost your senses? Here's this wonderful, model husband roaming the house like a zombie, and your children not knowing *what* to think, and the neighbors all atwitter, and the TV people and newspapers spreading our names across the state of Maryland—"

"It's been on TV?"

"Every station in Baltimore! Big color photograph flashing on the screen: 'Have you seen this woman?' "

"What photo did they use?" Delia asked.

"The one from Linda's wedding."

"That was years ago!"

"Well, most other times you were the one snapping the picture. We didn't have much to choose from."

"But that awful bridesmaid gown! With the shoulders that looked like the hanger was still inside!"

"Delia," Eliza said, "ever since Mr. Sudler phoned, I've been trying to figure out what could have made you walk away from us like that. Till now I'd thought you'd had it so easy. Baby of the family. Cute as a button. Miss Popularity in high school. Daddy's pet. It's true you lacked a mother, but you never seemed to notice. Well, you were only four years old when she died, and anyhow she was bedridden all your life. But now I think four years old was plenty old! Of course you noticed! You'd spent those afternoons playing in her room, for God's sake!"

"I don't remember," Delia said.

"Oh, you must. You and she had those paper dolls. You kept them in a shoe box on the floor of her closet, and every afternoon—"

"I don't remember anything about it!" Delia said. "Why do you keep insisting? I have no memory of her at all!"

"And then being Daddy's pet was kind of a mixed blessing, I guess. When he discouraged you from applying to college, took it for granted you'd come to work in the office . . . well, I wouldn't blame you for resenting that."

"I didn't resent it!"

"And then his dying: of course his dying would hit you harder than—"

"I don't see why in the world you're bringing all this up!" Delia said.

"Just hear me out, please. Dee, you know I believe that human beings live many lives."

Ordinarily, Delia would have groaned. Now, though, she was glad to see the talk veering in a new direction.

"Each life is a kind of assignment, I believe," Eliza told her. "You're given this one assigned slot each time you come to earth, this little square of experience to work through. So even if your life has been troubled, I believe it's what you're meant to deal with on this particular go-round."

"How do you know my assignment doesn't include Bay Borough?" Delia asked her.

A ripple of uncertainty crossed Eliza's forehead.

Delia said, "Eliza, um, I was wondering . . ."

"Yes?" Eliza said eagerly.

"Can you tell me if they brought the cat home from the beach?"

A mistake. Something closed over behind Eliza's eyes. "The cat!" she said. "Is that all you care about?"

"Of course it's not all I care about, but he *was* kind of skulking under furniture when I left, and I didn't know if they'd remember to—"

"They remembered," Eliza said shortly. "What for, I can't imagine. Durn creature is getting so old he snores even when he's awake."

"Old?" Delia said.

"They packed all your clothes and your casseroles too," Eliza said. "Poor Susie had to pack your— Delia? Are you crying?"

"No," Delia said in a muffled voice.

"Are you crying about the *cat*?"

"No, I said!"

Well, she knew he wasn't a kitten anymore. (Such a *merry* kitten he'd been—a kitten with a sense of humor, slinking theatrically around the forbidden houseplants and then giving her a smirk.) But she had thought of him as still in his prime, and only now did she recall how he had started pausing lately as if to assemble himself before attempting the smallest leap. How she had swatted him off the counter once this spring and he had fallen clumsily, scrabbling with his claws, landing in an embarrassed heap and then hastily licking one haunch as if he had intended to take that pose all along.

She widened her eyes to keep the tears from spilling over.

"Delia," Eliza said, "is there something you're not telling me? Does this have something to do with that . . . man back home?"

Delia didn't bother acting puzzled. She said, "No, it's not about him." Then she went to the head of the bed, causing Eliza to take a step back. She reached under her pillow for the toilet paper and blew her nose. "I must be going crazy," she said.

"No, no! You're not crazy! Just a little, oh, tired, maybe. Just a little run-down. You know what I think?" Eliza asked. "I think it took more out of you than any of us realized, tending Daddy's last illness. You're probably anemic too! What you need is plain old physical rest. A vacation on your own. Yes, this wasn't such a bad idea, coming to Bay Borough!

Few more days, couple of weeks, and you'll be home again, a new woman."

"Maybe so," Delia said unsteadily.

"And that's what I'm going to tell the police. 'She just went back to our people's place for some R and R,' I'll say. Because I do have to inform them, you know."

"I know."

"And I'll have to tell Sam."

"Yes."

"And then I expect he'll want to come talk things over."

Delia pressed the toilet paper to each eye.

"I'm not very good in these situations," Eliza said. She lifted one hand from her purse and placed it on Delia's shoulder.

"You're fine," Delia told her. "It's not your fault."

She felt saddened, all at once, by the fact that Eliza was wearing lipstick. (A sugary pink, lurid against her murky skin.) Eliza never bothered with makeup, as a rule. She must have felt the need to armor herself for this visit.

"I'll have Sam bring some of your clothes with him, shall I?" she was asking.

"No, thanks."

"A dress or two?"

"Nothing."

Eliza dropped her hand.

They left the room, Eliza walking ahead, and started down the stairs. Delia said, "So how's your *gardening*?" in a forced and sprightly tone.

"Oh . . . ," Eliza said. She arrived in the downstairs hall. "You'll need money," she told Delia.

"No, I won't."

"If I'd realized you weren't coming back with me . . . I don't have very much on me, but you're welcome to what there is."

"Honest, I don't want it," Delia said. "I'm making this huge, enormous salary at the lawyer's; I couldn't believe how much when he told me." She ushered Eliza out the door. "And you know I took the vacation cash. Five hundred dollars. I feel bad enough about that."

"Oh, we managed all right," Eliza said, eyeing a fibrous area in one porch floorboard.

Delia could have walked her to her car, or at least as far as the office, but that would have meant prolonging their parting. She had left her handbag upstairs, therefore, and she stood on the porch with her arms folded, in the attitude of someone about to go back indoors. "I'm sure you *managed*," she told Eliza. "It's not that. It's just that I feel bad I didn't start out with nothing. Start out . . . I don't know. Even."

"Even?"

"Even with the homeless or something. I don't know," Delia said. "I don't know what I mean!"

Eliza leaned forward and set her cheek against Delia's. "You're going to be fine," she told her. "This little rest is going to work wonders, take my word. And meanwhile, Dee—" She was about to turn away, but one last thought must have struck her. "Meanwhile, remember Great-Uncle Roscoe's favorite motto."

"What was that?"

" 'Never do anything you can't undo.' "

"I'll bear it in mind," Delia told her.

"Uncle Roscoe may have been a grump," Eliza said, "but he did show common sense now and then."

Delia said, "Drive safely."

She stood watching after Eliza—that short, economical, energetic figure—until she disappeared down the sidewalk. Then she went back in the house for her bag.

Climbing the stairs, she thought, *But if you never did anything you couldn't undo*—she set a hand on the splintery railing—*you'd end up doing nothing at all*, she thought. She was tempted to turn around and run after Eliza to tell her that, but then she couldn't have borne saying goodbye all over again.

8

Her book that night was *The Sun Also Rises*, but she didn't manage to finish it because she kept getting distracted. It was Friday, the start of the weekend. The traffic beneath her window had a livelier, more festive sound, and the voices of passersby were louder. "Hoo-*ee*! Here we come!" a teenage boy cried out. Momentarily, Delia lost track of the sentence she was reading. Around eight o'clock someone crossed the porch—not Belle but someone in flat-soled shoes walking slowly, as if weary or sad —and she lowered her book and listened. The front door opened, he entered the house, the stairs creaked upward one step at a time. Then the doorknob across the hall gave a rattle, and she thought, *Oh. The other boarder.*

She returned to her book, but every now and then a sound would break through her concentration—a hollow cough, the sliding of metal hangers along a closet rod. When she heard the shower running, she rose and tiptoed over to her door to make sure it was locked. Then she climbed back into bed and reread the paragraph she had just finished.

An hour or so later, Belle arrived. She had a man with her. Delia heard his hearty, booming laugh—not a laugh belonging to anyone she knew. "Now, be serious!" Belle said once. The TV came on downstairs, and the refrigerator door slammed shut with a dull clunk.

Mr. Lamb turned out to be an emaciated man in his forties, with straight
brown hair and sunken eyes. Delia met him in the upstairs hall as she
was setting out on some errands the following morning. "Hello," she
said, and passed on, having resolved in advance to keep their exchange
to a minimum. But she needn't have worried. Mr. Lamb flattened his
back against the wall and smiled miserably at his shoes, mumbling something unintelligible. He was probably no happier than she about having
to share the bathroom.

She was looking for a bank that kept Saturday hours. She wanted to
cash Friday's paycheck. The check was drawn on First Farmers', just
north of the square, but she found First Farmers' closed, and so she
walked on to Bay Borough Federal. It was a cool, breezy day, with dark
clouds overhead that turned the air almost lilac; and this part of town,
which she had not seen since the afternoon she arrived, now looked
completely different to her. It looked out of date, somehow. The buildings
were so faded they seemed not colored but hand tinted, like an antique
photograph.

"Would you be able to cash this for me?" she asked the teller at Bay
Borough Federal.

The teller—a woman in squinty rhinestoned glasses—barely glanced
at the signature before nodding. "Zeke Pomfret? No problem," she said.

So Delia signed over the first real paycheck of her life and received
a few crisp bills in return. She was surprised at how much the taxes and
whatnot could eat away from a salary.

Weber Street, East Street. Diagonally across the square. She carried
her head high and set her feet down with precision. She might have been
the heroine in some play or movie. And her intended audience, of course,
was Sam.

It wasn't that she looked forward to his visit, certainly. She dreaded
having to explain herself; she knew how lame and contradictory all her
reasons would sound to him. And yet as early as yesterday afternoon,
some part of her mind had been making its devious calculations. *Let's
say it's two hours to Baltimore. Eliza could get home around, oh, say,
four-thirty, so Sam could be here by six-thirty. Maybe seven. Or supposing
he decided to finish up at the office first, supposing he had to buy gas
. . .* And then later that night: *He must be waiting for the weekend.
That would be much more sensible.*

Imagine if he came upon her this minute, heading toward the library for Saturday's book. Or pausing on the way home to rummage through a table of mugs in front of Katy's Kitchenware. Or stepping out of the Pinchpenny with the navy knit dress in a bag. Imagine if he were watching from the boardinghouse porch as she rounded the corner of George Street. He would see her skimming along, wearing professional gray, entirely at ease in this town he had never laid eyes on before. He would think, *Could that really be Delia?*

Or imagine if she climbed the stairs and found him waiting at the door of her room. "Why, Sam," she would say serenely, and she would draw her keys from her handbag—so official-looking, room key and office key on Mr. Pomfret's chrome ring—and open the door and tilt her head, inviting him inside. Or he would be inside already, having persuaded Belle to admit him. He would be standing at one of the windows. He would turn and see her entering with her burdens—her library book and her tea mug and new dress—and, "Here, let me help you with those," he would say, and she would say, "Thanks. I can manage."

But he wasn't there after all, and she set her things on the bed in total silence.

She went downstairs to pay her rent. Belle was home, she could tell. She heard sounds from behind the celery-colored door leading off the hall. She knocked and Belle called, "Come in!" meanwhile squeaking something, whirring something. It was a stationary bicycle, Delia discovered when she stepped inside. Belle was pedaling madly, flushed and overheated in a pink sweat suit strewn with tiny satin bows. "Whew!" she said when she saw Delia. Her living room, like the rest of the house, seemed furnished with pieces earlier tenants had discarded. A dingy plush sofa faced the TV; the coffee table bore a loopy design of ring-shaped water stains.

"I just wanted to pay my rent," Delia told her.

"Oh, thanks," Belle said, and without slowing her pedaling she stuffed the folded bills up one sleeve. "Everything all right?"

"Yes, fine."

"Great," Belle said, and she leaned diligently over the handlebars as Delia closed the door again.

Delia planned to go next to the Gobble-Up for some lunch things, but just as she was leaving the house a young man in uniform arrived on the porch. She thought at first he was some kind of soldier; the uniform was a khaki color, and his hair was prickly short. "Miz Grinstead?" he said.

"Yes."

"I'm Chuck Akers, from the Polies."

It took her a moment to translate that.

"Think I could have a word with you?" he asked.

"Certainly," she said. She turned to lead him inside and then realized she had nowhere to take him. Her bedroom was out of the question, and she couldn't very well use Belle's living room. So she turned back and asked, "What can I do for you?" and they ended up conducting their business right there on the porch.

"You *are* Miz Cordelia F. Grinstead," he said.

"Yes."

"I understand you came here of your own free will."

"Yes, I did."

"Nobody kidnapped you, coerced you . . ."

"Nobody else had anything to do with it."

"Well, I surely wish you had thought to make that clear before you left."

"I'm sorry," she said. "Next time I will."

Next time!

She wondered when on earth she supposed that would be.

Saturday, Sunday. The elaborate filling of empty white hours, the glad pounce upon the most inconsequential task. Saturday evening she ate at home, little cartons of Chinese takeout, and she read *Daisy Miller* late into the night. Sunday breakfast was tea and a grocery-store muffin in bed, but she made an event of lunch. She ate at the Bay Arms Restaurant, a stodgy, heavily draped and carpeted establishment, where all the other tables were occupied by families in church clothes. Her inclination was to get the meal over with as fast as possible, but she forced herself to order a soup course, a main course, and a dessert, and she worked her way through all this in a measured and leisurely fashion, fixing her gaze upon a point in the middle distance.

Once Susie had announced, during a particularly feminist stage in her life, that every woman ought to learn how to dine alone in a formal restaurant without a book. Delia wished Susie could see her now.

In fact, maybe Sam would bring the children with him when he came. Maybe they would walk right into the Bay Arms; it was not impossible that they would track her down. She was wearing her new navy dress from the Pinchpenny. It looked very becoming, she thought. She requested a second cup of coffee and sat on awhile.

Out of nowhere, she longed for a cigarette, although she had not smoked since tenth grade.

When she left the restaurant she headed north to the library, planning to choose that night's reading. But the library door was locked tight and the venetian blinds were slanted shut. She should have realized the place would be closed on Sundays. Now she would have to *buy* a book—invest actual money.

In the pharmacy on George Street, she found one rack of paperbacks—mostly mysteries, a few romances. She chose a romance called *Moon Above Wyndham Moor.* A woman in a long cloak was swooning on the cover, precariously supported by a bearded man who encircled her waist with his left arm while he brandished a sword with his right. Delia hid the book in her purse after she had paid for it. Then she continued toward Belle's, taking quick, firm steps so that anybody watching would think, *That woman looks completely self-reliant.*

But there was no one watching.

She remembered how, as a child, she used to arrange herself in the front yard whenever visitors were due. She remembered one time when her great-uncle Roscoe was expected, and she had placed her doll cradle on the grass and assumed a pretty pose next to it till Uncle Roscoe stepped out of his car. "Why, looky there!" he cried. "It's little Lady Delia." He smelled of cough drops, the bitter kind. She had thought she retained no mental picture of Uncle Roscoe, and she was startled to find him bobbing up like this, shifting his veiny leather gladstone bag to his other hand so he could clamp her shoulder as they proceeded toward the house. But what had the occasion been? Why had he come to visit, wearing his rusty black suit? She suspected she would rather not know the answer.

"I was singing my doll a lullaby," she had told him in a confiding tone.

She had always been such a *false* child, so eager to conform to the grown-ups' views of her.

———

Moon Above Wyndham Moor was a disappointment. It just didn't seem very believable, somehow. Delia kept lowering it to stare blankly at the dim, far corners of the room. She checked to see how many pages remained. She cocked her head toward the sound of Mr. Lamb's radio. He had been playing it all weekend, though never so loudly that she could decipher the announcer's words. On the porch overhang outside, raindrops were falling one by one. She missed the noises of the family across the street. They must have closed their windows against the weather.

Is he not going to come at all, then?

On Monday morning Mr. Pomfret let her know, in a roundabout way, that he had learned the truth. "I see you have a new dress, *Mrs.* Grinstead," he said, eyeing her significantly. But she pretended not to understand, and by noon he had drifted back to "Miss." Not that she much cared. She felt oddly lackluster today. The rain didn't help. She had been forced to buy an umbrella at the pharmacy, and during lunch hour she went to the dime store and purchased an inexpensive gray cardigan made of something synthetic. Miss Grinstead's standards were slipping, it appeared. She poked her hands dispiritedly through the clingy, tubelike sleeves.

Because of the rain, she couldn't picnic on her usual park bench, and she wasn't up to the social demands of Rick-Rack's or the Bay Arms; so she took her cup of yogurt back to her room. She opened the front door, stepping over the mail, and started up the stairs. Then she halted and turned to look back at one of the envelopes on the floor.

A cream-colored envelope—or more like custard-colored, really. She knew that shade well. And she knew the name embossed in brown on the upper-left-hand corner: SAMUEL A. GRINSTEAD, M.D.

He would settle for just writing her a letter?

She stooped to pick it up. *Mrs. Delia Grinstead*, the address read (Miss Manners would be appalled). *George Street, house w/ low front porch next door to Gobble-Up Grocery. Bay Borough, Maryland.*

She took it to her room before she opened it. *Delia,* he wrote. No *Dear. Delia, it is my understanding from Eliza that* . . .

He had used the office typewriter, the one with the tipsy *e*, and he hadn't bothered to change the margins from when she'd done the bills. The body of the letter was scarcely four inches wide.

Delia, it is my understanding from Eliza that you have requested some time on your own due to various stresses including your father's recent death, etc.

Naturally, I would much rather you had forewarned us. You cannot have been unaware of the anxiety you would cause, simply strolling off down the beach like that and disappearing. ~~Do you have any idea how it feels to~~

Nor am I entirely clear on what "stresses" you are referring to. Of course I realize you and your father were close. But his death after all occurred four and a half months ago. ~~and frankly I feel~~ Perhaps you view me as one of the stresses. If so this is regrettable but I ~~have always tried to be a satisfactory husb~~ vowed while I was growing up that I would be a rock for my wife and children and to the best of my belief I have fulfilled that vow ~~and I don't understand what~~ but if you have any complaints against me I am certainly willing to hear what they are.

In the meantime you may rest assured that I will not invade your privacy. ~~xxxxxxxxxxxxxxxxxxxxxxxxxxxxxxxxxxxxxxxxxxxxx~~ ~~xxxxxxxxxxxxxxxxxxxxxxxxxxxxxxxxxxxxxxxxxxxxxxxxxxx~~ ~~xxxxxxxx~~

Sam

He had made his first four corrections with the hyphen key—easy for Delia to read through—but the fifth was so thoroughly x-ed over that she couldn't figure it out even when she held the letter up to the light. Well, no doubt that was for the best. It was probably something even more obtuse than his other remarks, and Lord knows those were obtuse enough.

Not invade her privacy! Just sit back and give up on her, as if she were a missing pet or mitten or dropped penny!

She might have known, she reflected. All this proved was how right she had been to leave.

Her teeth were chattering, and her new sweater was no help. Instead of eating her lunch, she slipped off her shoes and climbed into bed. She lay shivering beneath the one blanket, with her jaw set against the cold and her arms wrapped around her ribs, hugging her own self tightly.

9

No wonder she'd been unable to picture winter in Bay Borough! Underneath, she realized now, she had expected Sam to come fetch her long
before then. She resembled those runaway children who never, no matter
how far they travel, truly mean to leave home.

So anyhow. Here she was. And the entire rest of her life was stretching
out empty before her.

She took to sitting on her bed in the evenings and staring into space. It
was too much to say that she was thinking. She certainly had no conscious
thoughts, or at any rate, none that mattered. Most often she was, oh,
just watching the air, as she used to do when she was small. She used
to gaze for hours at those multicolored specks that swarm in a room's
atmosphere. Then Linda had informed her they were dust motes. That
took the pleasure out of it, somehow. Who cares about mere dust? But
now she thought Linda was wrong. It was air she watched, an infinity
of air endlessly rearranging itself, and the longer she watched the more
soothed she felt, the more mesmerized, the more peaceful.

She was learning the value of boredom. She was clearing out her
mind. She had always known that her body was just a shell she lived in,

but it occurred to her now that her mind was yet another shell—in which case, who was "she"? She was clearing out her mind to see what was left. Maybe there would be nothing.

Often she didn't begin the night's reading till nine or nine-thirty, which meant she could no longer finish a novel in one sitting; so she switched to short stories instead. She would read a story, watch the air awhile, and read another. She would mark her page with a library slip and listen to the sounds from outdoors—the swish of cars, the chirring of insects, the voices of the children in the house across the street. On hot nights the older children slept on a second-floor porch, and they always talked among themselves until their parents intervened. "Am I going to have to *come upstairs?*" was their father's direst threat. That would quiet them, but only for a minute.

Delia wondered if Sam knew that Carroll was scheduled for tennis lessons the middle two weeks in July. You couldn't depend on Carroll to remember on his own. And did anyone recall that this was dentist month? Well, probably Eliza did. Without Eliza, Delia could never have left her family so easily.

She wasn't sure if that was something to be thankful for.

The fact was, Delia was expendable. She was an extra. She had lived out her married life like a little girl playing house, and always there'd been a grown-up standing ready to take over—her sister or her husband or her father.

Logically, she should have found that a comfort. (She used to be so afraid of dying while her children were small.) But instead, she had suffered pangs of jealousy. Why was it Sam, for instance, that everybody turned to in times of crisis? He always got to be the reasonable one, the steady and reliable one; she was purely decorative. But how had that come about? Where had she been looking while that state of affairs developed?

She read another story, which contained several lengthy nature descriptions. She enjoyed nature as much as the next person, but you could carry it too far, she felt.

And was anybody keeping an eye on Sam's health? He had that tendency, lately, to overdo the exercise. But, *It's none of my concern*, Delia reminded herself. His letter had freed her. No more need to count cholesterol grams; pointless to note that the Gobble-Up carried fat-free mayonnaise.

She called back some of the letter's phrases: *You cannot have been unaware* and *Nor am I entirely clear*. Bloodless phrases, emotionless phrases. She supposed the whole neighborhood knew he hadn't married her for love.

Again she saw the three daughters arrayed on the couch—Sam's memory, originally, but she seemed to have adopted it. She saw her father in his armchair and Sam in the Boston rocker. The two of them discussed a new arthritis drug while Delia sipped her sherry and slid glances toward Sam's hands, reflecting on how skilled they looked, how doctorly and knowing. It might have been the unaccustomed sherry that made her feel so giddy.

Just a few scattered moments, she thought, have a way of summing up a person's life. Just five or six tableaux that flip past again and again, like tarot cards constantly reshuffled and redealt. A patch of sunlight on a window seat where someone big was scrubbing Delia's hands with a washcloth. A grade-school spelling bee where Eliza showed up unannounced and Delia saw her for an instant as a stranger. The gleam of Sam's fair head against the molasses-dark wood of the rocker. Her father propped on two pillows, struggling to speak. And Delia walking south alongside the Atlantic Ocean.

In this last picture, she wore her gray secretary dress. (Not all such memories are absolutely accurate.) She wore the black leather shoes she had bought at Bassett Bros. The clothes were wrong, but the look was right—the firmness, the decisiveness. That was the image that bolstered her.

"Whenever I hear the word 'summer,' " one of the three marriageable maidens announced (Eliza, of course), "I smell this sort of melting smell, this yellow, heated, melting smell." And Linda chimed in, "Yes, that's the way she is! Eliza can smell nutmeg day at the spice plant clear downtown! Also anger." And Delia smiled at her sherry. "Ah," Sam murmured thoughtfully. Did he guess their ulterior motives? That Eliza was trying to sound interesting, that Linda was pointing out Eliza's queerness, that Delia was hoping to demonstrate the dimple in her right cheek?

The washcloth scrubbing her hands was as rough and warm as a mother cat's tongue. The squat, unhappy-looking young woman approaching Miss Sutherland's desk changed into Delia's sister. "I wish . . . ," her father whispered, and his cracked lips seemed to tear apart rather than separate, and he turned his face away from her. The evening after he died, she went to bed with a sleeping pill. She was so susceptible to drugs that she seldom took even an aspirin, but she gratefully swallowed the pill Sam gave her and slept through the night. Only it was more like *burrowing* through the night, tunneling through with some blunt, inadequate instrument like a soup spoon, and she woke in the morning muddled and tired and convinced that she had missed something. Now she thought what she had missed was her own grief. Why that rush toward forgetfulness? she asked herself. Why the hurry to leap past grief to the next stage?

She wondered what her father had been wishing for. She hadn't been able to figure it out at the time, and maybe he had assumed she just didn't care. Tears filled her eyes and rolled down her cheeks. She made no effort to stop them.

Didn't it often happen, she thought, that aged parents die exactly at the moment when other people (your husband, your adolescent children) have stopped being thrilled to see you coming? But a parent is always thrilled, always dwells so lovingly on your face as you are speaking. One of life's many ironies.

She reached for her store of toilet paper and blew her nose. She felt that something was loosening inside her, and she hoped she would go on crying all night.

In the house across the street, a child called, "Ma, Jerry's kicking me." But the voice was distant and dreamy, and the response was mild. "Now, Jerry . . ." Gradually, it seemed, the children were dropping off. Those who remained awake allowed longer pauses to stretch between their words, and spoke more and more languidly, until finally the house was silent and no one said anything more.

Independence Day had passed nearly unobserved in Bay Borough—no parades, no fireworks, nothing but a few red-white-and-blue store windows. Bay Day, however, was another matter. Bay Day marked the anniversary of George Pendle Bay's famous dream. It was celebrated on the first Saturday in August, with a baseball game and a picnic in the town square. Delia knew all about it because Mr. Pomfret was chairman of the Recreation Committee. He had had her type a letter proposing they replace the baseball game with a sport that demanded less space—for instance, horseshoes. The square, he argued, was so small and so thickly treed. But Mayor Frick, who was the son and grandson of earlier mayors and evidently reigned supreme, wrote back to say that the baseball game was a "time-honored tradition" and should continue.

"Tradition!" Mr. Pomfret fumed. "Bill Frick wouldn't know a tradition if it bit him in the rear end. Why, at the start it was *always* horseshoes. Then Ab Bennett came back from the minors with his tail between his legs, and Bill Frick Senior got up a baseball game to make him look good. But Ab doesn't even play anymore! He's too old. He runs the lemonade stand."

Delia had no interest in Bay Day. She planned to spend the morning on errands and give the square a wide berth. But first she found everything closed, and then the peculiar weather (a fog as dense as oatmeal and almost palpably soft) lured her to keep walking, and by the time she reached the crowd she felt so safe in her cloak of mist that she joined in.

The four streets surrounding the square were blocked off and spread with picnic blankets. Food booths lined the sidewalks, and strolling vendors hawked pennants and balloons. Even this much, though, Delia had trouble making out, because of the fog. People approaching seemed to be materializing, their features assembling themselves at the very last instant. The effect was especially unsettling in the case of young boys on skateboards. Elated by the closed streets, they careened through the crowd recklessly, looming up entire and then dissolving. All sounds were muffled, cotton-padded, and yet eerily distinct. Even smells were more distinct: the scent of bergamot hung tentlike over two old ladies pouring tea from a thermos.

"Delia!" someone said.

Delia turned to see Belle Flint unfolding a striped canvas sand chair. She was wearing a vivid pink romper and an armload of bangle bracelets that jingled when she sat down. Delia hadn't been sure till now that Belle remembered her name; so she reacted out of surprise. "Why, hello, Belle," she said, and Belle said, "Do you know Vanessa?"

The woman she waved a hand toward was the young mother from the square. She was seated just beyond Belle on a bedspread the same color as the fog, with her toddler between her knees. "Have some of my spread," she told Delia.

"Oh, thanks, but—" Delia said. And then she said, "Yes, maybe I will," and she went over to sit next to her.

"Get a load of the picnic lunches," Belle told Delia. "It's some kind of contest; they ought to give prizes. What did you bring?"

"Well, nothing," Delia said.

"A woman after my own heart," Belle said, and then she leaned closer to whisper, "Selma Frick's brought assorted hors d'oeuvres in stacked bamboo baskets. Polly Pomfret's brought whole fresh artichokes on a bed of curried crayfish."

"Me, I'm with the teenagers," Vanessa said, handing her son an animal cracker. "I grab something from a booth whenever I get hungry."

She reminded Delia of those girl-next-door movie stars from the 1940s, slim and dark and pretty in a white blouse and flared red shorts, with shoulder-length black hair and bright-red lipstick. Her son was over-dressed, Delia thought—typical for a first child. In his corduroys and long-sleeved shirt, he looked cross and squirmy, and for good reason; Delia could feel the heat of the pavement rising through the bedspread.

"How old is your little boy?" she asked Vanessa.

"Eighteen months last Wednesday."

Eighteen months! Delia could have said. Why, she remembered that age. When Ramsay was eighteen months, he used to . . . and Susie, that was when Susie learned to . . .

Such a temptation, it was, to prove her claims to membership—the labor pains, the teething, the time when she too could have told her baby's age to the day. But she resisted. She merely smiled at the child's shimmer of blond hair and said, "I suppose he gets his coloring from his father."

"Most likely," Vanessa said carelessly.

"Vanessa's a single parent," Belle told Delia.

"Oh!"

"I have no idea who Greggie's father might be," Vanessa said, wiping her son's mouth with a tissue. "Or rather, I have a few ideas, but I could never narrow it down to just one."

"Oh, I see," Delia said, and she turned quickly toward the ball game.

Not that there was much to look at, in the fog. Apparently home plate lay in the southeast corner. It was from there she heard the *plock!* of a hit. But all she could discern was second base, which was marked by a park bench. While she watched, a runner loped up to settle on the bench, and the player already seated there rose and caught a ball out of nowhere and threw it back into the mist. Then he sat down again. The runner leaned forward with his elbows on his knees and stared intently toward home plate, although how he hoped to see that far Delia couldn't imagine.

"Derek Ames," Belle informed her. "One of our best hitters."

Delia said, "I would think the statue would get in the way."

"Oh, George plays shortstop," Belle said, giggling. "No, seriously: there's a rule. Bean the statue and you walk to first. It used to count as an automatic run till Rick Rackley moved here. But you know professional athletes: they excel at *any* sport. It got so every time Rick came to bat, he laid old Georgie low."

"Rick Rackley's a professional athlete?"

"Or was, till his knee went. Where've you been living—Mars? Of course, his game was football, but believe me, the Blues are lucky to have him on their side. That's who we're watching, in case you didn't know: the Blues versus the Grays. Blues are the new folks in town; Grays have been here all along. Whoops! That sounds to me like a homer."

Another *plock!* had broken through from the southeast corner. Delia gazed upward but saw only opaque white flannel. In the outfield, such as it was (a triangle of grass behind second base), one player called to another, "Where's it headed?"

"Damned if I know," the second player said. Then, with a startled grunt, he caught the ball as it arrived in front of him. "Got it," he called to the first man.

"You see it?"

"I caught it."

"It came down already?"

"Right."

"Bobby caught that!" the first man shouted toward home plate.

"What say?"

"He caught it," someone relayed. "Batter's out."

"He's what?"

"He's out!"

"Where is the batter?"

"*Who* is the batter?"

Vanessa fed her son another animal cracker. "Fog on Bay Day is kind of a rule here," she told Delia. "I don't believe anyone's ever once got a good look at that game. So! Delia. How do you like working for Zeke Pomfret?"

"Well . . . he's okay," Delia said. She supposed she should have expected that her job would be common knowledge.

"He's a real fine lawyer, you know. If you decide to go ahead with your divorce, you could do worse than hire Zeke."

Delia blinked.

"Yes, he did just great with my ex-boyfriend's," Belle told her. "And he got Vanessa here's brother Jip out of jail, when Jip hit a spell of bad luck once."

"I haven't given much thought to, um, divorce," Delia said.

"Well, sure! No hurry! And anyhow, my ex-boyfriend's case was totally different from yours."

What did they imagine Delia's case was? She decided not to ask.

Belle was rummaging through her big purse. She pulled forth a pale-green bottle and a stack of paper cups. "Wine?" she asked the others. "It's a screw top. Don't tell Polly Pomfret. Yes, Norton's case was so straightforward, for one thing. He'd only been married a year. In fact, we met on his first anniversary. Met at a Gamblers' Weekend Special in Atlantic City, where he'd brought his wife to celebrate. He and I just sort of . . . gravitated, you know?" She passed Delia a cup of white wine. "It helped that his wife was one of those people who end up soldered to their slot machines. So one-two-three I move to Bay Borough, and we rent a little apartment together, and Zeke Pomfret goes to work on Norton's divorce."

The wine had a metallic aftertaste, like tinned grapefruit juice. Delia cradled the cup in both hands. She said, "I'm not really planning anything that definite just yet."

"Well, of course you're not."

"I'm really feeling sort of . . . blank right now. You know?"

"Of course you are!" both women said simultaneously.

In the square, the inning must have ended. The players they had been watching vanished and new players took shape, a new second baseman floating up by degrees and solidifying on the bench.

She dreamed Sam was driving a truck across the front lawn in Baltimore and the children were playing hide-and-seek directly in his path. They were little, though; not their present-day selves. She tried to call out and warn them, but her voice didn't work, and they were all run over. Then Ramsay stood up again, holding his wrist, and Sam climbed out of the truck and he fell down and tried to get up again, fell down and tried to get up, and the sight made Delia feel as if a huge, ragged wound had ripped open in her chest.

When she woke, her cheeks were wet. She had thought she was starting to lose her habit of crying at night, but now tears flooded her eyes and she gave in to wrenching sobs. She was haunted by the picture of Ramsay in those little brown sandals she'd forgotten he'd ever owned.

She saw her children lined up on the lawn, still in their younger versions before they'd turned hard-shelled and spiky, before the boys had grown whiskers and Susie bought a diary with an unpickable brass lock. Those were the children she longed for.

One evening in September, she returned from work to find several envelopes bearing her name scattered across the hall floor. She knew they must be birthday cards—she was turning forty-one tomorrow—and she could tell they were from her family because of the wordy address. *(House w/ low front porch . . .)* The first card showed a wheelbarrow full of daisies. *A BIRTHDAY WISH*, it said, and inside, *Friendship and health / Laughter and cheer / Now and through / The coming year.* The signature was just *Ramsay*, with the tail of the *y* wandering off across the page in a halfhearted manner.

She carried the rest of her mail upstairs. No sense facing this in public.

Susie, the next card was signed. *(Heartiest Congratulations and Many Happy Returns.)* And nothing at all from Carroll, though she riffled through the envelopes twice. Well, it was easy to see what had happened. These cards were Eliza's idea. She had coaxed and cajoled the whole family into sending them. "All I'm asking," was a phrase she would have used. Or, "No one should have to pass a birthday without . . ." But Carroll, the stubborn one, had flatly refused. And Sam? Delia opened his envelope next. A color photo of roses in a blue-and-white porcelain vase. *Barrels of joy / Bushels of glee . . .* Signed, *Sam*.

Then a letter from Linda, in Michigan. *I want you to know that I sincerely wish you a happy birthday*, she wrote. *I don't hold it against you that you absconded like that even though it did mean we had to cut short our vacation which is the twins' only chance each year to get some sense of their heritage but anyhow, have a good day.* Below her signature were Marie-Claire's and Thérèse's—a prim strand of copperplate and a left-hander's gnarly crumple.

Dear Delia, Eliza wrote, on yet another rhymed card.

> *We are all fine but we hope you'll soon be home. I am taking care of the office paperwork for now, and all three kids have started back to school.*
>
> *Bootsy Fisher has phoned several times and also some of the*

neighbors but I tell everyone you're visiting relatives at the moment.
I hope you have a good birthday. I remember the night you
were born as if it were just last week. Daddy let Linda and me
wait in the waiting room with the fathers, and when the nurse
came out she told us, "Congratulations, kids, you can form a
singing trio now and go on Arthur Godfrey," and that's how we
knew you were a girl. I do miss you.

Love, Eliza

Delia kept that one. The others she discarded. Then she decided she
might as well discard Eliza's too. Afterward she sat on her bed a long
while, pressing her fingertips to her lips.

On her actual birthday, a package arrived from Sam's mother. It was
roughly the size of a book, too thick to fit through the mail slot, so it
stood inside the screen door, where Delia found it when she came home.
She groaned when she recognized the writing. Eleanor was known for
her extremely practical gifts—a metric-conversion tape measure, say, or
a battery recharger, always wrapped in wrinkled paper saved from Christmas. This time, as Delia discovered when she took the package upstairs,
it was a miniature reading light on a neck cord. Well, in fact . . . , she
reflected. It would probably work much better than her lamp. She tucked
it under her pillow, next to her stash of toilet paper.

There was a letter too, on Eleanor's plain buff stationery:

Dear Delia,
This is just a little something I thought you might find helpful.
On the few occasions when I've traveled myself, the reading light
has generally been miserable. Perhaps you're having the same ex-
perience. If not, just pass this along to your favorite charity. (Lately
I've been most dissatisfied with Goodwill but continue to feel that
Retarded Citizens is a worthwhile organization.)
My best wishes for your birthday.

Love, Eleanor

Delia flipped it over, but all she found on the back was RECYCLED
PAPER RECYCLED PAPER RECYCLED PAPER running across the bottom. She
had expected indignation, or at least a few reproaches.

She remembered how, when she and Sam were first engaged, she had entertained such high hopes for Eleanor. She had thought she was finally getting a mother of her own. But that was before they met. Eleanor came to supper at the Felsons', arriving directly from the Home for Wayward Girls, where she volunteered as a typing teacher twice a week. Once the introductions were over, she hardly gave Delia a glance. All she talked about was the terrible, terrible poverty endured by the wayward girls and the staggering contrast of this meal—which, by the way, was merely pot roast sprinkled with onion-soup mix and an iceberg lettuce salad. "I asked this one poor child," Eleanor said, "I asked, 'Dear, could your people buy you a typewriter so you could work from your house after the baby arrives?' And she said, 'Miss, my family's so poor they can't even afford shampoo.' " A basket of rolls appeared before her. Eleanor gazed into it, looking puzzled, and passed it on. "I don't know what made her choose that example, of all things," she said. "Shampoo."

(Why was it that so many voices came wafting back to Delia these days? Sometimes as she fell asleep she heard them nattering on without her, as if everybody she'd ever known sat around her, conversing. Like people in a sickroom, she thought. Like people at a deathbed.)

Another present Eleanor had once given her was a tiny electric steamer gadget to freshen clothes during trips. This was some years back; Delia couldn't remember what she'd done with it. But the thing was, here in Bay Borough she could have put it to use. She could have touched up her office dresses, both of which had grown somewhat puckery at the seams after repeated hand laundering. It would certainly have been preferable to buying an iron and ironing board. Oh, why hadn't she kept the steamer? Why hadn't she brought it with her? How could she have been so shortsighted, and so ungrateful?

She didn't answer any of the birthday cards, but etiquette demanded a thank-you note to Eleanor. *The little light is very convenient,* she wrote. *Much better than the goosenecked lamp I've been reading by up till now. So I've moved the lamp to the bureau which means I don't have to use the ceiling bulb and therefore the room looks much softer.* In this manner she contrived to cover the entire writing area of a U.S. postcard without really saying anything at all.

The next morning, while she was dropping the card in the mailbox near the office, she was suddenly struck by the fact that Eleanor had once worked in an office. She had put her son through college on a high-school secretary's salary—no small feat, as Delia could now appreciate. She wished she had thought to mention her job in her thank-you note. But maybe Eliza had said something. "Delia's employed by a lawyer," Eliza might have said. "She handles every detail for him. You should see her all dressed up for work; if you met her on the street, you wouldn't know her."

"Is that so?" Sam would ask. (Somehow, the listener had changed from Eleanor to Sam.) "Handles everything, you say. Not mislaying important files? Not lounging around the waiting room, reading trashy novels?"

Well, she'd spent more than half her life trying to win Sam's approval. She supposed she couldn't expect to break a habit like that overnight.

October came, and the weather grew cooler. The square filled up with yellow leaves. Some nights, Delia had to shut her windows. She bought a flannel nightgown and two long-sleeved dresses—one gray pinstripe, one forest green—and she started keeping an eye out for a good second-hand coat. It was not yet cold enough for a coat, but she wanted to be prepared.

On rainy days, now, she ate lunch at the Cue Stick 'n' Cola on Bay Street. She ordered coffee and a sandwich and watched the action at the one pool table. Vanessa often wheeled her stroller in to join her. While Greggie lurched among the chair legs like a brightly colored top, Vanessa would offer Delia thumbnail sketches of the players. "See the guy breaking? Buck Baxter. Moved here eight or ten years ago. Baxter as in Baxter Janitorial Supplies, but they say his father's disowned him. No, Greggie, the man doesn't want your cookie. Now, her I don't know," she said. She meant the diminutive, dark-haired young woman who was leaning across the pool table to shoot on tiptoe, her purple canvas pocketbook still slung over her shoulder. "Must be from outside. Leave him *alone*, Greggie. And the fellow in the cowboy boots, that's Belle's ex-boyfriend, Norton Grove. Belle was out of her mind to fall for him. Fickle? That man put fickle in the dictionary."

Delia was gathering an impression of Bay Borough as a town of misfits. Almost everybody here had run away from someplace else, or been run away *from*. And no longer did it seem so idyllic. Rick and Teensy Rackley were treated very coolly by some of the older citizens; the only two gay men she knew of seemed to walk about with no one but each other; there was talk of serious drug use in the consolidated high school; and Mr. Pomfret's appointment book was crammed with people feuding over property lines and challenging drunk-driving arrests.

Still, she felt contented here. She had her comfortable routine, her niche in the general scheme of things. Making her way from office to library, from library to café, she thought that her exterior self was instructing her interior self, much like someone closing his eyes and mimicking sleep in order to persuade sleep to come. It was not that her sadness had left her, but she seemed to operate on a smooth surface several inches above the sadness. She deposited her check each Saturday; she dined each Sunday at the Bay Arms Restaurant. People nodded now when they saw her, which she took not just for greeting but for confirmation: *Ah, yes, there's Miss Grinstead, exactly where she belongs.*

Although every so often something would stab her. A song from Ramsay's Deadhead period about knock-knock-knocking on heaven's door, for instance. Or a mother and a little girl hugging each other in front of the house across the street. "She's leaving me!" the mother called mock-plaintively to Delia. "Going off to her very first slumber party!"

Maybe Delia could pretend to herself that she was back in the days before her marriage. That she didn't miss her children at all because they hadn't been born yet.

But in retrospect it seemed she had missed them even then. Was it possible there had been a time when she hadn't known her children?

Dear Delia, Eleanor wrote. (She addressed her letter to 14 George Street this time.)

> *I was so pleased to get your postcard. It's good to know that my little gift came in handy, and I'm glad you're doing some reading.*
>
> *I myself find it impossible to sleep if I don't read at least a few pages first, preferably from something instructive like biography or current events. For a while after Sam's father died I used to read the dictionary. It was the only thing with small enough divisions to fit my attention span. Also the information was so definite.*
>
> *Probably Sam has been marked by losing his father at such an early age. I meant to say that in my last note but I don't believe*

I did. And his father never had a strong personality. He was the kind of man who let all the bathwater drain away before he got out of the tub. Maybe it would worry a boy to think he might grow up to do the same.

I hope I haven't overstepped.

Love, Eleanor

Delia didn't know what to make of that. She understood it better when the next note came, some two weeks later. *Please forgive me if you felt I sounded "mother-in-lawish" and that's why you didn't answer my letter. I had no intention of offering excuses for my son. I've always said he was forty years old when he was born, and I realize that's not easy to live with.*

Delia bought another postcard—this one the kind with a picture on it, a rectangle of unblemished white captioned *Bay Day in Bay Borough*, so there was even less space to write on. *Dear Eleanor,* she wrote. *I'm not here because of Sam, so much. I'm here because*

Then she sat back, not knowing how to end the sentence. She considered starting over, but these postcards cost money, and so she settled, finally, for *I'm here because I just like the thought of beginning again from scratch.* She signed it, *Love, Delia,* and mailed it the following morning on her way to work.

And after all, wasn't that the true reason? Truer than she had realized when she wrote it, in fact. Her leaving had very little to do with any specific person.

Unlocking the office door, she noticed the pleasure she took in the emptiness of the room. She raised the white window shades; she turned the calendar to a fresh page; she sat down and rolled a clean sheet of paper into the typewriter. It was possible to review her entire morning thus far and find not a single misstep.

Mr. Pomfret sometimes employed a detective named Pete Murphy. This was not the swaggery character Delia would have envisioned, but a baby-faced fat boy from Easton. It seemed he was hired less often to locate people than to *fail* to locate them. Whenever a will or a title search required his services, Pete would plod in, whistling tunelessly, and trill his pudgy fingers at Delia and proceed to the inner office. He never spoke to her, and he probably didn't know her name.

One rainy afternoon, though, he arrived with something bulging and struggling inside the front of his windbreaker. "Got a present for you," he told Delia.

"For me?"

"Found it out in the street."

He lowered his zipper, and a small, damp gray-and-black cat bounded to the floor and made a dash for the radiator. "Oh!" Delia said.

Pete said, "Shoot. Come out of there, you little dickens."

Beneath the radiator, silence.

"It'll never come if you order it to," Delia said. "You have to back away a bit. Turn your face away. Pretend you're not looking."

"Well, I'll let you see to that," Pete decided. He brushed cat hairs off his sleeves and started for the office.

"Me! But . . . wait! I can't do this!" Delia said. She was speaking now to Mr. Pomfret; he had come to his door to see what all the fuss was about. "He's brought a stray cat! I can't take care of a cat!"

"Now, now, I'm sure you'll think of something," Mr. Pomfret said genially. "Miss Grinstead was a cat in her last incarnation, you know," he told Pete.

"Is that a fact," Pete said. They walked into the office, and Mr. Pomfret closed the door.

For the next half hour, Delia worked with one eye on the radiator. She watched a gray-and-black tiger tail unfurl from behind a pipe, gradually fluffing as it dried. She had a sense of being under surveillance.

When Pete reemerged, she said, "Maybe the cat belongs to someone. Have you thought of that?"

"I doubt it," he told her. "I didn't see no collar." He trilled his fingers and left. When the door slammed behind him, the tail gave a twitch.

Delia rose and went to the office. "Excuse me," she said.

Mr. Pomfret said, "Hmm?" He was back at his computer already. This morning he had discovered something called Search-and-Replace that was apparently very exciting. *Tap-tap*, his fingers went, while he craned his sloping neck earnestly toward the screen.

"Mr. Pomfret, that cat is still under the radiator and *I* can't take it anywhere! I don't even have a car!"

"Maybe get a box from the supply closet," he said. "Damn!" He hit several keys in succession. "Just see to it, will you, Miss Grinstead? There's a good girl."

"I live in a boardinghouse!" Delia said.

Mr. Pomfret reached for his computer manual and started thumbing through it. "Who wrote this damn thing, anyhow?" he asked. "No human being, that's for sure. Look, Miss Grinstead, why don't you leave early and take the kitty wherever you think best. I'll lock up for you, how's that?"

Delia sighed and headed for the supply closet.

Pet Heaven: they might help. She emptied a carton of manila envelopes and carried it to the other room. Kneeling in front of the radiator, she placed a palm on the floor. "Tsk-tsk!" she said. She waited. After a minute, she felt a tiny wince of cold on the back of her middle finger. "Tsk-tsk-tsk!" The cat peered out at her, only its whiskers and heart-shaped nose visible. Gently, Delia curved her hand around the frail body and drew it forward.

This was hardly more than a kitten, she saw—a scrawny male with large feet and spindly legs. His fur was almost startlingly soft. It reminded her of milkweed. When she stroked him, he shrank beneath her hand, but he seemed to realize he had nowhere to run. She gathered him up and set him in the carton and folded the flaps shut. He gave a single woebegone mew before falling silent.

It was still raining, and she didn't have a free hand to open her umbrella, so she hurried along the sidewalk unprotected. The carton rocked in her arms as if it contained a bowling ball. For such a little thing, he certainly was heavy.

She rounded the corner and burst through the door of Pet Heaven. A gray-haired woman stood behind the counter, checking off a list. "You wouldn't happen to know if Bay Borough has an S.P.C.A.," Delia said.

The woman looked at her a moment, slowly refocusing vague blue eyes. Then she said, "No; the nearest one's in Ashford."

"Or any other place that takes homeless animals?"

"Sorry."

"Maybe *you'd* like a cat."

"Gracious! If I brought home another stray my husband would kill me."

So Delia gave up, for now, and bought a box of kibble and a sack of litter-box filler, the smallest size of each just to get her through one night. Then she lugged the cat home.

Belle was there ahead of her, talking on the phone in the kitchen. Delia heard her laugh. She tiptoed up the stairs, unlocked the door of her room, set the carton on the floor, and shut the door behind her. In the mirror she looked like a crazy woman. Tendrils of wet hair were plastered to her forehead. The shoulders of her sweater were dark with rain, and her handbag was spotted and streaked.

She bent over the carton and raised the flaps. Inside, the cat sat hunched in a snail shape, glaring up at her. Delia retreated, settled on the edge of her bed, looked pointedly in another direction. Eventually, the cat sprang out of the carton. He started sniffing around the baseboards. Delia stayed where she was. He ducked beneath the bureau and returned with linty whiskers. He approached the bed obliquely, gazing elsewhere. Delia turned her head away. A moment later she felt the delicate denting of the mattress as he landed on it. He passed behind her, lightly brushing the length of his body against her back as if by chance. Delia didn't move a muscle. She felt they were performing a dance together, something courtly and elaborate and dignified.

But she couldn't possibly keep him.

Then Belle's clacky shoes started climbing the stairs. Belle almost never came upstairs. But she did today. Delia threw a glance at the cat, willing him to hide. All he did was freeze and direct a wide-eyed stare toward the door. *Knock-knock.* He was smack in the center of the pillow, with his bottle-brush tail standing vertical. You couldn't overlook him if you tried.

Delia scooped him up beneath his hot little downy armpits. She could feel the rapid patter of his heart. "Just a minute," she called. She reached for the carton.

But Belle must have misheard, for she breezed on in, caroling, "Delia, here's a—" Then she said, "Why!"

Delia straightened. "I'm just trying to find a home for him," she said.

"Aww. What a honey!"

"Don't worry, I'm not keeping him."

"Oh, why not? Er, that is . . . he is housebroken, isn't he?"

"All cats are housebroken," Delia said. "For goodness' sake!"

"Well, then! Not keep this little socky-paws? This dinky little pook-ums?" Belle was bending over the cat now and offering him her polished fingernails to sniff. "Is it a prinky-nose," she crooned. "Is it a frowzy-head. Is it a fluffer-bunch."

"Mr. Pomfret's detective found him out in the rain," Delia said. "He just dumped him on me; nothing I could do. I mean, I knew I couldn't keep him myself. Where would I put a litter box, for one thing?"

"In the bathroom?" Belle asked. She started scratching behind the cat's ears.

"But how would he get out to use it?"

"You could leave your door cracked open, let him go in and out as he likes," Belle said. "Ooh, feel how soft! I don't know why you ever lock it, anyhow. Little town like this, who do you think's going to rob you? Who's going to creep in and ravish you?"

"Well . . ."

"Believe me, Mr. Lamb couldn't gather up the enthusiasm."

Belle stroked beneath the cat's chin, and the cat tipped his head back blissfully. He had one of those putt-putt purrs, like a Model T Ford.

"I don't know if I want my life to get that complicated," Delia said.

"Is he a complication. Is he a bundle of trouble."

Belle was holding an envelope in her free hand, Delia saw. That must be what had brought her upstairs. Eleanor's stalky print marched across the front. Delia felt suddenly overburdened. Things were crowding in on her so!

But when Belle said, "Are you going to keep this itty-bitty, or am I?" Delia said, "I am, I guess."

"Well, good. Let's call him Puffball, what do you say?"

"Hmm," Delia said, pretending to consider it.

But she had never approved of cutesy names for cats. And besides, it seemed that at some point she had already started thinking of him as George.

She was in bed that night before she got around to reading Eleanor's letter. It was more of the same: a thank you for Delia's last postcard, news of her Meals on Wheels work. *I can certainly empathize with your desire to start over!* she wrote. (That careful word, *empathize*, revealing her effort to say just the right thing.)

> *And I'm relieved it's the reason you left. I had assumed it was Sam. I've wondered if maybe he expressly wanted a flighty wife, in which case you could hardly be held to blame.*
>
> *But when you've finished starting over, do you picture working up to the present again and coming home? Just asking.*
>
> > *All my love, dear,*
> > *Eleanor*

A furry paw reached out to bat the page, and Delia laid the letter aside. The cat had found a resting place next to her on the blankets. He had eaten an enormous meal and paid two visits to the makeshift litter box in the bathroom. She could tell he was beginning to feel at home.

She reached for her book—Carson McCullers—and turned to where she had stopped reading last night. She read two stories and started a third. Then she found she was growing sleepy; so she set the book on the windowsill and clicked off her little reader's light and placed it on top of the book. Light continued to shine through the partly open door, sending a rod of yellow across the floorboards. She slid downward in bed very cautiously so as not to disturb the cat. He was giving himself a bath now. He pressed against her ribs with each movement in a way that seemed accidental, but she could tell he meant to do it.

How strange it was, when you thought about it, that animals would share quarters with humans! If Delia had been out in the wilderness, if this were some woodland creature nestling so close, she would have been astounded.

She yawned and shut her eyes and pulled the blanket up around her shoulders.

One of the stories she had read tonight was called "A Tree, a Rock, a Cloud." A man in this story said people should begin by loving easier things before they worked up to another person. Begin with something less complex, he proposed. Like a tree. Or a rock. Or a cloud. The rhythm of these words kept tapping across Delia's mind: tree, rock, cloud.

First a time alone, then a casual acquaintance or two, then a small, undemanding animal. Delia wondered what came after that, and where it would end up.

10

The Sunday before Thanksgiving, Belle waylaid Delia at the bottom of
the stairs. "Say, Dee," she said. "What're you doing for the holiday?"

"Oh, um . . ."

"Want to have dinner at my place?"

"Well, I'd love to," Delia said.

"I'm serving this real hokey meal: turkey and dressing, cranberry
relish . . ."

"I didn't know you cooked!"

"I don't," Belle said grimly. "It's a plot. I'm trying to look domestic
for this fella I've been seeing."

At the moment, she looked anything but domestic. Sunday was always
a busy day at the real estate office, and she was dressed to go out in her
huge purple coat, the one with the shoulders not just padded but flaring
to sharp points like an alien's space suit. Lilac trousers swam beneath it,
and the smell of her fruity, overripe perfume freighted the air all around
her.

"Vanessa is coming with Greggie," she said. "Nice touch to invite a
child, don't you think? And these out-of-towners I just sold a house to,
married couple; that's always good. . . ."

"And I would help in the food department," Delia guessed.

"Oh, I'm bringing in the food from outside, just between you and me. But I was thinking you could add a little, call it, class. I need for this guy to see me as all proper and respectable. And also you could advise me on the wifely touches: the centerpiece and et cetera. You must've used to do that stuff back home, didn't you? Do you have one of those baskety things that look like a cornucopia?"

"Well, not right handy," Delia said. "But I'll be glad to do what I can."

"Great," Belle said. She toed the cat aside—he had followed Delia downstairs—and opened the front door. They stepped out into a chilly, tin-colored day. "This fella's name is Henry McIlwain, did I mention that?" she asked. "We've been dating several weeks now and I'd like to start getting more purposeful. I don't want him thinking I'm just a good-time gal! Maybe you could drop a few remarks in front of him. Something like, 'Gosh, Belle, I hope you made your famous brussels-sprout dish.' "

"You're serving him brussels sprouts?"

"I don't have any choice. It's the only green vegetable Copp Catering offers that will fit in my toaster oven."

Delia said, "How did you manage the meals when you were living with Norton?"

"We ate out. But this time I want to do things differently. Maybe while Henry's listening you could ask me for one of my recipes."

"I can hardly wait to hear how you'll answer," Delia said.

"Dinner's at one, but could you come down a bit early to help set up? And wear your gray pinstripe. Your gray pinstripe is so . . . gray; know what I mean?"

On Thanksgiving Day Delia slept late, and she idled the morning away drinking tea and reading in bed, with the cat curled up beside her. Across the hall, in Mr. Lamb's room, an announcer's voice droned steadily. This was a TV announcer, Delia had figured out; not radio. Now that she kept her door cracked open, she could hear how the music swelled and diminished without apparent reason, responding to some visual cue; and today she caught distinct phrases each time she emerged for more tea water. "The mother bear leads her cubs . . . ," she heard, and, "The female spider injects her victims . . ." Evidently Mr. Lamb was watching nature shows.

Shortly after noon, she rose and started dressing. It was a pity she didn't have a string of pearls to add a festive note, she thought. Or at least a scarf. Didn't she own a paisley scarf with gray commas around the edges? Yes, she did—back in Baltimore. She could see it lying folded in her grandmother's lacquer glove box.

She applied an extra-bright coat of lipstick, and then she leaned toward the mirror to smooth her hair. It was longer now, which made her curls look flatter and somehow calmer—very suitable for Miss Grinstead. Although when she stepped back to gauge the total effect, the person who came to mind was not Miss Grinstead at all. It was Rosemary Bly-Brice.

She turned sharply from the mirror and picked up the vase of autumn flowers she had bought the day before.

The cat came along when she left. He scampered after her down the stairs, and he tumbled around her ankles while she knocked at the living-room door. When nobody answered she tried the other door, the one to the right, and finally she turned the knob and poked her head into the dining room. "Anybody home?" she asked.

Goodness, Belle did need her services. The table—one of those long, narrow, wood-grain affairs you see at PTA bazaars—was not even spread with a cloth yet. Delia put her flowers down and walked on into the kitchen. "Belle?" she said.

Belle was leaning against the sink. Her arms were clamped across the bosom of a violently frilled white apron, and tears were streaming down her face.

"Belle? What's happened?" Delia asked.

"He's not coming," Belle said thickly.

"Your date?"

"He's back with his wife."

"I didn't know he *had* a wife."

"Well, he does."

"Oh, I'm sorry."

In fact, she was shocked, but she tried not to show it. No wonder Belle had been so eager to look respectable! Delia gave her a tentative pat, just in case she wanted consoling. She did, it turned out. She fell into Delia's arms, sobbing hotly against her neck.

"He was perfect for me!" she wailed. "He was exactly what I wanted! And then this morning he calls up and—oh, I should have known from how low he was speaking, mumbly low secretive voice like he was scared somebody might hear him—"

She drew back from Delia's embrace to snap a paper towel off the roll above the sink. Blotting first one eye and then the other, she said, " 'Belle,' he tells me, 'about today. Something's come up,' he tells me. 'Oh?' I ask. 'What's that?' Thinking maybe he couldn't start the car, or wanted to bring a friend. 'Well, it's like this,' he tells me. 'Seems like Pansy and I have gotten back together.' "

"Pansy would be his wife," Delia guessed.

"Yes, and the baby's name is Daffodil, can you believe it?"

"There's a baby?"

"And it wasn't even a springtime baby! It was born in October!"

"You're talking about . . . this *past* October?"

Belle nodded, loudly blowing her nose.

"So the baby is, what, a month old?"

"Six weeks."

"Ah."

Belle's apron was so new that the pinholes still showed from the packaging. Her hairdo was even larger than usual, and she wore the first actual dress Delia had ever seen her in—or presumably it was a dress, for her legs were visible beneath the apron, encased in nylon stockings with a frosty white sheen like the bloom on plums. But her face was a disaster—blurred lipstick and blackened eyes and gray dribbles of tears. "You'll have to get in touch with the others," she was saying as she dabbed the tears. "I can't possibly go through with dinner."

"But everything's all ready," Delia said. She was taking stock of the foil-wrapped, disposable pans covering one counter, and the plates and silver heaped on the kitchen table, and the empty serving dishes waiting to be filled. Through the oven's lighted window she could make out a brown turkey, although she wasn't able to smell it, for some reason. "That turkey looks about done," she told Belle.

"It arrived done. I'm just reheating it. I had to keep it in the fridge overnight."

"So, why not go ahead with your party? Maybe it'll cheer you up."

"Nothing could cheer me up," Belle said.

"Oh, now, you sit here and I'll see to things."

"I wish I was dead and buried," Belle said, pulling out one of the kitchen chairs. She sank into it and picked up the cat. "I'm getting too old to be jilted! I'm thirty-eight years old. It's *tiring* to keep going on first dates."

Delia didn't answer, because she was hunting a tablecloth. No telling where Belle kept her linens. This was one of those fifties kitchens with shiny bare walls and enormous white appliances and rust-specked white metal cabinets and drawers. She slid open every drawer with a clanking sound. Most were empty. Eventually she located a jumble of fabrics in the space below the sink. "Aha!" she said, shaking out a wrinkled damask cloth. She carried it into the dining room and spread it over the table, resetting her flowers in the center. "I know you must have candlesticks," she called.

"We met last spring," Belle said. "I was the one who sold off their house. They were moving to a bigger place on account of the baby coming. And wouldn't you know it took me six months, with the market the way it's been."

Delia opened all the drawers of the apple-green bureau that served as a dining room buffet. She found two brass candlesticks lying in a nest of extension cords, and she placed them on either side of the flowers. Meanwhile, in the kitchen, Belle had sold the house just as Daffodil arrived. "Settlement date was two days before due date," she said. "Kid was born three days later. So naturally I stopped by the hospital with a giftie; these things are tax-deductible. And there was Henry all proud and fatherly, took me down the hall to that baby window they have and showed me how smart and cute and blah-blah-blah. Well, he just got to me, you know? I stood there not hearing a word he said, watching how his mouth moved, and all at once I thought, *Suppose I was to step forward and kiss him, what do you guess he'd do?*"

"Candles?" Delia asked.

"Try the broom cupboard." Belle blew her nose with a honking sound that caused the cat to spring off her lap. "And this was not even my usual style of man," she said. "He was skinny! And pale! And computerish! But there I stood, thinking, *Suppose I unbuttoned my blouse right here in front of the baby window, staring at his mouth the whole time and running the tip of my tongue across my lower lip.*"

The candles were not in the broom cupboard but on top of the refrigerator, in a yellowing white box. Even the candles were yellowed, and also a bit warped, but Delia fitted them into the holders anyway. Then she collected the dishes and silver from the kitchen table and dealt them out. Belle proceeded through the baby's colic, the new parents' cranky quarrels, her own warm-eyed, cooing sympathy. "I schemed and plotted, I lay in wait," she said. "I told him my door was always open.

Two, three, four o'clock in the morning he would leave that spit-up milk and dirty-diaper smell and find me here in my spaghetti-strap nightie from Victoria's Secret."

And to think all this had been going on while Delia was sound asleep! She checked the turkey. It appeared to have caved in around the breastbone. She found the brussels sprouts in their foil pan and set them in the toaster oven at 350 degrees. There were biscuits too, but she would wait to warm those till the very last minute.

"Two weeks ago, Pansy goes back to her mom's," Belle said. "Takes Daffodil and leaves. I was in heaven. Didn't you notice I've had this radiant glow about me lately? Oh, Delia, how can you stand it, going without a love life?"

Holding a pack of paper napkins printed all over with pilgrims, Delia paused to reflect upon the question. "Well," she said, "I do miss *hugs*, I guess. But nowadays when I think about, um, the rest of it, I just feel sort of perplexed. I think, *Why did that seem like such a big deal, once upon a time?* But I suppose it's only—"

The doorbell rang.

"Oh, Lord, we didn't call off dinner," Belle said, as if she had not been sitting in the midst of Delia's preparations. "Shoot! I can't cope with this! See who's there, will you, while I try to fix my face."

As Delia walked through the dining room to the hall, she felt drab and thin and virginal, like somebody's spinster aunt fulfilling her duties.

It was Vanessa at the door. She wore a leather blazer and blue jeans, and she toted Greggie on one hip. Behind her, just stepping out of their car, were a man and a woman who must have been Belle's married couple. Delia barely had time to whisper the news to Vanessa—"Henry McIlwain's gone back to his wife"—before the couple arrived on the porch. "Why! What have we here!" the husband told Greggie. He was young, no more than thirty, but as staid as a middle-aged man, Delia thought, with his receding tuft of black hair and his long black formal overcoat. His wife was a trim, attractive brunette in a tidy red woolen suit that reminded Delia of a Barbie-doll outfit. "I'm Delia Grinstead," Delia told her. "This is Vanessa Linley—do you know each other?— and Greggie."

"We're the Hawsers," the husband said for both of them. "Donald and Melinda."

"Won't you come in?"

She planned to lead them into the living room, but when she turned she found Belle at the door of the dining room. She was showing all her teeth and adjusting the plunging neckline of a flowered, button-front dress. "Happy Thanksgiving!" she sang out. Whatever repairs she had made to her face had not done much good. Gray tracks still ran down her cheeks, and her eyes were pink and puffy. But she caroled, "So glad you could come! Step in and have a seat!"

There was nowhere to sit but around the table. "Donald, you're on my right," Belle said, "and Vanessa's on my left. I've put Greggie next to you, Vanessa. Get some phone books from the kitchen if he needs a booster. And Melinda's on the other side of Greggie."

Well, maybe this was the local custom: proceeding directly to the food. But even Vanessa seemed taken aback. And the husband (still wearing his overcoat) stood frozen in place for a moment before approaching his chair. "Are we . . . late?" he asked Belle.

"Late! Not at all!" she said, and she let out a cascade of musical laughter. "Delia, you'll sit next to—"

She broke off. "Oh!" she cried. "Delia! Honestly!"

"What's the matter?" Delia asked.

"You've gone and laid too many places!"

It was true. Delia had doled out all she'd found on the kitchen table, and that must have included a setting for Henry McIlwain. Belle gazed toward the chair at the far end, her eyes brimming over with fresh tears.

"I'm sorry," Delia told her. "We could just—"

"Run fetch Mr. Lamb," Belle ordered.

"Mr. Lamb? From upstairs?"

"Hurry, though. We're all waiting. Tell him we'll eat without him if he doesn't get down here pronto."

What they would have eaten Delia couldn't imagine, since there wasn't a morsel of food anywhere in sight. But Vanessa, returning from the kitchen with several phone books, told Delia, "Go ahead. I'll get the meal on."

Delia went out to the hall, which seemed very quiet after the bustle in the dining room. With the cat twining underfoot, she climbed the stairs and knocked on Mr. Lamb's door. "Desperately, the salmon fling themselves against the current," a stern voice announced. The door opened on a sliver of Mr. Lamb's rag-and-bone face. "Yes?" he said, and then, "Oh!" for George had somehow managed to wriggle through the crack.

Delia said, "Belle sent me up to invite you for Thanksgiving dinner."

"But it seems your animal's got into my room!"

"Sorry," Delia said. "Here, George."

She reached in for the cat, and Mr. Lamb grudgingly opened the door another few inches. Delia caught the hazelnut smell of clothes worn once and then stuffed into drawers unwashed. The television's icy light flickered in the dimness. She scooped George up and backed away.

"I've been meaning to mention the toilet arrangements under the bathroom sink," Mr. Lamb told her.

"The . . . ?"

"Couldn't your animal use the outdoors?"

"Not in the middle of the night," Delia said. She clutched George more tightly and asked, "Are you coming to dinner, or aren't you?"

"What time?"

"Um . . . now?"

"Well, I suppose I could make it," Mr. Lamb said.

He looked down at what he was wearing—a limp T-shirt, baggy dark pants—and then sadly closed the door in her face.

Delia wondered how a man so fond of nature programs could object to a harmless cat.

Downstairs, Vanessa had finished setting everything on the table— turkey, brussels sprouts, cranberry relish, mashed sweet potatoes dotted with marshmallows, all in their original pans. Still wearing her leather blazer, she was spooning the stuffing out of the turkey. Greggie lolled on the stack of phone books, sucking his thumb and watching his mother with heavy-lidded eyes. It must be naptime.

Belle was discussing Henry with the Hawsers. "What I can't figure," she was saying, "is when all this came about. Last night as of ten o'clock, everything was jim-dandy. Henry and I had a real nice dinner over in Ocean City. Then this noon on the phone—poof! He's a totally changed man."

"So his wife showed up in the morning," Donald Hawser said sagely. He had draped his coat over the back of his chair, and he was lighting the warped candles with a silver lighter. "She got out of bed this morning and, 'Here I am,' she must have said, 'away from home on Thanksgiving. A family holiday,' she said."

Delia placed the cat on the floor and sat down next to Donald. A *family holiday*, she thought, *and I'm eating a store-cooked turkey with strangers*. She felt madcap and adventurous.

" 'Here I am with my mom when I ought to be with my husband,' she said, and she packed her suitcase then and there and went back to him, but he couldn't let you know till noon because what was he going to do—excuse himself and run phone you the minute she walked in?"

"Donald has an expert opinion to offer on every subject," his wife announced with a brittle laugh.

She was sitting very tensely, her spine not touching the chair. Her hair was scrolled upward at the ends like the sound holes in a violin.

"Yes; you might call it a gift," Donald agreed, unruffled. "I'm able to envision. See, first there's the business of settling her into the house. Don't forget she has that baby with her, and a diaper bag no doubt and one of those infant car seats—"

"But he could have just turned her away!" Belle exploded. "He doesn't even love her! He told me he didn't!"

"Well, of course that's what he would claim," Donald said, leaning back expansively.

By now Vanessa was carving the turkey. Delia began passing around the other foods. The brussels sprouts were barely warm, she discovered. The sweet potatoes were refrigerator cold, but everybody took some anyhow.

"You're right," Belle said. "Oh, when will I learn? Seems this happens to me about every other week. Norton Grove was the only one who actually divorced his wife for me, and look how that ended up!"

"How *did* it end up?" Delia asked.

"He fell in love with a lady plumber who came to unstop our sink." Donald nodded, implying he could have predicted as much.

"It's just the way Ann Landers keeps saying in her column," Belle told them. "She says a man who would leave his wife will most likely leave you, too, by and by."

"Maybe you ought to look for someone who doesn't *have* a wife," Vanessa suggested, handing her son a turkey wing.

"Yes, but it's kind of like I lack imagination. I mean, I can't seem to picture marrying a man till I see him married to someone else. Then I say, 'Why! He'd make a good husband for *me*!' "

The hallway door opened and Mr. Lamb stood on the threshold, wearing a shiny black suit that turned his skin to ashes. "Oh, God, you have guests," he said.

"Yes, Mr. Lamb, and you're one of them," Belle said. "Donald

Hawser, Melinda Hawser . . . Vanessa and Greggie you've seen around, I bet. This is Horace Lamb," she told the others. She waved carelessly toward the one empty chair. "Have a seat."

"Well, I can't stay long."

"Have a *seat*, Mr. Lamb."

He entered the room with a skimming sound that made Delia glance downward. On his feet he wore the kind of backless paper slippers given out free in hospitals. "This afternoon will be sports, sports, sports," he said as he fell into his chair. "All regular programs are preempted. I'm reduced to the educational channels."

"Say!" Donald cried. "Who you going to root for?"

"Pardon? Weekday afternoons, I like to watch the soaps. Oh, I confess. I admit it. I make a point of stopping for *All My Children* every blessed day I'm on the road."

"What's your line of business, Horace? Okay if I call you Horace?"

"I sell storm windows," Mr. Lamb told him. He accepted the container of sweet potatoes and peered down into it. "This looks exceedingly rich," he said. His long front teeth were so prominent that his lips had to labor to stretch across them. His whole face seemed stretched, and too intricately hinged at the jawbone. He raised his deep-set eyes to Belle and said, "Regrettably, I'm afflicted with a touchy stomach."

"Oh, eat up, it'll do you good," Belle snapped. "We were discussing married men."

"Pardon?"

"Another problem I have is, I look at a married man and I can't believe he won't find me irresistible."

"Irresistible?"

"I'm speaking to the table at large, Mr. Lamb. Eat your dinner. I see a man with his wife, mousy boring wife who isn't even attempting to keep herself up, and I think, *Why wouldn't he prefer me instead? I'm a hell of a lot more fun, and better-looking to boot.* But it's like there's some—I don't know—some hold wives have, and I can't seem to break it. Is it a secret? Is it some secret you-all pass around among yourselves?"

She was asking Melinda Hawser, but Melinda just gave another shattered laugh and started crumbling bits of biscuit onto her plate. "Is it?" Belle asked Delia.

"Oh, no," Delia told her. "It's more like just . . . what's the word? The word from science class. Momentum?"

"Inertia," Mr. Lamb supplied.

"Right." She glanced over at him. "It's just a matter of people staying where they are."

"Well, if that's all it is," Belle said, "how come Katie O'Connell got to waltz off to Hawaii with Larry Watts? *She* must have found out the secret. Why, when Larry Watts was boarding here, he never even gave me a look! He almost seemed to be avoiding me. He acted like I was some floozy the one time I asked him downstairs for a friendly little drink!"

Her mouth collapsed, and she covered her eyes with one hand. Donald said, "Oh, now! Hey!" and Vanessa said, "Aw, Belle, don't cry," while Mr. Lamb started tugging ferociously at his nose.

"To be honest," Melinda said in a crystal voice, "I can't think what you want with a husband anyhow."

There was a pause, a kind of reconsidering among the other diners.

"Who first thought marriage up, do you suppose?" Melinda asked Greggie. He goggled at her from behind a greasy fistful of turkey wing. "Everyone pushes it so, especially the women. Your mother and your aunts and your girlfriends. Then after you're married you see how he's always so full of himself and always going on about something, always got these theories and pronouncements, always crowing over these triumphs at his business. 'I told them this,' and 'I told them that,' and you ask, 'What did they say back?' and he says, 'Oh, *you* know, but then I told them such and such, and I let them have it outright, I put it to them straight, I said . . .' And if you mention this to your mother and your aunts and so forth, 'Oh,' they say, 'marriage is a pain, all right.' 'Well, if that's the way you feel,' you want to ask them, 'why didn't you speak up before? Where were you when I was announcing my engagement?' "

"Ha. Yes," her husband said. He glanced around the table. "They're going to think you mean *our* marriage. Dear."

Everybody waited, but Melinda just speared a brussels sprout.

"Oh," Belle assured him, "we would never think that." She was sitting erect now, her tears already drying on her cheeks. "A gorgeous man like you? Of course we wouldn't." She told the others, "Donald and Melinda are customers of mine. They bought the old Meers place—lovely place. Donald's an important executive at the furniture plant."

Melinda was chewing her brussels sprout very noisily, or maybe it only seemed that way because the room was so quiet.

"*Mrs.* Meers had gone into the nursing home," Belle said, "but Mr.

Meers was still living there. Took us through the house himself; taught us how to work the trash compactor. Told us, 'Here in the freezer are one hundred forty-four egg whites, no charge.' "

"Folks who made their own mayonnaise," Mr. Lamb surmised.

Belle was about to go on speaking, but she stopped and looked at him.

"I don't guess you'd be in the market for storm windows," Mr. Lamb told Donald.

"Not really," Donald said, with his eyes on his wife.

"Ah, well, I didn't think so."

"That house needs absolutely nothing," Belle said. "The Meerses kept after it every minute. And Donald here, Don . . ." She smiled at him. "Don spotted that the first time he walked through."

"Melinda and I have a *fine* marriage. Married seven years." Donald said, still watching his wife. "We were one of those recognized campus couples at our college. Went steady, got pinned: the works."

"I know the type you mean," Belle said.

"Why, Melinda's known me so long she still calls me Hawk! Hawk Hawser," he added, turning at last to meet Belle's gaze. "I was on the basketball team. Kind of a star, some people might say, though I never had the height to go professional."

"Is that right!" Belle exclaimed.

"Hawk Hawser," he repeated lingeringly.

"I believe I might've heard of you."

"Well, maybe so if you were ever in Illinois. Jerry Bingle College?"

"Jerry Bingle. Hmm."

"I played center."

"Really!"

"And midway through my senior year—"

"Marshmallow," Greggie demanded.

He didn't have the usual small child's trouble pronouncing *l*'s. He spoke very precisely and daintily. "Mama? Marshmallow!"

It was Delia, finally, who plucked a marshmallow from the sweet potatoes and reached across the table to set it on his plate. Everyone else was watching Belle. Open-mouthed and breathless, miraculously recovered, Belle stroked her topmost button with a hypnotic, circular motion and kept her damp-lashed eyes focused raptly on Donald's lips.

II

Sometimes Mr. Pomfret ordered Delia to go out and feed the parking meter for a client. Sometimes he snapped his fingers when he needed her. Once, he tossed her his raincoat and told her to take it down the block to the one-hour cleaner's. "Yes, Mr. Pomfret," she murmured. When she returned, she placed the receipt on his palm as smartly as a surgical nurse dealing out a scalpel.

But now she began to feel a little itch of rebellion.

"Miss Grinstead, can't you see I'm *merging?*" he demanded when she brought in some letters to sign, and she said, "Sorry, Mr. Pomfret," but neutrally, too evenly, with her expression set in granite. And back at her desk, she seethed with imaginary retorts. *You and your crummy computer! You and your "merging" and your Search-and-Destroy or whatever!*

One Friday in early December, a stooped, gray-haired man in a baseball jacket arrived without an appointment. "I'm Mr. Leon Wesley," he told Delia. "This is about my son Juval. Do you think Mr. Pomfret might have a minute for me?"

Mr. Pomfret's office door was closed—it was early morning, his time to peruse new catalogs—but when Delia inquired, he said, "Leon? Why,

Leon resurfaced my driveway for me. Send him in. And make us a pot of coffee while you're at it."

It was impossible to avoid overhearing Mr. Wesley's reason for coming. He poured it out even before he was seated, speaking through the grinding of the coffee beans so Mr. Pomfret had to ask him to repeat himself. Juval, Mr. Wesley said, was scheduled to join the navy first thing after Christmas. He had a highly promising future; special interest had been taken on account of his qualifications, which seemed to involve some technical know-how that Delia couldn't quite follow. And last night, clear out of the blue, he had been arrested for breaking and entering. Caught climbing through the Hanffs' dining-room window at ten o'clock in the evening.

"The Hanffs!" Mr. Pomfret said. The Hanffs owned the furniture factory, as even Delia knew—the town's one industry. "Well, of all the doggone folks to up and burglarize," he said.

Delia went to the supply closet for more sugar, and when she came back Mr. Pomfret was still marveling at Juval's choice of victims. "I mean, here you've got Reba Hanff, who disapproves of jewelry and doesn't own a piece of silver," he said, "gives every cent of their profits to some religious honcho in India . . . What did the boy hope to steal, for God's sake?"

"And why, is what I'd like to know," Mr. Wesley said. "That's the part I can't figure. Was he in need of money? For what? He doesn't even drink, let alone take drugs. Doesn't even have a girlfriend."

"Not to mention the Hanffs own the only house alarm in all of Bay Borough," Mr. Pomfret mused.

"And with such a hotshot career ahead!" Mr. Wesley said. "You can bet that's all down the drain now. How come he went and ruined things, so close to time he was leaving?"

"Maybe *that's* how come," Delia spoke up, setting two mugs on a tray.

"Ma'am?"

"Maybe he ruined things so he wouldn't have to leave after all."

Mr. Wesley gaped at her.

Mr. Pomfret said, "You may go now, Miss Grinstead."

"Yes, Mr. Pomfret."

"Shut the door behind you, please."

She shut the door with such conspicuous care that every part of the latch declared itself.

In regard to the establishment of a designated fund, she typed, and then Mr. Pomfret emerged from his office, stuffing his arms into his overcoat as he walked, forging a trail for Mr. Wesley. "Cancel my ten o'clock," he told Delia.

"Yes, Mr. Pomfret."

He opened the outer door, ushered Mr. Wesley through it, and then closed it and came back to stand at Delia's desk. "Miss Grinstead," he said, "from now on, please do not volunteer comments during my consultations."

She stared at him stubbornly, keeping her eyes wide and innocent.

"You're paid for your secretarial skills, not for your opinions," he said.

"Yes, Mr. Pomfret."

He left.

She knew she had deserved that, but still she felt a flare of righteous anger once he was gone. She typed rapidly and badly, flinging the carriage so hard that the typewriter kept skidding across the desk. When she called to cancel the ten o'clock appointment, her voice shook. And when she left the office at lunchtime, she picked up a Bay Borough *Bugle* so she could look for another job.

Well, not that she would actually go through with it, of course. It was just that she needed to fantasize awhile.

The weather was raw and dismal, and she hadn't brought any food with her, but she walked to the square even so because she couldn't deal with the Cue Stick 'n' Cola today. She found the park benches deserted. The statue looked huddled and dense, like a bird with all its feathers reared against the cold. She wrapped her coat around her and sat down on the very edge of one damp, chilly slat.

How satisfying it would be to announce her resignation! "I regret to inform you, Mr. Pompous . . . ," she would say. He would be helpless. He didn't even know where she kept the carbon paper.

She opened the *Bugle* and searched for the classified section. As a rule she didn't read the *Bugle*, which was little more than an advertising handout—several pages of half-price specials and extremely local news, stacked weekly in various storefronts. She flipped past a choral call for the Christmas Eve Sing on the square, a two-for-one day at the shoe store, and a progress report on the Mitten Drive. On the next-to-last page she discovered four Help Wanted ads: baby-sitter, baby-sitter, lathe operator, and "live-in woman." This town must have unemployment problems. After that came the For Sale ads. A person named Dwayne wished to sell two wedding rings, cheap. Her eyes slid back to *Live-in Woman*.

> Single father desires help w/ lively, bright, engaging, 12-yr-old son. Must be willing to wake boy in a.m., serve breakfast, see off to school, do light cleaning / errands / shopping, assist w/ homework, provide transportation to dentist / doctor / grandfather / playmates, attend athletic meets & cheer appropriate team, host groups of 11–13 yr olds, cook supper, show enthusiasm for TV sports programs / computer games / paperback war novels, be available nights for bad dreams / illness. Driver's license a must. Non-smokers only. Room, board, generous salary. Weekends & most daytimes free except school holidays / sick days / snow days. Call Mr. Miller at Underwood High 8–5 Mon–Fri.

Delia clucked. The nerve of the man! Some people wanted the moon. She rattled the paper impatiently and refolded it. You can't expect a mere hireling to serve as a genuine mother, which was really what he was asking.

She rose and placed the *Bugle* in the trash basket. So much for that.

Crossing West Street, she glanced toward the shops—Debbi's and the dime store and the florist. How about a job in sales? No, she was too quiet-natured. As for waitressing, she used to forget her own family's dessert orders in the time it took to walk to the kitchen. And she knew from her talks with Mrs. Lincoln at the library that the town was having to struggle to support even one librarian.

Actually, she reflected, passing the sterile white blinds of the Fingernail Clinic, a hireling would in some ways be *better* than a mother —less emotionally ensnarled, less likely to cause damage. Certainly less likely to suffer damage herself. When the employer's child was unhappy, it would never occur to the live-in woman to feel personally responsible.

She turned into Value Vision and took another *Bugle* from the stack just inside the door.

"I wouldn't like for my son to think people are checking him over," Mr. Miller said. "Filing through to see if he's up to standard. That's why I asked you to come while he was out. Then if you find you're interested, you could stay on and meet him. He's eating supper at a friend's, but he'll be home in half an hour or so."

He sat across from her in a chintz armchair that he seemed to dwarf, as he dwarfed the whole overstuffed, overdecorated living room of this little ranch house on the edge of town. To Delia's surprise, he'd turned out to be someone she recognized. Joel Miller: he had consulted Mr. Pomfret several months ago on a visitation matter. She remembered admiring his undisguised baldness. Men who scorned the subterfuge of artfully draped strands of hair, she felt, conveyed an attractive air of masculine assurance; and Mr. Miller, with his large, regular features and his olive skin and loose gray suit, seemed positively serene. Underneath, though, she detected some tension. He had told her three times—contradicting the entire gist of his ad—that his son would be at school for the vast majority of every day, in essence *all* day, and that even when he was home he required not much more than a token adult in the wings. Delia had the feeling that no one else had applied for this position.

"He eats at friends' houses often, in fact," Mr. Miller was saying. "And in summer—I don't think I mentioned this—he spends two weeks at sleep-away camp. Besides which there's computer day camp, soccer clinic—"

"Summer!" Delia said. She rocked back in her chintz-padded rocking chair. Summer, with its soft, lazy afternoons, tinkling glasses of lemonade, children's peach-colored bodies in swimsuits! "Oh, Mr. Miller," she said. "The truth is, I seem to be in a changeable stage of life right now. I'm not sure I could get that . . . invested."

"And in summer I'm around more myself," Mr. Miller went on, as if she hadn't spoken. "Not the whole day, exactly—a principal doesn't have quite the same leeway his teachers do—but quite a lot."

"I probably shouldn't have come," Delia said. "A child your son's age needs continuity."

Then why did *you come?* he might reasonably have asked, but instead, poor man, he seized on her last sentence. "You sound experienced," he said. "Do you have children of your own, Miss Grinstead? Oh." The corners of his mouth jerked briefly downward. "I'm sorry. Of course not."

"Yes, I do," she told him.

"So it's *Mrs.* Grinstead?"

"I prefer 'Miss.' "

"I see."

He thought this over.

"But, so, you *are* experienced," he said finally. "That's excellent! And do you come from this area?"

Evidently he didn't keep up with Bay Borough gossip. "No, I don't," she told him.

"You don't."

She could see him reconsidering. Desperate he might be, but not foolhardy. He wouldn't want to hire an ax murderer.

"I'm from Baltimore," she volunteered at last. "I'm perfectly respectable, I promise, but I've put that part of my life behind me."

"Ah."

Oh, Lord, now he was envisioning some drama. He surveyed her with interest, his head slightly tilted.

"But!" she exclaimed. "As far as the job goes—"

"I know: you don't waht it," he said sadly.

"It's nothing to do with the job itself. I'm sure your son is a very nice boy."

"Oh, he's more than nice," Mr. Miller said. "He's really, he's such a good kid, Miss Grinstead. He's wonderful! But I guess I overestimated how well we could do on our own. I thought as long as we knew how to work the washing machine . . . But things have gotten away from me."

He waved a hand toward the room in general, which puzzled Delia, because it seemed painfully neat. Fat little cushions with buttons in their middles filled the skirted couch, each one propped at a careful angle. Glossy fashion magazines lapped at mathematical intervals across the coffee table. But Mr. Miller, following her glance, said, "Oh, the *surface* I can handle. I've posted a chart in the kitchen. Each day has its special job. This afternoon we vacuumed, yesterday we dusted. But it seems there are other issues. Last weekend, for example, he asked if we could have penny soup. 'Penny soup!' I said. Sounded kind of weird to me. He said his mother used to serve it for lunch when he was little. I asked him what was in it, and it turns out he meant plain old vegetable soup. I guess they call it penny soup because it's cheap. So I said, 'Well, I can make *that*.' I heat up a tin of Campbell's, he takes one look, and what does he do? Starts crying. Twelve years old and he falls apart, kid who didn't so much as whimper the time he broke his arm. I said, 'Well, what? What did I do wrong?' He said it had to be homemade. I said, 'God Almighty, Noah.' Still, I'm not stupid. I knew this soup had some meaning for him. So I haul out a cookbook and set to work making homemade. But when he saw what I was doing, he told me to forget it. 'Just forget the whole thing,' he told me. 'I'm not hungry anyhow.' And off he went to his room, leaving me with a pile of diced carrots."

"Sliced," Delia told him.

He raised his straight black eyebrows.

"You should have *sliced* the carrots," she told him, "and also zucchini, yellow squash, new potatoes—everything coin-shaped. That's why they call it penny soup. It's nothing to do with the cost. I doubt you'd find it in cookbooks, because it's more a . . . mother's recipe, you know?"

"Miss Grinstead," Mr. Miller said, "let me show you where you'd stay if you took the job."

"No, really, I—"

"Just to look at! It's the guest room. Has its own private bath."

She rose when he did, but only because she wanted to make her escape. What had she been thinking of, coming here? It seemed she could feel within the curl of her fingers the urge to slice those vegetables as they ought to be sliced, to set the soup in front of the boy and turn away briskly (twelve was too old to cuddle) and pretend she hadn't noticed his tears. "I'm sure it's a lovely room," she said. "Somebody's going to love it! Somebody young, maybe, who still has enough . . ."

She was trailing Mr. Miller down a short, carpeted hall lined with open doors. At the last door, Mr. Miller stood back to let her see in. It was the sort of room where people were expected to spend no more than a night or two. The high double bed allowed barely a yard of space on either side. The nightstand bore a thoughtful supply of guest-type reading (more magazines, two books that looked like anthologies). The framed sampler on the wall read WELCOME in six languages.

"Large walk-in closet," Mr. Miller said. "Private bath, as I believe I've mentioned."

In another part of the house, a door slammed and a child called, "Dad?"

"Ah," Mr. Miller said. "Coming!" he called. "Now you get to meet Noah," he told Delia.

She took a step backward.

"Just to say hello," he assured her. "What harm could that do?"

She had no choice but to follow him down the hall again.

In the kitchen (cabinets the color of toffees, wallpaper printed with butter churns), a wiry little boy stood tugging off a red jacket. He had a tumble of rough brown hair and a thin, freckled face and his father's long dark eyes. As soon as they entered the room, he started talking. "Hey, Dad, guess what Jack's mother gave us for dinner! This, like, cubes of meat that you dunk into this . . ." He registered Delia's presence, flicked a look at her, and went on. ". . . dunk into this pot and then—"

"Noah, I'd like you to meet Miss Grinstead," his father said. "Should we call you Delia?" he asked her. She nodded; it hardly mattered. "I'm Joel," he said, "and this is Noah. My son."

Noah said, "Oh. Hi." He wore the guarded, deadpan expression that children assume for introductions. "So the pot is full of hot oil, I guess it is, and each of us got—"

"Fondue," his father said. "You're talking about fondue."

"Right, and each of us got our own fork to cook our meat on, with different, like, animals on the handles so we could keep straight whose was whose. Like mine was a giraffe, and guess what Jack's little sister's was?"

"I can't imagine," his father said. "Son, Delia is here to—"

"A pig!" Noah squawked. "His little sister got the pig!"

"Is that right."

"And she cried about it too, but Carrie cries about everything. Then for dessert we each had a bag of chocolate marbles, but I turned mine down. I was polite about it, though. I go to his mom, I go—"

"Said."

"Huh?"

"You *said* to his mom."

"Right, I'm all, 'Thanks a lot, Mrs. Newell, but I'm so full I guess I better pass.' "

"I thought you liked chocolate marbles," his father said.

"Are you kidding? Not after what I know now." Noah turned to Delia. "Chocolate marbles are coated with ground-up beetle shells," he told her.

"No!" she said.

"No," Mr. Miller agreed. "Where'd you get *that* information?" he asked his son.

"Kenny Moss told me."

"Well, then! If Kenny Moss said it, how can we doubt it?"

"I'm serious! He heard it from his uncle who's in the business."

"What business—tabloid newspapers?"

"Huh?"

"There are no beetle shells in chocolate marbles. Take my word for it. The FDA would never allow it."

"And guess what's in corn chips," Noah told Delia. "Those yellow corn chips? Seagull do."

"I never knew that!"

"That's what makes them so crackly."

"Noah—" his father said.

"Honest, Dad! Kenny Moss swears it!"

"Noah, Delia came to talk about keeping house for us."

Delia shot Mr. Miller a frown. He wore an oblivious, bland expression, as if he had no idea what he'd done. "Actually," she said, turning to Noah, "I was only . . . inquiring."

"She's going to think about it," Mr. Miller amended.

Noah said, "That'd be great! I've been having to fix my own school lunches."

"Horrors," his father said. "Don't let on to the child-labor authorities."

"Well, how would *you* feel? You open your lunch box: 'Gee, I wonder what I surprised myself with today.' "

Delia laughed. She said, "I should be going. It was nice to meet you, Noah."

"Goodbye," Noah said. Unexpectedly, he held out his hand. "I hope you decide to come."

His hand was small but callused. When he looked up at her, his eyes showed an underlay of gold, like sunshine filtered through brown water.

Outside the front door, Delia told his father, "I thought you didn't want him to feel people were checking him over."

"Ah," Mr. Miller said. "Yes. Well."

"I thought you were trying to spare him! Then you went and told him what I was here for."

"I realize I shouldn't have done that," Mr. Miller said. He spread one hand distractedly across his scalp, like a cap. "It's just that I wanted so badly for you to say you'd come."

"And you haven't seen my references, even! You don't know the first thing about me!"

"No, but I approve of your English."

"English?"

"It kills me to hear him speak so sloppily. 'Like' this and 'like' that, and 'I go' instead of 'I said.' It drives me bats."

"Well, of all things," Delia said. She turned to leave.

"Miss Grinstead? Delia?"

"What."

"Will you at least think it over?"

"Of course," she said.

But she knew she wouldn't.

Vanessa said Joel Miller was the most pitiful man she knew of. "Ever since his wife left, the guy has been barely coping," she told Delia.

"Isn't anyone in Bay Borough happily married?" Delia wondered.

"Yes, lots of folks," Vanessa said. "Just not who you choose to hang out with."

They were sitting in Vanessa's kitchen the following morning, a cold, sunny Saturday. Really it was her grandmother's kitchen; Vanessa and all three of her brothers lived with their father's mother. Vanessa was filling out labels with an old-fashioned steel-nibbed pen. *Highly Effective Insect Repellent*, she wrote, in hair-thin brown script on ivory paper ovals. Highly Effective was an ancient family recipe. When Vanessa had finished her daily allotment of labels, her youngest brother would glue them onto the slender glass phials in which various dried sprigs and berries bobbed mysteriously underwater. Delia found it hard to believe that people could make a living this way, but evidently the Linleys did all right. The house was large and comfortable, and the grandmother could afford to travel once a year to Disney World. Vanessa said the trick was pennyroyal. "Don't let this get around," she'd told Delia, "but insects *despise* pennyroyal. The other herbs are mostly for show."

On the floor, Greggie was building a tower with stacks of corks. After Vanessa finished her labels, she and Delia were going to take him to visit Santa. Then Delia might do a little Christmas shopping. Or maybe not; she couldn't decide. She had always disliked Christmas, with its possibilities for disappointing her family's secret hopes, and this year would be worse than ever. Should she just, maybe, skip the whole business? Oh, why wasn't there an etiquette book for runaway wives?

Which brought her back to Mr. Miller. "How come his wife left him, does anyone know?" she asked Vanessa.

"Oh, sure; everyone knows. Here they were, together for years, sweet little boy, nice house, and one day last spring Ellie, that's his wife, found a lump in her breast. Went to the doctor and he said, yup, looked like cancer. So she came home and told her husband, 'In the time that I have left to me, I want to make the very best of my life. I want to do exactly what I've dreamed of.' And by nightfall she had packed up and gone. That was her deepest, dearest wish—did you ever hear such a thing?"

"So where is she now?"

"Oh, she's a TV weather lady over in Kellerton," Vanessa said. "The lump was nothing at all; they removed it under local anesthetic. Now Mr. Miller and Noah can turn on their TV and watch her every evening. Or you might have seen her in *Boardwalk Bulletin*. They ran a profile of her last August. Real pretty blond? Hair like that shredded straw we pack our bottles in. Course, no one here was impressed in the slightest —person who'd leave her own child."

Delia looked down at her lap.

"All the women in town have been trying to help Mr. Miller out," Vanessa said. "Bringing pans of lasagna, taking his kid for the afternoon. But I guess by summer he realized it wasn't enough, because that's when he put the ad in the *Bugle*."

"The ad's been in since summer?"

"Right, but his neighbor tells me the onliest answers were teenaged girls from the high school. Every girl at Dorothy Underwood's got a crush on Mr. Miller. I did too; it's part of being a student there. I was a senior the first year he was principal, and I thought he was the sexiest man I'd ever laid eyes on. But of course he can't hire some airhead, so he's just kept running the ad. It never crossed my mind you'd want the job yourself."

"Well, I don't, really," Delia said. She watched Greggie start a cork train across the linoleum. His little hands reminded her of biscuits, that kind with a row of fork holes pricked on top. She had forgotten what a joy it was to rest your eyes on young children. "It's just that I'm so fed up with Mr. Pomfret," she said. "Do you suppose they have any openings at the furniture factory?"

"Oh, the furniture factory," Vanessa said, dipping her pen. "All's they ever need there is oilers. Stand all day rubbing oil into chair legs with these big mittens on your hands."

"But they must have office positions. Typist, filing clerk . . ."

"How come you're not taking the job at Mr. Miller's?"

"I don't want to just . . . step into a little boy's life like that, in case I decide to leave," Delia told her.

"Do you always up and leave a place?"

Delia wasn't sure how that question was intended. She looked at Vanessa suspiciously. "No, not always," she said.

"I mean I never heard you speak a word against Zeke Pomfret. Now you want to quit."

"He's so bossy, though. So condescending. Also, the pay is ridiculous," Delia said. "I didn't realize how ridiculous when I took the job. And he doesn't even provide health insurance! What if I got sick?"

Vanessa sat back to watch her.

"Well," Delia told her, "yes, I *do* seem to up and leave a lot."

As she spoke, she saw a lone, straight figure marching down the coastline. It was strange, the feeling of affection the image summoned up in her.

For her family's Christmas, she decided to buy nothing at all. Maybe Greggie's trip to Santa had depressed her. He had appeared to grasp the concept before they went, but once they got there he started screaming and had to be carried out. Vanessa was crushed; even the Santa looked crushed. And their shopping expedition afterward was spiritless, with Greggie hiccuping tearfully and slouching in his stroller in a brooding, insulted manner. Delia told Vanessa she thought she would call it a day. "I need to go to the laundromat anyhow," she said—a flimsy excuse.

When she got home, Belle hailed her from the living-room doorway. "You had a phone call," she said.

"I did?"

Her knees seemed to melt. She thought first of the children, then of Sam's heart.

But Belle said, "Mr. Miller from the high school. He wants you to call him back."

"Oh."

"*I* didn't know you knew Joel Miller."

Delia hadn't mentioned him to Belle because working for him would mean moving out of this house, and how could she ever do that? This house was perfect. Even Mr. Pomfret had his good points. Somehow the visit to Santa had shown her that. So she nonchalantly accepted the number Belle had scrawled on the corner of a takeout menu. Might as well get this over with. She perched on one arm of the couch and reached for the phone and dialed. Meanwhile Belle hovered in the background, supposedly absorbed with the cat. "Is you a nice little kitty. Is you a sweet little kitty," she crooned. Delia listened to the ringing at the other end of the line, letting her eyes travel gratefully over the blank white walls and bare floorboards.

"Hello?" Noah said.

She said, "This is Delia Grinstead."

"Oh, hi! I'm supposed to tell you I'm sorry."

"Sorry? For what?"

"Dad says a guy shouldn't talk about seagull do in front of ladies."

"Oh. Well—"

A man said something in the background.

"Women," Noah said.

"Excuse me?"

" 'Women,' I meant to say, not 'ladies.' "

All pretext, of course. Mr. Miller surely didn't think she would be offended by seagull do. Or the word "ladies." This was mere strategy. But Noah himself probably had no inkling of that, and so Delia told him, "It's quite all right."

"Kenny Moss's uncle drives a snack truck; that's how Kenny knows about the you-know-what. But Dad claims his uncle was teasing him. Dad goes, 'Right, the corn-chip factory really does take the time to send their workers out to the beach with shovels.' "

Another mutter in the background.

"Okay, 'said.' He *said*," Noah told Delia. "And on top of that he *said*"—heavy stress, meaningful pause—"he said how come it's not in the list of ingredients, if they use seagull do? Oops."

"Oh, you know those lists," Delia told him. "All those scientific terms. They can cover up just about anything with some chemical-sounding name."

"They can?"

"Why, sure! They probably call it 'dihydroxyexymexylene' or some such."

Noah giggled. "Hey, Dad," he said, his voice retreating slightly. "Delia says it probably *is* on the list; it's probably dihydroxy . . ."

Belle had carried the cat over to the window now. She was holding him up to the glass, which was nearly opaque with dust. And cobwebs clouded the tops of the curtains, and the philodendron plant on the sill was leggy and bedraggled. The whole room seemed drained of color, as if, already, it had slipped into the dimmest reaches of Delia's memory.

12

Mr. Pomfret said, "Moving on, eh," without so much as a change of expression. (You would think she was a piece of office equipment.) All he asked, he said, was that she finish out the week—tie up any dangling odds and ends. Which of course she agreed to do, even though there were no odds and ends; just the usual busywork of rat-a-tat letters and robot phone calls and Mr. Pomfret's daily sheaf of marked catalogs.

It seemed he urgently required a pair of perforated leather driving gloves. A radio antenna the size and shape of a breakfast plate. A solid-walnut display rack for souvenir golf balls.

When she turned in her office key on Friday afternoon, he told her he might wait till after New Year's to replace her. "This time," he said, "I believe I'll hire a word processor, assuming I can find one."

Delia was confused, for an instant. She pictured hiring a machine. Just try asking a machine to debate his glove size with an 800 operator! she thought. Then she realized her mistake. But still, somehow, she felt hurt, and she shouldered her bag abruptly and left without saying goodbye.

———

All she owned fit easily in a cardboard carton begged from Rick-Rack's. The goosenecked lamp poked its head out, though. She could have left it that way (Belle was giving her a ride), but she liked the notion of a life no larger than a single, compact box; and so she shifted things until the flaps closed securely. Then she took her coat and handbag from the bed, and she picked the carton up and walked out.

No point sending one last look backward. She knew every detail of that room by heart—every nail hole, every seam in the wallpaper, and the way the paw-footed radiator, in the furry half-light of this over-cast Saturday morning, resembled some skeletal animal sitting on its haunches.

At the bottom of the stairs, she set down her load and put her coat on. She could hear Belle talking to George in the kitchen. He was staying here another week or two, just till Delia was settled. It was Delia's belief that she had to let her own smell permeate the new place first; otherwise he'd keep running back to the old place.

Mr. Miller had told her George was more than welcome. He'd been meaning to buy a cat anyhow, he said. (But notice how he'd used the word "buy," apparently unaware that true animal lovers would not be caught dead in a pet shop.)

Still buttoning her coat, she walked through the dining room to knock on the kitchen door. "Coming," Belle called. Delia returned to the hall. Upstairs, Mr. Lamb was creaking the floorboards, and his TV had started its level, fluent murmur. She wondered when he would get around to noticing she was gone. Maybe never, she thought.

It was still not too late to change her mind.

"I gave George a can of tuna," Belle said when she emerged. "That ought to keep him occupied."

"Oh, Belle, you'll spoil him."

"Nothing's too good for my whiskums! I'm hoping he'll refuse to leave me when it's time. 'No, no, Mommy!' " she squeaked. " 'I want to stay here with Aunt Belle!' "

Meanwhile she was flouncing into her winged coat, fluffing her curls, jingling her car keys. "All set?" she asked.

"All set."

They walked out to her enormous old Ford. Delia fitted her carton among a tangle of real estate signs in the trunk, and then the two of them got in the car and Belle started the engine. With the seat-belt alarm insistently dinging, they pulled away from the curb.

It was months since Delia had ridden in a car. The scenery glided past so quickly, and so smoothly! She gripped her door handle as they swung around the corner, and then *zip! zip! zip!* went the dentist, the dime store, the Potpourri Palace. In no time, they were turning onto Pendle Street and parking in the Millers' gravel driveway—a trip that had taken her at least ten minutes, walking.

"My parents live in a house like this," Belle said. She was peering through the windshield at the cut-out designs of covered wagons on the shutters. "In a suburb of York, P.A. Dee, are you sure you want to do this?"

"Oh, yes," Delia said weakly.

"You'll be nothing but a servant!"

"It's better than being a typewriter," Delia told her.

"Well, if you're going to put it *that* way."

Delia climbed out of the car, and Belle came around to help her maneuver her box from the trunk. "Thanks," Delia said. "You have my phone number."

"I have it."

"I'll let you know when's a good time to bring the cat."

"Or before then," Belle said. "Or supposing you want to move back! I'll wait a few days before I try renting your room."

They might have gone on this way forever, but at that moment Noah burst out the front door. "Delia! Hi!" he called.

"Ms. Grinstead to *you*," Belle muttered under her breath. She told Delia, "Don't you let them treat you like a peon."

Delia just hugged her and turned toward the house. How the Millers treated her was the least of her concerns, she thought. The question was how to treat *them*—what distance to maintain from this mop-headed, blue-jeaned boy. It was so easy to fall back into being someone's mother! She smiled at him as he lifted the carton from her arms. "I can manage that," she said.

"I'm *supposed* to carry your luggage. Dad told me. Don't you have anything more?" he asked. Belle was already backing the car out of the driveway.

"This is it," Delia said.

"Dad's over at the school, so I'm supposed to show you where everything is. We've got your room all made up for you. We changed the bedsheets even though they were clean."

"Oh, then why did you change them?"

"Dad said if they didn't still have their laundry smell you might think someone else had slept in them."

"I wouldn't think that," she assured him.

They walked through the living room, where the cushions lined the couch in last week's exact formation and the magazines had not varied their positions by an inch. The carpet in the hall was freshly vacuumed, though. She could see the roller marks in the nap. And when they entered the guest room, Noah placed her box on a folding luggage stand that had definitely not been there earlier. "It's new," he said, noticing her glance. "We bought it at Home 'n' Hearth."

"It's very nice."

"And lookit here," he said. On the bureau sat a tiny television set. "Color TV! From Lawson Appliance. Dad says a live-in woman always has her own TV."

"Oh, I don't need a—"

"Clock radio," Noah said, "decorator box of Kleenex . . ."

What touched her most, though, was how they'd turned the bedcovers down—that effortful white triangle. She said, "You shouldn't have." And she meant it, for the sight made her feel indebted, somehow.

She followed Noah to the closet, where he was displaying the hangers. "Three dozen matching hangers, solid plastic, pink. Not a wire one in the bunch. We had our choice between pink or white or brown."

"Pink is perfect," she told him.

Three dozen! It would disappoint them to find out how few clothes she owned.

"Now I'm supposed to leave you in private," Noah said. "But I'll be in my room if there's anything you need."

"Thank you, Noah."

"You know where my room is?"

"I can find it."

"And you're supposed to unpack and put your stuff in drawers and all."

"I'll do that," she promised.

As he left he glanced back at her doubtfully, as if he worried she wouldn't follow instructions.

Her carton looked so shabby, resting on the needlepoint webbing of the luggage stand. She walked over to it and lifted the flaps, and out floated the lonesome, stale, hornet's-nest smell of the room on George Street. Well. She took off her coat, hung it on one of the hangers. Draped her purse strap over a hook. Drew the goosenecked lamp from the box but then had nowhere to put it, for the room already contained two lamps, shaded in rigid white satin. Still holding the goosenecked lamp (with its helmet of army-green metal and the dent at its base from when the cat had knocked it over one night), she sat down limply on the edge of the bed. She had to brace her feet so as not to slide off the slick coverlet. It was one of those hotel-type beds that seem at once too springy and too hard, and she couldn't imagine getting used to it.

Elsewhere in the house she heard a door open, a set of heavy footsteps, a man's voice calling and Noah answering. She would have to rearrange her face and go join them. Any minute now, she would. But for a while she went on sitting there, clutching her homely little lamp and gathering courage.

At the rear of the house, divided from the kitchen by only a counter, lay what the Millers called the family room. Here the stuffy decorating style relaxed into something more casual. A long, low couch faced a TV, an office desk stood against one wall, and three armchairs were grouped in a corner. It was this room that became, within the next few days, Delia's territory. (She had always wanted a more modern house, without cubbies or nooks or crannies.) In the mornings, when she was through cleaning, she sat at the desk to write her grocery list. She went out for several hours then—usually on foot, even though she had a car at her disposal—but afternoons would find her puttering between family room and kitchen while Noah did his homework on the couch. Evenings, she read in one of the armchairs while Noah watched TV. Sometimes Mr. Miller watched too—or Joel, as she had to remind herself to call him—in which case she retired early with her book. She was a little shy with Mr. Miller: Joel. This was such an awkward situation, businesslike and yet at the same time necessarily intimate. But usually he had meetings to go to, or he spent the evening at his workbench in the garage. She suspected he felt the awkwardness too. He couldn't possibly have stayed away so much before she came here.

They liked plain food, plainly prepared—roast beef and broiled chicken and burgers. Noah hated vegetables but was required to eat one spoonful each night. Mr. Miller was probably no fonder of them, but he worked his way conscientiously through everything, and he always told her, "Dinner is delicious, Delia." She suspected he would have said that no matter what she served. He asked her several courteous questions at every meal (had her day gone well? was she finding what she needed?), but she sensed he didn't listen to her answers. This was a sad, sad man underneath, and sometimes even when his own son spoke there was a moment of silence before he pulled himself together to reply.

"Guess what!" Noah might say. "Kenny Moss just got a humongous golden retriever. Dad, can we get a golden retriever?"

Long pause. Clinking of china. Then finally: "There is no such word as 'humongous.'"

"Sure there is, or how come I just used it?"

And the two of them would be off on one of their arguments. Delia had never known anyone as particular about words as Joel Miller. He despised all terms that were trendy (including "trendy" itself). He refused to agree that something was "neat" unless it was, literally, tidy. He interrupted one of Noah's most animated stories with the observation that no one could be "into" mountain climbing. But he always spoke with good humor, which probably explained why Noah still ventured to open his mouth.

Fastened to Delia's bathroom door was a full-length mirror, the first she had faced in six months, outside of a changing booth; and she was startled to see how thin she had grown. Her hipbones were sharp little chips, and the tops of her dresses looked hollow. So she served herself large helpings at these suppers, and she breakfasted with Noah every morning, and she walked to Rick-Rack's each noon to dine on something hefty—even crab cakes, for she was making good money now and had nothing else to spend it on.

Rick also served pork barbecue, the vinegary kind she was partial to, as it turned out. "You know," she told him, "I never had much of a chance to try a real meal here. I knew you were a good cook, but I didn't know *how* good."

"And here you been taking your Sunday dinners at that la-di-da Bay Arms!" he said.

Was there anything about her this whole town didn't know?

After lunch, she crossed the street to pay a visit to George. He was in a snit with her for leaving. He showed up as soon as she let herself in but then turned his back pointedly and stalked off. "George?" she wheedled. No response. He marched into Belle's living room and vanished. Delia waited in the hall, and a moment later a telltale sprig of whiskers poked around the edge of the door. A nose, an ear, an accusing green eye. "Georgie-boy!" she said. He sidled out, dusting the door with his fur and seeming to hang back even as he drew close enough to let her pat him.

Why couldn't Delia's children miss her this much?

All around town the streets were festooned with bristly silver ropes and honeycombed red tissue bells. There was a wreath above Mrs. Lincoln's desk in the library. Vanessa had tied a red bow to Greggie's stroller.

The thought of spending Christmas with the Millers—poor Noah bearing the full weight of it—filled Delia with dread. But maybe they didn't celebrate Christmas. Maybe they were Jewish, or some kind of fundamentalists who frowned on pagan ritual. It was true that so far, with just a week remaining, they hadn't given a sign they knew what season this was.

Delia went out to the garage to talk to Mr. Miller. "Um, Joel?" she said.

He was measuring a board at his workbench, wearing a raveled black sweater and frayed corduroys. Delia waited for him to look up—it took a minute—and then she said, "I wanted to ask about Christmas."

"Christmas," he said. He reeled in his measuring tape.

"Do you observe it?"

"Well, yes. Normally," he said.

By "normally," he must mean when he still had his wife. This would be their first Christmas without her, after all. Delia watched the thought travel across his face, deepening the lines at either side of his mouth. But he said, "Let's see. Ah, you would get the day off, of course. Noah will be at his mother's, and some friends in Wilmington have been asking me to visit. School is closed through New Year's, so if you need more time in Baltimore—"

"I won't be going to Baltimore."

He stopped speaking.

"I just wondered how you celebrate," she told him. "Do you put up a tree? Should I take Noah shopping for gifts?"

"Gifts."

"Something for his mother, maybe?"

"Oh, God," he said, and he sank onto the high stool behind him. He clamped the top of his head with one large hand—his usual sign of distress. "Yes, certainly for his mother, and also for Nat, Ellie's father.

He and Noah are pretty close. And for me, I guess; aren't we supposed to encourage that? And I should get something for him. Oh, God Almighty."

"I'll take him tomorrow," she said. She hadn't intended to plunge the man into despair.

"That's a Saturday. Your weekend."

"I don't mind."

Seated on the stool, Mr. Miller was closer to Delia's eye level. He looked across at her for a moment. He said, "Don't you have any family around? For weekend visits and such?"

"No."

It was a mark of his isolation, she thought, that he had apparently not heard so much as a whisper about her past. For all he knew, Delia had dropped from the sky. Clearly he would have liked to ask more, but in the end he just said, "Well, thanks, Delia. As far as a tree goes, I figure since Noah won't be here for the day itself, we don't need to bother."

Delia would have bothered anyhow, if it had been up to her. But she didn't argue. When she left, Mr. Miller was still slumped on his stool, staring down at the measuring tape in his hands.

She and Noah did all his Christmas shopping at the hardware store—dark, old-fashioned, wooden-floored Brent Hardware, across the street from Belle's. Noah had very definite ideas, Delia discovered. For his mother he chose a screwdriver with interchangeable shafts, because she lived alone now and would need to make her own repairs. For his grandfather, who had trouble bending, a tonglike instrument called a "grabber" that would help him retrieve dropped objects. And for his father, a device to hold a nail in position while he was hammering it in. "Dad is all the time banging his thumb," Noah told Delia. "He's not a real great carpenter."

"What is it that he builds, exactly?" Delia asked.

"Shadow boxes."

"Shadow boxes?"

For an instant she pictured Charlie Chaplin shadowboxing in baggy trunks.

"Those, like, partitioned-up wooden shelves. You know? To hang on a wall?"

"Oh, yes."

"Because my mom collects miniatures. Teeny little kitchen utensils and furniture and like that, and he used to make these shadow boxes for her to keep them in."

And now? Delia wanted to ask.

As if he had read her mind, Noah said, "Now he just piles them behind the tires in the garage."

"I see."

She couldn't tell from Noah's tone how he felt about his parents' separation. He had mentioned his mother only in passing, and this coming visit would be his first since Delia's arrival.

"I want to pick out one more thing," he told her. "You go wait outside a minute."

So he was buying her a present too. She wished he wouldn't. She would have to act appreciative; she would have to make a big show of putting whatever it was to use, not to mention the necessity of buying something for *him* that was neither more nor less serious than what he'd bought her. Oh, how had she worked her way back to this? She should have stayed at Belle's; she'd known it all along.

But Noah was so gleeful as he hustled her out the door, she couldn't help smiling.

"Will you need money?" she asked him.

"I've been saving up my allowance."

He closed the door after her and made a comic shooing motion through the glass.

She waited on the sidewalk, watching the passersby. It was hard to resist getting caught up in the spirit of things. Everyone carried shopping bags and brightly wrapped parcels. From Rick-Rack's Café, next door, the cheering smells of bacon and hot pancakes drifted into the frosty air. When Noah rejoined her, hugging his own bag, she said, "How about I buy you a soda at Rick-Rack's?"

He hesitated. "You going to put it in the book?" he asked.

He meant the little notebook Mr. Miller had given her. She was supposed to keep a record of reimbursable expenses, and Noah always worried she might shortchange herself. (He viewed her as someone *less fortunate*, which she found both amusing and slightly humiliating.) "Today it's my treat," she told him firmly, and even as he opened his mouth to protest, she was nudging him toward the café.

Rick waved a spatula in their direction; he was busy at the grill.

Teensy, though, made a big fuss. "It's Delia! And Mr. Miller's boy. Look, Pop!" she chirped, turning to an old man seated at the counter. "This is Delia Grinstead! She used to live across the street! My father, Mr. Bragg," she told Delia. "He's come to stay with us awhile."

Teensy's father, Delia seemed to recall, was a snarky man who had not behaved very graciously toward his son-in-law; so she was unprepared for his timid, meek expression and wilted posture. He sat up close to his breakfast like a child. When she said, "Hello," he had to work his mouth a minute before the words formed.

"I'm having cocoa," was what he finally said.

"How nice!"

Her voice came out sounding as false as Teensy's had.

"That your boy?" he asked.

"This is . . . Noah," she told him, not bothering with a full explanation.

"Come sit here, boy."

"Oh, we'd better take a booth, with all we're carrying." Delia gestured toward Noah's shopping bag. The handles of his grandfather's grabber extended from it a good two feet.

In the rear corner booth, Mr. Lamb sat hanging his head over a bowl of cereal. Two teenage girls had a window table—Underwood students, Delia assumed, judging by how they perked up at the sight of Noah. (Already she had turned several away from the house, briskly thanking them for their plates of homemade fudge and pretending not to notice how they gazed beyond her for Joel.) One of them sang out, "Hey there, Noah!" Noah rolled his eyes at Delia.

"What can I get you?" Teensy asked, standing over their table.

"Coffee, please," Noah said.

"Coffee!"

"Can't I?" He was addressing Delia. "Dad lets me have it, sometimes on special occasions."

"Well, all right. Make that two," Delia told Teensy.

"Sure thing," Teensy said. Then she bent so close that Delia could smell her starched-fabric scent, and she whispered, "When you leave here, could you say goodbye real loud to Rick, so Pop can hear you?"

"Of course," Delia said.

"Pop can act so hurtful to him sometimes."

"I'd have said goodbye anyhow, you know that."

"I know, but . . ." Teensy flapped a hand toward her father. He still appeared harmless, the X of his suspenders curving with the hunch of his back.

Noah was one of those people who like gloating over their purchases even before they get them home. He was rustling through his bag, first pulling out the screwdriver, then burrowing to the bottom for a furtive look at something there and shooting a tucked, sly glance at Delia. When she craned across the table, pretending to be angling for a peek, he laughed delightedly and crumpled the bag shut again. His two front teeth were still new enough to seem too big for his mouth.

And see how his hair fell over his eyes—the bouncy thickness of it, the soft sheen that made her want to press it with her palm. And the tilt at the tip of his nose, the knobby cluster of little-boy warts that showed on the bend of his index finger when he gripped the mug Teensy brought him. One point of his jacket collar stuck up crookedly. The knit shirt beneath it bore scratches of ballpoint-pen ink. His jeans, she knew, were ripped at the knees, and his sneakers were those elaborate, puffy high-tops that could have been designed for walking on the moon.

He was telling her a dream he'd had—something boring and impossible to follow. His teacher changed into a dog, the dog came to visit at Noah's house, which was somehow the school auditorium too, if Delia knew what he meant . . .

Delia nodded, smiling, smiling, and folded her hands tightly so as not to reach across to him. When they left, she told Rick goodbye with such feeling that her voice broke.

Belle claimed the cat had developed an eating disorder. She brought him over in a Grape-Nuts carton late Monday morning, so he could adjust to the house while Delia was the only one home. Still in the carton, he was borne directly to Delia's room and set on the floor. "It's like he's bulimic," Belle was saying. She sank onto the edge of the bed to watch him nose his way out of the carton. "The minute his bowl is half empty he starts nagging me for more; I swear I never knew a cat could plan ahead that way. And if, God forbid, he should finish every bit of it, we have this heartrending melodrama the second I walk in from work. Great yowling and wringing of paws, and as soon as I fill the bowl he staggers over all weak-kneed to eat and makes these disgusting gobbling sounds and then darned if he doesn't throw up in a corner not ten minutes after he's done."

"Oh, George, did I do this to you?" Delia asked him. He was investigating the room now, sniffing daintily at the luggage stand.

"About six times a day he goes to the cupboard and looks up at his sack of kibble, checking to make sure I'm keeping enough in stock."

"All my life," Delia said, "I've been the ideal cat-owner. I lived in one place; I had a routine. I was motionless, in fact. Now I'm flitting about like a . . . He must feel so insecure!"

She bent to stroke the black M on his forehead, while Belle gazed around her. "This room is awfully small, isn't it?" she asked. "Your old one was a whole lot bigger."

"It's okay." Delia was trying to lure George into the bathroom now. "See? Your litter box," she told him. "Store-bought; not just cardboard."

"What're you doing for Christmas, Dee?" Belle called after her.

"Oh, staying here."

"Christmas with strangers?"

"They'll be gone, at least for the day."

"That's even worse," Belle told her.

"I'm sort of looking forward to it."

George stepped into the litter box and then out again, as if demonstrating that he knew what it was.

"Come along with me to my folks'," Belle told her. "They'd be thrilled to have you."

"No, really, thanks."

"Or get Vanessa to invite you to her grandma's."

"She already did, but I said no."

"Well, granted it's kind of hectic there," Belle said. "I'm a little peeved at Vanessa these days."

"Oh? How come?"

"You know what she had the nerve to ask me?" Belle stood up to follow Delia into the hall; they were heading for the bowl of cat food in the kitchen. George wafted after them in a shadowy, indecisive way. "I was complaining about my love life," Belle said. "Can't find a man to save my soul, I told her, and she asked why I'd never thought of Mr. Lamb."

"Mr. Lamb!"

"Can you imagine? That dreary, gloomy man, that . . . Eeyore! I said, 'Vanessa, just what sort of idea do you have of me? Do you honestly believe I would date a man who's spent his entire adulthood in rented bedrooms?' I mean, think about it: no one even calls him by his first name, have you noticed? Quick: what's Mr. Lamb's first name?"

"Um . . ."

"Horace," Belle said grimly. She plunked herself at the kitchen table. "I may be single, but I'm not suicidal. What's that I see on the fridge?"

She meant Mr. Miller's map of the household. "It's to keep things in the living room the way Mrs. Miller left them," Delia said. "He's charted all the doodads, exactly where she used to set them out."

Belle leaned forward for a closer look. On the rectangle representing the mantel, tiny block letters spelled *blue vase, pine-cone candle, sandbox photo, clock.*

"Well, that's just pathetic," Belle said. "And why would he need it? What makes him think these things would go and lose themselves, for Lord's sake?"

"You wouldn't ask if you could see him around the house," Delia said. "For someone so set on order, he's awfully . . . discombobulated. He's just plain incompetent! Oh, everything's fine on the surface, but when you look in the back of a cupboard you find pans with scorched bottoms that will never come clean, dish towels with big charred holes in them . . ."

Belle was peering at the diagram of the coffee table. "*Large paperweight, small paperweight, magazines,*" she read.

"He keeps these magazines that still come to the house in her name, all about clothing styles and cellulite and such."

"Ellie Miller never had a speck of cellulite in her life," Belle said.

"A new magazine comes, he fits it in the spot where the old one was and throws the old one away."

"That's what you get for worshiping a person," Belle said. "Poor man, he thought she walked on water! In fact, she was kind of silly, but you know how the smartest men will sometimes go so gaga over silly women. I asked him to a picnic after she left, and he said, 'Oh, I'm afraid I wouldn't know anyone; thank you just the same.' This is a high-school principal we're talking about! He ought to know the whole town! But he always depended on Ellie for that. Ellie was real outgoing and social, threw these parties with themes to them like Hawaiian Luau, Wild West Barbecue . . . and a Grade Mothers' Tea in the fall, but Joel hasn't kept that up. He just let the grade mothers flounder this year, when needless to say, every gal in town was dying to help him."

"I wish . . . ," Delia began.

She wished Sam Grinstead had felt like that about her, she'd been going to say. But she stopped herself.

"Oh, I'm sure he'll let *you* help," Belle said, misunderstanding. "You just have to do it inch by inch, you know? Pretty soon, you'll be indispensable."

"Well, yes, of course," Delia agreed.

That much she simply assumed. Already, only ten days into her stay, Mr. Miller had requested another of "her" meat loaves; he had wordlessly laid out a shirt in need of a button; he no longer left his compulsive lists of instructions on the breakfast table.

But wasn't it odd that she had assumed it? She seemed to have changed into someone else—a woman people looked to automatically for sustenance.

The cat wove around her ankles, purring. "See?" Delia told Belle. "He doesn't have an eating disorder. All he ate was a couple of kibbles, just to be polite."

"You're amazing, Dee," Belle said.

Belle had also brought Delia's mail—a package from Eleanor and a letter from Eliza. Eleanor's package contained a knitted jacket for reading in bed. Eliza's letter said she'd invited the Allinghams for Christmas dinner. *I won't press you but you know you're welcome too,* she wrote, and then she hurried on to news of Linda. *She says the twins are getting to the age where they want to spend the holidays at home, so I guess it will be just the Allinghams and us and then Eleanor too of course. . . .* The stationery gave off that faint scent of cloves (for positive thoughts) that always hung in the air of Eliza's bedroom.

Noah was very excited about the cat. He came straight home from school that day, and he flung his books any old where and raced through the house, calling, "George? George?" George, of course, hid. Delia had to explain to Noah how cats operated—that you shouldn't pursue them, shouldn't face them head-on; should do everything at a diagonal, so to speak, with a cat. "Sit at his level," she said when George finally showed himself. "Look a little sideways to him. Talk in a crooning tone of voice."

"Talk? What should I say?"

"Tell him he's beautiful. Cats love the word 'beautiful.' I guess it must be something in your tone, because they're not the least bit good at language, but if you draw out that *u* sound long and thin and twangy . . ."

"Bee-yoo-tee-ful," Noah said, and sure enough, George slitted his eyes in a sleek, self-satisfied smile.

On Christmas Eve, Delia picked Noah up at school and drove him to his mother's. The Millers' car was a Volkswagen Beetle. She didn't yet feel completely at home with the stick shift, so it was a rocky ride. Noah was nice enough not to comment. He sat forward and watched for the turnoff to Kellerton. "Most times Mom comes to get me," he said, "but her car's in the shop right now. She's had five wrecks in the last nine months."

"Five!" Delia said.

"None of them were her fault, though."

"I see."

"She's just, like, unlucky. This last time, a guy backed into her while she was looking for a parking spot. Here's where you turn."

Delia signaled and took a right onto a patchy highway that ran between fields of frozen stubble. This countryside was so flat, at least she didn't need to shift gears all that often. They were heading east, in the direction of the beaches. Mr. Miller had told her it was a half-hour drive.

"Tonight at six you want to watch WKMD," Noah said. "It's not like I'll be on it or anything, but at least you'll know I'm sitting there in the station."

It must feel eerie to see your absent mother deliver the weather report every night. Although Noah never did, to the best of Delia's knowledge. Six o'clock was *The MacNeil / Lehrer NewsHour*, which Mr. Miller watched instead.

The fields gave way to hamburger joints and used-car lots and liquor stores, implying the approach of a town, but soon Delia realized this *was* the town—this scattering of buildings flung across the farmland. Noah pointed out the television station beneath its Erector-set tower. He showed her where his mother did her grocery shopping and where she got her hair done, and then he directed her two blocks south to a low, beige-brick apartment building. "Should I come in with you?" Delia asked, parking at the curb.

"Naw. I've got a key if she's not there."

Delia was disappointed, but she didn't argue.

"When you wake up tomorrow," Noah told her as she unlocked the trunk, "look on my closet shelf and you'll find your present."

"And when *you* wake up, look in the inside end pocket of your duffel bag."

He grinned and took the bag from her. "So, okay," he said. "See you, I guess."

"Have a good Christmas."

Instead of hugging him, she tousled his hair. She'd been longing to do that anyhow.

By the time she got back to the house, Mr. Miller was waiting at the front window. They barely crossed paths in the doorway—Mr. Miller holding out a palm for the car keys, wishing her a Merry Christmas, saying he'd be back with Noah tomorrow evening—and then he was gone. The cat mewed anxiously and trailed Delia to her room.

On her bureau, she found a Christmas card with a check for a hundred dollars. *Season's Greetings*, the card read, followed by Mr. Miller's block print: *Just a token thank you for setting our lives back in order. Gratefully, Joel and Noah.*

That was nice of him, she thought. Also, he had shown tact in clearing out of the house when he did. It would have been a strain without Noah to serve as buffer.

She spent the afternoon on the couch, reading an extra-thick library book: *Doctor Zhivago*. The wind dashed bits of leaves against the picture windows. George slept curled at her feet. Twilight fell, and her lamp formed a nest of honey-colored light.

A few minutes before six, she took the remote control from the end table and clicked the TV on. WKMD had a one-eyed pirate advertising choice waterfront lots. Then a housewife spraying a room with aerosol. Then a deskful of newscasters—a bearded black man, a pink-faced white man, and a glamorous blonde in a business suit. Delia thought at first the blonde was Ellie Miller, till the black man called her Doris. Doris told about a bank heist in Ocean City. The robber had been dressed as Santa Claus, she said. She spoke in such a way that her lipstick never came in contact with her teeth.

Delia was disconcerted by the speed at which everything moved. She had lost the knack of watching television, it seemed. She felt her eyes had experienced an overload, and during the next round of commercials she looked away for awhile.

"Now here's Ellie with the weather," the bearded man said. "So tell us, Ellie, any chance of a white Christmas?"

"Not a prayer, Dave," Ellie told him in that sporty, bosom-buddy tone that TV people affect. Her face, though, didn't match her voice. It was too soft, too open—a pretty face with a large red mouth, surprised blue eyes, and circlets of pink rouge. Her hair was silvery fluff. Her white sweater, a scoop-necked angora, seemed uncertain around the edges.

Delia rose and went to stand in front of the TV. Ellie slid weather maps along an aluminum groove. Somewhere behind that painted backdrop of marsh and improbable cattails, Noah would be sitting, but at the moment Delia wasn't thinking of Noah. She was memorizing Ellie, trying to see what lay beneath her sky-blue, doll-like stare.

"Continued cold . . . gale-force winds . . ." Delia listened with her head cocked, her fingertips supporting her cheek.

The weather was followed by sports, and Delia turned and wandered out of the family room and through the kitchen, down the hall to the master bedroom. She opened the closet door and studied the clothes hanging inside. Mr. Miller's suits straggled across the rod toward the empty space at the right. The shelf above was empty on the right as well. It appeared that Ellie, unlike Rosemary Bly-Brice, had taken everything with her when she went. Even so, Delia next pulled out each drawer in Ellie's bureau. All she found was a button, trailing a wisp of blue thread.

Back in the family room, the TV was showing the national news. It was months since she had watched the news, but she could see she hadn't missed anything: the planet was still hurtling toward disaster. She switched the TV off in midsentence and went to make her supper.

When she woke the next morning, the sun was out. Something about the hard, bright light told her it was very cold. Also, George lay nestled close under her arm, which he wouldn't do in warmer weather.

Not until she was drinking her tea did she consider the fact that it was Christmas. Christmas, all by herself! She supposed that would strike most people as tragic, but to her the prospect was enjoyable. She liked carrying her cup through the silent house, still wearing her nightgown and beach robe, humming a snatch of "We Three Kings" with no one to hear her. In Noah's room she rooted through the top drawer for a pair of woolen socks to wear as slippers. Then she remembered he'd left her a gift, and she pulled it down from his closet shelf—a squarish shape wrapped in red foil. The tag read, *Because you don't have house-type clothes,* which puzzled her till she tore off the foil and saw a canvas carpenter's apron with pockets across the front. She smiled and slipped the neck strap over her head. Till now she'd been using the cocktail apron she'd found among the dish towels, which protected no more than the laps of her dresses.

Her gift to Noah had been a survival kit from Kemp's Kamping Store. Boys seemed to go for such things. And this kit was so ingenious—hardly bigger than a credit card, with streamlined foldout gadgets, including a magnifying lens for starting fires.

She fed George, and then she dressed and settled on the couch again with *Doctor Zhivago*. Periodically, she looked up from the book and let her eyes travel around the room. Wintry sunlight, almost white, fell across the carpet. The cat was giving himself a bath in a square of sunlight on the blue armchair. Everything had a pleasantly shallow look, like a painting.

At home they must be opening their presents now. It was nothing like the old days, when they used to rise before dawn. Now they ambled downstairs in midmorning, and they passed out presents decorously, one person at a time. Then for dinner they always had goose, a contribution from one of Sam's patients who hunted. For dessert, plum pudding with hard sauce, and they would complain it was too heavy but eat it anyhow and spend the rest of the afternoon moaning and clutching their stomachs.

Every so often it took her breath away to realize how easily her family had accepted her leaving.

Although it *did* seem acceptable, come to think of it. It seemed almost inevitable. Almost . . . foreordained. In retrospect she saw all the events of the past year—her father's death, Sam's illness, Adrian's arrival—as waves that had rolled her forward, one wave after another, closer and closer together. Not sideways, after all, but forward, for now she thought that her move to the Millers' must surely represent some kind of progress.

She had imagined that her holiday would not last nearly long enough, but when Joel and Noah turned into the driveway at dusk, she was already watching at the window. She dropped the curtain as soon as she saw the headlights, and she rushed to open the door and welcome them home.

13

Once a week, generally on Wednesday afternoons, Delia drove Noah a few miles west on Highway 50 to visit his grandfather. The old man lived in a place called Senior City—four stories of new red brick on the edge of a marshy golf course. Delia would pull up in the U-shaped drive, let Noah out, and leave, maneuvering past a fleet of gigantic Buicks and Cadillacs. She came back to collect him at the front door an hour later. It was an inconvenient length of time, just slightly too short to make returning to Bay Borough worth her while, and so she formed the habit of heading for a nearby shopping center. There she browsed in a bookstore, or picked up some treat for supper at the gourmet food store.

She was dropping Noah off one Wednesday in mid-January, when he announced that she should come in with him. "Me? What for?" she asked.

"Grandpa wants to see you."

"Well, but . . ."

She glanced down. Beneath her coat she was wearing a housedress, a dark cotton print she had bought at an after-Christmas sale. "How about next week?" she suggested.

"He asked me to bring you today. I forgot."

She pulled into one of the visitors' parking slots. "If you'd warned me, I would have dressed up," she said.

"It's only Grandpa."

"I look a mess! What's his name?"

"Nat."

"I meant his last name," she said, getting out of the car. Years of experience had taught her not to rely on children's formal introductions. "I have to call him Mister *something*."

"Everybody just says Nat."

She gave up and followed Noah past a row of Handicapped license plates. "Does he want to see me for any particular reason?" she asked.

"He says he doesn't know who to picture when I talk about you."

They approached the double doors, which slid open to admit them. The lobby was carpeted with some nubby, hard substance, probably to accommodate wheelchairs. It made a winching sound beneath their feet. On their right was a glassed-in gift shop, and through an entrance at their left Delia glimpsed a cafeteria, deserted at this hour but still giving off that unmistakable steamed-vegetable smell. Several old women waited in front of the elevators. One sat in a motorized cart, and two leaned on walkers. This was like visiting a war zone, Delia thought. But the women were elegantly coiffed and dressed, and at the sight of Noah their faces lit up in smiles. *Valiant* smiles, they seemed to Delia. She was familiar with old people's tribulations, having observed Sam's patients for so long.

The elevator opened to expose a slim, blue-haired old woman in a designer dress. "Sorry!" she caroled. "I'm going down."

"You *are* down, Pooky," the woman on the cart said. "This is the bottom floor."

"Well, you're welcome to come along for the ride, but I've pressed One, I regret to say."

"This *is* One, Pooky."

The others didn't bother to argue. They entered laboriously, most of them clinging to various surfaces for support. Noah and Delia came last. The door closed behind them, and they began rising. Meanwhile everyone beamed at Noah—even Pooky, who seemed unfazed that they were not, in fact, going down. At the second floor, a woman with a shopping bag got off. At the third floor, Noah said, "This is us," and he and Delia stepped into a long corridor. Several women followed, with metallic clanking sounds and a whirring of wheels. Pooky, however, remained on board, gazing contentedly straight ahead as the elevator door slid shut.

"She rides up and down all day sometimes," Noah told Delia.

Nothing here seemed any different from a standard apartment building, except for the handrails that ran along both walls. Blond flush doors appeared at intervals, each with a peephole at eye level. Noah stopped at the fourth door on the right. *Nathaniel A. Moffat, Photographer*, a business card read, with a Cambridge, Maryland, street address crossed out. When Noah pressed the doorbell, a single golden note sounded from within.

"Is that my favorite grandson?" a man shouted.

"Yes, it is," Noah called back.

"It's his *only* grandson," he told Delia with a giggle.

The door opened, but instead of the old man Delia had expected, a short, chunky woman stood smiling at them. She could not have been out of her thirties. She had a round apricot of a face and pink-tinted curls, and she wore an orange sweater-dress with a keyhole neckline. Her shoes were orange too—tiny, open-toed pumps, as Delia found when she checked, reflexively, for nurse shoes to explain the woman's presence. "Hi! I'm Binky," she told Delia. "Hey there, Noah. Come on in."

The living room they entered must have been as modern as the rest of the building, but Delia couldn't see beyond the furniture, which was dark and tangled, ornate, ponderously antique. Also, there was far too much of it, set far too close together, as if it had once filled several larger rooms. For a moment Delia had trouble locating Noah's grandfather. He was rising from the depths of a maroon velvet chair with viny arms. A four-pronged metal cane stood next to him, but he moved forward on his own to shake her hand. "You're Delia," he said. "I'm Nat."

He was one of those men who look better old, probably, than they ever did young—clipped white beard, ruddy face, and a lean, energetic body. He wore a tweed sports coat and gray trousers. His handshake was muscular and brisk.

"Thank you for coming," he told her. "I wanted to get a look at this person my grandson's so taken with."

"Well, thank you for inviting me."

"Won't you give Binky your coat?"

Delia was about to tell him she would keep her coat, she could only stay a second; but then she saw that the table in front of the couch was laid for tea. There were plates of cakes, four china cups and saucers, and a teapot already steeping in a swaddling of ivory linen. Thank goodness Noah had remembered she was invited.

She handed her coat to Binky and then sat where Nat indicated, at one end of the couch. Nat reclaimed his chair, and Noah took a seat in the little rocker next to him. Binky, when she returned from the coat closet, settled on the other end of the couch and bent forward to unwrap the teapot.

"Noah always likes mint instead of plain," she told Delia. "I hope you don't mind."

"Not at all."

Noah had this tea party every time he came here, then? Delia had imagined he was, oh, playing checkers or something. She looked over at his grandfather, who nodded gravely.

"Noah's been taking tea with me since the days when he drank from a training mug," he told her. "He's the only boy in the family! We men have to stick together."

Binky handed Delia her cup and said, "So how do you like keeping house for Noah's father, Delia?"

"Oh, very much," Delia said.

"Joel's a good man," Nat said placidly. "I make it a point not to choose sides in my daughters' domestic disputes," he told Delia. "Back when they were wee little girls, I swore an oath to myself I would approve of whoever they married."

Enough of a pause hung after his words so that Delia felt pushed to ask, "And do you?"

"Oh, absolutely," he said. His chuckle, filtered through his beard, had a wheezy sound. "I love my sons-in-law to death! And they think I'm just wonderful."

"Well, you *are* wonderful," Binky told him staunchly.

He bowed from the waist. "Thank you, madam."

"Maybe not quite as wonderful as they imagine, mind you . . ."

He grimaced at her, and she gave Delia a mischievous wink.

Was this Binky a paid companion? Was she one of the daughters? But her merry face bore no resemblance to Nat's. And she didn't seem all that connected to his grandson. "Have some butter," she was telling Noah, not noticing he had nothing to put it on.

"Have some low-cholesterol vegetable-oil spread," Nat corrected her. "First I wolf down my I Can't Believe It's Not Butter," he told Delia, "and then I go wash my hair in Gee, Your Hair Smells Terrific."

Delia found this remark mystifying, but Noah tittered. His grandfather glanced over at him; his lips twitched as if he were trying not to smile. Then he turned back to Delia. "You're from Baltimore, I hear."

"Yes," she said.

"Got family there?"

"Some."

He raised his eyebrows, but she offered nothing further.

"Ninety percent of the people in this building come from Baltimore," he said finally.

"They do?"

"Rich folks, retiring to the Eastern Shore. Roland Park and Guilford folks."

Delia kept her face blank, giving no sign she had ever heard of Roland Park or Guilford.

"You surely don't suppose all those chichi ladies are locals," he said. "Lord, no. I wouldn't be here myself if I hadn't married a Murray. That's Murray as in Murray Crab Spice. You think a two-bit, hole-in-the-wall photographer could afford these exorbitant prices?"

"They're going to raise the rates again in July, I hear," Binky told him.

Delia was looking around the room. The mention of photography had alerted her to the pictures hanging everywhere—large black-and-white photos, professionally framed. "Are these your work?" she asked him.

"These? If only."

He stood, this time reaching for his cane. "These were taken by the masters," he said, stumping over to a study of a voluptuous green pepper. "Edward Weston, Margaret Bourke-White . . ." He pivoted to inspect the picture at his left—factory chimneys, lined up like notes of music. "Me, I photographed brides," he said. "Forty-two years of brides. Few golden-anniversary couples thrown in from time to time. Then I started getting my, what I call, flashbacks." He gave a downward jab with his beard. Delia thought at first he was indicating the rug. "Old boyhood polio came bouncing back on me," he said. "Thelma—that was my wife—she'd passed on by then, but she had put our names on the waiting list when they first drew up the plans for Senior City. Just why, I couldn't tell you, since she refused to budge from our big old house long after the girls were grown and gone. She always said, what if they wanted to come back for any reason? And come back they did, you know they did: all four of them rushing home at every minor crisis, just because of the very fact they had a home to rush to, if you want my honest opinion. 'Lord God, Thel,' I told her, 'we can't be rearing those girls for all time! Look at how cats do,' I told her. 'Raise up their kittens, wean them, don't know who the hell they are when they meet them in the alley a few months later. You think humans should be any different?' "

"Well, of course they should!" Binky protested, and she and Delia exchanged a smile.

But Nat hissed derisively behind his beard. "Hogwash," he told Noah. Noah merely licked a dab of frosting from his thumb. "In any event," Nat said, "I started getting these flashbacks. Times the one leg would clean give out on me, along about the end of day. Reached the point where I barely made it up the stairs some nights; I knew I couldn't go on living where I was. So I phoned the people here and said, 'Listen,' I said, 'didn't my wife put our names on your waiting list once upon a time?' And that's how I happened to end up in Senior City. Senior City: God. Abominable name."

"It seems very . . . well-organized, though," Delia said.

"Precisely. Organized. That's the word!" He spun around (there was something explosive, barely contained, about even his most painful movements) and returned to his chair. "Like files in a filing cabinet," he said, reseating himself by degrees. "We're organized on the vertical. Feebler we get, higher up we live. Floor below this one is the hale-and-hearty. Some people there go to work still, or clip their coupons or whatever it is they do; use the golf course and the Ping-Pong tables, travel south for Christmas. This floor here is for the moderately, er, challenged. Those of us who need wheelchair-height counters or perhaps a little help coping. Fourth floor is total care. Nurses, beds with railings . . . Everybody hopes to die before they're sent to Four."

"Oh, they do not!" Binky said indignantly. "It's lovely up on Four! Have a cupcake, Noah."

" 'Lovely' isn't the word that first comes to *my* mind," Nat told Delia. "Not that I don't applaud Senior City in theory, understand. It's certainly preferable to burdening your children. But something about the whole setup strikes me as uncomfortably, shall we say, symbolic. See, I've always pictured life as one of those ladders you find on playground sliding boards—a sort of ladder of years where you climb higher and higher, and then, *oops!*, you fall over the edge and others move up behind you. I keep asking myself: couldn't Thelma have found us a place with a few more levels to it?"

Delia laughed, and Nat sat back in his chair and grinned at her. "Well," he said, "don't let me ramble on. I'm glad we finally got to meet you, Delia. Noah's told me how much you've done for the two of them."

She recognized her cue. "It was good to meet you too," she said, rising.

"From now on, stop in and have tea whenever you come for Noah, why don't you?"

"I'll do that," she promised.

She slid her arms into the coat Binky held for her, and Noah wrangled his jacket on. "Drive carefully, now," Binky said as she opened the door. Her keyhole neckline showed a teardrop of plump, powdered pink, bisected by the tight crevice between her breasts. Was it that, or was it the memory of Nat's roguish grin, that made Delia wonder suddenly whether Binky might in fact be his girlfriend?

Joel told her he had no idea who Binky was. He hadn't realized she existed, even. "Binky? Binky who?" he asked. "What kind of a name is Binky?"

They were eating supper in the kitchen, just the two of them. Noah had accepted a last-minute invitation to the Mosses'. At first Delia had contrived to be on her feet most of the time, but finally Joel said, "Sit down, Delia," in a kindly tone that made her feel he'd seen straight through her. "Tell me how you think Noah's doing," he said.

That took about three seconds. (Noah was doing fine.) Then they had to find a new topic, and so Delia thought to mention Binky.

"How old is she, would you guess?" Joel asked.

"Oh, thirty-five, thirty-six . . ."

"So: too young to be a fellow resident. And I doubt Nat needs a nurse. What did Noah say about her?"

"He said she's just 'around.' I asked who she was, and he said, 'I don't know; someone who's just around a lot.' "

"Hmm."

"Well, anyhow," Delia said. "It's really none of my business. I can't think why I brought it up."

But then she remembered why, because they were back to an uneasy silence.

"His wife was a paragon of virtue," Joel said while he was helping himself to another roll. "Noah's grandma, that is."

"Oh, really?"

"To hear *her* tell it."

"Oh."

"I never could abide that woman. Always interfering. Nudging into our lives. Inquiring after the welfare of her gifts. 'Do you ever use the such and such?' 'How come I never see you in the so-and-so?' "

Delia laughed.

"So if this Binky is his mistress," Joel said—the bald, bold word giving Delia a slight shock—"I say more power to him. He deserves a little happiness."

"Well, I didn't mean—"

"Why not? He's only sixty-seven. If it weren't for those damn flash-backs, he'd be out sailing his boat still."

Delia hadn't known that Nat sailed, but she could easily picture it: his spiky figure all over the deck, everywhere at once.

"She liked to say she was 'there' for people," Joel was reminiscing. He must be on the subject of Noah's grandma again. "First person I ever heard say that, though Lord knows it's grown common enough since. 'I'm always *there* for my daughters,' " he mocked. "You want to ask, 'Where's that, exactly?' It's one of my least favorite terms."

Delia hoped she hadn't used it herself. She was fairly sure she had not.

"That and 'survivor,' " Joel said. "Well, unless it's meant in the literal sense."

"Survivor?"

"Nowadays you're a survivor if all you did was make it through childhood."

"Ah."

"And another word I hate is . . ."

It was lucky he held so many strong opinions. Delia wouldn't need to make conversation after all. Instead, she sat watching his mouth, that long, firm, fine-edged mouth with the distinctive notch at the center of the upper lip, and she reflected that for someone so absorbed in questions of language, he certainly didn't reveal very much.

Now when she went to the gourmet food store after dropping Noah off on Wednesday afternoons, she chose some additional item—sour French cornichons, hot-pepper jelly—and paid for it with her own money and brought it to tea at Nat's. "How did you guess I like such things?" Nat would ask. "Most people come with chocolates. Fruit preserves. Sweet stuff."

She didn't tell him it was because her father, too, had been fond of pickly foods, for something gallant and slightly flirtatious in Nat's manner suggested he didn't view himself as all that old. Often he poked fun at Senior City, as if to prove he didn't really belong there. "House of the Living Dead," he called it. He claimed to believe that the seagulls drifting above the building were vultures, and he spoke jocularly of the "poor dears" on floor Four. And then there was his romance with Binky.

For Binky *was* his girlfriend; Delia couldn't doubt that. Three times Delia arrived for tea and found her perched on his couch, playing hostess. And the fourth time, when she was missing, Nat found it necessary to explain that she'd been called away at the last minute. Her son had chipped a tooth, he said.

"Binky has a son?" Delia asked.

"Two sons, in fact."

"I didn't know that."

"So Noah has been doing the honors today."

Delia settled on the couch, laying her coat over the arm. She watched Noah pour an unsteady stream of tea.

"I didn't even know she was married," she said.

She chose her words carefully; she didn't say *had been* married, because it could be that Binky was married still. And Nat's response left her none the wiser. "Oh, yes," was all he said. "To a dentist."

Inspired, she said, "Well, then, the chipped tooth should be no problem."

"Correct," Nat said. He sent her a glint of a look from under his tufted gray eyebrows. Then he relented. "Assuming she doesn't mind flying her son to an office in Wyoming."

"Oh."

"They're divorced."

"Oh, I see."

"*Bitterly* divorced," Nat said with some relish. "Months in court, lawyers and replacement lawyers, forty thousand dollars spent to win five thousand . . . you get the picture."

"I'm sorry to hear that."

"She ended up almost penniless, had to take a job in the Senior City gift shop."

"She works in the gift shop?"

"Well, for now."

He glanced over at Noah, who was passing around a plate of brownies at a perilous tilt. "Fact is," Nat said, "Binky and I are getting married."

Noah let the plate tilt more sharply. Delia said, "Oh! Congratulations," and bent to pick a brownie off the rug.

"Honest?" Noah asked his grandfather.

"Honest. But don't mention it to the girls yet, will you? I should have told your mom and your aunts before anyone."

"So then will you move out of here?" Noah asked.

"Afraid not, son." Nat turned to Delia. "Noah liked my old place better," he said.

"The old place had this real cool tree house out back," Noah told her.

"However, it did not have an elevator. Or a handgrip above the bathtub. Or a physical-therapy room for ancient codgers."

"You're not an ancient codger!" Noah said.

"Plus there's the little detail of my contract with Senior City," Nat told Delia. "Bit of a problem with the board of directors, as you might imagine. All my life savings are sunk in this apartment, but the minimum age of entrance is sixty-five. Binky's thirty-eight."

"And how about her sons?" Delia asked.

"Yes, that *would* have been a poser! Rock music in the cafeteria, skateboards down the halls . . . However, her sons will stay on with her parents. One is already in college, and the other's about to go. But even so, the board is having hissy fits, and then a few neighbors are mad at me too, because men are mighty scarce in these parts. Plan was, I would marry one of the residents, not some luscious babe in the gift shop."

"Well, I think you've made the perfect choice," Delia said.

She meant it, too. She had developed a liking for Binky, who edged all their conversations with a ruffle of admiring murmurs and encouraging remarks.

So when Delia stopped by the following week, she made a point of telling Binky that Nat was a lucky man.

"Well, thank you," Binky said, beaming.

"Have you set a date yet?"

"We've talked about maybe June."

"Or March," Nat amended.

Binky rounded her eyes comically at Delia. March was right around the corner; they were halfway through February. "He has no idea what goes into these things," she said.

"Oh, are you planning a big wedding?"

"Well, not *that* big, but . . . My first wedding, I eloped. I was a freshman at Washington College and wore what I'd worn to class that day. So this time I'd like all the trimmings."

"I'm going to be best man," Noah told Delia.

"You are!"

"I get to hold the ring."

"You'll come too, won't you, Delia?" Nat asked.

"If I'm invited, of course I will."

"Oh, you'll be invited, all right," Binky said, and she patted Delia's hand and gave her a dimpled smile.

But later, riding home, Noah told Delia that Binky had been crying when he got there.

"Crying! What about?"

"I don't know, but her eyes were all red. She pretended she was fine, but I could tell. And then when she was in the kitchen the phone rang and Grandpa shouted out, 'Don't answer that!' and she didn't. And he didn't either, just let it ring and ring. So finally I said, 'Want me to get it?' but he said, 'Nah, never mind.' Said, 'It's probably just Dudi.' "

"Who's Dudi?"

"One of my aunts."

"Oh." Delia thought that over. "But why wouldn't he talk to her?"

He shrugged. "Beats me," he said. "You want to watch your speedometer, Delia."

"Thanks," Delia said.

She'd been issued two tickets in the last three weeks. It was something to do with this open country, she believed. The speed just seemed to inch up on her, and before she knew it she was flying.

Back in Bay Borough, Joel was already home and waiting to hear the latest. He took a rather gleeful interest in Nat's wedding plans. "Noah's going to be best man," Delia told him as she hung up her coat.

"No kidding!" He turned to Noah. "Where are you throwing the stag party?"

"Stag party?"

"Have you thought out your toasts yet?"

"Toasts!"

"Don't you pay any attention," Delia told Noah. He was looking worried.

It occurred to her that she was bound to run into Ellie at the wedding. Scandalous that they hadn't met before; Delia was in charge of Ellie's son. What kind of mother entrusted her son to a stranger?

A couple of weeks before, passing through Nat's bedroom to use his bathroom, Delia had noticed a color photo of his daughters on the highboy. At least she assumed they were all his daughters—Ellie and three other blondes, linking arms and laughing. Ellie was the most vivid, the one you looked at first. She wore a cream dress splashed with strawberries that matched her strawberry mouth. Her shoes, though, were not very flattering. They were ballerina flats, *black* ballerina flats, papery and klutzy. They showed the bulges of her toes. They made her ankles look thick.

Why did Delia find this so gratifying? She had nothing against Ellie; she didn't even know her. But she bent closer to the photo and spent several moments hunting other flaws. Not that she found them. And not that she would have occasion, anyhow, to point them out to Joel.

14

On a Friday morning at the tail end of February—a day so mild and sunny that she would have supposed spring was here, if she hadn't known the tricky ways of winter—Delia walked to the Young Mister Shop to exchange some pajamas for Noah. (She had bought him a pair like an Orioles uniform, not realizing that for some strange reason, Noah preferred the Phillies.) And then, because it felt so pleasant to be out in nothing heavier than a sweater, she decided to walk to the library and visit with Mrs. Lincoln awhile. So she cut across the square and started up West Street. At the florist's window she slowed to admire a pot of paper-whites, and at Mr. Pomfret's window she slid her eyes sideways to check out his new secretary. Rumor had it he was limping along with a niece of his wife's who couldn't even type, let alone run a computer. But the way the light hit the glass, Delia would have had to step closer to see inside. All she could make out was her own silhouette and another just behind, both ivy-patterned from the sprawling new plant the niece must have set on the sill. Delia increased her speed and crossed George Street.

The window display in the Pinchpenny was little girls' dresses this week; so now the two silhouettes were made up of rosebud prints and plaids. She noticed that the second silhouette was storky and gangling, mostly joints, like an adolescent boy. Like Carroll.

She turned, and there he was. He looked even more startled than she felt, if that was possible. His expression froze and he drew back sharply, hands thrust into his windbreaker pockets, elbows jutting.

She said, "Carroll?"

"What."

"Oh, *Carroll!*" she cried, and the feeling that swept through her was so wrenching, like the grip of some deep, internal fist, that she understood for the first time how terribly much she had missed him. His face might have been her own face, not because it resembled hers (although it did), but because she had absorbed its every detail over the past fifteen years —the sprinkle of starry freckles across his delicate nose, the way the shadows beneath his eyes would darken at fraught moments. (Right now they were almost purple.) He raised his chin defiantly, and so at the very last second she merely reached out to lay a hand on his arm instead of kissing him. She said, "I'm so happy to see you! How'd you get here?"

"I had a ride."

She had forgotten that his voice had changed. She had to adjust all over again. "And what are you doing on West Street?" she asked.

"I tried your boardinghouse first, but no one answered, and then I happened to see you crossing the square."

He must not have told the family he was coming, therefore. (She had sent Eliza her new address weeks ago.) She said, "Is something wrong at home? Are you all right? It's a school day!"

"Everything's fine," he said.

He was trying, unobtrusively, to step out from under her hand. He was darting embarrassed glances at passersby. Much as she hated to, she let go of him. She said, "Well, let's . . . would you like some lunch?"

"Lunch? I just had breakfast."

Yes, it was morning still, wasn't it. She felt dizzy and disoriented, almost drunk. "A Coke or something, then," she said.

"Okay."

Turning him in the direction of Rick-Rack's gave her an excuse to touch him again. She loved that hard tendon at the inside crook of his arm. Oh, she might have known it would be Carroll who finally came for her! (Her most attached child, when all was said and done—her most loving, her closest. Although she would probably have thought the same if it had been either of the other two.)

"There's so much you have to bring me up-to-date on," she told him. "How's tenth grade?"

He shrugged.

"Has your father had any more chest pains?"

"Not that I know of."

"Ramsay and Susie all right?"

"Sure."

Then what is it? she wanted to ask, but she didn't. Already she was falling back into the veiled, duplicitous manner required for teenage offspring. She led him west on George Street, very nearly holding her breath. "Is Ramsay still seeing that divorcée person? That Velma?" she said.

Another shrug. Obviously, he was.

"And how about Susie?"

"How about her."

"Has she figured out yet what she'll do after graduation?"

"Huh?" he said, looking toward a Bon Jovi poster in the record store.

He was as frustrating as ever, and he hadn't lost that habit of ostentatiously holding back a yawn each time he spoke. She forced herself to be patient. She steered him past Shearson Liquors, past Brent Hardware, and through the door of Rick-Rack's.

"Dee-babe!" Rick hailed her, lowering his copy of *Sports Illustrated.* She would have known from his greeting alone that his father-in-law was sitting at the counter. (Rick always put on a display for Mr. Bragg.) "Who's that you got with you?" he asked.

"This is my son Carroll." She told Carroll, "This is Rick Rackley."

"Hey, your son!" Rick said. "How about that!"

Carroll looked dazed. Delia felt a prickle of annoyance. Couldn't he at least act civil? "Let's sit in a booth," she said brusquely.

Teensy was nowhere in sight, so Delia took it upon herself to grab two menus from the pile on a stool. As soon as they were seated, she passed one to Carroll. "I know it's early," she said, "but you might want to try the pork barbecue sandwich. It's the North Carolina kind, not a bit sweet or—"

"Mom," Carroll whispered.

"What."

"Mom. Is that *Rick*-Rack?"

"What?"

"Rick Rackley, the football player?"

"Well, yes, I think so."

Carroll gaped at Rick, who was topping off his father-in-law's mug of coffee. He turned back to Delia and whispered, "You know Rick-Rack in person? Rick-Rack knows you?"

This was working out better than she could have hoped. She said, "Yes, certainly," in an airy tone, and then, showing off, she called, "Where's Teensy got to, Rick?"

"She's over at House of Hair," he said, setting the coffeepot back on the burner. "You-all going to have to shout your order direct to me."

"Well, is it too early to ask for pork barbecue?"

"Naw, we can do that," Rick said.

Carroll said, "I just had breakfast, Mom. I told you."

"Yes, but this is something you wouldn't want to miss," she said. "Not a drop of tomato sauce! And it comes with really good french fries and homemade coleslaw!"

She didn't know why she was making such a fuss about it. Carroll was clearly not hungry; he was still staring at Rick. But she called, "Two platters, please, Rick, and two large Cokes."

"You got it."

Mr. Bragg spun his stool around so he could study them. His thin white crew cut stood erect, giving him the look of someone flabbergasted. "Why!" he cried. "What's happened with this *boy*?"

Delia glanced toward Carroll in alarm.

"How'd he shoot up so fast?" Mr. Bragg asked. "How'd he get so big all at once?"

She wondered if the old man had somehow read her mind, but then he said, "Last Christmas he was only yea tall," and he set a palm down around the level of his shins.

"Oh," Delia said. "No, that's Noah you're thinking of."

It was common knowledge by now that Mr. Bragg was failing, which was why poor Rick and Teensy couldn't send him back wherever he came from.

"Who's Noah?" was his next question.

"Who's Noah?" Carroll echoed.

"Just the boy who . . ." She felt rattled, as if she had been caught in some disloyalty. "Just the son of my employer," she said. "So! Carroll. Tell me all that's been going on at home. Has the Casserole Harem descended? Lots of apple pies streaming in?"

"You haven't asked about Aunt Liza," Carroll told her.

"Eliza? Is she all right?"

"Well. All *right*, I guess," he said.

"What is that supposed to mean? Is she sick?"

"No, she's not sick."

"Last Christmas you were just a shrimp," Mr. Bragg called. "You and her were drinking coffee together, tee-heeing over the presents you'd bought."

"Eliza *is* still taking care of the house, isn't she?" Delia persevered.

But Carroll seemed distracted by Mr. Bragg. He said, "Who's he talking about?"

"I told you: my employer's son."

"Is that why you've got that bag with you? 'Tasteful Clothing for the Discerning Young Man'? You buy this kid clothes? You tee-hee together? And what's that you're wearing, for God's sake?"

Delia looked down. She wasn't wearing anything odd—just her Miss Grinstead cardigan and the navy print housedress. "Wearing?" she said.

"You're so, like, *ensconced*."

Two plates appeared before them, clattering against the Formica. "Ketchup, anyone?" Rick asked.

"No, thanks." She told Carroll, "Honey, I—"

"I would like ketchup," Carroll announced belligerently.

"Oh. Sorry. Yes, please, Rick."

Carroll said, "Have you forgotten you have a son who puts ketchup on his french fries?"

"Honey, believe me," she said, "I would never forget. Well, maybe about the ketchup, but never about—"

A plastic squirt bottle arrived, along with their Cokes in tall paper cups. "Thank you, Rick," she said.

She waited till he had left again, and then she reached across the table and touched Carroll's hand. His knuckles were grained like leather. His lips were chapped. There was something too concrete about him; she was accustomed to the misty, soft-edged Carroll of her daydreams.

"I would never forget I have children," she told him.

"Right. That's why you sashayed off down the beach and didn't once look back at them."

Someone said, "Delia?"

She started. Two teenage girls stood over their table—Kim Brewster and Marietta something. Schwartz? Schmidt? (She brought Joel homemade fudge so sweet it zinged through your temples.) "Well! Hello there!" Delia said.

"You won't tell Mr. Miller you saw us here, will you?" Kim asked. Kim was one of Delia's remedial pupils; lately, Delia had been volunteering as a math tutor over at the school. "He would kill us if he found out!"

"We're cutting class," Marietta put in. "We saw you in here and we figured we'd ask: you know how Mr. Miller's birthday is coming up."

Delia hadn't known, but she nodded. Anything to get rid of them.

"So a bunch of us are chipping in on a present, and we thought you might could tell us what to buy him."

"Oh! Well . . ."

"I mean, you know him better than anyone. He doesn't smoke, does he? Seems like a lot of gifts for guys are smokers' stuff."

"He doesn't smoke, no," Delia said.

"Not even a pipe?"

"Not even a pipe."

"He's always so, you know, distinguished and all, we think he'd look great with a pipe. Maybe we should just get him one anyways."

"No, I really think he would hate that," Delia said firmly. "Well! It was good seeing you girls."

But Kim was studying Carroll now from beneath her long silky lashes. "You don't go to Old Underwear," she informed him.

Carroll flushed and said, "Underwear?"

"Our high school: Dorothy Underwood," she said, snapping her gum. "You must be from out of town."

"Yeah."

"I knew we hadn't seen you around."

Delia started eating her coleslaw; she felt it would be a kindness not to look at Carroll's face. But Carroll just picked up the ketchup and squirted it thoroughly and methodically over every single one of his french fries. "Well . . . ," Kim said at last, and the two of them moved on toward an empty booth, trailing crumbs of remarks behind them. "Thanks anyhow, Dee . . . ," they said, and, "If you think of something . . ."

Delia took a sip of Coke.

"So who's the guy?" Carroll asked, setting down the ketchup with a thump.

Confused, she glanced around the café.

"The guy with the pipe, Mom. The oh-so-distinguished guy that you know so extremely-emely well."

"Oh," she said. She laughed, not quite naturally. "It's nothing like that! He's my boss."

"Right."

He pushed his plate away. "It all fits together now," he said. "No wonder you weren't home for Labor Day."

"Labor Day?"

"Dad said you'd be back by then, but I guess it's pretty clear now why you weren't."

She stared at him. "Dad said I'd be back by Labor Day?"

"He said you just needed some time to yourself and you'd come home at the end of the summer. We were counting on it. He promised. Susie thought we should go get you, but he said, 'No,' he said, 'leave her be. I guarantee she'll be here for our Labor Day picnic,' he said. And look what happened: you went back on your word."

"*My* word!" Delia cried. "That was *his* word! I didn't have a thing to do with it! And what right was it of his, I'd like to know? Who is he to guarantee when I'll be home?"

"Now, Mom," Carroll said in an undertone. He glanced furtively toward Rick. "Let's not make a big thing of this, okay? Try and calm down."

"Don't you tell me to calm down!" she cried, and at the same time she caught herself wondering exactly how often she had uttered that sentence before. *Don't you tell me to calm down!* And, *I am completely cool and collected.* But to Sam; not to Carroll. Oh, it all came back to her now: that sense of being the wrong one, the flighty, unstable, excitable one. (And the more she protested, of course, the more excitable she appeared.) She gripped the edge of the table with both hands and said, "I am completely cool and collected."

"Well, fine," Carroll told her. "I'm glad to hear it." And he picked up a red-soaked french fry and threaded it into his mouth with elaborate indifference.

I'm glad to hear it was one of Sam's favorite responses. Along with *If you say so, Dee,* and *Have it your way.* After which he might serenely turn a page, or he would start talking with the boys about some unrelated subject. Always so sure he was right; and the fact was, he *was* right, generally. When he criticized people she liked, she would suddenly notice their faults; and when he criticized Delia, she saw herself all at once as the foolish little whiffet he believed her to be. Like now, for instance: he had promised she would slink home by summer's end, and the picture of that humbled return was so convincing that she almost felt it had happened. She couldn't even *desert* properly! Had only been off in a pout, anyhow. Just needed to get it out of her system.

Although, in fact, she had not slunk home. Not by summer's end and not afterward. Not to this day. She had actually made a life for herself in a town Sam had nothing to do with.

So when Belle sailed in, calling, "Hey, Dee, I *thought* that was you I saw," Delia made a point of rising to give her a flamboyant hug.

"Belle!" she cried, and Belle (her purple-clad figure a luxurious, pillowy armful) had the grace to hug her back.

"Who's your new fella?" she asked.

"This is my son Carroll. This is Belle Flint," she told Carroll. She kept an arm around Belle's waist. "How're you *doing*, Belle?"

"Well, you're never going to guess what, not in a million years."

"What?" Delia asked, a little too enthusiastically.

"Swear you won't tell Vanessa, now. This is just between the two of us."

But the whole demonstration went for nothing, because just then Carroll stood up and pushed his way out of the booth. "So long," he mumbled, head down.

"Carroll?"

She dropped her arm from Belle's waist.

"Tomorrow night," Belle was saying, "I've asked Horace Lamb to the movies."

Horace Lamb? Delia felt an inner hitch of surprise even as she went hurrying after Carroll. He lunged out the café door. "Carroll, honey!" she called.

On the sidewalk, Teensy was mincing toward them beneath a gigantic new busby of exploding red ringlets. Carroll almost ran her down. Teensy said, "Oh!" and took a step back, reaching up to feel for her hairdo as if she feared it might have toppled off. "Delia, tell me the truth," she said. "Do you honestly think I look silly?"

"Not a bit," Delia told her. "Carroll, wait!"

Carroll wheeled, his eyebrows beetling. "Never mind me, just tend to your pals!" he said. "Orphan Annie here and Mr. Distinguished and little Tee-hee Boy and Veranda or whoever . . ."

Vanessa, Delia almost corrected him, while behind her, Teensy asked, "Delia? Is everything all right?" and Belle, in the doorway, said, "Kids. But that's just how they are, I guess."

"I *was* going to do you a favor," Carroll said.

"What, honey?"

"I *was* going to tip you off to what's going on at home, but never mind. Just never mind now," he said.

Still, he didn't turn and leave. He seemed to be suspended, teetering on the squeaky rubber soles of his gym shoes. Cannily, Delia came no closer. She stayed six or eight feet away from him, her face a mask of smoothness. "What's going on at home?" she asked him.

"Oh, nothing. Not a thing! Except that your own blood sister is making a play for your husband," he said.

"Eliza?"

"And Dad's so out of it, he just laughs it off when we tell him. But *we've* all noticed, me and Susie and Ramsay notice plain as day, and we can guess how it's going to end up, we bet, too."

"Eliza would never do that," Delia said, but she was trying out the notion even as she spoke. She cast her mind back to the living-room couch, the row of marriageable maidens. *Whenever I hear the word "summer," I smell this sort of melting smell.* And now it seemed that Sam sent Eliza a quick, alert, appreciative glance, as he had not done in real life. It wasn't impossible, Delia saw.

But she told Carroll, "You must be imagining things."

"Oh, what do *you* care?" Carroll burst out, and he spun around again and started running toward West Street.

"Carroll, don't go!"

She followed at a fast walk. (How far could he get, after all?) He crossed George Street, halting briefly for a mail truck, and disappeared around the corner. Delia picked up her pace. On West Street she saw him loping south, passing Mr. Pomfret, who stood in front of his office speaking with a UPS man. She raced by Mr. Pomfret herself, with her face averted; the last thing she needed just now was another acquaintance calling out her name. She lost sight of Carroll for an instant and then spotted him near the florist's. He was jogging up and down on the curb as he waited for a break in the traffic. Evidently he was headed for the square. Good: they could sit on a bench together. Catch their breath. Talk this over.

But once he'd crossed the street, he stopped at one of the cars parked along the perimeter. A gray car, a Plymouth. *Her* Plymouth. With Ramsay at the wheel. She recognized his dear, blocky profile. Carroll opened the passenger door and got in. The engine ground to life, and the car swung out into traffic.

Even then she might have run after them. They were forced to drive very slowly at first. But she stayed where she was, brought up short on the sidewalk with one hand pressed to her throat.

Ramsay had been right here in town. He had driven all these miles and then not bothered to visit her. Susie too, perhaps, although Delia had glimpsed only two heads in the Plymouth.

She deserved this, of course. There was no denying that.

She turned and retraced her steps to Rick-Rack's, all but feeling her way.

An enormous amount had happened to her, but when she reached the café Belle and Teensy were still talking out front, Kim and Marietta were blowing sultry ribbons of cigarette smoke inside, and Rick was tucking her lunch bill under the ketchup container. She counted out her money in slow motion and paid, not forgetting to leave a tip on the table. She gathered her purse and her Young Mister bag and walked out the door, through the scorched, chemical smell of Teensy's hairdo, through the clack and tumble of Belle's chatter. "Have you ever noticed," Belle was saying, "that Horace Lamb looks the eentsiest little bit like Abraham Lincoln?"

At the corner, Delia turned south. The clock in the optician's window read eleven-fifteen—nowhere near time for lunch, and yet she regretted leaving that barbecue sandwich. And the coleslaw had been superb. It was the creamy kind, with lots of celery seeds. A seed or two still lodged in her mouth, woodsy and fragrant when she bit down. She savored the taste on her tongue. She felt the most amazing hunger, all at once. She felt absolutely hollow. You would think she hadn't eaten in months.

15

For a short while after Carroll's visit, half a dozen spots around town seemed haunted by his presence. Here was the ivy-filled window where he had first appeared, here the booth at Rick-Rack's where he'd sat, here Belle's front porch where he must have spent several minutes waiting for someone to answer the door. (Had he noticed the scaly paint? The hammocking of the floorboards under his tread?) In Delia's memory he seemed not surly now but sad, his porcupine behavior merely a sign of hurt feelings. She should have taken him with her when she left, she thought. Except that then she would have had to take Susie and Ramsay too. Otherwise it would have looked like favoritism. She saw herself striding down the coastline with her retinue—the two boys' ropy wrists in her grasp, Susie scurrying to keep up. *Where we going, Mom? Hush, don't ask; we're running away from home.*

Although her children had been partly what she was running from, as it happened.

Then she reflected that after all, Carroll had not appeared ruined by her leaving. He had survived just fine, and so had his brother and sister. And she remembered Nat's philosophy: we ought to forget our grown offspring as easily as cats forget theirs. She smiled to herself. Well, maybe not *quite* as easily.

Still, wasn't it true that over the past several years, her children had turned into semistrangers—at last even her youngest? That not only had she lost her central importance to them but they, in fact, had become just a bit less overwhelmingly all-important to her?

She sat stone still, staring into space, wondering how long ago she had first begun to know that.

Then, having watched her children slip free, she turned to what remained: her husband.

If he really did remain.

In her mind's eye he sat at the breakfast table while Eliza poured his coffee. Eliza wore her tan safari dress and even a bit of rouge. She was not unattractive, from certain angles. She had that smooth, yellowish skin that didn't go all fragile with age, and the rouge turned her dark eyes bright and snappy. She would insinuate herself into Sam's routine, take over his charts and bills, provide him with hot meals and a seamlessly organized household. "Why, thanks, Eliza," Sam would say feelingly. Men were so gullible sometimes! And he had more in common with Eliza than you might suspect. Granted, Eliza claimed she was living life over and over again until she got it right, while Sam said that for his part, he meant to get it right the first time. But both of them did assume that "getting it right" was possible. Delia herself had more or less given up trying.

Besides which, there was the fact that Eliza was Delia's sister. She had Delia's small, neat bone structure and her phenomenally sound teeth, her tendency to get out of hand after eating any sugar, her habit of letting her sentences trail away unfinished. Loving Eliza would come as naturally to Sam as appreciating a song he had already heard once before.

Delia felt an impulse to jump in the car and tear off to Baltimore, but she knew how trite that was—to want a man back the instant she learned he was wanted by someone else. She made herself sit still. *This is what you asked for*, she told herself.

This other woman's maimed husband and child, this too new ranch house with its walls that thunked like cardboard when you rapped them, this thin town propped on a countryside as flat and pale as paper.

Before dawn one morning, she came sharply awake, perhaps disturbed by a dream, although no fragments of it lingered. She lay in bed recalling, for some reason, the first dinner party she'd given after she and Sam were married. He had wanted to invite two of his old classmates, along with their wives. For days she had pored over possible menus. She had refused her sisters' offers of help; she had extracted her family's promise not to show their faces during the evening. It was essential that she prove she was a grown-up. And yet from the moment the first couple arrived, she had felt herself sinking back into childhood. "Hey, Grin," the husband had said to Sam. Grin! Would she ever feel so comradely as to call Sam that herself? she had wondered, twisting her skirt. "Hi, Joe," Sam had said. "Delia, I'd like you to meet Joe and Amy Guggles." Delia had not been informed of their last name ahead of time, and in fact had never heard the name Guggles in all her life. It had struck her as funny, and she'd started laughing. She slid into helpless cascades of laughter, her breath dissolving in squeaks, her eyes streaming tears, her cheeks beginning to ache. It was like being in sixth grade again. She laughed herself boneless, while the couple watched her with kindly concern and Sam kept saying, "Delia? Honey?"

"I'm sorry," she had told them, when finally sheer embarrassment had sobered her. "I'm so sorry, really I can't think what—"

At which point, the second couple arrived. "Why, here you are!" Sam had cried in relief. "Hon, these are my oldest friends, Frank and Mia Mewmew."

Oh, Lord.

But Sam had been very understanding. After the party, he had drawn her into his arms and told her, speaking warmly into the curls on top of her head, that these things could happen to anyone.

How young he'd been, back then! But Delia hadn't realized. To her he had seemed fully formed, immune to doubt, this unassailably self-possessed man who had all but arrived on a white horse to save her from eternal daughterhood. Around his eyes faint puckers were already evident, and she had found them both appealing and alarming. *If he dies first I don't want to go on living*, she had thought. *I'll find something in Daddy's office cabinet that's deadly poison.* In those days, she could say such things, not having had the children yet. She used to picture all sorts of catastrophes, in those days. Well, later too, to be honest. Oh, she'd always been a fearful kind of person, full of hunches and forebodings. But look what happened: the night of his chest pains, she hadn't felt the slightest premonition. She had sat there reading *Lucinda's Lover*, dumb as a post. Then the phone rang.

Although the news had not come as a shock, certainly. Listening to the nurse's diplomatic wording, she had thought, *Ah, yes, of course*, while a dank, heavy sense of confirmation had solidified inside her. *First Daddy, and now Sam.* He would die and they would bury him in Cow Hill Cemetery and he would lie there alone till Delia crept up to join him, as on those nights when she stayed awake watching some silly movie and then climbed the stairs afterward and slipped between the covers and laid one arm lightly across his chest while he went on sleeping.

She sat against her headboard, jostling the cat, and switched on the clock radio. They were playing jazz, at this hour. Lots of lonesome clarinets and plinkety-plonk pianos, and after every piece the announcer stated the place it was recorded and the date. A New York bar on an August night in 1955. A hotel in Chicago, New Year's Eve, 1949. Delia wondered how humans could bear to live in a world where the passage of time held so much power.

Nat and Binky were not going to have a June wedding after all. They moved the date up to a Saturday in March. Nat said he had exercised his seniority. "I used your basic how-much-longer-have-I-got approach," he confided to Noah and Delia. "Your take-pity-on-an-old-geezer approach."

Binky adapted cheerfully to the change in plans. "This way," she told Delia, "I'm Mrs. Nathaniel Moffat three months sooner, that's all. So what if we skimp some on the frills? They're not such a very big deal." The two of them were alone in Nat's kitchen when she said this, leafing through cookbooks. (The wedding cake was one of the frills she was skimping on.) "And I do mean to be Mrs. Moffat," she said. "None of this 'Ms.' business for me! He's the first man I've ever known who's just totally, totally loved me." Then the skin around her eyes grew pink, as if she might start crying, and she turned quickly back to her cookbook.

"In that case, you ought to marry him this instant," Delia said.

"Well, I wish his daughters agreed," Binky said. "You heard Dudi cut all her hair off."

"Cut her hair off?"

"Threw a tantrum when Nat announced our engagement; ran into his bathroom, grabbed up these little scissors he trims his beard with and cut every bit of her hair off."

"Goodness," Delia said.

"And Pat and Donna refuse to come to the wedding, and when I asked Ellie to be an attendant—purely out of niceness; I've already got my sister and my nieces—she said maybe she wasn't coming either, she couldn't be sure, she might or might not, so she'd better say no. Then she went and told Nat he ought to have his lawyer draw up a prenuptial agreement. I guess they all think I'm some kind of . . . gold digger. It doesn't occur to them what an insult that is to their father, not to believe a woman might love him for his own self."

"They're just a little surprised," Delia said. "They'll get over it."

Binky shook her head, smoothing a cookbook page with her palm. "They phone him and the very first thing, 'Is *she* around?' they ask. 'She,' they call me; they never use my name if they can help it. They hardly ever come to visit. Donna says it's because I'm always here. She says I don't allow them any time alone with him, but I try to; it's just that—"

She broke off, blushing, and Delia wondered why until Binky mumbled the end of her sentence. "I do sort of, kind of like, live here now," she said.

"Well, of course," Delia hastened to say. "What do they expect?"

"Oh, well, I didn't start out to bore you with all my troubles," Binky said. "You know why I like to talk to you, Delia? You never interrupt with *your* experiences. No wonder you're so popular!"

"I'm so popular?"

"Don't be modest. Noah's told us how you're friends with half of Bay Borough."

"Good grief! I hardly know anyone," Delia said.

Although she was startled to see how her friends did add up, now that she stopped to count.

"You're not just marking time while I'm speaking," Binky said. "Not jiggling your foot till you get a chance to jump in with your life history."

"Well, it isn't as if there's a whole lot I could jump in with," Delia told her.

Last week at supper, Joel had asked what part of Baltimore Delia hailed from. "Oh," she had said, "here and there," and he had dropped the subject—or so she'd thought. But a minute later he had said, "Strange, isn't it? A person who doesn't discuss her past is automatically assumed to *have* a past, I mean more of a past than usual, something rich and exotic."

"Is that right," she had said neutrally. It had struck her as an interesting theory; she had considered it until, noticing the silence, she looked up and found his eyes on her. "What?" she had asked.

"Oh, nothing."

Then Noah had reached between them for the salt—a disruptive swoop, a lunge forward on two legs of his chair—and the moment had passed.

Driving to the wedding, Delia kept glancing in the rearview mirror. She was afraid she might have put on too much makeup. "What do you think of my lipstick?" she asked Noah.

"It's okay," he said without looking.

He had worries of his own. Periodically he wriggled his fingers between the buttons of his winter jacket, checking for the ring in his shirt pocket.

"Are you sure it's not too heavy?" she asked him.

"Hmm?"

"My lipstick, Noah."

"Nah, it's okay."

"*You* look nice," she said.

"Well, I don't know why I had to get so dressed up."

"Dressed up! You call a shirt and no tie dressed up!"

"I look like one of those yo-yos who sing in the school chorus."

"You should just be thankful Nat didn't make you buy a suit," she told him.

"And what if I drop the ring? You know my hand will shake. I'll drop the ring and it will clink real loud and roll across the floor and fall into one of those grate things, *clang-ang-ang!*, and we'll never get it back again."

"I wish I had a fancier outfit," Delia said. "I look like an old-maid aunt or something." Under her coat she was wearing her gray pinstripe. "Or at least a necklace or a locket or a string of beads."

"You're okay."

In her jewelry box back in Baltimore was a four-strand pearl choker. Fake, of course, but it would have been perfect with the pinstripe.

How long before she could say that her Baltimore things would have gone out of fashion anyway, or fallen apart or been used up even if she'd stayed? When would the things she had here become her *real* things?

She flicked her turn signal and swerved onto Highway 50. "U-u-urch!" Noah squealed, grabbing his door handle.

"Sorry." She slowed. "So," she said. "I guess I get to meet your mother, finally."

"Yup."

"She did decide to come, didn't she?"

"Last I heard she did."

Recently, Delia had found the *Boardwalk Bulletin* profile buried in the back of Noah's closet. (*Who's the gorgeous new weather wench on WKMD?* the article began.) But to look at Noah now, you wouldn't guess he spared his mother a thought. He was yawning and gazing out his window at the remains of last week's freak snowstorm. The woods were a scrawl of black against white, like an arty photograph.

A snow warning or a hurricane watch can be a matter of life and death, Ellie had told her interviewer. *It gives me a lot of warm fuzzies to know I'm making a contribution to my community.*

Delia wondered what Joel would have said about "warm fuzzies."

The red-brick cube of Senior City rose before them. Delia signaled and turned into the parking lot. "What if they want me to make a speech?" Noah was asking.

"You won't have to make a speech."

"Or what if somebody faints or something? I'm supposed to assist."

"Believe me," Delia said, "this will be a breeze."

They got out of the car and crossed the lot, which was not as well plowed as it might have been. Delia, who didn't own boots, had to hang on to Noah's arm as they picked their way around icy spots. "See?" she told him. "Already you're assisting!"

His arm was thin but fiercely strong, like a band of steel.

In the lobby, they asked an old man the way to the chapel. "Straight ahead, then left at the end of the hall," he said. "You must be going to the wedding."

They nodded.

"Well, I'll be along directly; wouldn't miss it. Everyone in the building's been invited, you know."

Delia thanked him, and they proceeded down the hall. Passing the elevators, with their gleaming metal doors, she checked her reflection. It seemed to her she looked pale and draggled, her coat a dreary, wilted shape clinging too low on her shins.

Clothes are my biggest weakness, Ellie had told *Boardwalk Bulletin*. *But luckily my figure's the kind that everything hangs really well on, so I don't have to spend a fortune to look good.*

At the end of the hall they turned left and entered the side door of a small chapel, carpeted wall to wall in beige and lined with sleek beige pews. Already the pews were nearly filled with elderly women and three or four widely spaced men. Most of the women wore stylish dresses; a few wore bathrobes. Several people in wheelchairs formed an extra row at the rear. Delia and Noah stood gazing about until a dark young boy in a suit approached and offered Delia his arm. "We're seating everyone helter-skelter," he told her. "Wherever we can find room."

"Well, Noah here won't need a seat. He's the best man."

"Hey there, Noah. I'm Peter. Son of the bride," the boy said. He had not inherited Binky's small, pursed features or her rosy coloring; just her easy manner of talking to people. He told Noah, "You're supposed to go through that door up front. Your grandpa's already waiting."

Noah sent Delia one last imploring glance, and she grinned at him and brushed his hair off his forehead. "Good luck," she said.

Then she let Peter escort her to one of the few remaining seats, between a woman in a brown-and-white dress and an old man fiddling with his hearing aid. The old man had the aisle seat and merely moved his bony knees to one side so she could get past. It was the woman who helped her out of her coat. "Isn't this exciting?" she asked Delia. She had a freckled, finely wrinkled face lit with a gracious expression, and a crimp of orange-sherbet hair that must once have been red. "It's our very first Senior City wedding! We don't count Paul and Ginny Mellors; they eloped. Are you a relation?"

"Just a friend."

"The board is in a tizzy, I can tell you. They want to charge Binky higher rates because she's underage. Otherwise the young folks will be *flooding* in, they claim, on account of our security and our managed health care. My name's Aileen, by the way."

"I'm Delia."

"It's nice to meet you, Delia. What I say is, hell's bells, Binky's such a lambie-pie I think we ought to pay *her!* She'll be a huge addition to our Sunday Socials."

Just then, Ellie appeared at the side entrance.

Delia knew her immediately—the tinsel hair, the pulpy red mouth. She wore a long, cream-colored coat just one shade off from her skin, and she stood poised, looking somehow stiller than ordinary women, until an usher approached. This was not Peter but his brother, evidently—someone equally dark but more stockily built. Ellie took his arm and walked toward the front, the hem of her coat swaying classily. Where would she find a seat, though? All the pews were jam-packed. The usher seemed to be informing her of this; she listened, pooching her lips and frowning. They were crossing in front of the pulpit now. On the other side, several people—mostly kitchen staff, in aprons—lined the wall, and Ellie was deposited in their midst. What a pity, Delia thought, that the one daughter who'd shown up should have to stand!

But no, another daughter was here as well—a wan, wraithlike woman who rose from her seat and edged past a row of knees to join Ellie. The second woman had fair hair too, but it was cut so brutally short that in places it seemed scraped off her skull. Behind cupped fingers, she whispered something to Ellie. Then they both turned and looked straight at Delia.

Guiltily, Delia lowered her eyes. She should have smiled at the two of them, but instead she pretended to be absorbed in conversation with Aileen. "That's Mary Lou Simms playing the organ," Aileen was saying. Delia hadn't noticed there *was* an organ, but now she heard a wispy rendition of "Blessed Assurance." From the old man on her right came a piercing whistle, something to do with his hearing aid. "Oh, and there's Reverend Merrill," Aileen said. "Isn't he striking?"

Reverend Merrill was not all that striking in Delia's opinion, but he wore his black robe with a certain flair. He strode toward the pulpit, swinging a Bible in one hand. Behind him came Nat and Noah. Nat held himself rigidly erect; he was doing without his cane today. Noah was getting so tall, Delia realized. Now that he took his position next to Nat, she could see how he had shot up, just in the few months she'd known him.

The organ slithered into the "Wedding March." Everyone looked toward the rear.

First came a stouter, plainer version of Binky—the matron of honor, in a wide blue gown, with square-cut gray hair and a broad, pleasant face. Then Binky herself, in white. She looked lovely. She was carrying pink roses and beaming joyously as she floated down the aisle. Her two nieces, as bulky as their mother, plodded behind with fistfuls of her train.

"Oh, what a vision!" Aileen said. "Did you ever see anything sweeter?" Delia's other seatmate was gnawing open a blister pack of batteries. Over by the wall, Ellie's white face blazed fixedly, but it didn't seem to be Binky she was watching.

The bridal procession reached the front, and Nat, proudly stern, gave Binky his arm and turned toward the minister.

It was a very brief ceremony—just the vows and the exchange of rings. Noah did fine. He produced the ring on cue, and he didn't drop it. But all of this Delia observed with only part of her attention, while with another part—her tensed, wary, innermost part—she was conscious every moment of Ellie Miller's unwavering stare in her direction.

All the guests were invited to Nat's apartment afterward—anybody who wanted to come. There was a great press of frail bodies milling out of the chapel. Delia offered support to arms as withered and soft as day-old balloons. She packed mothball-smelling woolens into elevators, and then, upstairs, she settled more women than she would have thought possible onto the swampy cushions of Nat's couch. They were all looking forward to Binky's cake. It seemed they *preferred* homemade, and were glad she hadn't had time to order the towering pagoda she had dreamed of. "We get store-bought in the cafeteria all the time," one woman told Delia. "Sent over from Brinhart's Bakery. Tastes like Band-Aids."

Delia looked for Ellie but didn't see her, or Dudi either. Although in this crush, people were easily missed.

She threaded her way toward Binky, who was cutting squares of sheet cake, with her train looped over her arm. "Do you think it went all right?" Binky asked. Her headpiece of pink roses slanted toward one ear like a rakish halo.

"It went perfectly," Delia said. She started distributing the cake. Nat, meanwhile, was pouring champagne, which he sent around with Binky's two sons and her nieces. They ran out of stemware and had to open a pack of disposable tumblers.

When everyone was served, Nat proposed a toast. "To my beautiful, beautiful bride," he said, and he made a little speech about how life was not a straight line—either downward or upward, either one—but something more irregular, a zigzag or a corkscrew or sometimes a scribble. "And sometimes," he said, "you get to what you thought was the end and you find it's a whole new beginning." He raised his glass toward Binky, and his eyes were suspiciously shiny.

One of the women on the couch said Binky must have grated her own lemon zest. "I can always tell fresh-grated zest," she said. "It's no use trying to substitute that brown dust that comes in bottles." She licked crumbs off her fork in a contemplative way. Her face had gone past merely old to that stage where it seemed formed of disintegrating particles, without a single clear demarcation. Did there come a point, Delia wondered, after you'd outlived every one of your friends, when you began to believe you might be the first to escape death altogether?

She relieved Binky of her cake knife and cut more slices, which she carried around on a platter in case people wanted seconds. In the bedroom, a young woman in a nurse's white pantsuit was holding forth on various hospitals, referring familiarly to "Saint Joe" and "Holy Trin" while a circle of residents listened spellbound. Two men were playing chess in a corner; one of them asked Delia if he could take an extra piece of cake for his wife on Floor Four. Aileen, Delia's former seatmate, was nodding and smiling as a fur-stoled woman described other weddings she'd been to. "And then Lois: *she* was a lucky one! Married a man with all his major appliances, including convection oven."

Noah walked in with a glass of champagne, which he tried to hide when he saw Delia. "Give me that," she ordered.

"Aw, Delia."

She took it from him and set it on a passing tray. "By the way," she said, "where's your mother?"

"I don't know."

"She didn't come upstairs?"

He shrugged. "I guess she must have had other stuff to do," he said. Then he turned on his heel and left the room before she could comment—not that she would have been so tactless.

Binky's sister, the bearer of the tray, tut-tutted. "I saw her walk out directly after the vows," she said. "Her and her sister both. Doodoo, is that what they call her?"

"Dudi."

"All this brouhaha about *his* family's reaction! How about ours? We could have said plenty, trust me: marrying a man old enough to be her father."

"Well," Delia said, "I'm just glad she and Nat found each other."

"Yes, I suppose," the sister said, sighing.

Then Nat popped up at Delia's elbow. "Have you met my sister-in-law?" he asked her. "Bernice, my new sister-in-law. Can you imagine someone my age getting a brand-new sister-in-law?" He was exultant, his voice unsteady, his face so firm-skinned and glowing that he looked like a *pretend* old man made up for a high-school play. If he'd noticed his daughters' disappearance, it hadn't dampened his happiness.

During the drive home, Delia told Noah she thought his mother was very pretty. In fact, this was not strictly true. She had decided Ellie had a garish quality; the high contrast of her coloring went over better on TV than in person. But she wanted an excuse to mention her. All Noah said in response was, "Yeah," and he drummed his fingers and looked out the side window.

"And you looked mighty handsome up there, too," she said.

"Oh, sure."

"You don't believe me? Just watch," she teased him. "The next wedding you're in might very well be your own."

But he didn't so much as smile. "Fat chance," he said.

"What—you're not getting married?"

"Me and Dad have blown it with women," he said glumly. "There must be something about them we don't understand."

In other circumstances, she might have been amused, but now she felt touched. She glanced at him. He went on staring out the window. Finally she reached over and gave him a pat on the knee, and they rode the rest of the way without speaking.

16

"If x is the age Jenny is now, and y is the age she was when she went to California . . . ," Delia said.

T. J. Renfro put his head on the kitchen table.

"Now, T.J., this is not so hard! See, we know that she was three years older than the girlfriend she was visiting in California, and we know that when her girlfriend was—"

"This is not going to do me one bit of good in real life," T.J. informed her in a smothered voice.

He had the kind of haircut that seemed half finished—medium length on top but trailing long black oily strands in back. Both of his upper arms were braceleted with barbed-wire tattoos, and his black leather vest bore more zippers than you'd find in most people's entire wardrobes. Unlike Delia's other pupils, who met with her in the counseling room over at the high school, T.J. came to the house. He had been suspended till May 1 and was not allowed to set foot on school property; showed up instead at the Millers' back door every Thursday afternoon at three o'clock. Delia didn't want to know what he'd been suspended for.

She told him, "Real life is full of problems like this! Finding the unknown quantity: there's lots of times you'll need to do that."

"Like I'm really going to walk up to some chick and ask how old she is," T.J. said, raising his head, "and she's going to say, 'Well, ten years ago I was twice the age my third cousin was when . . .' "

"Oh, now, you're missing the point," Delia said.

"And how come this Jenny would visit someone three years younger anyway? That don't make sense."

The phone rang, and Delia rose to answer it.

"She probably just *claimed* she was visiting, and then hid out in some motel with her boyfriend," T.J. said.

Delia lifted the receiver. "Hello?"

Silence.

"Hello!"

Whoever it was hung up. "That's happened a lot lately," Delia said, hanging up herself. She returned to her chair.

"It's electrical backwash," T.J. told her.

"Backwash?"

"If you don't use your line awhile, it, like, develops all this pent-up power that spills out in this kind of like overflow and sets your phone to ringing."

Delia cocked her head.

"Happens at my mom's house once or twice a week," T.J. told her.

"Well, here it's been happening more on the order of once or twice a day," Delia said.

The phone rang again. She said, "See?"

"Just don't answer."

"It *kills* me not to answer."

He tipped back in his chair and studied her. The phone gave a third ring, a fourth. Then the outside door burst open and Noah tumbled in, bringing along a gust of fresh air. "Hey, T.J.," he said. He shed his school knapsack and picked up the receiver. "Hello?"

In the pause that followed, T.J. and Delia watched him closely.

"Naw, I don't guess I can," Noah said. He turned away from them. "I just can't, that's all." Another pause. "It's nothing like that, honest! Just I got all this homework and stuff. Well, I better go now. Bye." He hung up.

"Who was that?" Delia asked.

"Nobody."

He slung his knapsack over one shoulder and walked off toward his room.

T.J. and Delia looked at each other.

The next afternoon, a cool, sunny Friday, Delia went with Vanessa to a knitwear sale at Young Mister. Spring would be arriving any minute now, and Noah had outgrown all last spring's clothes. It was an excruciatingly slow trip, because Greggie was in the midst of his terrible twos and refused to ride in his stroller. He had to walk every inch of the way. Delia felt she had never seen Bay Borough in such detail—every plastic cup lid wheeling along the sidewalk, every sparrow pecking tinfoil in the gutter. They didn't start heading back until nearly three o'clock. "Oh-oh," Delia said, "look at the time. Noah will be home before I am."

"Isn't he going to his mother's?" Vanessa asked.

"Not this week."

"I thought he went every Friday."

"Well, I guess something must have come up."

They had reached the corner where they separated, and Delia said, "Bye, Greggie. Bye, Vanessa."

"So long, Dee," Vanessa said. "Let's ask Belle if she wants to get together over the weekend."

"Fine with me."

Belle was saving all her weekends for Mr. Lamb these days, but Delia had been ordered to keep that a secret.

At the grade school, children were already pouring onto the playground. Delia didn't try to find Noah, though. She knew he'd want to walk home with his friends. She sidestepped a runaway skateboard, smiled at a little girl collecting scattered papers, and politely ignored a mother and son quarreling next to their car.

But wait. The son was Noah. The mother was Ellie.

Wearing her cream-colored coat from the wedding but looking frazzled and disordered, Ellie was trying to wrestle Noah into the passenger seat. And Noah was pulling away from her, his jacket wrenched halfway off his arms. "Mom," he kept saying. "Mom. Stop."

Delia said, "Noah?"

They threw her an identical distracted stare and went on with their tussle. Ellie started mashing Noah's head down the way policemen did on TV, guiding their handcuffed suspects into squad cars.

"What's happening here?" Delia asked. She made a grab for Ellie's wrist. "Let go of him!"

Ellie flung her off so violently that she knocked Delia in the face;

her sharp-stoned ring grazed Delia's forehead. Noah, meanwhile, managed to yank himself free. He stumbled several steps backward and adjusted his jacket. His knapsack was gaping open and spilling papers. (*Those* were the papers the little girl was collecting!) He wiped his fist across his nose and said, "Gee, Mom."

Ellie stood straighter, breathing harshly, glaring at him.

Reverently, the little girl presented Noah with his papers. He took them without looking at them. Now Delia saw that two of his friends were loitering nearby—Kenny Moss and a second boy, whose name she couldn't remember. They were watching but pretending not to, kicking the sidewalk. The other children, passing in groups, seemed unaware that anything was wrong.

"I just wanted you to come visit! Like always! Just a normal Friday visit!" Ellie cried. "Is that too much to ask?" She turned to Delia. "Is that so—?"

Something stopped her. Her mouth fell open.

Noah said, "Gosh!" He was staring at Delia's forehead. "Delia! Golly! You're all bloody!"

Delia raised her fingers to her forehead. They came away bright red. But she didn't feel much pain—only the least little sting at that spot in her temple where the pulse beat. She said, "Oh, it's nothing. I'll just go home and—"

But Noah's eyes were huge, and Kenny Moss said, "Holy moley!" and gripped the other boy's sleeve, and the little girl said, in an informative tone, "I pass out if I see blood."

She did seem about to pass out—her lips had an ashy pallor—and so Delia, attending to first things first, said crisply, "Don't look, then." She herself wasn't dizzy in the slightest. This was plainly one of those wounds that appear much worse than they are. However, she was concerned about her clothes. "Somewhere here . . . ," she said, hunting through her purse for a tissue. Her Young Mister bag hindered her, and she passed it to Noah, leaving sticky red fingerprints across the scrunched top. "I know I must have a—"

Soft, blossomy mounds of tissue were thrust under her chin—an offering from Ellie. "I am so, so sorry," she was saying. "It was an accident! Believe me, Delia, I never meant to harm you."

"Well, I know that," Delia said, accepting the tissues. She found it oddly flattering that Ellie called her by name. She pressed the tissues to her temple, and her pulse began to throb.

"Oh, God, we have to get you to a doctor," Ellie said.

"I don't need a doctor; goodness."

"You're no judge of that! You're not in your right mind," Ellie said. Although it was Ellie who seemed unhinged, thrusting more handfuls of tissues at her (did she carry them loose in her pockets, or what?) and shrilly ordering the others about. "Move! Give us room. Noah, you ride in back; we'll put Delia up in front."

"Isn't there a school nurse or something? Why don't we look for the nurse?" Delia asked.

But Ellie said, "You don't want to end up with a scar, do you? An ugly, disfiguring scar?"

Which was something to consider; so Delia allowed herself to be shepherded toward the front seat. Noah, who had folded the seat forward so he could climb into the rear, straightened it for Delia. When she was settled, he leaned over her shoulder to offer her a gray sweatshirt from his knapsack. "Here," he said. "You're going through those hankies like a spigot."

She would have argued (blood was so hard to launder), but it was true she had used up the tissues. She pressed the sweatshirt to her forehead and breathed in its smell of clean sweat and gym shoes. Meanwhile Ellie slid behind the wheel and started the engine. "You'll probably need stitches," she said, pulling into traffic. "Oh, lately it seems everything I touch goes galloping off in every direction! Leaves me staring after it amazed!"

"I know exactly what you mean," Delia told her. She took a peek from under the sweatshirt. Up close, Ellie seemed more likable. Her lipstick was worn to a tired outline, and her eyes sagged slightly at the outer corners.

"I'm not myself these days," Ellie said. "You hear people say that all the time, but up till now I'd assumed it was a figure of speech. Now I stand off to one side looking at myself like a whole other person, and I ask, 'What could she be *thinking* of?' "

They turned left, onto Weber Street. Delia folded the sweatshirt to a new section. She was beginning to understand why you often saw red roses planted near gray stone walls. The bloodstains looked so vivid against the sweatshirt fabric, she would have liked to show the others. But Ellie was still talking away. "I admit it was me who walked out on the marriage," she said. (Delia replayed the last few sentences, wondering if she had missed some key transition.) "You don't have to remind me! I started picturing how I'd get to heaven and God would say, 'Such a waste; I sent you into the world and you didn't even make use of it, just sat there in one spot complaining you were bored.' So I walked out. But when I saw you at the wedding, when I saw how—well, I guess I thought you'd be older and fatter and wearing a zip-front dress or something. I know I made a scene, phoning Joel like I did. . . ."

Ellie had phoned Joel?

"In fact I watched myself dialing, and I said, 'What a dumb thing to do!' But I went right on doing it. And I'd planned to be Madam Iceberg. 'I've been thinking, Joel,' I'd say. 'Perhaps you should grant me custody, now you've got a female companion.' But I guess he told you how it came out. I hear his voice, I'm like a woman possessed. 'How dare you do this to Noah! Exposing an innocent child to that tawdry little love nest you've set up!' "

Love nest! Delia was thrilled.

"And if that wasn't bad enough, then I go and drag Noah in too. I'm sorry, honey!" Ellie said, addressing the rearview mirror. But she didn't wait for Noah's reaction. "And you know how heartless kids can be. The minute you show you're upset, they pretend you don't exist. They stare right through you. They make up all these excuses why they can't come and visit you."

"Mom," Noah said.

Delia was curious to hear how he would handle this, but all he said was, "Mom, you just passed Dr. Norman's."

"Yes, I know," Ellie said. They were on Border Street now, heading toward Highway 380. "Every morning I'd wake up saying, 'Today I'll get ahold of myself. I'll just put it out of my mind,' I'd say, but there you were, regardless: this mystery woman no one knew a thing about, the very type Joel would fall for. I bet you speak perfect English too, don't you?"

"You have it all wrong," Delia said, much as she hated to. "It's not the way you—"

But Ellie was turning north on 380, and Noah broke in to ask, "Mom? Where you going?"

"There are scads of doctors in Easton," Ellie said.

"Easton!" Noah and Delia said together.

"Well, you surely don't think we could use Dr. Norman. He's right there in town! Anybody in town will believe I did this on purpose."

"Can't we just tell him you didn't?" Delia asked.

"Ha! You don't know Bay Borough like I do. People there make a scandal out of the simplest little trifle."

"Maybe a drugstore, then," Delia said. She was beginning to feel uneasy. "All I need is a bandage."

"Oh, Delia, Delia, Delia," Ellie said. "You are so naive. Sure as you live, the pharmacist would be some Underwood graduate who couldn't wait to get on the phone and start blabbing. 'Guess what!' " she mimicked. " 'Mr. Miller's demented wife tried to murder his girlfriend.' "

"I'm not his—"

"I bet *you* never say 'share,' do you?"

"Share?"

"As in communicate. As in, 'So-and-so shared his feelings with me.' Joel used to gnash his teeth when I said that. And he had this thing about putting in the objects of my verbs. 'Enjoy *what?*' he'd ask me. Or, 'Take care of *whom?* Where's the end of your sentence, Ellie?' "

Delia watched a field of dead autos slide past. In back, Noah was silent.

"Funny how men always worry ahead of time that marriage might confine them," Ellie said. "Women don't give it a thought. It's afterwards it hits them. Stuck for life! Imprisoned! Trapped forever with a man who won't let you say 'parenting.' "

She braked; they had reached the stoplight at Highway 50. While they waited for it to turn green, she started digging through her purse. "Do you have any cash?" she asked Delia. "I don't want to pay with a check. Even over in Easton, my name might ring a bell."

She was crazy, Delia decided. So far she had been able to see Ellie's side of things—had sympathized, even. But now she had a sense of panic. And besides that, her cut was starting to hurt. She imagined she could actually feel its widening mouth, the edges hardening into a permanent scar.

They would have to make a run for it, as soon as she could safely snatch Noah out of the back. Maybe when they got to the doctor's. *If* they got to the doctor's; for here they sat, on and on, at this eternal red light. "Green light, green light," she urged. She leaned forward, as if that would hurry things.

Ellie, misunderstanding, said, "Oh, sorry," and took her foot off the brake. They zoomed onto Highway 50, and an oil truck, horn blaring wildly, swerved around them and careened down the wrong side of the road. Ellie screamed. Delia was too terrified to scream. They veered onto the shoulder and bounced over a stretch of dry grass before coming to a stop.

"I thought you said the light was green!" Ellie shrieked.

"I only meant—oh, Lord," Delia said. She turned to check on Noah. "Are you all right?" she asked him.

He swallowed and then nodded.

Surreptitiously, in a movement that might have been oiled, Delia felt for her door handle. She gave it a smooth nudge downward and let the door inch open. Then she shouted, "Out, Noah! Quick!" and sprang from the car, at the same time slamming her seat forward so Noah could follow. He did, luckily. He had good reflexes. He landed almost on top of her, because she happened to step directly into some kind of hole or ditch concealed by the flattened grass. Her right ankle twisted beneath her and Noah came bruising into her shoulder, and of course she still had the sweatshirt pressed to the wound on her head, but at least they were safe.

Ellie, meanwhile, had opened her own door, causing yet another truck to honk as it passed. The bleat of the horn traveled straight through Delia's chest. All at once her heart caved in, as if only now receiving word of the danger. Why, they had run a red light! Whizzed into high-speed traffic without a glance in either direction! Her skin began to tingle with the memory of it. She imagined that her outermost surface had actually been brushed by their near miss.

"We could have been killed!" she cried, and Ellie, rushing toward her, called, "I know! I can't believe we're still alive!" She flung her arms around Delia and Noah. Noah said, "Mom," and struggled free, but Delia hugged her back. Both women were slightly teary. Ellie kept saying, "Oh, God, oh, God," and laughing and dabbing her eyes.

"Mom," Noah said again, from the sidelines. "Can we just go to Dr. Norman, please?"

"We'll tell him I bumped my head," Delia said. "He won't think a thing about it."

"Well, you're right," Ellie said. "We'll do that. Come on, if I can get up the nerve to drive again."

So they all climbed back in the car, which turned out to be a Plymouth, just a year or two newer than Delia's Plymouth; and Ellie waited till there wasn't another vehicle in sight before inching out onto the

highway and executing a U-turn. Not until they were traveling back down
380 did she venture to speak, even; she was so intent on her driving.
Then she asked Noah what he planned to tell his father.

Noah let a long pause develop, but finally he said, "Same thing we
tell Dr. Norman, I guess. You gave us a ride home from school? Delia
banged her head some way?"

"I knocked against the car door as I got in," Delia suggested.

"Oh, good," Ellie said, and her hands relaxed on the wheel.

Most likely it was Delia she had been worrying about. She must have
known that Noah wouldn't tattle; he had that disconcertingly cold, stoic
secretiveness you often see in children of troubled marriages.

"And in fact that's almost what happened," Ellie said. "We just got
caught up in one of those, what you might call flurries of events, right?
Am I right?"

"Well, of course," Delia told her.

Ellie slowed for the turn onto Border Street. "You may not believe
this," she said, "but I'm a very stable person as a rule. It's just that lately,
I've been under a lot of stress. Oh, working in front of the camera is way
more pressure than I thought it would be! I have to watch my weight
every instant, make sure I get my full eight hours' sleep, take care of my
complexion. See this?" She was in the midst of parallel parking, but she
paused to grab a strand of her hair. "Bleached, stripped, body-waved,
color-treated . . ." She pulled the strand taut and released it. "See how
it stretches out so long and thin and then just snaps, *boing*? That's not
hair anymore; it's, I don't know, Silly Putty. And if only they'd give me
a leave of absence till my eyebrows can grow back in!"

One tire scraped the curb. "Besides which there's my nutso sister
losing her marbles over Dad's marriage," she said, "and this leak in my
apartment ceiling nobody knows where from, and not to mention Dad
himself. What business does he have, starting all over at his age? He's
sixty-seven years old and in constant pain to boot, were you aware of
that? Why do you suppose he keeps Noah's visits so short? His favorite
grandchild, but any more than an hour and Dad's exhausted!"

"Oh, the poor man," Delia said. She opened the door and got out,
still holding the sweatshirt to her head. Somehow the urgency of their
errand had receded, she noticed. She flipped the seat forward for Noah,
and he piled out after her.

"When I think how hard I worked moving him into that place!" Ellie
told her, slamming her own door. "All those boxes I packed! I felt like

I was sending him off to camp or something. 'Do you have the right kind of clothes for this? What will the other kids be wearing?' And now they're threatening to evict him."

"Evict him!" Delia said.

They were climbing the steps of a large frame house with a wraparound porch. Noah led the way. Delia trailed behind because her ankle was slowing her down. She called, "I thought they said he could stay on after he married."

"That was before they found out his wife was expecting," Ellie said.

Delia halted on the top porch step and stared at her. Even Noah stared. "Expecting what?" Delia asked foolishly.

"Use your head, Delia! Why do you suppose they moved the wedding up to March?"

"Well, because . . . did they tell you this? Or are you just surmising?"

"Darn right they told me," Ellie said. "Made a big announcement of it, just last week. Dad asks Binky, 'Angel? Are you going to break the news, or am I?' and Binky says, 'Oh, you do it, honeybunch.' Don't you want to just gag? That kind of talk seems so, I don't know, fake, when it's a second marriage. So Dad clears his throat and says, 'Ellie,' he says; says, 'you're going to have a sister.' Well, I was kind of slow on the uptake. I said, 'I *already* have a sister. Several.' He said, 'I mean another sister. We're pregnant.' That's an exact quote. 'We,' he said. You can bet he didn't word it that way the first four times around."

"But . . . when is this going to happen?" Delia asked.

"September."

"September!"

Majestically, Ellie sailed through the front door. Delia stood on the porch with her mouth open. Binky had always been a rotund little person, rotund in the stomach as well, but . . . She looked over at Noah. "Did *you* know about this?" she asked.

He shook his head.

"Well," she said. "So you'll have a . . . baby aunt! Imagine!"

As she limped through the door, she heard Ellie's humorless snicker.

This was the first time Delia had been to Dr. Norman's office, although his telephone number was posted next to the Millers' kitchen phone. The instant she smelled that mixture of floor wax and isopropyl alcohol, she was overcome by a settling-in sensation—a feeling that she had returned to her rightful place; that all other places were counterfeit, temporary, foreign to her true nature. She stopped short in the foyer (stringy Oriental rug, ginger-jar lamp on a table), until Ellie took her arm and steered her toward the waiting room. "Is he in?" she asked the woman at the desk. The woman was much older than Delia and fifty pounds heavier, but still somebody Delia could identify with, seeing her fingers poised on the chrome-rimmed keys of an ancient typewriter. "We've got an emergency here!" Ellie told her.

Oh, yes, the emergency. Delia had almost forgotten. While Ellie explained the circumstances ("sharp metal corner on the . . . nothing *I* could do . . . tried to warn her but . . ."), Delia unstuck the sweat-shirt from her forehead and discovered she was no longer bleeding. The bloodstains on the shirt had dried to a dull, blackish color. She glanced toward the other patients. Two women and a small girl sat watching her with interest, and she hastily clapped the sweatshirt back on her temple.

Dr. Norman was just hanging up the phone when the secretary led them in. He was a dumpy man with a flounce of white curls above his ears. "What have we here?" he asked, and he rose and came around the desk to peel away the sweatshirt with practiced fingers. His breath smelled of pipe tobacco. Delia would have liked to take hold of his hand and cradle it against her cheek. "Hmm," he said, peering. "Well, nothing you'll die of."

"Will it leave a scar?" Delia asked him.

"It shouldn't. Hard to tell for sure till I get it cleaned up."

"Of course I did everything humanly possible," Ellie said. "Warned her over and over again. 'Watch yourself getting in, Dee,' I told her; if I told her once, I told her half a dozen times—"

Dr. Norman said, with a touch of impatience, "Yes, fine, Ellie, I understand," and Ellie shut up. "Come next door," he told Delia. He ushered her into an adjoining room. Ellie and Noah followed, which may not have been what he had intended.

This second room held an examining table upholstered in cracked black leather. Delia boosted herself nimbly onto the end of it and settled her handbag in her lap. While Dr. Norman rummaged in a metal drawer the color of condensed milk, he asked Ellie about the weather; he asked Noah about his softball team; he told Delia he had heard she was a ba-a-ad tutor.

"Bad!" Delia said.

"Good, that means." He looked up from the rubber gloves he was slipping on. "In T. J. Renfro's language, 'bad' is good, and so is 'wicked.' You teach a wicked equation, he says."

"Oh," Delia said, relieved.

Ellie, who had been studying a poster on the Heimlich maneuver, looked over at her. "You tutor at Underwood?" she asked.

"Yes."

She sniffed. "Joel must be in heaven," she said. "He was always after me to volunteer."

Dr. Norman sent Ellie a quick glance that she probably didn't notice. Then he told Noah, "Excuse me, son," and stepped around him to peer again at Delia's forehead. She stilled her swinging feet as he came close. "This'll smart some," he said, tearing open an antiseptic wipe. The keen, authoritative smell filled her with longing. *I'm really not just a mere patient*, she could have told him. *I know this office top to bottom! I know you'll sit down to supper tonight and tell your family that that Ellie Miller sure acts mighty possessive of Joel, considering they're separated. I know you'll say you finally got to meet that live-in woman of his, and depending on how discreet you are, you might even voice some suspicion as to exactly how I was injured. Don't think I'm one of those outsiders who can't see beyond the white coat!*

But of course she said nothing, and Dr. Norman swabbed her wound and then laid dots of rubbery warmth on either side of it as he tested it with his fingertips. "What you've got," he said, "is a superficial scratch across the forehead, but a fairly deep gash at the temple. No need for stitches, though, and I doubt there'll be a scar if we keep the edges together while it heals." He turned back to the cabinet. "We'll just apply a butterfly closure. This nifty type of bandage that . . ."

Yes, Delia knew what a butterfly was—had plastered more than a few onto her own children's injuries. She shut her eyes as he set it in place. Next to her she heard Noah breathing; he was leaning in close to watch. "Cool!" he said.

"Now, if you want I could prescribe a pain medication," Dr. Norman said, "but I don't believe—"

"It hardly hurts at all," Delia told him, opening her eyes. "I won't need anything."

He scrawled a note for his secretary before he showed her out, and clapped Noah on the shoulder, and said, "Ellie, always good to see your clothes hanging so well on you."

"Oh, stop," Ellie said. She told Delia, "Everybody pokes fun at this remark I made in *Boardwalk Bulletin*."

Delia's only response was, "Oh?" because she didn't want to let on she'd read it.

"But I was misquoted!" Ellie said. "Or at least, I didn't mean it that way. What I meant was, I dress economically."

She was still going on about that—telling Noah that this skirt, for instance, had cost thirteen ninety-five at Teenage World—when they reached the reception desk, which left Delia to pay the bill. She did think Ellie might have offered. But she had planned to decline anyhow, and so she held her tongue.

Out on the porch, she folded the sweatshirt and stuffed it in her bag. Then she followed Ellie and Noah down the steps. Ellie was discussing the clothing budget of someone named Doris. Doris? Oh, yes, the anchorwoman at WKMD. "What she spends on headbands alone," Ellie said, "to say nothing of those scarves she wears to hide her scraggy neck . . ."

Delia was reflecting that she should have accepted that prescription after all, not for her forehead but for her ankle. She had completely neglected to mention twisting her ankle. She limped painfully to the car and fell with a thud into the passenger seat.

"So I guess you want to go home now," Ellie said.

"Yes, please," Delia told her.

But Ellie had been speaking to Noah. "Honey?" she said, watching his face in the rearview mirror.

"I guess," he said.

"Don't want to change your mind and visit *me*?"

"I've got this history test to study for."

Ellie's shoulders slumped. She didn't point out that he could do that anytime over the weekend.

They cruised down Weber Street, passing Copp Catering where Belle had bought Thanksgiving dinner, and the Sub Tub, where all the Underwood students headed for snacks after school. In Ellie's company, Delia felt that Bay Borough took on a different shading. It didn't look as happy as it usually did. The women walking home with their grocery bags seemed unknowingly ironic, like those plastic-faced, smiling housewives in kitchen-appliance ads from the fifties. Delia shook off the thought and turned to Ellie. "Well!" she said. "Maybe I'll run into you at your father's sometime."

"If I ever go back there," Ellie said gloomily.

"Oh, you have to go back! Why wouldn't you? He's such a pleasure to talk to."

"That's easy for you to say," Ellie said. "You're not his daughter."

She turned onto Pendle Street, braked for a jaywalking collie, and pulled into the Millers' driveway. (The glance she shot toward the front windows could have meant nothing at all.) "Bye, No-No," she said, blowing her son a kiss. "Delia, sorry again about the whatever."

"That's all right," Delia said.

Limping after Noah up the sidewalk, she remembered where she'd heard that phrase of Ellie's before. "Easy for *you*," Delia's sisters used to tell her. They said, "Naturally *you* get along with Dad. You arrived so late, is why. You don't have so much to hold against him."

But they never specified just what they held against him themselves. They hadn't been able to name it even when she asked, and she would be willing to bet that Ellie couldn't either.

When Delia changed into the shoes she wore around the house, she found that the strap of her pump had left a groove across her right instep. Her foot was so swollen, in fact, that she seemed to be wearing a *ghost* pump, pressing into her flesh. And her anklebone had become a mere dent. She doubted anything was broken, though. She could still wriggle her toes.

She drew a dishpan of cold water, added a few ice cubes, and sat down on a kitchen chair to let the ankle soak. And what else should she do for it? All those times she'd heard Sam advising his patients; you'd think she would remember. There was a mnemonic: R.I.C.E., he always told them. She tried it aloud. "Rest, ice . . ." But what was the C for? Caution? Coddling? She tried again. "Rest, ice . . ."

"Rest, ice, compression, elevation," Joel told her, setting his briefcase on the counter. "What happened to *you*? You look like a war orphan."

"Oh," Delia said, "you know that sharp corner they have on car doors . . ." Then she realized that this in no way explained her ankle. "It's just been one of those days," she finished vaguely.

He didn't pursue it. He opened an overhead cabinet and felt for something on the top shelf. "I know we have a first-aid kit," he said. "I had to take a course in— Here we go." He pulled out a gray metal tackle box. "When you're through soaking, I'll tape it."

"Oh, I'm through," Delia said. She should probably allow more time, but the ice was making her shiver. She lifted her foot and patted it dry with a dish towel. Joel bent over it. He whistled.

"Maybe you ought to get that x-rayed," he said. "Are you sure it's not broken?"

"Pretty sure. Everything works," Delia told him.

Moving aside the dishpan, he knelt and started unrolling a strip of flesh-colored elastic. Delia felt self-conscious about the puffiness of her ankle and the dead blue of her skin, but he showed no reaction. He began wrapping her foot, crisscrossing her instep, working his way upward in a series of perfectly symmetrical V's. "Oh, how neat! Tidy, I mean," Delia said. "You're very good at this."

"Part of a principal's education," Joel said. He wound the last of the bandage around her shin. Then he secured it with two metal clips the same shape as the butterfly closure on her temple. "How's that?" he asked. He took hold of her foot, as if weighing it. "Tight enough?"

"Oh, yes, it feels . . ."

It felt wonderful. Not just the bandage—although the support was a great relief—but the hand clasping her foot, the large palm warming her arch through the elastic. She wished she could push even harder against his grip. She was thirsty, it seemed, for that firmness. Till now she had never realized that the instep could be an erogenous zone.

As if he guessed, he went on kneeling there, looking into her face.

"Delia?" Noah said. "Can I invite—?"

Both of them jumped. Joel dropped her foot and stood up. He said, "Noah! I thought you were off at your mother's."

Noah stood in the doorway, frowning.

"We were just, ah, taping Delia's ankle," Joel told him. "It seems she must have sprained it."

Delia said, "Rest, ice, compression, elevation! That's the menon . . . menonom . . ." She laughed, short of breath. "Oh, Lord, I never can pronounce it."

Noah just watched her. Finally he said, "Can I invite Jack for supper?"

"Oh, of course!" she said. "Yes! Good idea!"

He looked at her a moment longer, looked at his father, then turned and walked out.

———

Joel wouldn't let her cook that night. He settled her on the family-room couch with her feet up and the cat in her lap, and he went off to order a pizza. Meanwhile Noah and Jack sprawled on the floor in front of the TV. Some kind of thriller was playing. During the more suspenseful scenes a piano tinkled hypnotically. Delia loosened her hold on George and leaned her head back and closed her eyes.

Behind her lids, she saw the gritty surface of Highway 50 rushing toward her. She saw the Plymouth darting across a stream of traffic, miraculously avoiding collision like a blip in a video game. She jerked awake, eyes wide and staring, shaken all over again by the narrowness of her escape.

17

The cut on Delia's forehead healed quickly, leaving just the faintest white
fishhook of a scar. The sprain, though, took longer. She favored her right
ankle for weeks. "This is not my actual walk," she wanted to tell passersby,
for she felt, somehow, at a disadvantage—second rate, inferior. She
wondered how people endured it when they knew they'd be disabled
forever, like some of the residents in Senior City.

Senior City was the one place where her limp attracted no attention.
She could proceed unhurriedly toward a waiting elevator, trusting the
other passengers to hold it for her. When she finally stepped inside, she
would find them conversing among themselves without a sign of impatience, one of them leaning absently on the Open button till Delia
reminded her to release it. No longer did their own infirmities seem so
apparent, either, or their wrinkles or white hair. Delia had adjusted her
slant of vision over the past months.

And what a contrast Binky made! For anyone could see now that she
was pregnant. By May she was in maternity clothes. By early June she
was cupping her belly like an apronful of fruit as she rose from a chair.
"Seems like things are *more so*, with this one," she told Delia. "When
I had the boys I hardly showed till the end. I used to wear unzipped
jeans and one of my husband's long-tailed shirts. But now I have to

squeeze through car doors sideways and I've still got three months to go."

There was no question that this baby was unplanned. Binky said she'd been twelve weeks along before she suspected a thing—had continued proclaiming her June wedding date to all and sundry. "Then I said, 'What *is* this?' and I went to see my doctor. When he told me I was pregnant I just looked at him. He said, 'But nowadays, thirty-eight is nothing. Lots of women give birth at thirty-eight.' I said, 'How about sixty-seven?' He said, 'Sixty-seven?' I said, 'That's the age of the father.' He said, 'Oh.' Said, 'I see.' Said, 'Hmm.' "

"I view it this way," Nat told Delia. "What better place for childbirth than a retirement community? Here we have all these doctors and nurses, just standing by twiddling their thumbs on Floor Four."

Delia was horrified. She said, "You would go to Floor Four for this?"

"He's teasing," Binky told her.

"We'll turn the cardiac unit into a labor room," Nat went on impishly. "Use one of those railed hospital beds for a crib. And Lord knows these folks have got enough diapers around. Right, Noah?"

Noah grinned, but only at his teacup. He had reached that age where any talk of bodily functions was a monumental embarrassment.

"The best part is," Nat said, "whoever drew up the bylaws for Senior City never dreamed of this eventuality. All our contract says is, 'Applicants must be sixty-five before entering,' but this baby isn't an applicant. However, we did lose the Floor Two dispute. You heard we asked permission to move down to Floor Two? Now that I have Binky to look after me, I said . . . but the board said no. Said it wasn't the way the place worked. Progression was supposed to be up, they said; not down."

"Well, perhaps it's for the best," Binky told him. "Our neighbors on Three would be heartbroken to lose us, now the baby's coming."

"Yes, she certainly won't lack for sitters," Nat said dryly.

He kept insisting that the baby was a girl, even though they had chosen not to learn the sex. Girls were the only babies he'd had experience of, he said. He tried to convince Noah that *all* babies were girls but metamorphosed, some of them, into boys at about the same time their eyes darkened.

"You wouldn't believe how many old ladies are working on booties right now," he told Delia. "Little knitted slippers, socks, embroidered Mary Janes . . . Kid is going to be the Imelda Marcos of the nursery set."

Still, both Nat and Binky must have misgivings, Delia thought. How could they not? She was awed by their determined good cheer—by Binky's habit of telling people, "We couldn't be more pleased," as if prompting them; and by Nat's solicitude, even as he hobbled around as fragile and easily overturned as something constructed of Tinkertoys.

"When my first wife was dying," he told Delia one afternoon, "I used to sit by her bed and I thought, *This is her true face*. It was all hollowed and sharpened. In her youth she'd been very pretty, but now I saw that her younger face had been just a kind of rough draft. Old age was the completed form, the final, finished version she'd been aiming at from the start. *The real thing at last!* I thought, and I can't tell you how that notion colored things for me from then on. Attractive young people I saw on the street looked so . . . temporary. I asked myself why they bothered dolling up. Didn't they understand where they were headed? But nobody ever does, it seems. All those years when I was a child, longing for it to be 'my turn,' it hadn't ever occurred to me that my turn would be over, by and by. Then Binky came along. Is it any wonder I feel I've been born again?"

Binky was present when he said this, and she leaned forward and kissed his cheek. "Me too, sweetheart," she told him.

Delia grew suddenly conscious of her own separateness—of her upright posture, her elbows pressed primly against her sides in an armchair all to herself.

Then it was summer, warm and green and buzzing with cicadas after a long, cool spring. School came to an end, and Noah started sleeping late and hanging around the house with his friends and complaining of boredom. Joel switched to vacation hours and was home by midafternoon. In the maple tree out back, a woodpecker couple built themselves a nest. Delia could hear their cries from time to time—high-pitched, excited squawks that reminded her of girls'-school girls attending their first mixed party. And on Highway 50, more and more cars sped toward the beach, their rooftops spinning with bicycle wheels, their back seats stuffed with children, their rear window ledges a coagulation of sand shovels, rubber flippers, and Utz potato chip cartons.

Would Delia's family be going to the beach themselves? she wondered. It was June, after all. It was a year since she had left them, although it seemed much longer. She had, by now, done everything at least once—observed a birthday alone as well as Thanksgiving, Christmas, and New Year's. Paid her income taxes (married filing separately). Registered to vote. Taken the cat to the vet. She was a bona fide citizen of Bay Borough.

Then a letter arrived from Susie.

The envelope bore the correct address, which meant that Susie must have consulted Eliza or Eleanor. The handwriting was so rounded that *Borough* resembled a row of balloons anchored by a single string. Delia lifted the flap almost stealthily, unsealing it rather than tearing it, as if this would soften the impact of whatever waited inside.

Hi Mom!

Just a quick note to fill you in! How you doing? Thanx for the graduation card! Commencement was kind of a drag but Tucky Pearson gave the most awesome party afterwards at her family's horse farm!

Nothing special to report except Dad is being so-o-o-o difficult right now! I know you'll see my side of things so could you maybe phone him and have a talk? Don't tell him I asked you to call— just say you got a letter from me and thought you should discuss my plans. You wouldn't believe how mean he's being! Or maybe you would! Honestly Mom sometimes I don't even blame you for going! See ya!

Luv, Susie

Delia had a sudden sense of exhaustion. She refolded the letter and put it back in the envelope.

Well.

She couldn't phone from the house. She didn't want the call appearing on Joel's bill. Nor did she want to reverse the charges, which would give an impression of needfulness. So first she had to scrounge through her handbag and various pockets for change, and then she had to walk to the pay phone at Bay and Weber Streets, a block and a half away. She walked as fast as her ankle allowed, because if she made her call between eleven-thirty and twelve, she had a better chance of reaching Sam directly. He always broke for lunch then. Unless, in her absence, things had altered more than she had predicted.

Inside the booth—just one of those above-the-waist, partially enclosed affairs that let in every traffic sound—she lined up her coins on the shelf and then dialed the grown-ups' number. She had never called long distance from a pay phone before, and she was distressed to find that she had to wait to deposit the coins till her party answered. First the phone at the other end rang twice, then Sam said, "Dr. Grinstead," and then a recording issued instructions and Delia dropped her quarters in. *Whang! Whang!* It was humiliating—very nearly as bad as calling collect, and made worse by the fact that Sam didn't grasp what was going on. "Hello?" he kept saying. "Is anyone there?"

His deep, level voice, his habit of slanting downward even on questions.

Delia said, "Sam?"

"Where are you?" he asked immediately.

He assumed this was a plea for help, she realized. He thought she was admitting defeat—calling to say, "Come get me." He must have been expecting it for months. She stood straighter. "I'm calling about Susie," she told him.

A dead silence. Then: "Oh. Susie."

"I wonder if you know what's troubling her."

"I believe my feeble brain can encompass *that* much," he said icily. "But I suppose you're going to tell me anyhow, aren't you."

"What?" Delia pressed her fingers to her forehead. "No, wait—I mean I'm honestly asking! She wrote me there was some problem, but she didn't say what it was."

"Oh," Sam said again. Another silence. "Well," he said, "this would have to do with her wedding, I suspect."

"Susie's getting married?"

"She wants to. I'm opposed."

"But—" Delia said. *But she didn't talk to me about this!* she wanted to protest. *Didn't even consult me!* Unreasonable, she knew; so she changed it to, "But Driscoll's a very nice boy. It is Driscoll, isn't it?"

"Who else," Sam said. "However, that's not the issue. She can marry whoever she chooses, of course, but I told her she'll have to live on her own for one calendar year beforehand."

"A year! Why?"

"I hate to see her jumping straight from school to marriage. From her father's house to her husband's house."

Her *father's* house? *He* hated to see? How about her mother? Oh, all right . . . but her *husband's* house?

And the biggest offense of all: what he meant was, he didn't want

Susie turning out like Delia. Who had never spent so much as a night on her own before *she* married; and just look at the results.

He'd been mulling that over all year, she supposed. Arriving at his own private theory.

"But if she lives alone," Delia said, "she'll be so . . . unprotected. And also she and Driscoll might . . . I mean, what if they end up, um, sleeping together or something like that?"

"Don't you suppose they already sleep together, Delia?"

Her mouth dropped open.

A taped voice said metallically, "To continue your call, please deposit another—"

"Hold on, I'm going to try to get these charges reversed," Sam told Delia.

She didn't argue. She was trying to reassemble her thoughts. Well, no doubt they *did* sleep together. On some level, she'd probably known that. Still, she felt bereft. She pictured herself waving goodbye while Susie and Driscoll dwindled into the distance, never once looking back.

"You know she doesn't have a job yet," Sam said when he'd dealt with the operator.

"I wondered about that."

Amazing, how easy it was to fall back into this matter-of-fact, almost chatty exchange of information. The *ordinariness* of it struck her as surreal.

"She sleeps till all hours," he was saying, "and then heads off to the swimming pool. No interviews set up, no mention of careers . . ."

But if she's getting married, Delia thought. That too, though, she censored. She asked, "How about Driscoll? Does he have a job?"

"Yes, he's hired on with his father."

Delia tried to think what Driscoll's father did, but she couldn't remember. Something businessy. She said, "Well, have you and Susie talked about this? Discussed what kind of work might interest her?"

"No," Sam said.

"And where could she afford to live? I mean, if she isn't earning money yet."

"We haven't gone into that," Sam said.

"Well, golly, Sam, what *have* you gone into?"

"Nothing," Sam said. He gave a slight cough. "It appears that we're not speaking."

Delia sighed. She said, "How about Eliza? I know Susie must talk to *her*."

"Not necessarily," Sam said.

"What do you mean?"

"I don't think they do talk, to tell the truth."

"They had a fight?"

"I'm not sure. Well, they did, I guess, but I'm not sure if it's still on or not. Actually, Eliza is out of town right now."

"Out of town!"

"She's visiting Linda awhile."

Delia digested this. She said, "Aren't you all taking your beach trip this year?"

"No, Delia," Sam told her, and the iciness was back in his voice. Delia understood his point as clearly as if he'd stated it: *Do you really imagine we'd go back to the beach, now that you've ruined it for all of us forever?*

Hastily she said, "So no one's sat Susie down and discussed her options with her."

"I fail to see how I can hold a discussion with someone who walks out of a room the instant I walk in," Sam said.

You follow her, is how, Delia wanted to tell him. *You walk out after her. What's so hard about that?* But for Sam it would be unthinkable, she knew. He wasn't a man who laid himself open to rebuff. He didn't like to plead, or bargain, or reverse himself; he had never made a mistake in all his life. (And was that why the people around him seemed to make so many?)

A delivery truck wheezed past, and she covered her free ear. "All right," she said, "here's what I propose. I'm going to write and tell her that if she wants you to pay for her wedding, she'll have to accept your conditions. And if she doesn't like those conditions, then she can pay for her own wedding. Either way, you will go along with it."

"I will?"

"You will."

"But then she might decide to marry him tomorrow."

"If she does, she does," Delia said. "That's up to her."

Sam was quiet. Delia's ankle had started to pound, but she didn't push him. Finally he said, "How about the not-speaking part?"

"How about it?"

"Could you tell her to talk all this over with me?"

"I could suggest it," she said.

"Thank you."

She felt uncomfortable in this new role. She said, "So! Everything else all right?"

"Oh, yes."

"Boys okay?"

"They're fine."

"Who's taking care of the office while Eliza's gone?"

"I am."

"Maybe *that's* a job for Susie."

"Never," he said flatly.

Another stab to the heart. *Never*, he meant, *would I let my daughter follow her mother's wretched example.* And she couldn't even argue with that. She said, "I guess I'll be going, then."

"Oh. Well. Goodbye," he said.

After she hung up, it occurred to her that on the other hand, maybe he was just saying Susie would be a disaster in the office. It was true that she was hopeless when it came to organizational matters. Unlike Delia, who had a gift for them.

Could that have been what he'd meant?

In her letter to Susie she included one request that she hadn't mentioned to Sam beforehand. *When you do get married*, she wrote, *whatever kind of wedding it may be, will you let me come? I couldn't blame you if you didn't, but . . .*

She wrote that afternoon, using the desk in the family room, choosing a time when she had the house to herself. Before she was finished, though, Joel came home. He said, "Oh, here you are." Then he stood about for a while, jingling coins deep in his pocket. At last she stopped writing and looked up at him.

"Was there something you wanted?" she asked.

"No, no," he said, and he moved away, went off to another part of the house. But as soon as she had finished the letter, he was back again. He must have heard her starting supper preparations. He stood in the kitchen doorway, once again jingling his coins. "Saw you on Weber Street today," he said.

"Weber Street?"

"Making a phone call."

"Ah."

"You know you're welcome to use the phone here," he said.

Delia had one of those flashes where she saw herself through someone else's eyes: huddling over the receiver and shielding her ear with one hand. She almost laughed. The Mystery Woman Strikes Again. She said, "Oh, well, it's just that I . . . had to call on the spur of the moment, that was all."

He waited, as if hoping for more, but she said nothing else.

Sometimes Delia noticed some detail in Joel—the play of muscles under the skin of his forearms, or the casual drape of his suit coat across his back—and she felt a pull so deep that she had to remind herself she hardly knew this man. In fact, they barely talked to each other. Ever since he'd bandaged her ankle they seemed to have grown tongue-tied and shy. And anyhow, they had Noah to think of.

Watchful, mistrustful Noah! Always lurking about, lately, scanning their faces for signs of guilt. One night when Joel and Delia came home from a Volunteer Tutors' Supper (potluck, each woman meditatively eating just her own dish, for the most part), they found him waiting at the front door with his arms clamped across his chest. "What took you so long?" he demanded. "That supper was supposed to get over at nine. It's nine forty-three, for gosh sake, and the Brookses' house is not but five minutes away!"

Well, think about it: in October he would turn thirteen. Not an easy age, as Delia knew far too well. Already there were signs. For instance, he had spurned those clothes she'd bought him this spring. And he wanted her to leave his laundry in the hall outside his room from now on, not bring it in. And one morning after his friends had slept over, he asked her, "Do you have to wear that beachy-looking cover-up at breakfast? Don't you own a bathrobe like normal people?"

Yes, it was clear where he was headed.

"He's getting so tall all at once; I went to kiss him the other day and his face was just about even with mine," Ellie said. (Often, now, the two of them talked on the phone awhile before Delia summoned Noah.) "Every time I see him, he's changed some way! He's started listening to this horrible music in the car, these singers who might as well be gossiping amongst themselves except every now and then you manage to overhear a stray word or two."

"And he says he's going to start a rock band," Delia told her. "He and Kenny Moss."

"But he doesn't play an instrument!"

"Well, *I* don't know. They've already got a name picked out: Does Your Mother Have Any Children?"

"That's a band name?"

"So he tells me."

"I don't get it," Ellie said.

"You're not supposed to, I guess. And you heard he doesn't want to go to camp this summer."

"But he loves camp!"

"He says it's babyish."

"What will he do instead, then?"

"Oh, he's going, willy-nilly," Delia told her. "Joel says he has to." She felt odd, mentioning Joel so familiarly to Ellie. She hurried on. "He's already paid the deposit, he says, and anyhow, I won't be here to tend him. I'll be on vacation."

"You will? Where?"

"Ocean City, the middle two weeks in July. Belle Flint set it up with this friend of hers who runs a motel."

"You and I should get together while you're there," Ellie told her. "Have dinner one night in my favorite restaurant. I hang out in Ocean City all the time!"

Evidently she no longer thought Delia was Joel's girlfriend. Delia wondered why. Was it seeing Delia up close that had changed her mind?

Delia felt a little bit disappointed, to be honest.

She dreamed she ran into Sam in front of Senior City. He was standing outside the double doors in his starched white coat, with his hands in his pockets, and she walked directly up to him and said, in her most positive tone, "At the Millers' I have a full-sized bike I built all by myself out of paper clips."

He gazed down at her thoughtfully.

"A working bike?" he asked.

"Well, no."

She woke up still squinting against the sunlight that had flashed off his glasses. He had been wearing a stethoscope, she recalled, looped across the back of his neck like a shaving towel. He hadn't worn a stethoscope since the first week he came to work for her father. It was a new-young-doctor thing to do, really, and new was what Sam had been then, in spite of his age, because he'd had to spend so long working his way through school. But he never would have given her such a stern and judging look when they were first acquainted.

Or would he?

Maybe he'd been that way from the start. Maybe Adrian had it right: what annoys you most, later on, is the very thing that attracted you to begin with.

For her trip to the beach she bought a suitcase—just a cheap one from the dime store, big enough to hold her straw tote. Belle was driving her over early Saturday morning. Noah was still home when Belle honked out front (he'd be leaving for camp around noon), and Delia gave him a quick goodbye hug, which he put up with. To Joel she said, "Don't forget to feed Vernon."

"Who's Vernon?"

She couldn't think why he asked, for a moment. Then she said, "Oh! I meant George." Silly of her: George and Vernon were not at all alike. She said, "George the *cat*!" as if it were Joel who had been confused. "Well, so long," she told him, and she rushed out the door, her suitcase knocking against her shins.

Belle wore enormous sunglasses, the upside-down kind with the earpieces hitched at the bottom. "I have the world's worst hangover," she told Delia right off. "I never want to see another drop of champagne as long as I live."

"You had champagne?"

"Did I ever. A whole entire bottle, because last night Horace proposed."

"Oh, Belle!"

"But he couldn't drink any himself because he's allergic," Belle said. "Just sat there watching *me* glug it down, following every swallow with those hound-dog eyes of his. Yes, that's the way we do things, we two. Still, it made a nice gesture. Champagne, a dozen roses, and a diamond ring: the works." She lifted her left hand from the wheel to display a tiny, winking glint. Then she pulled into the street. "Near as I can recall, I must have accepted. Think of it: Belle Lamb. Sounds like a noise in a comic book: *Blam!*" She was keeping her face expressionless behind the dark glasses, but there was something complacent and well-fed in the curve of her lips. "I guess now I'll have to go through with it," she said.

"Don't you want to go through with it?"

"Oh, well. Sure." She turned onto 380. "I do care about him. Or love him, I guess. At least, if he bangs his head climbing into my car I get this sort of clutch to my stomach. You reckon we could call that love?"

Delia was still considering this question as Belle went on. "But I can't help noticing, Dee: most folks marry just because they decide they've reached that stage. I mean, even if they don't have any particular person picked out yet. *Then* they pick someone out. It's like their marriages are arranged, same as in those foreign countries—except that here, the bride and groom are the ones who do the arranging."

Delia laughed. She said, "Well, now I don't know *what* to say. Am I supposed to congratulate you, or not?"

"Oh, well, sure," Belle said. "Congratulate me, I guess." And her left hand rose swaybacked from the wheel for a moment so she could admire her diamond.

The Mermaid's Chambers was a peeling turquoise motel on the wrong side of the highway, between a T-shirt shop and a liquor store. But Belle had got her a very good discount, and Delia wasn't planning to spend much time in her room anyhow.

Each morning, she crossed the highway carrying her tote and a motel bedspread, along with a Styrofoam cup of coffee. She rented an umbrella on the beach and settled herself amid a crowd that thickened as the day progressed—squealing children, impossibly beautiful teenagers, parents in assorted weights and ages, and stringy white grandparents. First she sat drinking her coffee as she stared out at the horizon, and then, when she had finished, she pulled a book from her tote and started reading.

Here in Ocean City she was back to romances, an average of one a day. They seemed overblown and slushy after her library books, and she read them almost without thinking about them, paying more heed to the yellow warmth soaking through her umbrella, the cries of gulls and children, the sunburned feet scrunching past her in the sand. One day, she started a book about a bride who was kidnapped by her fiancé's brother, and she realized partway through that this was what she'd been reading on *last* year's vacation. She checked the title: yes, *Captive of Clarion Castle*. She gazed toward the ocean. A mother was holding her diapered baby just above reach of the surf, and the radios all around were playing

"Under the Boardwalk," and Delia fancied she caught sight of her own self strolling south alongside the festoons of sea foam.

Toward noon she would stand up and head toward the boardwalk for lunch. She ate in one or another rinky-dink café—a sandwich shop, a pizza joint—blinking away the purple spangles that swarmed across her vision in the sudden dimness. Then she returned to her umbrella and napped awhile, after which she read a bit more. Later she took a walk down the beach, just a short walk because her ankle still sent out a little blade of tenderness every time she put any weight on it. And then she went for her one swim of the day.

She spent forever submerging, like someone removing a strip of adhesive tape by painful degrees. Arms lifted fastidiously, stomach sucked in with a gasp, she advanced at a gingerly, crabwise angle so as to present the narrowest surface to the breakers. Finally, though, she was in, and not a hair on her head was dampened if she'd played her cards right. She floated far out with a smug sense of achievement, sending a lofty, amused glance shoreward whenever the swell she bobbed on crashed against the shrieking throngs in the shallows. And she always waited for the most docile wave to carry her back to land—although sometimes she misjudged and found herself knocked off her feet and churning underwater like a load of laundry.

Then she staggered onto the beach, streaming droplets and wringing out the skirt of her suit. By that time all her sunblock would have been washed off, and her face grew steadily pinker and more freckled over the course of her vacation. Her first act when she returned to her room at the end of every day was to check the mirror, and every day a more highly colored person gazed back at her. When she peeled off her swimsuit, a second suit of fish-white skin lay beneath it. In the shower her feet developed scarlet smatterings across the tops.

She lounged on the bed in Sam's beach robe and toweled her hair dry. Filed her nails. Watched the news. Later, when the moldy-smelling, air-conditioned air began to chill her, she dressed and went out to dinner—a different restaurant each night. Her Sundays at the Bay Arms stood her in good stead, and she dined alone serenely, making her way through three full courses as she surveyed the nearby tables. Then she sat on the boardwalk awhile, if she could find an empty bench. The racket of video games and rock music pummeled her from behind; in front stretched the empty black ocean, fringing itself white beneath a partly erased disk of moon.

She was back in her room by nine most nights. In bed by ten. She turned off the air conditioner and slept under just a sheet, lightly sweating in the warm air that drifted through her window.

One day was cloudy, with scattered, spitting rain, and she stayed inside and watched TV. Talk shows, mostly: a whole new world. People would say anything on television, she found. Family members who hadn't spoken in years spoke at length for the camera. Women wept in public. By the time Delia turned the set off her face ached, as if she'd attended too many social events. She went out for a walk and bought a new book to read, not a romance but something more serious and believable, about poor people living in Maine. For her walk she wore her Miss Grinstead cardigan, which clung gently to her arms and made her feel like a cherished child.

Twice she sent postcards to Noah at camp. *Nice weather, nice waves,* she wrote. That sort of thing. She bought a card for Joel too but couldn't decide what to say. In the end, she wrote Belle instead. *This was a really good idea. Thank you for setting things up for me.* Belle's friend Mineola, a dyed brunette in pedal pushers and stiletto heels, always greeted her amiably but otherwise left her alone, which suited Delia just fine.

Occasionally some jolt to the senses—a whiff of coconut oil, the grit of sand in her swimsuit seams—brought to mind the old family beach trips. She was returning her umbrella to the rental stall one afternoon when a child cried, "Ma, make Jenny carry something too!" which swept her back into that packing-up moment toward sunset each day when children beg to stay a little bit longer and grown-ups ask who's got the rafts, where's the green bucket, will somebody grab the thermos? She remembered the bickering, and the sting of carelessly kicked-up sand against burned skin, and the weighty, soft-boned weariness. She recalled each less-than-perfect detail, and yet still she would have given anything to find herself in one of those moments.

Whose sneakers are these? Someone's forgetting their sneakers! Don't come to me tomorrow whining about your sneakers!

She bought a postcard showing a dolphin, and she wrote on it, *Dear Sam and kids, Just taking a little holiday, thinking about you all.* Then it occurred to her that they might assume she was referring to this whole past year, not a mere two weeks in Ocean City; and she wasn't certain how to clarify her meaning. She tore the card in half and threw it away.

On her last night, she was supposed to meet Ellie at The Sailor's Dream. She regretted having agreed to it. Carrying on a conversation struck her all at once as a lot of work. However, canceling would have been work too, so she showed up at the appointed hour in front of the restaurant. Ellie was already standing under the awning. She wore a white halter dress shot with threads of silver, the kind of thing you'd expect to see on cruise ships, and she carried a little white purse shaped like a scallop shell. Men kept glancing over at her as they passed. "Why, Delia! *Look* at you!" she called. "Aren't you all healthy and rosy!" Delia had forgotten how good it felt to have somebody know her by name and act glad to see her coming.

The Sailor's Dream had the padded-leather atmosphere of an English gentlemen's club, but with some differences. The carpet, for instance, gave off the same mushroom smell as the one in Delia's motel room. And all the waiters were deeply tanned.

"So tell me," Ellie said as soon as they were seated. "Have you been having a good time?"

"A lovely time," Delia told her.

"Was this your first vacation by yourself?"

"Oh, yes," Delia said. "Or rather . . ."

She wasn't sure whether traveling alone to Bay Borough qualified as a vacation or not. (And if it did, when had her vacation ended and her real life begun?) She met Ellie's eyes, which were fixed on her expectantly.

"Doesn't it feel funny going swimming on your own?" Ellie asked.

"Funny? No."

"And what about eating? Have you been eating in your room all this time?"

"Goodness, no! I ate out."

"I *hate* to eat out alone," Ellie said. "You don't know how I admire you for that."

They had to stop talking to give their orders—crab imperial for Delia, large green salad hold the dressing for Ellie—but as soon as the waiter moved away, Ellie said, "Did you practice beforehand? Before you left your, ah, previous place of residence?"

"Practice?"

"Did you *use* to eat out alone?"

Delia began to see what Ellie was up to here: she was hoping to gather some tips on how to manage single life. For next she said, "I never did, myself. I never even walked down a street alone, hardly! Always had some escort at my elbow. I was awfully popular as a girl. Now I wish I'd been a little less popular. You know how long ago I first thought of leaving Joel? Three months after we were married."

"Three months!"

"But I kept thinking, *What would I do on my own, though?* Everyone would stare at me, wonder what was wrong with me."

She leaned even closer to Delia. Lowered her voice. "Dee," she said.

"Yes?"

"Did you *have* to leave?"

Delia drew back slightly.

"Like, were you in just . . . an impossible position? Had to get out? Couldn't have survived another minute?"

"Well, no," Delia said.

"I don't want to pry! I'm not asking for secrets. All I want to know is, how desperate does a person need to get before she's certain she should go?"

"Desperate? Oh, well, I wouldn't say . . . well, I'm *still* not certain, really."

"You're not?"

"I mean, it wasn't an actual decision," Delia told her.

"Take me, let's say," Ellie said. "Do you think I made a mistake? There you are in that house with my husband; do you think I was overreacting to leave him?"

"I'm not married to him, though. There's a difference."

"But you must know what he's like, by now. You know how persnickety he is and how . . . right all the time and always criticizing."

"Joel, criticizing?" Delia asked. "Belle Flint says he worships you! He's trying to keep the house exactly like you left it—hasn't anyone told you?"

"Oh, yes, *after* I left it," Ellie said. "But while I was there it was, 'Why can't you do it this way, Ellie?' and, 'Why can't you do it that way, Ellie?' and these big cold silent glowers if I didn't."

"Is that so," Delia said.

And just then she saw Sam standing in front of the fridge, delivering one of his lectures on the proper approach to uncooked poultry. Sam was so phobic about food poisoning you'd think they lived in some banana republic, while Joel never mentioned it. No, Joel's concerns were more endearing, she thought—his household maps and his chore charts. They so plainly arose from a need for some sense of stability. All he was really after was *sureness.*

Or could the same be said for Sam?

Their food arrived, and the waiter flourished a pepper mill as big as a newel post. He asked, "Would either of you like—?"

"No, no, go away," Ellie said, waving a hand. As soon as they were alone again, she turned back to Delia. "Three months after our wedding," she said, "Joel went to a conference in Richmond. I said to myself, 'Free!' I felt like dancing through the house. I almost *flew* through the house. I played this kind of game with myself, went through all his drawers and packed his clothes in boxes. Packed what hung in his closet too. Pretended I lived by myself, with no one peering over my shoulder. He wasn't due home till Wednesday, and I planned to put everything back Tuesday night so he'd never guess what I'd done. Except he came home early. Tuesday noon. 'Ellie?' he said. 'What *is* this?' 'Oh,' I told him, 'it's just I wanted to picture what it would feel like to have more drawer space.' That's how women get their reputations for ditsiness. The real reason wasn't ditsy in the least, but who's going to tell him the real reason?"

She hadn't touched her salad. Delia plucked a piece of crab cartilage from her tongue and set it on the side of her plate.

"In a way, the whole marriage was kind of like the stages of mourning," Ellie said. "Denial, anger . . . well, it *was* mourning. I'd go to parties and look around; I'd wonder, did all the other women feel the same as me? If not, how did they avoid it? And if so, then maybe I was just a crybaby. Maybe it was some usual state of affairs that everybody else gracefully put up with."

Finally she speared a lettuce leaf. She nibbled it off her fork with just her front teeth, rabbitlike, all the while fixing Delia with her hopeful blue gaze.

"That reminds me of Melinda Hawser," Delia told her. "This woman I met at Belle's last Thanksgiving. The way she talked, I figured she'd be divorced by Christmas! But I run into her uptown from time to time and she's still as married as ever. Looks perfectly fine."

"Exactly," Ellie said. "So you can't help thinking, *Wouldn't I have been fine too? Shouldn't I have stuck it out?* And you get to remembering the good things. The way he loved to watch me put on my face for a party so I always felt I was doing something bewitching; or after the baby was born, when we weren't allowed to have sex for six weeks and so we just kissed, the most wonderful kisses . . ." Now the blue eyes were swimming with tears. "Oh, Delia," she said. "I *did* make a mistake. Didn't I?"

Delia looked tactfully toward a brass lamp. She said, "It's not as if you couldn't *un*make it. Jump in the car and drive back home."

"Never," Ellie said, and she dabbed beneath each eye with her napkin. "I would never give him the satisfaction," she said.

And what would have become of Delia if Ellie had answered otherwise?

Belle told Delia she hadn't missed a thing in Bay Borough, not a blessed thing. "Dead as a tomb," she said, driving languidly, one-handed. "Little fracas in town council—Zeke Pomfret wants to drop the baseball game from Bay Day this year, switch to horseshoes or something, and Bill Frick wants to keep it. But no surprises *there*, right? And Vanessa swears she's known about me and Horace all along, but I don't believe her. And we've set the wedding date: December eighteenth."

"Oh, Christmastime!" Delia said.

"I wanted an excuse to wear red velvet," Belle told her.

They left the glitter of the beaches behind and rode through plainer, simpler terrain. Delia watched shabby cottages slide by, then staid old farmhouses, then an abandoned produce stand that was hardly more than a heap of rotting gray lumber. She would never have guessed, the first time she traveled this road, that she could find such scenery appealing.

At the Millers' house, the front lawn was mowed too short and crisply edged, and each shrub stood in a circle of fresh hardwood chips. Evidently Joel had found himself with an abundance of spare time. Inside, the cat cold-shouldered her and then trailed her footsteps in a guilt-provoking way as Delia walked through the empty rooms. The house was tidy but somehow desolate, with subtle signs of bachelorhood like a huge wet dish towel instead of a proper washrag hanging over the kitchen faucet, and a thin film of grease coating the stove knobs and cupboard handles (those out-of-the-way places men never think to clean). On her bureau, a note read: *Delia—I've gone to pick up Noah. Don't fix supper; we'll all grab a bite out someplace. J.* Also, she had mail: a handwritten invitation on stiff cream paper. *Driscoll Spence Avery and Susan Felson Grinstead request your presence at their wedding, 11 a.m. Monday, September 27, in the Grinstead living room. R.S.V.P.*

What a lot could be deciphered from a couple of dozen words! For starters, the writing was Susie's (blue ink, running steeply downhill) and no parents' names were mentioned—certain proof that she was proceeding on her own. Sam must have acquiesced, though, because the wedding would take place at the house. The date was harder to figure. Why September? Why a Monday morning? And had Susie found a job or had she not?

Delia wished she could phone and ask, but she felt she didn't have the right. She would have to respond by mail, like any other guest.

Of course she planned to attend.

She looked up and met her own face in the bureau mirror—her eyes wide and stricken, her freckles standing out sharply.

When they told her that her firstborn was a girl, she had been overjoyed. Secretly, she had wished for a girl. She had planned how she would dress her in little smocked dresses; but Susie, it turned out, insisted on jeans as soon as she could talk. She had planned how they would share womanly activities (sewing, baking pies, experimenting with skin-care products), but Susie preferred sports. And instead of a big white wedding, with Susie swathed in antique lace and both her parents beaming as they jointly (in the modern manner) gave her away, here Delia stood in an Eastern Shore ranch house, wondering what sort of ceremony her daughter was inviting her to.

Noah seemed to have grown two inches while he was at camp, and the macramé bracelets he wore around both wrists pointed up the new brownness and squareness of his hands. Also, he'd developed a habit of saying, "Are you inputting that?" in a way that already seemed to be exasperating Joel. They sat in a booth at Rick-Rack's, Joel and Noah on one side and Delia on the other, and she could observe Joel's wince even if Noah couldn't.

"Take my word for it," Joel told him finally. "I have indeed managed to grasp your meaning, but I would certainly not choose to convey that fact in computer jargon."

"Huh? So anyhow," Noah said, "at camp they made us do fifty push-ups every morning. Fifty, are you inputting that? I guess they wanted to kill us off and keep our fees for nothing. So me and Ronald went to the infirmary—"

"Ronald and I," Joel said.

"Right, and tried to get a health excuse. But the dumbhead nurse wouldn't write one. She goes, like—"

"She said."

"She said, like—"

Their food came—burgers for Noah and Joel, pork barbecue sandwich for Delia. "Thanks, Teensy," Noah said.

"Sure thing," Teensy said cheerfully.

"Mrs. Rackley to *you*," his father told him.

Noah glanced across at Delia. Delia merely smiled at him.

"Daddy's been asking where you got to these last couple of weeks," Teensy said to Delia.

"I went to Ocean City."

"Yes, I told him so, but he couldn't seem to keep it in mind. He said, 'She never even mentioned it! Just walked on out and left!' His memory's a whole lot worse lately."

"Oh, I'm sorry to hear that," Delia said.

"He says things are coming at him too fast for him to take in. And Rick tells him, just trying to be nice, tells him, 'Oh, I know exactly what you—' but Daddy says, 'Don't you poke your black self into this!' and I said, '*Daddy!*'—"

Teensy broke off, glancing at Joel. "Well," she said. "I guess I better get back to work."

She slid her hands down her apron front and hurried away.

"Remarkable," Joel said.

He seemed to have no inkling that it was his impassive gaze that had sent her rushing off.

"Maybe Mr. Bragg should go live in Senior City," Noah said.

"I don't think he can afford it," Delia told him.

"Maybe they have scholarships. Or grants or something, are you in-putting that?"

Joel rolled his eyes.

"So anyhow," Noah said, picking up his burger. "Next thing, me and Ronald worked out that we'd pretend we were injured. Only we couldn't do it both at once, because it would look kind of fishy."

"You went about it all wrong," Joel told him. "Nothing good ever comes of resorting to subterfuge."

"To what?"

"Subterfuge."

"What's that?"

Joel stared across the table at Delia. His eyebrows were raised so high that his forehead resembled corduroy.

"He means something underhanded," Delia told Noah. "Something sneaky."

"Oh."

"He means you should have protested the rule openly. Or so I assume." She expected Joel to elaborate, but he was still gaping. "Is that what you meant?" she asked him.

"He doesn't know what 'subterfuge' is!" Joel said.

She took her sandwich apart and started spooning in coleslaw.

"He never heard the word 'subterfuge.' Can you believe it?"

She wouldn't answer. Noah said, "It's no big deal. Geez."

"No big deal!" Joel echoed. "Don't they teach kids anything in school these days? 'Subterfuge' is not all that arcane, for God's sake."

Delia watched Noah decide not to ask what "arcane" meant.

"Sometimes I think the language is just shrinking down to the size of a wizened little pellet," Joel told her. "Taken over by rubbish words, while the real words disappear. The other day, I discovered our cafeteria supervisor didn't know what cutlery was."

"Cutlery?" she asked.

"It seems the word has dropped out of use."

" 'Cutlery' has dropped out of use?"

"That's the only explanation I can think of. I told him we were ordering a new supply of cutlery, and he said, 'What's that?' "

"Oh, fiddlesticks," Delia said. "*You* know what cutlery is," she told Noah.

He nodded, although he didn't risk demonstrating.

"See there? It hasn't dropped out of use! Teensy," Delia called, "could we have more cutlery, please?"

"Coming right up," Teensy said, and behind the counter they heard the rattle of knives and forks.

Delia looked triumphantly at Joel.

"Oh. Well . . . ," he said.

Noah grinned. "Way to go, Dee," he told her. And eventually even Joel started smiling.

Delia smiled too, and put her sandwich back together and gave it a pat. Underneath her breath she was making a humming sound—a thin, sweet, toneless hum, not much different from purring.

18

Binky's baby was born on Labor Day—very fitting, Nat said. He telephoned that same afternoon; he spilled the news in a swelling voice that seemed about to break. "Eight pounds, eleven ounces," he crowed. "James Nathaniel Moffat."

"James!" Delia said. "It's a boy?"

"It's a boy. Can you believe it?" He gave one of his bearded chuckles. "I'm not sure I'll know what to *do* with a boy."

"You'll do fine," Delia said. "Noah's off on a picnic right now, but he'll be thrilled when I tell him. How's Binky?"

"Couldn't be better. She just *sailed* through this, and so did James. Wait till you see him, Delia. He's got the roundest face, little pocket watch of a face, and lots of blondish hair, but Binky says . . ."

To listen to him, you would never have guessed he had been through this experience four times.

Delia had overstated when she said Noah would be thrilled. Oh, he was interested, in a mild sort of way—wanted to know who the baby looked like, and what the board of directors had said. But when Wednesday morning rolled around, he asked if he couldn't put off his regular visit. School had just reopened, and he wanted to try out for the wrestling team. Delia said, "How about we look in on the baby for just a second, and then I drop you at tryouts afterward?"

"Can't we do it tomorrow?"

"Tomorrow I have tutoring, Noah, and the day after is the Grade Mothers' Tea, and if you wait too long your grandpa's going to think you don't care. I'll phone ahead and tell him you can stay just a minute."

"Well, okay," Noah said halfheartedly.

When she picked him up at school, he was trying to elbow Jack Newell off the sidewalk, and she had to tap her horn to catch his attention. He disentangled himself, jerked open the passenger door, and fell into the car. "Hi," she told him, but he just slid down in his seat and jammed his Phillies cap on his head. Then, out on the highway, he said, "I've got to stop doing this."

"Doing what?"

"I can't spend all my time visiting people! Mom, and Grandpa . . . I'm in the eighth grade now! I've got important activities!"

He cracked froggily on "activities," and Delia shot him a glance. His voice was about to start changing, she realized. Oh, Lord, here she was with yet another adolescent.

But all she said was, "Maybe you could switch your visits to weekends."

"Weekends I hang out with my friends! I'd miss all the fun!"

"Well, *I* don't know, Noah," she said. "Talk it over with Nat and your mom."

"And could you please drive something under ninety miles an hour? I'm not going to *live* to talk it over, riding with a maniac."

"Sorry," she said. She slowed. "Take a peek at what I found for the baby," she told him. "It's on the back seat."

He glanced back, but he didn't reach for it. "Why don't you just *tell* me what it is," he said.

"A little bitty pair of athletic shoes, not any bigger than thimbles."

"Huh."

In the old days, nothing could have stopped him from peeking at that gift.

The day was cool and cloudy, with a forecast of rain, but all they encountered during their drive was a stray drop or two on the windshield. Noah listened to a radio station where the singers screamed insults, while Delia played calmer songs in her mind—a technique she had learned with her own children. She was just starting "Let It Be" when they turned in at Senior City.

"You've got to be kidding," Noah said.

Next to the double front doors stood a four-foot-tall wooden cutout of a stork, sporting a pale-blue waistcoat and carrying a pale-blue bundle. Pale-blue balloons floated from the portico. The lobby bulletin board (which ordinarily bore cards of thanks from convalescents and sign-up sheets for bus trips to the shopping outlets in York) was plastered with color snapshots of an infant just minutes old. Three women wearing the regulation jaunty neck scarves stood peering at the photos and discussing the significance of hand size. One woman said large hands in infancy meant great height in adulthood, but another said that held true only for puppies.

In the elevator they found Pooky, taking one of her never-ending rides. Today, though, she seemed fully aware that she had reached Floor One, and she said, punching Three for them, "If you hurry you'll be in time for the burping."

"Oh, have you seen him?" Delia asked as they rose.

"Seen him twice. I was one of those in the lobby yesterday when they brought him home from the hospital. I hope that gift is not shoes."

"Well, sort of," Delia said.

"So far he's got Swedish leather clogs, inch-long flip-flops, and eentsy little motorcycle boots. And that's not even counting all we've knitted."

The elevator stopped with a lilt, and the door slid open. "I would come with you," Pooky called after them, "but I've got to get back to my apartment and finish childproofing."

It was Nat who answered when they rang the doorbell. "There you are!" he said. "Come in, come in!" He was using his cane today, but he walked rapidly and bouncily as he led them toward the bedroom. "James is just having a snack," he called over his shoulder.

"Should we wait out here?" Delia asked.

"No, no, everyone's decent. Bink, sweetheart, it's Noah and Delia."

Binky was sitting against the headboard of the bed, dressed but in her stocking feet. The receiving blanket draped over her bosom covered the baby's face, so all they could see was a fiery little ear and a fuzzy head. "Oh, look at him!" Delia whispered. It always seemed the bottom dropped out of her chest when she saw a new baby.

Noah, though, looked everywhere but. He stuck his hands in his back pockets and studied a distant corner of the bedroom till Binky, winking at Delia, asked, "Want to hold him, Noah?"

"Me?"

She removed the baby from her breast, at the same time adroitly rearranging the blanket. The baby's eyes were closed, and he made nostalgic little smacking movements with his lips, which were rosebud-shaped, tightly pursed. He did have big hands, with long, translucent fingers knotted just under his chin. "Here," Binky said, holding him out to Noah. "Just support the back of his head, like this."

Noah received him in an awkward, jumbled clump.

"He seems to be a very easy baby," Binky said as she buttoned up. "Most of the day he's slept, which is miraculous considering all the callers we've had. Your mother phoned, Noah; wasn't that nice? That was so nice. No word from the other three yet, but I hope—"

"Oh, forget it, just forget it, hon," Nat told her. "Who cares about them!" He gave an angry shake of his head, as he often did when his daughters were mentioned. "Let's go sit in the living room."

They followed him—Noah still carrying James, feeling his way with his feet—and settled amid an uncharacteristic clutter of slippers and afghans and gift boxes. Already the apartment had that rainy, sweet, baby-powder smell.

Binky unwrapped the athletic shoes and laughed and passed them to Nat, and then, at Delia's request, she brought out the baby's motorcycle boots. A present from her sons, she said; they claimed to be disgusted with her, but Peter had cut classes to deliver these in person. Then Nat reported on their ride to the hospital ("I said, 'Binky,' I said, 'didn't I say from the start we should have gone to Floor Four?'"), and Binky rehashed the birth, which all in all, she said, had been a cinch compared to her first two. ("I shouldn't discuss this in mixed company," she said, "but ever since Peter was born, I just never have known when I needed to tinkle. The best I can do is go every couple of hours, just in case.")

Noah looked downright queasy by now, so Delia stood up to collect the baby—an excuse to feel, for an instant, the limp, crumpled weight of that little body—and return him to Binky. "We have to get Noah to his tryouts," she told Binky. "Is there anything I can do for you? Grocery shopping? Errands?"

"Oh, no. Nat's taking wonderful care of me," Binky said.

Nat, Delia happened to know, felt the ache of his flashbacks most keenly when he was driving, but she couldn't point that out when he was looking so proud of himself.

Joel seemed very nervous about the Grade Mothers' Tea. He must be wishing for Ellie, Delia thought—for Ellie's clever, theme-party style of entertaining. But when she proposed phoning Ellie and asking for suggestions, he said, "Why should we do that? We're surely capable of a simple tea, for God's sake."

"Yes, but maybe—"

"All we need from Ellie is her recipe for lemon squares," he said.

"Lemon squares. I'll ask."

"The ones with the crispy glaze on top. Also her cucumber sandwiches."

"Well, *I* can make a cucumber sandwich," Delia snapped.

"Oh. Of course."

After that he let the subject drop—forced himself to drop it, no doubt. On Friday afternoon, though, he paced circles around her as she set up the party-sized percolator on the dining room buffet. "This group will be nothing but women," he told her.

"Well, so I gathered: grade mothers."

"There is a grade father, but he's away on business. It's one hundred percent women."

She went to draw the water for tea. He followed. "You do plan to help with the conversation, don't you?" he asked.

She hadn't expected to. She had envisioned herself biding her time in the kitchen, like those discreet lady housekeepers in nineteenth-century novels. She had been looking forward to it, in fact. She said, "Oh, um . . ."

"I can't do it alone, Delia."

"Well, I'll try."

But no help was needed, she found. Fourteen women showed up—two for each homeroom, minus the traveling father and a mother who couldn't get off work. All of them were acquainted, most since childhood, and they slid easily into topics so well established that they seemed to be speaking in code. "What did Jessie finally decide?"

"Oh, just what we figured all along."

"Darn!"

"Yes, but who can say—maybe this will turn out like the Sanderson girl."

"Well, that's a thought."

Delia wore her navy knit, on the assumption that teas were dressy, but the guests wore slacks or even jeans, and one had on a sweatshirt reading COMPOST HAPPENS. They all seemed unduly curious about her. They kept coming up to ask, "So how do you *like* it here? How is Noah handling all this? Has he adjusted?" When she answered, the voices nearby would trail off and others would edge closer. "Golly," one said, "Mr. Miller must be awfully glad to have you. And you help with the tutoring too! You tutor the Brewsters' youngest! Mr. Miller's always complaining he can't find enough math tutors."

Now she knew how new girls must feel on their first day at school. But she responded politely, keeping a smile on her face, holding the teapot before her like a ticket of admission. She liked Bay Borough very much, thank you, and Noah was getting on well, and she had probably learned more from her pupils than they had learned from her. The usual remarks. She could have made them in her sleep. Meanwhile Joel stood talking with two women at the other end of the room, nodding pensively and from time to time wrinkling his brow. He no longer seemed nervous. And when she approached with a plate of cookies, he said, "You're doing a fine job, Delia."

"Thank you," she said, smiling.

"It may be the best tea we've given."

"Oh! Well, the lemon squares were Ellie's, remember; Ellie was kind enough to—"

Then one of the women asked Joel what had been planned for the Fall Bazaar, and Delia escaped to the kitchen.

She straightened things up, wiped counters, put a few items in the dishwasher. The cat had taken refuge under the table, and she hauled him forth to cuddle him and scratch behind his ears. For a while she watched the minute hand of the wall clock visibly jerk forward: five-eighteen to five-nineteen to five-twenty. Time for the guests to recall that they should get home and fix supper. In fact, she could detect a certain shift in the blur of voices—the rising notes of leave-taking.

"Didn't I have a purse?"

"Has anyone seen my keys?"

And then, "Where's *Delia*? I should say goodbye to Delia."

She had to drop George and make another appearance, see them all to the door. ("It was good meeting you, too. I'd be happy to give out the recipe.") Then she returned to the dining room, and Joel unplugged the percolator while that woman who always has to stay longest (there was one at every party) fussily separated the clean spoons from the dirty ones. "Please," Delia told her, "just let them be. I've got a system." How quickly the old formulas came back to her: *I've got a system. Don't give these a thought. It won't be a bit of trouble.*

The woman was reluctant to leave and stood awhile gazing into her purse, as if searching for instructions on where to go next. She had triplets, Delia had overheard—all boys, all just starting to drive. Easy to understand why she wasn't rushing home. Finally she said, "Well, thanks, you two. This was a real treat." And darting a smile in Joel's direction, she told Delia, "Isn't he helpful! Why, if I asked *my* husband to clear, he'd think I was joking. He would just act . . . bemused and go off with his pals."

Joel waited till she was gone before he snorted. " 'Bemused'!" he echoed. "Discouraging, isn't it?"

Delia wasn't sure what he was objecting to. (At least, she thought, he hadn't seemed to notice the woman's apparent belief that they were a couple.) She carried a stack of cups to the kitchen and began fitting them into the dishwasher.

"You realize what's going to happen," Joel said. He set the percolator on the counter. "Bit by bit, more and more people will say 'bemused' in place of 'amused,' thinking it's just the twenty-dollar version, the same way they think 'simplistic' is a twenty-dollar 'simple.' And soon enough that usage will start showing up in dictionaries, without so much as a 'non-standard' next to it."

"Maybe she really did mean 'bemused,' " Delia said. "Maybe she meant her husband was puzzled; he was perplexed that she'd asked him to help."

"No, no. Nice try, Delia, but no, she meant 'amused,' all right. Everything's changing," Joel said. "It's getting so we're hardly speaking English anymore."

She looked over at him. He was winding the cord around the percolator, although it hadn't been emptied yet or washed. "Yes, I've noticed that's what bothers you, most times," she told him.

"Hmm?"

"Most times it's not grammatical errors—other than the obvious, like 'me and him.' It's the *new* things, the changes. 'Input' and 'I'm like' and 'warm fuzzies.' "

Joel shuddered. Too late, Delia recalled that he had never to her knowledge mentioned "warm fuzzies"—that it came from Ellie's interview. She hurried on. "But think," she said. "Probably half your own vocabulary was new not so long ago. Well, 'twenty-dollar,' for instance! These terms pop up for good reason. 'Glitch.' 'Groupie.' 'Nickel-and-diming.' 'Time-shifting.' "

"What's time-shifting?" Joel asked.

"When you record a TV program to view later. Mr. Pomfret used to say that, and I thought, *Oh, how . . . economical!* Don't you sometimes *wish* for new words? Like a word for, a word for . . ."

"Freckles," Joel said.

"Freckles?"

"Those freckles that are smaller than ordinary freckles," he said. "And paler. Like gold dust."

"And also, um, tomatoes," Delia said, too quickly. "Yes, tomatoes. You have the true kind and then you have the other kind, the supermarket kind, the same color as the gums of false teeth, and those should be given a whole separate name."

"And then," Joel told her, "that different sort of surface people take on when you really begin to see them."

She had nothing to say to that.

"They get so noticeable," Joel said. "It seems you can feel every vein and pulse underneath their skin. You think, *All at once she's become* . . . but what word would you use? Something like 'textured,' but textured to the vision, instead."

His eyes seemed a softer hue of brown now, and that long, notched mouth had grown shapelier, more tender.

"Goodness!" she said, spinning toward the door. "Is that Noah?"

Although Noah had gone to Ellie's and was not due home till bedtime. And anyhow, would be dropped off at the front of the house, not the back.

Sometimes when Delia said to herself, *Only x number of days till Susie's wedding,* she felt a clammy sense of dread. *This is going to be so embarrassing. How will I face them? It's not a situation I've been taught to handle.* But other times she thought, *Pshaw, what's so hard about a wedding? We'll have all those other people there as buffers. I can just breeze in, breeze out. Nothing to it.*

For a while she had an idea that Susie might ask her to come early, as much as several days early, to help with preparations. At least that way she wouldn't feel like a mere guest. She pounced hopefully on the mail every morning, cleared her throat before answering the phone, delayed notifying Joel of her plans till she knew how long she'd be gone. But Susie didn't ask.

And sometimes she considered not attending. What purpose would she serve? They wouldn't even miss her. A day or two after the wedding, one of them might say, "Hey! You know who didn't show up? Delia! I just now remembered."

And still other times, she fantasized that they could hardly wait to see her. "Delia!" they would cry, "Mom!" they would cry, running out onto the porch, letting the door slam behind them, flinging their arms around her.

No, cancel that. More likely they would ask, "What do you think *you're* doing here? Did you imagine you could waltz back in just as if nothing had happened?"

She should remember to bring her invitation, in case there was any question.

She broached the subject to Joel at Sunday breakfast, having waited till the very last day for word from Susie. Sunday was a good time anyhow, because Noah was there, wolfing down buckwheat pancakes; the conversation couldn't get too probing. She said, "Joel, I don't know if I mentioned or not"—knowing full well she had not—"that I'll need to take the day off tomorrow."

"Oh?" he said. He lowered his newspaper.

"I have to go to Baltimore."

"Baltimore," he said.

"Geez, Delia!" Noah said. "I promised my wrestling coach you'd give a bunch of us a ride to the meet tomorrow."

"Well, I can't," she said.

"Well, geez! *Now* what'll we do?"

"Your coach will think of something," Joel told him. "If you wanted to volunteer Delia's services, you should have asked her first." But he was keeping his eyes on Delia's face as he spoke. "Is this a, some kind of emergency?" he asked her.

"No, no, just a wedding."

"Ah."

"But it's one I'd very much like to attend, a family wedding, you know, and so I thought if you didn't mind . . ."

"Of course; not at all," Joel said. "Could I drive you to the bus station?"

"Oh, thanks, but I'm going by car," Delia said. "Baltimore's on Mr. Lamb's sales route, it turns out."

Joel probably had no idea who Mr. Lamb was, but he nodded slowly, eyes still fixed on her face.

"So!" she said. "Now, I assume I'll be back by evening. Maybe suppertime, but I can't be sure; I'm returning by bus; so I've left a chicken salad in the fridge. There's a tub of Rick-Rack's coleslaw next to it, biscuits in the bread drawer . . . But I bet I'll be back by then, anyhow."

"Should I meet your bus?"

"No; Belle's doing that. I'll call her when I get into Salisbury."

"You could call me instead."

"No, really, I have no idea when . . . it might be late at night or something. It could even be the next day; who knows?"

"The next day!" he said.

"If the reception runs very long."

"But you *are* coming back," he said.

"Well, of course."

Now Noah was watching her too. He looked up from his pancakes and opened his mouth, but then he didn't speak.

Toward noon she set out on a walk, planning to end at the Bay Arms for lunch whenever her ankle grew tired. It had rained in the morning, but now the sun was shining, and the air felt so thick and warm that she regretted wearing her sweater. She pulled it off and swung it loosely from one hand. Everywhere she looked, it seemed, she saw people she knew. Mrs. Lincoln waved to her from the steps of the A.M.E. church, and T. J. Renfro, roaring past on his Harley, called out, "What say, Teach!" and on Carroll Street she ran into Vanessa and Greggie, poking along in matching yellow slickers. "Delia! I was just about to phone you," Vanessa said. "Want to ride with me to Salisbury tomorrow?"

"Oh, I'm sorry, I can't," Delia said. "I have to go to Baltimore."

"What's in Baltimore?"

"Well," Delia said, "my daughter's getting married."

She'd told Belle this too, but nothing more, and now all at once she felt an urgent need to pour it all out. "She's marrying her childhood sweetheart and I'm so worried how to behave at the wedding but I really want to be there; her father thinks she's rushing things since she's only twenty-two years old and I say—"

"Twenty-two! How old were you when you had her: twelve?"

"Nineteen," Delia said. "I married right out of high school, practically."

Vanessa nodded, unsurprised. Well, most of the girls in Bay Borough married right out of high school, Delia supposed. And had babies at nineteen or so. And ended up mislaying their husbands somewhere along the line. Vanessa's only question was, "What'd you buy for a wedding gift?"

"I thought I'd wait to see what they needed."

"That's always smart," Vanessa said. "Greggie! Let the bug go where it wants to. That's what I did with my girlfriend," she told Delia. "I thought I'd get her a hand-held mixer but then I thought no, why not wait, and I'm so glad I did because the first time I went to visit her I saw she didn't have one single piece of Tupperware in her whole entire kitchen."

Vanessa's face, above the slicker, glowed with a fine film of sweat, and her eyes seemed very pure and clear, the whites almost blue-white. Delia suddenly felt like hugging her. She said, "Oh, I'd have loved to ride to Salisbury with you!"

"Well, another time," Vanessa said. "There's this place there we buy our barley in bulk, to make Grandma's gripe water recipe."

"Gripe water?" Delia asked.

"It's for babies. Soothes the colic and the afternoon frets and the nighttime willies."

Delia wished they made gripe water for grown-ups.

She dreamed she was in Bethany, walking down the beach. Ahead she saw a highway, a sort of narrowing and darkening of the sand until it turned to asphalt, and there sat her old Plymouth, baking in the sun. Sam encircled her upper arm to guide her toward it. He settled her inside.

He shut the door gently after her and leaned through the open window to remind her to drive carefully. She woke and stared at the motes of darkness swarming above her bed.

From Noah's room she heard a repetitive dry cough, beginning sharply each time as if he'd tried first to hold it in—one of those infuriating night coughs that won't quit. For half an hour or so, she lay debating whether to get up and bring him the lozenges from the medicine cabinet. Possibly he would stop coughing on his own. Or possibly he was asleep, in which case she hated to wake him. But the cough continued, pausing and then resuming just when she thought it was finished. And then she heard the creak of a floorboard, so she knew he wasn't asleep.

She rose and went to open her door. "Noah?" she whispered.

Instantaneously, almost, Joel was standing in front of her. She couldn't see him so much as feel him, as the blind are said to feel—a tall, dense, solid shape giving off warmth, his moon-pale pajamas only gradually emerging from the dark of the windowless hall.

"Yes, Delia?" he whispered.

He had misunderstood, she realized. "Noah" and "Joel" sounded so much alike. The same thing often happened when she called one of them to the phone. She said, "I thought I heard Noah."

"I was just going to see to him," he said.

"Oh."

"I'll bring him some of those cough drops."

"All right."

But neither one of them moved.

Then he stepped forward and took her head between his hands, and she raised her face and closed her eyes and felt herself drawn toward him and enfolded, surrounded, with his lips pressing her lips and his palms covering her ears so all she could hear was the rush of her own blood.

That, and Noah's sudden cough.

They broke apart. Delia stepped back into her room and reached for her door with trembling hands and shut herself inside.

19

Mr. Lamb's car was a dull-green Maverick with one orange fender and a coat-hanger antenna. Inside, several scale-model windows filled the back seat—wood-framed, double-sashed, none more than twelve inches tall. Little girls from the neighborhood were always begging to play with them. The bottom of his trunk was paved with panes of clear plastic, so that when Delia leaned in with her suitcase, she had an impression of bending over a gleaming body of water. Mr. Lamb told her the plastic was pretty near indestructible. "Slide your suitcase right on top," he told her. "It won't do the least bit of harm. That's where our product beats anything else on the market. When I go to a house that has pets? I like to lay a square of Rue-Ray on the floor and let a dog or cat march straight across, gritching with its toenails."

Rue-Ray, Delia knew, took its name from the married couple who owned the company, Ruth Ann and Raymond Swann. They lived above their workshop on Union Street, and Mr. Lamb was their one and only salesman. She had learned all this from Belle, but still she felt like laughing at the sound of those two slurred, slippery R's.

It also struck her as comical that Mr. Lamb turned out to be so talkative. Before they reached Highway 50, even, he had gone from storm windows (their noise-reduction powers) to the wedding gift he planned for Belle (a complete set of Rue-Rays, fully installed) to his philosophy of salesmanship. "The important thing to remember," he said, veering around a tractor, "is that people like to proceed through a process. A regular set of steps for every activity. For instance, the waitress wants to give you your bill before you hand her your credit card. The mechanic wants to tell all about your fuel pump before you say to go ahead and fix it. So I ask my customers, I ask, 'You notice any drafts? Northern rooms any colder than southern?' I know they've noticed drafts. I can hear their durn windows rattle as I'm speaking. But if I let folks kind of like describe the symptoms first—say how the baby's room is so cold at night she has to wear one of those blanket sleepers with the fold-over flaps for the hands—why, they get this sense a certain order has been followed, understand? Then I'm more apt to make the sale."

Unfortunately, he was one of those drivers who feel the need to look at the person they're talking to. He kept his muddy, deep-socketed eyes fixed on Delia, his scrawny neck twisted in his collar, while Delia glued her own eyes to the road as if to make up for it. She watched a column of cypress trees approach, then a long-dead motel as low to the ground and sprawling as a deserted chicken shed, then a strip of fog-filled woods where entire clouds seemed trapped in a web of branches. Only a few leaves here and there had developed a faint tinge of orange, and she could imagine that it was still summer—that it was last summer, even, and she had not lost the year in between.

"Many people don't realize that salesmen consider such things," Mr. Lamb was saying. "But salesmen are a very considering bunch, you'll find. I say it comes from traveling by car so much. Belle had an idea we should travel by car for our honeymoon, but I told her I just didn't know if I'd focus on her right, driving along with my own thoughts like I do."

Delia said, "Hmm." Then, because she felt she wasn't holding up her end of the conversation, she added, "*I* honeymooned by car."

"You did?"

She had startled herself; she very nearly turned to see who had volunteered this information. "I don't recall that it interfered with our focus, though," she said.

He glanced at her, and she gave an artificial cough. Probably he thought she'd meant something risqué. "Of course, my husband was not so attuned to driving as you must be," she said.

"Ah," Mr. Lamb murmured. "No, not many people are, I suppose."

Sam's car at the time had had a bench seat, and Delia had sat pressed against his side. He had driven left-handed, with his right hand resting in her lap, his fingers loosely clasping her nylon-clad knee, their steady warmth sending a flush straight through her. She coughed again and gazed out her window.

The passing houses looked arbitrarily plunked down, like Monopoly-board houses. The smaller the house, it seemed, the more birdbaths and plaster deer in the yard, the tidier the flower beds, the larger the dish antenna out back. A brown pond slid by, choked with grappling tree trunks. Then more woods. In Delia's girlhood, the very word "woods" had had an improper ring to it. "So-and-so went to the woods with So-and-so" was the most scandalous thing you could say, and even now the sight of winding, leafy paths conjured up an image of . . . Well.

Goodness, what was _wrong_ with her?

She forced her thoughts back to Mr. Lamb. He seemed to be talking about dogs. He said that after he and Belle were married they might just get themselves one, and then he went into a discourse on the various breeds. Golden retrievers were sweet-natured but sort of dumb, he said, and Labs had that tendency to whap a person's knickknacks with their tails all the time, and as for German shepherds, why . . .

Gradually the scenery began to have a different feel to it. Around Easton she started noticing bookstores and European-car dealers, neither of which existed in Bay Borough, and by the time they hit Grasonville, the road had widened to six lanes that whizzed past gigantic condominiums, flashy gift shops, marinas bristling with masts.

Mr. Lamb settled finally on a collie. He said he might name it Pinocchio if it had one of those long, thin noses. They crossed the Kent Narrows bridge, high above the grassy marshland. Delia could remember when crossing the Kent Narrows could use up the better part of an hour—long enough to get out of your car and stretch your legs and buy a watermelon, if you wanted—but that was in the days of that cranky old drawbridge. Now they were beyond the narrows in no time flat and speeding through a jungle of factory outlet stores, strip malls, raw new housing developments with MODELS NOW OPEN! DESIGNER TOUCHES! And then here came the lovely, fragile twin spans of the Bay Bridge, shimmering in the distance like something out of a dream, while Mr. Lamb decided that he might let Pinocchio have one little batch of puppies before they got her fixed.

The countryside seemed so green, so lush, after the scoured pallor of the Eastern Shore. Delia was surprised when they turned onto Highway

97—a road she'd never heard of—but then she relaxed in the glide of brand-new pavement not yet bordered with commercial claptrap.

She might have been away for decades.

Mr. Lamb said Belle was scared of dogs but he thought it was all in her head. Where else could it be? Delia wondered. Not that he gave her a chance to ask. He said women just got these notions sometimes. Delia smiled to herself. It amused her to see how quickly he had come to take his happiness for granted.

On the Baltimore–Washington Parkway, the lanes were so crowded that she gathered herself inward, as if that would help their car slip through more easily. She looked ahead and saw the Baltimore skyline—smokestacks, a spaghetti of ramps and overpasses, monster storage tanks. They began to pass gray-windowed factories and corrugated-metal warehouses. Everything seemed so industrial—even the new ballpark, with its geometric strutwork and its skeletons of lights.

"Mr. Lamb, ah, Horace," she said, "I don't know where you're headed, but if you'll drop me at the train station, I can grab a taxi."

"Oh, Belle told me to drive you direct to the door."

"But it's only . . ." She checked her watch. "Not quite ten," she said, "and I don't have to be there till eleven."

"No, no, you just sit tight. Belle would never forgive me," he said.

She would have put up more of an argument, but she was afraid her voice would shake. All at once she felt so nervous. She wished she'd worn a different dress. In spite of the gloomy weather, it was warmer than she had expected, and her forest-green was too heavy. It was also too . . . Miss Grinsteadish, she realized. Luckily, though, she had brought other clothes. (She had debated which was worse: wearing the wrong thing or lugging a suitcase to a wedding, and like the most insecure schoolgirl, she had opted for the suitcase.) Maybe once she reached the house she could duck into a vacant room and change.

Mr. Lamb was asking her a question. Which street to take. She said, "Up Charles," using as few words as possible. She didn't seem to have enough air in her lungs.

How intimate this city seemed! How quaint and huddled to itself! After all those superhighways, Charles Street threaded between tall buildings like the narrowest little river in a ravine.

She opened her bag and searched for Susie's invitation. Yes, there it was, safe and sound.

Mr. Lamb was admiring the Johns Hopkins campus now. He said

he had a cousin who had gone there for one semester. "Oh, really?" Delia murmured. He said he himself had not had the opportunity of a college education, although he felt he would have put it to good use. Delia wished he would stop talking. He was so irrelevant, so extraneous. She kept swallowing, but there was something in her throat that wouldn't go away.

When she told him to turn left he had to ask her to repeat herself. "Hah?" he asked, like a deaf old man. Like an irritating, deaf old man.

At a red light on Roland Avenue, a jogger ran toward them, a young woman with her long dark hair in a topknot and the fingers of her right hand delicately clasping two fingers of her left hand. A man in a tweed hacking jacket crossed with a tiny chihuahua. ("Now, there is a dog you couldn't pay me to put up with," Mr. Lamb said. "Might as well own a mosquito.") The air had a greenish, fluorescent quality, as if a storm were brewing.

She showed him where to turn next, which house to park in front of. (Was this how their house looked to strangers: so brown, so hunched, so forbidding?) She said, "I can get my things myself, if you'll just pop the trunk." But no, he had to unfold from the car, walk around to the rear, take forever hauling forth her suitcase. "Thanks! Bye!" she said, but even then she wasn't free to go. He kept on standing there, swaying slightly on his long, scuffed shoes and gazing at the house.

"We could easily manage the round one," he told her.

"Pardon?"

"The round little window up top there, what is it, over a stairs? Rue-Ray makes round windows all the time."

"Oh, good," she said, and she shook his hand, just to get him to leave. But an odd thing happened. Holding on to his bunched-twig fingers, meeting his bucktoothed, wistful smile, she unaccountably began to miss him. She felt like climbing back into the car with him and riding along for the rest of his trip.

Four vehicles stood in the driveway: Sam's Buick, a beat-up purple van, Eliza's Volvo, and a little red sports car. The mulberry tree had already started to scatter its chewed-looking leaves, and she had to step around acorns on the front walk. Evidently no one had thought to sweep.

The shutters had been repaired. The replacement louvers were a different color, though—a paler, flatter brown, as if they'd been given just a primer coat and then forgotten. There was a new sisal mat at the top of the porch steps, and a foil-wrapped pot of yellow chrysanthemums next to the door.

Knock, or walk in?

She knocked. (The doorbell would have been too much, somehow.) No answer. She knocked harder. Finally she turned the knob and stuck her head in. "Hello?"

For a house that was hosting a wedding in less than forty minutes, it didn't seem very welcoming. The front hall was empty, and so was the dining room, although (as Delia found when she advanced) the dining-room table was spread with a white tablecloth. She set down her suitcase, intending to continue into the kitchen, but just then Eliza walked through the kitchen door with a mug of something hot. She was concentrating so hard on the mug that it took her a second to see Delia. Then she said, "Oh!" and stopped short.

"I know I'm early," Delia told her.

"Oh, Delia! Thank heaven you're here!"

"What's wrong?" Delia asked. She was alarmed, of course, but also grateful to find herself in demand.

"Susie's changed her mind," Eliza called over her shoulder. She was proceeding toward the stairs.

Delia grabbed her suitcase and followed. "Changed her mind about marrying?" she asked.

"That's what she claims."

"When did this happen?"

"This morning," Eliza tossed back, starting upward. She wore a new dress, a magenta A-line Delia couldn't imagine her buying, and patent-leather shoes whose heels rang against the stair treads. "Last night she slept in her old room," she was saying, "and this morning when we got here I asked Sam, 'Where's Susie? Isn't she up yet?' and he said—"

Delia felt disoriented. Susie's *old* room? Where was her new room? And who were "we" and what place had they got there from?

There wasn't a sign of Sam. Not a sign.

They had reached the second floor now, and Eliza, holding the mug in both hands, was sidling through the partly open door of Susie's bedroom. "Look who I brought with me!" she said. Delia set her suitcase down and walked in after her.

The room itself was what she noticed first. Frilly and flowered and stuffed with chintz since the days when it had been Linda's, it was a hollow cube now, unsoftened by curtains or rugs, furnished only with a foldaway cot and an ugly, round-cornered bureau from the attic. Susie sat cross-legged in a welter of blankets, wearing striped pajamas. Surrounding her—seated on the cot as well but all dressed up, even overdressed—were Linda, Linda's twins, and a pudgy young woman Delia could almost name but not quite. They raised a flank of alerted faces when Delia entered, but Delia looked only at Susie. Susie said, "Mom?"

"Hello, dear heart."

She bent over Susie and hugged her, absorbing that unique Susie smell that was something like dill weed. Still holding on to her, she settled on the cot beside her.

"Mom, I don't want to get married," Susie said.

"Then don't," Delia told her.

"Delia Grinstead!" Linda shrilled. "We're trying to talk some sense into her, do you mind?"

Linda was wearing bifocals—a new development. The twins had grown several inches, and from their dresses—stiff, mint-colored lace that hardly touched their skinny frames—Delia suspected they might be bridesmaids. Everyone looked so detailed, so eerily distinct: she couldn't explain it. Her eyes kept returning to Susie, craving the sight of her uncombed hair and her sweetly round chin and her cushiony lower lip.

The other young woman wore mint lace too. Driscoll's sister, that's who she was. Spencer? Spence. Driscoll Spence Avery's sister, Spence Driscoll Avery. "This exact same thing happened with my cousin," Spence was saying. "You all remember my cousin Lydia. She cried the whole way down the aisle of St. David's, and now she's happy as a clam and her husband is a bigwig in D.C."

"What kills me," Susie told Delia ("kills be," was how it came out, as if earlier she had been crying), "is we just signed a two-year lease on this fancy-shmancy apartment near the harbor. I've been phoning the realtor ever since last night, but all I get is his answering machine. I don't want to say why I'm calling, because then he might not call back. I figure if I could just reason with him . . . I left three different messages; I told him it was urgent; I said could he please get back to me immediately? But he didn't! It's after ten and he hasn't phoned and I'm stuck with that damned apartment forever!"

She was wailing now. Eliza said, "Oh, dear, oh, dear . . . have some tea, why don't you," and Linda said, "Well, for God's sake, Susie, the realtor is the least of it!"

But Delia told Susie, "I'll take care of it. You just give me his number, and I'll keep calling till I reach him."

"Would you?" Susie asked. She jumped up, trailing blankets, and went over to the bureau. "Wait a minute, I'll find his . . . Here. Mr. Bright, his name is. Tell him I apologize and I know I said we wanted it but to please, please let me out of this if he has a shred of human decency."

"You may have to forfeit your deposit," Delia said, examining the business card Susie handed her.

"Delia! Honest to God!" Linda cried. "Could we address the issue here?"

"Well, I'm not getting married, Aunt Linda," Susie told her, "so why waste time discussing it? Has anyone seen my jeans?"

She was roaming the room now, rummaging under the cot, scooping up a T-shirt. How shiny the floor was! Delia couldn't help noticing. Then she recalled the refinishers from last year's beach trip, and she felt all the more like an outsider. She set her handbag primly on her knees, trying to take up less space. But Linda noticed her anyway. She said, "Tell her, Delia."

"Tell her what?"

"Tell her all brides go through this."

Did they? Delia hadn't. Before her own wedding, her one concern had been that Sam would die before she got to be his wife. *Groom Slain on Wedding Eve*, the papers would read, or *Tragic Accident En Route to Nuptials*, and Delia would miss her chance for perfect happiness.

She had never doubted for a moment that it *would* be perfect.

Susie was dressing now, nonchalantly facing the wall while she peeled off her pajama top and hooked a gray-seamed bra. (Accustomed to locker rooms, she evidently thought nothing of changing in public.) Her back was a beautiful butterscotch color, as sturdy as a tree trunk. She pulled her T-shirt over her head, shook her hair loose, sauntered toward a suitcase on the floor, and bent to study its contents. Everybody watched. Finally Eliza, still holding the mug, said, "Susie has a very nice wedding dress. *Don't* you, Susie. Show your mother your wedding dress."

"It's a dopey dress," Susie said, but she turned and crossed the room to fling open the closet door. White chiffon exploded forth. Both twins rose, as if pulled by strings, and floated toward the closet with their lips parted. Susie slammed the door shut again. A filmy white triangle poked through on the hinge side.

"And your veil? Show her your veil," Eliza urged.

Obediently, Susie stomped over to the wastebasket. *"Here's* my veil," she said, and she pulled out several tatters of gauze and a headband of white silk roses snipped into jagged shreds.

The two aunts sucked in their breaths. Spence said, "Great God Almighty!"

"Allow me to model it for you," Susie said. She clamped the headband around her neck, then let her head flop to one side and half closed her eyes and stuck out her tongue.

"Susan Grinstead!" Linda shrieked.

"So," Susie said calmly, removing the headpiece. "Driscoll and I are sitting downstairs last night, watching a movie. Folks had made this big federal case about how I ought to spend my final unwedded hours in my ancestral home."

"Well, how would it have *looked*?" Linda demanded.

Susie dropped the headband into the wastebasket. "So the two of us are in the study like old times," she said, "and the phone rings. It's this high-school-sounding boy; you can tell the call is taking all his courage. He clears his throat and says, 'Um, yes! Good evening. May I please speak to Courtney, please?' I tell him he has the wrong number. Not ten seconds later: *ring!* Same boy. 'Um, good evening. May I please—' 'You must have misdialed,' I tell him. So we're just getting settled again—Driscoll had rented *Nightmare on Elm Street*; he thinks it's the major motion picture of our time—when sure enough: *ring! ring!* Driscoll says, 'Let me handle this.' He picks up the receiver. 'Yeah?' he says. Listens a minute. Says, 'Tough luck, feller. Courtney doesn't want to have anything to do with you.' And slams the phone down."

"Oh! How mean!" Delia said involuntarily, and Eliza clucked her tongue. Then everyone looked at Driscoll's sister. "Well, sorry, Spence," Delia told her, "but really! That poor boy!"

"Yes, it *was* mean," Spence said complacently. She prinked her skirt out around her. "But that's how guys are, Sooze. What can you do?"

"It is not how guys are," Susie said. "Or if it is, all the more reason not to marry *anyone*. But for sure I'm not marrying Driscoll. And don't you defend him, Spence Avery! There is nothing you can say that will make him look good to me after that."

Thérèse said, "Couldn't he just apologize?"

"Apologize to who? Not to me; I'm not the one whose feelings he hurt. No, I see it all now," Susie said. She was drifting around the room without apparent purpose, wearing her T-shirt and pajama bottoms. She stopped in front of the mirror to yank at a handful of hair; then she continued her travels. "All these things I've been trying not to notice all this time. Like when we get ready to go out and he says, 'How do I look?' and I say, 'Fine,' he just goes, 'Thanks,' and never mentions how *I* look. Or when I'm telling him something that happened, he won't let me tell it my way. He always has to interrupt, to sort of . . . redirect. So I'll say, like, 'This patient of Dad's came into the shop today—' and right away he's, 'Wait a minute, you know who your dad's patients are? Isn't that a violation of confidentiality?' and, 'Now hold on, she asked for this by brand name? Or not,' and, 'What you should have told her is . . .' Till I feel like saying, 'Just shut up! Shut up! Shut up and let me get to the end of this story which I'm sorry now I ever began!' And speaking of my shop—"

What shop? Delia would have asked, except she didn't want to sound like Driscoll.

"He has never for one minute supported me on that. Oh, at the start he did because he thought it was just a whim, you know? He figured it would pass. But then when I borrowed the money from Gram—"

Eleanor had lent Susie money? (Eleanor didn't believe in lending money.) Susie must have noticed Delia's bafflement, because she said, "Oh. I've started this kind of like, business. House in a Box, I call it."

"A darling little business!" Linda chimed in.

"Got a mention in *Baltimore* magazine," Eliza said, "two and one-quarter inches long."

"I'd moved to an apartment," Susie told Delia, "after that bust-up with Dad. Me and Driscoll found a place on St. Paul Street. Well, I couldn't have afforded anything by myself. And I was looking for a job, but first I wanted to settle in, you know? Buy supplies for the kitchen and all. We had some furniture from home but no incidental stuff, skillets and stuff; didn't own so much as a spatula. So there I was, running around the stores, spending a fortune I didn't have, finding one thing one place and another thing another place. . . . I said, 'Wouldn't it be great if they sold a kitchen in a *box*? Kind of a one-stop purchase?' And that's what started me thinking. So now I've got this little showroom out past the fairgrounds; well, it's only about three feet square, but—"

"It's darling!" Linda said.

"And I sell these boxes: Kitchen in a Box, Bathroom in a Box . . .

just things I buy in bulk and combine in a kit and deliver, you know? I've tacked an ad on every campus bulletin board for miles around. I'm open seven days a week and I'm slaving away like a dog; that's why I set the wedding for a Monday. Didn't want to miss the weekend shoppers. As it is, I'm closed till Friday, which I hate. But Driscoll acts like this is some kind of hobby. When he heard about Gram's loan he was, 'Oh, you wouldn't want to get in over your head, hon.' He was, 'Wouldn't want to bite off more than you can chew, now, hon.' So discouraging and dampening; he doesn't think I'm up to this. Doesn't credit me with the brains to buy a simple shower curtain for college kids and a few damn rings to hang it with."

"Now, Susie, that is just not fair," Spence told her staunchly. "He's only trying to protect you."

"Plus he leaves spat-out fruit pits all over the apartment," Susie said.

Eliza suddenly set the mug on the bureau, as if this were the last straw.

"So I stopped *Nightmare on Elm Street*," Susie said, "and I gave him back his ring and sent him packing. And then I phoned the realtor, but I guess it was too late at night. And I'm sorry you all came for nothing, but I said to Dad, I said, 'Which is more trouble: calling off the wedding or suing for divorce?' "

"Where *is* Sam, anyhow?" Eliza wondered.

Delia was glad she hadn't had to ask that herself.

"He went to dress for the wedding," Susie said.

"But you did tell him—"

"I did tell him I'd changed my mind, but he just shut his eyes a minute and then he said he had to go dress for the wedding."

Yes, that was Sam, all right.

Delia stood up. She said, "I should get busy."

"Doing what?" Linda demanded.

"I have to phone the realtor."

She started for the door (the nearest phone was in Eliza's room), but Linda said, "Delia, my stars! Are you just going to accept this?"

"What else can I do?" she asked. "Drag her by the hair to the altar?"

"You could reason with her, for God's sake!"

"This is not a now-or-never proposition," Delia told her. (Really she was telling Susie, who stood leaning against the bureau, watching her with interest.) "If Susie isn't sure she wants to marry Driscoll today, she can marry him tomorrow, or next week, or next year. What's the hurry?"

"*She* can say that," Linda told the others. "*She* didn't fork over an arm and a leg for three airline tickets."

Delia latched the door quietly behind her.

At the same time, Sam's door, catty-corner across the hall, swung open and he stepped forth. He was tugging down his shirt cuffs. He caught sight of her and stopped still. They were separated by the stairwell, with its varnished wooden balustrade, and so she waited where she was. He said, "Why, Delia."

"Hello, Sam."

His suit was that slim, handsome black one they had bought on sale several years ago. His face looked thinner. It was all straight lines— straight gray eyes and an arrow of a nose and a mouth that seemed *too* straight until (she knew) you saw the upward turns at the corners. His glasses happened to be slipping, the way they had a tendency to do, and when he raised a hand to adjust them he appeared to be doubting his eyesight. She said, "Didn't you know I was coming?"

"I knew," he said.

"Well . . . I guess you heard Susie's not going through with the wedding."

"She'll go through with it," he said. He rounded the balustrade— no, not to approach her (though already she had taken her first step forward to meet him), but to start down the stairs. "We'll proceed as planned," he sent back as he descended. "She'll come around."

Delia gazed down at him over the railing. She could clearly see his scalp through the fair hair on top of his head. *If I glimpsed him in a crowd, I'd say he was just another worn-out, aging man*, she thought. But she didn't really believe that.

She made herself turn away and go into Eliza's room.

Here, too, she sensed a difference. The furniture was the same, but there wasn't a single object on the bureau, and only the gaunt, old-fashioned black telephone sat on the nightstand. Had Eliza changed rooms, or what? This one had been hers from the day she was born.

I knew, he had said. *We'll proceed as planned*, he had said.

Well, no point dwelling on it. Delia propped the realtor's card on the nightstand, lifted the receiver, and dialed.

"This is Joe Bright," a man announced thinly. "I can't come to the phone right now, but you may leave a message after the beep."

"Mr. Bright, this is Delia Grinstead calling, Susan Grinstead's mother. Could you please get back to me as soon as possible? It's very important. The number is . . ."

As she hung up, she heard the doorbell ring downstairs. "Hello, come in," Sam said, and next she heard one of those drawling, gravelly, Roland Park matron voices. Instantly, she lost all her confidence. She wasn't wearing enough makeup and her dress wasn't dressy enough, and when she looked in Eliza's mirror, her face seemed unformed and childish.

But she might have just imagined that, because when she started down the stairs (planting her feet just so and holding her head very high), everyone looked up at her with the most respectful attention. The pastor—a tweedy, shaggy man—said, "Mrs. Grinstead! What a pleasure!" and Driscoll's parents broke off their chitchat with Sam.

"It's a pleasure to see *you*, Dr. Soames," she said. (Considering she attended church only on major holidays, she was impressed that she remembered his name.) "Hello, Louise. Hello, Malcolm."

"Why, hello, Delia," Louise Avery said, as if they'd last seen each other yesterday. She was a leathery woman with a lion's mane of gold hair rearing back off her forehead. Her husband—older, smaller, crinkly-eyed—said, "I don't guess you could have brought some sunshine with you."

"Oh," Delia said, and she glanced past him toward the door. "Is it raining?" she asked.

"No, no, we're sure it will hold off till later," Louise said. "I was telling Malcolm this morning, I said, 'At least this is one good thing about a home wedding.' Can you imagine if they'd planned a big formal church affair? Or something out on the lawn?"

"No, I certainly . . . can't," Delia said.

She looked over at Sam, but he was fitting Dr. Soames's rolled umbrella into the umbrella stand, and he didn't meet her eyes.

Maybe they would just have this wedding without the bride, she thought. Was that the plan?

In the living room, all available chairs had been lined up facing the fireplace. That must be where Dr. Soames would stand. In the dining room, Linda and Eliza were setting out platters of pastries. In the kitchen, the twins were gazing enraptured at Driscoll; he was discussing the honeymoon. "I told Sooze we ought to just head to Obrycki's for crabs," he said. "Call *that* our honeymoon, in keeping with the general tone of the wedding. And she said, 'Or why not carry-out?' but in the end we settled for three days at— Oh, Miz Grinstead! Hey there!"

"Hello, Driscoll," Delia said. She was puzzled to see him looking so cheerful. He was dressed in a navy suit with a white rose in the lapel, and his face had a scrubbed, fresh, oblivious look. She said, "Ah, have you . . . talked with Susie this morning?"

"Oh, can't see the bride before the ceremony, Miz Grinstead!" he said, wagging a finger.

"Yes, but just to talk with her—talk on the phone, maybe," Delia said.

"Say! Where's those ushers of mine, Miz Grinstead? Any sign of them yet?"

"Ushers?"

"Ramsay and Carroll!"

"Well, no, I . . . gosh, I hope someone thought to wake them," she said. Neither one of the boys had yet lost the knack of sleeping till noon.

"Maybe you should give them a ring," Driscoll told her.

With her mind on wedding matters, she thought for an instant he meant the kind of ring you wear on your finger. She looked at him blankly. Then Eliza, sailing past with a three-tiered cake stand, said, "Why they need ushers anyhow, with no one but family attending and seats for not more than a dozen . . ."

"It's so these glamorous bridesmaids will have somebody's arm to hang on to," Driscoll said, winking at the twins. Marie-Claire giggled, and Thérèse sent him a solemn, worshipful stare and stood straighter inside her tepee of mint lace.

Delia gave up and left the kitchen. She would go see if Susie had decided to get married after all. Who knows, she might have. (For it was easy to believe, in such company, that she was at this moment adjusting her magically reconstructed veil.) And if so, then Delia would check on the boys, make sure they were awake and dressed.

But the boys were already downstairs, standing by the front door in their suits. They looked astoundingly grown-up—Ramsay square-jawed and almost portly now, Carroll as wiry as ever but taller, with something more carved about his face. With them were Ramsay's girlfriend, Velma, wearing an upside-down pink hollyhock of a dress that ended just below her crotch, and her little daughter (who? oh, Rosalie) in aqua. Ramsay said, "Hi, Mom," and kissed Delia's cheek, and Carroll allowed her to hug him, and Velma said, "Well, hey! How was your trip?"

"It was fine," Delia said.

So that was the way it would be, evidently. She had been settled into a convenient niche in people's minds: just another of those eccentric wives you see living year-round in an Ocean City condo or raising horses on a farm in Virginia while their husbands continue their workaday routines in Baltimore. Nobody gave it a thought.

She passed through the assembling guests, smiling and murmuring greetings. Sam's uncle Robert squeezed her hand but went on listening to Malcolm Avery rehash a recent golf game. Sam himself was helping his aunt Florence out of a black rubber raincoat that looked capable of standing on its own.

"How do we know when the ceremony starts?" someone asked at Delia's elbow.

It was Eleanor, in a gray silk shirtdress. "Oh, Eleanor!" Delia cried, and she threw her arms around Eleanor's spare figure.

"Hello, dear," Eleanor said, patting her shoulder. "How nice you came for this."

"Of course I came! How could I not?"

"I was wondering about the procession," Eleanor said smoothly. "Do they plan any kind of music? Susie has been admirably sensible about the arrangements, but how will we know when the bride walks in?"

"Eleanor, I'm not even sure there's going to *be* a bride," Delia said. "She claims she's reconsidered."

"Ah. Well, you'll want to go see to her, then," Eleanor said, unperturbed. "Run along; I can take care of myself, dear."

"Maybe I *should* go," Delia said, and she fled up the stairs.

Susie was alone now, dressed in jeans and sneakers, lounging on the cot and reading *People* magazine. She glanced up casually when Delia knocked on the doorframe. "Oh, hi," she said. "Are they having conniptions down there?"

"Well, they don't . . . exactly grasp the situation yet," Delia said. "Susie, should I send Driscoll up?"

"Driscoll's here?"

"He's here in his wedding suit, waiting for you to come marry him."

"Well, shoot," Susie said, lowering her magazine. "It's not like I haven't informed him in plain English."

"And his parents are here, and Dr. Soames—"

"Did you talk to the realtor?" Susie asked.

"I left a message."

"Mom. This really, really matters. If I don't get that lease revoked, it'll be me they come after for the money, do you realize that? I'm the one who actually signed my name. And I didn't want to say this in front of Driscoll's sister, but the fact is, I am dirt poor. I'm in debt for the wedding, even—four hundred twenty-eight dollars, no thanks to that father of mine."

"What did the four hundred twenty-eight dollars go for, exactly?" Delia asked out of curiosity.

"My dress and veil and the bouquet in the fridge. Aunt Eliza's footing the bill for refreshments. *Please* go call Mr. Bright. If he's still not there, tell his machine it's a life-or-death situation."

"Well, all right," Delia said. "And then should I send Driscoll up?"

"He knows where to find me."

Susie went back to her magazine. Delia started to leave, but in the doorway she turned. She said, "How come the house looks so different?"

"Different?"

"All the furniture's gone from your room, and Eliza's room seems . . . unlived-in."

"Well, it is unlived-in," Susie said, flipping a page. "Nobody lives here but Dad anymore."

"What?"

"Didn't you know that?"

"*No*, I didn't know that. What happened?"

"Well," Susie said, "let me see. First Ramsay and Dad got into a fight about—no, wait. First *Eliza* and Dad got into a fight. She claimed it was because he didn't let her know he'd be late for dinner, but the real truth is, she was making a play for him, Mom, like you wouldn't believe. It was pitiful. All us kids told her so, but she was like, 'Hmm? I don't know what you're talking about,' and meanwhile there was Dad, out of it as usual, just going about his business and paying her no mind. So one day she picks a quarrel about a totally nother issue and flounces off to visit Aunt Linda, and when she comes back she announces she's leaving for good. Now she lives on Calvert Street; that's where Linda and the twins are staying for the wedding. Okay, so *then* Ramsay and Dad got into a fight, on account of Dad calling Velma 'Veronica' by accident which Velma swore he did on purpose, and Ramsay moved to Velma's in a huff; and then Carroll moved there too because he missed his curfew one night and Dad was pacing the floor and picturing him dead on the road, he said. . . . And me: you know about me. I moved out in July, just before Ramsay."

"Yes, I suppose I . . . ," Delia said abstractedly.

"So are you going to call the realtor, Mom?"

"Oh. Right," Delia said, and after a brief pause, she walked out.

In Eliza's old room, she sat on the edge of the bed, lifted the receiver, and then stared into space.

Imagine Sam pacing the floor. Always before, it had been Delia pacing the floor, and Sam pooh-poohing her and telling her to simmer down. "How can you be so cool about this?" she used to ask him. "What have you got in your veins: ice water?" And it seemed to her that he had given a little smile at that, a gratified, sheepish little smile, as if she had paid him a compliment.

She dialed the realtor's number again. "This is Joe Bright," the machine said. "I can't come to the . . ."

"It's Delia Grinstead again, Mr. Bright. I'd appreciate your calling me at your earliest convenience," she said. And just to oblige Susie, she added, "It's a matter of life and death. Bye."

Downstairs, the voices were a woven mass, as if people had given up on the wedding and settled for a party instead. But when she descended to join them, conversation halted for a moment and people turned expectantly. She smiled at them. She was glad now she'd worn the forest-green, with the skirt that swung so alluringly just above her ankles.

She crossed the hall to the living room, and the others followed. Probably they thought this was a signal of some kind. In fact, Carroll, killingly attractive in his usher's suit, caught up with her to offer his arm and lead her to a front seat, and a moment later Eleanor joined her, escorted by Ramsay. "Put Aunt Florence in a straight chair," Ramsay muttered to Carroll. "She says her back is acting up." Delia heard the usual audience sounds—coughs and rustling skirts. Driscoll's parents settled on the couch. Dr. Soames took his place on the hearth, smiling benignly toward the room at large and extracting a folded sheet of paper from his breast pocket.

"Bridal jitters all over now?" Eleanor whispered to Delia.

"No, um, not exactly."

Velma's colorless child chose a wing chair so big for her that her Mary Janes failed to touch the floor. A young man Delia didn't know— some relative of Driscoll's, no doubt—deposited Eliza on the love seat, and Linda plopped next to her unescorted and eased her feet out of her pumps. "Is she coming?" she mouthed when she saw Delia looking at her. Delia merely shrugged and faced front again.

Now Driscoll was standing beside Dr. Soames, fidgeting with his boutonniere. And the bridesmaids were clustered at the foot of the stairs, where the ushers joined them when the very last guest had been seated.

Sam bent over Delia. She hadn't seen him coming; she drew back slightly. "Should I put the record on?" he asked her.

"Record?"

"Is she ready?"

"Oh," she said. "Well, no, I don't believe she is."

He straightened and stared down at her. He said, "Then shouldn't you be doing something?"

"Like what?"

He didn't answer. His lips were very dry and white. Delia smoothed her skirt and sat back to observe the next development.

She had never realized before that worry could be dumped in someone else's lap like a physical object. She should have done it years ago. Why did Sam always get to be the one?

Now he turned toward the record player, which was housed in a walnut cabinet at Delia's elbow. He clicked a button, and a moment later the sound of horns flared out. Delia recognized the theme from *Masterpiece Theatre*. Privately she found the selection a bit too triumphal, and she suspected from the sniff on her right that Eleanor felt the same way. Everybody else, though, sat in a reverent hush as Sam strode from the room. Delia heard his shoes crossing the hall and crisply mounting the stairs. Why, this wedding must have been planned to duplicate her own: the father of the bride escorting the bride down the stairs and through the double doorway to the center of the living room, to a spot directly beneath the gawky brass chandelier.

But suppose the bride did not stand waiting in the upstairs hall?

The footsteps must have continued, but the music drowned them out. Or maybe Sam had stopped at the top of the stairs, just beyond the guests' view, instead of going in to talk with Susie. That was more like him. In any case, the trumpets blatted on while people smiled at one another (*Isn't this so informal and so family*, they were probably thinking), and then the footsteps started down again. But anyone could tell that no bride was keeping pace with that rapid, noisy descent.

Sam marched to a spot directly in front of Dr. Soames. Delia wondered, for an instant, whether he planned to carry on regardless—take the vows in Susie's place. But he moistened his lips and said, "Ladies and gentlemen . . ."

It was Delia who reached over and lifted the phonograph needle.

That was the least she could do, she figured, since it was Sam who announced that he was sorry to have to say this, he hated to put people out like this, but the wedding had been postponed a bit.

"Postponed" was optimistic, in Delia's opinion. But people did seem to view it as the most minor readjustment in the couple's schedule. Linda announced crossly that she and the twins were reserved on a noon flight home two days from now, totally nonrefundable, which she damn well hoped Miss Susie would bear in mind. Dr. Soames, leafing through a pocket diary, muttered something about meetings, visits, Building Fund . . . but later in the week looked all right, he said; looked quite promising, in fact.

Even Driscoll's mother, who seemed more distressed than anyone, turned out to be thinking mainly of a reception she was giving after the honeymoon. "Will they be married by Saturday night, do you think?" she asked Delia. "Could you just, maybe, feel Susie out a little? We've got fifty-three of our closest friends coming; you too if you're still in town."

"Maybe Driscoll will know more when they've finished talking," Delia said. "I'll have him get in touch with you the minute he comes downstairs."

For Driscoll had at long last gone up to speak with Susie. He should have done that at the start, if you asked Delia.

The rain that had been threatening all day was falling now, and people scurried to their cars once they were out the front door. First Dr. Soames left, and then Sam's aunt and uncle with Eleanor, and Driscoll's sister with the unnamed usher, and finally Driscoll's parents. Then Eliza said, "Well! I thought that little sports car of Spence's had boxed me in for life!" and she swept out, with Linda and the twins in tow. But Ramsay and Carroll stayed on, dogging Delia's heels as she carried platters of food to the kitchen, which meant that Velma and Rosalie had to stay as well. They made themselves scarce, though, watching TV in the study. Meanwhile Sam set the living-room furniture in order, and Carroll told Delia the entire plot of a movie he and Ramsay had seen. This man, he said, had been stuck in some kind of time warp where he had to keep reliving the same one day over and over. Delia thought that with all the topics they could have been discussing, Carroll had made a mighty peculiar choice, but she just said, "Mmhmm. Mmhmm," as she flitted around the kitchen, swathing various platters in plastic wrap. Carroll followed so closely that she couldn't reverse direction without advance notice, and Ramsay wasn't far behind.

But then Sam brought in the tablecloth, bunched in a clumsy cylindrical shape, and the atmosphere changed. Carroll stumbled in his recitation. Ramsay got very busy shutting cupboard doors. Both of them seemed to be watching Delia even while they were looking away.

"Tablecloth," Sam said. He passed it to her.

Delia said, "Oh! Good! Thanks!" Then she said, "I'll just take it down to the . . . ," and she wheeled and walked through the pantry and down the basement stairs.

Not that that tablecloth had the slightest need of laundering.

At the bottom of the stairs the cat was waiting, gazing up at her intently. Vernon always escaped to the basement when there were guests. She said, "Vernon! Have you missed me?" and she bent to cup his round, soft head. "I missed you too, little one," she whispered. He was purring in that exaggerated way cats have when they want to put humans at ease.

Footsteps crossed the pantry and started down the stairs. Delia rose and went over to the washing machine. Vernon vanished into thin air. The machine was full of damp laundry, but she stuffed in the tablecloth anyhow and recklessly poured detergent on top.

Behind her, Sam cleared his throat. She turned. "Oh! Hello, Sam," she said.

"Hi."

She busied herself with the washing machine, selecting the proper cycle and rotating the dial with a zippery sound. Water started rushing; pipes clanked overhead. Outside the dust-filmed window, ivy leaves bobbed beneath the falling raindrops.

"As soon as Driscoll comes down," she said, turning again to Sam, "I'm going to call a cab, but I figured I'll wait till then so I can say goodbye to Susie."

"A cab to where?" Sam asked.

"To the bus station."

"Oh," Sam said. Then he said, "It would be silly to call a cab, with all these cars at hand. Or rather, I don't mean silly, but . . . I could drive you. Or Ramsay could, if you prefer. Ramsay's been using the Plymouth, you know."

"Oh, has he?" Delia asked. "How has it been running, anyway?"

"All right."

"No more electrical problems?"

He just looked at her.

"Well, thanks," she said. "I probably *will* ask for a lift, if it isn't too much trouble."

She left unanswered the question of who would drive her.

They went back up the stairs, Delia preceding Sam and moving with self-conscious gracefulness. The kitchen was empty now. The dining-room table had a naked look; Sam had not thought to replace the candelabra after removing the tablecloth. The hall was empty too, but they paused there a minute, gazing toward the silence overhead.

"I don't think he's going to change her mind," Delia said.

"It's only wedding-day nerves."

"I think she's serious. I think she really means this."

"You remember how she was when she was little," Sam said. "She used to get these fixations, remember? Like when she wanted to wear her cowboy pajamas to kindergarten. You said no and she came to breakfast in her underwear, but you pretended not to notice and by schooltime she'd put on a skirt."

"A skirt and her pajama tops, which I'd covered partway with a bandanna to hide the snaps," Delia said. "We compromised. There's a difference."

She was touched, though. She wasn't sure why. Maybe it was because she herself figured so prominently in his story, as if he had taken notes on what she'd done and then attempted, years later, to do the same.

She stayed in the hall a moment longer, in case he wanted to tell her anything more, but evidently he didn't. He turned away and made for the living room. Delia first smoothed her dress and adjusted her belt (not wanting to appear to chase him), and then she followed.

In the study, the lamps were unlit, and everyone sat in pewter-gray light watching TV—Velma and the boys on the couch, Rosalie on the floor between her mother's feet. They turned as Sam and Delia entered. "What's for lunch?" Carroll asked.

Delia said, "Lunch!"

"We're starving."

She checked the time. It was after one. She glanced toward Sam for some cue (the kitchen wasn't hers anymore; the household wasn't hers to feed), but he didn't help her. Then footsteps sounded overhead.

"Driscoll," Sam said.

Rosalie continued gaping at a soap opera, but the rest of them went out to the hall—Velma and the boys rising in an elaborately bored, stretching way, everyone moving slowly so as not to seem overeager. They gathered at the bottom of the stairs and watched Driscoll descend.

He looked distraught. His hair was raked and ropy, and his tie was wrenched askew. When he reached the bottom step he shook his head.

"No wedding?" Delia asked him.

"Well, I wouldn't say *no* wedding."

"What, then?"

"She says she hates me and I'm not a good person and now she sees she never loved me anyway."

"So, no wedding," Delia mused aloud.

"But if I want to change her mind, she says, I know what I should do."

"What should you do?"

"I don't know," Driscoll said.

Sam snorted and moved off toward the living room.

"Send flowers?" Velma suggested. "Send a singing telegram?"

"I don't know, I tell you. I said, 'Couldn't you give me a hint?' She said, 'It'll come to you. And if it doesn't,' she said, 'it's a sign we shouldn't get married.' "

"Send a Mylar balloon with a message printed on?" Velma pursued.

"Saying what, though?" Driscoll asked.

"Driscoll," Delia said, "I believe your mother wants to talk with you."

"Oh. Okay," he said dully.

He stood thinking a moment. Then he gave his shoulders a shake and let himself out the front door—no raincoat, no umbrella, nothing. The rain was falling so hard it was bouncing off the porch railing.

"Hire a skywriter!" Velma said after he'd gone.

"Mom," Carroll said, "could we just eat?"

"I'll fix something right away," she told him.

Might as well. Nobody else was going to do it.

Delia prepared a tray for Susie and brought it up to her room. She found her asleep on top of the covers—not all that surprising. Susie was the kind of person who retreated into sleep like a drug, losing whole days at times of emotional crisis. Oh, the *otherness* of Delia's children never failed to entrance her! She considered it a sort of bonus gift—a means of experiencing, up close, an entirely opposite way of being.

"Susie, honey," she said. Susie opened her eyes. "I thought you'd want something to eat," Delia told her.

"Thanks," Susie said, and she struggled blearily to a sitting position.

Delia placed the tray in Susie's lap. "It's all your favorites. Ginger cheesecake, Jewish-grandmother cookies . . ."

"Great, Mom," Susie said, shaking out her napkin.

"Lemon chiffon tartlets, chocolate mousse cups . . ."

Susie looked down at the tray.

"I had to use the wedding food," Delia explained. "There weren't a lot of groceries in the kitchen."

"Oh," Susie said. She said, "So is that . . . what everyone's eating?"

"Well, yes."

"They're eating up my wedding food?"

"Well . . . would you rather they didn't?"

"No, no!" Susie said too breezily. She picked up a tartlet.

Delia felt confused. She said, "Did you want us to save them? If you were planning on, um, rescheduling in the near future, why, then I suppose—"

"No, I said! It's fine."

"Well, what *are* your plans? I'm not trying to pressure you or anything, but Driscoll did mention . . . I'm just asking so I can make travel arrangements."

In the midst of taking a bite, Susie looked over at her.

"On account of my job and all," Delia explained.

"Oh, just *go*, if you're so set on it!" Susie burst out.

"That's not what I—"

"I'm amazed you came at all! You and your stupid job and your man friend and your new family!"

"Why, Susie—"

"Gallivanting off down the beach and leaving Dad just wandering the house like the ghost of someone, and your children . . . orphaned, and me setting up a whole wedding on my own without my mother!"

Delia stared at her.

"What did he *do*, Mom?" Susie demanded. "Was it him? Was it us? What was so terrible? What made you run out on us?"

"Sweetheart, no one did anything," Delia said. "It wasn't that clear-cut. I never meant to hurt you; I didn't even mean to leave you! I just got . . . unintentionally separated from you, and then it seemed I never found a way to get back again."

She knew how lame that sounded. Susie listened in silence, gazing over her tartlet, and now that letter she'd sent—the forced gaiety of all those exclamation points, the careful carelessness of *See ya!* and *Luv*— made Delia want to weep. "Honeybun," she said, "if I'd known you wanted help with the wedding, I would have done anything! Anything."

But all Susie said was, "Could you please phone the realtor again?"

"Yes, of course," Delia said, sighing, and she bent and kissed Susie's forehead before she left.

By a process of inaction, of procrastination (much like the one that had stranded her so far from home in the first place), Delia stayed on through the afternoon, waiting for Susie to come downstairs. But time passed, and when she went back up to check, she found Susie asleep again, the tray nearly untouched on the floor beside the cot.

Sam was in his office, presumably—doing what, she had no idea, since she hadn't seen any patients arrive. The others sat in the study watching TV, and she settled on the couch next to Velma and pretended to watch too. The good thing about TV was that everyone talked around it in an unthinking, natural way; they forgot that she was listening. She learned that Carroll had gone out three times with a girl from Holland; that Ramsay's history professor had a grudge against him; that Velma had promised Rosalie a beauty-parlor manicure if she would quit biting her cuticles. It reminded Delia of her car-pool days, when she'd been privy to all the latest gossip because children don't seem to realize that drivers have ears.

Nobody mentioned Susie.

Sam came to stand in the doorway, and when she looked over at him he asked if she would like him to go get some groceries for supper. She felt absurdly pleased. She said, "Yes, why not," and then everyone started requesting specific dishes—her tarragon chicken, her ziti salad. She went out to the kitchen and made up a grocery list. She waited for Sam to invite her along when he left, but he didn't.

Eliza phoned—her second call in two hours. "Now, where is Driscoll in all this?" she asked. "Don't tell me he's just letting her be."

"It does seem that way," Delia said. She was talking on the kitchen extension, so she didn't have to lower her voice. "I don't know *what* to think," she said. "Susie's fast asleep and Driscoll's disappeared and the rest of us are just sitting here, wondering what next."

"Mark my words," Eliza said, "they'll be married before sundown tomorrow. That's what I told Linda. I said, 'You won't even have to switch your airline reservations.' How about *you*? You're not leaving yet, are you?"

"I haven't decided."

"You can't," Eliza said. "You'd only have to turn around and come back."

"You may be right," Delia said.

The real reason she couldn't leave was Susie—her sad little face above the tartlet. But she didn't tell Eliza that.

As soon as they said goodbye she called Joel, but the telephone rang and rang. They had probably gone out for supper, ignoring what she'd left for them. They were probably at Rick-Rack's. She knew what they would order, even, and the tune of their conversation—Noah's exuberant spurts of words and Joel's neutral answers. His palms cradling her head. His mouth firm but not insistent. His body tensed as if, with every move, he had been gauging her response.

After the baby, Ellie said, *we just kissed, the most wonderful kisses* . . .

Delia hung up.

When Sam came back from the grocery store, she asked him (with her head in the fridge, tossing the question over her shoulder) whether he would mind if she stayed till tomorrow.

"Why would I mind?" he said.

It wasn't a very satisfying answer. But before she could go into it further, Ramsay and Carroll trooped through—off to the video shop, they said, to rent that time-warp movie again—and Sam left the room. Delia fixed supper by herself. Everything came back to her: those weird little nipples on the cabinet knobs, the squeak of the exhaust fan above the stove. But here she was, in Miss Grinstead's forest-green dress and old-maid shoes with the strap across the instep.

Susie did appear in time for supper. She sat at the table swaddled in a blanket, looking like a little girl awakened from her nap. But she didn't refer to the wedding, and nobody else brought it up. Then afterward they all watched the movie—even Sam, his glasses glinting in the dark. Although really it was Susie they were watching. Any time Susie made a moderately humorous comment, her brothers fell all over themselves laughing, and Velma gave a hissing titter, and Rosalie sent her a deadpan, penetrating stare.

At the end of the movie Ramsay and Velma collected Rosalie and said good night, but Carroll announced that he might as well sleep over. Delia went upstairs with him to put sheets on his bed. While she was plumping his pillow she heard Susie come upstairs too, and she knew that left only Sam in the study. She didn't go back down, therefore. Instead, she returned to the linen closet for another set of sheets, and she made up the bed in Eliza's room.

Much later, flat on her back in the dark, she heard Sam's shoes on the stairs. He crossed the hall to his room without so much as a pause, and she heard his door click shut behind him.

It was ridiculous of her to feel so wounded.

20

"This sugar caster," Linda told the twins, "was a gift from your great-great-aunt, Mercy Ramsay, when her sister married Isaiah Felson in 1899."

Delia couldn't imagine how Linda knew that. The twins, however, seemed unimpressed. They were busy admiring Carroll, who was shaking the caster upside down over his bowl of cornflakes. It was eleven-thirty in the morning, and he was only now eating breakfast. Linda and the twins had had breakfast earlier, after Eliza dropped them off on her way to work. Sam, presumably, had fixed himself something before he went into his office, and Susie wasn't awake yet. It was going to be one of those days when the tail end of one person's meal ran into the start of another's from morning to night. Delia herself was just sort of munching along with every new shift.

"Mercy Ramsay was a huge concern to her parents because she never married," Linda was saying. "She had a job as a 'typewriter,' was what they called them then, at a law office down near the harbor."

Delia glanced over at her.

Carroll was shoveling in cornflakes now, and Marie-Claire appeared to be warming her hands on the sugar caster—which was not, to tell the truth, very imposing: a chesspiece-shaped urn of dulled and dented plate.

Thérèse was setting an index finger here and there on the table to mash stray crystals of sugar and transfer them to her tongue.

Linda said, "In every generation of our family, there's been one girl who never married."

"This generation it'll be Thérèse," Marie-Claire said.

"Will not," Thérèse said.

"Will so."

The phone rang.

"If that's the school, I'm sick," Carroll told Delia.

"Carroll Grinstead! I refuse to fib for you," Delia said. She dumped the cat off her lap and rose to answer. "Hello?"

"Delia?" Noah said.

Delia turned away from the others. "What's wrong?" she asked, as quietly as possible.

"I've got a cold."

"Are you in bed?"

"I'm on the couch. Where'd you *get* to? Why aren't you back yet?"

"Well, I did try to telephone last night, but you were out," Delia said. "How'd you know where to call, anyway?"

"And that's another thing! You didn't leave a number! I had to phone Belle Flint and she said you'd gone to your family's so I told Information, 'Look for Grinstead,' and the first Grinstead turned out to be this lady and she said, 'Oh, that's my daughter-in-law you want,' and she had me write down the . . . But you said you'd be back yesterday!"

"Or today," Delia reminded him. "I'll probably catch a bus, oh, maybe this afternoon; I'll know more as soon as—"

"Is that the *realtor*?" Susie called from upstairs.

Delia covered the mouthpiece of the receiver. 'No, it's not!" she called back. Then she told Noah, "You just stay on the couch. I'll be home soon. Bye."

When she hung up, she turned to find everyone watching her. "Well!" she said vivaciously. "So!"

From their expressions, you would have thought she'd been caught in some crime.

Then Sam walked in, wearing his white coat. He was taking his lunch break, and here they were, still at breakfast. In fact, Linda had his chair, which she made no move to give up. "If it isn't the good doctor," she said in an acid tone.

Delia said, "Sam, what would you—?" and then she stopped. It wasn't her place, really, to offer him lunch. But he didn't seem to realize that, and he sat in Susie's usual seat and said, "Anything would be fine. Soup."

Soup must be what he lived on, because it was just about the only thing in the cupboard—his special salt-free, fat-free, taste-free brand, with a dancing heart on the label. She opened a tin of soya-milk mushroom and poured it into a saucepan.

Now he was asking Carroll why he wasn't in school. He was going about it all wrong, taking a drilling-in approach that would only raise Carroll's hackles, and Carroll was hunching belligerently over his cereal bowl. Both of them, Delia noticed—in fact, everyone in the room—had become less perceivable to her since yesterday. Already they had lost that slick exterior layer of the unaccustomed.

Sam said that the distant likelihood of a sibling's wedding was not sufficient grounds for playing hooky. "What do *you* know about it?" Carroll asked him. "Some of the kids in my class take off for Orioles games, for Christ's sake."

"Watch your language, young man," Sam said. Delia merely stirred the soup. She pictured Sam shifting in midair like some kind of kite or streamer, like a wind sock changing shape with changes in the wind. From one angle he was gentle and reserved and well-meaning; from another he was finicky and humorless. She remembered all at once that when she had gazed across her desk at him the morning they first met, there had been a split second when his fine-boned face had struck her as *too* fine, too priggish, and she had faltered. But then she had brushed that impression aside and forgotten it forever—or at least, until this moment.

"Please, Uncle Sam?" the twins were coaxing. Marie-Claire said, "Can't he stay home just this once? For our sakes?"

The front doorbell rang before he could answer. Everybody looked at one another, and the cat made a dash for the basement. "I'm not here," Carroll said with his mouth full. Finally Delia lowered the flame beneath the soup and went to see who it was.

In the sun-glazed windowpane at the center of the door, Driscoll Avery stood gazing off to one side and whistling. Whistling! Goodness. Delia opened the door and said, "Hello, Driscoll."

"Hey there, Miz G.!" he said, stepping inside. "Super weather."

It was, in fact. Autumn had moved in overnight, nippy and hard-edged, and Driscoll's cheeks glowed pink. He wore fall clothes, weekend clothes even though this was a Tuesday. Delia shut the door against the chill. "Come into the kitchen and have some breakfast," she said. "Or lunch, or whatever you're on."

"No, thanks. I just need to talk to Susie a minute."

"Well, I think she must be awake, but she hasn't come downstairs yet," Delia told him.

"Okay if I go up?"

"Oh, I don't know if she—"

"Please, Miz Grinstead. I believe now I've got it! I know how to get her to marry me."

Delia gave him a skeptical look, but he said, "All right?" and without waiting for her permission, he wheeled and bounded up the stairs.

It took real character not to listen for what happened next.

Back in the kitchen, everyone was waiting. "Well?" Linda demanded.

"That was Driscoll."

"Driscoll!" both twins said.

"He's gone up to speak with Susie."

The twins scooted their chairs away from the table. Linda said, "Stay right where you are."

"Can't we just—?"

"They'll never sort things out with you two making pests of yourselves."

Delia returned to the stove. She stirred the soup until it started dimpling, and then she poured it into a bowl—a bleak gray liquid that reminded her of scrub water. "Taupe soup," she said as she set the bowl before Sam. The phrase tickled her, and she gave a little snicker. Sam glanced at her sharply.

"Thank you, Delia," he said in his deliberate way.

The twins were badgering Linda about their bridesmaid dresses. Could they put them on right now? Could Linda iron their sashes where they'd wrinkled from before? Delia placed a spoon beside Sam's bowl, and he thanked her all over again and picked it up. "You go get your books together," he told Carroll. "A half day of school is better than none."

"I'm just waiting to hear what Driscoll says," Carroll told him.

"Driscoll has nothing to do with this."

"He does if the wedding is on again. And anyhow, I don't *have* my books. They're at Velma's place. So there."

Sam started spooning soup, ostentatiously composed.

"I've been in charge of getting my own self to school all fall," Carroll told him. "How come the minute I'm under your roof I'm treated like a two-year-old?"

"Because you're behaving like a two-year-old," Sam said.

Carroll pushed back from the table. His chair scraped across the floor, and he very nearly slammed into Driscoll, who arrived at that moment in the dining-room doorway. "Hi, all," Driscoll said.

"Driscoll!" the twins screeched. "What'd she say?" "Did she say yes?"

They should have known she hadn't. Driscoll had come back down far too soon, and if that were not enough, they could have read the bad news in his face, which was somber and no longer pink-cheeked, somehow thicker through the jaw. He gave a deep sigh and then turned and—it seemed for an instant—took his leave; but no, he was fetching a chair from the dining room. He dragged it back to the kitchen and placed it next to Carroll and sat down heavily. "She says I've got to do it myself," he said.

"Do what?"

"See, all night long I thought and thought," he said. He seemed to be addressing Delia, who had reclaimed her own seat at the end of the table. "I thought, *What is it Susie wants?* And it came to me: I had to set things straight with that kid who called on the phone. But the only person who might know his name was the girl he was trying to reach—Courtney. So this morning I started dialing every possible variation on you-all's number, looking for Courtney."

"Lord have mercy," Linda said.

"Well, it's simpler than it sounds. Turns out I had to transpose two digits, that was all. About my tenth or so try, I get Courtney's mom, I guess it was, and she tells me Courtney's at school."

"Ah," the twins said together.

"So I say, 'Well, I was supposed to drop off her history notes, so what I'll do, if you don't mind, I'll bring them by her house after school, is that okay? And could I please have that street address again?'"

"Cool," Carroll said.

Even Sam looked mildly interested. He had stopped eating his soup and was watching Driscoll, with his eyebrows raised.

"Lucky for me, the mom fell for it," Driscoll said. "Gave me their address straight off—place right here in the neighborhood." He paused, struck by a thought. "Carroll," he said, "*you* don't know any Courtneys, do you?"

"I know six or seven Courtneys," Carroll said.

"Any on Deepdene Road?"

"Not that I'm aware of."

"Well, anyhow," Driscoll said, "all I have to do now is ask her who her caller was."

"But what if she has no idea who he was?" Delia said.

"She might have *some* idea. If he's been hanging around her a lot, giving her, like, signals or something."

Sam was spooning up soup again, shaking his head.

"So next I go talk to Susie. Ask her to come with me to Courtney's after school. You know I can't do it alone! Strange guy showing up full of questions . . . Except Susie says no."

"No?" Linda echoed.

"No. Sends me straight downstairs again. Says I'll have to manage without her. Bring her the boy in person, was how she put it, if I want her to forgive me."

If you want to win the princess's hand, Delia thought to herself, because the errand did have a certain fairy-tale ring to it. She began to feel slightly sorry for Driscoll, although he himself seemed to be recovering his good spirits. "So now it's up to you, Miz G.," he said almost jauntily.

"Me!"

"Could you come with me to Courtney's after school?"

"Why, Driscoll, I—"

"I'll go!" Thérèse said.

"Me and Thérèse'll go!" Marie-Claire said.

Driscoll didn't seem to hear them. He said, "Miz Grinstead, you can't imagine what I feel like. I feel like I've got this . . . cloud in my chest! You think at first it's some snit she's having, some temporary snit, and you're mad as hell and you figure if you ignore it . . . but then it starts to get to you. You start to feel really, I guess you'd say, sad, but still mad besides and also eventually just, almost, *bored*, I mean so sick of it all, so sick of going over it and over it, sick of your own self, even; and you say to yourself, 'Well, look at it this way: you ought to be glad you're free of her. She always did act kind of irritating,' you say. But then you say, 'If she'd give me one more chance, though! I mean, how did things get so out of hand here? When did they start to go wrong that I didn't even notice?' "

Sam set down his spoon. Linda gave a sudden sigh. Delia said, "Well,

I . . . well, why *don't* I come with you? I doubt I'd be much help, but certainly I could try."

"Oh, God, thank you, Miz G.," Driscoll said.

"I don't know if this will work, though," Delia told him.

"It'll work," he said, standing up. "If school lets out, say, two forty-five, three o'clock, and I come pick you up by . . ."

That wasn't what Delia had meant. She'd meant that in her opinion, Susie might reasonably refuse to marry him even after he apologized. But she changed her mind about saying so. She didn't even say goodbye to him, because just as he was leaving, the telephone rang.

This time it was Joel. He said, "Delia?"

"Yes," she said evenly. She glanced toward her family. They were all watching her—everyone but Sam, who seemed to be studying the table.

"Where *are* you?" he asked.

This was such an illogical question that she couldn't think how to answer it. She said, "Um . . ."

Where are you? Sam had asked in another phone call, months ago, and she wondered now if he had meant the question in the same way Joel did.

Then Joel, as if recollecting himself, said, "I came home to have lunch with Noah and he told me you haven't left Baltimore yet. I just thought I should find out if everything's all right."

"Oh, yes. Fine," she said.

She wished the others would resume talking, but they didn't.

"But you do plan to be back, don't you?" Joel asked. "I mean, eventually? Because I see from your closet . . . I wasn't trying to pry but I did just, so to speak, glance in your closet, and I noticed all your clothes are gone."

"They are?" she said.

"I thought you might have left for good."

"Oh, no, it's just . . . things are taking longer to finish than I expected," she told him.

Sam rose and walked out of the room.

From upstairs, Susie called, "Mom? Mom?"

"It's *not the realtor!*" Delia called back.

Joel said, "Pardon?"

"Sorry, Joel, I'd better go," she said. "See you in a while."

She hung up.

"Well, aren't *you* the popular one," Linda said.

Delia gave what she hoped was an offhand laugh and started clearing the table.

It was true, she saw when she went upstairs, that she had brought all her clothes. Well, not really all. Joel would have found enough in her bureau to reassure him, if he'd looked. But what with one thing and another— the iffy season, the dither over a wedding outfit—she had packed as if she'd be gone for days. She pictured Joel standing in front of her closet, his broad forehead creased in perplexity as he surveyed the empty hangers. Abruptly, she closed her suitcase and snapped the latches shut.

Then she crossed the hall to Sam's room. Here she had left plenty behind. How odd that when she was debating what to wear for the ceremony, she hadn't considered her old wardrobe! Or maybe not so odd—all that froufrou and those nursery pastels. She turned away. She went to her bureau and found, in the top drawer, a draggled blue hair bow, safety pins, ticket stubs, everything hazed with talcum powder. A pair of sunglasses missing one lens. A fifty-five-cent hand-lotion coupon. A torn-out photo of a fashion model in a stark, bare sliver of black. She couldn't imagine ever wearing such a style, and she studied the photo for some time before recalling that it was the model who'd caught her eye, not the dress. The sickle-shaped model with the same snooty haircut as Rosemary Bly-Brice.

Footsteps climbed the stairs, and she closed the drawer as stealthily as a thief. She turned and found Sam halting in the doorway. "Oh!" she said, and he said, "I was just—"

They both broke off.

"I thought you were seeing patients," she said.

"No, I'm through for the day."

He put his hands in his trouser pockets. Should she leave? But he was filling the doorway; it would have been awkward.

"Mostly now I keep just morning hours," he said. "I don't have a lot of patients anymore. Seems half of them have died of old age. Mrs. Harper, Mrs. Allingham . . ."

"Mrs. Allingham died?"

"Stroke."

"Oh, dear, I'm going to miss her," Delia said.

Sam very kindly did not point out that she'd lost all touch with Mrs. Allingham sixteen months ago.

His bed was made, but like most men, he seemed unable to grasp the concept of tucking a fold of spread beneath the pillows. Instead, a straight line of fabric slanted dismally toward the headboard. Just for something to do, Delia set about fixing it. She turned down the spread and whacked both pillows into shape.

"I guess you think I've destroyed your father's practice," Sam told her.

"Pardon?"

"I've run it down to a shadow of its former glory, isn't that what you're thinking?"

"It's not your fault if people die of old age," Delia said.

"It's my fault if no one new signs on, though," he said. "I lack your father's bedside manner, obviously. I tell people they have plain old indigestion; I don't call it dyspepsia. I've never been the type to flatter and cosset my patients."

Delia felt a familiar twinge of annoyance. *I would hardly consider "dyspepsia" flattery,* she could have said. And, *I don't know why you have to use that bitter, biting tone of voice any time you talk about my father.* She stalked around to the other side of the bed.

But then Sam asked, "What is that limp you've got?"

"Limp?"

"It seems to me you're favoring one foot."

"Oh, that's from a couple of months ago. It's almost healed by now."

"Sit down a minute."

She sat on the edge of the bed, and he came over to kneel in front of her and slip her shoe off. His fingertips moved across the top of her foot with a knowledgeable, deft precision that shot directly to her groin.

In her softest voice, she told him, "Your patients never minded, that I was aware of. They always called you a saint."

"They don't anymore," he said. He was gazing out the window while he traced a tendon, as if he expected to hear the injury rather than see it. "The other night Mrs. Maxwell phoned with one of her stomach problems, and I told her, 'If I let myself think about it, Mrs. Maxwell, I could list quite a few complaints of my own. My eyes burn and my head aches and my knee is acting up,' I said. Which of course offended her. It seems I've lost my tolerance. Or maybe I was never all that tolerant to begin with. I don't have a very . . . wide nature. I'm short on, you might call it, jollity."

The very word, in connection with Sam, made Delia smile, but he was prodding her ankle now, and he didn't notice. "Does this hurt? This?" he asked.

"A little."

She thought of how Joel had held her foot in exactly this way. But Joel's touch had felt so foreign, so separate from her—not quite real, even, it seemed as she looked back.

"I suppose that's why I married you," Sam was saying. Had she missed something? "You were extremely jolly when we met," he said. "Or more like . . . lighthearted. Now I see that I chose you for all the wrong reasons."

She drew back slightly.

"There you sat on that couch," he said, "next to your two scary sisters. Eliza preaching sea kelp and toxic doses of vitamins; Linda tossing off words like *louche* and *distingué*. But you were so shy and cute and fumbly, smiling down at your little glass eyecup of sherry. You were so wavery around the edges. You I'd be able to handle, I thought, and I never stopped to ask why I needed to believe that."

He dropped her foot and sat back on his heels. "Stand up, please," he told her. She stood. He narrowed his eyes. "It does seem there's a bit of swelling," he said. "I would guess you've torn a ligament. Ligaments can be very slow to mend. How'd you do it?"

She'd done it acting fumbly, acting wavery around the edges, but she didn't want to say so. He was continuing, anyway, with his original train of thought.

"When you left," he said, "the police were sympathetic at first. But then they figured out you'd left of your own accord, and I could see them beginning to wonder. Well, you can't blame them. I was wondering myself. I asked Eliza, when she came back from seeing you: 'Was it me? Did I have any part in it?' Maybe I hadn't phrased it right about that man friend of yours. Or I nagged too much about sunblock, or you hated how my chest hair had grayed. Or the angina; I know the angina business must have gotten tedious."

"What?" she said. "Now, that is just not fair!"

"No, no, I did go overboard for a while. Checking my pulse rate every two minutes. I think I had it in mind I was going to drop dead like my father." He rose, carefully brushing his knees even though they weren't dusty. "But Eliza said it wasn't any of those things. She said you were suffering from stress. I'm still not sure what she meant."

Nor am I entirely clear, he had written, *what "stresses" you are referring to.* Delia wished now she hadn't thrown that letter away. Had its tone, perhaps, been less cold than she had imagined? She reflected on the deletions; she recalled how they had increased near the end and how the commas had fallen away, as if he had been hurtling headlong toward his final sentence. Which he had then crossed out so thoroughly that she hadn't been able to read it.

The phone on the nightstand started ringing, but neither of them reached for it, and eventually it stopped.

"The thing of it is," he said, "you ask yourself enough questions— was it this I did wrong, was it that?—and you get to believing you did it *all* wrong. Your whole damn life. But now that I'm nearing the end of it, I seem to be going too fast to stop and change. I'm just . . . *skidding* to the end of it."

Susie called, "Mom?"

"It's like that old Jackie Gleason show on TV," Sam said. "The one that used to open with a zoom shot across a harbor toward a skyline. Was it Miami? Manhattan? That long glide across the glassy water: my picture exactly of dying. No brakes! No traction! No time to make a U-turn!"

"Mom, telephone!"

Delia didn't take her eyes from Sam's face, but Sam said, "You'd better get that."

Still she didn't move.

"The phone, Delia."

After a moment, she picked up the receiver. "Hello?" she said.

"Delia?"

"Oh, Noah."

Sam's shoulders sagged. He turned toward the window.

"Haven't you even started out yet?" Noah demanded.

"No," she said, with her eyes on Sam. He was setting his forehead against the panes now, looking down into the yard. "I won't know what my arrangements are till afternoon," she told Noah.

"But it's afternoon now, and I'm lonesome!" he said. Sickness, it seemed, had turned him into that open-faced child she'd first known.

"I've got no one taking care of me! Grandpa came but he wouldn't stay, and now I've finished the cough drops."

"Well, there's another box in the . . . your grandpa? Came to Bay Borough?"

"For about a nanosecond."

"What did he want?"

"He said he was just riding around, and then he left. I told him I was sick, but what did *he* care? And Dad claims I don't even have a fever and Mom can't come till after work and also something's wrong with the television set."

"Read a book, then," she told him. "I'll be home before long. Either this evening or maybe tomorrow; tell your father, will you?"

He was in the midst of a theatrical groan when she said goodbye.

"Sorry," she told Sam. "That was just—"

But Sam said, "Well, it's obvious you have things to attend to," and he started toward the door.

"Sam?" she said.

He stopped and turned.

"It was just the little boy I'm taking care of," she told him.

"So I gathered," he said, somehow not moving his lips.

"He's sick with a cold."

"And you have to get 'home' to him."

His voice had that pinched, tight, steely quality that always made her shrivel inside, but she forced herself to say, calmly, "Well, it *is* where I happen to live."

"I may not be perfect, Delia, but at least I don't delude myself," Sam said.

"What is that supposed to mean?"

"I don't go around trying to roll the clock back," he said. "Shucking off my kids as soon as they turn difficult and hunting up a whole new, easy, *little* kid instead."

Delia stared at him. "Well, of all the preposterous theories!" she said. "What do you know about it? Maybe he's not easy at all! Maybe he's just as difficult!"

"If that's the case," he said, "you can always shuck him off too."

"I didn't shuck him off!" she shouted. "I just came for Susie's wedding and then I'm going back—and not a moment too soon, might I add. I have no intention of shucking him off!"

Sam studied her impassively. "Did I say you did?" he asked. And while she was grabbing for words, he left the room.

One of Delia's handicaps was that when she got angry, she got teary, which always made her angrier. So there she was, banging around the kitchen and fighting back tears as she washed the dishes, while Linda followed behind, trying to console her. "There, there," she said. "We love you, Dee. Your blood kin loves you. Careful, that's Grandma's last soup bowl. We'll stand by you."

"I'm all right," Delia said, dabbing her eyes impatiently with the heel of one hand. She ran water over a sponge. It had a horrible cilantro smell, as if it had soured in the cupboard.

"You shouldn't put up with him," Linda said. "Give him the boot! Send him packing. This is our house, not Sam's. It's you who ought to be living here."

Delia had to laugh at that. "Really? On what money?" she asked. "If not for Sam, we'd have lost this place long ago. Who do you think pays the property tax? And the maintenance, and the bills for all those improvements?"

"Well, if you call uprooting every last shrub an improvement," Linda sniffed. "I call it high-handed! And did you know he's got plans to paint the shutters red?"

"Red?"

"Fire-engine red, is what he told Eliza. Though she says he's sort of petered out on his projects lately. But think of it! Like an old, old man with his hair dyed, that's what red shutters would look like. You notice he only started doing this after his heart attack."

"Chest pains," Delia corrected her mechanically.

Susie wandered in, dressed in her jeans and a navy pullover of Carroll's. "When's lunch?" she asked Delia.

"Lunch! Well . . ."

"A gold digger's what he is," Linda said. "He had his eye on you from the moment Daddy hired him."

"Who did?" Susie asked.

"Sam Grinstead; who do you think? He schemed to marry your mother before he ever laid eyes on her."

"He did?"

"Oh, Linda," Delia said. "If you get right down to it, I schemed to marry him, too. I sat behind that desk just pining for someone to walk in and save me."

"Save you from what?" Susie asked.

Delia ignored her. "Look at our own grandmother," she told Linda. "Marrying Isaiah to escape TB. Look at the woodcutter's honest son, marrying the princess for her kingdom!"

"Who was T.B.?" Susie demanded. "What woodcutter? What are you two *talking* about?"

Linda went over to Susie and draped an arm across her shoulders in a chummy, confiding way that made Delia feel excluded. "If your mother had half the sense you do," she told Susie, "she would kick your father out and get herself a job and move back to Baltimore."

"I already have a job," Delia said. "I have a whole life, elsewhere!"

And Bay Borough seemed to float by just then like a tiny, bright, crowded blue bubble, at this distance so veiled and misty that she wondered if she had dreamed it.

"Here's what I'm hoping," Driscoll told Delia. "When Courtney hears somebody's phoned her, she'll know right off it's got to be this guy she gave her number to. I mean, he did call you-all's house three times. So you know he didn't get the number from the phone book; he must have written it down wrong. Don't you think?"

"Well, it's possible, I suppose," Delia said. In fact, it seemed very likely, but she couldn't work up the energy to tell him so. For the past forty-five minutes they'd been standing out here in the cold. From time to time she sent a longing glance over her shoulder at Courtney's white clapboard house, but they had already rung the doorbell and no one had answered. "Driscoll," she said, "has it occurred to you that Courtney might have after-school sports? I mean, Susie used to come home in the dark, some days."

"Then we'll wait here till dark," he said.

Other students were passing—Gilman boys in their shirts and ties, and teenage girls in Bryn Mawr aqua or Roland Park Country School blue. "We should be holding up one of those signs," Delia said, "the way they do at airports."

Driscoll scowled at her.

"Couldn't you have brought Pearce for this instead?" Delia asked him.

"Who's Pearce?"

"Your sister, for heaven's sake!"

"You mean Spence?"

"Spence. Sorry."

She gave a little laugh. He scowled harder.

"Spence is at work," he told her. "But I doubt she'd have come anyhow. She doesn't think I ought to get married."

"She doesn't!"

"Well, why is that such a shock?" he asked. "You're not the only one who's against this."

"Did I say I was against it?"

"You sure act like you are. Dragging your heels every step of the way, wishing I'd brought someone else."

"I'm just getting cold, is all," Delia told him.

"For your information, my whole family claims I'd be better off single."

Delia felt stung. She said, "Well, thanks a lot!"

"Oh, they like Susie," he said. "But, you know . . . 'Why get mixed up with those Grinsteads?' my mom is always asking."

"There's nothing wrong with Grinsteads!"

"No, well, but . . ." He followed a knot of passing schoolgirls with his eyes. "You've got to admit," he said, "you-all are so . . . you do things such a different way. Not mingling or taking part, living to yourselves like you do; and then you pretend like that's normal. You pretend like *everything's* normal; you're so cagey and smooth; you gloss things over; you don't explain."

Delia breathed again. He could have named flaws much worse, she felt, although she didn't know exactly what. "Well," she said, "those sound to me like good qualities, not bad."

"See there?" Driscoll demanded. "That's exactly what I mean!"

"Look who's talking!" Delia said. "Someone who had his wedding canceled and then showed up for it anyway! How's that for glossing over?"

"At least *I* didn't make believe I was nothing but a guest," Driscoll told her. "Walking in at the very last minute like the bride was some passing acquaintance."

"I would have come earlier! But nobody asked me!" she told him.

"See what I mean?" he said.

"What *do* you mean?"

A car drew up at the curb, a station wagon teeming with faces. A girl got out with an armload of books. "Thanks!" she called, and the car honked and pulled away.

"Courtney?" Driscoll asked.

The girl paused on the sidewalk. Delia had known, somehow, that Courtney would be a blonde. She was tall and slim and golden-skinned, and her clothes were just the right degree of unstudied—her blazer expertly tailored but her knee socks falling down. "Yes?" she said.

"My name is Driscoll Avery," Driscoll said, "and a couple of nights ago I believe I answered a phone call that was meant for you."

Courtney tilted her head. Her pageboy swung prettily to one side.

"Some guy called, a wrong number," Driscoll told her, "and now my fiancée is mad because I was, um, maybe a little bit rude. So I need to ask if you know who might have called you."

Courtney looked over at Delia.

"I'm his fiancée's mother," Delia explained. The word "fiancée" brought to her mind someone in a pillbox hat, nothing at all like Susie. She felt herself assuming the flat-faced, wide-eyed expression of a liar. She said, "Driscoll's telling the truth; I swear it. A boy phoned, asking for Courtney, and Driscoll said you didn't want to talk to him."

"You said *that?*" Courtney asked Driscoll. The smile was gone now. "What if it was someone I was dying to hear from?"

"Well, like who?" Driscoll said. "I mean, *was* there someone?"

"There's Michael Garter."

"Did you give Michael Garter your number?"

"No, but it's in the book."

"You think he's the one who called you?"

"Well, maybe. He could have. Well, sure!" She seemed to be warming to the idea. "In a couple of weeks, there's this dance?" she told Delia.

Delia said, "But you didn't actually tell him your number."

"Well, no."

"We were thinking it might be someone you'd told."

"No, but there's this big homecoming dance? And Michael Garter's this guy I know? He's the second-strongest guy in his school."

"But—" Delia began, at the same time that Driscoll said, "Well, great! Let's get moving!"

"But *was* there someone you told?" Delia asked.

"Oh, gosh, guys are always wanting my number. You know? And I give it to them, but, like, I just do it to be nice. I would never actually go out with them."

"Would you give them the *wrong* number?" Delia persisted.

"Well, sure, if they're, like, totally not of interest."

"You'd just transpose a couple of digits, say."

"I might."

"Did you do that recently?"

"Well, maybe to this guy at my Christian fellowship group."

"What's his name?"

"But I think it's more likely Michael Garter," Courtney said.

"But the name of the boy at your fellowship group . . ."

"That's Paul Cates. But he's, like, a dork. You'd know what I meant if you saw him."

"I bet anything it was Michael Garter," Driscoll said soothingly.

Courtney sent him an appreciative look.

"Well, whoever," Delia said, "you just tell Driscoll all the possibilities, and then he can track down which one it was."

"And maybe I could come along," Courtney said. "I could show you exactly where Michael Garter has football practice."

Anybody with half a brain would look for Paul Cates first. Hoping to convey that, Delia screwed up her eyes at Driscoll. "Huh?" he asked her, and then, "Ah. Does, ah, Paul Cates play football too?"

"Are you serious?" Courtney asked. "Paul Cates? Play football?"

Delia collected herself to go, hitching her handbag strap onto her shoulder. "Good hunting," she told Driscoll.   .

"What, you're not coming with us?"

"You'll do better by yourselves."

He opened his mouth to argue, but Courtney said, "Nice meeting you!"

Delia waved and walked off.

She was glad to have some time alone. Had family life always been so cram-packed? she wondered. How had she kept her wits about her? But then she remembered she hadn't, at least not in Sam's opinion.

Skimming south on Roland Avenue, she passed Travel Arrangements, the Mercantile Bank, Eddie's Supermarket. She was careful not to look toward the other pedestrians, in case they were people she knew. Suppose they asked where she'd been all these months and what she planned to do next. Or suppose—here was a thought—she met Adrian Bly-Brice.

The funny thing was that she couldn't picture Adrian's face anymore, although she tried.

"Delia," Linda whispered at the front door, "you've got someone waiting for you."

"I do?"

Delia felt herself flush, but Linda said, "An *older* gentleman. Name of Nat?"

"Oh," Delia said.

She followed Linda through the dining room and into the kitchen. Nat was sitting at the table with Susie and the twins, but he rose to his feet when Delia entered. "There she is!" he said.

Away from Senior City, he seemed older. His hair was so white that it glittered, and he was leaning very heavily on his cane. This must be one of his flashback days. She said, "Nat? Is everything all right?"

"Oh, yes," he said, "quite all right. Hello, my dear." He gave her a courtly kiss on the cheek, prickling her with his beard. "I just happened to be tootling around in the car," he said. "Thought I'd offer you a lift back."

"Tootling around . . . Baltimore?"

"Yes, well, hither and yon."

This was puzzling, but she didn't pursue it. "That's nice of you," she said, "but I'm not sure exactly when I'll be leaving." She glanced toward Susie, who was watching her over her coffee mug. "Driscoll is still working on that telephone matter," Delia told her.

The twins nudged each other. Nat said, "Oh, I know all about that! Your sister here has filled me in. So how is it progressing? Have we located the hapless young man?"

"Well, we've narrowed the field some," Delia said. "Nat, is anything wrong at home?"

"Wrong! Why do you keep asking that?" he said. "Can't a man take a little drive on his own these days?"

Linda placed a mug of coffee on the table in front of him, and he lowered himself back onto his chair with a thud. "Thank you, my dear," he said. He set his cane aside. It stood on its four little legs in a perky, independent manner.

"Cream?" Linda asked him. "Sugar?"

"Just black, thanks." He told Delia, "You never mentioned you had a sister. And such a charming daughter! And two gorgeous nieces!"

There was something feverish about his enthusiasm, but none of the others seemed to notice. "She doesn't only got a daughter," Marie-Claire told him. "She's got two boys besides."

"Two boys!" Nat marveled. "Where does she keep them hidden?"

"Well, Carroll's hiding upstairs, on account of this fight with his dad. And Ramsay lives with his tacky girlfriend at a place we don't know the address of."

Nat shot Delia a questioning look. "Yes," she said with a laugh. "You'll have to excuse us, I'm afraid. Nobody here is on speaking terms."

"They seem to *me* to be speaking," he said reasonably.

"Oh, speaking, yes. But . . ."

She gave up and went to pour herself some coffee. Nat resumed quizzing the twins. "And do all of you live in this one big house? All except Ramsay, that is, and his tacky girlfriend?"

"Oh, no, none of us live here! Just only Uncle Sam."

"Uncle Sam! This is government property?"

The twins chortled. Thérèse said, "Silly! Uncle Sam is Aunt Delia's husband."

Delia sensed Nat's glance in her direction, but she didn't turn around, and the twins moved on to the topic of Eliza. "She burns weeds in little bowls," Marie-Claire told him. "She has a bottle called Forbearance, to smell from when she's feeling fed up."

"Where would one buy that, I wonder," Nat said wistfully.

Delia went to the silverware drawer for a spoon and found Susie all at once lounging in front of it, waiting for her, one sneakered foot cocked across the other. Her nonchalant expression didn't fool Delia for a second. "So," Susie said. "Driscoll did get hold of Courtney, sounds like."

"Yes."

"And narrowed down who the boy was, you said."

"Well, Courtney gave him a couple of possibilities."

"So I guess now he's gone to talk to them."

"He's working on it," Delia told her.

She reached toward the drawer, and Susie slid infinitesimally to one side. "Looks to me like you would have gone with him," Susie said.

"Well, you can see I'm right here," Delia snapped.

She supposed that Susie must care for Driscoll; and in that case, well, all right, they should probably get married. How simple-minded Delia had been, to take their breakup seriously! And how sage and mature and practical Susie seemed in comparison! Delia flashed her a radiant smile. Susie examined her warily.

People always talked about a mother's uncanny ability to read her children, but that was nothing compared to how children could read their mothers.

The twins were describing their bridesmaid dresses. "Big floppy bows—"

"Puffy shoulders—"

"Exact same color as Crest fluoride toothpaste."

"They must be stunning," Nat told them. "And when do you plan on wearing them?"

"Maybe tonight," Marie-Claire said, while Susie, overlapping, said, "Tomorrow."

Everyone looked at her. She met Delia's gaze defiantly. "Well, if Driscoll brings me that boy, I mean."

"But he could do that in the next five minutes!" Linda told her. "You could get married this evening, if he hurries."

"Yes, but Dr. Soames can't fit us in till ten a.m. tomorrow."

"He told you that?" Delia asked. "You talked to him? When?"

"Oh, um, just a little while ago."

"But if our flight home is tomorrow at noon," Linda said, "and the drive to the airport takes, let's see . . ."

Nat told Delia, "Sounds as if you won't be riding back with me tonight."

He spoke cheerfully enough, but Delia hadn't lost her suspicion that something was troubling him. She glanced toward the others, who were still discussing schedules, and then she said, "Nat, what brought you here? Really."

"Nothing, I tell you!"

"You just drove two hours for no reason."

"Two and a half, actually," he said. "Little backup on the bridge."

She scrutinized him. "How's the baby?" she asked.

"He's thriving."

"And Binky?"

"Healthy as a brood mare."

"Does she know you're in Baltimore?"

"I called her a few minutes ago. Your sister let me use your phone."

"And Noah has a cold, I hear," she said, still ferreting.

"The merest sniffle," Nat assured her. "I looked in on him this morning while I was driving around. Found him playing Tetris. Hardly on his deathbed, I'd say."

"It's true he didn't sound very sick," Delia said. "Maybe he just needed a day off."

"Yes," Nat said. "We could all do with a day off, from time to time."

Something bumped against the back door, and then Sam walked in bearing two bags of groceries. A long stick of French bread poked forth from one of them. "I found the ginger," he told Linda, "but they were fresh out of shallots."

"Well, never mind; we'll make do with green onions," Linda told him, taking the bags. "Is that okay, Delia?"

"Is what okay?"

"Can you make your Chinese dish using green onions?"

"I always use green onions anyhow," Delia said. "But—"

"Oh, good. Because we're going to be so many, you know, I thought you could fix your . . . Oh, Sam, you haven't met Nat, have you. Nat Moffat, this is Sam Grinstead. I certainly hope you plan to stay for supper, Nat. Delia's Chinese dish feeds an army, believe me."

"I would love to stay for supper," Nat said, to Delia's surprise. He had risen during the introductions, and now he stood holding on to the back of his chair. Sam, who must have had no idea where Nat had materialized from, wore a pleasant, slightly blank expression as they shook hands. "Good to meet you," he said.

"Good to meet *you*," Nat told him. And then he added, darting a mischievous glance at Delia, "I've heard so much about you."

This was lost on Sam, of course. He just smiled politely and asked Linda, "Have I got time for a house call before supper?"

"Ask Delia; she's the cook," Linda said.

Sam turned to Delia. "I promised Mr. Knowles I'd check on him," he said.

"You have plenty of time," she told him.

They spoke without letting their eyes meet, like people in a play, whose words are meant for the audience.

No one had to tell Delia which boy had turned out to be Courtney's caller. She knew it was Paul Cates as soon as she saw him—sweet-faced and naive, with a tousle of rust-colored curls. His jeans were a little too short for him, his sneakers too thin-soled and childish, his plaid wool jacket the kind boys wear in elementary school. He followed Driscoll over to Susie, who was perched on a stool chopping water chestnuts for Delia's Chinese dish. Behind him came Courtney, of all people. She took her place close behind Driscoll and Paul, tucking her hands into the pockets of her blazer and regarding Susie with undisguised curiosity. Susie, who had turned from the counter at their approach, looked only at Driscoll.

"Susie," Driscoll said, "this is Paul Cates." Then he faced Paul Cates and said, "Paul, I'd like to apologize. When you phoned here by accident the other night, I let you think you'd reached Courtney's house, but I was wrong, wrong, wrong."

Paul was beaming. "That's okay," he said.

Formally, Driscoll faced Susie again. "*Now* will you marry me?" he asked.

Susie said, "Well, I guess."

One of the twins said, "Hot dog!" and the other said, "Kiss him! Kiss him, Susie!"

Susie planted a kiss to one side of Driscoll's mouth. She told Paul, "It's nice of you to be so understanding."

"Oh, I don't mind a bit!" he said, and he sent Courtney a shining glance from under his long lashes. Courtney just surveyed him coolly and then turned back to Susie.

"And Courtney, it was nice of you to come along," Susie told her.

"No problem. Me and your brother Carroll met last spring at a party."

"Oh, really?"

"My girlfriend asked him to her birthday party; I put it all together when your fiancé told me your name."

Paul was looking less happy now; so Delia broke in and said, "Can you two stay for dinner? We're having this Chinese dish that's infinitely expandable."

"Well, I *might* could," Courtney said.

Paul said, "I'll just need to phone my mother."

"Right over here," Delia told him, and she cupped his elbow protectively as she led him toward the phone. How cruel and baffling—how tribal, almost—young girls must seem to boys! Somehow she hadn't realized that when she was a young girl herself.

"I propose a toast," Nat said. He raised his coffee mug. "To the bridal couple!"

Driscoll said, "Why, thanks"—not having the dimmest notion, of course, who this old man might be, but adapting with his usual good humor. "Hello, Ma?" Paul said into the phone, and then Carroll appeared from the dining room just as Eliza stepped through the back door; so both of them had to be filled in on the latest developments. Eliza hadn't even heard yet what Driscoll's magic task was. She kept saying, "Who? He brought who?" with her eyebrows quirked in bewilderment, her pocketbook hugged to her chest, and Courtney was sidling toward Carroll to ask, "Carroll Grinstead? I don't know if you remember me," and the twins were insisting that this time they should wear lipstick to the wedding.

Delia took her cutting board to a less populated area, and she started chopping ginger. Her Chinese dish required eleven different bowls of ingredients, most minced no bigger than matchstick heads, all lined up in a row for rapid frying. So far she had finished only bowl number four. She was thankful to be occupied, though. She chopped rhythmically, mindlessly, letting an ocean of chatter eddy around her. *Tick-tick*, the knife came down on the cutting board. *Tick-tick*, and she slid all her thoughts to one side as she slid the mounds of ginger into a bowl.

With every one of its leaves in place, the table filled the whole dining room. ("This tablecloth came from your grandma's hope chest," Linda told the twins. "The stain is where your aunt Delia set a bowl of curry. *She* doesn't give a damn; she was your grandpa's favorite; she treats these things like Woolworth things.") Twelve place settings marched the length of it—five at each side, one each at head and foot. There had been talk of inviting Eleanor, but Susie didn't want to jinx her entire marriage with thirteen at table; and no one answered the phone when they called Ramsay.

"Courtney, I'll put you in the middle here," Delia said. "Then Paul, you're next to Courtney . . ."

Courtney, however, had obviously made up her mind to sit with Carroll, which left Paul stuck between the twins; not that the twins weren't delighted. And the others remained standing while they continued a discussion they'd started in the living room—something about Mr. Knowles's tingly arm. "Didn't Daddy always say the same thing!" Eliza was exclaiming. "He used to say he wished he had a dictionary of pains. Those symptoms people came up with—'Pepsi-bubble stomach' and 'whiny argumentative back'!"

"Driscoll, you're beside Linda," Delia said, but Driscoll, feigning engrossment in the conversation, kept his face turned toward Eliza and sneakily drew out the chair beside Susie. Delia gave up. "Oh, just *sit*," she told Nat, and Nat sat down where he was, which happened to be exactly where she'd intended, at her right hand. "Help yourself to some rice," she said, passing him the bowl, and she told the others, "Everything's getting cold!"

Eliza settled at Sam's left, shaking her head at what Sam was saying. "Who knows, anyhow?" he was saying. "Maybe it's all equal: hangnail for one, cancer for another. Everything on the same level, just barely within endurance."

"Sam Grinstead, you don't believe that for a minute!" Linda squawked. "What a bizarre suggestion!"

Delia said, "Paul, will you have some rice and pass it on, please? Everybody! Sit down!"

Very suddenly, the rest of them sat. They seemed to have run out of steam, and there was a pause, during which Paul dropped the serving spoon to the table with a loud clunk. He bared all his teeth in embarrassment and picked it up.

Nat said, "Do any of you know the photographs of C. R. Savage?"

The grown-ups turned courteous, receptive faces in his direction.

"A nineteenth-century fellow," he said. "Used the old wet-plate method, I would suppose. There's a picture I'm reminded of that he took toward the end of his life. Shows his dining room table set for Christmas dinner. Savage himself sitting amongst the empty chairs, waiting for his family. Chair after chair after chair, silverware laid just so, even a baby's high chair, all in readiness. And I can't help thinking, when I look at that photo, *I bet that's as good as it got, that day. From there on out, it was all downhill, I bet.* Actual sons and daughters arrived, and they quarreled over the drumsticks and sniped at their children's table manners and brought up hurtful incidents from fifteen years before; and the baby had this whimper that gave everybody a headache. Only just for that moment," Nat said, and his voice took on a tremor, "just as the shutter was clicking, none of that had happened yet, you see, and the table looked so beautiful, like someone's dream of a table, and old Savage felt so happy and so—what's the word I want, so . . ."

But now his voice failed him completely, and he covered his eyes with one shaking hand and bent his head. "So anticipatory!" he whispered into his plate, while Delia, at a loss, patted his arm. "I'm sorry! I'm sorry!" he said. Everyone sat dumbstruck. Then he said, "Ha!" and straightened, bracing his shoulders. "Postpartum depression, I guess this is," he said. He wiped his eyes with his napkin.

"Nat has a three-week-old baby," Delia explained to the others. "Nat, would you like—"

"Baby?" Linda asked incredulously.

Sam said, "I thought Nat was *your* friend, Linda."

"No, he's mine," Delia said. "He lives on the Eastern Shore and he's just had a baby boy, a lovely boy, you ought to see how—"

"Most irresponsible thing I've ever done in my life," Nat said hoarsely. "What could I have been thinking of? Oh, not that it was anything I planned, but . . . why did I go along with it? I believe I thought it was my chance to be a good father, finally. I know it was, or why else did I assume it was a girl? All my others were girls, you see. I must have thought I could do the whole thing over again, properly this time. But I'm just as short-tempered with James as I ever was with my daughters. Just as rigid, just as exacting. Why can't he get on a schedule, why does he have to cry at such unpredictable hours . . . Oh, the best thing I could do for that kid is toddle off to Floor Five."

"Floor Five? Oh," Delia said. "Oh, Nat! Don't even think it!" she said, patting his arm all the harder.

She should have realized at his wedding, she told herself, that someone so elated would have to end in tears, like an overexcited child allowed to stay up past his bedtime.

"Yes. Well," Sam said, clearing his throat. "It's really very common now, this more senior class of parent. Why, just last week I was reading, where was it I was reading . . ."

"The important thing to remember is, this is your assignment," Eliza said in ringing tones. She was all the way up near Sam, and she had to lean forward, bypassing a row of tactfully expressionless profiles, to search out Nat's face. "It's my belief that we're each assigned certain experiences," she said. "And then at the end of our lives—"

"*The New England Journal of Medicine!*" Sam announced triumphantly.

Nat asked Delia, "Do you have a place where I might lie down?"

"Yes, of course," she said, and she slid her chair back and handed him his cane. "Excuse us, please," she told the others.

Everyone nodded, abashed. As she and Nat crossed the hall, she could almost feel the furtive exchange of glances behind their backs.

"There's a flight of stairs," she warned Nat. "Can you manage?"

"Oh, yes, if you'll hang on to my other arm. I'm sorry, Delia. I don't know what got into me."

"You're just tired," she told him. "I hope you're not thinking of driving back tonight."

"No, I suppose I shouldn't," he said. On each stair step, his cane gave a tinny rattle, like a handful of jacks being shaken. His elbow within his tweed sleeve was nothing but knob and rope.

"I'm going to make up a bed for you," Delia told him when they reached the second floor, "and then you should call Binky and tell her you're staying over."

"All right," he said meekly. He hobbled through the door she held open and sank into a slipcovered chair.

"This used to be my father's room," Delia said. She went out to the hall closet and came back with an armload of sheets. "There's still a telephone by the bed, see? From the days when he was in practice. Even after he stopped seeing patients, he could pick up his receiver whenever Sam got a call; chime in with a second opinion. He just hated to feel left out of things, you know?"

She was babbling aimlessly as she bustled around the bed, smoothing sheets and tucking in blankets. Nat watched without comment. He might not even have been listening, for when she went to Sam's room to borrow a pair of pajamas, she returned to find him staring at the blue-black windowpanes. "In fact," she said, placing the pajamas on the bureau, "I can't tell you how often I made up his bed just the way I did tonight, while Daddy sat where you're sitting now. He liked for his sheets to be fresh off the line, oh, long after we switched to an automatic dryer. And he would sit in that chair and—"

"It's a time trip," Nat said suddenly.

"Why, yes, I suppose it is, in a way."

But he'd been talking to himself, evidently. "Just a crazy, half-baked scheme to travel backwards," he said as if she hadn't spoken, "and live everything all over again. Unfortunately, Binky's the one who's left with the consequences. Poor Binky!"

"Binky will be fine," Delia said firmly. "Now. That door right there is the bathroom. New toothbrushes on the shelf above the tub. Can I get you anything more?"

"No, thank you."

"A tray of food, maybe? You didn't touch your supper."

"No."

"Well, you be sure to call me if you need me," she said.

Then she bent to press her lips to his forehead, the way she used to do with her father all those nights in the past.

Delia was the next to go to bed. She went at nine-thirty, having struggled to keep her eyes open ever since dinner. "I am *beat*," she told the others. They were all sitting around, still—even Courtney, although Paul had been picked up by his mother at some point. "It seems this morning took place way back in prehistory," Delia told them, and then she climbed the stairs to Eliza's room, so weary that she had to haul her feet behind her like buckets of cement.

Once she was in bed, though, she couldn't get to sleep. She lay staring at the ceiling, idly stroking the curl of warm cat nestled close to her hip. Downstairs, Linda and Sam were squabbling as usual. A Mozart horn concerto was playing. Eliza said, "Why *wouldn't* he, I ask you." Wouldn't who? Delia wondered. Wouldn't do what?

She must have slept then, but it was such a fitful, shallow sleep that she seemed to remain partly conscious throughout, and when she woke again she wasn't surprised to find the house dark and all the voices stilled. She sat up and angled her wristwatch to catch the light from the window. As near as she could make out, it was either eleven o'clock or five till twelve. More likely five till twelve, she decided, judging from the quiet.

She propped her pillow and leaned back against it, yawning. Tears of boredom were already edging the corners of her eyes. It was going to be one of those nights that go on for weeks.

Let's see: if the wedding began at ten tomorrow, she supposed it would be finished by eleven. Well, say noon, to play it safe. She'd reach the bus station by half past, if she could catch a ride with Ramsay. Or with Sam. Sam had offered, after all.

She saw herself riding in the passenger seat, Sam behind the wheel. Like two of those little peg people in a toy car. Husband peg, wife peg, side by side. Facing the road and not looking at each other; for why would they need to, really, having gone beyond the visible surface long ago. No hope of admiring gazes anymore, no chance of unremitting adoration. Nothing left to show but their plain, true, homely, interior selves, which were actually much richer anyhow.

Where was she? Bus station. Catch a bus by one o'clock or so, reach Salisbury by . . .

The tears seemed not exactly tears of boredom after all. She blotted them on her nightgown sleeve, but more came.

She folded back the covers, mindful of the cat, and slid out of bed and walked barefoot toward the door. The hall was lit only by the one round window, high up. She had to more or less feel her way toward Sam's room.

Luckily, his door was ajar. No sound gave her away as she entered. But she knew, somehow, that he was awake. After all these years, of course she knew, just from that bated quality to the air. She stepped delicately across cool floorboards, then scratchy rug, then cool floorboards once again—terrain she had traveled since the day she first learned to walk. She sat with no perceptible weight upon the side of the bed that used to be hers. He was lying on his back, she saw. She could begin to sift his white face from the flocked half-dark. She whispered, "Sam?"

"Yes," he said.

"You know that letter you wrote me in Bay Borough."

"Yes."

"Well, what was the line you crossed out?"

He stirred beneath the bedclothes. "Oh," he said, "I crossed out so many lines. That letter was a mess."

"I mean the very last line. The one you put so many x's through I couldn't possibly read it."

He didn't answer at first. Then he said, "I forget."

Her impulse was to stand up and leave, but she forced herself to stay. She sat motionless, waiting and waiting.

"I think," he said finally, "that maybe it was . . . well, something like what Driscoll was wondering earlier. Was there anything that would, you know. Would persuade you to come back."

She said, "Oh, Sam. All you had to do was ask."

Then he turned toward her, and Delia slipped under the blankets and he drew her close against him. Although, in fact, he still had not asked. Not in so many words.

———

Long after they went to sleep, the telephone rang, and Delia resurfaced gradually. This late, it had to be a patient calling. But Sam didn't even change the rhythm of his breathing; so she inched out from under his arm to reach for the phone.

"Hello?" she said.

"Mrs. Grinstead?"

"Yes."

"It's Joe Bright."

A voice as bright as his name, wide awake and chipper at the ungodly hour of—she peered at the alarm clock. One twenty-three.

"Um . . . ," she said.

"The realtor?" he prompted.

"Oh!"

"You called me? You and your daughter? Left a whole bunch of messages?"

"Oh! Yes!" she said, but she was still floundering. "Um . . ."

"I would never phone so late except you did say it was life and death, Mrs. Grinstead, and I only now got in from out of town. Wife's mother died, spur of the moment."

"Oh, I'm sorry to hear that," she said. She sat up straighter. "Um, Mr. Bright, why I called was . . ." She shifted the phone to her other ear. "My daughter has been wanting to know," she said. "Yes . . . will she be allowed to pound nails in the walls?"

There was a silence.

"Just in case they need to hang some pictures, say, or a mirror . . . ," Delia said, trailing off.

"Nails," Mr. Bright said.

"Right."

"She wanted to know if she could pound in nails."

"Right."

"Well," Mr. Bright said. "Sure. I reckon. Long as they spackle the holes upon vacating."

"Oh, they will!" Delia said. "I can promise. Thank you, Mr. Bright. Good night."

There was another silence, and then, "Good night," he said.

Delia replaced the receiver and lay down again. She had assumed Sam was still asleep, but then she heard him give a little whisking sound of amusement. She started smiling. Outside, far downtown, a train blew past. In the house, a floorboard creaked, and a moment later a foggy cough broke from the room where Nat slept.

"It's a time trip," Nat had said.

She thought of her attempt, that afternoon, to picture Adrian. She had begun with his resemblance to her high-school boyfriend, and only now did she realize that the image she had come up with happened to be Sam's, not the boyfriend's. A younger Sam, earnest and hopeful, the day he'd first walked through the door.

It had *all* been a time trip—all this past year and a half. Unlike Nat's, though, hers had been a time trip that worked. What else would you call it when she'd ended up back where she'd started, home with Sam for good? When the people she had left behind had actually traveled further, in some ways?

Now she saw that June beach scene differently. Her three children, she saw, had been staring at the horizon with the alert, tensed stillness of explorers at the ocean's edge, poised to begin their journeys. And Delia, shading her eyes in the distance, had been trying to understand why they were leaving.

Where they were going without her.

How to say goodbye.

ABOUT THE AUTHOR

ANNE TYLER was born in Minneapolis in 1941 but grew up in Raleigh, North Carolina. She graduated at nineteen from Duke University and went on to do graduate work in Russian studies at Columbia University. Anne Tyler's eleventh novel, *Breathing Lessons,* was awarded the Pulitzer Prize in 1988. She is a member of the American Academy and Institute of Arts and Letters. She lives in Baltimore.